Failed State

ALSO BY CHRISTOPHER BROWN

Tropic of Kansas
Rule of Capture

Praise for *Rule of Capture*

"This one is fresh, intelligent, and emotional, with a plot that envisions an alternate reality hard to dismiss as unreal. It's a legal thriller, with a big twist, stirring and imaginative, brimming with skulduggery, that will have you asking: is this possible?"

—*New York Times* bestselling author Steve Berry

"A kind of madcap Texas Gothic dark comedy, as the Houston good ole boy network is displayed like a courtroom scene in an unpublished Hunter S. Thompson novel. . . . It moves, rocketing along at a ferocious pace—and then it lingers, haunting you."

—Cory Doctorow, for *BoingBoing*

"Christopher Brown looks to be cornering the market on future dystopias. . . . *Rule of Capture* is not just sci-fi, it's also a legal thriller. Its author is himself a lawyer, just like John Grisham, and he has a grip on detail that full-time sci-fi authors can't match."

—*Wall Street Journal*

"*Rule of Capture* is a taut, smart legal thriller set five minutes into the future in a dystopian postwar America that looks scarily plausible from the vantage point of 2019, and marks Brown as one of our most tuned-in science-fiction writers."

—Adrian McKinty, Edgar– and Ned Kelly Award–winning author of *The Chain* and *Rain Dogs*

"Peel back the dystopian and science-fiction layers of this fast-moving and entertaining story, and what remains is a smart, taut legal thriller bound to keep readers turning pages deep into the night."

—Robert Bailey, bestselling author of
the McMurtrie and Drake legal thriller series

"Interpersonal drama fuels the story as much as legal maneuvering, and Brown keeps tight control of his narrative even as this alternate America slips its gears."

—*Publishers Weekly* (**starred review**)

"This dark, dystopian story will appeal equally to readers of John Grisham and Cory Doctorow."

—*Booklist*

"Put this one on the shelf next to Orwell."

—*Locus*

"An exhilarating, all-too-real journey into a scary place, where the fall of democracy is sure to be streamlined: the courts. Chris Brown's frenetic prose will keep you turning the pages, make you laugh, and fill you with horror—it's the long-awaited, judicial dystopian thriller for our times."

—Fernando Flores, author of *Tears of the Trufflepig*

"If this first installment is any indication, I will buy the others the day they appear on shelves, mute my phone, and cancel all appointments for the next couple of days."

—*Lone Star Literary Life*

"Read this! A dark, funny novel of homegrown revolution, constitutional crisis, and edgelands biology [deponent affirms he could not stop reading]."

—*Endless Bookshelf*

"I can't remember a legal thriller having made me cry before—though I suppose terrifyingly near-future compassionate dystopian SF is another story. *Rule of Capture* is both."

—*The Mossy Skull*

Praise for Tropic of Kansas

"Futurist as provocateur! The world is sheer bat-shit genius . . . a truly hallucinatorily envisioned environment."

—William Gibson, *New York Times* bestselling and award-winning author

"The great American novel about the end of America. This book is marvelously propulsive, bighearted, and whip-smart."

—Kelly Link, Pulitzer Prize–nominated author of *Get in Trouble*

"This vision of the future is violent, unforgiving, and bleak: Cormac McCarthy meets Philip K. Dick. It's disturbing because of how believable it is. . . . It's remarkably effective. Recommended for fans of Paolo Bacigalupi and China Miéville."

—*Booklist*

"Timely, dark, and ultimately hopeful: it might not 'make America great again,' but then again, it just might."

—Cory Doctorow, *New York Times* bestselling and award-winning author of *Homeland*

"*Tropic of Kansas* is like a modern dystopian buffet. . . . It is, in this particular moment in history, frighteningly prescient. It is the nightly news with the volume turned up to 11."

—NPR

"This funny, heart-wrenching book cuts through genre expectations with the speed of a jackhammer."

—*Seattle Times*

"This book is a powerful vision of an America that might be, an America that some nights seems as though it is all too likely to be, filled with powerful characters and a chilling presentiment of how far our country could fall . . . a novel well worth reading."

—*San Francisco Book Review*

"*Tropic* [*of Kansas*] is a knockout first novel, paradoxically solemn yet exuberant, restrained yet inventive, as attested to by well-deserved encomiums from William Gibson, Bruce Sterling and Cory Doctorow."

—*Locus*

"A new mutation of the alternate-history novel."

—Norman Spinrad (*Asimov's Science Fiction*)

"This stunning novel of a time all too easily imaginable as our own highlights a few of the keen-voiced, brave-souled women and men who balance like subversive acrobats on society's whirling edges. . . . Read it to burn with the joy of realistic hope."

—Nisi Shawl, Tiptree Award–winning author of
Everfair and *Writing the Other*

"A unique blend of Philip K. Dick, Kafka (just a smidgen), and a whole lot of Christopher Brown. Adventure novel meets political satire and the finest elements of realistic sci-fi, and it's so well written it goes down like a greased eel. It's hopeful dystopia. What a book."

—Joe R. Lansdale, author of the Hap and Leonard series

"*Tropic of Kansas* is the tale of a politically desperate USA haunted by a sullen, feral teen who is Huck Finn, Conan, and Tarzan. Because it's Chris Brown's own imaginary America, this extraordinary novel is probably more American than America itself will ever get."

—Bruce Sterling, award-winning author of
Islands in the Net and *Pirate Utopia*

"*Tropic of Kansas* is a great novel. Brown's writing is tightly composed, and flows nicely. . . . Definitely recommended."

—*Civilian Reader*

"Fun, fast, violent, smart, and with enough adventure and science-fiction elements to keep fans of both genres happy, this was more than a superb novel: it was the kind of book that announces the arrival of an author at the top of his game."

"*Tropic of Kansas* is savvy political thriller meets ripping pulp adventure—a marriage made in page-turning, thought-provoking heaven. . . . It's a vision both frighteningly prescient and already too real, and a story of valiant heart and brain up against the worst architectures of greed and power."

Failed
State

A NOVEL

Christopher Brown

HARPER Voyager
An Imprint of HarperCollinsPublishers

FAILED STATE. Copyright © 2020 by Christopher Brown. All rights reserved. Printed in the United States of America. No part of this book may be used or reproduced in any manner whatsoever without written permission except in the case of brief quotations embodied in critical articles and reviews. For information, address HarperCollins Publishers, 195 Broadway, New York, NY 10007.

HarperCollins books may be purchased for educational, business, or sales promotional use. For information, please email the Special Markets Department at SPsales@harpercollins.com.

Harper Voyager and design are trademarks of HarperCollins Publishers LLC.

FIRST EDITION

Designed by Paula Russell Szafranski

Interior art © by Ricardo Reitmeyer/Shutterstock, Inc.
Interior art © by justhavealook/GettyImages
Interior art © by Konstantin Kirillov/Dreamstime

Library of Congress Cataloging-in-Publication Data has been applied for.

ISBN 978-0-06-285910-5

20 21 22 23 24 LSC 10 9 8 7 6 5 4 3 2 1

For Octavia and Ajin

Failed State

PART ONE

Things Fall Apart

THE FAILURE OF THE AMERICAN LEGAL SYSTEM TURNED OUT TO BE good for the lawyers. It was not so good for the clients, but in those first few years after the uprising, everybody had to adapt.

For Donny Kimoe, the hardest thing about adapting was that he had to spend a lot of time in Dallas. That he had grown up there only made it worse. But it was where what passed for justice in those days could be found, far enough from the disappearing coast that they only had to close the courthouses during tornado season. As a bonus, Dallas still had real food, if you could afford it. And the air conditioning still worked, which was more than you could say for most cities in those days, when the infrastructure that hadn't been destroyed in the fighting or died of old age and inattention was often out of juice, or saved for when it was really needed. Half the people Donny knew back home in Houston, and all the ones with money, had bailed for Big D over the past decade, the same way they had vacated New Orleans as it drowned. And so Dallas was still rich, or at least good at making you think so, by keeping things as shiny as it could with available materials. As shiny as the waxed BMWs and Benzes you could still find proud corporate execs driving down the increasingly empty freeways, usually with armed chauffeurs who were also the ones they paid to wait in the gas lines.

Those execs were the ones Donny came to hunt. Them, and their investors, assets, and insurance policies, and what-

1

ever else they had managed to hold on to through the years of dictatorship, blight, and civil strife that burned up the hard-earned savings of most. Donny did not have a BMW, a Benz, or even a Chevy. He did have a locked file drawer crammed full of jewelry and expensive watches he had accepted as payment in lieu of fees from the political dissidents he had represented during the long emergency. The contents of that drawer could be enough to retire on, if the economy ever recovered enough for people to afford such luxuries again. Or to really care what time it was, in an America where the idea of the future was a form of nostalgia rarely discussed outside of corner bars and neighborhood marijuana dispensaries. And where most people, including Donny, were focused on settling the scores of the past.

The judges still cared what time it was, but there were not enough Rolexes in the world to correct Donny Kimoe's knack for showing up late. Even when his own future was on the line.

As he stepped through the courtroom doors that Friday morning at 9:27 A.M., Donny found the Honorable Laura O. Larriva already seated at her bench, and every other player at their place. When she saw Donny, the judge broke away from her off-the-record sidebar with defense counsel, and then pulled back the sleeve of her black robe to look at her own Rolex, a gesture whose real purpose was as clear as the big government clock on the wall.

"You know being a lawyer isn't like being a musician, Mr. Kimoe," said the judge, addressing him with the formality the courtroom and its transcript required, even though they had known each other on a collegial if not chummy first-name basis for more than a decade. "Keeping them waiting does not make them want to hear from you more."

"I should have had the good sense to scalp my tickets while

there was still demand," said Karen Keller, the lead lawyer for the private prison company Donny was suing, who was sitting at the opposite table with her pinstriped entourage from Polson & Chevalier. Donny felt a tremor of anxiety wondering what Karen and the judge, who knew each other even better, had been talking about off the record while they waited for him.

The judge laughed. "And now you have me trying to remember if I have ever heard Donny Kimoe sing."

"I did once," said Karen. "Three years ago, when they had the bad idea to host karaoke night at the state bar convention."

The self-disgust that came on as the scene cued up in Donny's head was driven not so much by the cringeworthy memory of his wasted performance as the reminder that he spent so much time fraternizing with the enemy during his years fighting the regime.

"What did he sing?" said the judge.

"'Ebb Tide,' if you must know," said Donny, embracing the fool. That was the role the system liked him to play—sometimes to his advantage. "A prescient and underappreciated evocation of amorous melancholy in a drowning world."

"That was just the warm-up," said Karen. "Before he got all punk rock. And then degenerated into political rants like some mic-hogging Oscar winner. Best performance as a burned-out lawyer who can't win a case and blames the system."

Judge Larriva and Karen both chuckled. They had probably been joking about him before he got there. They had worked together at P&C before the judge went on the bench, and now Karen and her partners were the judge's most reliable campaign contributors. The only good thing about that setup was you knew the only bribes Judge Larriva took were legal ones.

Donny shrugged. "There may be a few videos still out there in circulation if you really want to see it, Your Honor. And I'm pretty sure there's one from the same night, of Ms. Keller and Bridget Kelly channeling the Red River Girls, big-hair wigs and all."

Karen smiled, and the judge joined her. And Donny realized he was doing it again.

"But the only thing either of us should be embarrassed about," he added, "is that we were partying while Ms. Keller's client was busy killing people for their politics."

"Save it for the press conference, Mr. Kimoe," said the judge. "Because you have a long way to go to make that case, and there are no cameras in here. Now, let's get on the record and see if we can make up some of the time you wasted. I have a full docket of people with real problems lined up behind you."

She gaveled them in with a barely audible tap, and her staff attorney, court reporter, and bailiff kicked into gear with the energy of a middle-aged cover band ready to play the same old song one more time.

This was the kind of hearing the clients don't show up for. And it was the kind of case the clients might even forget, as the years rolled by with depositions and document requests and discovery fights but no real progress. Donny had been a different kind of defense lawyer, the kind who tries to keep guilty people alive and out of jail, so he could appreciate Karen's gifts for delay and jurisprudential misdirection. But looking over at her and her squad, he was reminded that while P&C was billing enough every month to pay the full salary of one of those associates, Donny would only get paid if and when he won. In the meantime, every hour he put into working on this case, and every buck he spent on travel and discovery, was a sunk cost. That each of the junior lawyers sitting there with Karen made more money in one year than Donny made in the last three added to the rub, even before you remembered that one of them commanded that salary in part because she had clerked for Judge Larriva. But Donny had finally compelled them to produce the witness who, if Donny's information was good, could break the case open. If the morning went well, he might even get Karen to talk about writing a check that would keep the real story wrapped up in a confidential settlement agreement. Donny would get a third of that check, and it would be just enough to make up for the guilt he would feel at failing to get the true story out there. It would have to be, because this was the only real case Donny had worked on for the past year. He had debts to pay, real ones and karmic ones, and he had put all his chips on this hand.

The witness was sitting right there in the first row behind the defense table, a twitch in his eye as he inadvertently caught Donny's gaze. Behind him was the lone reporter who had shown up for the show, if you could call her that—a blogger who had been covering the case from the beginning. The only other people in the gallery were two unfamiliar faces in the back row, a man and a woman who could have passed for feds but for the architect glasses the guy wore. Maybe they were real journalists. Or maybe that was wishful thinking. The time when Donny could command mainstream press attention for his cases had passed with the prior regime, and his last big criminal case had made him a different kind of news.

The fasces embossed on the wall behind them was a good reminder of whom the 299th District Court really served, even if it was the minor leagues, and an unlikely place to seek justice for war crimes. It was a state civil court, normally the venue for small-time business disputes, divorces, and personal-injury cases. And it looked the part—a small, drab courtroom, the kind of setup that county bureaucrats had deemed nice enough back in the days when most of the budget went to locking up unruly refugee kids from more climate-ravaged states, locals who violated the emergency restrictions on public assembly, and the people from both groups that managed to get classified as domestic insurgents. Maybe it was Donny's memories of handling those cases that made the courtroom seem so claustrophobic as he pulled out his files and took his place at the plaintiff's table.

Donny looked back up at Judge Larriva, who was watching him attempt to get organized while the clock ticked.

"We're ready," he said, even though the "we" was just him, and the main evidence of his preparation was a dog-eared yellow pad on which he had overwritten layers of notes in three different colors, most of the pages embellished with bold geometric doodles.

"All right," said the judge. "We are back for another installment in *Harrison v. AMR*, case number 12–247893. And hopefully getting close to the finish line. Trial is set for one month from today. I have Mr. Kimoe's amended complaint—this is the fifth amended complaint, I believe—"

"That's correct, Your Honor," said Donny. "We uncovered new facts that required us to add additional claims."

"Some rather incendiary claims, if I may say so," said the judge. "You've gone from saying people died under the defendant's care due to negligence to saying they were murdered."

"That has always been our belief, Your Honor," said Donny. "That the resettlement farms were used as cover for a secret program to disappear opponents of the regime. But we had not wanted to state our claim in those terms until we had the evidence to back it up."

"Well, it's the only claim you have left," said the judge. "Last time you were here, I ruled your negligence claims were precluded by AMR's contract with the government. And today

I have déjà vu. Not just because you are late again but also because we have essentially the same issue—that your wrongful-death claims are exempt from suit under last year's general immunity included as part of the cease-fire. A finding Ms. Keller wishes me to make today and grant her client summary judgment."

"That's correct, Your Honor," said Karen. "We dispute all of the allegations in the complaint, which read like they were copied from one of the conspiracy sites. Accidents did happen on the farms AMR helped operate, and some people died. No real evidence has been provided that any camp residents were deliberately killed for their insurrection. But even if they were, such claims are barred by the Interstate Compact for the Cessation of Hostilities, which provided amnesty to combatants on both sides of our recent troubles. We all lost blood and treasure in the conflict. Many of us lost loved ones. And we all agreed to move on in the interests of peace. Mr. Kimoe does not get to make exceptions just because he filed this case before the Compact was signed."

"As you have copiously briefed," said the judge. "And Mr. Kimoe has less copiously, but quite colorfully, rebutted in his response. So at the outset let me tell you all that I am inclined to agree with Ms. Keller on the amnesty question. If employees of her client, acting as representatives of the former government, killed insurgents who had taken up arms against that government, whether in the urban battlefield or in the seeming sanctuary of a resettlement farm, that conduct is exempt from suit just as those same insurgents have immunity for their attacks on federal personnel and contractors. But I have also noted the defense's resistance to providing Mr. Kimoe access to its personnel for depositions."

"Your Honor," said Karen, "most of the personnel Mr. Kimoe

sought testimony from are no longer in the company's employ, and it is not our responsibility to locate them. But we have the latest witness Mr. Kimoe requested with us ready to testify today."

"Which witness you made us subpoena," said Judge Larriva. "And who Mr. Kimoe claims will persuade me that the immunity does not apply."

"You have that right, Judge," said Donny. "And I believe he will also help show there is a more active concealment of evidence going on with respect to the other witnesses we've identified. Especially the guards."

"I'm all ears," said the judge. "So you can take what's left of this hour to convince me I shouldn't dismiss this case and stop wasting the court's valuable time."

Six years of work, riding on minutes you could watch roll by on the clock.

"You will want to hear more than that, Judge."

"I don't have time to hear more than that, Mr. Kimoe. So let's get after it."

"Your Honor," said Karen. "Before we get to that, can we discuss our Rule 123 motion?"

Donny did not recall any such motion. He could not even remember what Rule 123 was.

"The one you filed at ten P.M. last night?" said the judge.

Donny pulled his laptop out.

"Yes, Your Honor," said Karen. "For which we are sorry to have burdened the court, but it's a procedural matter that only ripened over the weekend, and your consideration of which could save us all some time."

The judge was looking at her benchtop screen.

Donny was trying to find a network connection with one

hand while the other pulled his beat-up copy of the rules from his bag.

"Let's discuss this after plaintiff's counsel presents his witness," said the judge. "Are we ready, Mr. Kimoe?"

Donny looked back up at the judge, and stood.

"Yes, Your Honor."

As she called the witness to the stand, he looked back down at the page he had flipped to.

RULE 123.
SUGGESTION OF DEATH.

He didn't have time to read the rest of the rule, or to guess why Karen was invoking it. All he knew was the only viable strategy he had was to try to turn the shifty-looking middle manager standing there in the box into a ventriloquist's dummy. One that made more than a suggestion of death.

THE WITNESS DID not look hostile, though that was what Donny had been allowed to designate him. One of those all-American white guys who looks to have been raised in a cubicle on a diet of soda pop and paternal admonitions. Forty-three, according to the personnel file, but somehow resembling an oversized kid despite the suit—maybe because of the way the suit looked too big and too small at the same time, punctuated with a red tie that brought out the blood in his pink face.

"Good afternoon, Mr. Bagley. I'm Donald Kimoe, the lawyer for Daryl Harrison, the lead plaintiff in this case. Thank you for coming today."

"You made me," said Bagley.

"We only sent the subpoena after your employer made us. But I'm sure you don't share their desire to cover up the truth, and I appreciate you being here to testify. Could you please state your name for the record?"

"Richard Bagley."

"Who is your current employer, Mr. Bagley?"

"PDL."

"An acronym for Prairie Dog Logistics, am I right?"

"That used to be the name," said Bagley.

"Maybe before the animal in question became extinct," said Donny.

"I wouldn't know."

"I hear you. It's hard to keep up with the species count, even when they run it in the Sunday paper. PDL is a private transportation company, correct?"

"Transportation and logistics, yes."

"But not like Greyhound. I can't just go buy a ticket for a ride to Houston or Chicago."

"That's right. We move cargo for governments and businesses."

"Some of it human cargo."

"Correct."

"Who is your biggest customer?"

"That would be our parent company, AMR—the American Management and Retraining Company."

"Such a big customer that they bought you so they could get a better deal."

"I guess so. They bought us three years ago, after PDL had become one of their main suppliers."

"And their biggest customer is the federal government?"

"Was," said Bagley. "Now I'm not sure who the biggest customer is."

"Business is off, I take it."

"Their business is."

"And what business is that?"

"They operate detention, resettlement, and skills-training facilities for governments and other companies. Or did. Most of the federal contracts got canceled after the takeover."

"By the takeover, you mean the popular revolt that restored the Constitution?"

"No, I mean the foreign-backed revolt that shredded the Constitution."

"Compliance with international law hasn't been bad for your business, has it?"

"No. The bus business and cargo volumes have really taken off since the air-travel bans."

"How long have you been working for PDL?"

"Nine years, since before the buyout."

"That's a long run. What is your current position?"

"I'm the VP of operations for District Four."

"What territory does District Four cover?"

"Most of the Central US—the Dakotas and Minnesota south to here in Texas, and as far east as Mississippi."

"So your region covers most of the resettlement farms and crop labs."

"Pretty much."

"Where are you based?"

"Oklahoma City."

"'The Crossroads of America.' Good hub for a bus company."

"It works well for us."

"How long have you been the VP of operations?"

"Around two years."

"Since the cease-fire?"

"Pretty much."

"And before that you managed the operation at Fort Hood down in Killeen, correct?"

"I was one of the managers."

"Is PDL paying you to be here today?"

"I guess. I'm on a salary, and this ain't vacation."

"No, it's not. You sent some folks on vacation, though, didn't you? Permanent vacation."

"Objection, Your Honor," said Keller. She didn't need to explain the basis.

"Mr. Kimoe," said the judge.

"Sorry," said Donny. "That's not what they called it. But we'll get to that in a bit. At Fort Hood, you were assigned to help support the AMR account, before AMR bought PDL, correct?"

"They were our main customer. But we were all really working for Tripto Labs, who hired AMR. And for the federal government, who gave Tripto Labs the contract to grow their New Corn on a production scale."

"So this was after Fort Hood was designated as a resettlement farm, where Tripto Labs planted their next-gen GMO crop and the prisoners provided the labor."

"They were not prisoners," said Bagley. "Maybe some of them. Most were just refugees. Refugees from other states."

"From the 'Tropic of Kansas.' States where the old corn wouldn't grow anymore."

"Not like it used to. Some were resettled because of blight, or drought. Others because of the fighting up there."

"Did they come voluntarily?"

"I don't know," said Bagley. "My understanding was they got compensation. Food and shelter, some money. And the chance to help develop the crops that could restore the places they came from and fix our food crisis."

"By working the fields of a genetically engineered grain that can grow in spent fields, suck a third more carbon from the air, and get twice as big as regular corn—just as long as you have a small army of workers to pollinate it by hand."

"Look, I just handled the transportation to and from," said Bagley.

"Fair enough, Mr. Bagley," said Donny. "May I ask how many buses you dispatched, during your three and a half years supporting the AMR account at Fort Hood?"

"How many buses?"

"Yes. How many buses."

"I don't know. Usually about one a day."

"Every day?"

"Most days. When things got really busy, there might be two or three. And they weren't always buses."

"What do you mean, they weren't always buses?"

"We ran out sometimes. So to fulfill our contract we had to find alternate transportation. Trucks."

"What kind of trucks?"

"Tractor trailers, mainly."

"Air-conditioned?"

"Just ventilated, usually. Livestock trailers. We were using all the grain trailers to move product."

"You used livestock trailers to ship people off to resettlement farms."

"Only when we had to. And when we did, we cleaned them up real good. Put a port-a-potty in there, plenty of water. Still better than the conditions where most of these people were coming from."

"Cattle cars, but business class," said Donny. "So these trucks, and buses, they were used to transport internal refugees to work at the farms."

"Yep."

"And also people who were actual detainees?"

"They kept the insurgents in a separate section of the camp. More secure. Same with the transportation."

"And who was in charge of moving these people around?"

"Federal emergency relief authorities. FEMA, Coast Guard, other branches of the Motherland Guard."

"The same agencies in charge of the camp."

"Correct, but not the farms where they worked."

"Tripto Labs ran the farms. And oversaw the security AMR provided there."

"Pretty much."

"And you moved the people and material in and out of there."

"That's right."

"Did you ever go into the camp?"

"Behind the wire? No. I didn't have clearance. Closest I got was the transit depot across the highway, where we loaded and unloaded passengers."

"What were they like?"

"Just like anybody, I guess. Skewed pretty young. Young guys, especially."

"Those were the actual prisoners. Or detainees. Suspected insurgents."

"Correct. Otherwise it was just like a cross section of folks from that part of the country. A lot of farm people."

"Even old folks and young kids?"

"Yes, a cross section. That's what I saw, at least."

"Were they happy?"

"How would I know? They looked poor and hungry."

"Did they cooperate? Did they start fights?"

"Sometimes people would mouth off. Maybe a young punk

would try to pull something. If they did, the guards got them back in line real quick. Mostly people were cooperative."

"Like livestock."

"I wouldn't know."

"You mentioned unloading *and* loading. Sometimes you sent people away. Were they going home?"

"Not usually."

"Where were they going?"

"Other facilities, usually, as they started more farms. Places like Bartlesville, Joplin, Sugarland, Irving, New Orleans. Sometimes they even got to go back home, with seed licenses, to help start new farms."

"What was in New Orleans?"

"Camp Zulu, and the Superdome."

"The Superdome was more like an actual prison."

"Sort of. It was an emergency detention facility. And the people we sent there were the most dangerous insurgents."

"So you were told."

"Sometimes by the insurgents themselves, yeah. But mostly by the Camp Administrator's Office."

"So the camp administrator decided who qualified as an insurgent combatant?"

"I don't know. Could have been they got their lists from the Guard."

"Were you provided a list?"

"They just brought us the passengers, and names for the manifest."

"And those passengers had to be sent on more secure buses. With bars on the windows, and bars you could tie their chains to."

"Yes, we outfitted a prison transport bus for that."

"So you would load it with prisoners—"

"The guards would load it."

"So the guards would load it, and take them to New Orleans, to the Superdome, as far as you understood. And then the bus would come back in a day or two?"

"That's right."

"Did you get confirmation the passengers had been delivered to their destination?"

Bagley shifted in his chair. "No. Once they boarded, we had done our handoff to AMR and the manifest was closed."

"But your drivers knew."

"Those weren't 'our drivers.' They were AMR personnel, with security clearances, working on contract for Motherland."

"You knew most of them, though, right? You worked with them all the time. Many had been PDL employees before, and toward the end you shared a corporate parent."

"I knew some of them."

"Did you ever hear any of them talk about 'dropping the kids off at the pool'?"

Donny glanced at the judge. She was listening closely, eyes on the witness.

"I can't remember," said Bagley.

"You don't remember anyone talking about what happened to prisoners who left on those buses but never showed up at the Superdome?"

"I heard some stories about that, but only later. After the raids."

"Were you there when the bus came back on the Friday before Memorial Day four years ago?"

"That was a long time ago."

"Let me refresh your recollection." He handed copies of a document to the judge and Karen, which they had both seen before and the judge admitted without objection. Then he handed it to Bagley. "This is your ops log from that month, correct?"

"Yes," said Bagley. He shifted in his chair again, like suddenly the weight of his extra flesh was heavier than it had been.

"That's your handwriting on there, making additional notes?"

"Looks like it."

"Do you see the entry for May 22, on the second page? The one you highlighted in yellow?"

"Yes."

"So if I'm reading this correctly, that bus was scheduled to depart for New Orleans at six-fifteen A.M., with Mr. Gannon as the driver and Ms. Lee and Mr. Peña as the guards."

"That's what this says, but I don't remember which guards were on it."

"Is that because they have disappeared?"

"Excuse me?"

"You didn't know that Mr. Gannon, Ms. Lee, and Mr. Peña are all missing and presumed dead?"

"I heard something about Gannon, not so much about the other two. But we all know a lot of people who were lost, or just lost track of."

"Or silenced," said Donny. "Do you remember who was on that bus when it went out?"

"I'd need to see the manifest."

"Turn to page six."

Bagley flipped the pages, and read.

Donny held up his copy, and pointed at the spot Bagley was reading. "Do you see that blank space where the names are supposed to be?"

"Yes."

"So did the bus go out empty, or did you white out the names?"

"I didn't blank anything out. Someone else must have done that, after I filed it."

"But you were the one who highlighted the bus in yellow."

"I don't remember what I highlighted or didn't highlight four years ago."

"What if I told you one of our sources says there were just two prisoners on the bus who were supposed to be transferred to the Superdome."

"Objection," said Keller. "That testimony isn't in the record."

"Noted," said the judge. "You can answer, Mr. Bagley."

"That wouldn't be unusual. Sounds right."

"Do the names Gil Harrison and Juana Croat ring a bell?"

"Yes."

"Why do you know those names?"

"They were the poisoners. The ones who tampered with the corn."

"That was what you believed."

"Still is."

"Not your kind of people."

"Objection," said Keller.

"Withdrawn," said Donny. "Do you remember seeing them on the bus when it went out that day?"

Bagley took a minute to consider his answer. He didn't look at the judge, but you could see he felt her gaze. "Yes," he said.

"And the bus came back the same day."

"Yes."

"Before dark."

"Yes."

"Is that enough time to get to New Orleans and back?"

"No."

"But there were no prisoners."

"No, sir."

"Where did they go?"

"I don't know."

"Did you ask?"

"No."

"Why not?"

"I don't know."

"Sure you do."

"Objection," said Keller. "Argumentative."

"Overruled," said the judge. "But let's stick to questions, Mr. Kimoe."

"Yes, Your Honor. Is it fair to say you didn't ask where the prisoners went, Mr. Bagley, because you didn't want to know?"

"I guess."

"Did you ever find out? Hear anybody talk about it?"

"No."

"Not even the driver? Who worked for the same company as you?"

"He said he couldn't talk about it. And then they transferred him the next week."

"He got a promotion, from bus driver to vice president, and a big raise. I guess he was a really good driver."

"Is that a question?"

"No. But this is. Did you inspect the bus after it returned?"

"Yes."

"Was it clean?"

"Not really."

"What was wrong with it?"

"There was some blood."

"How much blood?"

"I wouldn't know how to measure it."

"Try."

Bagley looked at the judge.

"Go ahead, Mr. Bagley," she said.

Bagley looked back at Donny. "A lot," he said, almost looking like he wished it was Donny's.

Donny glanced at the judge, and wondered if that was enough blood for her to rule in his favor. Then he looked at the clock.

"Pass the witness," he said.

"Ms. Keller," said the judge, turning to Karen.

"No questions," she replied.

Donny wanted to give the bailiff a high five when he heard that, but instead looked back to make sure the reporters were still there.

"All right then," said the judge.

Bagley began to stand, but the judge stopped him. "Hang on, Mr. Bagley," she said. "I have just a couple of questions for you, if you don't mind."

"Yes, ma'am," said Bagley. He didn't expect the judge to ask her own questions.

"I want to know more about how these special passengers were picked. The ones who went on the buses to nowhere. Or took trips to the pool or whatever euphemisms were used. You said they gave you a list?"

"Just names for the manifest."

"But they had a list, didn't they? There's always a list."

"I don't know, ma'am."

"Really?" said the judge. "Do you understand the oath you just took? Did you ever hear anyone talk about such a list?"

"There was some talk."

"I bet. Did the list have a name?"

Bagley nodded. "They called them Code Yellows."

"Why yellow?"

"I guess because of the kind of people they were."

The judge nodded, putting together pieces Donny was missing.

"People who hadn't committed acts of what the government considered terrorism, but who it suspected would in the future," she said. "Do I have that right?"

Bagley shifted.

"Answer the question, please," said the judge.

"That's not how they put it," said Bagley.

"How did they put it?"

"They were 'predictively guilty.' People whose behavior in the camps and on the farms showed they were likely to commit acts of violence against the government in the future. And this was the only way to prevent that."

"In other words, they were noncombatants."

"Not as our customers saw it," said Bagley.

"Well, contrary to popular opinion," said the judge, "the customer is not always right."

She looked at Karen. Karen kept her poker face on.

"You can step down now, Mr. Bagley," said the judge.

She leaned back. She looked over at her clerk. She looked at the monitor on her desk, and punched a couple of keys. Then she looked at Donny.

"You have my attention, Mr. Kimoe. There is more to this case than I appreciated."

"A lot more," said Donny.

"Maybe. Certainly enough for me to let you proceed to trial."

"Your Honor," said Karen, standing. "Before you make a decision on that, can we finish the discussion of our Rule 123 motion?"

"Right," said the judge, as she scrolled back through the

files on her desktop monitor. "Mr. Kimoe, what do you have for me on this?"

"I'm sorry, Your Honor," said Donny, reaching for the rules. "I understood you to say this was just filed late last night, and I haven't even had a chance to look at it."

"The file shows it was served on you a little over two months ago, Mr. Kimoe." She looked at the whiteboard calendar on the wall behind her bench, the one she called her reconstruction docket. "Which means the sixty days you had to respond with a substitute plaintiff expired on Friday."

"I'm sorry, Your Honor. What was served?"

"The defense's Suggestion of Death," said the judge. "Maybe they have an extra copy they can provide you."

"We do, Your Honor," said Karen. She looked at Donny as one of her associates handed him a two-page document. "Your client is dead. And your case is dead with him."

"What are you talking about? I just talked to him."

That wasn't exactly true. It had been months. Maybe close to a year. This wasn't the kind of case where you needed to talk to the client often. But Daryl was a real person, one Donny had known since he was a teen. And the only one Donny had to build his case on, so far.

"You just talked to him?" said Karen, raising her eyebrows as she looked at Donny. Then she turned back to the judge. "Maybe counsel used a psychic for that, Your Honor. Because we have a death certificate showing he died four months ago."

"That's impossible," said Donny. "He was—"

"He was killed," said Karen. "And we have proof." She held her hand in the air, and her paralegal handed her a stack of paper from one of the bankers boxes. "May I?" she asked the judge.

The judge nodded, and Karen approached the bench with

the document, then handed Donny a copy. There were multiple pages, stapled together.

"What is this?" said Donny.

"Defense Exhibit 317, with the court's permission," said Karen.

"I'll admit it provisionally for now," said the judge. "I need to read it, and you'll need to authenticate it."

"That's fair, Your Honor," said Karen. "But you'll see it's pretty straightforward. And the main thing is the second page, which is already self-authenticated in part: a Certificate of Death from the New Orleans Coroner's Office, attesting that Daryl Harrison died on January 3. Cause of death: blood loss resulting from gunshot wounds."

Donny flipped ahead.

"Where's the autopsy report?" he asked.

"There was none performed," said Karen.

"Because there was no body," said Donny, holding up the death certificate and pointing at one of the notes.

"Is that true?" said the judge, looking to Karen.

"It is," said Karen. "Mr. Harrison was killed in a firefight, while attempting to serve what the new government in New Orleans calls an 'extraterritorial arrest warrant' and the rest of us call an illegal kidnapping order. Here in Dallas, right after the New Year. He was shot by private security guards. Killed in action. And left behind by his colleagues, who finished the mission."

"I see that now," said the judge, flipping the pages.

"'Suggestion' of Death is right," said Donny. "This isn't proof."

"Of course it's proof," said Karen. "The coroner did not have the body. But they did have photos, taken by the security team before they disposed of the body. We are working on obtaining copies of those as well."

"So the body's in Dallas?"

"I believe there are cremains in possession of the municipal government, Your Honor, but no family has claimed them."

Donny looked back at the death certificate, searching for defects, signs of alteration. But it was the real thing. He felt cornered.

He threw Karen's document down on the table. "Your Honor," he said. "You can't throw this out over this. You heard the testimony just now. This is about hundreds of innocent people, maybe more, who were murdered for their peaceful resistance to the regime."

"I just heard your evidence, Mr. Kimoe. There is more to your allegations than I thought. But I don't have a choice. The rules are very clear."

Donny held up his copy of the rules, and pointed at the provision they were citing. "The rule gives me ninety days."

"That was amended last year," said the judge, beating Karen to it. "An effort to help clear the glut of cases from our backlog." She gestured at her reconstruction docket. Every day was fully booked, including a few nights.

Donny looked at the worn cover of his copy, and was reminded it was three years old. The fact that each edition cost several hundred bucks was no excuse, especially when the rules were also available online for free.

"I didn't receive this notice, Your Honor," said Donny. The more accurate thing to say was that he had not seen it.

"We have a file-stamped copy right here showing that you did," said the judge. "And you also got a copy of what was filed last night. It's a shame that you weren't able to attend to this, as all you would have needed to do is give me a notice from the estate. Or provide another plaintiff, which you have made a persuasive case there are many to choose from. But now I have to dismiss your case entirely."

"With prejudice, Your Honor," said Karen.

"Don't rub it in, Counselor." With prejudice meant the case could not be refiled. "I'm only doing this because I know I would be wasting my time otherwise, as you would have the Court of Appeals overrule me. You'll have to keep your own counsel about the consequences for the victims."

Donny wanted to sit down. His legs felt wobbly. He looked at Karen, containing her competitive satisfaction at the gotcha. He looked at the perfectly balanced scales of justice inlaid into the wood paneling behind the judge, which failed to show how rigged the system really was. So rigged the only way to rebalance it sometimes was with made-up bullshit.

"What if I can prove he's still alive, Your Honor?" said Donny, turning back to the judge.

The judge raised an eyebrow. "How do you propose to do that?"

"Just give me a few weeks, Judge. There's something fishy about this."

"Looks pretty straightforward to me," said the judge.

"It's backed up by news reports, Your Honor," said Karen.

"There's no body, Judge. What if you throw this case out, only to later learn, too late for us to do anything, that the information was bad? Just give me a couple of weeks to look into it. Please."

The judge leaned back, considering that scenario.

"Your Honor," said Karen, "the rules do not permit that."

The judge looked at Karen. "They do not," she said, registering some annoyance at being instructed in the bounds of her discretion. "And I have your form of order here ready for me to sign. But I am going to take a week to review it myself, and prepare my own order. Mr. Kimoe is free to consult whatever reanimators he wishes in the meantime. And if he can prove himself Lazarus by, say, a week from Friday, I will be free to tear that up."

"That's your decision, Your Honor," said Karen. "The outcome will be the same."

"That may be."

"Thank you, Your Honor," said Donny, already wondering what better angle he could come up with in that time to keep the case alive.

"And don't try to come back in here with some other strategy to delay," added the judge, as if reading Donny's mind. "You have now officially exhausted our patience for your inability to manage your own mess. Can you manage that, at least?"

"Absolutely," he lied.

IN A JUST WORLD, IT WOULD NOT MATTER THAT DONNY'S CLIENT was dead. All that would matter would be whether the crimes he alleged had been committed. And those crimes would be dealt with by the state. But Donny had made his living, such as it was, fighting for justice from an unjust system. Most of it fighting a state that no longer really existed, and had worked hard to cover its tracks while it could. Maybe it was because of all the cases he lost that he couldn't stop fighting now that the war was over. Even as most people had moved on to dealing with the fact that, while they were fighting, nature died.

It took a few years after the coup they called the state of emergency before the scope of the deeper crisis became apparent. Donny should have seen it coming. He started his practice representing detainees they had rounded up from the refugee camps, and he heard the stories about the barren breadbasket they had left behind up north. But when the price of corn started to lap the price of oil and outpace the rising temperatures and rising seas, the strain to the system became more evident. Even Donny realized it really was an emergency. And not just because he could no longer afford a cheeseburger, except on special occasions.

You could agree it was an emergency without agreeing that the implementation of authoritarian population controls was an acceptable solution. Especially if you could see how the new system they implemented was rigged to make sure a shrinking elite was able to keep extracting fat profits from a starved economy. Donny ended up making what he called a living defending the people who dared to resist the authorities, trying to work with a Constitution they were amending on the fly, one secret ruling at a time. It wasn't easy, the clients were usually broke, and sometimes your own safety was at risk. But he got pretty good at it, and even learned how to clean himself up enough to argue his cases on the evening news, in the court of public opinion.

The jury of the silent majority probably figured Donny was as guilty as his clients, if not more so. At least in the beginning. The need for labor to work the new farms gave perfect cover to the "resettlement" programs that were really just euphemisms for camps to lock whole populations up before they could start a revolution. The farms, if you believed the propaganda documentaries they streamed across the networks, were the secret to bringing back a healthy and well-fed future. New food that would feed the people, sustain the livestock, fuel the cars, and help clean up the mess, maybe even rehabilitate the exhausted fields to where they could once again grow the heritage crops that had failed. And people never really wanted to know where their food came from.

So as much as Donny and his colleagues in the dissident bar liked to credit their work for helping bring the system down, in the end it was the overreaching by the people in charge of the system that led to the uprising. The pie kept shrinking, and the government controlled who got their piece, through official channels and unofficial ones, all of them equally corrupt. The president, who had been elected as a reformer who would heal the nation's scars, became a self-dealing autocrat, and the accumulation of power brought out the mad king. When he began to piss off the wealthy donors who had given him that power, they turned on him. They made pacts with the underground networks who had been resisting him all along, and the exiles who had been seasoning the population with an alternate narrative, waiting for such a moment. And when the spark of revolution finally ignited, the uprising coalesced so fast, after so many years of repressed yearning for real change, that you couldn't help but wonder what had taken it so long.

They got more than they bargained for.

The president who provided the regime's public face and insane personality was gone, removed from office by a mob, tried for his crimes, and then assassinated before he could serve his sentence. International peacekeepers moved into the vacuum and brokered a cease-fire, immunizing the combatants from criminal prosecution. The resettlement farms survived, under new management. Now it was up to the people to renegotiate the social contract and come up with a new Constitution. In the meantime, the federal government was officially broken. The president had no replacement, and if the radical factions got their way, never would. Congress was short on members, with the former majority party having been outlawed, and met only infrequently. The courts still worked, except that most of the federal judges had been appointed by the deposed regime, and the only way they had to enforce their judgments was through the Marshals Service.

That meant if you wanted to get justice for what had gone down in the dark years that preceded the uprising, you had to get creative. Jail was no longer a remedy. Money was. But if you picked your defendants well, that would hit them where it really hurt.

"What would Njal do?"

That was what his old colleague Miles jokingly said when he started this case, teasing Donny about one of his favorite books, saying the name so it sounded just like "y'all." It was an old book, the only one of the Icelandic sagas whose hero was a lawyer rather than some ax-swinging Viking raider. A lawyer in a society that had no real government other than lawsuits, which would be settled every summer at a national camp-out presided over by the elders. Like the Anglo-Saxons who ruled England with their schedules of fees people could be made to pay for causing an injury: this much for an eye, a finger, a limb, a life. Tort law was the ur-law, the law that was older than the idea of the state that enforced it, rooted in ancient customs designed to temper the destructive forces of revenge that powered ever-escalating blood feuds.

When Donny and Miles joked about Njal in those days, they didn't know they were predicting the future. That the blood feuds were already happening on their watch, and would continue after the government was deposed. Hopefully by means other than the spilling of more blood. That Donny's motivation in chasing this case was partly about avenging the spilling of Miles's blood was something he tried to keep to himself. And as he sat there staring at the death certificate while everyone else in the room stood for the judge's exit, hearing Miles ask him the question in his head, Donny knew one thing: Neither Miles nor Njal would let himself lose a case with these kinds of facts just because the client who actually suffered the injury no longer existed. If there was a real wrong, there was a way to make the law correct it, even when the law was designed to make that hard for a private party to do. Even when it was supposed to be impossible.

Donny put the death certificate down, facedown, and looked over at the victorious defense team packing up their portable war room to the sounds of paper shuffling, clasps locking, and bungee cords snapping into place.

"Hey, Karen," he said, calling across the aisle.

Karen looked at him with a smile that was equal parts predatory and friendly.

"You know it's not too late to settle," said Donny, momentarily convincing himself that he believed it.

Karen laughed. "Not if you'll take five figures." That would be enough to cover what most people made in a year, but less than Karen's client was paying her every month, and a tiny fraction of what would be fair.

"What a chickenshit way to try to get rid of this case. You know what really went down here."

"Spare me the lecture, Donny. It was war. And we all agreed to make it part of the past. Hell, you defended some of the worst so-called war criminals."

"*The* worst. But that was different, and you know it," said Donny.

"Whatever," said Karen. "I'm not the one trying to profit from the dead. If you'll excuse me, I am going to take my clients over to Bullion for a celebratory lunch."

"Steaks paid for by the dead."

"Fuck off, Donny. There's plenty of that to go around and you know it."

"I'm not kidding about settlement. You heard what I got on the record today. There's more of that to come. A lot more. If you wait, it will be too late."

She laughed in his face. She had Donny—and his case—nailed, like a frog pinned to the dissection table.

As he watched them leave, he tried to convince himself there was a way out. Instead, he felt the floor disappear under his feet as he stood to gather his papers. The win-lose extremes of litigation always put high mileage on the souls of the lawyers. Especially a lawyer like Donny, who was both emotionally and financially invested in the outcome. But bad verdicts from runaway juries and adverse rulings from mercurial judges were to be expected. This was like going to the doctor for your annual physical and finding out you're already dead.

He looked at his files spread out there on the table. He had been so proud of what he had pulled together on this, a clear chronology that fleshed out his theory of the case and was actually supported by evidence he could show the company had been trying to suppress. Now it just looked like crazy man stuff, all his outlines and charts and sticky note palimpsests that theorized a lot but proved nothing.

He picked the death certificate back up, but couldn't stomach looking at it again, and just shoved it in his bag with the rest of the files, only barely resisting his urge to toss it all in the government-issue trash bin.

He needed to get back to the sanctuary of his office and regroup. But first he had to get past the blogger from *Detention Watch*, who was waiting for him outside the courtroom.

"Hello, Sarah," he said.

"Donny, can I ask you a couple of questions?"

"Sure," said Donny, stopping there in the hallway by the sign that listed the day's docket, and trying to summon his composure as he thought how to frame it. Sarah's readership was small, but sometimes her content got picked up by others.

"That was wild," said Sarah. "I for sure didn't see that coming."

"You heard the testimony that witness gave, right?" said Donny.

"Yes, that was some really scary stuff."

"It was more than scary. And it's just the tip of the iceberg. You should be asking them the questions. See if they can explain that away. We need to keep the pressure on. The truth will out."

"Yeah, but what about your client?"

"Daryl Harrison earned the nickname Slider for a reason," said Donny, summoning the inner spin doctor he had developed handling political trials. "During the long dark years when he was a valued member of the resistance that finally liberated this country from the tyrant and his enablers, they could never catch him. Not with drones, or undercover agents, or tracking devices, or dogs. News of his demise has come before, and every time he turns back up. I expect to be able to prove that what AMR pulled this morning is just another trick in their years-long cover-up. If Daryl is really dead, you can bet the murderers of his parents killed him. But what you can be certain of is that next Friday he will be back here with me, in person or in spirit, to hold AMR to account for their role in the murder of innocent citizens whose only crime was to hold contrary political opinions. I hope you will be here too. Now, if you'll excuse me, I need to go get to work."

It was good bullshit. So good that it rallied his own morale. Not so much that he actually believed it, but enough that he thought there had to be some way he could salvage the case. He walked toward the stairs with fresh determination.

Only to be stopped again, by another verbal shirt-tugging.

"Mr. Kimoe!" said a man's voice calling from behind him. The guy had a foreign accent.

Donny pretended not to hear, striding forward. Then it repeated, louder.

Donny glanced over his shoulder. It was the guy with the architect glasses. The woman was with him.

The guy was flashing some kind of ID. The law-enforcement kind, with one of those hologram badges that seems to flicker in the light like a handheld semaphore.

Donny pretended not to see or hear them. He ducked into

the stairwell marked FIRE EXIT, and ditched them. He had seen a couple of Dallas County deputies pop through that door the month before, and was relieved the alarm was still busted—another piece of broken government infrastructure that would probably never be repaired, just like the surveillance cameras that still hung from all the streetlamps even though their network connection had been severed at the hub.

He didn't know what the Eurocops wanted, but it probably wasn't good, and he definitely didn't have time for it. The sound of his beat-up wingtips echoing off the old concrete floors as he found his way to the street made him feel like a fugitive.

The feeling was unexpectedly liberating.

3

DONNY'S DALLAS OFFICE WAS HALFWAY BETWEEN THE COURT-
house and the jail, in a beat-up old strip mall that also housed
a combination liquor store and secondhand electronics shop.
Donny had taken down the big "Law Office" sign he'd inherited from the prior tenant, a local criminal-defense lawyer
who got tired of losing to the government and retired early to
Costa Rica, so now the front of the building was dominated
by the sign for the business next door, the name CRAZY RIVER
in big, red, illuminated caps. The name was not as crazy as
it sounded, because right there on the other side of the jail
flowed the Trinity, which had always been a crazy river, even
crazier now than it used to be, no matter how hard the town
fathers worked to tame it.

Right behind the building was another sort of river, the
overpass where Interstate 35 passed downtown on its route
between Laredo and Duluth. Behind that was Dealey Plaza,
in the shadows of the dome-topped Reunion Tower and the
rest of the Dallas skyline. Dallas was the town that proudly
invented the triple underpass, a city where the freeways came
first. The high-rises where the freeways pretended to end were
the sort that worked hard to fake you, pretending to be the bea-
cons of a promising and prosperous future while they helped
to hide the relics of a more complicated past, and pushed the
poverty and repression of the present into their shadows. Like

the shanties people had built up along the riverbanks, hidden from view by the levees and the jails.

The traffic on the overpass above Donny's office was not what it had been, now that driving your own car was a retro luxury, and the conflicts with Mexico had eliminated most of the Texas truck traffic. But it was still loud. It didn't stop the guy zonked out at Donny's door from sleeping his way through the lunch hour. So Donny decided to let him be, and entered through the back.

The radio was on inside when he opened the door. That alarmed him, until he remembered he had left it on the last time he was up here a few weeks earlier, on the advice of a burglar client who told him that's a good cheap substitute for an alarm. One of the fortunate by-products of the government collapse was that the media controls had collapsed along with it, and now you could tune the dial to any number of eclectic stations operated by microbudgeted indies trying to make a meager buck in the ruins. This one was an alt-classical program, at that moment playing some raging bummer of a baroque guitar solo that sounded like an old man remembering the plague. Donny went to turn it off, but then decided it suited his mood.

He grabbed the pile of mail that had accumulated where the slat dumped it just inside the front door, and took it to his desk. It was junk mail, mostly, the kind of stuff it was hard to believe people still wasted the postage on. Flyers for lawyer seminars on topics like habeas corpus after dictatorship, conflicts of law in times of interstate military conflict, and federalism under the new Constitution that still only existed in draft form—several different drafts, depending on which faction you talked to. There were three of those mailers offering preapproved ways to get out of debt by getting into more debt, two garish pamphlets for antiaging nutritional supplements, and one solicitation from the North Texas Gun Club that came with a stack of return address labels preprinted with Donny's name and business address and a little icon of a black-powder rifle. Donny saved the window sticker, which was one of those things meant to signal some fraternal code to any officer of the law that might pull you over. If only he had a car to put it on.

He sorted the pile there on his already-messy desk, tossing the junk mail to the floor after inspecting whatever looked interesting, and making a new chronological stack of what looked like actual business correspondence. And there at the bottom of that pile, earliest to have been received, was the fine white envelope printed with the letterhead of Polson & Chevalier.

"Suggestion of Death." That about captured how Donny felt as he read it again, and realized how majorly he had fucked up by not having all notices and pleadings sent to his Houston office, which was the one where he actually worked most days, even though his cases were all over the state and sometimes across the country. This office was just a cheap sublet from the prior tenant, who owed Donny for agreeing to take on his cases after he decided to throw in the towel. Donny used it mainly to meet with those clients, and most of those cases had now run their course. This one was his last big one, and the one that would pay his ticket to never have to come to Dallas again. Or that was the idea.

Abogado Harry Martinez Jr. had left Donny his library as well. It was meager, a couple of shelves of basic books, but it did include a current copy of the *Rules of Civil Procedure*. It was sitting there under a gift-shop bust of Socrates, the inventor of mansplaining. Donny pulled that, and reread the rule about what happens when your fucking client gets himself killed and your last chance at real justice and the retirement money you have been busting your ass to make dies with him. You had to read between the lines to get it, but the part that mattered was as clear as anything in the law ever got.

Donny searched his electronic inbox and confirmed he had received the same notice there, even earlier. How he missed that was only partly explained by the even larger volume of unread inbounds that showed up in the queue. Donny wasn't the kind of lawyer who could afford a secretary. And working in a system that had long been broken, he had learned to focus on what seemed to really matter for the clients. Sometimes at their expense, and more often at his own.

The most surprising thing about the news that Slider was dead, before the age of twenty-five, was how little it surprised Donny. The kid was a battle-hardened revolutionary who had processed his anger over what happened to his parents by taking up arms against the state. And he had been an effective one, a wannabe Robin Hood whose actions during the resistance and uprising got their share of public attention. He also earned more than his share of enemies, even among his supposed comrades. That was something he and Donny had in common. But more than anything, Slider was a risk-taker, reckless with his own life, and the idea that he had lost it on the job was entirely plausible. So much so that Donny had considered the risk when he first put the case together, convincing himself that he would quickly be able to identify other disappeareds and build up his class action to insure against that risk.

That calculation had not factored in Donny's failure to adhere to basic business hygiene like checking your mail and keeping up your docket. He had let a simple delaying strategy by the defense ripen into a fatal trap. He had a week to try to come up with a way to slash his way out, but there was no obvious way to do it. It would have to start with trying to find the full story.

He grabbed his bag and found his Swissfōn, the mobile device he had to keep in his briefcase because it was too big for his pockets. The phone he'd had to get one of his former clients to help him sneak into the country, a baggage handler in Houston whom Donny had helped get a commutation for a crate of more lethal contraband he had leapfrogged past customs. They claimed the official surveillance was a thing of the past, and the phone was legal now, and could even be registered with the network without having to pay way too much to a crazy ex-BellNet guy to mask it behind an alias. Now and before, it was designed to be surveillance-free, protected by military-grade encryption, active countermeasures, and guaranteed no back doors. It was also, as a consequence, huge and ugly. The first time his grandma saw him pull it out when he visited her, she busted a gut, and made a crack about shoe phones.

The shoe phone had saved his ass more than a few times over the past few years, and he was not going to give it up that easily. Maybe it could save his ass again.

The number he needed to call was one of the first ones he had programmed into it—the number for one of his oldest clients, which was really an alias for whatever forwarded line she was using at the time.

Xelina wasn't there, and the message he left was brief.

It's Donny. Call me. It's about Slider.

He had an urge to call Slider, just to shake his last bit of disbelief, but Slider didn't do phones when he was alive. Said they were the ultimate tracers. Even the blackphones like Donny had.

He went online, looking for news about the events Karen had described in her ambush that morning. It took him a while to figure out where and how to find it. Information channels were tricky in those days. Through platform standards and censorship both soft and hard, the prior regime had mostly managed to turn the media into several hundred versions of the same channel, most of it propaganda, even when it was propaganda disguised as sports, or sitcoms, or nature shows. When it died, the atrophied remains of what had once been a vigorous free press had trouble filling the vacuum. Especially since they no longer had a viable way to pay the bills. Most of the myriad factions pushing their agendas for what the new regime should look like had media organs they used to spin their take, and there were a handful of wire services that still cobbled together updates. Beyond that, it was like the radio stations—a lot of irregularly programmed and often eccentric perspectives. So mostly you had to go to the foreign sources for the real news, assuming you could cough up the digital snow-flakes to get through the paywall.

What was most annoying to Donny was that, when he finally found a solid recap of the story Karen had spun, it was on *Detention Watch*. No wonder Sarah had shown up. She already knew.

Heiress Arrested by New Orleans Justice Tribunal
Casualties on Both Sides as Firefight
Precedes Extraterritorial Seizure

Dallas, Feb. 3—Texas heiress Heather Hamilton-Green was seized tonight from her family home by paramilitary deputies of the Free City of New Orleans, who claim Hamilton-Green and HG Enterprises are responsible for damage to the environment there and must be prosecuted before their new truth and reconciliation tribunal. This is the third such arrest by agents of the People's Council of persons residing outside of their jurisdiction, in states that do not recognize their legal authority, and the first such arrest in which the deputies faced armed resistance. It follows a series of burglaries from corporate offices around the region, including at HG affiliates Promethean Resources and Tripto Labs. Three are reported dead.

The raid occurred in the predawn hours in the Highland Park neighborhood. The deputies managed to breach the security of the family compound where Hamilton-Green, an investor and activist, was staying for the holidays. Private security forces in the family's employ were caught off guard, but managed to put up a fight. One of the deputies was killed, along with two of the guards, but the mission was successful and Hamilton-Green is now reported to be in custody in New Orleans.

Since the signing of the Interstate Compact for the Cessation of Hostilities, New Orleans has been occupied by the demilitarized remnants of the Popular Front, the guerrilla band that originally formed during the federal occupation of the city under the Mack regime, and later coalesced into one of the forces that led the uprising that ultimately removed President Mack from power. The Compact gave New Orleans a measure of independent governance that has allowed it to serve as a foothold for efforts to undo some of the strictures of the Compact, and last fall the government there established a new truth and reconciliation tribunal for the declared purpose of holding accountable "not just the current generation of criminals and klepts, but all the generations that came before them and stole the fortunes their heirs are now hoarding." The arrests are among the first judicial acts of this new body, which has announced its plans to begin its first trials as soon as April.

The family of Ms. Hamilton-Green could not be reached for comment.

Donny was pretty sure he could reach the family of Ms. Hamilton-Green, because he knew them. Her father, Lou, had been one of Donny's closest friends, a former colleague who had stayed on to become a star partner at the firm where they both started their careers. Politics got in the way of their friendship, as it began to take over their lives, each of them on opposite sides of the conflict that consumed the country.

Donny knew the daughter too. Not as well. But the things he knew about her made the pieces of the story that was now coming together seem incongruous.

Donny went to find the documents Karen had proffered that morning, but was interrupted by a loud knock on his front door. He got up, expecting to see the guy who had been sleeping there.

Instead, he found the detectives who had been hounding him outside the courtroom that morning.

"CAN I HELP YOU?" SAID DONNY.

"I'm Inspector Blonk," said the guy, holding up his badge. When the light hit it, you could see the lenticular of the agency logo layered over the identifying info, a ring of stars in a blue field with a tiny map of the world. "This is Deputy Commissioner Abboud. We are with Interpol."

Donny looked up at the guy when he said that. Blonk was tall, a few sizes taller than Donny, more than a few years younger, and a good bit whiter. His English was almost perfect, but you could hear the waffles in the vowels.

"Interpol?" said Donny. "Does that even still exist?"

Donny didn't leave the country much. For most of the last decade, it had been illegal to do so without a special visa.

"Oh, yes," said Deputy Commissioner Abboud, in crisp but French-accented English. She was shorter than Donny, and darker. Closer to Donny's age, with the years in her eyes. "More than ever."

"We would like to ask you some questions," said Inspector Blonk.

"About what?" said Donny. He looked at his watch, as if he had somewhere to go.

"We are detailed to the UN Office of the Special Rapporteur for Extrajudicial Executions," said Blonk.

"The what?"

"We investigate war crimes," said Abboud.

"Excellent," said Donny, realizing how much he meant that, excited and relieved at the possibility of some help with his case from real investigators with real resources. "Come on in."

He took them to the conference room. It was small and messy, but not as messy as his office. He grabbed the files he had spread out on the table and set them atop one of the stacks of file boxes along the wall. There was one piece of art hanging there, a black-and-white photo of a man in nineteenth-century clothing standing by a wooden bridge with a big hammer in his hands and a funny-looking cowboy hat on his head.

"That is Victor Considerant," said Abboud, pointing at the photo. "The Frenchman."

"How did you know?"

"There was a little exhibit about him in the hotel. Very interesting bit of local history."

"He was on to something," said Donny. "Some days I like to imagine if the Dallas he had tried to build had become real."

"It was real, for a while, from what I read," said Abboud.

"Not for long," said Donny. "Dallas is about as far from a socialist utopia as you can get."

"Yes, well, utopia does not exist," said Abboud. "Because people are thieves at heart. Or you and we would not be able to make a living."

"They're making a pretty good run at it in New Orleans," said Donny.

"You think so?" said Abboud. "They may be good at the rewilding, but their justice system is a step backwards if you ask me."

"That's partly my fault. I used to work with them, and helped them come up with the basic outline for their new code.

But we had a falling-out, and they took it in their own direction."

"They share your American proclivity for violence, and that will be their undoing, just as it was for the prior regime."

"You may be right," said Donny. "And I assume the violence of the prior regime is why you were in the courtroom today. If you are looking for some of the information I have pulled together about these atrocities, I'd love to share it with you, and I bet you have some information I don't. With your investigative resources, we could really up our game, maybe even expand the scope."

They looked at the boxes piled up around the room, all labeled in black marker with the name of the case, the year in which the files were compiled, and other identifying scribbles. Then they looked at each other before Abboud looked back at Donny and spoke.

"Yes, well, that is an intriguing project, and one that may be of interest to our commissioners, but that is not what we wish to speak with you about."

"Oh," said Donny.

"We are investigating the death of President Mack."

Donny sat back, trying to process that.

"We have learned you were on the team of lawyers that defended him after his arrest by the new government."

"Calling them a government is generous," said Donny. "And I only helped with the sentencing." Admitting that out loud still made him blush with shame, even as he knew he had done the right thing.

"We understand," said Abboud. "Very honorable of you, to fight against the death penalty even when the defendant is someone who has killed your friends."

"Tell that to my other friends," said Donny. He didn't mention that he had also lost family to the regime. "That's why they kicked me out of New Orleans."

"Well, he got the death penalty anyway," said Blonk.

"No," said Donny. "He got life. Several life sentences, in fact. We won that. But then he was murdered."

"He was assassinated," said Blonk. "When he was to be delivered into our agency's custody to be prosecuted for his crimes against humanity."

"So I heard," said Donny. "And I really wish that hadn't happened. Because we needed that trial. Our own prosecution was too hamstrung by our broken politics, and people's desire to 'move forward.'"

"Is that why you helped them kill him?" said Abboud.

"*What?*" said Donny.

He looked at them. You could see they meant it.

"That's nuttier than French socialists in Dallas," he said.

Abboud smiled.

"Maybe even nuttier than these people who say he's still alive, tanning on some faraway beach," added Donny. "Waiting for his comeback. I saw them kill him, just like you did. And when it happened, I was a thousand miles away in Houston, working. What are you suggesting?"

"Well, we are not suggesting you are a hit man," said Abboud. "We have been investigating this for close to a year now. And we have good information that there was a team of assassins sent by the Popular Front. A group which you already acknowledged you have been associated with in the past."

"The Popular Front never really existed as more than a name," said Donny. "That's like talking about a bunch of competing gangs and calling them the Mafia. And to the extent the factions had an alliance, it broke up after the uprising petered out."

"Maybe," said Abboud. "What we know is your client was on the team."

"What client?"

"Daryl Harrison."

"Slider?" said Donny. "That's why you came to the courthouse today? That's preposterous."

It wasn't preposterous. Donny just had never considered the possibility.

"Is it?" said Blonk, clearly thinking what Donny was already coming around to. "The man was a hardened guerrilla, a veteran of the fighting in New Orleans, and a committed ideologue. He had already done several 'special missions' for the Front's leadership during the years of resistance. And now he has been killed on a very similar mission for the People's Council, most of whom came from the Front."

"What do you want from me?" said Donny. "I kind of have my hands full, as you may have noticed at the courthouse this morning. And I have nothing to do with any of this."

"Who else knew about the plans for the prisoner transfer, and was also in contact with Harrison and others in the movement?"

"Oh, come on," said Donny, trying to convey the most dismissive possible expression.

"You look a little squirmy," said Abboud. The way she said the last word, with that accent, made him actually squirm.

"I know how to keep my clients' secrets," said Donny.

"You met with Harrison a week before the assassination," said Blonk. "Are you sure you didn't talk about the president's case?"

"How do you know my calendar?" said Donny. "Never mind—I don't even think that timeline's right."

"Oh, it's right," said Abboud. "We have our sources. We just want you to be one of them. Come clean with us about Daryl and whoever else in your network as counselor to the revolution you told about this. And we, in turn, will be able to avoid having to treat you as a co-conspirator."

"You're fishing in the wrong hole, Deputy Commissioner," said Donny. "That's a fascinating theory, but it's fiction. And even if there were truth to it, you'd be out of your jurisdiction. I suppose you could report it to the feds, but they have their hands full trying to keep the country from falling apart. Did you hear they're starting to auction military equipment off to corporations and NGOs?"

"All the more reason why we need to step in to fill the vacuum," said Abboud. "And we do have jurisdiction, by treaty and international law, over what was an incident involving our prisoner. I can send you the authorities if you don't believe me."

Donny didn't need to look it up, because he realized it was true the moment she said it.

"That won't be necessary," he said. "Because I'm not your leaker. Now, speaking of missing bodies, I need to go find Mr. Harrison. And when I do, you can talk to him yourself."

"Good luck with that," said Abboud. She stood to leave. "Here is where you can contact us if you remember anything you think we might be interested to hear. It would be much easier if you would tell us anything you know now, rather than having us find out through other sources that you haven't been truthful."

When Abboud smiled as she handed him her business card, Donny realized that she was probably the type who could get him to say whatever she wanted, given the right interrogation setup.

But that would never happen. Because Donny was pretty sure that the people who could pin him for what they were sniffing out were either dead or in a place where no Eurocop will ever find them.

5

DONNY WENT THROUGH HIS CALENDAR, TRYING TO PIECE IT TO-
gether.

Donny was probably the last lawyer left in America who kept his calendar on paper. It was a habit he had formed during the prior administration, when he was working the secret cases, representing people under government surveillance. He had learned the hard way that the federal agents fighting what they viewed as a revolutionary insurgency did not let attorney-client privilege get in the way. And the judges backed them up, most of the time. That meant anything you recorded in digital form on a device connected to the network was likely to be caught in the net. And they even had ways of getting into devices that were off-network. So Donny carried a hardbound daily calendar just like his grandma used to. They could search that, too, if they wanted to harass him in person—something they often did. What they couldn't do was make him write legibly. And it would take a lot more than some Motherland men in black to get him to read his own handwriting. Assuming he could if he tried. The legibility of his own scrawl had a rapidly diminishing half-life even to its author, such that the older the entry the harder it was for him to fill in the gaps.

That worked great, until he found himself needing to dig into last year's calendar and put together a chronology of his meetings with Slider.

Normally, he would have billing records to help him. But

Slider's case was on a contingent fee, meaning he didn't need to generate a bill, at least not at this stage of the case. So all he had were his chicken scratches.

He looked at the case file, to find the documents the client had had to sign.

Putting all that together, he realized the last time he had met with Slider was almost a year earlier, when they were in the initial stages of drafting their pleadings in this case they called *Harrison II*. Donny dug through the file and found his hand-written notes from that meeting. They were high-level, because he hadn't needed much information from Slider, but looking at those and the documents Slider had signed helped him remember quite well the discussion they had had.

SLIDER REFUSED TO meet Donny at his office, which was a pain in the ass. Getting around Houston had been bad enough under martial law. Now, even though the checkpoints were gone, the damage from heavy weather and sometimes heavier fighting meant so many streets were closed and sections of town blocked off that most trips took twice as long as they used to, if not longer. Luckily Donny had managed to get himself loaned a pretty nice bicycle from one of his clients, a courier for the underground who had been locked up for information smuggling and was free now but trying to get his record expunged. Donny hadn't ridden it much, but he did that day, when he decoded Slider's message and saw where he wanted to meet. He never would have thought riding a bicycle would be the fastest way to get around Houston, or that doing so wearing a suit would improve his mood. He wished he had the time and the knees to take his old skateboard.

Slider had never been willing to come to a law office, unless it was the only path to liberty. So instead, Donny always said why don't I come to your place. It was only after they had been working together awhile that Donny realized Slider didn't *have* a place. He just couch-surfed. Stayed with people in his network. A habit he had developed when he was a wanted man. Sometimes he stayed outside, something he had done as an intermittently homeless kid after his parents were arrested and disappeared, and before he got connected with the Front.

The directions took Donny to a little bungalow just south of downtown, in a spot near a paved stretch of bayou. Donny knew that area because he had fished it after the floods a few times, and seen you could ride it like a Veloway when the water was down. And that day there was just a trickle, though that didn't stop the overflying geese from following its path north.

The house looked almost abandoned, with a lawn gone wild, the way Rovers liked to keep it, and all the windows blocked with heavy curtains, which was also how they liked to keep it. But the mastodon was there stenciled on the doorjamb. And when you walked up onto the porch, you could see signs that people had been hanging out recently—a saggy old couch, an old crate turned into a stool, empty beer cans, two burned-down candles, a book that had been set down open to save the page. Donny looked and saw it was a copy of Brigada's prison notebooks, another sure sign of a Rover.

The door opened before Donny even knocked.

"Can I help you?" The woman standing there was young and black, probably mid-twenties, big braids pulled back in a bright-red band, wearing a plain black T-shirt, blue jeans, and boots. The jeans were held up with a thick black belt, and tucked into them was a handgun she made no effort to hide. Among the liberties the change in government had secured was to make Texas an open-carry state again, now that the federal firearms controls that restricted ownership to licensed militias, deputized posses, and registered hunters had been suspended. The international peacekeepers had tried to impose their own ban, but it didn't stick in Texas.

"I'm looking for Slider," said Donny. "Name's Donny Kimoe."

"Yeah, I recognize you," said the woman. "You're the lawyer who switched sides. And I can see now you look the part."

"We all have a job to do," said Donny. "And I never switched sides."

"Whatever," she said. "He said to let you in, and you wouldn't stay long." She ushered Donny through. "Hey, Slider!" she yelled back into the house as she triple-bolted the door behind them.

The living room was simple and bare, like a furnished apartment. Nothing on the walls but a beat-up old poster of Maxine Price screaming to a crowd, and ancient wallpaper fading from green to brown.

Slider stepped out of the shadow of the hallway. He moved like an athlete, or an actor, or both, with a healthy dose of moody teen. And he looked like a rock star. Lithe but strong, wearing his revolutionary couture—tight jeans, some crazy patterned vintage dress shirt, a leather necklace strung with shiny little totems of his war and roams, and lace-up leather boots that looked like something a British officer would have worn in a colonial war in some other timeline. And those green eyes on brown skin working its way to black, with inky hair just long enough that it always looked like he just got out of bed, or was ready to take you there.

"Hey," said Slider, friendly enough in his gaze when their eyes met. Donny liked to think he had earned Slider's trust after successfully helping him out of a few jams, yet every time they met, he could never be sure.

"Holler if you need me," said the woman. "I'll be in the shed."

Slider nodded.

"Can we sit?" said Donny.

Slider nodded again, in the direction of the living-room furniture. Slider took the armchair, and left Donny the love-seat, which tried to swallow him when he sat in it.

Slider laughed.

"For my next trick I will step right onto the trapdoor," said Donny.

"We actually have one," said Slider. "This safe house has a basement."

"Really," said Donny. "Doesn't sound like such a great idea here in the city of underwater freeways."

"Yeah," said Slider. "That's what I thought, but this spot is pretty high and dry. Not much of a basement, just kind of a rough cellar, but a good place to cache stuff."

"What do you keep down there?"

"Better if I don't tell you," said Slider. "Even if you are my lawyer."

"Maybe your lawyer isn't even sure he wants to know why you still need a safe house. The fighting is over, in case you missed the memo. You won."

"That's a matter of opinion," said Slider.

"How so? We were both there, when the people took over Washington."

Slider nodded. "Yeah, and that was awesome. But just the beginning."

"I hear you," said Donny. "We still need to work out what the new Constitution is going to look like—"

Slider rolled his eyes like Donny didn't get it.

"That kind of thing takes a while," said Donny. "Especially

when you want to make sure executive power is never concentrated in the hands of a single individual ever again."

"Man, I thought you were smarter than that," said Slider. "The change we need is so much more radical than what any of those do-gooder dorks think. The only ones who half get it are in New Orleans, and even they don't have the balls to take it far enough."

"Your parents would have been pretty happy with it," said Donny.

"What do you know about what my parents wanted? Give me a fucking break."

"Maybe you're right. I've just been reading up on their work. Watched some old interviews, found their manifesto. I feel like their ideas helped us get here. And I think I've figured out a way to get justice for what happened."

"You mean lawyer justice? For what they did to my parents? The amnesty deal your friends in Washington cooked up is what that is. Fucking nada, sorry, thanks for playing. In case you didn't get that memo. That's what killed the case your buddy Miles Powell tried after he gave me the same speech."

"I know. I helped Miles and Percy with that case."

"I miss Percy being my lawyer."

"I don't blame you. She's the best. Maybe even better than Miles. But maybe I *should* blame you, because from what she told me you had a big part in converting her into a true believer. You and my ex-girlfriend. Do you still see her?"

"I see both of them. Percy more than Joyce. And I didn't have anything to do with Percy quitting her job and moving to New Orleans. She did that when she heard Joyce was back in-country, helping to reboot the project."

"Say hi for me next time."

"Yeah, maybe not. You're not so popular there, Donny."

Donny nodded. He didn't like to acknowledge it.

"But I did talk to Percy about the case. She said it's a waste of time. That they all got amnesty."

"She doesn't know the facts I have."

"Oh yeah?" said Slider, reddening a bit. "You gonna be my white knight now?"

"Come on," said Donny. "You don't have to like me, but I'm here to finish what we started, and make them pay. I got a new source. A good one. Inside the company. I think I can expose the whole thing."

Slider's demeanor shifted. He was more interested now.

"I got the names of the guys who did it," said Donny. "I can put all the facts together when I file the lawsuit."

"Bullshit," said Slider.

"You don't believe me?" said Donny. "Hang on."

He opened his briefcase, pulled out his working file on the case, found the page with those notes, and showed it to Slider.

"Is that shorthand or something?"

"No, just shitty handwriting. They're right here." Donny put his figure right on the three names, and read them aloud to Slider:

Gannon

Peña

Lee.

Slider listened, and stared at the paper for a long moment, like he was recording it. Then he looked Donny in the eyes.

"You for real?"

"Absolutely," said Donny.

"Who's the source?"

"Can't tell you," said Donny. "Just like you can't tell me what's in the basement."

"Where are these guards?" he asked, pointing at Donny's scribbles.

"Two guards, one driver," said Donny. "And the answer is, I don't know yet. But I'm going to find out. First, I want to get this case on file. If we wait much longer we could have a statute-of-limitations issue. We're coming up on the five-year anniversary, and if we miss that they can bounce the whole thing."

"Okay," said Slider. "But what about the amnesty?"

"That's the thing—I don't think it applies on these facts. Your parents were pranksters, not fighters. And with these names, we can put together the real story. Of the real reason they killed your parents, and a lot of other people who got disappeared for their politics."

"You gonna be able to put them away?"

"No," said Donny. "I can't do that. That's up to the prosecutors. Most of whom can barely keep up with the dockets they have, and don't want anything to do with war-crimes cases. In Washington they're talking about giving *all* these guys amnesty."

"I heard about that, man. What bullshit."

"Well, the good news is that bullshit would apply to you too. At least for stuff you did fighting the government. Not to suggest you committed any crimes, of course."

Slider smiled, which was kind of creepy.

"We might be able to feed the information to the international courts," continued Donny. "See if they will pursue war-crimes charges. But there are other kinds of justice. When I say make them pay, I mean make them pay. With money. Lots of it."

"What kind of money do prison guards and bus drivers have?"

"Not their money. The company's money. We just have to show the company was in on the whole program."

"So the dudes who actually did the deed walk."

"We can bankrupt them too, but that's not really the point."

"Your system sucks," said Slider.

"I agree," said Donny. "But I'm making the best of what we've got."

"How much money are we talking?"

"Seven figures, I think," said Donny. "Maybe more. Definitely more if we can really build the case for a whole class of people they disappeared. There are hundreds of cases. Some say thousands."

"That's a lot of money," said Slider.

Donny nodded.

"How much do you get?" said Slider. He could do the math.

"Just a third. Assuming the judge signs off."

"*Just* a third?"

"A lot of lawyers would take half," said Donny. "Understand: I only get paid if I win. And I will have to invest a lot in the case to do that. The risk is all mine."

"I'm the one who has to put his name on there as suing these guys." He pointed at the draft pleadings Donny had pulled out and left on the coffee table.

"We both have to put our names on it," said Donny. "And I'm the one who has to sign the actual lawsuit. I know these are dangerous people we are taking on. The last lawyer who sued these guys ended up dead. You just need to sign this letter appointing me as your lawyer. If you want, I can even file with you as a John Doe, and keep your name out of it for now. But you never seemed the type who scares easily. Especially when it comes to seeking justice for what happened to your parents."

Donny pushed the document over to Slider, open to the flagged signature block, and held out a pen.

Slider looked at the document, then looked at Donny. Then he took the pen.

"You can put my name on it," said Slider, grabbing the document and signing it. "Just don't fuck this up, man."

"I promise you," said Donny. "I'm going to win this."

Donny knew better than to make promises. But he meant it.

"I hope so," said Slider. "And at least you'll be on the right side on this one. Fighting the killers instead of helping them."

This was two weeks after the ex-president's sentencing.

"I guess everybody heard about that. Even the people like you who don't have phones or TVs."

"You definitely got people talking with that gig," said Slider. "People are pissed."

"How about you?"

"I guess I know you too well. You gave me enough lectures about how you didn't want to have to defend me against the death penalty that I know you really mean it."

"Thanks," said Donny. "He got what he deserved. And now he's going to face the international war-crimes tribunal."

"Yeah, screw that. What do those people in Switzerland or India know about what he did? We need to take care of that shit right here."

"It's how it needs to work," said Donny. "We need a global system. Rules for everyone on the planet to follow. How else are we going to build a future people can live in?"

"Fuck people. The animals and plants will be fine without us."

"I don't think it's that bad yet."

"Maybe not down in your fancy office. I mean offices."

"There's nothing about my offices anyone would call 'fancy.'

And besides, they kicked me out of my New Orleans digs. The radicals are seizing power."

"So I heard. They're even more pissed about what you did than I am."

"Makes sense you'd know." Digging, he said, "You're probably in on the takeover."

"Well, your ex-girlfriend definitely is. She's hardcore, man, even if she just says she's our mentor, not our leader. But yeah, I'm all-in on that program. It's our turn. Time for a new generation. And a new idea of liberation. One that starts with the creatures that don't have a voice. You want rules for the whole planet? Wait till we get done."

"Good luck with that," said Donny.

"My luck's going to improve if you can really win me that kind of money. I could do a lot of good with that. When are you going to file it?"

"Soon," said Donny. "Hopefully first thing Monday."

"They don't need you back in Washington?"

"No," said Donny. "They're done with me, and El Presidente's case is done. Our part, at least. They're getting ready to transfer him to UN custody for the international case."

"Oh yeah? When?"

"A week from Friday," said Donny. "But you didn't hear that from me."

Slider pulled an invisible zipper across his lips.

"Seriously," said Donny.

"Relax," said Slider. Then he looked to the door at the sound of footsteps on the porch.

Donny turned. The door opened, and a young blond woman stepped in.

"Hey, baby," said Slider.

The woman was looking at Donny, her poker face not quite containing her surprise.

It took a minute for Donny to realize who she was. The last time he had seen her, she was still in school.

"Hello, Heather," he said. "How's your dad?"

DONNY HAD BEEN AROUND HEATHER A FEW TIMES OVER THE years. The one he remembered best was a dinner party Donny and his then-girlfriend Joyce had attended at the home of Heather's parents, Donny's old colleague Lou and his wife, Helen.

On the golf course and at the bar, they used to only half-jokingly ask Lou why in the hell he was still billing 2,300 hours a year when he was married to one of the richest women in Texas. His replies were always half-true, you could tell.

She makes me.

I love what I do.

I need to get out of the house.

I love the view from my office.

I need to model a good work ethic for my daughter.

Only their closest friends knew that Heather had an older brother, a boy whose name no one said anymore, because he had died as a toddler. It happened when Lou and Helen were out entertaining a client, and the kid was home with the nanny. The boy drowned in the pool. There was even some suspicion that it was not an accident, that the eccentric English nanny was crazier than the background check had revealed. Lou and Helen decided to channel their grief into the joy of a new kid, and making sure nothing bad ever happened to her.

Some kids are born with a silver spoon. Heather was born with a trust in her name worth more than $10 million. And when her mother's life was taken, she became a billionaire, if you counted all of the family holdings that traced back to her through the labyrinth of shell companies the corporate lawyers hid it in. The money that went into her trust upon the probate of her mother's estate was old money, money that had been hard-coded before World War II by different lawyers—ones with white shirts under three-piece, three-button suits and wire-framed glasses—to never leave the lineal descendants of the man who first earned it. Even Lou couldn't touch it.

Now we know why you still practice law when you could be playing tennis all day, they teased Lou, when he first told them that he was the only dude they knew who had to sign a prenup.

Heather had it all, and then some. More than money. She had the constant, unconditional love and support of two exceptionally well-educated parents, each with their own vibrant careers, Dad as a litigator and Mom as a professional investor, a rare woman at the top of the venture-capital business who helped ignite the biotech boom that was one of the bright spots in an otherwise war-worn economy. Heather was beautiful, in a stereotypically American way, a naturally blond and blue-eyed icon of Western white femininity, and also in a more classic way—chiseled and international, with her natural looks enhanced by the kind of grooming, wardrobe, and diet that privilege affords. Every time Donny had seen her, she had that sort of rich-girl tan that reminded him of a perfectly browned marshmallow. Maybe because she was outside so much. She was a great athlete, on the soccer and tennis teams, winning second in the girls' singles at the state tournament her senior year in high school. The boys loved her, though most were also secretly afraid of her, which was fine with her. The girls loved her too, and mostly envied her.

One of the other girls was with her the night of the dinner party. A friend you could tell was something more, a dark-haired French exchange student who was on the soccer team with Heather. They showed up just in time for dessert, which was served by another French-speaker, the Haitian chef named Aimée whom Helen had hired as the guest worker in charge of her kitchen. They lit up the room with the glow of health, very fine edibles, and the sacred sex of pure-strain teenagers. Heather already knew who all the guests were, greeted each in turn, introduced Chantal, and produced two more chairs when Dad invited them. They talked about the game that day, Dad bragging about the goal Heather scored and Heather bragging about Chantal's assist. Lou opened some fancy German dessert wine that tasted like grapes that had been preserved in Alpine ice from an epoch before air pollution, maybe even before cities. His guests soaked up that libation somehow less enthusiastically than the vibrantly red-blooded youth—like vampires, Donny had thought, even as he himself indulged— but you could tell Heather was in charge, and controlling the dose.

When Aimée came out of the kitchen with the insane torte she had made, like something you would see on one of those baking shows Joyce liked to binge, Heather put her own cherry on the evening by breaking out the French, which she had learned in school and polished in her own junior year abroad, as the kind of girl who could afford to learn a mostly useless and now politically suspect language. Heather, Aimée, and Chantal got going in a long aside that no one else in the room understood. Or so they thought, until Joyce dialed in, the lady who spent her Saturday mornings reading obscure works of Continental theory in the original. The way Joyce said it sounded like cranky snark, but it got Heather, Chantal, and

Aimée laughing so hard that everyone wanted to know what the joke was.

"It's a secret," said Heather, looking right at Joyce.

Joyce nodded and smiled, and changed the subject by complimenting Helen and Lou on their parenting skills.

On the way home, Donny asked Joyce what they had talked about.

Joyce explained that they were talking about the Haitian revolution. Not the one that had happened two years earlier, inciting the US invasion and occupation, but the one that happened two centuries before, when Haiti was a French colony. The revolt in which the slaves killed their masters and took over the whole country.

So what was the joke?

Heather was asking Aimée if she could help her secure her own freedom. Freedom from her indenture.

Doesn't sound very funny to me.

I know, but it was the way Heather said it. Funny, liberating, and a little bit sexy.

So what did you say?

Something about wanting to be free from men. Except I said it in a more vulgar and meaty way.

Teach me.

It means something like bag of dicks, but as big as the world.

DONNY REMEMBERED THE INTERACTION A YEAR EARLIER MORE clearly now.

"My dad?" said Heather as she stood there in the doorway of Slider's safe house.

"He and I used to work together," said Donny. "We met when you were a kid."

"Donny's my lawyer," said Slider. "He got me out of detention, twice. Now he's helping me with my parents' case. He's okay."

Heather looked like she wasn't persuaded.

"Sorry, I don't remember you," she said.

"It's okay," said Donny. "It was a long time ago. And a lot has happened in the intervening years. To all of us."

She nodded, warily. "I don't talk to my dad much anymore," she said. "Politics kind of got in the way."

"Sounds like my family," said Donny, trying to make light of it. But what happened to both of their families wasn't very funny.

"Uh-huh," said Heather.

"I'm sorry about your mom," said Donny.

She didn't answer. She just gave Donny a look.

"I should get going," said Donny.

"Sounds good," said Slider. "We need to get going too."

"Where are you headed?" asked Donny.

"New Orleans," he said. "Back to work for me."

Donny looked at Heather. She didn't need to work. But you could see which side she was on.

INSPECTORS BLONK AND ABBOUD LEFT DONNY ALONE WITH THESE and other thoughts. What he needed to do was start digging through those boxes of research for other plaintiffs who could replace Slider as the anchor of his lawsuit. But instead he found himself replaying the untrustworthy reels of his own memory, wondering what story lines he had missed in his self-absorption.

The idea that Slider had been on a team to kidnap Heather, even if they called it an arrest, was hard to believe. They had tried to downplay it that day when Heather walked in on Donny talking to Slider. But he saw how Slider looked at her. And even if they weren't hooking up, or weren't anymore, the suggestion that they or their leaders treated Heather as an enemy of the people seemed a stretch when you could see where her sympathies lay. Then again, loyalties were mercurial in those days, especially among the radical factions. You never knew what you might do or say that would have your face erased from the class photo. Donny knew. They had erased him from the roster of friends of the revolution, for doing what he thought the same principles that had first compelled him to help those people out required.

Was it really possible that, rather than saving the President from execution, he had sealed his fate by revealing his whereabouts to Slider? The official story, supported by separate reports from both the Secret Service and the Justice Department inspector general, was that the President had been murdered by his own former loyalists—security personnel inside DOJ and the Bureau of Prisons acting on orders from others within what remained of the President's party, to keep him from incriminating them for helping him suppress the opposition and enrich themselves through illegal and often murderous means. It made sense. But so did the idea that the President's former victims would want the punishment Donny and his colleagues had persuaded the court to withhold.

Free of his Interpol guests, Donny logged back in to the research web to see if he could find better answers. Maybe they had been hiding in plain sight all along.

He had his own archived copy of the *Drake Report*, which synthesized the multi-agency investigations into the President's death, and when he pulled it up he found his way into the findings, and then into the labyrinth of footnotes. Hoping to see the concrete foundations for the report's conclusions, he found only provisos and obfuscations, when the details weren't covered up with actual redactions. But they had confessions from two of the guards who had been part of the conspiracy, confessions that had them and one other colleague now serving time in Quantico, the secret prison that the rebels had pledged to close but instead had maintained "temporarily" to house the most dangerous counterrevolutionaries. It was too elaborate and consequential to be a cover story. But there was one other guard who had escaped arrest, and who some sources said was hiding in New Orleans.

Finding no real answers there, Donny turned his attention back to Slider himself. He looked for more reports on the raid in which Slider had been allegedly killed, but there were only squibs with essentially the same information. He sought information about the underlying case against Heather, which was really against the family business holdings. The best material on that was, to Donny's surprise, in the business press, handicapping the seemingly small risk of a financially crippling outcome in the series of cases the people's prosecutors had initiated against them and several other closely held conglomerates. Donny understood the novel legal theories underlying the cases, because he had helped conceive them back when he was still welcome in New Orleans.

That was a deep rabbit hole to go down, and when he finally looked up, it was after five. He had spent the afternoon at the books, and accomplished little other than to make himself hungry and more confused than when he started.

He went next door to Crazy River and grabbed a cricket taco to go. Insects had become a growing part of the American diet, usually processed to remind you of the meat you used to be able to afford. But these were prepared to a recipe older than America, a really good one. And as he sat there at his desk wiping hot sauce from the corners of his mouth, he looked over at Socrates and waited for him to ask the question that would turn the tumblers and solve Donny's problems. But he couldn't think anymore, so he decided to stretch his legs.

He walked across the street and past the jail, which was really a complex of jails, all built up atop the levee that held in the Trinity. It was a very Dallas sort of thing that the river on which the city had been founded, its core geographic and ecological feature, had been engineered into near invisibility. They had channeled it to try to control it, moving it away from downtown. They had shaped the banks into terraced levees so sharply angled you would have mistaken them for pavement were it not for the neatly mowed grass. They had built a dozen bridges and overpasses so no one would ever have to enter that zone. And then they located all the nastiest land uses along the perimeter. Like the jail.

Most of the jail buildings had been built in the last decade to house people rounded up by the prior regime—some for their politics, some for stealing what they needed in a city that operated on the "eat what you kill" ethos of unregulated competition. But one tower had been there since Donny was a kid. Thirteen stories of red dirt brick with castle slat windows behind chain link and concertina. Donny had visited it many times as a lawyer, and he had also spent a night there as an inmate, the summer after his junior year in high school. His dad had used his connections to get the charges dropped and the arrest expunged from Donny's record, which came in handy a decade later when Donny was applying for his law license, but the experience had proven useful.

The cell they put him in for those thirty-six hours had a view of the spot where they had busted him, tagging the support columns of the bridges down there in the floodplain while in possession of a felonious quantity of acid. Dallas acid was a special blend, especially back then, a liberatory concoction designed to turn freeway interchanges into paths of astral travel, taking advantage of the city's love of shine and its surprisingly atemporal way of hiding the past in plain sight to unleash its latent capacity for unicorn sparkle and dimensional distortion. Donny took so much of it that summer that he was pretty sure the residue still kicked in every once in a while, and he was waiting for the day when the portal would open during one of his melancholic twilight saunters and let him step into a more rainbow-based version of the world.

Instead, when he stepped over the levee, he found himself in Rivertown. It wasn't much of a town—it was a long band of shelters built into the grade with desperate ingenuity, a patchwork village made from salvaged materials, most of them timber, trash, and other flotsam left behind by the river at flood stage. It looked like the set from some old western, crossed with the set from one of those movies about life after the end of the world. Donny spotted a trio of teenagers holding sticks over a tire fire, and they looked back at him like you would look at a cop who has walked up to your back porch. Donny wondered how long it would be until the next flood, and if the shantybuilders' guesses as to how high it would flow would prove correct.

Donny remembered when kids like that first started showing up, all those years before. It took a while before people started realizing that what they thought were homeless bums were climate refugees. Refugees from their own country. Often from not far away.

In the early days, there were no FEMA camps or FHA resettlement projects. Just people displaced by a bad situation where they came from in Nebraska, New Orleans, or someplace in between. Crop failures, dead fields, dying towns. Places that used to be wet gone dry as a desert, and places that were always wet now underwater and battered by hurricane winds. And the fires that burned long and hard, all through the year, sometimes scorching off the edges of the big cities.

Donny remembered when he was starting out at the law firm, and the people you would see camped out under the overpasses started to change. The white kids were the real giveaway. Milk-fed and freckled like you'd see in some sitcom from the century before, gone dirty, hungry and gaunt. It got pretty bad like that, until some of them started getting organized. Donny realized now what an ass he'd been for only paying attention when the people suffering looked like him.

Taking people away from the land where their families

have lived for generations turns out to be politically destabilizing. Americans kind of perfected that model. They just never considered the possibility that it would happen to them, in no small part because of how they had abused that land.

It was in the most wasted-out rural corners of the Midwest that the insurgency first brewed. No one even realized that's what it was, when it was just a news report about somebody blowing up a bank or vandalizing the big ag-bots or burning one of the GMO granaries. Not until they started putting out statements to the press, signed with names like the Platte River Posse or the Hawkeye Freedom Network. Donny had never expected that the idea of a Cornhusker could be so scary. But he also knew better than most that it was the government's treatment of restless people as a threat that turned them into bona fide rebels.

Having invented segregation zoning a century before, Dallas quickly restricted the refugees to designated zones, far from the nice parts of town. It had been very effective during the long emergency, when there were legal and martial means to enforce it. But now there was a new wave of displacements in the aftermath of the rebellion. And one of the new nationwide rules was that no one could be prohibited from sleeping on public property as long as they were not impeding some other recognized use. In Dallas, that meant the refugees who refused to live in the camps congregated in the natural areas that the city had otherwise mostly forgotten. And the floodplain of the Trinity River was one of the biggest urban greenbelts in Texas, even if people rarely remembered it was there.

Until they had no choice but to remember it—and remember they didn't like what was happening there.

Donny followed the trail down the bank, scouting the remains of his favorite outlaw skate ramps and spots where he had left graffiti tags back in the day. The columns that held up the Commerce Street overpass were still covered in street art, but it was all new, much of it telling the story of environmental blight and internecine conflict through beautiful pictograms, the kind of street art some kid raised under the big skies of a Kansas farm makes to let her mind fly free after she's been locked up in a Texas refugee camp. He found remnants of the prior batch of shanties here and there, bits of plywood flotsam and shreds of Tyvek in the bare trees that were left behind when the last flood washed most of the shelters away, after the town fathers and their vigilante sons had cleared it with force and fire, saying they were there to save them. While a few newcomers had resettled farther up the banks, the displaced persons were now mostly congregated in two big camps out by DFW, one at a new biofarm and the other in a former shopping mall. And some were getting resettled for real, finally, in the brownout zones that had been partially revitalized, or at least cleaned up enough for people to safely move back in.

Donny continued toward the river, which was so well hidden in its engineered channel that you really could only see it clearly from a plane, unless you had the nerve to walk on one of those bridges that denied the possibility of pedestrians. But it was definitely there, flowing fast over the concrete boulders. The city's founders had the nutty idea that Dallas would be a port city, moving goods up and down the river from where it emptied into the Gulf above Matagorda Bay, but it proved to be navigable only seasonally. Not anymore, now that the volatile weather had regularly filled it with enough water to keep the flow just below what used to be considered flood stage. With air travel and long-haul trucking restricted by the emergency emissions controls finally imposed too late to do any good, there was talk about reviving that idea. An idea so nuts you had to love it. Donny wondered if he was too old to become a ship's captain, or a river pirate, now that he had proved to be such a failure as a plaintiff's lawyer.

As he sat down there on a big chunk of rubble, watching the river run past a calm little pool that had formed, Donny remembered when he used to be able to catch some decent bass in that stretch. He tried to imagine what kind of mutants could survive in there now, but all he found from looking into those dark currents was the suffocating anxiety about his own immediate future.

He tried to let the water take it away, without the aid of Dallas acid, watching time flow, thinking about how ancient the river was and how it will still be flowing after he—and everyone else—was long gone.

Then he noticed movement on the opposite bank. He looked. There was a big green dumpster there, out in the middle of the wide floodplain but not far from the overpass. You could hear the sound of someone hitting the metal from the side. Then he saw who the someone was: three big raccoons, stepping out into the beginning of night. The dumpster was already open on one side, and all three of them peered down into it. Then one dove in while, to Donny's astonishment, another one grabbed its back legs to let it dangle down there. And then pulled his mate out, holding a pizza box.

The amazing thing was, there was only one slice in there, and they shared it.

Donny had filed a lawsuit once trying to protect the nutria of Houston from a countywide program to cull their population. He had a soft spot for urban wildlife, even those big greasy water rats, and he liked the challenge of asserting they had rights. The judge threw the case out at the first hearing, despite Donny's epic briefing, but he refused the county attorney's request for sanctions. At the time, Donny wondered if the case would have better odds if he had picked a more sympathetic animal. Now he wondered if the real trick would be to pick a smarter one. Imagine what would happen if you could win one of those cases.

The sunset was peaking as Donny walked back to the office, lighting up the skyline with an intense swath of pink working on purple. You could see the contrails of the transcontinental jets that still flew the affluent Europeans and Asians above the American flyover, laying their seams in the stratosphere like strands of cotton candy. Even the Reunion Tower looked good in that light, so good you could almost imagine it had been created by the French commies who lived there in the 1850s, instead of the 1970s Chamber of Commerce.

As he got a little farther, Donny could see the old Dallas County Courthouse there in the shadows of the tower. In the crazy light, the red sandstone forms from which it had been carved looked almost alive, even while—at the same time— the building looked like an ancient ruin. You could imagine when it was the biggest and most important building standing there on the banks of the river, as people cleared trees and built roads from what had been raw wilderness just a few generations earlier. That hallucinatory shimmer made you wonder what it would be in the generations to come. After us.

Donny's twilight daydream of sentient raccoons taking over the ruins led to the revelation that to salvage his case he needed to go to New Orleans. The official story about the circumstances of Slider's death didn't add up. He might not be able to get justice for the kid's parents, but he could at least get justice for Slider. And if private-security goons really killed him while he was helping a team of constables, there might be an easy opportunity to make their employer pay. New Orleans was also the one place where Donny knew people who might be able to step into Slider's shoes. And the place where a different idea of the future was taking shape. Maybe even his own future, if he could talk his way back in.

He had something fresh in his step as he walked back to the office, just as the pink in the sky finally went to black, and he noticed the gold BMW parked outside his office. He only knew one guy who had a car like that, and he was the last guy Donny wanted to see.

9

THE CAR WAS A BIG G-SERIES SEDAN, AN ALL-ELECTRIC MODEL that ran on batteries so small the interior was as roomy as a living room. G for green—zero emissions and minimum power despite the maximum size and weight. G for *Gepanzert*, which meant armored, armored like a tank, armored for the conflict-ridden future bequeathed by a heritage in which consideration of our ecological footprint was an afterthought. And G for gold, with the body plates made from ballistic aerospace-grade brass polished to a gleaming shine. The really annoying thing was that you couldn't help but think they were cool, even though they cost a quarter-mil without options. Or even when the sight of it outside your place caused a reflexive panic to run through your nerves.

As Donny sucked it in and tried to walk right past the car like it wasn't there or must be waiting for a passenger, the driver's window rolled down just enough that Donny could see the guy's face. It was a hard face, a face that had been in some fights, gray buzz cut coming down below the line of his cap and the tail of some tattoo peeking up above his white collar.

"Mr. Thelen is waiting for you inside," said the driver.

"What the fuck?" said Donny, as if anyone was listening.

As Donny stepped toward the front door of his office, he heard the car door open and close behind him. He looked back, and saw the full frame of the chauffeur.

"I'll follow you in," he said. "If you don't mind."

"Suit yourself, Sarge."

He found Thelen sitting in his office chair, reading one of Donny's law books.

"I thought this would put me to sleep, but it's fucking awesome," said Thelen. "The shit people fight about!"

Thelen was dark prep, a well-bred local with chocolate hair slicked back tight and a sharp-looking blue suit. An account manager with edge, in his thirties, but the lines were starting to show around his eyes.

"What the hell do you think you're doing in here?" said Donny.

"We own the building, Donny," said Thelen.

"Since when?"

"Since last month. We've been diversifying pretty heavily into real estate this year, especially with all the new no-go zones they're declaring. And Dallas is hot. The boss asked me to come check this place out, as we're allowed to do under your lease. Thinking we might do something a little nicer and bigger here. Plus, we have some pending business we need to talk about, right? Come on in. Have a seat and let's talk."

Thelen gestured at the chair opposite Donny's desk.

Donny looked at the bust of Socrates, and wondered if it was heavy enough to serve as a weapon. Then he looked at the driver body-blocking him in the doorway, and sat down.

"I gotta say, this place is a disaster, Donny. No wonder you can't pay your bills."

Thelen was the fastidiously tidy sort. Donny had seen his office.

"I make my rent every month."

"Not the bills I'm talking about, Donny. Come on, don't give me that crap."

Donny sighed.

"You owe us a hundred grand, Donny. Which we're okay with. But not when you go six months without making a payment."

The original loan was for a third of that.

"I know, Terry, I know. I've just been totally invested in this case, a big one. And I should be able to get it wrapped up next week."

"Yeah, Donny, we've been following that case too. Got a report this afternoon. That's the other reason I wanted to stop by."

"Who's your source?"

"We have a lot of friends at the courthouse, Donny."

"Probably one of those Poindexters from P&C."

"Good guess. But no, someone more impartial."

"Uh-huh."

"Donny, we helped you out when you were desperate."

"I wasn't desperate. You know that. It wasn't about me."

"Yeah, yeah, I know, you needed to save your honey."

"My friend."

"Your ex, whatever. She got in trouble, and you couldn't lawyer your way into getting her sprung, so you needed to make a deal. We understand. If you recall, we even helped you set the table on that one. No extra charge."

"You're a regular fucking Santa Claus, Terry."

"Sometimes I am," said Thelen. "I don't like hearing about people being tortured, even if I don't agree with their politics. But that was three fucking years ago, Donny." He hit three hard beats on the table with his index finger when he said that. "And this year, you haven't been very good. I even hear you're spending what money you have in all the wrong places."

"Fuck off, Terry, I'm too busy to party."

"And a little too old, if you don't mind me saying. It's starting to show, bro."

Donny looked in the glass of the frame on the wall, but the only reflection he saw was Thelen's.

"What's the plan, Donny?"

"I'm going to get my client to get his ass up here next week, and then I'm going to get AMR to settle for enough to pay you guys twenty times over."

"That's a nice plan, Donny. Except for the part about your client being dead."

"Don't assume he's dead. That kid just has a knack for disappearing whenever he smells trouble. He's like a coyote, man. And even if he is dead, I have a backup plan."

"I guess I don't share your flair for the mystic, Donny. Our guys read the report. And looked over your whole file. They tell us you have no client, and nobody you can replace them with. Come next week, your whole deal goes poof."

"So wait till then, and you can collect."

"Collect from what?" He held up his hands to gesture at Donny's accumulated business assets piled up around them. "The boss doesn't like those odds. We need a better plan, Donny."

"You guys have all those researchers," said Donny. "Why don't you help me find a substitute plaintiff?"

Thelen put his hand on his chin. He and his boss weren't like the loan sharks of old. They were corporate. Money managers, running a firm of family investment offices, with a few billion under management. The personal loans were a way of expanding their influence network, and extracting obscene profits in the process. The other difference: they were legal. In no small part because half the legislators in the Texas state-house were borrowers, usually under much more generous terms than Donny.

"That's an interesting idea, Donny. But I thought you said you have a plan B, and we'll all have a happy ending."

"That's right," said Donny.

"So let's stick with that. We just need to make sure you have some real skin in the game. Give us a little more confidence in the outcome."

"You think I don't have skin in this game, you slick fuck?"

"Hey," said the bodyguard. The hand on Donny's arm felt like it could snap his bones like a pretzel.

"It's okay, Buzz," said Thelen. "Donny, we need some additional surety, is what I'm trying to say. I can't leave without it. Got any ideas?"

Donny looked at Thelen leaning back in Donny's swivel chair with his arms behind his head like he owned the place, which evidently he actually did.

"I'd love to hook you up with a new watch," said Donny. "A guy with your style should have something more singular than that Rolex. I have a Time Master in the lock box that would look great on you."

Thelen watched Donny as he said that, then busted out laughing. "You hear that, Buzz? Donny Kimoe's gonna give me a new watch!"

"Priceless," said Buzz.

"Yeah, no kidding," said Thelen. "Donny, the one who needs a new Time Master is you! Preferably one that enables actual time travel, so you can go undo this pathetic fucking mess you have made of your life."

"Ouch," said Buzz.

He was right. Donny felt the blush, equal parts shame and anger. He looked at his own office with fresh eyes. Rewound what had happened that day. What had got him to this point.

"I'm sorry, Donny," said Thelen. "I remember you telling me about your collection. But we deal with more liquid assets. I have an idea."

Thelen leaned forward.

"You have this real estate you own out in Plano, right?" he said.

"Oh, man," said Donny. "You can't do this to me."

"Let me remind you who is fucking who in this particular situation, Donny. That's you, the guy who hasn't made his payments, mistreating my boss and my company, who were generous enough to set you up in a tough situation even though they knew you were a high credit risk, relying on your good word. Which has now run out."

Donny remembered a takedown Joyce once riffed on the debtor economy and the whole idea of the time value of money. Then he remembered what she said when he got her free with the loan that was now past due.

"Thelen, that's my grandma's house," said Donny. "She's retired. With nowhere else to go."

"We understand that, Donny. But she won't need to go anywhere, right? Because you are going to make this all happen."

"What are you proposing, exactly?"

"You are going to give us the property in escrow. You deliver by the end of next week, we're all set, all is forgiven. She won't even need to know. You screw up, it's ours, we sell it to cover what you owe us, and Grandma can come stay with you in that sweet apartment I heard you have in Houston."

"That house is worth a lot more than what I owe."

"Yeah, well, there's a premium for this kind of risk. Come

on, Donny. Buzz here is also one of our paralegals, and he has the papers for you to sign."

Donny turned to look at the bodyguard, who had the tablet and stylus out. He could tell it wasn't an option, even before he let Donny see the gun.

10

LOOKING BACK ON IT, DONNY WISHED HE HAD KNOWN AT THE TIME
he bought Joyce's freedom that in just a few months the country would break out in revolution, and all the political prisoners would be freed. He also wondered if it would have made any difference in the decisions he made.

It wasn't the first time he had sprung Joyce from jail. It was the third, not counting the time they both got picked up together for driving while high, back before the coup. But it was definitely the most expensive.

That he was able to buy her freedom revealed just how corrupt the administration was in the later years. Corrupt in many layers, like some kind of rotting meat pie, every official focused on using their office to their own personal benefit. It was a sign of the imminent end, he now realized. But at the time, he took it as a sign of permanence. The natural endpoint of a society founded on appetite, self-interest, money, and mirrors.

It wasn't Donny's responsibility to obtain Joyce's freedom. She was in a mess of her own making, the radical academic turned public agitator turned expat talking head, on TV and in her open letters from abroad, pushing for regime change and a radical reinvention of the American model. But somehow, he felt like it was his fault. That if he hadn't bailed on her when they were supposed to leave the country together the day of the coup, she would never have been picked up the first time, and would have taken a different path after she crossed the border.

They could have forgotten it all, in a permanent buzz on some Mexican beach. But Donny got the idea in his head that he needed to stay in Texas, and fight the power. A decidedly quixotic path that had its wins, as long as you radically recalibrated your victory conditions.

His old client Ward Walker was the one who hooked him up with the loan. That was the easy part, at least if you had Donny's gift for willfully ignoring the future. He was on his own when it came to finding a public official to help, though a few friends pointed him in the right direction.

He had to go to Washington to seal the deal, carrying all that cash in his briefcase, five times the amount of cash it was legal to carry. Not just to Washington, but all the way to the Capitol Building, where his contact arranged the meet-up. He wasn't even an executive branch official. He was a fucking Senate staffer. Wesley O'Brien, deputy staff director of the Committee on Motherland Affairs, working for Senator Grinsley, the guy from Georgia who had been a big opponent of the president in his first term and then switched parties when he saw the writing on the wall.

O'Brien had Donny wait for him there in Statuary Hall next to the marble likeness of Vice President Tower, watching the pols give their stand-ups. About five minutes after he was supposed to show up, he called Donny from a secure line and gave him an address on New Jersey Ave., S.E. That turned out to be seven blocks away, a townhouse on the House side that belonged to an outfit called the Foundation for American Freedom. A lobbying shop, which was really just a back door for the collection of political contributions, most of which you could smell were bribes like the one Donny came to pay.

In person, O'Brien looked the part: extra-white version of a white guy, mid-thirties, bit of a baby face, kind of a dorky jacket-and-chinos combo, necktie striped with the colors of a regiment he had never been in. A hall runner who had found his way to the most lucrative hall there was to run.

They called him "The Bundler." The deal was, he only kept 20 percent. The rest went to others in the chain of custody, as it were. People whose names Donny didn't need to know. He even gave Donny a receipt, for the 10 percent portion that was allocated to the campaign fund. A surprise that annoyed Donny more than anything because he would show up on the public list of contributors. That, and the realization that federal detention had now become little more than a high-dollar kidnapping racket run by well-educated goons with nice suits and maybe even MBAs.

Where do I get my money back if you don't deliver, asked Donny, as they sat there in O'Brien's little office with a view of the freeway. There was a picture on the wall behind O'Brien, of the General and the President laughing together on the golf course, like a still from a commercial, or a freeze-frame from the end of a heist movie where they celebrate what they just got away with.

No refunds, said O'Brien. But you don't need to worry.

Donny considered power-vomiting on the guy there in his office. He definitely had it in him at the moment. The photo was bad enough, before he smelled the cologne. But he didn't do it. He didn't even lay any snark.

The worst thing was, he didn't even find out they had released her five days later until he heard it from friends. She was on a plane to Managua before he even figured out how to reach her. And that's why she didn't even know that he was the one who hooked it up.

But he knew that was how it was meant to be.

Even still, when the revolution came, he made sure to

tell his insurgent clients about the Foundation for American Freedom.

Slider was the one who collected the refund from O'Brien, but he spent the money on other things they needed at the time.

THELEN'S VISIT SHOULD HAVE HELPED DONNY FOCUS, BUT IT mostly had the opposite effect.

After Thelen left, the first thing Donny did was try to tally up his available assets. He had less than twelve grand in cash on hand, most of that fees recently collected from clients and deposited in his business account. More pathetic was that he only had another seventeen in his 401(k). At one point it had been close to four times that, when he'd had a nice chunk of the fee on a case he shared with Miles and Percy, but it only took a few months before Donny started dipping into it. That some of the dipping was to advance loans to clients did not persuade the IRS auditors that Donny should be released from the excise tax, especially since loaning money to clients was also against the rules—and since they figured out that Donny had spent three grand of the money on clothes. "Business attire." Including the suit he had worn to court that morning, and was still wearing, a suit that had started to fray, just like the suits it had replaced a few years earlier. It might have been a good investment if it had helped him make money. But the time and effort he had invested in his caseload was proving to be the worst investment of all, judging from his balance sheet, and the dismissal that morning of the one case into which he had sunk it all.

Donny had one car back home, but it wasn't his to sell. It was the vintage Lincoln Town Car Miles had bequeathed him, which Miles had inherited from his dad. Everything else he rented or borrowed, including his apartment and his offices. He had his books, but they weren't worth much to anyone but him.

What he did have was the bling. Most of the watches and jewelry were in Houston, but he had a decent stash right there in the locked cabinet in his office.

He opened the cabinet. There wasn't as much as he thought, and he already knew what the pawnshops were willing to pay.

There was no choice: he would have to lawyer his way out of this one.

He dug back into his case files on *Harrison II*, looking for alternate plaintiffs. He had begun a list of possibles months earlier, mostly compiled from the message boards where the families shared information. So he sat down and made a new list of missing persons on those lists who had Texas residences associated with their names, until he had a dozen names. Then he looked for the names and contact information of family members. The message boards operated by the detention survivors networks were good for that, because the bereaved usually left complete details on where they could be reached with information about their missing kid, sibling, partner, or parent. When he was done with that, Donny had two phone numbers, three messaging handles, and one mailing address.

He drafted a letter on firm letterhead, explaining the case and why he was contacting them, and then sent tailored versions out to each of the four, three electronically and one in an envelope he would drop at the courier in the morning. He looked at the clock on the wall. Then he dialed the first of the numbers anyway. He didn't have time to worry about the time.

The first number went to voicemail. He left a message. A long message.

The second number, he got an answer.

"Hello," said a man's voice.

"Is this Mario Walsh?"

"Who's calling?"

"My name is Donald Kimoe. I'm a lawyer, investigating the case of Clarissa Walsh."

"Clarissa is gone. Please leave us alone."

"I understand, Mr. Walsh. Clarissa and a lot of other people. That's why I sued AMR, and all their execs, to prove what they did, what really happened on the farms. And I think I have them by the balls. Now I just need the people who were most affected to help me make the case."

"What did you say your name was?"

"Kimoe. Donald Kimoe."

"You're calling me at eleven at night so you can make a buck off the death of my daughter, you fucking shyster? I remember you now. I just looked you up. You're the one who used to be on TV all the time, helping out the idiots who got us into this mess. Led my daughter and a lot of other kids down the Yellow Brick Road to nowhere."

"I'm trying to get justice, Mr. Walsh."

"Go fuck yourself, you parasite. Justice is what will happen if I ever meet one of those bastards on a dark street or an empty road. And maybe what will happen after I report your sleazy ass to the state bar."

"Mr. Walsh, please, let me just—"

Click.

As Donny looked at the phone, wondering if it felt as dirty as he did, he considered trying to recall the other messages he had sent. He tried to convince himself he really was doing the right thing, and one of them would understand. Maybe he could even get Mario Walsh to reconsider.

Instead, he found himself reconsidering a lot of his own choices, aided by what was left in the bottle of cheap mezcal he found in the drawer. It tasted like Clorox for the brain, but felt better than that sounds.

He was already on the waiting-room couch by the time he got to the worm, and when he finished swallowing it, he lay back and tried to forget his worries. Instead, they rushed him, all at once, at the edge of sleep, the ghosts of the dead and the ghosts of the living.

When he finally started to get some ideas about how to solve his problems, he nodded off.

He dreamed about raccoons in suits. When the raccoons started talking, Donny realized they were in court. And they were arguing against him. When he got up to object, he woke up.

It was still dark in the office, the room pulsing with the glow of Donny's screen saver in the next room. Five after midnight, but he was wide-awake.

He realized that in the dream, the courtroom the raccoons were in was the one in New Orleans. A real courthouse Donny had been in, back when it housed the US Court of Appeals for the Fifth Circuit, and that now was used for the truth and reconciliation tribunals they called the Tributary. The main difference, other than the talking raccoons, was that in the dream the courtroom looked like the one in the old *Perry Mason* TV show, complete with the gallery full of 1950s Americans in black and white. But the case they were arguing was a real one. It was Heather's case.

He got up, made some fresh coffee, and looked the case up.

It was too late to call when the idea really took root and he got the nerve to try it, even though he knew it was probably a bad idea, the kind of idea that a brain in a corner comes up with in a reckless effort to save itself. So he sent a message instead, to an old friend who was a different sort of victim from the ones he had been calling earlier.

To his surprise, he got an answer, just as he was getting ready to lie back down.

Can u talk now?

WHEN HE HEARD THE VOICE, HE REALIZED HOW LONG IT HAD BEEN since he last heard it.

"Lou?"

"Hello, Donny."

In the long pause that followed, Donny remembered the rest of the story. Not all of it, but most of it. The details they mostly kept out of the news.

"I didn't expect to hear back from you right away," said Donny.

"Well, I was up working. And you said you had information about my daughter."

Donny already felt guilty for doing that. Even though it worked.

"What's got you working this late?"

"I'm in Washington. Advising the Texas delegation to the Constitutional Convention."

"How's that going?"

"Slowly. I'm stuck in this working-group session right now that promises to go all night."

"Jesus, it's two in the morning there."

"No shit. We're up against a deadline, but we're deadlocked, about what the threshold will be for calling a national referendum. These direct-democracy people drive me up the wall. They have no idea what a mess this will be."

"I'm surprised you're able to work," said Donny.

"Keeps my mind off it. And we need to get this done, so the country can get back to work."

"Sounds like you never stopped. I should have figured you'd only get busier the more messed up the country got."

"I'm fortunate to have clients who keep me busy. Mostly with work like this. More lobbying than lawyering, figuring out what the new rules are going to be. Surprisingly rewarding, in fact. A chance at a fresh start."

"Are you happy?"

"Am I happy? What kind of stupid fucking question is that?" Queens still came through strong in Lou's voice, even after a couple of decades in Texas.

"I mean, is this the life you wanted?"

"Not since your motherfucking clients seized the golf courses."

"Come on," said Donny. "You know what I mean."

"We're lawyers, Donny. We're not supposed to be happy."

Donny laughed. "Now I remember why I never talk to you—because you're always so uncomfortably right."

"Last time I talked to you, you gave me a twenty-minute, expletive-laden screed about how I was a 'house pet for klepto-crats' with blood on my hands. Now you tell me you have news about my kid, and then you give me this bullshit. I guess you must want something."

Donny remembered that argument. It wasn't long after Lou helped Donny pay the bribe that had freed Joyce. Donny had waited to vent until Joyce was actually free. He could tell from Lou's voice now that the bridge between them had been successfully burned. They had been colleagues, once. But now it was like two guys who had fought in the same unit, only to realize they had been on different sides in the war.

"I'm sorry about Heather, Lou. But I think I can help."

"Don't patronize me, you snake. What's your game, Donny? You're their number-one lawyer, for Christ's sake."

The bitterness in his voice was real, and raw. Drawing it out was a shitty thing to do. But it seemed to be working.

"Not lately," said Donny. "If ever. My most famous client kind of messed that up."

"Whatever. I know who your other clients are. Some of the big ones. The real nasty ones. So don't try to tell me you care."

"Come on, Lou. You know it's not that simple. You never bought into the propaganda. You just went where the money is. Since I guess marrying the dirty money wasn't enough."

The last part of that didn't come out quite as Donny intended. He wished his phone had the seven-second censor delay they used to have in the counterinsurgency courts.

"Sorry," said Donny, before Lou could reply, or hang up. "None of those people were my clients."

"They could have been."

That was true. And the truth was, one of the terrorists *was* one of Donny's clients. But Lou didn't need to know that.

Donny had remembered the incident vividly even before he read up on it again that evening. He had seen the news clips when it happened. He meant to send Lou a note, but couldn't get past his own lingering animus over everything else that had gone down.

It happened the autumn before the uprising. The rest of Lou's family was at the Aransas Club, a former national wildlife refuge south of Galveston that had been turned into a private resort for the superrich. Water, sun, and fun, and wildlife to kill all year round, surf or turf. While Lou was back in Houston working a case, leaving his wife and daughter with his brother and family in their lodge, the club got raided by insurgents. Frogmen who came up out of the water in the night, but not like the ones in the propaganda movies. Angry class warriors who said they were there to free the refuge and its rightful inhabitants, by which they meant the animals. Lou's brother was back in the administration then, working as a deputy secretary in the Commerce Department responsible for economic recovery in the blighted heartland, which made him a high-value target. That he was with his sister-in-law, heiress to the Promethean Resources fortune and the main backer of Tripto Labs, was an unanticipated bonus.

They made Lou watch while they made Helen eat her own diamonds, on a live feed they beamed out from their phones. That was after they shaved her blond hair off, and made her clean the toilets and bathe the feet of three of the guest workers. The diamonds were not crazy big, but they were big enough, and so were the guns, so she swallowed them all, no doubt hoping they would let her live.

They did not. At the press conference the next day, the government agents said the terrorists had shot them all, in the end, all the adults, in a big group. Then they fed them to the sharks.

Blood in the water.

They let the children go. One of children gave the press a different story. Said the insurgents had only asked for a small ransom and the release of three political prisoners. And that the hostages were killed when the government attacked. The government said the kid was a liar. A sympathizer.

That kid was Heather.

"Lou, just because I opposed the regime, and fought for due process for people who opposed it by other means, doesn't mean I agree with all the actions taken. Especially not after things started getting really crazy."

"You represented murderers, Donny."

"Including the President. The violence started on your side, Lou. Or maybe you forgot about the first roundups. Right now I'm sitting in Dallas two blocks from where the vigilantes strung up those kids in Dealey Plaza. But I'm not here to talk about the past—I'm calling to see if I can help make sure it doesn't happen again. Because I just heard about Heather. I can't believe they took her. Especially since, last I heard, she was on their side."

Donny listened for the reaction.

Some people whispered that Heather was in on what went down. That she had helped the guerrillas access the camp, told them where they could find the people they wanted. Donny didn't buy it. Especially now.

"Heather is her own woman," said Lou. "But she's not a terrorist. And they're not going to get away with it this time."

"And that's why I want to help," said Donny. "I know I can get them to release her."

Heather had been arrested for contempt of court, for failing to pay a default judgment the courts of the breakaway regime in New Orleans had awarded against her family's holdings. That case was based on charges arising out of her family's three generations of crimes against the planet, things that had not been crimes until the insurgents took New Orleans as the liberated territory they won in the war and made their own new laws. The family, like the other companies that had been sued in that court, denied its jurisdiction and refused to even show up. The result was damages in an amount not even that family could afford to pay. Damages that were more like reparations. And now if they didn't pay, Heather would pay. Maybe with her life.

"You piece of shit," said Lou. "You're in on this fucking shakedown, aren't you?"

"No, Lou. I told you, I don't work for those people anymore. They fired me. But I *know* them. I understand them. I even helped them set up this new court. They will listen to me."

Lou groaned. It was the sound of someone who really wants to end the conversation, wishes it had never begun, but now knows it can't stop.

"We already have this covered, Donny."

"Let me help. I have a plan. A better plan than whatever you have. Listen."

Donny told him his plan. To his surprise, it sounded pretty good. Better than when he had thought it up an hour before.

"How can you do that?" said Lou. "Those are your clients you would be going up against."

"It won't be the first time."

Lou grunted in agreement.

"It's not a conflict," Donny continued. "Not technically. There's nothing they can do to stop me. Trust me."

He could almost hear Lou thinking. There were voices in the background. One calling Lou's name.

"Come on," said Donny. "It can't hurt. And I'm pretty sure I can pull it off."

"It's tempting, Donny. Even if it's very unorthodox, and a little wacked. The thing is, I'm not calling the shots on this one."

"What do you mean? It's your kid."

"Yeah, but it's not my money."

"It's her money."

"It's more complicated than that. There's another guy you'll need to talk to. And he may be harder to convince than me."

"Who's that?"

Lou told him.

"I know him," said Donny. "We go way back."

"Okay, then maybe it will work."

"Maybe," said Donny, more convincingly than he actually believed.

13

AS HE RODE IN THE SELF-DRIVING CAB HEADED TO THE MEETING
Lou had set up, Donny watched the news feed on the seatback.
It wasn't news, really. Just a curated freak show of videos they
ran to try to hold your attention until the next ad. The newly
wedded actors Newton Towns and Lauren Stern showing the
crossbred giant vegetables they were growing in the urban farm
they started at an old dump site, Lauren talking about what the
crumbling old concrete does for the soil, how the pill bugs eat
the hard metals right out. Some guys walking into a clearing in
the Siberian forest, claiming they have found a landing site of
ancient aliens. And a new sighting of Donny's most famous—
and most hated—client.

It was a blown-up photo of a guy on the deck of a yacht.
He was with two topless women and one topless dude, holding
instruments the overdub said were the assault rifles of bodyguards, but could just as easily have been fishing gear. The image was too grainy to tell, but at just enough resolution for you
to see it kind of looked like it could be him, there in the Medi-
terranean sun off the coast of Ibiza.

"Hey, driver," said Donny.

"Yes, sir," said the voice of the bot. It was a perfectly pitched
androgyne, with just a hint of an English accent to make it
sound classier. Donny preferred it when they had German ac-
cents, which made the cars feel safer. "How can I help you?"

"Where is the president of the United States?"

A pause while it searched for the answer. "There currently is no president of the United States."

"Smart answer. Where is former President Thomas Mack?"

Another, longer pause. "President Mack is dead, according to a plurality of government and media sources."

"You're no fun," said Donny.

"I'm sorry," said the bot.

"What about the sources that say he's not dead? Like the one you just played for me on the TV. Any other recent sightings?"

A short pause. "Yes. Would you like to hear the sightings from this year to date?"

"Definitely."

Outside the window, they were passing through a district of warehouses. Dallas remained a logistics center and distribution hub, where the products Americans still made that people wanted in other countries, like guns, televisions, and marijuana, were gathered for export. And one of the main places where international relief supplies were received for distribution to the slowly recovering heartland.

"In January," said the bot, "a family returning from vacation in Cancun said they had seen him in the casino, playing blackjack. Also in January, a truck operator claimed to have found him running a Kum & Go convenience store on Interstate 70 in western Nebraska. In February *The Fort Report* republished a network post from user charliefiefortyfive that breakaway elements of the Department of Defense have him in an old missile silo in North Dakota. They also noted earlier speculations that the online self-help guru Jeremy Hardman is actually President Mack with plastic surgery and a beard. In March *La Nación* carried an interview with a ranch hand who said the President is in Paraguay as a guest of the regime on a big ranch stocked with game and guarded by the military. And two weeks ago the Chinese government released photos of him in one of their prisons."

"I saw that," said Donny. "Those were totally fake. Where do you think he is?"

"I don't understand your question. Would you like to stop for lunch? I have a coupon for you for Karl's Quick Grab, which is at the next corner and would only take you an extra twelve minutes to get to your destination."

"I'm not buying anything other than this ride," said Donny. "I asked you where the President is."

The bot was still working on an answer when they arrived.

THE NEIGHBORHOOD WHERE CHARLES LECKER HAD HIS OFFICE
was unofficially known as New Versailles among the locals.
Officially, it didn't have a name—it was just the zone between
Highland Park and downtown that had been built up with
new office buildings and hotels in the last decade, when Dallas had boomed under the prosperity the Mack administration had brought its way while most other parts of the country
declined. The nickname came from the fact that most of the
new structures were designed in a consciously French style,
eighteenth-century Parisian models reinterpreted by expres-
sive but collared architectural AIs and their human assistants
working with advanced materials and additive manufacturing.
Dallas had always had French affectations, from the strip-mall
buffets that masqueraded as brasseries to the electric Citroëns
that had become popular more recently, and somehow managed to make its Francophile appropriation seem perfectly
compatible with the engorged suburban sprawl of the fat years.
Maybe those lefty settlers had planted seeds that persisted, but
mutated to adapt to the place the civic boosters used to call the
"City of Splendid Realities."

The suite occupied by Liberty Advisors Limited was on the
top floor of the Savane Building, which was really three almost-
identical buildings around a courtyard of parking spots and
topiaries that looked genetically engineered to resemble the
animals into whose images they had been clipped. By the main

entrance of the central building grew a fox and a hedgehog. It was hard to tell which one was winning, but the hedgehog looked a little cocky the way it held its head up like it was about to proudly squeal.

The secretary who came down to escort Donny from security was an old white guy who reminded Donny of the retirement-ready marshals at the federal courthouse in Houston, but more Rotary Club than Shriner. He even had the lapel pin that signified his club membership. Donny wanted to ask him if he missed the memo, that the organizations that had incubated the dictatorship were now banned. But he caught himself, or more accurately the man's steely look preempted Donny's quip. And when they got up to the office, you could see it was still a safe place for allegiance to the Ancien Régime, which maybe helped explain the architecture as well.

The lobby walls hosted a gallery of war criminals. The General, Governor Jackson, Justice Korb, and the like, all pictured in a way that made them look both strong and kind. Patriarchally kind. One wall was devoted to young martyrs from Dallas's finest private schools who had turned in their football and lacrosse uniforms for the kind of uniforms that came with guns, as captains of militia brigades or officers in the Guard.

"Please take a seat," said the secretary, in a way that made it clear it wasn't optional.

Donny complied, opting for the big couch. There was a peach-colored *Financial Times* on the table, with headlines above the fold about catastrophe-bond traders shorting the future, the Australian walkout from the Port Moresby talks on the rights of seaborne refugees, and rogue Prince Harry's purchase of enough Honduran dirt to turn the small island he had bought into a new military airfield in the Gulf. Donny opted for one of the dog-eared back issues of *American Heritage*, from the years when it was edited by restorationist patriots. That magazine had been one of Donny's transgressive vices in college, mostly for the illustrations that were perfect for perusing while stoned—paintings by artists of the Norman Rockwell school channeling the garish subject matter of men's adventure pulps. The cover of the issue Donny grabbed featured a shirtless and bloodied dude shoving a large animal bone into the input drive of a wall-sized computer, under the headline MY WAR WITH A CHINESE MACHINE INTELLIGENCE. Donny flipped to the classifieds in the back, with political recruiting ads that had seemed so laughable at the time, a decade before the networks they helped create managed to seize control of the nation-state. The memory of how clueless he had been caused him to put the magazine back. He looked at his watch, and then noticed the nearby display case full of vintage oral-surgery instruments polished to a stainless sheen, and remembered when Dr. Lecker had a very different office nearby, and Donny was one of his teen patients.

"Mr. Kimoe," said the voice, older and harder than Donny remembered, but somehow less scary, maybe because he didn't have Donny in a dental chair and his hands in Donny's mouth. Dr. Lecker had retired from that practice, though there were stories that he still dabbled in a more experimental mode of oral surgery—or had before the Compact was signed.

"Thanks for seeing me, Doc," said Donny, turning to face his childhood torturer.

Dr. Lecker didn't look that different. Old but fit, with what appeared to be the same black-framed glasses. He still had his hair, but it was all white now, and the lines in his face cut deep, making the gray-blue of his eyes seem even colder. And when he shook his hand, Donny could remember one of those hands holding his head from squirming while the other pulled out the noncompliant tooth with dental pliers.

"It's always nice to see an old patient," said Dr. Lecker. "Even when they have failed to follow your advice."

"Are you talking about your medical advice, or the political lectures you gave along with them?"

"They were all grounded in the same philosophy," said Lecker. "And in your case, it was the mouthing off about politics that caused you to lose your tooth. Much to your father's disappointment, as I recall."

"Yeah, well, as much as we looked alike, what was inside our heads was as different as could be."

"That's what you think," said Dr. Lecker. "He did great things, as a businessman. And you've accomplished remarkable things in your profession, even if your choice of clients reflects the misguided politics of your adolescence. And as we all learned, he and you weren't as far apart in those matters as we once thought."

"Let's not go there, Doc. Okay? I came to talk with you about a different father and child."

"Right," said Dr. Lecker, smiling the smile of the lay pastor who plans to get his way with you. "Let's go down here."

He led Donny down a long hallway, passing private offices occupied by busy-looking people, presumably the investment professionals who helped support what had become Lecker's core business. They ended in a surprisingly large conference room that took up a corner of the building, with windows on two sides running from the floor to the double-height ceiling. Lecker opened the door in one of the windows, stepped out onto the balcony, and looked back at Donny.

"Not afraid of heights, are you?"

Donny shook his head.

The balcony was ample, with a long view to the north and

west. Along the railing a half dozen orange trees were arrayed in big planters.

"Let's share one, shall we?" said Lecker, reaching for a big ripe fruit. "These are the last of the winter season. And very sweet, thanks to the freezes we had."

"Is that from one of the family recipes?"

"Dr. Sava's Great Plains Valencia, actually. So yes. One of the hardiest varietals the citrus division has developed. I'm what you might call a beta tester. Perk of being an early investor, and a board member."

Donny put his hand on one of the oranges. The fruit was smaller than the oranges of his youth, with a more washed-out color. But it was still the first real orange he had held in a long time.

"Of course, it's a very finicky plant, like most of the Tripto Labs hybrids. But those leaves suck forty percent more carbon from the air. And gardening help is even less expensive than it used to be. Come."

He showed Donny to a wrought-iron chair at a glass café table, and took the opposite seat. Donny stood at the railing before sitting, taking in the view.

"It's weird seeing the airport so dead," said Donny, focusing in on the empty runways off in the distance.

"It's ridiculous, if you ask me," said Lecker. "We need to be upgrading the power plants to the new low-emissions models, not grounding flights. That just slows down development. And further delays the day when we can get those people new homes."

"Those people" were in the mosaic of color made out by the tents of Camp Lincoln—and past that, the green acres of Tripto Labs' flagship farm. Donny had seen it up close. But from this vantage, you could see that it took up more space than the airport.

"Your clients, I take it," said Lecker.

"Most of those cases were dropped after the uprising," said Donny, taking his chair. "But what happened there and on the farms is what has me here in Dallas."

"You mean the AMR case?"

"That's the one," said Donny.

"You know we used to work with that company," said Lecker. "They were our security contractor."

"I know all about that," said Donny. "And there are some Tripto execs with dirty hands too. But if you're on the board I guess we shouldn't talk about that. Not without your own lawyer present."

"You never struck me as the sort who lets the ethics rules get in your way."

"Said the guy getting rich off refugee labor."

"The international relief orgs manage the labor now," said Lecker. "And we pay a fair wage."

"And the uppity 'workers' have stopped disappearing in the cornfields."

"Accidents do happen. But you're right, there were excesses in the effort to save the country. Which is why we ended up on the same side in the end."

"Better late than never," said Donny.

Lecker laughed. "You have your father's odd sense of humor too." He had peeled the orange, and offered half to Donny.

"I'm sure he kept his executioners chuckling right up until they flipped the switch," said Donny.

"Well, he stuck to his principles, which is more than I can say for many of those who capitulated to the administration as its leadership became unmoored from the principles we put them in there to uphold, and forgot its loyalties to its original supporters. I'm glad to have known him."

Donny savored the first slice of the orange. It tasted good.

"He was an asshole," said Donny. "But nobody deserves to die for that. Or for being born rich."

"Some of your clients disagree."

"True, but they'll listen to me. I can get them to free Heather, with your backing."

"So Lou told me. And the answer is of course we all want her freed from those lunatics."

"You can help make that happen, Dr. Lecker. Just give me some realistic parameters to work out a deal."

"Are you asking me for money, Donny?"

"No. The people holding your ward are asking for money. And you and I both know they have a legitimate case. Even if you don't concede that they have jurisdiction."

"I don't concede anything," said Dr. Lecker. "Especially not to those communists."

Donny noticed the scorch sanded into the wood of the table at which they sat. Redwood, singed with the badge of the unique method of timber harvesting Heather's family business had developed.

"Do you concede that they have her in their custody, and the power to determine her fate?"

"I understand they claim to have 'arrested' her. But I don't trust anything those people say. And I don't even know if I trust Heather. She has been lost for a long time. Not unlike you, but of an even more radical generation."

"A kid who dares to ask where the money comes from."

Lecker raised a derisive eyebrow.

"Just let me go work out a deal," said Donny.

"My sources tell me you have your own reasons to want to get to New Orleans. You just want me to buy you a ticket."

"Well, New Orleans is on lockdown. Closed to outsiders, unless you have a transit visa. I think I could talk my way through, but having an official purpose, like being appointed to represent Heather in front of the Tributary, would definitely help me get in. I wouldn't propose it if I didn't care about Heather, or honestly believe I could get her home."

"Or need the money," said Lecker.

"That too." Donny shrugged.

"Well, I might be persuaded to take you on, if you can get after a very different sort of deal," said Lecker.

"What's that?" said Donny.

"The City of New Orleans are the ones who owe *me* money. Seven hundred million and counting. Money I paid for the repurchase and remediation of the toxic zone they call Echo Sector. Debt which your friends in the new government there repudiated."

"I thought you were supposed to be a smart investor. Everybody knew what crooks the administration had running that project. I bet most of that money was skimmed right off the top."

"About a third of it," said Lecker. "As we expected and understood. I'm not counting that. The rest of it is there in the cleaned-up soil, and in the seeds we gave them to grow in it."

"You want them to pay that? They're broke."

"If they want to give us the land back, I'm positive I can make my money back."

"They're not giving New Orleans back, and you know it. That was the deal," said Donny. "The price of getting them to leave Washington and take their AK-47s with them."

"I'm not talking about the whole city," said Lecker. "Just the part I already paid for."

Donny bit into another slice of the orange. It had a big seed in it. He pulled it from his mouth, and then looked at it. Then he held it up.

"This is what you really want, isn't it?"

Lecker almost smiled. "It's not all we want, but the most important thing. They are growing our seeds. Patented organisms that we own just as we own the land on which they are grown. And they are giving them away."

"Their law rejects the idea that you can own a living thing," said Donny. "Especially a thing that can feed the world."

"We won't be able to feed the world unless we can raise the funds to continue our research. Because our designs are still not hardy enough to really propagate."

"Not without an army of free labor."

"Basically. Tell them we can work out a deal where they share in some of that. As a proper licensee."

"And then they will remind me the reason they have detained Heather. That Promethean Resources owes New Orleans a lot more than they owe you. The value of seven hundred million trees in the forests, or something along those lines."

"A fanciful narrative wrapped in a simulation of law," said Lecker. "You know that. They want us to pay for things Heather's grandfather did, because some egghead came up with a half-baked theory that trees should have rights?"

"If corporations have rights, why not trees?"

Lecker harrumphed at that one.

"You don't have to buy it," said Donny. "But I think the better argument is that you can't make the shareholders pay out of their own pockets for things the management did."

"Yes, absolutely," said Lecker. "Go with that."

"They already awarded the judgment, though," said Donny. "So the deck is stacked. But what if I got them to forgive it? You forgive the repudiated debt in exchange."

Lecker leaned forward. "I didn't agree to meet with you, Donny, because I wanted to work out some loser's version of a 'win-win' deal. I agreed to meet with you because Lou made a very smart point to me, the kind of strategic insight only a first-rate trial lawyer like *him* can provide: that with you, we have an opportunity to enlist on our side someone the other side thinks is on their side. I am persuaded that is worth a try. But if you want me to pay you, as I know you do, then you will need to help me win. The Council needs to stop giving away our seeds. And they need to drop this retributive case against the company. In exchange, we will help them feed their people and achieve prosperity beyond their crunchy little imaginations."

"Don't forget about Heather," said Donny.

"Of course not," said Lecker. "That's an essential part of the package. The most important part."

Donny wondered if Lecker would be happy to have Heather out of the way.

He looked at the old dentist, sitting atop his virtual billions, the man who helped install the regime that had trashed the country in its misguided effort to save it, and now was angling to make a new fortune feeding the people he had helped starve. Donny tried to imagine presenting his list of demands to the new leaders in New Orleans, a junta of battle-hardened guerrillas and ideologues determined to liberate entire ecosystems from people like Lecker.

"I think I can do that," he lied.

"Excellent," said Lecker.

"I'll need some hazard pay in addition to my usual fee."

"I thought we could keep it simple. I hate hourly billing

arrangements, all the wrong incentives. I propose a success fee. Say, a hundred thousand dollars."

Donny wondered if Lecker knew about his deal with Thelen. It should have been a lot of money to Donny, even though it would have been small potatoes for the lawyers like Lou he had come up with, and chump change for a master of the universe like Lecker. But for Donny, it was just enough to cover his immediate needs. Which made him feel all the more pathetic when he found himself begging for a little more, from this guy who was going to pay him to betray the people who trusted him. Betray them again.

"We can start there," said Donny, trying to project confidence. "But I'll need a bit more to cover my expenses."

"Excellent," said Lecker. "We can throw in another ten thousand up front for per diem. I will have our lawyers draw up the paperwork."

"While you're at it, have them send a notice to the court in New Orleans adding me as counsel on your case."

Lecker nodded.

"And maybe see if you can throw in some life insurance," said Donny. "Because not everyone there will be happy to see me."

"You seem like you can be pretty persuasive when you need to get out of a jam," said Lecker. "And assuming you're referring to what I think, I for one appreciate you standing up for your principles. A rare thing these days. And the other part of why I was willing to consider this proposal."

"Plenty of people stand up for what they believe in," said Donny. "More than ever, I'd say. Like the people you want me to persuade to compromise just that. The problem is that what most people seem to believe in the most these days is the need for people who believe in something else to die."

Lecker laughed, a sincere guffaw from deep in the belly.

Donny didn't think it was funny.

"Strong punishments have their place," said Lecker. "Especially in undisciplined societies. But you were absolutely right that our president, for all his failings, did not deserve to be executed for his politics."

"He ordered the illegal execution of his own people, Doc. You can call it politics if you want, but it's murder. The penalty should have been death. I just stood up for my belief that the state does not have the right to murder anyone. And I made my point, even if they killed him anyway."

Lecker nodded. "Of course," he said, wearing a knowing grin.

"Is this where you open the door and the disappearing president walks in, tanned, rested, and ready?"

Lecker smiled big, revealing his excessively white dentist's teeth. "And then he can help me toss you from the balcony!"

"Save that for after I get your money," said Donny.

"Yes, right." Lecker laughed. "But no, nothing would be worse than if the urban legends came true and he reappeared. To my surprise, an ungoverned country suits me quite well. Suits the country quite well."

"How's that?" said Donny.

"We can do what we want," said Lecker.

Donny nodded. He had a pretty good idea who the "we" was. And it made him wonder if the restoration wouldn't be such a bad thing after all.

DONNY MET WITH HIS MOST-HATED CLIENT JUST ONCE BEFORE the sentencing hearing, at the offices of the lead lawyers on the case, Weitz, Weldon & Hogan.

It was early in the year before, late winter, less than a year after the uprising. Donny remembered how cold it was that morning as he walked to the meeting, trying to make a Texas-weight trench coat keep the mid-Atlantic winds of February at bay.

The President was a prisoner of the new government. Prisoner number one. But the new government wasn't much of a government. The situation in Washington was kind of like Donny imagined it had been when the General was in power and the students would take over a college campus. Some of the faculty and staff were still there, and everybody was secretly waiting for the National Guard to show up and restore the old order. So the deposed chief executive, who hadn't been replaced yet and never would be if the radical wing of the rebellion had their way, lived under house arrest in a brownstone at Logan Square, guarded by English troops detailed to the peacekeeping coalition that was responsible for keeping the Americans from killing one another—and keeping their nuclear arsenal secure until the decommissioning was complete.

Donny's responsibility that day was to keep his fellow Americans from killing just this one American. One he wouldn't mind killing himself, if he weren't so sick of killing.

Donny had watched the trial that determined his guilt. Everybody did. It was on all the channels.

Donny's old colleague Percy, who had gone on to become an A-league plaintiff's lawyer and then a member of Congress, was on the prosecution team. Percy had a personal stake in the case, and the scars and mementoes of dead friends to prove it.

Among the discoveries after the people took Washington was that the President had maintained a closed-circuit television system on his desk in the Oval Office and in the presidential bunker, through which he could access live feeds from the interrogation center that had been established at Quantico under Emergency Executive Order 37541. There had been leaks about this before, not that those kinds of leaks ever made it into the mainstream domestic press in those days—the censors mostly kept that sort of news contained to the underground whispernets. What the leakers hadn't known was that all of those feeds were automatically recorded by the bots that managed the White House archive. An AI named Publius X, whose programming included ideological parameters that caused it to see that footage as things patriots of the future would wish to see. Would even enjoy.

While evidence from the system logs showed that the federal AIs were swapping these videos and similar content with one another, even the President himself did not know that what he watched had been encoded in the permanent record. Or that such records included the sound of his voice providing instructions to the interrogators. Instructions, suggestions, jokes, descriptions, and orders, sometimes in a dictatorial scream, other times in a distracted aside.

The prosecutors spent the second day of their case playing excerpts from these. Seven hours of excerpts.

One involved a client of Donny's. An editor at the *Houston*

Current who had been arrested for allegedly serving as a conduit between members of the underground. Hearing the familiar voice of the President, but a more private version of the voice—a casual conversational tone you had never heard—suggest which interrogation enhancement to deploy from the menu of techniques that had been cleared as not technically constituting "torture" was more than unsettling. For Donny, who knew the precise clinical methods each of the code words described, just the audio alone would have been bad enough. Hearing the President sing the chorus for "Yellow Submarine" in a half-assed and slightly deranged-sounding Liverpudlian accent over a speakerphone mic, and then watching the grainy footage as the interrogators in their white-room suits and masks grab the naked prisoner by the hair and dunk his head in a urine-filled toilet until he suddenly and apparently unexpectedly drowned in it, actually made Donny puke.

There was much debate in the pretrial hearings regarding whether such footage should be seen by the public, with the defense arguing it would prejudice the fact finders and some arguing it would violate the privacy rights of the prisoners and their families. But the louder voices in the cacophony fighting to direct where things went in those days argued more convincingly that all courtroom proceedings must now be conducted on camera, with all evidence available for all to see. And that everyone in the American public, especially those who had supported the President, needed to confront those truths as a first step in their reeducation and national reconciliation.

Ann Landis was the partner at WWH who had made those pretrial arguments, and the truth was, she was right. It certainly prejudiced Donny. So much so that when Ann escorted him to meet his new client, and he saw the two SAS operators in their black berets guarding the conference-room door, he felt an intense and almost eldritch sense of fear well up in him as he prepared to step through.

"Good morning, boys," said Ann, who obviously *liked* having them around. Ann was a former federal prosecutor Donny had a case against some years earlier, and the member of the President's defense team who suggested they bring Donny in to help with the sentencing.

Donny had thought it was a good idea, until he saw the motherfucker sitting there at the conference-room table, and wondered if there was a way to kill a man with a porcelain coffee mug. If he could stab El Presidente's eyes with his ballpoint pen deep enough to reach the brain before His Majesty's Stormtroopers got to him.

"Happy Monday," said Ann. "I believe most of you know Donald Kimoe."

There were five other lawyers in there, from three different firms. They all shook hands, and introductions were made where needed.

The President remained seated there in his blue swivel armchair, sizing up Donny. They had told Donny beforehand that the President no longer shook hands, for fear of poisoning and general germaphobia. Donny said that works for me.

The President wore a very nice blue suit, with a pocket square, a red silk tie embroidered like the scales of a dragon, and the blue-black American-flag lapel pin of his officially disbanded political party. He no longer looked scary, though he still looked a little dangerous. He had been reduced to human scale. Without the klieg lights and regal trappings of office, he looked like a CEO who had just been unexpectedly fired, and now sat in the office of some HR flunkies as they collected his company phone and told him all the things he could no longer do. Maybe it was that image in his head, or maybe it was the anger and grief he felt bottled up inside, that made Donny walk right up to the guy, reach down, and remove the pin from his lapel.

"You can't wear this anymore," said Donny, holding up the pin. "Not if you want to live."

You could feel it in the room when he said that. But Donny didn't look to see the faces of the other lawyers. He just looked at the President and waited.

The President smiled, the smile of someone who still believed he had power, or would soon get it back. Power to punish anyone who angered or disrespected him.

Donny held out the pin, waited for the President to put out his hand, and dropped it in his palm. The President slowly closed his hand around the pin, then slid it into his jacket pocket.

There was a blond woman seated next to the President, in a suit of her own, but with a more feminine cut and an open collar. She stood up when Donny approached her boss, and when she did you could see how tall she was, and how strong. She had been introduced as the President's in-house counsel, but you could see she was also his bodyguard, and maybe his paramour.

"It's okay," said the President. "Mr. Kimoe and I go way back. Even if we've never met in person. And I'm sure he's right."

"If you want to wear the flag, wear your uniform," said Donny. The President was a war hero before he ran for office, a navy pilot who had been shot down in Korea during the war with China, and managed to escape. "Maybe your old one, if it fits, not the commander-in-chief one."

"I'll wear whatever you tell me, as long as you're there."

Donny poured himself a coffee and sat across from his new client. Who actually wasn't his client, yet. Donny had wanted to wait until they had this meeting before he formally agreed to the engagement, which technically would be as co-counsel to WWH. What was crazy was how well rested the guy looked. Fit, even. Out of power, but confident and relaxed, the kind of rogue alpha who is already angling what his next gig will be. Not at all the way you would expect someone facing the choice between death by public hanging and three consecutive life sentences would be.

"They say Charles the First was like this," said Donny.

Not much of a reaction to that.

"He got a cozy house arrest too. Until he tried to escape, at least. But acted regal right up until they lopped off his head and held it up for the crowd."

"Fortunately you are going to make sure that doesn't happen in this case," said Ann, trying to redirect the tone.

"That depends on how this meeting goes," said Donny.

The other lawyers in the room looked tense. They were on the client's side without reservation. Pinstriped restorationists who'd be glad to put their own lapel pins back on if they could get this guy back in power.

"I like your analogy," said the President. The guy had an intense stare, in person. Almost hypnotic. Donny had heard the stories, but never believed them until that moment, when he lived it.

"Yeah?" said Donny. "History is always good, because it lets you see some of the other ways things could have gone. Like if King Charles had negotiated an exile."

"Real leaders don't give up the fight," said the President. "Especially not when the other side is breaking the law. As was the case then, and now."

"Is this the part where you tell me how you're still the President?" said Donny.

"Sounds like I don't have to. Just like you don't have to tell me you're on their side. Always have been."

"I don't have a side," said Donny.

"Sure you do. It's just your own side. Lawyers are all alike. Morally malleable and ethically elusive. At least your clients know where they stand. You're just here because you know they're about to drive the economy into the ditch and this may be your last chance at a nice fee. Ann tells me they're going to pay you more just for putting your name on the briefs than you made in all of your cases last year."

"That's wrong too. Because I'm doing this the same as I did a lot of those cases. For free."

"For free?" said the President. "That's the most retarded thing I've ever heard. Sorry."

"I don't want your apology. And I don't want your money," said Donny. "That's stolen property, as far as I'm concerned. I just want to see you rot in jail."

The President scowled at him, the mask finally falling. When he did, you could see the scars more clearly, little white lines on the left side of his face from the bomb blast that had come close to doing the job, but not close enough.

"Donny, maybe this was a bad idea," said Ann.

"It was a great idea," said the President, his glare never leaving Donny. "One of your best. It's perfect. And it's totally going to work. The fact that he hates me as much as I hate him and his clients and every filthy thing they stand for means this is going to totally get the result we want. Because for the first time in his life this weasel defender of terrorists is going to stand up for what he actually believes in. I don't need him to understand what it means to believe in the idea of America. Because I know enough patriots are still out there to keep up the fight. And because he's going to make sure I live to fight another day."

"Are you, Donny?" said Ann.

"I'll argue for what I believe in, like I always do," said Donny, feeling his own bullshit detector go off as he talked. "In my own words. And that means I will do everything I can to persuade them that this tyrant should serve a lifetime in maximum-security prison for every life he stole. Down in the hole, at the inescapable Supermax he built to lock up the real patriots. The ones who fought for a future we can all live in."

The president watched Donny with a smile on the edge between sincere and sarcastic, and then he started clapping. A slow clap, a clap of derision and ridicule, but a real one. Except that it was when he started clapping that Donny remembered the left hand was fake, a prosthesis that was another relic of the bombing. And when he clapped with it, it sounded like rubber. Donny looked at the fake hand, and wondered if it was capable of giving him the finger. And then he thought about how in prison, they would not let him keep it.

16

DONNY WAS TELLING HIS GRANDMOTHER THAT STORY AFTER HIS meeting with Lecker, as they sat on her porch and enjoyed the takeout he had brought.

"You want some?" she said, proffering the brownie from which she had just taken a hearty bite.

"No thanks, Carol," said Donny. "I can never keep up with you."

"Suit yourself," said Carol. Carol was Donny's maternal grandmother. The first lawyer in the family, and the best, and the most ethical. And the most likely to be high, even in her eighties. Especially in her eighties.

Her place was in Plano, an old farmhouse that had somehow survived as suburbia boomed around it. And then outlasted them all, as the diminishing future pushed everyone back downtown. From the back porch where they sat, she had a view of a stretch of abandoned freeway. A surprisingly large herd of deer were gathered at the landscaped pond out in front of the former offices of a telecommunications software company, as the sun began to flash out behind the slowly collapsing shopping mall. When it was backlit like that, but there was still enough light that you could see the mustang vines growing up the sides and poking out through the windows, the modernist concrete blocks of the old JCPenney store looked every bit like a Mayan ruin.

It was a special house—and was now being secretly mortgaged to pay for his mistakes.

"I'm happy to just enjoy the view," said Donny, trying to defer a difficult conversation. "Hard to believe this was a refugee camp."

"And you helped shut it down," said Carol.

"And got a great deal on this place, before that news broke. But I can't believe how quickly it got ruined."

"Once the water started to get through, nature took over."

"Have you been inside?"

"Hell, yes," said Carol. "It's pretty dang awesome, if you ask me. Especially in the food court, where they had this big skylight. The exotic plants in the planters have gone all Pleistocene, and some of the local species have gotten in there and joined in the party. A couple are blooming right now. You should spend the night; we can go check it out in the morning. It's like visiting the future."

"Are those bats?" asked Donny, looking at a grainy black cloud emerging from the roofline and spreading out against the darkening sky.

"Yep," said Carol. "Mexican freetails. They moved in a few years ago. You should come check it out while you can."

"I wish I could, Grandma. But I need to head back to Houston. I'm going to try to catch the night bus. This case I'm supposed to take to trial next month is falling apart on me."

"No wonder you look so wound up. How come you can't learn not to take the work home with you? Maybe you should try one of these brownies. Get a little perspective."

"Knowing your brownies I'd be tripping for a couple of days. But I'm already so burned out I can barely muster the energy to keep fighting. Just when I'm this close to closing the damn deal. Real justice, right there, right in my grasp, and I feel like some kid trying to grab the moon."

"We all know what that feels like." She took another bite,

and watched the hummingbird working its way through the yucca by the door. "What's the case again?"

"The only good case I have left—against AMR, the private-prison-camp people."

"I thought you said you had the witnesses you need. What happened?"

"Not so bueno, Granny. I found the names, but most of the witnesses I need seem to have disappeared—or been disappeared. And now my lead plaintiff is dead. Killed on a mission, according to the news."

"They probably killed him."

"It's possible," conceded Donny. "But if they had done that, you can bet they would have made sure the body showed up, so there would be no doubt."

"What did the judge say?"

"That she is required to dismiss the case. She gave me a week to come up with a reason to convince her otherwise. But I'm running out of options."

"She'll give you more time than that."

"I'll tell her you said so when I blow her deadline. It's in the rules. She doesn't have any flexibility."

She didn't need to know that he'd already blown the deadline that really mattered, because of his own negligence.

Carol took another bite, and watched the cloud of bats slowly disperse into the dimming light.

"Don't you have people who can help you find him?"

Donny shrugged. "I have people who will know if he can be found. Family and friends, fellow fighters. But I can already tell they don't know. Especially since none of them are answering my calls."

"Maybe I can help."

Donny looked at her. She was serious.

"Grandma, you're too sick to work on my stupid cases."

"Might take my mind off the pain," she said, rubbing her left collarbone. "Focus it on someone else's pain. Do you know any better lawyers?"

"No." It was true. There was one who was as good, but that was why they killed him. And when that happened, the only other one he would put on that list gave up the law for politics. He wouldn't wish either outcome for his grandma. "I wish I could take your help. God knows I have enough on my plate."

"What else?"

"Well, I'm supposed to be back in federal court in Houston week after next. Hearing on a motion for a new trial. A woman who got locked up before the uprising and should have been released as part of the amnesty."

"Good luck. They aren't wasting any time rolling back the clock."

"Depends on the court. And the judge."

"Who'd you get?"

"Broyles."

"Great."

"He's actually mellowed."

"It's your mother's influence."

"Don't remind me."

"You always wanted an evil stepfather."

"Very funny, Grandma."

"Have you talked to her lately?"

"Not in a long time."

"She really went all-in, didn't she?"

Donny nodded. He had seen politics drive people to violence, but somehow losing a loved one over it was harder. That she had shacked up with Donny's mentor-turned-nemesis Judge Broyles added a layer of uncomfortable weirdness.

"I miss her."

"So call her."

"Not yet. I'm too busy to mess with that drama right now."

Grandma Carol nodded. Then she groaned and rubbed herself along the left side of the ribs. "You'd think with these edibles having been legal this long they could at least figure out a way to get them to kick in earlier."

"FDA won't let them."

"I'm surprised. I heard it's now the USA's number-one export. Which kind of makes sense."

"Marijuana Republic."

"Exactly. I hear they're about to tear down that old mall down there and build a brand-new greenhouse. Partly owned by the state."

"How convenient for you."

"Right?" she said. "They keep calling wanting to buy this place, but I told them we're staying."

Donny sank inside, but evaded the topic. "Maybe if they can get everyone high, we'll be able to keep the peace for a while."

"I couldn't sleep last night and turned on the TV and they had a bunch of Dutch soldiers evacuating from South Carolina, headed home. Blue helmets off, back to orange."

"I can't believe they think it's safe to go."

"They don't. They just think they're starting to get infected with what we've got. Especially after the assassination of that French opposition leader. Franz Ferdinand all the way. But bigger. Even the Indians are mobilizing. So our minders are leaving us in our quarantine and locking the doors behind them. And probably half hoping we'll finish what we started."

Donny knew what she meant. Carol always knew what side

she was on. She'd been on the right side before anyone even knew it was a side.

"Are you helping?" he asked.

"I gave them all my money, and the best advice I could."

"How did you never get arrested, Grandma? Or at least sanctioned?"

"Some of us know how to be more subtle than you. You get too emotional for a lawyer."

Donny shrugged. "Only when they really get under my skin."

"If you say so, sweetie."

Donny eyed the chunk of brownie she had left uneaten. There was a grackle in the nearby tree who looked like he had the same idea.

"There's something else, Grandma."

She looked at him. She could tell, even before he said another word.

"Uh-huh."

He told her. About Thelen. About the money he owed. About the lien on her house.

"Goddamn you, Donny," she said. "How could you?"

"I didn't have a choice, Grandma."

She sneered at him. "Give me a fucking break. You'd fuck up a two-car funeral, like your great-grandpa used to say."

"I made enough money to buy you this place, didn't I? And I did it doing the kind of work you said was work worth doing, for people who need the help. I just didn't do it legal aid–style like you. I did it in a way where you actually get paid. And you watch me, I'm going to do it again, and make enough money to buy you that whole damn mall so you can pet the bats and feed the butterflies till your dying days."

"Is that right?" she said. "And how are you going to pull that off?"

"Well, if I can just get myself a plaintiff, I'm pretty sure I can settle this AMR case. I got some great stuff on the record before they pulled the trapdoor on me. If I can come up with some other victims willing to sign on, maybe the judge will make a way to keep it going. But in the meantime, I need to focus on a sure thing. And I think I have a Plan C that will cover our immediate needs."

"Will you send me the file?"

Donny considered it. "Are you sure?"

"You always were bad at accepting help from people who love you. Like that professor you went out with."

Thanks for bringing that up, Grandma. He hadn't told her that was what he had borrowed the money for.

"Well, I'm going to need some help this time, unless I can figure out a way to clone myself. Because now it looks like I need to go back to New Orleans."

She looked at him, with eyes operating at a higher level of lucidity.

Donny told her the rest of it. His explanation was more complicated than it needed to be, because he was busy trying to convince himself. When he was done, he could tell he hadn't convinced her.

"Are you seriously going to help those fuckers?" she said, without pause.

Donny shrugged. "We need the money, Grandma. And I think it might help us keep the peace."

"First off, *you* need the money. I was doing just fine, remember? Second, they don't want peace."

"Maybe not. But I think I can persuade them."

"You ate one of these brownies when I was in the bath-room, didn't you?"

He moved over to her side of the picnic table and pulled her close. She smelled like Grandma always smelled. But there was something else, almost like you could smell the cancer.

"I can't stand to lose you, too, Grandma. You're all the family I have left."

She hugged him back.

"I'm not going anywhere," she said. "Not unless you fuck this up."

"No pressure," said Donny.

"Lots of pressure. This is my house, so in this case, a little pressure is good. Especially if it makes you get some help. So get me the files, and we'll get to work. See if we can come up with the money the right way. But first you promise me you're telling me the whole deal."

"Totally," he said, which was not really an answer.

"You know I can read your mind, you little shit."

"Then you know I know what I'm doing," he said. "Because I learned it from you."

She stared at him, then ate the rest of the brownie, and then started telling him stories about the revolution that came before. He had heard them all before, but he still liked them. They were good stories, and they were true.

17

ON SEVERAL OCCASIONS OVER DONNY'S LIFETIME, TEXAS HAD the opportunity to connect its cities with high-speed rail. It was such an obvious thing to do, especially since the rights of way were already there. Building out the railroads was what had brought the first big money to the state, before Spindletop and the discovery of big oil deposits in the ground. The last proposal was for one of those hypertrains that would make the Houston-to-Dallas run in twenty minutes. But the politics always killed it. Until it was too late. By the time it was no longer economically or ecologically viable to fly people distances that could be driven almost as fast, and then driving your own car was even more expensive, the money wasn't there to build a better, smarter, greener transportation infrastructure. So most people, including Donny, took the bus.

At least the Greyhound station was close to the courthouse. The station had no newsstand, but they did have doughnuts and coffee. The buses were mostly biodiesels, which meant they smelled like fast-food, but at least they had onboard network connections and room to work.

Donny had taken the bus all the time when he was in college and law school. After his dad dumped his mom, their war meant Donny was on his own financially, and he decided to get by without having a car, especially since the only car he could afford was the kind guaranteed to die somewhere outside of Waco if you had the bad idea to actually head to another town. So the bus was how he would get to and from school, and on weekends he figured out how to make the run for the border on the Mexican buses, which were cheaper and cooler, the poor man's idea of exotic travel. That was before the Mexicans closed the border to most American traffic.

Donny always managed to end up on the night bus, especially when he was headed home. That night he left his grandmother's the 10 P.M. bus was ninety minutes late. He tried to get some work done in the station, with coffee and a slightly stale cruller, but ended up giving free legal advice to the old lady sitting next to him, first about how she might clear her son's record, then about her war with her neighbors over the fence line. He tried working again once the bus finally got going, but only managed to wake up at 3 A.M. with drool drying along the corner of his mouth.

He watched the view from his window seat as they rolled into town. The Woodlands, once the most attractive suburban development, had been mostly abandoned as people moved back into town, though some folks who could afford it kept weekend places up there in the pines, tearing down the fat tract homes that the elements had already started to rot and replacing them with these little prefab eco-cabins. The area around the international airport had been heavily militarized, first by the feds during the long emergency, then by units of UN peacekeeping troops. The flag was still up over one of the camps by the freeway, but you could see most of the troops were already gone.

Donny saw the sign for the big Walmart just north of 610, with the whole property fenced off behind chain link, the building a charred ruin that had been destroyed in the riots.

When the bus finally exited at the edge of downtown, it stopped at the first light in three hours. And when Donny looked out into the predawn cityscape, he saw a couple of hungry-looking kids rummaging in a dumpster, just like those raccoons he'd seen. Behind them was a big lawn, something you never expected to see along the side of the feeder road in the shadow of the elevated expressways. And then he realized it was the funeral home where they had taken Miles.

Miles just had the one brother left when he died, his older brother, Milton III, who opted for medicine instead of law. Beyond that, the closest thing he had to family were his workmates. That's how Donny and Percy ended up going to the funeral home with Milton to see the body.

Percy had become Miles's only law partner by then, after she started out a decade earlier as Donny's part-time legal assistant while she was still in law school at U of H, only to be poached by Miles and his then-partner, who had since retired. Donny was never formally affiliated with the firm. Miles said that was partly for cultural reasons, but mostly because of the quote his malpractice carrier had given him when they were talking about that possibility and Donny filled out his part of the questionnaire. So they ended up working as co-counsel on a lot of cases, and trading notes on others, as the courts went crazy and the country went crazier.

Through all that craziness, Percy had worked hard to stay focused on what she said were the real people's cases—traditional criminal work, instead of the political cases Donny gravitated toward. After a couple of years, she discovered personal-injury work. She was picky about those cases, too, determined to find the real wrongs. She succeeded, and one of those cases, a wrongful death action involving a black kid killed by private-security forces for trespassing on an empty lot next to their client's polyethylene plant, delivered a big payday. One Percy got a third of, close to a million bucks. And turned around and gave most of it away, while even Miles sided with Donny in pleading her to hold on to more.

She said that verdict made her see what Donny was always saying. That all the cases were political cases, if you looked at them right. And then she said there's a lot more money where that came from.

Donny said be careful who you piss off, and she just said I'm not as reckless as you, Donny.

Miles took all the cases. At least all the ones that deserved him. He was so good at it, one of those lawyers in the mold of the ones who only seem to exist in fiction, the champion of the underdog who manages to make a nice living without ever breaching his own strict ethical code.

As the bus sat there annoyingly long at the light, Donny remembered how depressing he had thought it was that his friend had to begin his journey to the place where lawyers don't have to argue anymore with a stop along a Houston frontage road in the shadow of the elevated freeway. The lawn didn't really help, and the fountain tended by angels carved from black stone just made it look like some cheap amusement-park imitation of the Isle of the Dead. When they walked up that morning, the fountain was off, but the pool was full, with what looked to be rainwater, and one big miserable-looking koi. Milton was already there when Donny and Percy arrived, and the owners of the place, friends of the family, greeted him and took them up to the room where Miles lay for visitation.

"We didn't have time to do much to prepare him," said the funeral director, a middle-aged woman. "The wounds were pretty bad."

"It's okay," said Milton. "We're not having an open casket."

Donny looked at Percy.

The room was small, and quiet. You could hear the freeway

traffic, but close enough to white noise that you didn't mind. There was a reproduction of a painting on the wall, a still life with white flowers, some actual flowers in a vase, and four boxes of Kleenex around the room.

Miles lay on a tall table against the near wall as you entered. Milton had insisted they leave him in the same suit he had been wearing when those motherfuckers shot him outside the courthouse, a classic Miles tropical-weight gray flannel with a light-blue button-down and a bright-green tie. He looked good in it, the way the color of the tie seemed reflected in his dark skin. There was some blood spatter you could see on the left shoulder of the suit, and they had leaned his face toward the wall so you would have to work to look at the wound on that side. Milton straightened his tie while he talked to him, and then let Donny and Percy come up close.

Miles was such a fucking hero. Looking at his waxy face with the eyes you could tell had been closed by someone else's hands, Donny tolled a list in his head of the times he had let his friend down, and the times Miles had delivered even when Donny didn't deserve it. Donny managed not to cry until he grabbed Miles's right arm, and it felt like a block of wood.

"I wish we could light him up," said Donny, looking at the way they had him laid out there on the table.

Percy looked at him through her tears, like her anger at the unknown perpetrators had just been partially transferred to Donny.

"That's what they do," she said. "I don't know what you're going to do, but I'm going to make sure we help get these yahoos moseyed along to whatever redneck Valhalla they think awaits them."

You could tell she meant it. That something had changed in her. In how she saw things, and how she felt.

"I'll help you," said Donny.

And he did. At first, at least.

They divvied up Miles's caseload, and shared a few of the cases. They tried to find who had killed Miles. They suspected it was tied to the AMR case, but evidence in support of that theory was hard to come by. The courthouse where the shooting happened was blanketed with electronic surveillance, and the incident was captured on two camera views, but neither showed the faces of the perpetrators. And their ability to get more evidence through discovery was cut off when the judge dismissed the case six weeks after the killing.

That only made Percy more motivated. She put together a new case against AMR on similar facts, harvesting from the detailed file Miles had assembled on the case. She filed other cases against friends of the administration, having figured out that the civil courts were not yet entirely suborned by the powers in Washington and Austin who had successfully rigged other parts of the mechanics of justice in favor of them and their allies. She figured out the best judges and courts to chase down those cases. But it didn't move fast enough for her.

"People are dying while we take depositions," she said, the day she told Donny she was leaving the practice to run for office. He couldn't argue. Even though he knew the reason she could make that move was that she had managed to settle one of those cases she had filed, and banked enough this time to live on for the next decade, even if she decided instead she wanted to blow it on political ads.

She let Donny pick which of her cases he wanted. AMR was the easy one. If he could get it far enough along, not only could he expose what was going on in the farms but maybe also help bring down the regime, and make a nice payday in the process.

He might even find who ordered the hit on Miles, and who carried it out, and make them all pay.

The other thing about that case was, Miles had taken it on in the first place only because of Donny, when one of his oldest clients asked for help for her nephew. Maybe if he had taken it on himself at the beginning, instead of saying I only do criminal defense, Miles would never have ended up embalmed by the frontage road.

The light changed, but his thoughts stayed on his old friend.

"IT'S BEEN A LONG TIME," SAID DONNY, GREETING THAT OLD CLI-
ent and her partner at his Houston office later that morning.

"That it has," said Xelina.

Clint was behind her, casually guarding her. You could see
the war in their eyes.

"Thanks for coming down here to meet," said Donny.

"Wouldn't miss the chance to see you in your native habitat," said Xelina, sizing up the conference room. She had a
little bit of gray in her hair, coming in early, and her rebel style
had mellowed. The clothes were more minimalist, black cotton and denim, and the jewelry that looked like it could hurt
you had been replaced by pieces that looked like they could
put a spell on you.

"My native habitat is the courtroom, and you've already
seen me there."

She nodded. You could see she still didn't want to talk about
what she went through back then, almost a decade ago. "Where
did all this wood come from?" she said, putting her hand on the
paneling like it was the fossil of some extinct pterosaur. "Look
at that grain."

"I don't know," said Donny. "No doubt Miles had the full
provenance, but he never told me."

"I'm still sorry about what happened to him," said Xelina.

"Thanks," said Donny, looking at the ghosts in the room. "I
suppose taking over his lease wasn't the best way to cope with

his loss." Donny didn't mention that he had missed the last two payments on that lease.

"It was the right way to honor his memory," said Xelina. "To carry on his work."

Donny nodded.

"He was a good dude," said Clint, looking out the window. "Sucks that they never could figure out who killed him."

"We haven't given up yet," said Donny. That was true, except there wasn't much of a "we" anymore.

"At least you finally got justice for this guy," said Xelina, looking at one of the photos on the wall.

It was a picture of Donny standing with Sig, one of his most famous clients from the uprising. Slider had started out in one of Sig's gangs in New Orleans. Sig went on to build a bigger gang that led a series of cross-country raids and even helped liberate the White House, only to be jailed as a scapegoat for having the balls to rob the Federal Reserve and keep the money instead of giving it to the cause. Killing politicians was one thing. Taking the banks' money was a whole different deal.

"Yeah," said Donny. "That was actually easier than you would think. Mainly because his sister called in some favors, along with some powerful backers. I just came up with the idea to offer up his leaving the country in exchange for an early release."

"Such bullshit," said Xelina. "It's not what we fought for."

"I know," said Donny. "But I think he was actually kind of happy about it. He's a freeborn man. More of a Rover than any of you ever were, like literally born to roam. He told me he was happy to see the world across the ocean. I even paid for his upgrade to a nicer berth on the ship."

"He's lucky they didn't put him with the live animal cargo," said Clint. "I miss him. Is it true he's in Russia?"

"That's what I heard," said Donny. "Hanging out somewhere in Siberia, with actual nomads. But that's mostly word of mouth. Sig's not the kind of guy who sends a lot of postcards."

They sat.

Donny had his working file on Slider's case on the table in front of him, which was as thick as a couple of dictionaries stacked on top of each other. He put his hand on it.

"I don't need to tell you I have a lot invested in this case. Enough to be very close to getting the outcome we all want."

"You've told us that before, Donny," said Xelina.

"It's closer this time," said Donny. "For real. Trial is set for next month. I have finally found real evidence of AMR's complicity in the killings at the resettlement farms. At least the Killeen camp. Including Juana and Gil. This could bring the company down. We'll get to dissolve it, liquidate the assets, and pay them out to the families of all those who died or were injured behind the wire. Or that was the plan, until Monday, when the defense lawyers sprang their trap on me: Slider is dead. Killed during an op."

Clint sipped his coffee, watching Xelina. She had her soldier face on, but you could see the sad welling up.

"I can't imagine how hard this must be," said Donny. "He's y'all's nephew. You're the closest thing he has to parents, and he's the closest thing you have to a child. It's too late to save him, but maybe not too late to keep his case alive. And to do that I need to figure out what really went down."

Clint took Xelina's hand and held it. He looked even more emotional about the subject than her.

Donny looked at their hands.

Both had the scars of fighters who had been members of the resistance and been detained by the old regime. Her scars were finer than his, but older, and maybe deeper.

"Who did he piss off?" said Donny. "I know it's hard to talk about. But if I can put the real story together, I just might be able to convince the judge to give me a break. Or, failing that, get justice from whoever took him out."

"Daryl was an angry kid," said Clint. "He pissed off a lot of people."

"I know," said Donny. "I helped him get away with the things he did in the struggle."

"Can't I substitute for him in your case?" said Xelina. "Juana was my sister."

"Not in the eyes of the law, Xelina," said Donny. "You may have shared a house as kids, but there are no ties of blood or marriage. Nothing that will support you standing in as the injured party."

"Fuck the law and its bullshit ideas of what makes a family," said Clint.

"I agree. And we may have a chance to change that yet. But not in time to save my case. I need answers."

"You should leave it alone, dude," said Clint. "You need to come up with another angle."

"Did he piss off someone on the Council? He was always talking about how he had better ideas than them."

"Maybe," said Clint. "We got out of there, and I'm not going back anytime soon. That's some Reign of Terror shit they got going."

Donny looked at Xelina.

"I don't know what happened, Donny," she said. "Like Clint said, we haven't been back there in a while, and most of our people there have left too. We're tired of fighting. The only thing I do know that might help you is that some blue neckties have been sniffing around asking questions about Slider."

"A couple of them dropped in on me the other day," said

Donny. "Asking some pretty wild questions. I figured they were crazy. But now I want to know what he did."

"Then you know as much as we do," said Clint.

"Are you really going to New Orleans?" said Xelina.

"Yeah. To try to save the rich girl they were arresting when Slider was killed."

They looked at each other. Clint raised an eyebrow.

"I know what you think," said Donny. "But her dad is an old friend."

"Be careful," said Clint. "The war's not as over as people like to think. And last time I checked, you're on the payback list."

"I know. But I have to believe they'll talk to me. There's got to be a shot at a deal. And if I don't go, I'm afraid things will be a lot worse for all of us."

"You may be right about that," said Clint.

"When are you going?" said Xelina.

"In the morning. There's a hearing scheduled for Friday, and I'm hoping we can work a deal and make it a short trip."

"Good luck with that," said Xelina. "The people on the Council can't even figure out what to have for lunch without two days of argument."

"I'm counting on the fact that they know me. And they need to work something out just as badly as my clients do."

"Sounds like the time you told us you had the case all figured out, and then Xelina ended up spending a week on that fucking prison boat," said Clint.

Donny didn't remind him that he also got her freed. "It's worth a shot," he said. "To be honest, I don't really have a choice."

You could see it in their eyes, how their estimation of him suddenly dropped when they realized how desperate he really was. That it wasn't about the client's problems. It was about his problems.

Xelina reached for Donny's hand.

"Remember when we thought we were going to build a better future?" said Donny.

"Yeah, well, don't call us when you need a rescue from that," said Clint.

19

AFTER AN AFTERNOON AT THE FEDERAL COURTHOUSE CALLING IN a favor that would help him get Heather's jailers to the bargaining table, Donny checked his messages one last time for responses from the prospective class members he had contacted. Two bouncebacks, and a crazy-long message from a conflicted mom, the main point of which was how her late son's treasonous politics got him the punishment he deserved.

His grandma left him a message, asking him to send more files. And so he did.

Bone-tired, before he went home he made one more stop: at the safe house where he had last seen Slider. But the mastodon was gone, and the only person there was an old black lady who said those people moved out a year ago.

That night, Donny packed light for his trip to New Orleans. Xelina was right about negotiating with the committee, but he couldn't afford to be there more than a couple of days. With luck, by the time he got back, his grandma would have found a new plaintiff, and they would be back in business.

On the bed were two suits. One to wear on the way there, one to wear to the negotiation he had in mind. He took three shirts, four ties, and five pairs of underwear. You never knew.

He looked at his shoes. Lawyer shoes, nice ones he had bought when he raided his savings, now with rubber soles the cobbler put on when he wore holes through the original leather.

The TV in the next room was tuned to RT5, the French

channel. One of their US correspondents was touring New Orleans. Nassra al-Balushi, who had reported from the region off and on through the fighting, and knew how to make rubber boots look good. Even when she was standing calf-deep in the water that flowed down what used to be a major street.

Donny went to his closet, the one by the front door where he kept his fishing gear. He pulled out his rubber boots. They were the cheap kind from the neighborhood hardware store, unstructured, mainly used by Donny to get to his car when it flooded.

He reached farther back, and found his old waders. Maybe not.

Then he remembered the other boots. But he wasn't even sure if he still had them.

He went to the back closet. Pulled over a chair, and reached up onto the high shelf. Three boxes fell on him, full of old papers. Tax files and letters from dead friends.

He reached farther.

The next box was dusty. But you could still make out the Maschen logo.

When she bought them, Joyce explained how they were made on the French-German border. The inventor was on the German side and his factory was on the French side. Or maybe it was the other way around. The point was that the place had been on both sides. That the shoes were from a place that knew borders are a lie, even when they define your world.

No wonder they look so funny, said Donny.

They look great, she said. They work with a suit, or in the field. Try them on.

He did, and they fit perfectly. Joyce was always good that way.

It was the only time he wore them.

On TV, Nassra was in Jackson Square now. The rebel leader Gertrude Almeida was giving a speech to the gathered crowd.

Donny had the sound low, and he couldn't read the captions from that far away, but you could see Gertie was mad.

Gertie made her name by being mad, about things she had every right to be mad about. She was mad before they locked her up for talking about those things, and she was a lot madder when she got out, after the riot in the Superdome that freed all the prisoners.

You could just hear what she was saying.

First they stole our future. Then they stole our present. So now we are going to take their past.

It was a good line. She got it from Donny, at the meeting where he pitched the idea for the truth and reconciliation tribunals. An idea they had grabbed on to, and then taken in a totally different direction than he had in mind.

Donny tried on the boots. After he got the dead bugs out. Then he walked over and turned up the volume.

A group of purple-hooded paramilitaries made some middle-aged white guy in a green-and-blue golf outfit kneel in front of Gertie. They pulled a noose around his neck. Or that's what it looked like, until they made the guy take off his clothes, and you could see the rope was a leash.

Nassra explained that the man was a real-estate developer. One who had sold off foreclosed acreages in the Midwest at a huge profit to Tripto Labs and its biofuels partners.

He did not look good naked.

They had tried him for the destruction of the habitat of the animals that had lived on those lands, and for the poisoning of the Mississippi River watershed that the fuel producers caused.

The man did not produce enough money to satisfy the judgment, which meant he had to give back to nature in accordance with the old laws. By which they meant the laws of nature.

146

That part of it they didn't get from Donny.

Maybe it was the way the camera caught it, but Gertie's accusatory finger was a powerful and scary thing, especially close-up.

She asked him one more time to pay. He just got red in the face and started accusing her right back. So the hoods pulled the leash to take him away.

Donny looked at his feet. The boots still fit.

On the TV, Gertie and the others watched the man crawl.

Nassra cut to an exterior shot. Deep swamp, cypress and black water, sounds of birds and bugs. The developer is on a little boat with three of the guards. Still naked. The boat is a shallow-water punt. One of the guards is poling.

Nassra explains how the prisoner tried to bribe his guards.

Now he is just begging.

They have a banker's bag full of money. Cash and coins. They tie it to his leg with a length of cord.

Then they make him jump into the water.

He is screaming, spazzing, water up to his thighs. You can tell his feet are stuck in the muck of the bottom, weighed down by the money bag, which is stuck even deeper.

The camera reveals other motion in the water.

When you see the gator eyes move, you can also see the skyline of downtown New Orleans in the far background.

The man tries to grab on to the punt, but the poler pushes him back on his ass. And then he starts poling away.

The camera shows a montage of motion in water, bird sil-houette, sundown. The sound of night.

They do not show the man being pulled under, but they make you think that is what happened.

Donny looked at his boots. He read once that the holes in brogues were originally made for bogs and swamps, so the water drains off more easily. Maybe time to find out if that's really true, he thought. It sounded pretty ridiculous to him when he heard it, like the kind of thing the catalog copywriters come up with to make you think you are doing something more adventurous than going to an office.

Donny wished he could just go to his office, but then his ride called.

And while he was telling the guy where to pick him up, he continued to stare at the boots Joyce had given him, and wondered if he'd see her in New Orleans.

Seven Years Earlier

IT WAS A FIVE-HOUR DRIVE FROM HOUSTON TO BROWNSVILLE when Donny went to save Joyce, down coastal highways that were getting more coastal every year, especially with the downpours that weird winter was delivering. Donny headed out crazy early, aided by coffee he brewed the night before and the old-school lawyers' answering service he sometimes used as a wake-up call. His car was driving a little funny since he got it back from the feds who had tried to forfeit it on his last case, so he just drove it harder until the noise of the rain overpowered the noise of the weird knock down in the suspension. Not getting there was not an option.

This was right after the coup, when the only things playing on the radio were the FM version of Eagle News Network and the robot tones of the Emergency Broadcast System giving citizens instructions on how to protect themselves from their neighbors. Donny was not good at taking instructions from robots or anyone else, not even clients, really, so as he tooled along in his Chinese sedan that had seen better days, he scanned the AM band until he finally picked up one of the Mexican border blasters, this one out of Reynosa, playing some punk-ass corrido that as best Donny could tell was about the coyotes who helped smuggle Americans out. The chorus recited some kind of Spanglish network code mnemonic you could apparently use to get in contact with the dudes IRL. Donny sang along, hoping it would stick.

He was singing it back into his phone when he saw the first convoy coming the other direction. Troop carriers, maybe thirty of them, and a train of those loudspeaker vans with the LRAD cannons on top. Houston, we have a crowd-control problem.

Donny remembered the last time Joyce and he had gone out to Alpine for the long weekend, not that long before the first time she dumped him. On the last night, they got high and drove through the high desert to the Marfa Lights viewing area. They almost ran over some ghostly looking animal that Donny insisted was a Chupacabra and Joyce said was a feral dog. As they sat there listening to spacey music on the station out of Presidio, they argued about the future—the future of America and the future of them as a couple, both of which sounded bleak. Donny said I need to take a leak, which was really his way of taking a break from the low-intensity argument, and when he stepped out into the dark, cloudless night he heard the rumble of a big heavy train blowing down the tracks on the other side of the highway. He watched it until his eyes adjusted and he could see what freight it had: tanks, Humvees, and light artillery, painted that new army green that was almost black, headed east, destination unknown.

After midnight is when the secret cargo rolls.

Not long after the convoy drove by he saw a school bus loaded with prisoners, headed north on the Victoria bypass, maybe to one of the big camps outside of Houston.

In a fight between a lawyer and a tank, who would win?

As the sun came up over Corpus, you could see the miles of refineries along the coastline, and the interceptors taking off from the naval air station. It took him forty minutes to get through the checkpoint there at the I-37 interchange, and when he told them where he was going and why, Donny could see the guy phoning ahead as he pulled away.

When he finally got to Brownsville, he hit the last checkpoint. The one no one was supposed to be able to cross, six short blocks from the border and the freedom it represented. Between there were the old warehouses and commercial buildings that had been taken over by the Motherland Guard. One of which, a windowless former Kmart, was where they were holding Joyce.

The story was they had a new interrogation technique they were trying out. The Blue Light Special.

JOYCE HAD FLED the country on the day they seized power. Donny was supposed to go with her. Not as lovers, but as friends. She liked the idea of a lawyer helping her get across. And maybe she wanted more, but she could be hard to pin down on such matters.

Donny had even driven to her place that morning, all packed and ready to go. But by the time he got there, he had changed his mind. Or more accurately, the world had changed it for him. He had a duty to stay back and fight the regime in court. Fight to eke out what justice he could for the regime's enemies and victims. Lawyers in exile are useless. Joyce said you should write a book, a history of how we got here, but Donny said first we have to fix the future.

That same day, as Joyce went to cross at Brownsville, which she had been told was the safest, Donny was in court with Miles, trying to challenge the President's increasingly brazen use of his emergency powers with the domestic deployment of military forces they called police but anyone could see were soldiers and private military contractors. She didn't get across. She was detained at the border, even though she had one of the new passports.

The things she had written had gotten her on the list. As did some of her friends who had already been detained. Male academics, Donny later read in one of the memos that cleared the interrogation enhancements, were the easiest subjects to get to rat out their friends. The theories for why that was varied.

They had detained her three days before Donny even got the news. And that he only got because Judge Broyles let him know, in confidence. Probably the day after Broyles signed the order allowing her interrogation to proceed.

They had had her three weeks before Donny could get the order for her release. And even then, it wasn't entirely clear her release was due to Donny's efforts, or because they just decided they were done with her. But they said Donny could come pick her up.

Donny had told her not to try to take her pistol across with her, but Joyce was ornery that way.

"I'M HERE TO retrieve a prisoner," said Donny. "My client."

He handed the guard a business card. You would be surprised how often that works.

"Wait here," said the guard, and then he stepped out of his kiosk and walked back toward the nearby building.

The gate in front of him was a wall of steel on wheels. Some local kids had managed to tag it, with a red stencil of an armadillo holding a spray can in one hand and a hammer in the other. A guy in fatigues was on his knees trying to rub the graffiti out with some chemical that required him to wear a respirator. He wasn't having much luck.

Standing in front of that guy was a more serious-looking dude in the blue and orange of the Guard, waiting for Donny to give him an excuse to use the South African assault rifle he had slung to his tactical vest. Donny looked to his right, and saw the

K-9 officer walking the perimeter of his car, with a dog that was too short for Donny to see. In the rearview mirror were two more guards, one with the mirror on a stick they used to search the undercarriage for bombs. Behind them was an armored truck that had been pulled up to block Donny from backing out.

Donny had his arm up on the open driver's-side window. He looked that way, and noticed for the first time the cluster of cameras and microphones there, right about where the box would be at the drive-through of a fast-food joint.

"Hey, do you all have any breakfast tacos?" said Donny, speaking to the box.

The sixth member of the detail attending to his arrival standing there in the kiosk, who had been reading whatever it was the screen said about Donny, looked at him with something more confounded than a cop stare.

"Excuse me?" he said.

"No?" said Donny. "How about a latte."

The guy shook his head in disgust.

The dog was right there now, sniffing Donny's quarter-panel at the end of a short leash. It wore a black vest velcroed with morale patches of urban combat service in Nicaragua, New Orleans, and Nebraska. Its handler was a young white guy with an ugly beard made uglier by his service branch's regulations of its personnel's facial hair. Donny imagined the actual regulation that existed in a book each of those men had been issued, there with all the other rules ensuring conformity of their grooming and hygiene.

"What kind of dog is that?" asked Donny.

The K-9 handler just looked at him, then looked back at the dog.

"What kind of dog are you, Titus?" Donny asked the dog, whose name was also patched on its vest, in GI Joe letters.

"Don't talk to the dog," said the handler.

Donny could see it was one of those Doberman–pit bull mixes the Secret Service had bred back in the day for its combination of nose and attack aptitudes.

That was when the lead guard returned with Donny's business card still in his hand. He walked up to Donny and handed the card back.

"We have no record of that release, and you're not on the list."

"What list?"

"You can turn your vehicle around, and follow Officer Sullivan here to the return path."

"I'm not going anywhere without my client. I have an order from a federal judge."

"Did you hear that, Sully?" said the guard. "He has an order from a federal judge."

"All right, Burger King," said Donny. "Have it your way."

Donny opened his car door.

"Stay in the car," said Burger King.

Donny disregarded that order.

As soon as his feet touched pavement, the klaxon rang. And almost as soon as he stood up to face the guards, Titus took him down, paws on suit flannel.

When he looked up at the fangs, and the three gun barrels backing them up, Donny wondered if this was really the best way to get inside.

THEY TOOK ALL of Donny's stuff, everything but his clothes, and put him in a holding room. It reminded him of the interrogation suite at the federal detention in Houston—painted cinder-block walls, a metal bench bolted to the concrete floor, a picture of the President on the wall next to a poster in seven languages that explained how travelers have no Fourth Amendment rights in the borderzone, no matter what passport they carry. In the middle of the steel door was a little slat to look through from the other side. In the middle of the floor was a drain, which only made you wonder what fluids they planned to spill.

At least the air conditioning was working. They had it extra cold, on purpose.

They had left Donny uncuffed. They usually went a little easier on lawyers, he had learned, because lawyers were more effective than their usual victims at whining to judges about their treatment in detention.

"Fuck you," said Donny, to the face of the President staring at him from across the room. It was one of those official portraits where he had that almost-smile. The wily executive who will let you choose between serving him or fighting him.

He got up and tried to pull the picture off the wall, but they had attached it to where it was like a part of the wall. So he tried smashing it, and scratching it, with his bare hands. And right as he was about to give up, it came unmoored from the wall. Just a crack, but enough to be able to pry it all the way, pulling out some chunks of cinder block as it came free. Then he cracked it against the steel door, and shoved it through the slit. The metal frame clanged loudly as it hit the floor outside.

Then he sat back down and waited. He had already been there more than an hour, every minute one more that Joyce was still in their custody.

The door burst open, as fast as a door secured with five different locks can open. In came two uniformed guards and one suit.

"What the fuck's going on in here?" said the older of the guards, a beefy white Texan with a name tag that said Stevens.

"Just waiting for you idiots to obey the law and produce my client," said Donny.

Stevens grabbed Donny by the lapels and shoved him up against the wall.

"The only idiot in here is you," said Stevens, up in his face with teeth bared like he was going to bite him for real. "Disrespecting our President."

"He's not the president, Jethro. He lost the election. Maybe that was above your pay grade. And this fight isn't over yet."

"That's what you think," said Stevens, slamming Donny against the wall.

"Up yours, fat boy," said Donny, winded. "Every time you hit me is another year of time you're going to do when we wake up from this bad dream. And then I am going to bankrupt you and your family."

In those weeks after the coup, before everyone adjusted to the new normal, Donny actually believed that. In a way, he never stopped believing it. Even though it ended up taking another six years to get there, after they figured out elections and lawsuits weren't going to suffice.

"I want to speak with a supervisor," said Donny. "The customer service in this place sucks."

The guy in the suit actually chuckled at that.

"Lay off him for a minute, Stevens," said the suit.

Stevens dropped Donny back onto the bench.

"What's the deal, here, Mr.—" The suit grabbed the clipboard the other officer was holding and looked at the top sheet. "Mr. Kimoe?"

"The deal is I have an order from a federal judge for the release of a prisoner, and you guys are giving me the runaround."

The suit flipped the pages on the clipboard. "That would be Prisoner 11–07043–091?"

"Her name is Joyce." Donny repeated it, with her full name.

"Uh-huh," said the suit. "Do you understand why she was detained?"

"Yes. For her politics, which is why the judge ordered she be released."

"The judge got it wrong."

"Why don't you tell the judge that."

"That's not my job," said the suit. "And the orders we have say the orders of judges don't apply during the emergency. At least not here in the borderzone."

"Do you really want to defy the order of a federal judge?" said Donny. "Just to keep one college professor with a valid passport from exercising her right to leave the country and never come back?"

The suit looked like he was thinking that one over.

"What goes around, comes around," said Donny. "Someday everyone in this building is going to be held accountable for what is happening right now. I don't know if it's going to take two days or twenty years, but it's going to happen. And following orders from up the chain of command will not excuse illegality. Especially not illegal detention and interrogation techniques that we all know are torture."

"Don't listen to this snake, Perez," said Stevens.

"Each of you are personally in contempt of court, and liable for the unlawful imprisonment of my client," said Donny. "And I don't even want to know what other crimes you may be perpetrating on her. But you can be goddamned sure I will hold you accountable for them. Especially if you do not free her right now. So ignore me at your own risk, Mr. Perez."

"He's Special Agent Perez to you," said Stevens.

Donny corrected himself, and watched Special Agent Perez cogitate over the situation.

They heard the faint sound of a very loud scream muffled by sound baffling. Stevens nodded at his uniformed colleague to close the door.

"Is there someone with some decision-making authority I could speak to?" said Donny.

"Wait here," said Perez. He pulled out his phone.

"Who are you calling?" said Stevens.

Perez didn't answer. He stepped out into the hallway.

"Keep your hands where I can see 'em," said Stevens. He had his truncheon out now.

Donny gave Stevens the finger, with both hands.

They waited there for what felt like a long time. He thought he heard the sound of Perez's voice, but the air conditioner kicked on and muffled it through white noise.

Perez came back in.

"Come with me," he said.

Stevens looked disgusted, and gave Donny one last shove from behind for good measure as they left the room.

WHEN THEY FINALLY brought Joyce out, she was wearing the red jumpsuit of a noncompliant detainee. Donny almost wanted to make a smartass remark about it, but saw the shackles and thought better of it.

"Where's her stuff?" said Donny, and Perez had the guards remove her shackles. "She needs her passport."

No answer.

"And what about her car?" asked Donny.

"Maybe you should just go while you can," said Perez. "Deal with those things later."

Joyce looked at Donny and nodded.

"Fine," said Donny.

And then Joyce walked over to him, and they hugged for long enough that Perez said you need to go. He opened the door for them, and said follow me.

Perez led them outside into the Texas heat, light so bright even under the covered walkway that you had to squint. They passed checkpoints and stepped around barricades. And then they were standing at the beginning of the bridge, on the other side of which was Mexico.

Donny held Joyce's hand, and they walked. She was a little slow.

You could see a cantina there right past the bridge, painted with a big cartoon of the sun with a smiling human face, the logo of an old lager beer of the Mexican coast.

Before they could get there, they had to get past the Mexican checkpoint without a passport. It used to be there wasn't even a checkpoint on the Mexican side, not for pedestrian crossers, until the refugees started coming in droves.

The guards stepped out when they saw Joyce's prison jumpsuit.

"*Buscamos asilo,*" said Donny.

Asylum.

WHILE THEY WAITED for the Mexicans to complete their paperwork, Donny tried to convince Joyce that the first thing they should do when she was released was get a medical examination.

"There's an Amnesty office right here," he said. "We can file a human-rights complaint at the same time."

"No, Donny," was the answer.

They went straight to a hotel instead. The most Mexico-looking hotel they could find in the row lined up there along the main thoroughfare leading into Matamoros. Donny offered to get his own room, but Joyce settled on two beds.

"It's good to have someone close. Just not that close. Okay?"

Okay.

Donny went shopping while Joyce took a very long bath. He got her three sundresses, a western shirt, cheap sunglasses, some jeans, and a T-shirt advertising Playa Bagdad. She went with the jeans and the T-shirt, and the cheap tequila he got at the store next door. She put on the sunglasses, and you could tell she planned to never take them off again. They sat there all afternoon at the tiny table by the window, watching the sun slowly work its way across the square and hardly saying a word as they let the Cuervo work its way through their anxious minds. From where Donny sat you could see the border crossing, with the flag billowing there above the walls. The real purpose now was to keep people in on the other side. Maybe it always had been.

It wasn't until they went out for dinner that Joyce finally was willing to talk about what happened. That she had not been tortured, just questioned, and humiliated in a menu of ways that were not in any way actionable. That she did not want to sue anybody. That the American courts were not where the fight could be won. That the way to fight these fascists was not with lawsuits.

Donny decided not to argue with her.

In the morning, Joyce's application had already been approved. She was known. Donny didn't apply for asylum, just a tourist visa. They took the new train to Mexico City, the one that ran on magnets or whatever and produced zero pollution.

Her friends met her there at the station, a cabal of people that a later historian explaining their role in what was going on in the world would call intellectuals but Donny called fucking professors and fucking writers. Donny knew one of them, Howard Moritz, a philosopher Joyce had worked with at Rice until he got a new job in Dallas and then a political secondment to UNAM. The other expat in the group was someone Donny had heard of but never met: Wade Camacho, the singer-songwriter from Austin who had the distinction of being the first musician ever to be denaturalized for the treasonous lyrics of his songs. They all had a dinner for her, and nobody really had much to say to Donny. Maybe it was the suit, even though he left the tie in his bag, because Mexico. They knew he was still a lawyer. Agent of the state, even if a double agent. Even if he was the one who got Joyce there in the first place.

Joyce sat next to Wade, and soon she was smiling, the first real smiles Donny had seen on her in a while. He couldn't complain.

Donny hung out in Mexico City for a couple of days. He called up an old colleague from B&E, one of the guys who had been fired the same day as Donny in the purge. Hector was bilingual, and worked the US asylum cases from there. They had coffee at the library where Hector was working. Hector tried to recruit Donny to help with the project, but Donny said I have my own projects.

The next day was when he told Joyce he had to go back. She said I know. They both knew it was over, even if neither of them said it. Something had changed in the world that made what they thought they could get back gone forever.

He flew home. It would be a few years before that became impossible. He tried as hard as he could to get the immigration officer at the port of entry to arrest him, but no such luck.

Joyce got busy in a hurry, but Donny didn't find out about that until a lot later. After she had disappeared for good.

PART TWO

The Borders of Utopia

THE CONSOLATION PRIZE FOR SPENDING THE DAY TRAVELING across Cancer Alley by bus, train, and boat was the discovery that they sold souvenir T-shirts in utopia. Donny didn't buy one. But it was pouring rain when he stepped off the barge, and when he saw the canopied merch booth at the landing also sold hot coffee, he took shelter. He was paying for his cup and asking the kid for directions and whether there were any dry modes of local transportation available when he saw the little sign that said the proceeds from all sales went to the fund for the new school. So Donny blew eight bucks on a hand-tooled lapel pin. And when he got up the next day in his spartan room at the inn they called the Library, he put it on, the way some of his colleagues used to put the flag pins on when they wanted the judge to know which side they were on. This one was made from salvaged metal instead of industrial lacquer, with an image of a raccoon holding a book. Donny wasn't sure what it really meant, but he liked raccoons. And when he looked in the mirror, he convinced himself it would work, and set out to save his ex-friend's kid.

It had stopped raining that Friday morning when Donny headed to court in the flooded ruins of New Orleans. The locals didn't call them ruins. They called them liberated territory, and the law they applied in their new court, which they called the Tributary, was a new kind of law no judge had ever seen, even though they said it was the oldest and truest law in the world. Most of the so-called locals were people from some-place else, veterans of the uprising or latecomers who wanted to help beta-test a different kind of future. Donny used to feel like an honorary local, even when the city was under siege, and he expected to soon be reunited with some of his old comrades. But as he waited for the streetcar in the muggy morning air, he knew they might not be happy to see him. Especially when he was showing up on the other side of the case.

And when he checked his phone for news on the case he had left behind, all he got was the warning that he had no sig-nal. Because one of the first things his old clients did when they took over the city was to climb up the towers and replace all the corporate phone cells with birdhouses. They had their own network, which they said was free and open, if you could figure out how to get in. So Donny cursed them, and then tried to convince himself that it was a good thing to be offline for a day, and just focus on the immediate task at hand.

He looked down the median that cut through St. Charles, first light on the dewy grass that had been allowed to go long, and noticed how quiet the city had become. No engines. No cars, no trucks, no honking, no grinding, no screeching brakes, no air conditioners, no amplified music, no overflying jets or choppers. Just birdsong—the sound of a tropical city gone back to green.

It looked and sounded pretty, but it mainly made him sweat, a sweat that started under his arms and in the small of his back, the kind of mugtown sweat you can tell by breakfast is going to make you want a shower and change of clothes by noon. He would have to make it until evening, when his trans-port was scheduled to take him back to his true habitat.

The thought of what awaited him back home if he failed made him look at his watch anxiously, wondering if they even had a timetable here in the city that capitalism forgot. He reflexively straightened his tie, even though he should have been taking it off.

And then, after what seemed like an hour standing there—but wasn't even half that—he heard the bell of the approaching streetcar before he even saw it. Maybe because the front light was off, something that was no surprise given that the streetcar was the only means of independently powered transportation still running in New Orleans, off the power of the sun.

When she opened the door, the driver, a twentysomething white lady who wore a green jumpsuit and a revolver, gave him the look you would give a marooned time traveler you found at the side of the road.

"I hear this is the way to the future," said Donny.

She laughed. And then she held out her hand.

"I thought it was free," said Donny.

"Not for outsiders," she said. "Unless you have a pass."

"On my way to pick mine up now," he said. It was almost true.

"Come on," she said, not laughing anymore. "We need the funds. It's for a good cause."

"Hang on," said Donny.

"Open your fucking wallet, man!" yelled a voice from inside the trolley. Donny looked back at the crowd of passengers, who were all looking at him. You could spot the tourists from their cameras, and the sandals, visiting from Asia or Europe to check out the big experiment. You could spot the American refugees from their luggage, here to punch in their hard-earned ticket out, headed for a better life at the other end of a long cruise. You could spot the locals from the way they looked at Donny.

The one who was yelling at him was a white-haired older

lady sitting in front. She had a gun, too, sticking out of the purse on her lap, which looked like she had made it herself from found scraps.

"Cough it up, dude! We can't afford your coat-and-tie bullshit."

"Jeez," said Donny. "Hang on. How much?" He set down his briefcase and reached for his wallet.

"Five," said the driver.

He pulled out a worn five-dollar bill. Crisp ones were hard to come by these days, and not because they weren't printing them.

"Rupees, hon," said the driver. "Five hundred rupees. Money we can use. If you're paying greenbacks, I need twenty."

"How about pesos?" said Donny, digging into the secret stash.

"Bueno," said the driver, grabbing the cash and pocketing it.

The car lurched forward, and Donny stumbled his way to the back, almost tripping over the suitcases in the aisle. The bags and their owners were on their way to board ships for Guyana, Goa, or Godthab. Nodes in the network of newly minted sovereignties of which New Orleans was the newest, pockets of recovered ecological health in a blighted world that welcomed new settlers, especially if they had skills. Some were clutching their travel documents as Donny stepped over their bags. He found a seat in the very back, by the window, next to a nervous-looking couple telling each other stories of people who had been turned away after making it all the way here.

The streetcar clickety-clacked its way down the wide boulevard, through a city that had spent most of the past decade as a war zone. Along the avenue, it looked more like a city that had been abandoned, in no small part because much of it was, even there in those big old houses on what passed for high ground. Nature had always been winning in New Orleans, a city built on lush riverbanks and wetlands ever-ready to overgrow and devour any structure that didn't put up a fight. Green fungus on stucco, levees failed, yards gone wild. It was hard to know how much of this de-domestication of the urban environment resulted from inattention and how much from intention. The new regime was running the city on a different model, one that treated the lawn mower as a weapon of mass destruction, and believed in letting the water go where it wanted. The human inhabitants supported by an infrastructure that followed nature's paths instead of trying to control it.

It had been a long time since anyone conducted a census, at least of the living, but you didn't need statistics to know that the population was a fraction of what it had been before. Maybe because when the wild came back out, the human wild, you knew that was how things had always really been.

As they trundled on past Napoleon, picking up a passenger here and there, the signs of fighting became more evident. Long blocks of empty lots, many of them burned, a few of them leveled. Graffiti like fresh petroglyphs encoding a secret history of all the back-and-forth between the different factions. Parking lots and side streets taken over by weeds coming up through cracks in the blacktop. A city whose true rulers were the feral cats and dogs that patrolled the nights, and were reportedly being displaced by the new breed of coyotes that had mixed with the big dogs. Through the window, Donny saw one dog lope off into the tall grass at the sound of the trolley, too fast to see closely but with something pink and fleshy hanging from its mouth.

They were still adding to their serve count under the Golden Arches, but the arches were shattered, just the flimsy aluminum frame left, all the wiring stripped out for salvage. Under new management by the customers, who started the morning off with fair-trade chicory and fried dough liberally seasoned with the sugars of free peoples. The staff at the inn that morning had told Donny that was a good option for breakfast, but he didn't have time. Nor the inclination—until he noticed the garden they had grown where the drive-through used to be, and the gang of children spread out on a giant picnic blanket while their teacher handed out strawberries the size of baseballs. Something about that happy scene opened up the valve that contained his grief, a valve whose welds were cauterized by the cynicism of a lawyer who had seen some of the worst things people were capable of.

The nervous-looking woman in the seat next to him caught him crying, and gave him a look of understanding, if not of sympathy. And when she saw Donny's eyes, she clutched her travel papers tighter, pushed her suitcase closer to her husband, and looked past him at the old billboard by the roadside. A worker was up there pasting a new poster over the palimpsest.

COME TO GREENLAND

And the thing was, it was actually green. Even the new houses of the model village. And the people were wearing shorts.

The one thing he didn't see through the window were the blue helmets of the international peacekeeping troops. They had left New Orleans six months earlier. He opened up his briefcase, and dug back into the file he had not had enough time to study on the unexpectedly complicated trip down.

He was rereading the French news report on the Tributary when the streetcar stopped at Lee Circle for the security check.

Lee Circle, which no longer had that name, marked the western boundary of the secure zone beyond which outsiders were restricted. When the streetcar turned into the roundabout and stopped, two paramilitaries boarded the bus.

"Good morning, travelers," said the younger of the two, a twentysomething black woman wearing a purple beret and a Kalashnikov. "If you are not already known to us as a member of our community, please have your IDs and travel papers out. I know it's a hassle, but we've had a lot of infiltrators lately. And if you are headed to the port, please get off here and wait for the cart that will take you down there."

While she spoke to the passengers, her colleague, a bearded old white guy with a beat-up Saints cap and a shotgun slung low, was already sizing them up. Donny looked away.

Through the window he could see the monument at the heart of the Circle, the one that had once vaulted the Confederate general a hundred feet up in the air to watch for invaders from the north, not knowing the real danger came from the people at his feet, people who had finally gotten tired enough of the power he stood for that they were willing to do something about it. When the column that held him was toppled, they ritually buried the general in the muddy fathoms of the river. In his place, in the stump of rubble that was all that was left of the column, they planted a tree. It was some kind of oak, one that had been a sapling when they first liberated the city, but had grown remarkably fast since Donny's last visit, big enough to create some shade under which a trio of young people were sitting and talking.

Donny watched from the corner of his eye as the old rebel guard, who Donny now realized actually looked a little bit like Robert E. Lee, made a pair of young guys get up out of their seats for handoff to the other guards waiting outside.

Donny looked back out the window, as if he had nothing to worry about.

Beyond the tree, Donny could see the high-rises of the old Central Business District. Most of them were still standing, especially the older ones that had been built with more lasting bones, but you could also see the vegetation coming through the cracks and holes that brought the rain and sun. As he sat there in the long minutes waiting his turn for interrogation, one ear listening to the questions Old Boy was asking the other passengers and trying to think of clever responses while the other ear tuned in to the world outside the open window, he was struck again by the quiet of the city, even as they were at the edge of downtown. But it wasn't silent. Now you could hear the sounds of people working, hammers and blocks and men yelling, building a new place that was something different from a city, without the aid of power tools. And just then Donny heard a screech in the sky, and when he looked up he saw a bald eagle soaring over the ruins of Downtown, a thick, shiny catfish in its talons. He watched it fly home, right into the open window on the top floor of the brutalist tower that had once been the US headquarters of Royal Petroleum.

The building where, the French magazine profile reported, the diligent scriveners of the Tributary were preparing their cases, mining forgotten sins and distributed profits from the well-maintained and regularly audited books and records of vanquished petrocapital.

"What's your business inside the Circle?" said the old guy, now standing over Donny. He did not sound at all like Robert E. Lee, unless Robert E. Lee sounded like a guy from Brooklyn crossed with a guy from France.

Donny looked up at the guy. He did not look especially hostile, despite the gun.

Donny decided to try the honest approach. He reached into the side pocket of his suit coat, pulled out a business card, and handed it to the guy.

DONALD F. KIMOE
Attorney at Law
Washington • Houston • ~~New Orleans~~
1–800-Freedom

"I'm headed to the courthouse," said Donny. "The Tributary, on Camp Street."

The courthouse was just a couple blocks away, right past the barricades that demarcated the true bounds of the Circle.

The man read Donny's card and looked him over.

Donny tried his best smile. The trust-me smile, as Percy used to call it when they worked cases together, always reminding him it usually achieved just the opposite.

The man tucked Donny's card into one of the bib pockets of his overalls, behind the brass and red plastic of a ten-gauge shell. Then he pumped the shotgun.

"Get up," he said.

Donny complied, and stood in the aisle, both hands on the handle of his briefcase.

"I'll take that," said the man, grabbing the briefcase and setting it on the empty seat next to him.

The other passengers were all watching. Even the ones who had stepped off the trolley with their luggage and were now lined up on the street outside, under watch by other guards.

"I got him!" yelled the man to his colleague.

The woman with the purple beret walked down the aisle to join them, while the driver left her seat, drew her gun, and guarded the remaining passengers.

Old Boy handed Beret Girl the business card. She read it, then gave Donny her own lookover, followed by a pat-down.

"Easy," said Donny, which produced the opposite response. When she was done, she made him sit back down.

She had his wallet out, and looked through its contents.

"My bar card's right there."

"I have it," she said, holding it up along with his Texas driver's license. She looked at her colleague. "Did you get his phone?"

He shook his head.

She signaled Donny to hand it over.

"Open it up," she said.

"I don't have to do that," said Donny. "Not without a warrant."

She raised her eyebrows. "Give me the phone."

Donny handed it to her, still locked.

"You're coming with us," she said.

She pocketed his wallet and phone. Then she tried to open his briefcase, but found it was locked too. A simpler lock than the phone, a physical one with a three-digit code.

"What's the combination?"

Donny didn't answer. Beret Girl took out her knife. Preparing to carve open the gift from his grandmother.

"Fine," said Donny, holding up his hand to halt her. "One-one-one."

She opened it, and leafed through Donny's files.

"You know that material is protected by attorney-client privilege," said Donny.

"Whatever," she said. She flipped through the file he had on the Tributary. Pictures of the judges, who were also the jury. Not all 501, but the ones thought to be most influential. The pictures of Heather. The background material her family had provided, which included some reports by private investigators whom you could more accurately call corporate spies.

"Seriously?" said Donny. "This is what we fought for?"

"Doesn't look to me like you did too much fighting," said Old Boy. That was when Donny took a good look at the tattoos on the guy's forearms, some of which evidenced uniformed service in the wars of Donny's youth, others the fresher ink of the uprising and the secret battles that preceded it. The right arm had a puckered scar carved into the muscle.

"He played a role," said Beret Girl, putting the papers back in the folder. "But looks like the reports are true. He's switched sides."

"It's not like that," said Donny.

"Uh-huh," said Beret Girl. She dug deeper in the briefcase and pulled out the inlaid little wooden box he kept in the inside pocket. A souvenir from the tourist shop in Matamoros, that day he got Joyce across. "What's in here?"

"Medicine," said Donny.

You could tell she knew what he meant. She put the box down, and waved the files on the Tributary at him.

"Where did you get these?"

"That's confidential," he said.

He wondered which gun butt would hurt more, and settled on the metal folding stock of Beret Girl's AK-47. But so far these two were more restrained than the government paramilitaries he had gotten used to in the years before.

"Let's go," she said, signaling him to get back up.

"I don't have time for this," said Donny, not budging. He thought about what was really at stake, and corrected himself. "*We* don't have time."

"We have all the time in the world," said Old Boy, smiling. Then he nudged Donny with the barrel of his shotgun. "Come on, dude."

"Am I being arrested?"

"We are taking you to the courthouse," said Beret Girl.

"Okay," said Donny, standing. "Thank you."

Old Boy chuckled.

"Not like you think," said the woman. She grabbed his briefcase, with all its precious contents, and tossed his wallet and phone in there with them. "Come on."

They marched him off while the other passengers watched, some in fear and some in judgment, maybe some with both. One German-looking dude in fresh Birkenstocks took his picture. As he stepped through the door and felt the sun on his face, Donny realized he had already sweat through his suit coat.

They watched as the streetcar started back up and trundled on. The transit passengers still lined up nearby watched Donny try to maintain his lawyerly composure. You could tell it wasn't working, and they just wanted to look away and avoid catching whatever he had.

"This way," said Beret Girl. They hadn't cuffed him, but Old Boy kept the shotgun in his back as Beret Girl led the way. They followed the tracks through the checkpoint, past the emplacement of guards who waved them on from the machine-gun nest while the snipers watched from the rooftops.

Inside the Circle, the streets were mostly gone. Concrete dug up, replaced with dirt and gravel, grass coming up in patches. Donny gawked, until Old Boy shoved him on.

The last time Donny had argued in the Fifth Circuit was three years earlier, when the city had been occupied by the troops of the prior regime, and the appellate courthouse was used for the federal tribunals that adjudicated the internments of rebel fighters in the Superdome. Those were hard fights, and he had won more than most. Some of his clients from those days were now on the Council that ran the city. Its leaders, not that they used that term. When he called Lou to offer to help, to go back to what they now called the Free City but everyone outside worried was something very different than that, Donny had convinced himself those relationships would at least earn him safe passage. That they would give him a hard time, but they would talk to him, and work out a deal. But when they walked into the square and he saw the scene in front of the courthouse, he could feel that confidence drop while the butterflies in his stomach started knifing their way out.

"What the fuck?" said Donny.

In the middle of the muddy lawn that used to be called Camp Street, three human-sized cages hung from steel armatures. Two were occupied, by a man and a woman. The middle cage was open. Donny looked more closely. The guy stood. He was young, wearing chinos and a white Izod shirt. No shoes. The woman was slumped, in shadow, eyes closed. Hard to see. But it had to be her.

"Heather!" he yelled.

She didn't respond.

"Help me!" said the dude.

"Quiet," said Old Boy.

"HEATHER!" yelled Donny.

She opened her eyes. She looked out of it.

Izod dude started rattling his cage.

"Get me out of here, you freaks! I want to leave with that guy."

"You need to let that woman go," said Donny.

"What if she doesn't want to go?" said Beret Girl.

"Let me talk with her," said Donny. "She's my client."

"That is not your client," said Beret Girl.

"What do you mean?"

"Lawyers are forbidden here."

"Then how will these people be defended?"

"By the People's Defender."

"I want to talk to her."

"She doesn't want to talk to you. Not until it is your turn in the box."

"I want to talk to someone on the Council."

"You will only talk to them when it is time for judgment."

Izod guy started shaking his cage again. The whole thing was swinging.

"Careful!" yelled Beret Girl.

The cage door popped open as he shook it, and Izod guy fell to the ground, which was mostly pavement. He hit hard, and stopped screaming. Stopped moving.

"Jesus," said Donny.

"Take him to the infirmary!" yelled Beret Girl to the other guards standing closer to the courthouse.

"Come on, son," said Old Boy, pushing Donny toward the middle cage. "You can lose the coat and tie if you want. It's gonna be hot today."

Donny looked at the guy to make sure he really meant it.

"You have got to be kidding," said Donny.

The shotgun was pointed right at Donny's guts.

"Come on, man!" pleaded Donny. "I don't have time for this. I came to meet with the Tributary. I need to do that and get back to Houston. If I don't—"

"Don't make me gag you, lawyer. We all know that tongue in your mouth is the one that freed the president from the punishment he deserves. Now, go on and get up there. Or I'll cut your tongue right out of your mouth, toss it up there, and let you go chasing after it."

Donny looked the man in the eyes and decided to stop talking.

The ladder was a lot shakier than it looked.

22

WHEN THE TREATY NEGOTIATORS LET THE REBELS KEEP THE TERritory they had occupied in New Orleans, it was damaged goods. A big chunk of the eastern part of the city—the property whose remediation Lecker had funded—was a toxic site that had been cleared out for as long as most folks could remember. The north and the middle were underwater much of the year. And the rest of it had been emptied by hurricane, uprising, and occupation, a cycle that repeated until most of the infrastructure was shot and the buildings abandoned.

The new owners would be so busy trying to get the city functioning again that they couldn't cause any more trouble for their neighbors. That was the idea.

For the rebels, it was everything they had fought for. Real autonomy. A chance to prove their ideas in action.

They invited Donny to help the working group that would develop the new legal code. It was a volunteer gig, but one he was happy to take.

They all liked the idea of starting their own truth and reconciliation tribunal, but they were bound by the general amnesty. El Presidente was the only one of the domestic war criminals who would face real justice. So they got creative.

Donny told them about the work he had done representing the nutria of Houston. About the smattering of cases over the years that had flirted with the idea that animals, plants, and even entire ecosystems might have rights under the law.

Others on the committee had similar ideas, informed by their own work helping build the fresh constitutions of other newly liberated territories elsewhere in the hemisphere. As it took shape on a big blackboard in the old church where they met, the Tributary looked more like a tree, with elaborate branches of sources and outputs at both ends. In action, it would be a different kind of truth and reconciliation commission. One where the genocide was not of a people, but of a place. An entire ecology of diverse lifeforms that had been extinguished by human appetite.

The committee couldn't agree on what penalties their new court should impose. In the beginning, that didn't matter.

This was the third Tributary to be held. The first was right after the uprising, and did not garner much attention. Donny had watched it. It was more like a lecture than an actual trial, because the accused were tried in absentia. The second had not gathered much more attention, until the deals were announced. By seizing property, including drilling platforms in the area under its government's control, which extended from New Orleans out into the Gulf, the Tributary managed to extract substantial sums from the companies that owned the property. That had helped generate some funds—almost $20 million, which helped pay for much-needed solar cells and other infrastructure on the list. But it didn't produce much of a sense of justice, let alone authentic reconciliation. And they soon ran out of property to seize inside their territory, and with it, the means to enforce their judgments.

Some argued they should drop the project entirely and focus on the more important work of proving their new way of living in the rewilded city. Donny suggested that they let private lawyers like him sue on behalf of the city, and take a chunk of the reward after they figured out how to collect it. But the more strident contingent said what they needed to do was rewild the court. "Give the law some real teeth." So instead of seizing property, the Tributary decided to try seizing people.

It was the killer app they had been looking for.

Some were the usual suspects. CEOs, disaster capitalists, enforcers of dark patents. But the real genius, especially for a project whose précis was to achieve present-tense accountability for centuries of wrongdoing and destruction, was to go after mere shareholders. Owners who were not managers. The people who took the profits from the exploitation, even if their stakes were acquired through inheritance from dead ancestors. American law had long treated shareholders as immune from culpability for the acts of the companies they owned, so challenging that basic premise of the system was truly radical. And if the Tributary succeeded in making that stick, it would pull the thread on the sweater of the whole system.

If you want to end capitalism, make capitalists pay the real price of what they legally steal. Of the life value they take from the world, not just from people, on terms that are fundamentally devoid of equal exchange. A taking that does not give back in return, especially when the long-term costs are taken into account.

And if you want to make them pay for what they steal, steal them. Take their liberty away from them. Take their anonymity away from them, and put their gluttonous extravagances on public display.

That was how Joyce put it, in the press conference announcing her return to New Orleans to join the Council, not long after they kicked out Donny. It was an idea she'd advocated for a long time. What used to be the daydream of an idealistic young academic now was in practice, with the backing of a small but fierce guerrilla army.

It was from Donny that they got the idea to go after the lawyers, after he pissed them off so bad they made him the first one they went after. In the expulsion decree, they told him they would suspend the sentence. As long as he never returned to New Orleans.

23

AS DONNY STOOD IN THE HANGING CAGE, A CROWD GATHERED IN the square.

They were even younger than he remembered. A rainbow mob of the new generation, the ones who decided to take their future back by any means necessary. Most of them openly carried the tools of their revolution: the small arms that had enabled them to liberate the city, and the picks, shovels, and hoes they were using to reshape it. They were kids from all over the country, and some from other countries. Kids of every color, wearing every color, some of them wearing the colors of other species—the feathers of big birds, the bones of wild animals, the leaves of noble trees, like postapocalyptic Aztecs. Girls and boys and others who made their own categories or rejected the idea of categories entirely.

Donny had loved being around them, when he was their lawyer. Being their captive was different.

"Hey, Peter Pan!" he yelled, picking out the tall guy in the green ball cap who was waving a fringed machete at Donny like he was getting ready to throw it. "Who's in charge here?"

There must have been around two hundred of them by that point, some standing, some sitting, some climbing up the statue of Benjamin Franklin that had been painted over to let Ben's underappreciated freak flag fly. There was a slogan painted across Franklin's chest in purple letters:

Donny definitely felt like a creature, there in the cage, which seemed designed to challenge his basic ability to present himself as a biped. Every one of his movements caused it to rock and sway, putting him off balance, and worsening the problem. He grabbed the bars with both hands and straightened his posture, trying to look authoritative.

The crowd only laughed at him.

"Who's in charge of *you*, man?" yelled one woman in the back.

"Help me, Daddy!" screamed another.

"You heard me!" yelled Donny. "I want to speak to whoever is in charge here!"

Donny knew that wasn't how it was supposed to work, but in his panic he couldn't help but lapse into a reflexive search for patriarchal authority structures to navigate. The sun was all in the day now, the heat of midmorning that felt the way midafternoon used to. Donny felt the sweat soaking through his clothes.

The louder he yelled, the louder they laughed.

Some of them had cameras out, recording the spectacle like kids at the circus.

He looked over at Heather. She was curled up on the floor of her cage, wrapped in a ragged blanket.

"Is this what we fought for?" said Donny, trying to conjure dignity. "So we could keep fighting? So we could kidnap each other's kids?"

"Yes!" yelled two voices in the crowd, one of them laughing.

"I want to speak to the People's Defender! I'm here to defend this woman before the Tributary."

"You're too late, dude," yelled Peter Pan. "She was already sentenced."

"What do you mean? There's a hearing scheduled for today! I saw the notice."

"They moved it up," said the guy. "There's a big storm coming."

"Without a lawyer to defend her? What a joke. I thought you all stood for freedom."

"Freedom!"

Feathers fluttered. Hats and articles of clothing were tossed in the air. Some of the kids were making out. Others were passing around some of their special crop.

"Freedom is a lie!" yelled a boy.

"We are all servants of the Earth," yelled a girl. "Free to fly, but always connected to the sky."

"Free to work!"

"Free to die!"

"Free to wear a tie!"

Donny looked down at his bright-green tie, which was the closest thing he had to a feather. Then he heard the raucous sounds of birds. Donny looked, and saw the parakeets in flight over the square. They had the same kind in Houston—the descendants of illegally imported exotic pets that had escaped and gone native.

He cowered as they flew over, but felt the impact on his shoulder.

"Goddammit," he said.

The floor of the cage was caked with filth, not just from birds. But what had hit him was just a peanut shell, discarded by a bird who already got the prize.

By the time he realized it, the cage was swaying intensely from his spaz-out, knocking him to his knees.

Now they were really laughing.

He tossed the peanut shell at them, and they just laughed harder.

Looking out at their bright colors, he realized how hot he was getting. The sun was shining right on him now. He was red in the face and wet all over.

He took his suit jacket off. When he went to hang it through the grate, the cage swung, and the jacket fell, flapping toward the ground. One of the freaks caught it and put it on. Then she pranced around for her friends and the camera, strutting and melodramatically gesticulating in imitation of a man who takes himself too seriously.

Among the Mbuti people, nomadic hunter-gatherers of Zambia, the only specialization that is encouraged in members of the band who display the talent is miming, in order to lead the clownish ridicule that is the principal means of behavioral sanction in a group that functions without leaders. Donny was trying to remember what that anthropologist said was the best counter when he heard a phone ring.

His phone, with the ringtone he had adopted to know its sound amid a crowd, a ringtone ripped from his grandma's favorite old lawyer show, to know when she was calling.

The possibility that he might pick up a stray signal was why he had left it on, constantly trawling for the network.

"That's my phone!"

The phone kept ringing, a call he knew he needed to take, from the person he really came there to save, while the freaks he had helped secure their own freaky freedom laughed their asses off, repeating everything he said in a way that succeeded in making it sound ridiculous. It infuriated him, made him feel the panic spill over, and found him preparing to leap from the cage. He knew it was not as far as it looked, and that the guy he had seen fall hurt himself because he wasn't paying attention. And what better way to frustrate the camera eyes' efforts at ridicule.

There was Beret Girl, pulling his phone from his bag and looking around.

Then there was a group of older women. Some really old, some just grown-ups amid the mob, a few of them familiar faces. And one woman who was pretty young, at least on the calendar. Someone Donny realized he knew well, and knew to have an older soul. That was who took the phone from Beret Girl, pushed the button, and put it to her ear.

"Percy!" he said.

She was looking right at him while she talked on the phone.

"I'm sorry, he's not available at the moment. May I ask who's calling?"

The thing was, she already knew who was calling. And what was at stake.

DONNY SHOULD HAVE KNOWN SOMETHING WAS UP THE NIGHT when Percy said to meet her at her house instead of the office. She had been talking a lot about how they needed a different strategy. He hadn't appreciated just how different she had in mind.

"Is that a gun?" said Donny.

It wasn't really a question. Even disassembled into its components and laid out on a cloth on Percy's kitchen table, you could see what it was. An AK-47, the twentieth-century heritage totem of armed revolution. Clint was cleaning it.

"Almost as good as new," said Clint, inspecting the boring with the keen eye of a gunsmith. "Maybe better than new. Field-tested."

Donny looked at the crates over by the wall. Three of them, stacked one atop the other. The top one had been opened, its lid laid up against the side of the stack. The wood was stenciled in an alphabet Donny could not read. He didn't need to peek inside the open crate to know what was in there. And frankly, he didn't want to look—he might be able to survive interrogation by the feds if he could honestly state he only saw one gun instead of an arsenal.

Xelina, who was standing by the crates reviewing the manifest she had pulled from the top one, looked liberated and terrified at the same time.

"You have got to be fucking kidding me," Donny said. That wasn't a question either.

"It wasn't an easy decision," said Percy. She was sitting there at the head of the table, the big brass lacquered pin signifying her status as a member of Congress still buttoned to her lapel.

"It is for me," said Donny. "Count me out."

"We need to protect ourselves," said Percy. "You saw what they did to Miles."

Donny looked at the crates. "This is about more than self-defense. I wish I hadn't come."

"You're wrong," said Xelina. "And you know it's the only way. What else are we supposed to do when they rig the elections?"

"I didn't come to this decision easily, Donny," said Percy. "None of us did."

Clint raised his eyebrows like maybe that wasn't true in his case.

"I helped you get elected to office so it wouldn't come to this, Percy," said Donny. "You just got sworn in for your second term. I didn't think you were the type to give up so easily."

"I'm not," said Percy. "And I haven't. This is just the backup plan."

"The backup plan."

"Yeah."

"Meaning you don't plan to use them."

"Right. Basically."

"What do you mean, 'basically'?"

"I mean we won't use them unless we need to. But we need to be ready."

"What are you going to do with them in the meantime?"

"She said you could keep them for us," said Xelina.

For a minute he believed her. Clients often asked him for favors like that, based on a wishfully expansive idea of what the attorney-client privilege could cloak.

"We're going to distribute them," said Percy, and Clint laughed at the look on Donny's face.

"Please don't use that word," said Donny.

"Give them to friends," said Xelina.

"Exercise our Second Amendment rights," said Clint.

"Yeah, well, you may want to bone up on the case law on that one," said Donny. "Unless you want to ask the powers that be in Washington or Austin to license you three as a militia."

"We know what our true rights are," said Xelina. "And so do you. As for the law, the law is what we make it."

He sized up his friends, sitting there in the dining room of Percy's little old house in the Fifth Ward, the one she had bought when she was still an associate at Miles's firm.

"There's more of them than there are of you," he said.

"We have a big network of people ready to do what it takes," said Clint. "More than you think."

"And we have a smarter lawyer," said Xelina.

"Come on," said Donny. "I'm not even smart enough to sense that I shouldn't have come here. Now you've made me into your co-conspirator."

"Our lawyer," said Percy.

"Uh-huh," said Donny. "You and I both know they would love nothing more than to show that the defense lawyers, the last line holding up some tattered remnant of justice, are actually terrorists. That we're in on it with our clients."

"I'm taking a bigger risk than you, Donny," said Percy.

"You took a bigger risk than me when you decided to run

for office as a member of the opposition. That makes you an endangered species. I just want to be a lawyer. Not a politician. And definitely not a revolutionary."

"That's all we want," said Percy. "Be our lawyer."

"Who's the client?"

"The Gulf Liberation Front," said Xelina.

"Oh, you have got to be fucking kidding me," said Donny.

"Each of us," said Percy. "And the group of which we are a part."

"Like a neighborhood association," said Donny. "But with assault rifles. And probably bombs."

"Exactly," said Clint.

"The reason we need you," said Percy, "is we need to build the legal arguments to support our case. Our cause."

"Good luck with that."

"Come on, Donny," said Percy. "How many times have you spouted your theory about the right to revolt? You convinced me. You even convinced Miles. There's real law there to grab on to."

"Not in these courts."

"Maybe not today. But this isn't about today. It's about tomorrow. Building precedents, even if we start small."

Donny looked at her. She appeared to really believe in that idea.

"It's about fighting for a future you would actually want to live in," said Xelina.

She had a point.

"Or maybe you like watching your friends and clients disappear," said Clint.

Donny knew the truth of that better than most.

"While the planet dies," said Xelina.

"What do you want from me, exactly?" said Donny. "A memo?"

"I mean, maybe," said Percy. "Maybe that's part of it. I want to build our defense."

"Before you even do anything."

"Why not? They arrest people before they commit crimes."

"True."

"Build the best case you can. Like a cross between a memo and a manifesto."

"Kind of like the Declaration of Independence," said Clint.

"Yeah," said Donny. "Not exactly that easy. The Founders kind of had their revolt and ate it. But—" He paused. "This is interesting."

"Great," said Percy. "Put that together. And then we go find an international body that can help us make our case."

"Like the UN Court of Claims, the one that took our reparations case."

"Right."

"And then if we succeed, who enforces the judgment?"

Percy looked at the crates full of guns.

"Self-help," said Clint.

"I knew you were going to say that."

"Betcha wonder where we sourced these," said Clint, snapping the weapon back together.

"I'd rather not know," said Donny. That was true and false at the same time. He already had an idea. He'd seen the news reports a few days earlier, about the busload of asylum-seekers Percy had escorted to the Mexican border, part of a deal she had cut to allow them to leave the country. When she came back over, the bus must not have been as empty as they thought.

"Good idea," said Percy. "Are you still in touch with that ex of yours in Mexico City?"

"You mean Joyce?" said Donny.

"Yeah," said Percy. "You two still talking?"

"It's complicated."

"I thought maybe she could help. I've been reading her open letters. It's powerful stuff—puts all the pieces together in new ways. And she's very plugged in with the expat opposition."

"She's the minister of information for the so-called government in exile."

"Yeah. We could use their help."

"Let's start with the memos, okay?"

"Fair enough," said Percy.

"So who's paying me?" said Donny.

"We don't have much money," said Percy.

"How did you pay for those?" said Donny, nodding at the crates.

"Maybe they were a donation," said Percy.

"There's no such thing as a free lunch," said Donny. "Or a free Kalashnikov. Definitely don't tell me what strings are attached to that. Or who's holding them."

"We'll take care of you," said Xelina.

"Last time I represented you, I had to get paid by the court," said Donny.

"Not money," said Xelina. "Personal services."

Donny raised his eyebrows.

"Protection," said Clint, snapping the banana clip into the rifle, which was now fully assembled.

"That could work," said Donny. Life was dangerous in those days, when the cops were as likely to shake you down as the robbers.

"Great," said Percy. "Now I need to get my speech ready for tomorrow. Just as soon as the sisters get here for the pickup."

And on cue, there was a knock at the door.

EVEN FROM A DISTANCE, DONNY COULD SEE HER SCARRING.
Percy had grown up dodging bullets, and had the right instincts
when her fight for political change turned into a shooting war.
The transformation from radical lawyer to elected official to
rebel leader was hardwired into the history of democratic revolution, and made perfect sense, after it happened. It suited her.
Even with the blanching on the left side of her face that she
earned the hard way.

It definitely gave her credibility with her people. You could
see it as she stepped up onto a little platform made from salvaged wood, the way they encircled her and suddenly quieted
as they waited to hear her speak again. Percy's mother had been
a preacher, and it showed. But her dad had been a fighter, and
that showed too. She was their prosecutor, now—the enforcer
of the new rights they had fought so hard to obtain, and the
protector of those who couldn't stand up for themselves. Some
of them because they weren't even human.

But Donny couldn't help but talk to her like his old employee.

"Percy!" he yelled. "Get me down from here and give me
my phone!"

The crowd turned on him. "Respect for the Defender!"
they yelled. Whoever held the tether attached to Donny's cage
shook it.

"Congresswoman," said Donny, trying to change his tone despite his panic. "I need to speak with you. Please."

Percy held a finger in the air while she listened to the voice at the other end of the phone. "Okay, that sounds bad," she said. "He's not available now but I will let him know."

She handed his phone to one of the other women.

"She says you need to call her," said Percy. "Something about some guys coming by the house to take pictures."

Donny imagined that scene. It scared him even more than the one before his eyes.

"Why are you doing this, Percy?"

"You may only speak in response to our questions," said the gray-haired woman holding the phone. Donny realized he recognized her, too, across the distance—Claude Darjine, one of the only members of the revolutionary committee who had been there since the very beginning, when the people first took control of the city in the aftermath of Superstorm Zelda. "And no one wants your help."

"Fine," he said, steadying himself with his hands on the bars and looking out through the open door. "What do you want to know?"

Donny tried to size Percy up. To see if she was really all-in on the new program. The last time they communicated, it was in a letter: the expulsion order she signed in her official capacity. He couldn't tell.

"What are you doing here, Donny Kimoe?"

"I came to help her," he said, pointing at Heather, still curled up in her cage.

"You can't help her," said Percy. "You are banished. Barred from ever entering our community. I told you as much. Why have you violated our laws?"

On the copy of the expulsion order they sent to him, Percy

had handwritten a note below her signature. *Please understand this is the decision of the entire community, and please respect our need to enforce it.*

"Heather needed my help. And I thought me doing so would help you."

He could see the anger coming up before he even finished.

"What makes you think anyone needs your help, Donny Kimoe? We told you to go away and never come back. And I know Heather didn't even ask for this, did she?"

Donny looked at Percy, and then looked over at Heather. Heather was sitting up now, hooded by her blanket, but watching him with lucid eyes.

"She—"

Percy cut him off. "You were hired by her trustee!" She was waving a piece of paper—the notice of his appointment, from Lecker's office. "Not even family. You work for the money, Donny! And the men who control it, or want to. Money they made from raping Mother Earth, nonstop, for more than a century. And who act like it's all their right. Like there's nothing wrong with them controlling Heather's money, or controlling Heather, or paying some lawyer whatever it takes to get him to sell out his friends and the clients who made him."

"Percy, that's not fair," said Donny. "You know I only take clients I really believe in. I've known Heather since she was a kid."

He glanced at Heather. She was squinting now.

"I don't know this guy," she said.

"You're lucky," said Percy. "He's a snake. He betrayed the revolution. Just like he betrayed his partner, his colleagues, and his clients. He says he just wants to help, but he really just wants to take care of himself, while convincing himself what's good for him is good for everyone else. And the saddest thing is, only now can I really see it clearly."

199

Donny didn't have anything to say to that. He didn't want to believe it, but it had the ring of truth.

"Punish him!" yelled one of the young men in the crowd, and others joined in the chorus.

His cage dropped abruptly, knocking him on his ass. Then they pulled it back up, higher than it had been.

Donny tried to straighten out. His spine felt bent. He tried to ignore the mob and focus on Percy. He could see the anger. It was personal. She was right. His mind flashed a list of some of the occasions on which he had let her down while thinking at the time what a great example he was setting.

"What if I told you I took on Heather's money as a client so I could free it too?" said Donny.

"What do you mean?" said Percy.

"You said it yourself. I'm 'ethically flexible.' I know how to see both sides. Why can't I work both sides?"

"The only side you really care about is your own," said Percy.

"That's not really true, and you know it," said Donny. "I came here to get justice for everyone."

"Justice for your clients only comes in the form of punishment."

"That may be. And that may be what you do to me. But before you do that, you need to give me a chance to make my case."

"The people have already heard enough from you," said Percy.

"They haven't heard about the accounts we seized."

"What accounts?"

"The three operating accounts in the name of the City of New Orleans you have at UZB and two other Swiss banks. The ones you use for payments from your international trading partners, and all these refugees who pay the vig to get their boat rides out of here."

Percy looked over at her entourage of elders, and crossed a hand across her throat.

Donny reflexively put his hand over his own throat. It was too late to cover his mouth.

WHEN THEY WERE DONE HUMILIATING HIM ON CAMERA, THE crowd dispersed, they turned the cameras off, and they let Donny and Heather down.

Except that Heather let herself down. And looked a lot fresher than she had when she was in the cage.

"What the hell?" said Donny.

"It was hot up there today, y'all," she said. "But that was awesome."

"You're in on this?"

"Trying to do my part to help," she said.

"White girls make good bait," said Percy. "Especially rich ones."

"I knew it," said Donny. "Are the sacrifices real?"

Percy raised her eyebrows and looked away.

"Stick around and find out for yourself," said Heather. A friend was rubbing her shoulders now, and helping her clean up from her performance.

"I'm going to stick around until you leave with me," said Donny.

"That'll never happen," said Heather. "And right now, I need to get to my other job. See ya."

She and her friend started walking away, just as one of the guards brought Donny his suit coat.

"Heather!" he yelled, as he dusted the filth off. "Please! I just need a few minutes. I have a message from your dad."

"Buzz off," yelled Heather, not even looking back. "I don't want your help. Not unless you want to help get them to pay what they owe."

"We need to talk!" said Donny. "That's exactly why I came."

She had already disappeared around the corner. Percy walked up as Donny pulled his jacket on. Her colleagues were standing nearby, conferring.

"Goddamn you people," said Donny.

Percy grabbed him by the lapels and shook him, hard. Percy was strong, Donny was not, and it felt like she might pick him up and throw him across the square.

"You son of a bitch!" she yelled. "How could you do this to us? To me! Do you have any idea what's at stake?"

Donny grabbed her hands, but she pulled them loose. Then she shoved him with one hand and smacked him with the other. And kept smacking, with both hands, until he was down on the ground covering his face.

When the smacking stopped, he peeked out and looked up at Percy standing there over him, red in the face and breathing hard. She had three armed guards behind her.

"Watch him," she said. "I need to go find Kendra, and see if she can check on our accounts."

"It's true what I said," said Donny, half expecting to provoke a gun butt to the head. It wouldn't be the first time. "But we have to be able to work something out. Is there someplace we can talk? Or someone else I need to talk to? Because I came here to make a deal."

"What possible basis could you have to seize our accounts?"

"Well, I can only take partial credit for that. But the basis is patent infringement."

"What patents? That money is our lifeblood. At least until we're fully self-sufficient."

"They say those are the proceeds from stolen property. Seeds."

Percy looked at her colleagues.

"No one can own a seed," said Claude. "The design of life belongs to nature. Even if you try to reengineer it."

"Yeah, I hear you," said Donny, standing up and feeling his face for cuts and bruises. "But that's the law. A law most of the world follows. And that even applies here, at least on paper."

"You're representing Tripto Labs too?"

"Technically just Heather's trust, but they own a big stake, and so the trustee was able to call in a favor. And the craziest thing is they didn't even need a court order. I guess the licenses, and your accounts, are all coded into the Chain. And all they needed to do was transmit a few commands. Kind of ironic that the digital money system developed by the underground to finance the revolution turned into the smart contracts regime that lets companies enforce their rights without having to go through lawyers."

"Fucking bullshit, is what it is," said Claude.

"Can you go talk to Kendra and her team?" said Percy. "I'll interrogate him in the meantime."

"We'll come with you," one of the guards said to Percy.

"That won't be necessary," said Percy, looking at the cut on her hand from punching Donny.

PERCY LED DONNY into the ruins of the courthouse, down a long hallway to a big room in the back, where they sat at a wooden table on which a few file boxes had been stacked. You could see Percy had been working on the files, with three of them open by her notepad. This room had been the library for the judges and the clerks. But the books and even the shelves were all gone now. Probably burned for fuel.

"Sit down right here," said Percy, pointing at one of the chairs. It was wobbly. She pulled up another one, and sat across from him, close enough to hit him again. Then she started looking through his briefcase, which the guards had given her.

"Any chance I can see my phone?" said Donny.

She looked at him. "Sure," she said, and pulled it from the briefcase.

It really was his grandma who called. But no other messages, and no more signal. Only the clock worked now, reminding him how much of his window he had already blown.

"Don't suppose you have a phone I could borrow," said Donny.

She ignored his question. And you could tell she had seen enough of the work papers he carried.

"What the hell, Donny?"

"I don't even want to be here, Percy. Not under these circumstances. But I have to be. You can't kidnap people like this and not expect there to be consequences."

"We didn't kidnap anybody, Donny."

"You kidnapped me."

"We *detained* you. A lawful arrest under our law, for violating our expulsion order."

"Heather?"

"We arrested her for contempt. But she would have surrendered if her family hadn't locked her up. And now she is cooperating with us."

"What about the others? That guy I saw them wheel away. The people I saw on the news, sent off to die in the swamp. This is crazy, Percy. You've become as bad as they were."

Percy looked away, at the cracked windows of the big room.

"You might as well roll out the guillotines," added Donny.

"We know you don't like killing tyrants," she said, looking back at him.

"I don't like killing anyone."

"And we don't like killing any*thing*. But they killed most of the wildlife on this planet, Donny. And we need to restore some balance. It's not exactly how I would do it if it were my decision. But the people want justice. So does the Earth. We've run out of time for screwing around. We need to change the program before it kills what's left. And until others wake up and start following the same rules, these arrests are the fastest way to get people to pay attention."

"It's hostage-taking, Percy, and you know it."

"Something they've been doing with their laws for centuries. Putting people in prison for their debts. For refusing to follow their rules. All for a system to enslave their real hostage—the land and the creatures that live on it."

Donny considered that calculus. He thought about the dead fish, the vanishing bees, the silence of the mornings once filled with song.

"I should have known you would actually stoop to helping those criminals," said Percy. "Probably desperate to make a quick buck. Are you using again? You look like hell."

"It's more complicated than that."

"That's what you always say."

"Yeah, well, this time I mean it."

"I'm sure. I bet you have a great story of why you had to betray us again so you could save your own ass."

Her eyes had him even more nailed than the words she said.

"You say you want real justice," he said. "Well, so do I. Remember Slider's case? The mess you and Miles left me to sort out?"

She knew.

"I have it nailed. With just one little catch. Well, two."

"Come clean with me, Donny."

He looked at her hands. At her strong arms. At those eyes, which could see through bullshit.

He told her the whole deal. About Slider. About his debts. About Carol. About his pitch to Lou. And Lecker.

"I really thought I could put together a settlement that would actually help you," he said.

"Well, Slider's dead, Donny. Which you already know. It's sad, but at least he was fighting for the cause. I know other people here who lost loved ones in those camps, or were on the list and survived, but I don't think any of them will want to work with you. Not after what you've done. As for putting together a deal, that's not how we work. We don't compromise on the principles that matter."

"What if I got them to put up a bond, in exchange for you letting Heather go?"

"You're assuming she wants to go."

"Can I talk to her at least?"

"I don't know. Not right now. I don't even have time to screw around with you. I need to go attend to the problems you've already caused." She paused. "If we let her go, can you release the funds?"

Donny shifted in his chair.

"We also need to deal with the seeds," he said.

"Do you even understand what you're talking about? The world is starving, and you walk in here like the fucking waiter bringing the bill to the people in the alley begging for leftovers? I should just give you back to the guards and let them take you to the swamp."

"I'd rather see the farm," said Donny. "They wouldn't even let them show footage of it on that French documentary. I could tell Lecker covets it, but doesn't even really know. What's the secret?"

"I can't tell you. Not when you're working with them."

"I saw some of the strawberries."

"Pretty amazing, right? That's just a glimpse of what I'm talking about."

"So let me help you. We can shake those monopolists down together. I think I know how we can do it."

"They're your clients!"

"That doesn't mean I can't try to persuade them to make a deal. And like you said, technically Heather's money is my client. The trust. Not any of the companies they own. So let me in on your case. We can make them pay up. As long as we deliver Heather."

"What do you mean, let you in on our case?"

"Show me what you've got. So I can tell them why they need to settle."

"I don't know, Donny."

"You know what the alternative is. They come and repossess all y'all and all your New Corn and all your giant strawberries and shut down your whole project. The USA is dead, and the age of self-help is upon us. You may enforce your laws by kidnapping, but these companies have figured the same thing out. And they have a lot more firepower at their disposal."

"We're ready for them."

"But what if we could avoid that?"

Percy was thinking it over.

"Joyce would understand what I'm proposing," said Donny.

"That's what you think," said Percy. "But what the hell. Let me take you. And then we can decide how to send you back."

"Thank you, Percy," said Donny, standing and checking his watch. "Will they have food there?"

PERCY WALKED DONNY NORTH FROM THE COURTHOUSE DOWN
the wide path of what had been Poydras Street, past trees in
bloom. You could smell it in the air, the smell of the fruit that
would come with summer.

"Are you sure you don't want back in on any of your cases?"
said Donny. "If I could add your name to the pleadings, I'm pretty
sure we could extract a settlement for Slider. Even without Slider."

He meant it. Percy's reputation intimidated the defense
bar. She's the one they should have used in the ads.

"No, thanks," said Percy. "You can donate my share to what
we're doing here. Now, listen."

Donny soaked it in some more. He heard birds.

They walked farther along, to where the path opened up
on a wide clearing. Several blocks wide on either side, with no
buildings, more like a park. Tall grass popping with orange and
red poppies, around a wide depression in the center that had
filled with water.

"Wow," said Donny. And a dozen ducks took to the sky,
quacking their complaints at having to do so.

They had black bellies, orange beaks, and brown bodies.

"Recognize it?" said Percy.

He looked. There was something familiar, but he couldn't
place it. He looked at the wetland. It was almost a perfect circle.
He looked back at the direction they had come from. The buildings that marked the way.

"Oh," he said, looking back at the wetland.

It was the site where the Superdome had been. The arena. "The stadium where the fans learn to scream," as the lawyers who defended its inmates used to call it. The "temporary" detention camp lasted a lot longer than the temporary autonomous zone the rebels had briefly established. Right up until the riot, when a few prisoners, including one of Donny's old clients, led an uprising that burned the building badly enough that they had to demolish what was left.

Donny had never been inside it. Not since that one year in the good old days when he went to the Sugar Bowl with Joyce and some other friends. When it was an emergency jail and the prisoners were insurgents, they didn't need to let the lawyers visit their clients. They didn't even need to let the clients have lawyers.

Now it was this. A pocket of wild heaven coming up in the spot where man-made hell had been.

Donny saw a deer crossing the shallow water.

"Watch where you walk," said Percy. "It gets pretty wet. But there's a dry path, if I can find it."

"It's okay," said Donny.

"Suit yourself, but be careful. Sometimes the remains come up in the boggy parts."

He looked down at the footprints he had just left, the imprints of his boot tread filling with water. The water made the little pieces of debris in the dirt glisten.

"Who's buried out there?" he said, looking over the swamp.

"You know who, Donny. The biggest mass grave was farther up there," she said, pointing north. "Close to the Fairgrounds, where Camp Zulu was. Under a few feet of water now."

"Jesus," said Donny, looking toward the horizon line, seeing only damaged buildings. "I'll follow you."

Percy led them down a path that was mostly dry. As you walked in there, you could see the rubble. Big chunks of busted-up concrete, half-hidden behind tall grass and wild weeds. A garden of rebar.

He heard the whistle of an osprey, looked that direction, and saw its wide-winged profile against the silhouette of the I-10 overpass terminus, a road to nowhere since it was blown up by the rebels six years earlier.

His attention returned to the trail when he felt his foot sink into the mud, and the water filled his boot.

"You okay?" said Percy.

"I thought I was," said Donny, fighting to pull his foot free. When it finally came out, half expecting to find a skeletal hand wrapped around his ankle, he just saw his naked white foot.

"Crap." He squatted down, reluctantly reached into the hole, and fished out his boot with an airy slurp. The sock was dripping over the side.

"Up here," said Percy, looking back and laughing, then pointing at a little hill made from rubble. "You go first."

Donny climbed up there, holding the boot in his hand and favoring the other foot.

It wasn't especially high, maybe fifteen feet. But it was a good perch, complete with a big curb cut that served as a nice place to set your butt down and stare out at the beautiful post-apocalyptic swamp with your feet dangling off the edge.

They sat there and soaked it in.

Percy pulled out an orange, and began to peel it. It was a lot bigger and healthier-looking than the one Lecker had shared.

Donny took off his other shoe and emptied the water over the edge. He wrung out his socks and laid them in the sun. The fear of corpses had left him for the moment, superseded by anxious thoughts of Thelen's deadline. But even that stress seemed to bleed off in the moment.

"You know we're going back the same way, right?" said Percy.

Donny shrugged. "I'll be more careful. Or I'll do it again."

"Nice toes," she said, laughing.

"They don't get out much," said Donny.

Donny pointed to the east. The area north of the Quarter had been mostly razed, and you could see a long way from their perch. In the distance were fields of green.

"Are those the farms?" said Donny.

Percy nodded. "Some of them." She put her hand to her ear.

He listened along and heard the bugs. A cacophony, when you really paid attention. Thousands of them singing at one another. Maybe tens of thousands, maybe more.

A huge heron was there in the water, dinosaur strutting through the shallows like some predatory supermodel.

"Should have brought my fly rod," said Donny.

Percy didn't say anything. She just handed him some of the orange.

It tasted good.

"They say the first human settlements were at places like this," said Percy.

"In the ruins of the future?"

"In the wetlands of the past. Like in the 'fertile crescent.' Biodiverse swamps, full of all sorts of self-replenishing foods."

"Makes sense. If you can stand the bugs."

"They would drain them. Once they stopped moving, and started harvesting from one place, growing the population, pressures would build to focus on one or two grain crops. Easier to manage the group, and grow it, around a food that could also serve as a medium of exchange. Pretty soon, they were making people work the fields. People who had just wanted to roam free, the way nature meant."

"Sounds like another hokey 'state of nature' theory of the bucolic past to me. You can bet they were all killing each other and eating their way to oblivion all the way back to Eden."

"Said the guy airing his gnarly toe claws out in the open air of a city gone back to wild."

Donny smiled. He let his worries dangle out there with his feet for all the birds and bugs to admire. He spread out his toes. He opened his ears to the sound of the world he thought they had erased.

"I could get used to this," he said.

"You can start by fixing the mess you already made. Because this is just the beginning. And if we get cut off, it's all over."

"I understand," said Donny.

"Do you? Do you understand this is where real justice comes from? Not courtrooms, or legislatures. Out here, in the fields."

"Courtrooms are about all I can handle, Percy. You should see me with houseplants."

"You got off to a pretty good start when you had that land-reform case for Xelina, way back when."

"You remember that?"

"How could I forget? Basically arguing that all the land in the USA was stolen? Too bad you had to settle it."

Donny nodded, and looked out over the wetland. "That's kind of what you are putting into practice here."

"I didn't really understand it until the uprising," said Percy. "When I saw the whole country. Saw what we had done, saw the history laid out there in plain sight, that it finally clicked.

How all the injustices I had been fighting my whole life—the vestiges of slavery, the murder and dislocation of indigenous peoples, inequality, exploitation, all the shitty things people do to each other—that all of them are rooted in the damaged relationship we have with the land. All because people are allowed to take from it, to treat it as their exclusive property. The reason people kill for it, enslave each other to work it, and suck every ounce of value they can from it until it's dead."

"How do you fix that?"

"You seek justice for it. Value every life, not just ours. Make the case for a different kind of reparations—for the pillaging of the planet, the destruction of wilderness, the rape of the future. Then take what you can win from that, and put it to work on real healing."

"The only healing we need right now is to bring the people who murdered our friends to justice," said Donny. "I could use your help, Percy."

"We both know that doesn't fix anything," she said. "This does. You can feel it."

Donny had a stem of grass in his hand, idly picked as they walked. He pinched off one of the seeds, held it up in his fingers, and wondered if it was the key to justice, or the real key to slavery.

"Come on," said Percy. "I have more to show you."

AS THEY WALKED FARTHER IN, PERCY EXPLAINED TO DONNY HOW none of the people they saw out working had "jobs"—not as Donny would think of it. The community was divided into groups of 50 to 150 who occupied and tended to different zones, each with its own urban farm plots and restoration projects. The idea was to mimic the structure of the earliest human bands. Everyone took their share of the chores, and had plenty of time left over to pursue their own other interests. Members of the groups who were so inclined could even go out on hunting excursions or forages. Necessary tasks were dealt with based on skill and availability. But specialization was resisted.

"People need to live full lives," said Percy. "I am a lawyer, but I'm also a teacher, and a gardener, and a politician."

"Are you happy?" asked Donny, repeating the question he had asked Lou just days earlier, in a very different world just hours away.

"I now understand I never realized what happy even meant," she said. "This is a different kind of happy. Like a collective happiness that infects you, gets you out of your own head."

They walked along Canal Street, which had been turned into a long grassland. A crew was out there tilling one section, and planting new seed. Percy explained how some of the grasses were hybrids with seed crops that would both restore the land and produce production-grade wheats.

"Are they from Tripto?" asked Donny.

"I didn't ask," said Percy.

Farther along, a bunch of kids were out playing.

"They're from my school," she explained, walking over to say hello to the students. Donny had expected to see hungry, shabby creatures, but they were the happiest and healthiest-looking kids he had seen in a long time.

"How do you have time to do this and do your job?" asked Donny, crouching down to receive an interesting-looking rock from a four-year-old girl.

"We don't think of it that way. We especially don't think about time that way. Your time is your own, and you spend it the way you need, or the community needs, which hopefully are the same thing."

"No deadlines? No dockets?"

"Oh, I have plenty of those." She laughed. "Mostly because I manage all of our litigation in other forums, outside the community. But I have a lot of help. That's where we're going now."

She pointed up at one of the old skyscrapers of the Central Business District, a modernist edifice made of steel and local limestone. It was the Royal Petroleum Building, the one he had seen the eagle roosting in that morning. Donny had been there before, maybe fifteen years earlier, for document review on a big commercial case. This had been the company's US headquarters then, before they relocated to Houston. But walking up now was the first time he really noticed that the building was made out of fossils. You could see them there in the exterior limestone as you waited at the door, the first secure door Donny had seen in the whole city.

"What do you keep in here?" said Donny, watching the security protocols.

"The secret history of the world," she said.

"Now you sound like Joyce," said Donny.

Percy smiled. "I'm probably repeating her," she said. "Because this is her project more than anyone's. You can ask her about it yourself."

AS HE SAW HER STANDING THERE IN THE TALL DOORWAY, WHICH made her look tall, too, even though she was not, Donny felt the shudder, and shut it down as quickly as he could.

"Hello, Donny," said Joyce. She smiled as she sized him up, revealing the lines in her face, lines that had been etched by more than smiles. She still had the freckles on her brown skin, and some new spots where the sun had taken its toll. And yet the age only made her more beautiful. Maybe because he knew some of the story behind how it had been earned.

"Joyce," he said.

She proffered no embrace, nor even a handshake.

"I guess you heard I was coming," he said.

"I was the one who proposed we shoot you on sight," she said. "But I got outvoted." It was hard to tell if she was joking.

Donny looked at Percy, whose face suggested it was true.

"We compromised on the cage," said Percy. "A little shock treatment to help open your mind."

"Percy thinks we can turn you," said Joyce, raising her eyebrows. "I told her we can probably educate you, but that you are too mired in the world that's dying to be able to come unstuck."

"I just think we should be able to work out a deal," said Donny.

"Exactly what I'm talking about," said Joyce. "So we have come up with a new plan. I talked with the other members of the Council and they agree."

"What's that?" said Percy.

"There will be no negotiations. But we are going to have a rehearing of the case against Ms. Hamilton-Green's trust. As long as Donny here agrees on behalf of his client that whatever decision we come up with after we hear his side will be enforceable in any jurisdiction."

"I can't agree to that. I don't have the authority."

"Sure you do," said Joyce. "It says as much in the notice of appointment they sent the Tributary." She looked at Percy.

"That's true," said Percy.

"And if we have that, Heather can go free, whether or not you win. If she wants to."

"How do I know it will be a fair trial?" said Donny.

"I guarantee you it will be a lot more just than the courts you are used to. The jurors will all have their opinions coming in, but they are honest people and they will listen. And you have all day to review the evidence we have collected, to prepare your case. We have nothing to hide."

Donny looked over the room.

The ground floor had been taken over by the scriveners of the apocalypse. It looked like a scene from some old office farce, dozens of people at desks buried under mountains of paper, murmuring along to the clickety-clack of manual typewriters and a few beat-up data terminals. Except that they wore T-shirts and fatigues and the intensity of people with a real cause. Hardened veterans of dictatorship and civil war, now fighting a revolution by other means. A war across time, with facts, history, and law as their weapons.

"You want to do that tomorrow?" said Percy, reading between the lines.

"Yes," said Joyce. "Before the carnival. What do you say, Donny?"

"I'll take that deal. But I need to meet with my client."

"She's not really your client, and that's up to her, but we can arrange a visit," said Joyce.

"What about the bank seizures?" said Percy.

"Our customers have us covered," said Joyce. "Fronting what we need. They know what the real stakes are."

"Well, then I better get back to the office and get prepared for the morning," said Percy.

"You do that," said Joyce. "I'll make sure your prisoner gets back to his minders."

"WHERE DID YOU get all those old machines?" asked Donny as Joyce led him through her typewriter brigade.

"It's not hard," she said. "They last forever. Those things were just made better. And they are simpler to start with."

"No power."

"No software. Code degrades. Like memory. Like the things you said."

"Like what things I said?"

"Not 'you' you, Donny."

"Oh," said Donny, relieved and not relieved, wondering if she really meant it the way he originally understood it. He tried to read her face, but she wasn't letting him in. Instead, she was proudly looking over her team. "So what are they researching?"

Even as he said it, his mind was busy remembering some of the things he had said. The things they had said.

"A different kind of fossil record," said Joyce.

"Can you ever just say it straight?"

"Said the best liar I have ever known."

Donny shrugged. For a lawyer, it was the kind of insult

that is also the highest compliment. "If you're not going to have me killed, can you just explain what this is?"

"This," said Joyce, "is the infinite source of the Tributary. Sources, really, and maybe not truly infinite, but enough to keep us busy for years. The records of American business."

"Like accounting records?"

"That's one element, maybe the most important one. But also contracts. Lots and lots of contracts. Abstracts of title. Secured transactions. Payroll. HR records. Golden parachutes to unpack. And all the sins covered up in confidential settlements—a whole secret history of America ready to be reassembled and revealed."

Donny looked at the piles with new eyes. He looked at the stacks around the desk closest to them, close enough that he could read what they were. Royalty reports on an oil well. A bank loan for the purchase of exploration equipment. A confidentiality agreement between a software company and an investment bank. A severance agreement with a terminated CEO.

"Where do you get all this?"

"Some of it was left here. But by your definition, we steal most of it," said Percy. "By our definition, it's document production."

"That's what the office raids are about."

"Mainly. They are also fun. But the people who did the things documented here are the real thieves. Thieves who keep detailed records of their crimes. Records that go back decades, sometimes centuries, sometimes even farther than that."

"Do you really think they're going to let you all get away with this? Everything is already so broken. What good does this do?"

"What good does it do to make the living inheritors of a beautiful continent pay for some of the atrocities by which they have profited? Put a stop to their hedonistic orgy in penthouses while people suffer and animals die outside their gated communities? It's justice, Donny. Real justice. Not your bogus *mano a mano* adversarial justice, which does no more than codify and perpetuate the old system, all testosterone-fueled taking, I win, you lose. We are setting up a real reckoning this time. A restoration of true equilibrium. True equality."

"Economic justice through environmental justice."

"Right. It's not just about liberating labor, or abolishing private property. It's about creating a system that gives voice to the voiceless. And it's not just class or race or gender that makes you voiceless. Some don't have a voice at all."

"Not in a language humans can understand."

"You understand. Even if you choose to stick to the world you know. That one that gives you your privilege."

Donny looked at the army of researchers compiling their reports.

"You should come back and join us," said Joyce. Her hand was on his arm. "You helped find this path."

"I thought you said I should be shot on sight."

"I did, actually. But now I can see you half get it."

"Emphasis on half."

"At least spend some time here in the archive. You should make sure you know about Heather's family business before you get up to defend it."

"That sounds like a really bad idea."

"Who knows," said Joyce. "Maybe you'll find something we missed. Something exculpatory."

You could see she expected a different outcome. But as smart as she was, she never thought like Donny. He wished he could still believe that gave him an advantage.

30

DONNY KNEW A LITTLE BIT ABOUT HEATHER'S FAMILY BUSINESS,
even before they hired him. Everybody did, really, everybody
who had been around long enough to know how they had gotten here. But Donny had even read the book—a copy of Helen's
dad's memoir that Lou gave him when they were still associates
at B&E. He could never forget the title: *Keepers of the American
Flame*.

If you went all the way back, it started as a lumber company in East Texas. That grew into Diboll Timber Harvest-
ers, a diversified wood and paper products company that even
managed to go international. Helen's father, Hank, was the one
who'd had the idea to rename the company Promethean Resources, when he wanted to diversify into more scientific ap-
plications. He had a good intuition for where the zeitgeist was
going.

Like the Bible, the classics were good sources for people
who liked their history ahistorical, or even better, with a fa-
vorable spin. *The Aeneid* became popular a little later, after a
new translation that drew out the American ultranationalist
themes you didn't know old Virgil had been so keen on. One
of Donny's early cases had involved a company called Pallan-
tium, named after the mythical new home of the Trojans created when Aeneas planted the flag on Italian soil. Donny had
made the point to one of the lawyers involved with that deal

that Aeneas and his crew were refugees. The analogy was not well received.

The Spartans didn't have an epic poem of their own creation myth. They profited from the empty vessel of enigma, one that exploited the layers of hagiography that had been built by outsiders, from the Athenians who crafted the myth of Thermopylae to the early Americans who named their towns after them. There were Spartas in Wisconsin, Tennessee, Kentucky, Illinois, North Carolina, New Jersey, and Michigan, and a Spartanburg, South Carolina. The Gonzalez battle flag popular with Texan gun nuts, the one with the picture of a cannon that dared the Mexicans to "COME AND TAKE IT," was one of thousands of American adaptations of the purported battle cry of the 300. Many of which were printed into the morale patches and shoulder flesh of the paladins of American imperium. And a few decades earlier, when the general and his wonks put mercantile trading brigades under the control of military merchant commanders, the idea of Sparta became the namesake of a hundred paramilitary start-ups.

Hank was part of that generation. When he was younger he had become obsessed with an old Vietnam War movie, *10 Clicks from Laconia*, about a group of American soldiers who hold back a Chinese tank invasion with a wall of fire made from a single can of fuel. Being a preppy rich kid, Hank was well educated. But he also came from a long line of DIY Texas tinkerers. He bought himself one of the chemical plants that made napalm, along with most of the outstanding patents. He hired a couple of smart chemists to help him develop the crazy idea he had. And when they had a good beta version, he showed it to the Pentagon.

One of the generals in the original pitch meeting called

it "the neutron bomb of napalm." But it was better than that.

Titan Jelly® could burn the forest and leave the wood.

And when it was time to exterminate the green rebellion that had taken root in Central America, they made the decision to deploy Hank's new product.

That was forty years ago. Only now did people really understand what the price had been. The razing of jungles the size of entire countries caused climate change that was already under way to accelerate and morph in ways none of the models anticipated. Across the hemisphere, fertile farm regions became deserts, glaciers melted, rivers dried or overflowed, wildfires raged, storms became more frequent and more intense, and coastal cities drowned.

In the United States, some of those climate-ravaged regions became the breeding grounds for unrest.

But it was only when the unrest had erupted into a full-blown rebellion that the federal forces deployed Titan Jelly domestically, to burn the rebels out. It was supposed to be a targeted application on a handful of encampments, but when the fires started they couldn't be contained, and big swaths of old-growth forest in Louisiana, Mississippi, and Virginia burned. And among the consequences was that the rivers that fed into New Orleans and DC were poisoned—in the case of New Orleans, adding to the poisons that had already been draining out of the heartland for decades.

Joyce was not the first to make the case that someone should pay for those damages. But she was the first to say the ones who should pay are the ones who really made money from it.

In a way, it was very similar to what he was trying to do with Slider.

In another, it was very, very different.

Slider was one dead kid who lost his parents. Joyce and Percy and their comrades were suing on behalf of forests. He wanted to ask how it was they got their client to sign up for their program, but he couldn't afford to spend any more time in the cage.

JOYCE LEFT DONNY AT A BIG TABLE WITH THREE OF THE RE-
searchers helping Percy prepare her case. Their names were
Petra, Lupe, and Dan.

The idea of sharing files with the people you would be arguing against the next day was weird. To Donny. Obviously not
to them. They smiled, welcomed him, and proceeded to show
him their whole case, document by document.

When they were done, he understood why they were so
confident.

They had only fragments of the core elements, but it was
enough to know they were right. The work they had done on
the ecological damage was extensive. Not quite down to the
tree, but close enough. A narrative of the long life of the forests,
constructed from a mix of scientific reports, photographs, field
notes of anthropologists and explorers, lore of the first peoples
of the regions that had been razed, and so on. Stories of the
lives of the trees.

Donny had seen trees that old before. He had been to Oa-
xaca once, with Joyce, and they visited a village at the heart of
which was a tree so big and old that you could not take a picture of it. No lens could capture it. It was like a cross between
a redwood and a cypress, taller than a giant of your juvenile
imagination, but also drooping, enveloping, a canopy under
which you could live. Climb right up in there and return to
your simian roots. It was older than Columbus for sure, maybe

older than Christ. The more recent arrivals had built their cathedral on one side of it and the town hall on the other, as if to appropriate its magic. At least they knew better than to cut it down for lumber to burn or build.

Donny remembered being told by his mom that the ranch house they lived in before Dad left was made from old-growth redwoods. It sounded cool at the time. Now that lumber was probably sitting in some South Dallas landfill, after the house was torn down to make room for a builder home.

Joyce's team had records in there that you could use to count basically every tree that had been cut. Not its age, but its circumference. The sum of which was a number beyond Donny's capacity to really visualize, but behind the numbers on paper was an atrocity you could feel in your bones as you sifted the data. An atrocity of a scale far beyond the human injuries to one another that Donny pursued in his own cases.

It wasn't that trees could not scream, said Lupe. It was that we don't have the senses to hear them. Because they are senses that don't involve that kind of hearing.

And when you looked at the pictures laid out on the table and considered the entire forest as an interconnected thing, it was hard to argue.

They didn't even show him the files on the animals that lived in the forest. They did show him a summary sheet laying out how two-thirds of the wildlife population of the world had been exterminated in his lifetime.

There was a document in there, an email from a senior executive to his colleagues, reporting from a trip to the field. In it he described what it smelled like there, after the Jelly fire and before the big machines came in and took the trees. Like woodsmoke and oil and charred flesh and a chemical stink that he could taste for weeks after.

Then there were the documents that traced the money that flowed from the trees.

Not just to the company. But from the company to its owners. The profits that were realized by those who provided the capital to develop Titan Jelly and everything else the company did.

"Is this the list?" asked Donny, looking at a sheet with names, addresses, and numbers.

Lupe nodded.

"The top thirty current holders of the profits generated by Promethean Resources," said Petra. "We are working our way down."

"So where do I find her?" said Donny, pointing at Heather's name at the top of the sheet.

Petra looked at her colleagues.

"Joyce said it was okay," said Lupe.

"Let me see if I can explain how to get there," said Petra.

DONNY LIKED TO THINK HE KNEW HIS WAY AROUND NEW ORLEANS.
The years he had a New Orleans office were when the city was occupied, first by the federal troops and then by UN peace-keepers, a period that altered the geography with barricades and checkpoints. The geography had changed again since then, in ways that confounded his ability to navigate. Entire blocks gone back to wild, like the swamp that was the Superdome. Bodies of water allowed to accumulate, breach the banks, sub-merge the old roads, with creeks that had been buried now uncovered, and creeks that had been paved slowly restored. Vegetation allowed to consume what remained of old buildings already damaged beyond recovery. Green voodoo practiced through a mix of negligence and intention.

And everywhere he went, people working, and seeming to enjoy it. Or just hanging out. Percy hadn't been bullshitting: people seemed genuinely happy here.

Heather, it turned out, was serving a kind of house arrest that allowed her to live as a provisional member of the com-munity. She had offered to be a donor, and a scientist, and a soldier, but for now was working as a member of one of the restoration crews.

Donny noted the irony of a society that claims to have mostly abandoned private property holding people hostage for funding.

We may not use money inside these borders, said Petra.

But we need it to survive. Until more of the world becomes like us.

Donny got lost pretty quickly trying to find his way to Bywater, with entire swaths of the old city razed and overgrown with wild foliage. So he found the one landmark he knew they couldn't change.

But as it turned out, even the river had changed. The boardwalks were gone, and Mississippi had recovered something closer to its natural condition. The water was sick, but not as sick as it had been, and the banks now hosted tall grasses crowded with green and blue dragonflies. As he walked, one of the big tankers was chugging out toward the Gulf and the open ocean beyond, carrying its load of seeds for planting and refugees for resettlement, many of whom were there on the deck waving their goodbyes to the broken country they would probably never see again.

Donny wondered what it would be like to do that, to leave. He had passed on one such opportunity, at a time when it was much more attractive. He had thought seeing Joyce would heal the tumors of regret he had nurtured, but it only made them flare up. The hardness in her eyes amplified it, reminding him that his failures as a lawyer and lover had allowed her to undergo the traumas that got her to that place.

As he walked along the banks, he began to notice little artifacts in the mix of rock and mud at his feet. He stopped to investigate some. The best ended up in his briefcase. A quartz crystal. A shard of pottery with a floral pattern that looked like it could be two hundred years old. A piece of flint that you could tell when you held it had been knapped by human hands, probably thousands of years earlier. A big shell that turned out to be a fossil, the remains of some sea creature that had died millions of years ago. A tooth, the fang of some unknown mammal, still shiny white. He watched the river flow, and thought about what Percy said, about how time works differently there. He could feel it, and feel the freedom in it. But then he thought about what he needed to do. The deadlines that were waiting on him back in the real world. Especially the deadline Thelen had imposed.

In a proper utopia, they would not let any lawyers in.

After a while, Donny found his way to where the old Industrial Canal emptied into the river. The canal was the landmark he needed to find Heather, in the area just east of there, which had now morphed into a wide bayou full of wild plants growing along the waterline. The zone on the other side had been a toxic no-go zone since an industrial accident many years earlier, even before the coup. Now it was a farm. Not just for crops, but for plants that clean the air and heal the soil.

Phytoremediation, Lupe called it.

The nearest field was a spring garden full of tall grasses and wildflowers. The biggest butterfly garden you have ever seen.

Beyond that, the prairie got even taller, with acres of leafier grains. All of the plants hybrids, aided in their adaptation to the new world we had made. Most of them obviously succeeding. Closer to the river shined the solar roofs of the warehouses in which the products of those plants were stored for shipment.

They had been busier than he could have imagined. No wonder Lecker was worried about his monopoly.

The old footbridge across the canal was covered in foliage, mostly vines, some of them grown tree-trunk thick as they wrapped around the metal armature. It was only when he stepped onto the bridge and felt the give that he realized the vines had entirely replaced what was there before. The well-trod path was smooth and polished, but still glistening with life, and the rest was clumped with leaves and strands of bright-red flowers. At the end, he could see where the fast-growing trees were rooted at the waterline and then bent over to lean into their role, meeting their cousins with intertwining branches at midway.

When he stepped off, he found a group of young teachers seated in a meadow with a younger herd of kids. One of the teachers was Heather. And as he walked up to meet them, he knew how the repo man must feel.

33

WHEN MAXINE PRICE DIED, THE INHERITORS OF HER LEGACY WENT through her papers and found more than they expected.

Maxine Price had been a college professor, a novelist, a radical activist, vice president of the United States for one truncated term, and fugitive convicted in absentia for conspiring in a plot to assassinate the president who succeeded her former boss. Surprisingly, the novelist part was what really stuck, even though what she wrote was mostly what people considered science fiction. Donny had read a couple of the stories when they were assigned by one of his more far-out teachers in college, but they were not his kind of thing.

Now they had incorporated it into their new gospel.

It started with the tapes. Old-school cassette tapes, pure analog tech, guaranteed surveillance-proof, a medium Donny could get fully behind even if he was uncertain about the content. Of which there were evidently hundreds of hours. Lectures to the people who would save the future, dangerous propaganda of a seditious radical who would lead the nation to ruin, or the solitary rants of a crazy old lady, depending on your point of view. Donny figured it was some variation of all the above.

There were the notebooks, full of casual jottings, plans for her nerdy war games, dreams, scribbles of ideas big and small, field notes from garden and town, plans for real war, or at least direct action. All of them treated by their discoverers as presumptive profundities, even the entries detailing when she had composted her rooftop garden. Or the List, the one with her Nine Rules.

And then there was the book.

WE THE CREATURES was the title, which they always wrote in all caps, the way she had pounded it out on the typewriter she used, just like the ones at the archive.

They called it a novel, but Donny had read it, and didn't think so. It was something new, something that mixed fiction and nonfiction, fact and fantasia. Manual for a new alchemy, green Anthropocene *brujería*, a utopian conjuring. The chapters were almost like meditations, but they had story, anecdotes that started to accrete into an even bigger story as you read them. One that, when it settled in and took root in your brain, started to spin another story, a story about the whole world.

Donny thought it was all pretty crazy. He was pretty sure his cynicism about it was part of the reason they had banished him. Pretty soon he started seeing people hawking self-published copies on the street corners. Friends started asking him if he'd read it. The way he remembered friends in the old days asked him if he had asked the lord for forgiveness. Then he remembered how Joyce used to say the only way you can really change people's behavior is with a new religion or an old cult.

There was a picture of Maxine Price on the wall of the shed where they were letting Heather stay. The photo presented her at her most charismatic, backlit by the sun in a way that almost gave her a halo. Below the photo was a plaque, with one of her rules:

5. *You can take from nature, but you must give back in equal measure.*

This was not the only reason the shed reminded Donny of a chapel. From the outside, it just looked like a garden shed, albeit with a kind of high roof. Inside, it opened up and filled with light from the windows. No stained glass, just a view of the water on one side and the prairie on the other. On the wall hung relics of things that had died. The bones of animals, the wood of ancient trees, dried flowers, a giant shell washed in from the deep sea.

Below the wall, it was more like a florist's shop—a wide wooden table with metal instruments, test kits, and cuttings of plants. On a plastic cutting board in the center was a section of green stalk from which extruded a crown of red tendrils coated with some snotty film.

"What kind of mutant is that?" said Donny.

"That's a native, actually," said Heather. "A landrace. Sierra Mixe corn, from southern Mexico. Most of it was razed in the wars, but we found some seeds."

She sat in a simple wooden chair opposite him, wearing work pants, a plain black T-shirt, and ropers. Her hair was damped with sweat and matted from the ball cap that she now held in her hands, which were worn and dirty, with thick black under the nails. She seemed happy to discuss the work, even as she looked annoyed that he was the one she had to talk to.

"But what are those things sticking out of the side?" said Donny, looking back at the specimen like he was afraid it might leap from the table and attach to his face.

"Roots. This is a maize that extracts its nitrogen from the air. An adaptation to crummy soils. Of which we have plenty. We've already had some luck developing hybrids. It's what we're planting today."

She pointed at the window. A crew was working a fresh-plowed field with hand tools.

"Supposed to rain tonight," she said. "Hopefully it will give them a nice kick-start."

"What are those kids doing?" asked Donny, pointing farther in the distance, in the direction of the river.

"Testing water and counting birds," said Heather.

"How's the water?"

"The water in the channel is nasty. The water in the springs is better. Mostly they use rainwater here, though. Want some?"

She poured them each a glass from a nearby pitcher. The pitcher was made from clay, the glasses from the bottom halves of old soda bottles.

"Thanks," said Donny, savoring the drink. "I thought maybe you were training them to pollinate the New Corn."

"We don't need to do that."

"Is it true they're designing tiny drones to replace the bees?"

"I don't know. Probably, but that's not the solution. The solution is to help nature fix itself. So we improved on Mom's design. Crossed it with some of these wild grains, and came up with a self-pollinating varietal."

Donny processed that. "So you won't need an army of people to get it to grow?"

"Yes, and it's hardier all the way around."

"And you're just giving it away?"

"We will once we know it's ready to share. That's the real reason you're here. Even if you didn't know it."

"I'm here because your dad wants you home and he knew I could help make that happen." It was basically true, but he was beginning to understand more clearly what Lecker's real agenda was.

"I don't want to talk about him," said Heather.

"I guess you'd rather talk about her," said Donny, nodding at the picture of Maxine Price on the wall.

"She's the reason I dropped out of Rice," said Heather. "I wanted to help."

"I saw her in person once."

"Really?" said Heather. It was like telling some kid you saw a long-dead rock star at their peak.

"Back home, in Houston."

"Not with my dad."

"Definitely not," said Donny. "Though he's more open-minded than you give him credit for, or at least was back then. But no, he was not a fan. I went with my girlfriend at the time, who was. And still is. You know Joyce. We met at your parents' house that one night."

"She's more memorable than you. I even took her class."

"The one on how the richer people are the more they live like nomads?"

Heather nodded. "I guess you weren't converted the way Joyce was."

Donny shrugged. "I don't know. She was definitely better than the alternative, but I'm just not much of a joiner. I got tagged anyway. Lost my job just for going to that dang rally. Your dad knows all about it."

She nodded. "He used to tell me I was going to cost him his job, when I was in school."

"I'm sure you gave it your best shot. Which reminds me. He gave me something to give you."

She rolled her eyes.

"Come on," said Donny. He opened his briefcase and rummaged around until he found what he was looking for. "Check this out," he said, holding up a bar of chocolate. Not just any chocolate. A Gold Bar, from the Johnson Head, the super-luxury artisanal English stuff made from rare small-batch cacao in British Honduras. Fair trade it was not.

You could see her suck in the smile.

"I don't want that," she said. "We have better stuff here."

"Really?" said Donny.

"Do you know how they make that?"

"No idea. I just know your dad said this was your mom's favorite as well as yours."

He slid it across the table.

"No thanks," she said. Her look turned mean.

"I know you didn't do it, Heather. Your dad doesn't think so either. You're too much like her. You're like who she really wanted to be. Healing the damage your forebears did with science and privilege."

"How would you know," said Heather, talking down to him now. "I just realized, you're the guy that used to have those cheesy billboards. 'I fought the law and you won'?"

"I know," said Donny, sampling the chocolate. "But it worked. I was able to help a lot of people. Some of whom are here now, a lot freer than they were."

"If you're so woke, why are you helping Lecker?"

"Honestly? Because I have bills to pay. I spent the better part of a decade helping the cause, and all I have to show for it are unpaid debts and stopped watches. The other reason is this is the only way I could get to see you."

"What do you want from me?"

"I thought maybe we could help each other."

"I don't need any help. Not from some sleazy lawyer."

"I know what you want: that money old Dr. Lecker is hoarding. Money your mom and granddad said is yours. Money you can use to advance the cause. And from what I see, it's a cause worth investing in."

"You don't know anything. And what I know is you're here working for them, and everything you say is a trick."

"I'm here to defend *you*, Heather. You are my client. You call the shots. I have a way we can break the money loose. Different than the craziness they are pursuing in the Tributary, which is a great idea but will never work."

"I get it," said Heather. "You think I'm going to write you a big check."

"No, Heather," said Donny, playing a hunch. "I think you're going to tell me where Slider is."

34

"SLIDER'S DEAD," SAID HEATHER QUICKLY.

"That's what everybody keeps telling me," said Donny.

"It's true," she said. "And it's my fault."

"How's that?"

"He died trying to rescue me."

"That's not what the newspapers said. They said he died trying to arrest you. Got shot by your dad's bodyguards."

"That's what they thought. But he was killed by friendly fire. People from here, assigned to kill him for what the people that run this place call treason."

"Treason? I thought he was a loyal soldier for the cause."

"He was. But they said he had gotten too violent. Taken actions that put the community in a bad light."

"Too violent for this crowd? I thought that was a job requirement."

"It was, when they needed it. But they don't want their wild boys in the house anymore."

"Who's 'they'?"

"The old ladies who run the Council. They decided that they need to keep men of fighting age segregated. The most violent of the fighters were expelled. In Slider's case, he did something that made them decide he needed to be killed."

"What was that?"

"The last big job he did before they came for me. But I don't know what it was, or what went down. He couldn't tell me before he left, and when he got back he was even more secretive about it."

"How long was he gone that time?"

"About ten days."

"Do you know who he was working with? Who else was on the team?"

Heather shook her head.

"I suppose your relationship with him was also a secret."

"Kind of," she said. "Not something the people he worked with needed to know about. Some of our friends in Houston knew. But it wasn't exclusive, and we all have pretty open connections in our network."

"I bet. But you're telling me this was a special enough connection that he wanted to volunteer for a kidnapping squad to come rescue you from his own bosses."

She reddened.

"Nothing gets young love amped up like a little danger," said Donny.

Donny tried to dodge the glove she threw at his face, but Heather was too fast. "He died for me, you fucking shyster. No wonder Dad talked about you that way."

Donny could imagine Lou trying to use his bad example to teach kids valuable lessons at the dinner table.

"Tell me the real story, and I really will get you out of here," said Donny.

"What if I don't want to leave?" said Heather.

"That's what I was afraid of," said Donny.

But the truth was, he didn't believe that either.

DONNY FOUND A PEDICAB THAT WOULD TAKE HIM CLOSE ENOUGH
to Joyce's place that he was unlikely to encounter any wildlife.
The cab rode uptown, along Magazine Street, which was still
paved, and still aboveground, but most of the old shops and
restaurants were abandoned. The cabbie explained that there
wasn't much infrastructure past the Garden District, except
around the college campuses that still had their own genera-
tors, and so the places that were dark, most of which also had
no water, were left to the more intrepid resettlers.

The place where she let Donny off was near the end of
Magazine Street. To the north was Audubon Park, which had
always been verdant, but now was untamed, a literal urban
jungle. You could see paths leading back in there still, where
once there had been paving, but even that had mostly been
overtaken by foliage. The sound of the birds was intense, even
in afternoon, like a chorus of cackling little dinosaurs. The
smell of spring was more intense, an acrid intoxication of exotic pollens.

In the other direction was the river. And on the stretch of
land between Magazine and the river was the site of the old
zoo. There was even a sign still there, but the only letter you
could see through the vines that covered it was one fungal-
looking O. The cabbie pointed at a cluster of buildings back
there, behind the trees, and said that's where she stays.

Donny said how do I get back, and the cabbie said there

should be a bike around to borrow, and if not you can walk up through the park to the streetcar. Should be fine as long as you get going before the sun starts to set.

What happens then? asked Donny. She laughed and then did the weirdest meow-meow cat sound he had ever heard.

Donny tried to laugh with her, then tried to pay her, but she said it's free. So he gave her a business card and said let me know if you ever need help. No thanks, she said, handing the card back.

He hadn't walked far before he heard the music coming from the direction of the buildings. He recognized the song. An old song Joyce liked to play that always put him to sleep or made him cry.

He followed the sound, down an overgrown but well-used and not quite feral walkway. There were pomegranates growing along both sides, and flowering vines in the trellis above. At the end, he saw them, there on the porch of one of the buildings.

Saw her, sitting in the afternoon light playing her old guitar for two companions.

"Hey, Joyce," said Donny.

All three of them looked.

"Hello, Donny," said Joyce, a tired smile on her face. "How did you find me?"

"Everybody around here seems to know who the real boss is, and where she can be found."

"We don't do bosses here," she said.

"If you say so. Percy told me where I could find you. And then I heard the song. Bach, right? I remember you used to play that one when you were sad."

"I play it a lot, now. Trying to get it right. And it's not by Bach. He did a version, and his wife, Anna Magdalena, did some better versions, but it was already an old song by then.

One that had traveled a long way, across time and space. I call it the Sara Band."

"Still making shit up as you go along," said Donny.

She smiled. "You would know. Come on up and visit with us," she said. "Meet Patricia and Sig."

Donny walked up the steps. Patricia was a white lady about his and Joyce's age, with wiry salt-and-pepper hair on the edge of unkempt and wire-framed glasses, an old hardback book under her arm. Donny already knew Sig. He was a little older than the last time they had been together. But still young, small but strong, with long black hair and tanned skin that looked like some race of man from the ancient past or the far future. He dressed simply, in T-shirt, jeans, and generic sneakers, but he had a weird gravity, at the same time that he was as close to caveman as you would ever meet this early in the third millennium.

"Sig and I go way back," said Donny, greeting his old client. "I thought you were in Russia."

"They kicked him out for trying to start a revolution," said Joyce.

"And they might arrest him if they find him in the US," said Donny.

"You told me here was okay," said Sig.

"It is. Wrote it into your early release deal, so you can settle right back in. Looks like you already did."

"I'm not staying long." The way he looked at him was kind of like the way a wild animal looks at you in the woods.

"I guess that's why they don't make you stay out there with the other fighting-age men."

"We make an exception for Sig," said Joyce. "He's helping me on a special project. Patricia has lived here longer than me." Joyce hadn't got up to greet him, and kept quietly playing as they spoke.

"Sit down," she said, pointing with her chin.

Donny did, there on the top step. There were no other chairs.

"You've gotten a lot better," said Donny, meaning her guitar playing.

"I have a more attentive audience now," she said. "And more life lived to put into it."

Donny nodded. And for once, he shut up and listened.

It was like the blues, but a different blues, one that knew math, and the sound that comes from minarets, and the sounds of the horses of European wars. He could also hear the sound of more recent wars, in the way she played it.

"That's really beautiful," he said when she was done.

"Thanks," she said.

"I'm gonna go get us some dinner," said Sig. When he stood, Donny noticed the knife for the first time, hanging from his belt. Maybe because he put his hand on it when he said that, as if the knife was what he was going to use to get it.

"Is this still a zoo?" said Donny.

Joyce looked at him. In the outdoor light, he noticed she had more gray than him. She had earned it.

"We don't cage any animals here anymore, if that's what you mean," she said.

"What do you do, Patricia?"

"I'm a writer," she said.

Whenever Donny heard someone say that, it sounded more like a pose than a job.

"Patricia is a philosopher," said Joyce. "And a landscaper, and a birder, and an outstanding masseuse."

"You'll have to help me ID some of these crazy birds I keep hearing," said Donny. "Where did you two meet?"

"Mexico City," said Patricia. "Right after the coup."

"Of course," said Donny. He remembered the resentment he felt the last time he visited there and saw exiles talking politics at sidewalk cafés under the Aztec sun while others endured the dark years of dictatorship back here. "When did you come back?"

He already knew when Joyce had come back.

"Fuck off, Donny," said Joyce.

"Sorry," said Donny, even though he really wasn't.

"I came back after the Compact was signed, and it was safe," said Patricia. "There were no easy paths. But here we are now, finally on the path we were meant to find."

"Right on," said Joyce. Which was a weird phrase to hear her use.

"There are those birds," said Donny, pointing at his ear.

"They know Sig is coming," said Joyce. "They can smell him."

"So can I," said Donny.

"How was the archive?" said Joyce. As she set her guitar down, he noticed the new tattoo on her forearm. Rover-style, like Xelina used to wear, trading cards of extinct North American animals. This one a saber-toothed cat to match the more primitively inked giant armadillo she had gotten in prison.

"It was interesting," he said. "I'm impressed with what you all have pulled together there. I didn't even know records like that existed."

"We're just getting started. Are you ready for tomorrow? Or did you come to try to convince me we should make a deal?"

"I know better than that. And I don't think my clients are in any more compromising a mood than you. I wanted to come ask you about something else. But it can wait until after the hearing."

He looked at his watch, and regretted coming all the way

out there. Especially as he realized it was later than he had thought, and the sun was already starting to work its way behind the river.

"Is it safe to walk back from here?" he asked.

"I don't know," said Joyce. "I don't go out at night much anymore. But Sig always comes back. And I'm sure he'd be happy to help you find your way if you think you need it."

He looked back toward the trees to see if he could see the feral kid stalking his prey. He just saw the ruins of the zoo, back there behind the foliage gone wild. Then he heard a scream, or maybe a holler, like the sound of some big ape. It might have even been a man.

"It's a bird," said Joyce.

"A big heron," said Patricia. "She's ready to mate."

"Or she heard Sig is coming," said Joyce.

Donny tried to read the look on Joyce's face, and kept his quip to himself. He couldn't tell who was sleeping with whom in this house, but he knew it was none of his business. He was an asshole for coming in the first place, and for letting himself think Joyce would have anything more than business to talk with him.

"I should go," said Donny.

"That's probably a good idea," said Joyce.

36

DONNY HAD SEEN JOYCE JUST ONE OTHER TIME SINCE SHE FLED the country. In Mexico City, for lunch, about three years after she left. He was there to interview a witness, another expat. She picked the place, on a side street off the main drag in Roma.

"We need to be careful," she said in the message she left at his hotel. "Even here."

He didn't know what that meant, even though he sort of did. There had been a change in government in Mexico, and the new regime was said to be trying to improve relations with its northern neighbor.

That was the reason she had a table for them in the back, instead of out on the sidewalk enjoying the gorgeous weather. It was the reason she entered from the back.

"I'm afraid to even hug you," she said, half laughing and half scowling. "Like I'll catch one of your bugs."

"I'm not sick," he said.

"I don't mean that kind of bug. I just mean you are the biggest surveillance magnet I know."

He couldn't argue. "I just try to bore them."

"Maybe we should try to entertain them."

He looked her in the eyes, but couldn't tell if she was fucking with him.

"Should we eat first?" he asked.

"Definitely."

She ordered Donny a dish that looked like orzo pasta but

was in fact the eggs of some oversized species of ant. She ate blood-marrow tacos, and when he finally got her laughing for a moment she looked like a lioness enjoying her fresh kill.

It helped that she was laughing at him as he told a story of how he had accidentally tricked a federal prosecutor and a federal judge into putting into the public record a classified document about a new program for the monitoring of wayward journalists.

It wasn't until they were stoned on margaritas and carving the face of George Washington into a shared block of flan that Donny learned Joyce wasn't even based in Mexico City anymore.

"I'm in Managua, Donny. Mexico City isn't safe any longer. Too many CIA mofos show up at the parties here, and too many federales on the payroll. I shouldn't even be here, but we decided one of us needed to be here for the meeting."

"Who's the we?" said Donny.

"It's Wade, Donny. You know that."

She meant Wade Camacho, the singer-songwriter whom Donny decided had been deported for being too cute. Cowboy cute, with his denim shirts and five-day beards and annoying yodels about injustice.

She was right. He did know that. But the mind had a way of trying to convince you other things were possible. Even when you were separated by borders. By borders fortified with walls, guns, surveillance, and law. By the borders we build in our own minds, from language and feeling and our inability to ever really understand each other.

"How's that going?" said Donny, doing his best to let the envy go, reminding himself that he was the one who chose to stay behind.

"It's nice," said Joyce. "Nice enough. We share a common

cause, which is worth a lot. He's entertaining. I mean, he's a musician."

"So are you."

"Not like him."

"No."

"He's kind of an airhead, which works very well for us, to my surprise."

Donny smiled. "An airhead who's a pretty good poet," he admitted.

"Not bad," said Joyce. "But the most important thing is that he makes me feel safe. Not just because he's so tall. Cops and soldiers and politicians are all scared of him. You can tell."

"That's why I figured the White House deported him," said Donny. "They were afraid he would sell dissidence as the sexiest thing around."

"He is good at that," said Joyce.

She looked around, sizing up the crowd for suspicious eyes.

"Is he with you?" said Donny. "On this trip?"

She looked at him with a hint of scorn in her eyes and the hint of a smile on her face. And then she shook her head.

"Do you love him?" asked Donny.

"Do you even know what the fuck that word means, Donny?"

Donny wasn't sure if she was asking that as an accusation, or a genuine question, like some existential version of asking if you know what time it is.

"Not the first clue," said Donny. "How about you?"

She shrugged. "I bet your grandma knows. She also knows how important it is to police one's tendencies toward animalistic territoriality."

Donny nodded. "I bet you're right," said Donny. He pushed ant eggs around on his plate, and then changed the subject.

"What's it like there now?" he asked. "In Nicaragua."

Nicaragua was a free state, liberated by a coalition of revolutionaries, urban elites, and foreign backers who had installed an experimental new government six months earlier.

"It feels like a future you would actually want to live in," said Joyce. "True freedom, equal rights for all, a sense of real community. Even for an outsider."

"They won't put up with that for long. Anything that makes you not cynical is way too dangerous."

"Well, one thing you learn when you leave the country thinking you have found sanctuary is that there is no such thing. Not with the virus of power and dominion that infects the world."

"So when are you coming home?"

"Another word whose meaning you don't really understand. Because it doesn't really mean anything. We're all nomads, Donny. It's in our genes."

"I don't know," said Donny. "I really like my apartment."

She laughed. "You really like your books. I'm just saying, we need to be thinking about our problems on a planetary scale. And locally, at the same time, at least tactically. But dream big, for change that is real, and permanent."

"How do you do that?"

"It has to be almost like a religion. Like a religious movement. Like when Christianity or Islam or Buddhism swept over a swath of the planet. Like that, but green. Transcendent and grounded at the same time. A deep politics of the whole planet and every living thing. Even every inanimate thing in the natural world, which has its own kind of life."

"We the Creatures," said Donny.

"Exactly," said Joyce. This time the smile was real.

She raised her glass, and Donny joined her. Then she turned more serious.

"You should help us," she said.

"What do you mean?"

"Just what it sounds like."

Now Donny was looking around for eyes and ears.

"I can't leave my practice," said Donny. "You know that. I made that decision three years ago, when I missed my chance to stay here with you."

"We're not asking you to leave your practice, Donny. Quite the opposite."

"Who's 'we,' Joyce?"

"We have been following your work. You've gotten really good at it. And we think you can help the cause in new ways. Especially with your access to people in our network who have been detained. People with whom it is very hard for us to communicate."

"Are you recruiting me, Joyce?"

She just smiled, and fed him George Washington's brain.

They ended up a little later in a room upstairs, sating other hungers, ones that had been building up over a much longer time. She said it was where she stayed when she was in Mexico City. It was a studio apartment, spartan but comfortable, with a bed just big enough for the two of them to fit in at the same time, watched over by a cheesecake Aztec warrior woman in the calendar on the wall. Donny wondered whether that guardian would be enough to protect them, but not enough to restrain himself from reuniting with the only woman he had ever really loved, even as he knew that politics and the pain it can cause had pulled them apart in irreconcilable ways, and neither of them could any longer be trusted to be true with the other.

They stayed up late that night talking, sharing confessions with each other about the lovers they had had since they broke up. Donny had more, but Joyce's were more real. Joyce told him what nature was like in Nicaragua, where the decades of war had kept the developers at bay. She described some of the birds she had seen, with juvenile wonder in her eyes and invented words rolling off her tongue. Donny told her the developing taxonomy of lies he had invented to get people free, from a society that no longer really believed in the idea of freedom, unless freedom could be like a team mascot that everyone identifies with as the trademark of their tribe, without ever even giving any thought to what it is really supposed to mean. Like the American city, said Joyce, that has a picture of an Indian on its ball caps.

It was only when they woke up late, but not late enough, that they talked more about what Joyce had brought up at dinner. About how Donny could help the cause, with his contacts inside. He made promises. The kind of promises you make in code that lets you deny they were any such thing later. At least if they are read back to you from a surveillance transcript, at a deposition, or an interrogation.

The kind of promises a lawyer makes.

Donny was at the airport the next night, waiting for his flight back to Houston, when he saw the news of Joyce's arrest and extradition. Hooded perp walk, with Mexican Marines and American agents on either side as they took her to her own flight home.

As he started working the phones, too busy to consider what it meant for him, he remembered what she said about the lie that is the idea of home.

37

DONNY HAD MADE IT INTO THE CANOPY OF FLOWERS WHEN HE stopped and turned.

"Joyce," he said.

"Yes, Donny."

"I'm sorry."

She stopped playing her notes, but took a while to answer.

"I'm sure you are, Donny."

He walked back to the porch. It was just the two of them now.

"I mean, I'm sorry about Wade."

"We all are," said Joyce. She always was good at cauterizing her psychic wounds and hiding them from others.

Donny remembered the footage the government had leaked of Wade's execution. The way the President's goons had made him sing. Not Wade's protest songs, but the songs of the so-called patriots.

Freedom isn't free.

Joyce set her guitar against the wall. That was when Donny noticed the gun she had holstered to the front of the belt that held up her jeans.

"And I'm sorry I let you down," said Donny.

"It's okay, Donny. At least I wasn't the only one. Ask Sig."

Donny looked at his boots. They were beginning to look broken-in.

Donny had worn out his shoe leather when they kidnapped Joyce and brought her back to a cold cage in Dallas, on charges of treason and conspiracy. He called in every favor he had. He learned what had happened. How, while Donny and Joyce were in Mexico City, Wade had come to New York to play a show, on a special visa that turned out to be bait. How they arrested him during his performance, the better to strike fear into the hearts of his fans and followers, to show the price of dissent. How quickly he had broken during interrogation. Telling them everything he knew. Including where they could find Joyce.

Donny's efforts to free Joyce were not successful. Not at first.

Donny's efforts to build a network with himself as the conduit, between the people that were inside and the people that were outside, were more successful. Joyce was not a node in that network. He only heard stories, more like fragments of stories, about what she was doing. Making her new gospel, which like any good gospel, mostly just told the truth, spiced with the kind of mythic bullshit people like to hear. In Joyce's case, by beatifying dead American dissidents and a few live ones, and turning one story of separatist utopia into a model for others to follow.

"I wasn't meant to be free, Donny," said Joyce as she watched him ruminate there to the sound of the awakened night birds and one foghorn blowing on the river. You could see she didn't even recognize the boots she had bought him, and he realized how very long ago that had been. "I'm a teacher, remember. A college professor. My best work was done inside. First time it ever felt authentically meaningful."

He looked at her. You could see she meant it. You could also see the pain in her eyes. The memory of the things they had done to her while she was their captive, and the worse things they had done to others.

"And I'm still here, Donny," she said. "I'm alive."

She was smiling, but you could see the anger that hid behind the smile. Maybe it was the way her teeth looked momentarily feral.

"I'm glad for that, Joyce," said Donny. "I honestly wasn't sure."

"I've learned to keep a low profile," she said. "Took me long enough."

They both laughed.

"Don't feel sorry for me, Donny. I'm happy. For real. I have finally found a place I'm comfortable. A way to maintain the balance."

"Home?"

She nodded, in a noncommittal way. "Something like that. Sure."

"This is a good spot," said Donny, looking around. "What happened to the animals?"

"Some are still around," said Joyce. "The ones that have become too much like us, and no longer know how to be free."

Donny considered that. "What about the other ones?"

She just smiled.

Donny looked back toward the swamp from which he came. He couldn't see it, but he knew it was there. It had always been there, even when they drained it.

"Do you know how to be free, Donny?"

"Nope."

She laughed. And then she leaned forward, and took his hand.

"Stop blaming yourself for what happened, Donny. In the final reckoning there was really only one guilty person. And he has met his fate. No thanks to you."

"Did you kill him?"

"Do I look like I could kill him? They broke me, Donny.

You should see the pathetic rehab yoga I have to do just to get my ass out of bed in the morning."

"You know what I mean."

"And you don't seem to be able to figure out that the dead don't want their remains to be disturbed. Running around with your cathode-ray delusions of justice, imagining yourself as some white savior of the downtrodden victims to make up for the fact that you've fucked up your career and your relationships and every chance at happiness that came your way. Maybe the victims know how to take care of themselves."

It stung, but somehow their fights always energized Donny, and the more they got going the more he wanted to get into it.

"Is that what happened to Slider?" he asked.

She scowled at him. "Actually, yes. He wanted to avenge his parents. He came to me, knowing you would never get anywhere close to real justice. I helped him find where the goons were who had killed Juana and Gil. Living under new identities arranged by allies of their former employer, supported by a black pension, off the books. And he went and found them, and killed them."

Donny had tried to find those same guards. They were ghosts. Like they had never even existed. Employment records expunged.

"How did you find them?" asked Donny.

"I asked the right people," said Joyce.

"Did you have him killed too?"

She made a sour face. "Of course I didn't have him killed. I'm like you, Donny. I don't believe in the death penalty. I just don't volunteer to help real murderers evade it. And if you're wondering why he would go help arrest his little rich white honey—yes, don't look so surprised, of course I know—the reason is it was a fucking rescue operation, you fool. Her father, your friend, was keeping her prisoner."

"So I heard. Not sure I buy it."

"Well, it's true. Now she is free. And with her fortune, she is going to help us free the whole fucking world."

Donny stared at her there, sitting on her porch, happily ripping the duct tape from his eyes. He could see she believed every word she said. He also had one other question coming into his head. But Patricia had come back now, standing on the porch with a gun instead of a pen this time, giving Donny the look that said, *It's time for you to go.*

THE ARCHIVISTS OF NEW ORLEANS DID HAVE TWO FUNCTIONING copy machines. They would not, however, let Donny use them, saying the resource was too precious to their work and saved for the most important files. Nor would they let Donny check any of the materials out, saying he was not trustworthy. But when they confirmed he was staying at the Library, a lodging operated by people known to the Council, they offered to send files there. He didn't believe them, until he got back to the place and when he went to the desk the clerk on duty told him they had three file boxes set up in a carrel for him. Donny expressed his appreciation, but the truth was that all Donny wanted to do after seeing Joyce was find an expeditious way to self-medicate and worry about work in the morning.

The Library was one of the main lodgings for guests of the new government, and it stayed pretty full. Donny figured the only reason he got a room was so they could keep an eye on him. And when he got to his room, he saw that someone had been looking through the files he left out on the little desk, and made little attempt to hide the fact, and he doubted it was the housekeeping staff.

In the evenings at the Library, after enjoying the bounteous meals of real food on offer in the mess, people hung out in the common areas. New Orleans still had a nightlife of sorts, but nothing like before, so visitors mostly had to come up with their own entertainment. When Donny went back down thinking he could sit in a comfortable chair and have just one drink and a quick dinner before returning to his prep for the day to come, he found the lobby had been taken over by the international association of hydrological engineers. They weren't an official association—just a dozen experts in the field from around the world who were excited to help out with this experiment in learning how to coexist with a massive river that had burst its banks and would never go back. Volunteers, basically, given room and board, interesting work, a small stipend, and the joy of being part of the project. An equal mix of men and women, nice but kind of dorky. So he tried sitting there for a while devouring his meatless muffuletta while they shared a bottle of bespoke Bywater absinthe and quickly got to work on driving Donny crazy with a guitar and melodica duo playing folk songs of the world. When they started playing the Wade Camacho songs, and really getting into it, Donny decided it was time to go into the actual library part of the Library and get to work.

They had his three boxes of files on loan set up there at one of the old library tables. First, he pulled out the notes he had made while looking over the files with the researchers that afternoon.

The notes were mostly jottings of ideas that came into his head as he reviewed the files. Potentially exculpatory factual nuggets, ideas for alternative theories and creative defenses, possible counterclaims. The problem was, the law this court was enforcing was so upside down in its premises that it was hard to know where to even start. In essence, it was retroactively criminalizing things that had always been legal. The underlying idea wasn't really that different than the wrongful-death claims Donny was pursuing in the Harrison case. Except that it was totally different, because the deaths it was treating as wrongful were the deaths of trees and animals, not people. And the only way to argue with the idea that cutting down an old tree is murder is to point out that it is not and never has been under any law known to Donny. Things that exist in nature do not have rights, and if you want to change that, fine, but you can only do so prospectively. A perfectly reasonable argument. This wasn't about reason, though. And it wasn't really about the past. It was about the future. About the future the current generation was supposed to have, a future of general environmental health, something it was reasonable to argue they have a right to. About how that future had been stolen, by people who razed the past. Long past the tolling of any statute of limitations, but very recently in the measure of geological time. And about how some people had gotten rich from that theft of the future, enjoying a decadent and pampered present while the rest of the world suffered—and was likely to suffer even more as the long-reaching consequences cascaded.

It was hard enough to prepare for a hearing in a kangaroo court, one whose rules you had no familiarity with. It was even harder when you realized you really were on the wrong side of the case. Donny had helped whiteboard the idea, but he never expected them to take it this seriously—any real judge would throw it out without so much as a hearing. But Percy and her colleagues and clients were right about the merits, at least in terms of real moral justice. And they were prosecutor, judge, *and* jury. They knew it, too, just as they knew they were tearing up centuries of precedent to make a radical new law codifying that justice. It was then that Donny decided there wasn't much point in preparing an actual defense. The best strategy would be to plead mercy, warn of imminent danger, and try to work out a deal. Maybe Percy would help him with that, but somehow he didn't think there was much of a chance. If Heather really wasn't a true prisoner, maybe it wouldn't matter—if he could figure out a way to persuade her.

So he didn't even open the boxes. Instead, he decided to take the remains of his drink and see what other kind of reading the library had.

The shelving system did not follow any of the established methods. No Library of Congress numbers or Dewey decimals. No decimals at all. It was more intuitive. Books grouped together by subject matter, mostly, and sometimes by size, or color. Donny looked at the oversized shelves. A photo book about the long wars of his youth, when the General was in charge. Intense black-and-white shots of marines in their fallout suits going in to the Iranian blast zone to clear out the remnants of the "outlaw state." Jungle fighters working the border between Costa Rica and Panama, policing the US colony at Chiriquí, with fetishes on their machetes and fangs and tails and maybe even human ears around their necks. And then the fire patrols who went into Brazil to clear the rebels from the jungles with napalm, mortar, and man traps, followed by the military merchant companies who cleared the rain forest with Titan Jelly, chainsaws, bulldozers and fire, destroying the habitat of a lot more than the neo-nationalist nomads of ODA they were fighting, and paving the way for the accelerated warming of the atmosphere that followed.

When he put that away he found the older books. Dusty classics, some of them actual classics, including a three-volume re-compilation of the Greek myths by Hugh de Lavis, an English writer whose short novel about love in the trenches of the Somme Donny had read in college. He pulled up the entry on Demeter, thinking maybe there would be something there in the legends of the harvest that he could use to embellish his begging in the morning. And there was some of that, but then he got distracted reading about the wrath of Poseidon, stories that seemed equally applicable to storm-ruined New Orleans.

He went back to the boxes, trying to find the file that he remembered. Files, more accurately, a trove of binders that had been stolen by the outlaw archivists from Donny's old law firm, Barker & Eames. Donny had requested it more out of curiosity than any sense that it would help his case—wondering what kinds of deals his former colleagues were up to these days, and thinking he might find something in there on Lou, who was now one of the firm's senior partners.

It took him a while, but he found it. He worked his way through the merger agreements and the NDAs and the tender offers and the private-placement memoranda, and after a while he thought maybe it was a dumb idea after all.

Until he found the stock-purchase agreement.

It was only six months old, from late the year before. The buyer was a company called New Bourbon Investments LP, which Donny had never heard of. But the seller was AMR. And what they were selling was a majority stake in the company. With all of its assets, and all of its liabilities.

The most interesting thing was, when you flipped to the back, to where they always put the address to mail notices and lawsuits, the address for the buyer was the same as the address of Lecker's office.

Donny kept digging, looking for more AMR material, but everything else was what he had meant to pull—material on Promethean Resources. And none of that seemed worth his time anymore. Or didn't, until he found a file containing a five-year-old demand letter from Miles, asserting a different claim than the one Donny had been chasing in the case Miles bequeathed him. It was addressed to both Promethean and Tripto

Labs, as affiliated companies. It accused them of violating the labor laws and the Thirteenth Amendment's prohibitions on involuntary servitude. His clients, Miles said, were John and Jane Doe detainees who had been prohibited from organizing their fellow farm laborers. The letter referenced a draft of a lawsuit that was attached, but the attachment wasn't in the file. And it was dated just a couple of weeks before his death.

Donny copied the text of the letter longhand, on a separate page from his notes about the stock-purchase agreement. And then he tried to think of the fastest way to get back to his office after the hearing.

The engineers were still partying in the lobby when Donny got up from his work, and he decided to join them, thinking maybe a little bit of Bacchus would help him process it all. It was a good while and no small quantity of absinthe later that Donny was singing the vocals to the song he had persuaded the Croatian civil engineer named Dr. Elena to play on her guitar: "Thirteen Tortuga Suite," from the second solo album by Electric Hephaestus bass player Rodney Jobson. Donny wasn't sure exactly what the song was about, especially since it was in three totally different parts, but it was something like being a homeless stowaway who finds paradise only to get evicted in the most brutal way. One of those eccentric hits with some staying power, enough that three of the crew knew the song and Donny had them joining in. Who knew absinthe could make you ebullient. But then Donny found himself crying, in the part where it's hard to tell but it seems the narrator of the song is dead, and then Donny started laughing as he remembered how much Miles hated folk music by white people, especially Rodney Jobson.

That's when Donny spied Marianne Abboud standing there in the hallway, watching them and smiling.

"HELLO, MR. KIMOE," SHE SAID.

"Chief Inspector Abboud," said Donny.

"Marianne," she said. "I'm off-duty."

"Donny."

"You are quite an enthusiastic singer," said Marianne.

"Usually I have the good sense to only do that in the privacy of my own shower."

"I am sure that is even better. I love this song. My flatmate had the record in college."

"It's an acquired taste. My roommate sold my copy so I'd stop playing it."

"Well, it's better this way anyway."

"I don't know," said Donny. "Whenever I sing in public I usually get in trouble. This is the first time it will have gotten me arrested by Interpol."

"Don't worry," she said. "I left my handcuffs upstairs in my room."

Donny considered asking where that was, but he was too busy admiring how confidently she expressed the lines around her eyes when she smiled.

"And I'm not here to arrest you," she added. "Your story checked out."

"Well, that's a relief," said Donny, acting like he was joking.

"I would like to ask what you are doing here, though," she said.

"I have a hearing tomorrow. Different case than the one you were at. Trying to get the Council to free a prisoner. The daughter of an old friend."

"I see," she said, with sudden gravity on her face. "The Tributary. Good luck with that."

"Thanks," said Donny. "I don't think the odds are so good. That's why I decided to join the band when I should be cramming."

"I thought maybe you would say you were here looking for Mr. Harrison."

"I kind of hoped that was how it would work out," said Donny. "But every source I've talked to has me convinced it's true. He's dead."

"That is what we have concluded as well. So we are going up the chain, to see if we can find who organized the operation."

"Still chasing the same basic theory, then?"

"Absolutely. We have a source."

"May I ask who?"

"You may ask, but I cannot tell."

"Too bad," said Donny.

"Maybe we should just have a drink instead," she said. "I am tired of working too."

"Okay," said Donny. He wanted to look at his watch, but not as much as he wanted to talk to the chief inspector and see what other questions she had.

Forty-five minutes later, after the engineers had sensibly gone to bed, Donny and the chief inspector were into their second drink and laughing hard trading notes on their favorite bad album covers of their youth. It started when Donny discovered the shelf they had there in one of the alcoves off the lobby, a little music room that had a bin of old records, a ton of cassettes, and the means to play both. Chief Inspector Abboud produced a joint from her purse, to Donny's immense surprise. She seemed slightly embarrassed at first, or maybe just wary of letting down her prosecutorial guise so completely, but Donny encouraged her, even as the atrophied but still dutiful part of his brain that was mindful of his ethical duties as a lawyer reminded him of what was coming in the morning. It had rarely stopped him before, though, and soon they were lit up, and Marianne was rummaging through the tapes until she found one she liked better than what was playing and popped it in. Traumfunk's *Journey to the Far Side of the Sun*. Marianne did not even know that the album was a soundtrack. In her defense, the movie was made in East Germany. Donny gave her something approaching a free-verse synopsis of the plot, which involved a coed crew of astronauts with burnt-orange bell-bottomed uniforms traveling in a ship made from mixed-up plastic model parts to a mirror Earth in which cats have evolved to be the most intelligent species and dominate the planet. Marianne said that sounds like a place I would like to visit, and Donny said just as long as you're not mistaken for a big bird like the first human who stepped off the ship.

They talked about their work, about the mileage you put on the engine of the soul dealing with the dead and the caged, no matter which side of the courtroom you are on. Marianne said do you think the reason we all always talk about the past is because there's no more future? Donny said there's no question about it, but at least there's a right now for us to live in, which he thought was pretty clever until he could see her slyly laughing, like a cat that prefers to play with its toys at the end of a string. So he changed gears, and talked about his hearing the next day, about the theory behind the case, and what it would be like if you could really build a new legal system in which trees and cats and every other living thing had rights on parity with our own. Marianne said that only gets you so far, that the only way you can really fix this mess is if everyone can find their own way back to the grove. Donny asked what she meant by that and she said why don't you look it up. He said I would if I could get a signal on my damn phone. That's when she laughed at him for the first time, grabbed his phone, said she had the same model, and showed him how to change the setting from the US standard to Open 7.

When she did that, his phone pinged with the sound of electric popcorn, alerting him that he had twenty-seven new messages. That's when he finally looked at his watch.

It's okay, said Marianne. Maybe we can talk some more tomorrow.

Donny started to say how there won't be a tomorrow, but decided to leave it, even though he had lost the right-now.

And he definitely didn't want to tell her that what he was about to do was go back to his room alone and call his grandma.

PERCY HAD CUT HER TEETH DEFENDING YOUNG BLACK MEN IN THE
criminal courts of Houston, helping juries see each of her clients as the embodiment of all the black men whose bodies were
shackled and cut down or strung up over the dark centuries
of American history. Donny saw her make a closing argument
once in a felony murder case that somehow managed to get
you to envision every one of those lives in your head, to briefly
glimpse the quantum of feeling and dignity destroyed through
a violence that you knew could never be sated unless you radically changed the whole architecture of the society. That morning before the Tributary, she did the same thing. But instead
of black bodies, she talked about big trees. And she was really
good at it. Because to her, it was all connected.

You could see it on the faces of the jurors. All 501 of them.

That probably wasn't an accurate count, but it could have
been. The jury comprised any members of the community who
wanted to participate. They filled the courtroom and the gallery that morning, sitting wherever they chose, many of them
sitting right there on the floor near Donny. The litigants did not
have designated spots, but Donny had arrived early enough to
grab a chair, on which he set his briefcase while he stood behind it, hands on the frame.

In the Tributary, there were no judges, just more forceful
personalities among the chorus of jurors. It was a sharp contrast with the last time Donny had appeared in that courtroom,

when the only people there other than the lawyers were three federal appellate judges, two of whom were pretty sympathetic to Donny's case, despite the black robes and funereal demeanors. It was Donny's fourth effort to challenge the constitutionality of the suspension of habeas corpus. Others had already litigated the big issues, including the basic questions around the circumstances in which the power could be invoked, and who had the power to invoke it. Donny was then making the argument that five years was too long a period to qualify as an emergency.

He knew it was a loser when the chief judge interrupted him three minutes into his argument, quoting Justice Davidoff's holding in *United States v. Moro* that the president has the exclusive power to determine when conditions of domestic insurrection exist, and who qualifies as an insurgent. You could see they wanted Donny to help them find a loophole, and he tried, but in the end they didn't have the nerve. Members of the federal bench back then served the state, the way priests serve the church, at its mercy almost as much as Donny's detainee clients, if more pampered, subject only to existential tortures that don't really earn that name.

The other big difference in those days was the courtroom had a functioning roof. This one was dripping puddles in a half dozen spots, from the storm that had blown in the night before as Donny worked into the wee hours trying to put together the pieces. The dilapidated appearance seemed like it would undermine the credibility of the court. But then he watched as Percy stood there in a shaft of morning light and unspun a millennial saga of arboreal holocaust in a thirty-minute address, and cursed the advantage she had from knowing the quirks of this room down to the way if you stood in the right spot at the right time it would even let a lawyer serve as the sundial of redemption.

She had more than stories. She had facts. The facts they had filled a skyscraper with like you'd fill a silo with grain, woven together in a way that supported her story, visualized in slides she screened on the wall.

She talked about numbers on papers. Big numbers. Money.

She grounded the numbers in the earth. In the price per tree, triangulated with the long lives cut short, the promising futures extinguished. Her short history of the deforestation of the hemisphere made you feel the fire and hear the chainsaws. She nailed the connections between wars that were fought before they were born and the massive crop failures they had witnessed just as they were coming into adulthood. She explained how the wars against the guerrilla armies of the hemispheric south were just extensions of the much longer war against nature. And she built a model that showed how much of the damage to the environment could be attributed to Promethean Resources and its predecessors. It was tiny as a percentage of the total—mere basis points. But the number that translated into in dollars, when she flashed it on her screen for all to read, was bigger than the numbers they were talking about in Washington as reparations for slavery.

The amounts known to be in Heather's diversified trust were a fraction of that, and only a smaller fraction could be traced back to the bulldozers and Titan Jelly. It almost seemed small, until Percy showed what that would translate to in real profit per tree, and what it would be if you divided it up among every member of the community to invest in their restoration efforts.

This didn't even count the value of her ownership stake in Tripto Labs, which may have been conceived by Helen as a different way to compensate for the damage her family business had caused, but also profited from that damage.

It was hard to read a crowd that big, even as you knew the biases they had coming in. Donny had plenty of experience arguing to the mob—during the emergency, making your case to the cameras outside the courtroom was usually a more effective way to get justice for a political dissident than the rigged game they played inside. But he didn't even know the rules that applied in this courtroom, and what rules they had they seemed to be making up as they went along, with an unstructured informality that was like a classroom without the teacher. He was pretty sure they didn't really understand the stakes. The message from Carol he picked up the night before included a warning, relayed from a reliable source Donny trusted. Lecker was already preparing his backup plan: a rescue op that could reignite the fratricidal war that had ruined this city and taken down most of the nation with it. Donny's debts and Carol's imminent eviction were the least of their problems now. So Donny watched how Percy did it, and tried to focus on the faces in the crowd that he actually knew.

There were four of them there when he arrived: Bettina Borges, the bespectacled librarian with blond hair turning blue who was the real brains behind the archive; Col. Ellen Franco, a fortyish ex-soldier in carbon-colored coveralls who had led the liberation and now managed the battalions of young fighters camped at the edge of town; Carl Denis, the gray-haired builder who had been a successful architect before he joined the underground and became one of their principal designers of DIY weaponry; and Gertie Almeida, the youngest and most strident member of the Council. Two other Council members had walked in after Percy had already started: Claude and Joyce. Half of them were ex-clients of Donny's. But that wasn't an advantage. And just how rigged the setup was against him became more apparent when Bettina took the stand to help

Percy establish the documentary basis for all her numbers, and then went right back into the jury.

Heather was seated nearby, on the top of the old judges' bench, her worn ropers dangling over the edge.

Donny had a plan. He would attack them on the facts, challenging Bettina and her climate-scientist teammates on the oversimplified causal connections they distilled from an ecological system too complex for anyone to really even understand. He would attack them on the law, showing their jurisdictional and temporal overreach in making people outside their territory liable for actions that had been legal during the time when they were taken. And he would attack them for their hubris in presuming they were the ones who could speak for the trees.

But when the sun had moved on and it was finally Donny's turn, he got a different idea. Not just because he knew their minds were made up. And not because he realized, listening to Percy's case, that if they didn't stand up for the trees, no one would—the case needed to be made, and there needed to be an accounting, even if it was too late to repair the damage done. His victory condition was different from theirs—he just needed to figure out the most certain way to get Heather freed from their custody and on a plane back to Dallas with him. So instead of making the case they expected from him, he stood up, straightened his tie, and tried something different.

"I would like to call Heather as a witness," said Donny.

"What for?" said Bettina.

"To help all of you understand what's at stake more clearly," said Donny. "And do it in a way that does not try to undermine the compelling arguments Percy made."

"That sounds a little nonstandard," said the Colonel.

"This whole process is way beyond nonstandard," said

Donny. "I may have helped come up with the idea that morphed into this, but I can see that you got your ideas of due process from the emergency courts I used to defend some of you from."

The jurors who were not judges looked at one another. Especially the ones he was addressing, the ones who had been hauled in front of those courts.

"This is a waste of time," said Gertie.

"The least you can do is let my client tell her side of the story. Even if the case isn't really about her, but about the things her dead relatives did. Especially because of that, you need to let her speak."

"It's fine," argued Carl Denis. "I actually want to hear this. We all should. Even if I don't trust this traitor. I can't believe we let him back in after what he pulled."

Donny decided not to remind Carl of the time he got him out of detention after they busted him downloading 3-D printable mortar plans. He had his eyes on Heather, who looked simultaneously scornful and squirmy.

"Let her talk!" said some voices in the crowd.

"Set up a chair," said Ellen.

And they did. A group of the jurors put one of the chairs there in the middle of the room, and another group led Heather to it.

"What if I don't want to talk?" said Heather.

"Why wouldn't you want to let us hear your side?" said Ellen.

"I don't trust this guy either," said Heather, pointing at Donny.

"Come on," said Donny. "I just want to ask a few questions. All you have to do is tell the truth. How hard can that be?"

"Your truth and ours may no longer be the same thing, Donny," said Bettina.

"I think you'll find we can all agree on the facts I want to get on the record," he said.

"She needs to answer the questions," said Joyce, speaking up for the first time. "She's still our prisoner, even if we call her a guest, and our rules are premised on total transparency."

"Fine," said Heather. "I have nothing to hide. You already heard for the second time the sins encoded in my name."

"We heard a lot about your grandfather and great-grandfather this morning," said Donny. "Now can we talk about your mother?" he asked.

She visibly tensed at the subject.

"I know it must be difficult," said Donny. "And I think everyone here knows you helped cause what happened to her and the rest of your family."

"Come on, Donny," said Carl. "This is just cruel."

"Well, then why don't I ask you, Carl? Did she help your team that took those hostages?"

"That wasn't 'our team,'" said Ellen. "Those were independent actors."

"Was Slider one of them?"

"You would know better than we," said Ellen. "You were the one who defended him, I hear."

"The case I have for him involves the death of his parents," said Donny. "He's just the plaintiff. And now it's too late to ask him. So I'm asking Heather."

"What does this have to do with the case before us?" said Carl.

"Give me a minute and you'll see," said Donny. "Heather, please just tell us. Did you help the cell that kidnapped your family?"

Heather looked at Donny with a different kind of scorn. "Yes," she said.

"You told them the information they needed about how to get into the club, where and when they would find their targets, things like that."

She nodded.

"You had been aligned with the underground for a long time," said Donny.

"Have you been to that place? The 'refuge'?" You could hear the scare quotes in her voice.

"I never got invited," said Donny. "But I know people who have. They say it's like the Garden of Eden."

"An Eden where they slaughter the animals. That place needed to be liberated."

"Did you know they were going to take hostages?"

"No," said Heather. "They told me they just wanted to arrest my uncle, for crimes against the people. He worked for the administration."

"That's your dad's brother."

"Yes." You could see she was keeping the feelings bottled, trying to maintain her strength.

"That's what your friends in the cell told you."

"Friend," said Heather. "Singular."

"Was it Slider?"

She nodded.

"Did he betray you?"

"No," said Heather. "It just got out of control. Other people on the team that he hadn't worked with before. He wasn't even there—he was running the boat, out there in the water. They were supposed to just take Uncle Bob, bring him back here. But the weather turned on them. A storm was coming in. So they improvised. And then the feds caught up with them."

"Did you see it all?"

"Just some of it," said Heather.

"I'm sorry about your mom," said Donny.

"So am I," said Heather. She was crying, but lucid. "I loved her. But I also had come to see how corrupted she was, by her fortune."

"Your fortune," corrected Donny.

"I disclaim it," said Heather. "I don't want it. And I proved that by disclaiming my whole family."

She had the crowd's attention.

"That's very brave," said Donny.

"Is that what you think?" she said, reddening. "Fuck you. What do you know about courage? Fucking lawyer, presuming to stand there and talk to me like some professor or priest or patriarch who thinks he knows what's good for us. Don't you get it? The world is dying, Donny." She said it like a derisive nickname. "To save it, to save the future, we need to take radical action."

"More radical than even the elders of this rather radical community are willing to take," said Donny.

"That's right. And we're just getting started. The only real problem this planet has is people. And that's an easy problem to fix."

"Is that what you and Slider were working on?"

"I don't want to talk to you anymore," she said.

"But they took Slider away from you, didn't they?"

Now she looked really mad.

"Have you ever heard the story of Erysichthon?"

"Who?"

"I'm probably not saying it right. I'd never heard of it until last night, when I came across it in an old book."

"Where are you going with this, Donny?" said Carl.

"Let him talk," said Joyce.

"Thank you. Erysichthon was a king in ancient Greece.

A rich guy, basically—owned a lot of land. He thought that meant he could do whatever he wanted with that land. Including cutting down the trees to build himself a sweet new house. But he cut down the most precious trees. The oldest ones, even as his guys tried to get him to stop. What he thought was some great lumber was the sacred grove of Demeter. The goddess of the harvest, who got so pissed she cursed him with famine. Hunger so bad he ended up eating his own leg."

"Sounds like justice to me," said Heather.

"Sounds like your family to me," said Donny. "Or maybe our whole big American family. And I haven't even got to the part about his daughter. His beautiful daughter. He was so hungry he sold her. First to the sea god, but then over and over to others. Do you know how?"

"She was a shapeshifter!" yelled Joyce.

Donny looked. Joyce had already rendered her verdict on Heather.

"Are you a shapeshifter?" asked Donny.

"I'm exactly what you see," said Heather.

"A rich and powerful young woman who thinks she knows what's good for others."

"I'm a worker in the fields. Carrying on the good part of the work my mom started, but in a spirit of service instead of profit."

"Do your coworkers know you're a spy?"

"What?"

"Explain it to the others here, how you've been pretending to assimilate while you work as a clandestine source for those who would have the people leading this work locked up."

He had their attention.

"You know all about lying to your friends and allies," said Heather.

"Maybe. I also know that someone here has been serving as a confidential informant for both Interpol and private interests. Providing intelligence about the clandestine operations of the Council and its teams, in support of its judgments, including the sentences it delivers in secret. Information that will be used to develop prosecutions of some of the people sitting here in this room right now. And to bankrupt this project."

"What evidence do you have of that?" said Ellen.

"It's circumstantial," said Donny. "But Heather can tell us."

He looked at Joyce. She looked authentically surprised at the revelation, but also surprisingly pleased.

Heather looked like a rich girl suddenly ready to defend her privilege.

"I understand, Heather," said Donny. "Slider was the only person left that you were close to. Other than maybe your dad."

"You can't prove that was me," said Heather. "Because it wasn't."

"I can't prove it, until you admit it here before your comrades. But I can tell it was you. You certainly had the motive. They killed your lover. What better motive than that?"

Bettina and Ellen were looking at Joyce now.

"They will understand, Heather. And they will let me take you home."

"This is my home," said Heather.

"This is not your home," said Ellen. "You are our guest. And I can see that you have betrayed our trust."

"I am not going to argue with the case Percy made," said Donny. "To the contrary, I agree. Let me take Heather back to Dallas with me, to her family. And I will do everything in my power to work out a deal."

The judges who weren't judges looked at one another. A look of tentative agreement.

The crowd had a different idea.

"No deals!" yelled one voice. And you could tell, as soon as the words got out there bouncing around the room, that they had captured the spirit that animated the room.

The echo was not just from the cavernous chamber, but from the people repeating the declaration of uncompromising judgment.

"Banish her!"

You could see how Heather felt about that.

"Banish him!" said Heather, pointing at Donny.

"We already did," said Ellen. "And we're about to kick him out again."

Donny was relieved. "We can leave right now," he said.

"No, Donny," said Ellen. "You can leave. But Heather's banishment must be handled according to our law."

"You can't do that," said Donny. "Do you understand what her family will do? Not only will you never get the settlement you want. This could mean war. They're preparing as we speak."

"That may be," said Ellen. "But that is the law. And we are ready."

41

WHEN HE GOT BACK TO THE LIBRARY, DONNY ALREADY HAD HIS bag packed—everything but the work papers he had left out the night before.

As he tried to put those away with some semblance of organization, he found a copy of one of the stories about his work for the President. He remembered how he had wrestled with the decision to take that case, convincing himself he would save the revolution by standing up for its best values, and showing that they were better than the people they had defeated. He didn't know that one of the costs of the revolution was that the revolutionaries would learn from their enemies that the value of individual human lives can be easily trumped by the needs of the group. That they valorized nonhuman lives was small comfort.

He crumpled up the clipping and tossed it.

It hit the feet of Marianne Abboud, who was standing at the threshold, smoking a cigarette.

"I saw your door was open," she said. "I guess it didn't go well."

Donny shook his head. "They banished her."

"Oh," said Marianne. "That's not helpful."

"I know," said Donny. "I'm sorry to blow your source."

"I'm sorry I tipped you off. I hadn't meant to. But she's not my only source."

"She's not?"

Marianne shook her head.

"Who is?"

Marianne pulled an invisible zipper across her mouth.

"When will they administer the sentence?" she asked.

"Day after tomorrow," said Donny. "Monday, when I should be back in Dallas with her."

"They don't want to spoil the May Day celebration in the morning."

"Right," said Donny. "I guess there's some big parade to-night. They're even letting her ride one of the floats. They put me in a cage right away, but she gets to rage. Last hurrah of the damned, I guess."

"I hear it's quite the party. Like Mardi Gras, but with better politics. We should go."

"I can't. I need to go try to salvage my case, and face up to the mess I left back home, which I thought I was going to fix with what I just messed up here. I have someone helping me, but it's not looking good for Donny. Any chance you all are looking to hire any burnt-out war-crimes lawyers?"

"What if I told you the source you just burned gave me information that could help your case about the camps?"

"I'm listening."

"She told me where they disposed of his remains."

"The president?"

She nodded. "It's here. In New Orleans."

"Why would they go to the trouble of moving him so far?"

"For the same reason that you will find this information helpful. They buried him in the same spot where the AMR guards disappeared the prisoners. And we are not hiring, but I could use some help finding this spot."

"Let's go," said Donny, standing.

"There's just one problem," said Marianne. "It's underwater now."

"So am I. Come on."

42

WHAT THE CREW AT THE LIBRARY WERE ABLE TO COME UP WITH BY way of watercraft was not the fastest thing, but probably the one that could go the furthest into the shallows: a dinged-up old aluminum canoe still tagged as property of the concessionaires at City Park, on a trailer attached to a pedicab. There were no paddles, but someone had left a long wooden pole that worked to operate the canoe as a punt.

That meant that Marianne could concentrate on the search, seated in the bow, while Donny stood close to the middle, pushing against the bottom and scanning wide.

And so they worked their way from their put-in in Mid-City up to the heart of City Park, to where they could see the neoclassical columns of the Museum of Art sticking up out of the water. Donny half expected to see the banner of whatever the last exhibition was, but there was only vegetation hanging from the chipped cornice. He pushed them in closer, hoping to be able to see in through the shadows. A big night heron flew out from back in there, startling them with its primordial squawk before they even saw it.

"We don't have time for your apocalypse tourism," said Marianne.

"We also don't have time to be in a hurry," said Donny. They were both right.

That was when they saw the alligator, sunning itself on the roof of the old coffee shop. They saw it when Donny clumsily knocked the side of the boat with the pole, waking the beast with the noise.

"He looks a little cranky," said Donny. "Or she."

"What do they eat?" said Marianne.

"Anything that moves," said Donny. "So don't get any ideas about getting in the water."

The gator slid into liquid. They tracked its eyes and notches for a while as it picked up speed, swimming parallel to them and then away, and then they lost it as it seemed to head toward the neighborhood to the south.

"Maybe it went under," said Donny. "You got that map?"

She handed it to him. It was a map she had taken from the Library. New Orleans from before the floods, even before the fighting. A motorist's map to a perfectly normal American city, one of those maps from the era when you could get away with never thinking about geography. When you could think of the city as a static thing, made by people, to their design. Instead of a product of nature, organic, dynamic, entropic.

A map that did not anticipate that the waterline could change, let alone so dramatically.

A map that did not tell you this entire neighborhood was built on what had been, when Europeans first arrived, a swamp. Land below sea level, a bowl designed to hold vast quantities of water when the river broke free of its banks.

So they paddled out into it, navigating by the street signs that remained, green and white markers from the past poking up from the water.

They paddled past flooded blocks of big twentieth-century houses under ten to twelve feet of water, now occupied mostly by wildlife, if at all. Supposedly a handful of members of the community were living out here now, establishing shelter in attics and rooftop shanties, showing a way to live when the coastal settlements of the world were underwater. But they didn't see any of them.

They did see more alligators. And snakes.

They saw a rat the size of a small dog, swimming, looking not at all freaked out.

"Adaptation," said Donny.

He looked at the water to see if it was poisoned. The reptiles and birds didn't seem to mind, but they were hardier species, and ones that didn't need to spend all their time in the water.

"Over here," said Marianne. "See it?"

There was a sign in the near distance, marking the entrance to the Fairgrounds. It had been a very long time since they had a fair, or a music festival. This had most recently been a refugee camp—as so many such places seemed to end up in recent years—one of the biggest in the hemisphere. Camp Zulu was the place where many people found they had hit a wall. The place where they were trucked after illegally crossing a border or a state line, and made to live behind the wire, if they were lucky enough to stay out of the Superdome. A place where people had lived long enough for kids to grow up in there, and have kids of their own. Some of them Donny's clients. The place—or one of them, at least—where the real spark of revolution was ignited. And where the atrocities of war were buried underwater.

Only, not exactly there, according to Marianne. Closer to the bayou that flowed between there and the park.

"Up in there," said Marianne. "The big tree."

The directions they had were not the kind that involved a street address.

The tree Marianne was pointing at was a huge live oak that stuck up out of the water, on a high point that was no more than an inch or two submerged.

"How old do you think that tree is?" said Donny.

"Very old," said Marianne. "Older than the city."

He pushed the boat to it as Marianne stood up in the prow, and they both peered into the dark water spectrally illuminated by flashes of morning sun, and looked for the faces of other specters, of bodies put here to hide the evidence.

MARIANNE WAS RIGHT: THE PARTY THAT NIGHT AFTER THEY RE-
turned from their excursion was like Mardi Gras.

Just without the rich people.

Marianne said she would catch up with him later, after she finished updating her report.

Donny made his own mask, sacrificing one of his neckties to the project with the aid of a borrowed pair of scissors.

Donny had been to Mardi Gras in the good old days, before the floods and the fighting. Back then the way it worked was that parades were organized by different insider circles, most of them the elites, in a city built from elaborate social codes of class and ancestry. The rich people, usually rich white people, were the ones on the floats. Throwing plastic jewels and coins to the gathered mob below. Misogynistically expecting women to expose themselves for those trinkets, and making sure they were liquored up enough to comply.

At the new May Day parades, they threw real money, and real jewels.

And half the people were in some state of undress already.

The money came from the buildings they had seized during the uprising: banks, federal buildings, corporate offices. The gems came from the jewelry stores. The catch was, the money had no independent value there, in a community where most property was shared—or at least that was what they said the deal was. So throwing wads of cash to the mob for the new New Orleanians was just pure Dionysian play.

Bacchus liked to run up his credit card, and then walk the bill.

For Donny, however, the money was very real. And if he hustled, he might even get enough to get Thelen off his back for a while.

That's how he found himself chasing after a twenty-five-foot-high white heron, an insanely beautiful thing that looked to have been made from real feathers. Riding up at the top of its long neck was a beautiful brown girl with storybook long hair, naked but for the golden bling that adorned her bosom and arms, smiling and tossing hundred-dollar bills a little boy in a toga was handing her from a big saddlebag that sat between the wings. Donny was convinced the heron was alive, and that if he called out the right words both it and the girl would see him and want to give him a ride. But then he stumbled in the crowd and found himself on the ground, pulling bills from the scrubby turf and stuffing them in his already-full pants pockets.

He had already drunk the Kool-Aid back at the hotel, and also devoured the fungi the front desk clerk had hooked him up with, an offer Marianne wisely declined, but one that Donny was glad he had accepted. The best remedy for failure was self-medication, and the prescriptions they had on offer here were like nothing he had ever sampled.

He got up, and saw himself in the window glass of an old storefront. Shirtless and loco, tribally colored, silk necktie repurposed as Zorro mask, insane grin on his face, money falling out of his pants.

"Show me your dick!" yelled some female-sounding voice, and Donny, being a guy, assumed they were talking to him. But when he turned he just saw some bearish-looking dude with a ring in his nose, a big beard, a lethal-looking codpiece, and even less on than Donny. The guy grabbed Donny and gave him an aggressive French kiss, and then walked on.

Kim grabbed him, and kissed him even harder.

His mind needed a moment to register who "Kim" was, and how he knew her name. It came back to him: After he and Marianne split up at the hotel, Donny's evening had started out with that front desk clerk, Kath, and a pair of her young researcher friends, Earl and Kim. They invited him over to their place on Chartres Street, where they ate even more mushrooms and broke out the paints. That was how Donny had ended up mostly green from head to toe, with blue speckles, like some simian gecko. Earl and Kath were a couple, and Donny and Kim were acting like one, for the moment.

He grinned with unabashed psychotropic joy, and Kim grinned back, their hands lingering on each other, delighting in the sensory explosions popping along their fingertips.

"The snake is coming!" yelled another voice, and people turned and started moving farther down the parade line.

A flock of wild parrots flew through, so close to his head it felt like they were in his hair, their cackling chatter like crazy flying monkeys. And then there was an actual flying monkey, some naked furry dude with artificial wings who glided after them and alighted in the crowd not far from Donny. People started eating the wings, and Donny kept moving.

"We are all bonobos on acid!" yelled a voice in the crowd.

And the snake came into view.

It was four blocks long, this thing, made of some flesh-like material lubricated in a way that made it glisten. It had no wheels, or visible means of vehicular propulsion. It moved like a real snake. Maybe there were people inside it, moving like a human centipede. There were people on top of it for sure, a lot of people, naked and feasting and throwing strawberries the size of pomegranates to the crowd.

Donny finally caught one, and dove his face into it. It tasted even better than it looked. He even ate the leaves at the top.

"Get in!" yelled one of the eyes, which was a human face, the face of a cute black woman with green irises and lips painted real black. She was looking right at him.

Donny ran to the front, ahead of the snake, Kim forgotten.

"Come on!" said the woman.

"How?" said Donny.

"Feed me, baby!"

Donny ran after the snake, half-naked and shoeless, until he realized he was dropping the money.

He was on his knees trying to recover it when he felt his tie back around his neck. And then a jolt as it pulled taut, choking him.

When he looked up, he saw a beaked Venetian mask. But it revealed just enough of her face to see it was Heather.

And the smile on the wolf standing next to her was unmistakable. It was Slider, holding Donny's tie like a lasso.

44

WHEN DONNY WOKE UP, HE COULD STILL HEAR THE MUSIC, BUT IT was far away.

He could also hear the sounds of the swamp. Those sounds were closer.

"Where am I?" he said.

He was still tripping. He still had no shoes, and his shirt was torn and wet. The tie was still around his neck, knotted too tight. The room around him was moving. The bars of the undersized cage in which he was locked did not move.

His question received no answer. Just the sound of faraway brass, and crickets that sounded like they were inside his head.

"I knew I should have left town," he said.

"You should have never come," said Slider.

Slider had peroxide-white hair now. He also had some new tattoos, one of which, the image of some kind of cosmic coyote pounded out in luminescent ink, looked to be moving independently of Slider.

"I knew it," said Donny. "How'd you do it?"

"My squad helped me, just like they helped me spring Heather last night," he said. "And Heather paid off two of the guards, told them she wanted to split. I needed to disappear, or they were going to disappear me."

"Good to see that bribery still works even in a propertyless society."

"Only because they had the stupid idea to let the lawyers in," said Heather.

Donny saw her now, in the background. She was sitting at a table, working on something Donny couldn't see.

"Joyce says you killed the guards who disappeared your parents, Slider."

"Joyce is almost as big a liar as you," he answered. "I didn't kill anybody. Kind of wish I had now. But she wouldn't even tell me where to find those guys."

"What do you mean?"

"They found a trove of documents from the camps," said Heather. "Some of the secret blacklists of prisoners tagged for the detour, and the names of the guards who killed his parents."

"I have those names," said Donny. "The names of the guards."

"Not their new names," said Heather.

"New names?"

"New identities. Names, birthdays, Social Security cards, jobs, hometowns."

"Some of them even got new teeth!" said Slider. "So they could fake their own deaths."

"Joyce has all this info?"

"She's sitting on it," said Heather. "Says she wants to build cases to prosecute them all here, since the other courts won't do it."

"She's wrong," said Donny. "I *was* doing it. There's a way. Let me out. I can persuade her."

"Haven't you fucked enough shit up already?" said Slider. "If you would just mind your own damn business, I wouldn't have to grab you in the first place."

"I'm just trying to keep my promises," said Donny.

"Yeah, right. Promises to your banker, maybe. You're a sell-out, dude. Taking her dad's dirty money. And then fucking up our whole deal. We just want to be together. Can't you understand that?"

"I guess." He could, even if their Romeo and Juliet bit was hard to take. "This world we've made makes it hard."

"No shit."

"And I thought she was a hostage, Slider," said Donny.

"Man, you are such a sucker." He actually laughed. "Next thing, you're gonna tell us how her daddy loves her."

Donny could finally make out what Heather was doing at the table. Making bombs.

"Dad doesn't give a fuck about me," she said, not looking up. "It's just about the money."

"Well, Lecker's the one with the money."

"That freak. I can't believe you don't even know how they're using you."

"Let me out of here and tell me all about it."

He realized the cage was a kennel, for a medium-sized dog.

She laughed at his request, and kept talking. "All the patents for the Tripto Labs seeds are in my name. Mom kept them, separate from the trust, and licensed them to the company. But the license expired a month ago."

"While you were here, incommunicado."

"They need my signature to transfer them over. And then make sure no one uses their designs, or anything derived from them."

"Just say no. They can't get away with it."

"Sure they can. Don't you understand how things work now? Either I sign, or I'm likely to have an accident. And then the patents go to my sole heir: Daddy."

Slider was balancing a knife on his hand while he watched Donny and listened.

"Dad is getting a nice payday from Lecker out of the deal. Enough to stop working. Maybe enough to leave the country."

"I don't believe that," said Donny. "That's not how your dad works."

"Sure it is," she said, inserting wires into a bag of Titan Jelly. "He probably thinks it's for the good of the country."

"If what you're telling me is true, then why are you helping them?"

"Because we need to draw them out," said Slider.

"Huh?" said Donny.

"And because the people running this place have sold out the cause," said Heather. "You talk about justice the same way they do. Like it's something we can get from talking. But the creatures who have been murdered can't do any talking. We need to get this planet back to equilibrium."

"Using the same mode of ecocide your granddad used to get us into this mess?"

"This stuff works a lot different when you use it on a building instead of a forest," said Heather.

"You wouldn't do that," said Donny. But as he looked at them, he knew they would.

"Maybe we're just going to do what it takes to persuade Lecker to sign over Heather's trust funds, instead of her signing over the patents. And then we're going to finish what we started, before the lawyers and do-gooders and so-called peacekeepers got in the way."

"How much time do we have before they get here, baby?" said Heather.

"A few hours," answered Slider. "Terrell said he'd be here before sunup."

"Where are you going?" said Donny.

"Wouldn't you like to know," said Slider. He held up Donny's

Swissfōn. "What I do know is this thing will work wherever I take it."

"Oh, man, don't take that," said Donny. "Come on."

"You're not going to be needing it where you're going," said Slider.

"Where's that?" said Donny.

"Out there," said Slider, pointing at the open window. "Where they were going to send her."

"Where the wild things are," said Heather.

"At least you're giving me a chance," said Donny.

They both laughed.

"You both should come with me. Back to Dallas."

They both laughed harder.

"Slider, I am on the verge of getting the outcome you wanted in the case for your parents. For your parents and all the other victims. We will be able to make them pay."

"With what?" said Slider. "With money?"

"Yeah," said Donny. "Enough to shut down the company. Kill it, for all intents. And make them accountable. Names, dates, how and why. The truth will come out. We will publish their records, shame the perpetrators, and honor the victims. And hopefully prevent something like that from ever happening again."

"Money won't bring my parents back," said Slider.

"Neither will killing people," said Donny. "What if I told you I found where their bodies are?"

"You don't know shit," said Heather.

"Slider knows. Because he's dumped bodies there himself."

"What are you talking about now, Donny?" he answered.

"Out there by City Park. In that culvert."

A weird look came over Slider's face. The first time Donny had seen him look scared.

"What's he talking about, Slider?"

"I'm talking about where they buried the President. Or what was left of him. In the same place as his victims."

Slider looked at him with those crazy blue eyes, the tattoos dancing on his shirtless frame. Then he lifted up the cage Donny was in and tossed it over as hard as he could. It felt like wrecking a very small car.

"Don't make all that noise!" said Heather.

"You're lucky I don't stick you," said Slider, poking the knife through the bars. "It's time, anyway."

He came over, opened the door, and dragged Donny out by the tie around his neck, keeping the knife in his other hand.

"Sit here," said Slider, pushing him up against the wall. From there he could see the guns lined up against the opposite wall, underneath the posters of Maxine Price and the red armadillo.

"I know you did it, Daryl," said Donny.

"You don't know shit, Donny."

"Who helped you?"

"Fuck off."

"I don't blame you for doing it."

"You have no idea, dude. You and your fucking mind tricks don't work on me anymore."

"All I ever tried to do was help you."

"You tried. And you failed."

"Where's the body?"

"Why don't you ask Heather's daddy," he said. "They're probably keeping him there on display, in the middle of their mall church."

"Come on," said Donny.

"What's this about, baby?" said Heather. "Is it true?"

Slider looked at her. Then he looked at Donny.

"You really want to know?" he said to Heather.

She nodded.

"I was on the squad that intercepted that fucker. And I helped deliver the sentence."

"You really killed the President?" said Heather.

Slider nodded. "Me and four others. I'm the only one left. The rest all got out of the country. I had unfinished business. I needed to get you. But then the people who sent us to do the job decided we knew too much. And that's the real reason I had to disappear. But that's not his body. Because there is no body. We broke it down in acid. Dissolved it down to the bones. Now, stop asking about it. Leave it alone. And get the fuck out of here."

"I can go?"

"You *have* to go. Out there, like I said. I'm sorry, Donny. That's just how it is."

Donny looked at them. Then he stood up, grimaced at the pain from being locked in the box, and looked out at the landscape through the window.

Black water, the silhouettes of lush trees, and the sound of predatory wild.

"Okay, Daryl," said Donny. "But can you at least spare me some shoes?"

45

DONNY WALKED, BAREFOOT, DRAGGING OVERSIZED SNEAKERS through thigh-high water, waiting for when the pull on his leg was not the muck swallowing his feet, but a gator on his leg.

He had not been that high in many years, and the cocktail of intoxicants he had been enjoying from sundown to midnight mixed with the jolt of adrenaline he felt as he stepped out into it had a weird effect, simultaneously altering his senses and sharpening them. He felt the bite on his toe and the sting on his neck and the muggy sweat soaking through the T-shirt Slider had let him take. He heard the frogs laughing at him and wild dogs taking in his scent and the snakes moving his way, or maybe moving away. The moon was out, a new moon, but with a clear sky and just enough light that Donny swore he could see the glisten on the scales of the fish in the water, scattering at the sight and sound of his lumbering legs.

He saw other lights. Lights in motion, man-made. Trucks, he thought, before realizing they were boats, moving on the river, not too far away.

He saw the rooftops of submerged houses, like he and Marianne had seen earlier in the day. The water would be deeper. But maybe he could find shelter until the sun came up.

He was chest-deep when he saw the eyes on the waterline, reflecting his shape back at him in the moonlight.

He panicked.

He swam, a spaz-stroke wanting to be freestyle, splashing

enough to wake up every creature anywhere near that water. But it worked. He had never swum that fast in his life, but soon he was pulling himself up on the shingles of what must have been a very nice home before the world started to drown.

He scrambled up to the top, to the chimney. He grabbed onto the chimney like the mast of a sinking ship, panting, spewing swamp scum from his mouth and nose.

And then the gators came up to follow him. Three of them that Donny could see. Maybe more that he couldn't.

First they circled around. There was a couple of feet between the roof edge and the waterline. Too far for an alligator to climb up.

Or so he would've liked to think. Because then the first one did just that, with its snout and those stubby little legs.

The teeth that hang outside the mouth, and the claws at the end of the toes that look like meat hooks.

Donny screamed, a banshee scream, a scream to scare off dragons and summon forgotten angels of protection.

It didn't work. It looked like the gator was smiling. Those fucking jaws.

Donny looked down the chimney.

46

WHEN DONNY WAS A KID, BEFORE HIS PARENTS SPLIT UP, HIS FAM-
ily belonged to a country club. Dad liked to play golf, and Mom
liked to play tennis. Donny liked to hang out at the pool, lie in
the sun, and read books.

When he took a break and got in the water, one of the
things Donny liked to do was see how long he could hold his
breath at the bottom of the deep end. He got so good at it that
he would freak out the lifeguards, to say nothing of the moms.

The lung capacity he developed from this weird, dorky
pastime proved handy when he got to high school and college,
long after he learned the only way he could get back in the club
was as a caddy, which he did a few summers. His capacity for
sucking down long bong hits became legend in certain circles.
People were not as impressed with that particular talent when
Donny got to law school.

A girl who actually kind of liked him once taped one of his
answers to the professor in a second-year civil procedure class,
and it became almost as famous, especially for the digressions
about imaginary rules Donny invented as if that would make
up for his inability to remember the real ones through the fog.

Maybe it was the mushrooms that had brought that girl's
face into Donny's head as he came out of the fireplace into the
underwater living room full of what his fuzzed-out eyes were
sure were glow-in-the-dark catfish, waiting for the gator teeth
to pull him back. He kept swimming, trying to remember her

name, trying to remember what he had said, trying to find a way out of that house and into the open water.

It was the fish that showed him, as they tried to get away from him the same way he was trying to evade the gators.

Nature was helpful that way, if you paid attention.

So he followed them, as far as he could, until he knew he could no longer pretend to have gills.

And when he came up, he never knew he could be so happy to see concrete.

47

DONNY FOLLOWED THE OLD ELEVATED FREEWAY UP OUT OF THE
water. He looked back for his predators, but saw only the
moonlight on dark water.

His felt a weird tingle on his skin, like every hair on his
body was dancing to try to keep whatever toxins were in that
nasty water from finding their way through. He tried to ignore
it. He tried to tell himself he hadn't swallowed too much.

He scanned up ahead, seeing where the freeway came to
an abrupt end in a mess of twisted rods and concrete crumble.

He looked off to the left, and saw solid ground. Another
roadway coming up out of the water, this one up onto the soil
and turf, which was mostly covering the old pavement.

And down the middle of that muddy trackway, he saw an
animal in motion. A raccoon. It was carrying something. And
then it disappeared, down into a hole.

No sign of the gators. Donny hung himself from the edge
of the ruined overpass and dropped down onto the other road.
His ankle lit up when he landed, and he lost his footing, curled
in pain. Then he got up and walked over to where the animal
had been.

There were more than one set of tracks in the mud. Mostly
raccoon, recognizable from the opposable thumbs and the long
little claws.

Donny had seen a lot of raccoon tracks in his life, especially as one who liked to fish in urban creeks. But he had never seen tracks that big.

And the smell. The smell of smoke. Like barbeque.

Donny looked around. The path was an old right-of-way that ran through this stretch of higher ground, parallel to the road. A natural gas pipeline sign was still there, with the number to call before digging. Apparently no one had told the raccoons, judging from the track that converged around an old valve box someone had left open.

Donny squatted down and peered into the hole. What he saw was a bigger space than he expected. A little cubed steel cave buried in the ground, big enough for a small work crew. Sticking out of one wall was something like a pilot light. A flare. That was lit. And around the flame were three raccoons. In the weird light, they seemed the size of seventh graders.

Even weirder, Donny could have sworn they were cooking food on sticks.

But as he rubbed his eyes to make sure it wasn't the mushrooms, one of them noticed Donny, snarled, and screamed at him.

Those eyes stayed with him as he ran, trying to find the lights of the boats. The eyes, and the heads, which he could swear looked bigger than any raccoons he had ever seen.

48

DONNY'S HEAD WAS CLEAR BY THE TIME THE SUN BEGAN TO WORK its way up over the ragged skyline. It was Sunday, and his case wasn't as dead as he had thought. But if he wasn't on his way back to Dallas by the time the sun started to go back down, it would be.

Donny looked around to gather his bearings. It wasn't hard to figure out where he was. On the river, way uptown, looking at the opposite bank and wondering if he could swim it. He also wasn't far from Joyce's. And Joyce had information he needed, and other things to answer for.

He cut in from the river along one of the side streets that fronted the park. Some of the houses were still occupied, and Donny saw an old woman out tending her wild garden.

He found the backside of the fence that surrounded Joyce's place, the high fence that had kept the animals inside the zoo. The gate was locked, with a triple chain, which was odd in a community where all doors were usually open. He looked for Joyce or Sig back in there where the house was. But the only sign of people he saw was a truck, an old pickup. That was an even weirder thing to see, in the city that had banned cars. The french-fry smell told him it was one of those biodiesel conversions. It had an oversized camper top in the bed and a cargo trailer at the hitch.

The fence was steel, about ten feet high, only vertical bars. Not easily climbable, not without gecko feet or a simian athleticism Donny did not have. There was an old sign warning of high voltage, but he wasn't buying it, and a tentative touch with his left pinky did not shock. He tried to climb it and fell on his ass twice, tearing his shirt the second time, before he got the idea to use one of the stubby trees that had grown up along the outside of the fence. That got him up there and over, at the cost of a couple more tears.

He walked to the house, up on the porch.

"Joyce?"

There was no one there. Not that he could see. But he smelled fresh-baked bread, and coffee.

He looked at the other path and decided to walk back down there toward the old zoo buildings. Maybe they were doing their morning chores.

Donny remembered the joke the pedicab operator made, about the big cats that come out at night. He didn't believe it. At least not until he walked back in there and noticed for the first time how loud all the birds suddenly were. Alerting one another, and all the other creatures who knew how to interpret their signs, to Donny's presence.

Donny looked around, and listened.

"Joyce!" He wanted to yell, but only had the nerve to whisper. There probably weren't any zoo animals on the prowl. But Sig was around for sure, and he was probably more dangerous, and had even better reasons to have it in for Donny than Slider. He decided to keep quiet.

He saw a shadow off in the near distance to his right. Something low to the ground, but big.

He decided to walk back to the house.

The kitchen door was open.

"Hello?" he said, just loud enough. There was no answer. No sound of anyone about.

He tore off a piece of bread and scarfed it down as he stepped into the study.

It was a small room, furnished with plush old furniture and thick drapes over all the windows. There were bookshelves, but not enough for all the books, many of which were piled on the floor. There was an old rifle leaned up against the wall. And even though all the exterior light had been blocked out, the room was glowing.

When he stepped into the room, he found the source: a small video monitor on the desk. The screen showed a dimly lit room. The bars in the background revealed it was one of the old cages, refurbished to look like something more humane than a place to imprison animals. There were someone's things there. A couple of books. A notebook and pencils. Some postcards on the wall. A fighter jet. A map. A menagerie of animals.

On the right side of the frame was a door.

It opened.

Joyce walked in. She had a tray of food in one hand, and a Taser in the other. The gun was still holstered at her side.

From the shadows at the side of the room emerged a figure. Donny saw now there was a bed there, on which the figure had been lying.

It was a man. Donny expected to see Sig, but this was someone else. Middle-aged, wearing old coveralls. When he sat up, his bare feet glowed in the ambience of the surveillance feed.

It was President Mack.

49

JOYCE SET THE FOOD ON THE LITTLE TABLE.

She had more food in a bag over her shoulder. Not people food.

The President looked at the food. Donny could smell the bread. The President could, too.

The President stood. He didn't have his prosthetic arm anymore. He looked at the bag of food, picked it up with the one hand he had, and then poured the contents into a big metal bowl on the floor. He took some of the hot water from the tray Joyce had brought, and mixed it in.

He whistled.

A moment later, an old-looking lioness sauntered in, sliding past Joyce. And went to eat from the bowl.

While the lion ate, the President drank his water.

"Did you read your assignment last night?" asked Joyce.

He nodded. He didn't look like the guy Donny had met in that conference room that day not two years before. He wasn't cocky. He wasn't sure. He wasn't even unconsciously malevolent. He looked like a tired old man, tired beyond his years.

"We're leaving today," said Joyce.

"Why?" he said.

"We have to go. Sig is getting provisions now. We'll leave as soon as he returns."

"What about her?" said the President, meaning the big cat. "And the others."

"We can't take them," said Joyce.

"We can't just leave them," said the President.

"They'll be fine," said Joyce.

"Then just leave me with them," said the President.

"I wish I could," said Joyce. "I know you're doing a lot better. You've done good work with these animals."

"I feel better," he said. "Everything before . . ." He drifted off. "Like it's not real."

"It was real. Very real. And while you are encouraged to become better, you are not allowed to forget. We are taking those with us."

There were more postcards on the wall, back in the shadows around the cot. Donny zoomed the monitor to see. They weren't postcards. They were pictures. Of people. Headshots, mostly.

Donny recognized one of them. Wade Camacho. He looked at more, and started to recognize others.

Donny pulled back the drapes to the right of the desk and looked out over the yard. He could see the building back there.

He grabbed the rifle and went outside.

50

AS HE STOOD THERE STARING THROUGH THE OPEN DOOR, DONNY
realized the President was staring back at him.

"Kimoe?" he said.

Joyce saw him now.

For once, Donny didn't know what to say, so he didn't say
anything.

The only sound for a long minute was the sound of the old
lion devouring its food.

Joyce was looking at the gun. "Do you even know how to
use that?"

"No, but I bet I can figure it out." He looked down at the
weapon and realized he was aiming it at the President.

"You wanted him to get a life sentence," said Joyce.

Donny looked at the scene. He half expected the President
to beg for help. He barely even paid attention.

Donny looked at the photos on the wall. Wade, and all the
others.

"Please just go," said Joyce.

51

THE LAST TIME DONNY SAW JOYCE BEFORE HER RELEASE, SHE was gardening in chains.

They had expanded the Superdome detention camp to envelop the small park across the street. There, they had installed a small experimental farm growing some new Tripto Labs varietals better suited to tropical climates. So when the guard let Donny through the gate, he stepped into a little orchard of orange trees. And in the middle stood Joyce, pruning one of the trees with shackles around her ankles. Three other prisoners were doing the same nearby, under the watch of an equal number of guards.

"Go ahead," said the guard. "The boss said it's okay." Lawyers were not allowed inside the Superdome, but he had convinced one of the prosecutors to make this arrangement for him.

Joyce declined the hug, but she looked like she appreciated the visit.

"How are they?" said Donny, nodding at the oranges. They were small, and a little gnarly, but they still looked precious.

"We aren't allowed to eat them," said Joyce. "Only to tend them. And that's considered a special perk."

"You must be on good behavior."

"As far as they know." She looked over at the guards. When she had the attention of one, she pointed at the small picnic table in the clearing. The guard nodded, and they sat.

"I'm working on getting you out," said Donny.

"How do you propose to swing that?"

"It's not easy. Those 'open letters' you've been publishing got a lot of attention. Not just with people who are sympathetic to your position. Our position."

She raised a tired, incredulous eyebrow.

"You're on the Enemies List," said Donny. "That's a hard list to get off."

"You mean that's a hard list to get off alive. The other way is easy. And maybe easier on the soul."

"I'm sorry about Wade."

"What are you going to do about that?"

"We're working on that too. Some colleagues in Austin are in touch with his family there. He had a wife and kids."

"I know."

"They're looking at a wrongful-death case."

"So the wife and kids and the lawyers can get some money out of the deal. Classy."

"Even that will be hard to get anywhere. Not until there's real change. But it's something. The money, yes. But also the exposure of what's happening."

Joyce looked at the wall, then looked back at him.

"What do you think qualifies as real change, Donny?"

"Getting him out of office. A new government."

"You really think that will do the trick?"

"It would be a good start."

"And he gets to go back to his Park Avenue penthouse?"

"We could try to get him indicted."

"They'll never do it. People are too chickenshit. They're afraid of real justice. Because they know if we get it, it might come for them next."

Donny considered that.

"People suck, Donny. Especially if you give them power, or money. They will hoard it, and never be satisfied."

"So I noticed. But here we are. And I am here to tell you I am going to get you out of here so you can do whatever it is you think will fix it."

"It's not fixable. I mean, not unless you want to get way more radical. Like undoing-the-agricultural-revolution radical. Which is obviously not possible."

"I know, you have your own theory about revolution. I was one of the first ones to hear it."

"I was wrong about that. I didn't appreciate it until I started working this plot, and the big cornfields they are planting farther east. It's not about oil, Donny. It's not about high finance. It's about grain. That's where it starts, at least. Bending nature to serve man. Building permanent settlements devoted to it. Forcing people to work on it. All to accumulate surplus. Cities, money, all the foundations of civilization and culture—all that is rooted in our dominion, and comes with inequality and injustice preprogrammed. You just can't fix it. And the other thing it's preprogrammed for is collapse. Because people can never get enough."

"We can change. Build better systems and come a lot closer than we do now. Do a better job of making sure everyone gets their fair share."

"Maybe," said Joyce. "Probably. But it's hard to care about people once you see what they're capable of. And once you learn what these guys have taught me."

"What's that?" asked Donny.

"That the only thing that people really respond to is pain, or the fear of pain."

"I'm so sorry, Joyce. I feel like it's my fault."

"It's a gift. Now I'm cauterized to it. And I know better what can be done."

"What's that?"

"The human race is doomed. And that's a good thing. The planet will be better off without us. I'd give it a few hundred years to extinction, based on where we're at today. Maybe it's a few millennia. But other species will rise. And hopefully they will turn out better."

"What do we do in the meantime?"

"Hasten that along. Break the state." She looked at the guards. "It's coming," she said. "Right under their noses."

The Superdome was behind her. He could see the guards silhouetted on the roofline. He heard the sound of a chopper coming in from the north.

"I don't want to know."

She told him anyway. The chopper was loud now, loud enough that no one could hear them.

"Maybe someone will take him out first," said Donny. "He's pissed off a lot of his former allies. Costing some of them big money."

"We can't kill him, Donny. That just perpetuates the cycle. You don't get it."

She was right, he didn't. Not then, "I'm still going to get you out, Joyce, even if you talk like that."

"Don't bother, Donny. I need to find my own way out. Please."

PART THREE

We the Creatures

52

WHEN DONNY WAS IN LAW SCHOOL, THERE WAS A BIG HIT MOVIE called *Wrath of Atlantis*. It was one of those fantasy movies that always sounded stupid to Donny, lots of dudes in metal underwear flexing with swords while the women grimaced at the wind machine when they weren't flexing with their own swords. But he went with a group of friends who wanted to see it because of the hype and because of all the stars, and to his surprise he kind of liked it.

Part of why he liked it was because they all got high in the car before heading into the mall where the theater was. But that wasn't the only reason.

What was really cool about the movie was that they used stop-motion animation instead of CGI. It was like being a kid again and seeing your toys come to life. Except these models looked more real. All those mythological creatures. One of the characters got to fly on Pegasus, while another fought the hydra, and another had to talk her way past Cerberus, the three-headed dog that guarded the underworld. And the smile on that minotaur, so real it reminded him of Vice President Lane, the one who pushed through the interrogation-enhancements program.

It was kind of a Greek mythology smorgasbord. The plot, as best Donny could remember, was something about a war between Atlantis and Sparta. Atlantis was a lush, green city of beautiful, happy people, watched over by Athena and guarded by her giant steampunk owlbot, full of benevolent sorcerers.

There was a scene set in this library that literally looked like it went on forever and contained every book in the world. The music for them was kind of lame, like Renaissance faire meets turbopop, but it was forgivable.

The Spartans were heavy metal all day. They had robots, too, but more like horses. One of the Spartan horsebots was supersmart, not from the gift of any god, but because the old Spartan warrior engineer who had created it was just such a good maker and had endowed it with the finest clockwork brain ever made. Horsebot started to tell the future, and because they were so awed by this talking metal horse, they believed it must know. And what it predicted was that the world would soon end in a flood. And that the only way to stop the flood would be to capture the owlbot of Atlantis and dissect it to extract its knowledge of how to speak to the gods.

The Spartans won, because of the things the goddess Aphrodite did to trick the Atlanteans and please her lover Ares, the god of war and electric guitars, under whose patronage the Spartans had thrived.

Aphrodite also seduced Hephaestus, the R&D lab of the gods, into serving Ares and equipping the Spartans with the gear they needed for their mission.

Toward the end of the movie, there was this awesome scene where the waves dispatched by the angry Poseidon deluge Atlantis. That was stop-motion, too, with this insanely detailed model that looked around the same scale as the plastic kits Donny had built as a kid but big enough to fill a hotel ballroom. Watching it Donny imagined the guys standing there with hoses slowly drowning the beautiful thing they had made, and enjoying it.

We are all waiting for the big wave to wash it all away.

Way down, below the ocean.

Donny's buddies loved *Wrath of Atlantis* so much they got the companion video game. There was a whole semester Donny's second year when he was trying very hard for once to get decent grades and the sound from the main room every night was a continuous stream of electronic sword swings, magic gun bursts, kung-fu kicks and meaty punches, all to the soaring but repetitive and tinny power riffs of the soundtrack excerpt that played in the background. Every half hour or so there would be a pause, and you would hear the watery burble of the bong rip, and then it would start again.

What was weird to Donny about all this was how much the guys gravitated to the Spartans. As if *they* owned the future. Maybe it was because America had developed such a Sparta fetish in those days, at least among guys of a certain flesh tone, that they brought that preference with them. Donny liked the Atlanteans, though, with their trees inside the temples and mythical wild animals roaming the streets like furry neighbors and their magic spells and their libraries without end. The Spartans were so corporate, the little warlord band that wanted to raid and pillage and run the world. And it was the Spartans, with their machines, who pissed off Poseidon. Atlantis just happened to be in the way. And then the Spartans had the last laugh, when their horsebots showed they could transform into seahorses and carry their warriors to safety.

LECKER'S PEOPLE HAD arranged a charter flight for Donny on a small-engine prop charter out of Baton Rouge. The idea was that he would be returning with Heather. Things had not quite worked out as planned.

As he looked out the window in the back of the little

six-seater, engines rattling so loud you would hardly be able to hear your own voice if you tried to talk to the person next to you, Donny thought about how life never quite lived up to the version they storyboarded for you when they told you what to expect. Whether your own life, or the life of the people. Like what America actually did with the promise of a bountiful wilderness that had survived into the so-called Age of Enlightenment without being marred by the imprint of human engineers and architects and extractors, the way the landscape was that he saw out the window. The way the stories of valor and honor and love of the land usually masked not-so-secret histories of conquest and cheating and exploitation. The way his own desire to try to do something reasonably good with the particular tools life had bequeathed him more often than not caused him to fuck everything up for the people he cared about.

Seen from the window of an airplane, the landscape between Louisiana and Texas showed all the promise and betrayal of that paradox. All the old oil towns along the coastline that had never really been a line, more like a place where dry land slowly morphed into ocean. Many of those towns had been taken back by nature now, but you could still see their remains from up at ten thousand feet, the scaffolds of industrial-scale chemistry sets poking out of the water, flare-offs long extinguished, but the product they once processed into the plastic comestibles of capital now being sucked back into the subsurface, the muck beneath the water that rose just a little bit more every day. He saw highways that ended in standing water at the edge of the wide brown-blue expanse. Where the waterways emptied into the Gulf, you saw the stains of the things they carried with them, the sediments and toxins of faraway farmlands trying to exorcise the artificial stimulants that had been used to make them make more grain to feed the machine. And the patches of swampy forest trying to come back where they had been razed. Those once-verdant wetlands were where Audubon's greatest birds had made their home. More than half the species he documented were now gone.

It looked like a stop-motion hellscape out there, like a zone where the rubber suit monsters of his childhood matinees had been rampaging. And the thing was, it had always basically looked that way, even before they noticed, even before the climate started avenging itself. For all the time he spent mediating feuds between people and sometimes starting them, the real feud was between human beings and the land on which they lived. And maybe the real way to get people to stop doing shitty things to one another would start with getting them to stop doing shitty things to the Earth. Reground that relationship on a basis of reciprocity, of mutuality of exchange, of the kind of balanced principles that the law claimed to stand for, and maybe the other relationships would follow suit.

The Tributary was a start in the right direction, if an extreme one, and maybe too late to make any difference. But even in all his hard-earned cynicism about people, he couldn't give up on them like Joyce had. Not when they included people like Percy, or those kids she taught.

America was Sparta and Atlantis at the same time. But it had meant to be something different entirely. Not a city on a hill, even. More like an archipelago of small towns in a vast ocean of green, blue, and gold. And as he looked out the window at the scarred and depopulated but still-resilient landscape, he could almost imagine a future that realized that vision, or that at least tried to incorporate its aspirations.

But then Dallas came into view.

53

DONNY WAS CALLING FROM A NEW PHONE, WITH A LOUISIANA area code, so he had to leave a message and wait for Lou to call him back.

"Are you back from DC?"

"Yes. The talks broke down. I'm hoping you'll tell me you had a better outcome."

"Yeah, well, my psycho terrorist client stole my phone and ran off with your daughter."

"What?"

"It's not as bad as it sounds," said Donny.

"You fucking clown. Goddamn you. I'm an idiot for thinking you could help."

"Calm down, Lou. Let me explain."

Donny told him the story.

It was not as effective as he thought it would be.

"That does it," said Lou. "I guess we have to do this Lecker's way."

"No, Lou. I told you, Heather's free."

"It's obvious you don't know that. She's a prisoner of this fucking Harrison kid."

"No, Lou. It's not like that."

But Donny already knew where that was going. The feelings of fathers about their daughters had their own logic.

"Just give me one more day," said Donny. "Trust me."

"I *did* trust you, against my better judgment. I knew this

was a stupid idea, to let you get in the middle of this. I am going to have to take care of this myself."

"Better you than Lecker. He has his own agenda."

"He just wants to make sure we can feed our people, Donny. Heather may be a little lost right now, but she'll come around. I just need more time with her."

"Be careful, Lou. She and her friend are pretty wild. And I think they may be coming your way."

That caught him up short. "She wouldn't do that."

"You would be surprised. Listen. I'm here. In Dallas. We need to meet in person. It will be safer. And maybe we can all sit down and work something out."

"I'll talk to you later, Donny."

"Suit yourself," said Donny. "But be careful. Don't assume the guards protecting your gated compound there are actually doing their job. And if you change your mind, I'm going to meet with Lecker first thing tomorrow."

He wanted to ask Lou if he had ever played *Wrath of Atlantis*, but he knew he wasn't the type.

54

FROM THE AIRPORT, DONNY WENT TO VISIT HIS MOM AT HER condo in downtown Dallas. It was Sunday night. Before politics pulled them apart, Sunday night was when they used to always try to talk or, if they were both in town, have dinner. And because it was the weekend, Mom's boyfriend was there.

"Hello, Judge," said Donny, when he opened the door.

"Hello, Donny," said the father figure Donny least wanted to see.

It was since the uprising that the Honorable Harold W. Broyles had been dating Donny's mom, a turn of events that was more surprising to Donny at first than the uprising itself. And then Donny saw them together and realized it was actually a pretty good fit. Both lawyers, around the same age, with a similar social background—his mom, like Broyles, was blue-blood Houston. And with similar politics, though his mom was more loyal to the now-lost cause than Broyles was, the allegiance of a convert to the cause—where Broyles had just adapted his immutable values to the situation at hand.

"Is she here?" said Donny.

"No, Donny," said Broyles. "Catherine is out. She went to a movie with Ellen."

Donny didn't know who Ellen was.

"Okay," said Donny. "It was a stupid idea anyway."

"What was a stupid idea?"

Broyles was an old man now, but a fit one, and while his face showed its age his eyes still had that same edge.

"Coming here. I just thought—"

He had thought maybe he could hit his rich mom up for the money he owed Thelen. It was an idea so obvious that he had considered it before he went to New Orleans, only to convince himself that his elaborate scheme would be easier than swallowing his pride and his political disagreement along with it. And now that his scheme had crashed and burned like some ill-designed early flying machine, and he looked for gold BMWs around every corner as he snuck back into Dallas, coming here also seemed like a good way to evade his creditors.

"I'm sure she'll be happy to see you," said Broyles. "She should be back soon. Come on in. I was just reading."

Broyles, like Joyce, had a proclivity for Bach. But where she preferred guitar, Broyles liked the piano. You could hear the record playing from inside.

"You sure it's cool?" said Donny.

"It's cool," said Broyles, making fun of the phrase at the same time as he meant it.

The condo was nice, not big. It had a view to the west, high enough up that you could see the outline of downtown Fort Worth backlit by the little bit of light that was still in the western sky, and the green of the Tripto Labs farms fading to black. There was only one contrail arcing across the overburned sky, a late-breaking reminder of the things they had done to get them here, and the habits they had tried to break too late for it to do much good.

"Can I get you a drink?" said Broyles.

"Whatever you're having," said Donny.

"I suppose you want ice?"

"Only if it's the cheap stuff. Not cored from the time of the Trojans."

Broyles laughed.

"Sit down," he said.

The decor in his mom's living room was modernist, which was paradoxical in a way since her ideas were not, at least to Donny's sensibility, modern. Unless by modern you meant the thinking of the heart of the century before, that thought of itself as forward but was really just streamlining very old thinking.

Maybe Donny's newer ideas of what a better future could be like were no more than an updated version of the same thing. Whenever people set out to make things better by design, to improve on nature, they almost always made things worse. Joyce was right about that.

"Here you go," said Broyles, handing him a glass of scotch and sitting across from him.

Donny recognized the record now. It was one of those performances by Raquel Wang, the Baltimore-born prodigy who had been such a big deal a few years earlier for her electric piano interpretations of Bach's organ works. People said that you could hear the sound of the artist crying into her instrument if you listened closely, but Donny never listened closely. He was too distracted by her politics. By what they liked to call at the time "the sound of the coming age." The coming age that was now long gone.

"What are you reading?" said Donny.

Broyles held up his book. *Burr*, by Edward Alvarez.

"Heard of it?" he asked.

Donny shook his head. "No, but leave it to you to read a book about a treason trial in your spare time."

"It's not so much about the trial," said Broyles. "It's a new history of what led to the arrest and prosecution. But more than that. The writer has an agenda. Starts out making you think he's a revolutionary, like your old clients, or a fellow traveler, like you."

The way Broyles said that now, it was more like talking about which football team you liked, even though they all carried the scars of what had gone down.

"He seems to be building a kind of interesting thesis. About national rebirth. About the idea that the nation can be many nations. Or no nations at all. Just communities, but all connected."

"You're a little late to the party, Judge."

"I didn't say I buy it."

"Neither do I. But you have to admit it has a certain appeal."

"I suppose. But the problem is when you leave everything fragmented like that, people end up fighting. You need unification to maintain order. And that has to come from above."

You could hear the order in the music.

Looking across the coffee table at this old man in his wool cardigan and wide-wale corduroys peering at him over the rim of his glasses with those incisive eyes, Donny had a flashback to when he would peer down at him from the bench. Those same eyes were scarier when they were wrapped in black robes and backed by the penal power of the state.

"How long have you had those glasses, anyway?" asked Donny.

Broyles took the silver wire-frames from his face, and held them up to look at.

"Lord," he said, as if he had never even considered that. "Since my last year in law school. I came home for Christmas break, went hunting with my dad, and realized when I went to aim that the vision had degenerated in my right eye. Doctor said the eye was essentially permanently focused at the distance of a book. Which I thought was rather annoying, until Christmas dinner when my uncle the investment banker said don't you know the rule, Harry? Never trust a lawyer who doesn't wear glasses."

"I don't wear glasses," said Donny.

"Exactly," said Broyles, smiling.

Donny was going to make the argument that sunglasses should count, at least for certain types of lawyers, but the door opened.

"Look what the cat drug in, Catherine," said Broyles.

"Oh," said Donny's mom.

Donny was ready for her to turn red and point her finger at the door. And it looked like the thought crossed her mind. But then she smiled, a more adult variation of the "I should ground you for a year, but I'm glad you're home" smile.

"Come here," she said.

As Donny got up to hug her, he noticed the frames on the wall behind her in the hall. A picture of Donny, at his law school graduation. And next to that, an official portrait of the President.

It didn't stop him from asking her for help, and a place to crash.

55

LECKER SENT A LIMOUSINE TO PICK UP DONNY EARLY THE NEXT
morning. When they set out, instead of heading toward Highland Park, the limo drove west through Dealey Plaza, crossed the Trinity, and got on the freeway headed in the direction of Fort Worth.

"Why aren't you taking me to Dr. Lecker's office?" said Donny, looking out the window at the shanties along the river.

"I am taking you to Dr. Lecker's office," said the limo.

"Dr. Lecker's office is in another direction. Uptown, off Turtle Creek."

"I am taking you to Dr. Lecker's other office," said the limo.

"And where is that?" said Donny.

"I'm sorry, I can't tell you that."

"Well, I'm going to see it right through the window, and on your screen there."

"I'm sorry, you can't do that," said the limo.

The screen display went dark. And then the windows dissolved to black. Even the windshield. Donny had never known that was a possibility, but it immediately made sense.

Another screen dropped from the headliner, and an ad came on for commemorative plates featuring vignettes of country life before the droughts.

"Turn that off please," said Donny.

It did.

Around thirty minutes later, the limo let Donny out with a

click and a hiss, the door sounding almost like an airlock as it opened. The sun was bright. Fortunately, Donny had thought to bring his sunglasses.

He was in the middle of some kind of airport, out on the tarmac. But there were no airliners. At least, not with the logos on them. And no terminal—just hangars and blocky old one- and two-story buildings. You could hear the whine of the jets, the clanking of metal on metal, and the sound of men yelling.

"Mr. Kimoe!" yelled one voice. Donny looked. It was Lecker's secretary. He had gone from business casual to combat casual—a flight suit, a sidearm, and a black ball cap with the company logo. He looked fitter than he had before, like an aging wrestler who could still take you down if you pissed him off. He was waving at Donny from across the tarmac, walking in the direction of an executive jet. "Over here!"

Donny headed that way. It was hot out there. As he walked Donny looked around. He saw helicopters being fitted with what looked like the ziplock bags of the gods, secured with frames and filled with some kind of fluid the color of cheap whisky. There was a prop plane, maybe a crop duster, getting some tubular variation of the same thing. There was a big jet-liner painted matte black with no identifying insignia other than the call sign on the tail. A fuel truck was there under the wing, while other linemen loaded the luggage compartment with what looked like big metal foot lockers rolling up a mobile conveyor belt. It took two guys to load each locker onto the belt, and even then it looked heavy. Farther back was a big cargo plane, ass end open to make a ramp, up which the crew were driving a bunch of off-road-ready pickups.

"What the hell is this place?" yelled Donny over the engine noise as he met Lecker's secretary at the bottom of the collapsible stairs that led up into the Dornier-G.

"Carswell Field," the secretary yelled back. "After you." He gestured up the ramp to the open door.

Donny took another look around before stepping up. He'd heard of it—Carswell Field was an old air force base that had been one of many sold off to military merchant companies during the Mack administration. It was supposed to be primarily a logistics hub, but you always heard rumors about other stuff.

Inside, the plane looked like a cramped living room, with leather armchairs for seats. Lecker was there on the phone. He signaled Donny to sit down.

The secretary, it turned out, was also the copilot. The pilot, who glanced back as they entered, was a short and stocky blond woman who looked like she was made for kicking ass in low gravity.

Donny took the seat Lecker had pointed at, which faced Lecker on the opposite side of a small table that folded out from the fuselage. On the table were a tablet computer, a tumbler fizzing with club soda and lime, and an aviation map of the Mississippi River delta, with New Orleans there in the upper-right-hand quadrant. The map had been annotated by hand, in a way that reminded Donny of the diagrams the coaches used to draw on the whiteboard after football practice. Diagrams Donny was so bad at understanding that they kicked him off the team before the first game sophomore year, which was not really a bad thing because Donny seriously sucked at the game, but in those days was still trying to do things that would please his dad instead of actively seeking the things that would piss him off.

Donny looked at his onetime dentist, and onetime friend of his dad's, sitting there planning some kind of corporate invasion of the neighboring state, and wondered which strategy he would take with this representative of the collection of fucked-up patriarchs Donny had collected in his life. A type, as he and Joyce had once joked, that America was very good at producing, Donny had a knack for getting tangled up with, and Joyce had a desire to exterminate. Of course, back then, she wanted to exterminate them with ideas.

Through the window, Donny saw the soldiers unloading from the bus that had brought them out from one of the buildings, and then boarding the big passenger jet. They weren't dressed like soldiers. More like the world's biggest rich-guy hunting party, in their high-end technical gear and field wear, but each carrying an Armalite rifle along with whatever gear of their own they had brought.

"Thank you, Governor," said Lecker. "I will send you an update as soon as I can."

Then he hung up. And looked at Donny with the same kind of disappointed face as when Donny had allowed the perfectly fine tooth God had given him to get knocked loose by someone he had given lip to.

"So you have come back empty-handed," said Lecker.

"I wouldn't put it that way," said Donny.

"You are alone. Our stolen seeds are still shipping. Heather is still in their custody. You have nothing for me."

"Heather is free. I told Lou."

"Where is she?"

"I don't exactly know. She took off with her boyfriend."

"Oh."

"Who is my client. The lead plaintiff in my lawsuit against a company in which I just learned you are the controlling shareholder."

"In which Heather's trust is the controlling shareholder," he corrected.

"She told me the real deal."

334

"Did she? And what makes you think she even knows what the real deal is? She's a lost child. A runaway. She's lucky those treasonous terrorists haven't killed her."

"I don't know. It had the ring of truth to me. All I know is she's free, I helped make that happen, and I want my fee."

"That's not our deal at all," said Lecker. "Lawyers are so good at changing the deal as soon as you have them write it down."

"Come on, Doc. You owe me and you know it. But I guess I shouldn't expect you to honor a deal." He gestured out the window, at the corporate army mobilizing to steal its own sovereignty. "By what right do you think you can do this, in bald violation of the Compact?"

"The right of he whom no one will dare to stop," said Lecker. "We have an invitation from the governor, who has deputized us members of his state guard. The state is not party to your revolutionary compact, and the territory we are repossessing belongs to the state."

"I have everything I need to stop you."

"You can tell me on the way there, then," said Lecker.

"Never mind," said Donny. "I have a better idea."

He stood to leave. And it was only then that he realized the plane was in motion.

He grabbed the seatback and turned toward the forward part of the cabin. The door was closed. And between Donny and the door stood the beefy secretary, with a metal club in his hand.

Donny looked back at Lecker.

"I know about your ratline, Doc."

"Excuse me?"

"Bruce here probably was one of the camp guards I've been looking for," said Donny, nodding at the secretary. "That freaky TV pitchman grill of his should have given it away."

"You really do talk too much," said Lecker.

"That may be, but you are not going to shut me up about this one. Because I have the documentation to prove it."

Lecker laughed. "That's impossible."

"Is it? I wasn't surprised to learn a guy like you keeps such fastidious records, however much you try to code them. That's probably the real reason you're headed to New Orleans with your napalm posse. Not because they walked their debts, or because you want the real estate. You know they got their hands on enough of your files to put it together. Well, you're too late, because they did. And they gave me a copy. And I made more copies. I brought one just for you."

Donny opened his briefcase and handed the document to Lecker.

"The part about pulling their teeth and giving them new implants was a beautiful touch," said Donny. "Too bad it achieved the opposite effect of what you intended. That was the initial key that unlocked the whole program. Now we know where every one of these bastards is."

Lecker was flipping the pages as Donny spoke, taking in the information.

"What do you plan to do with this?" he asked.

"I thought maybe we could revisit our deal."

56

DONNY HAD SEEN LECKER'S VISION OF THE FUTURE. THERE WAS A whole TV show about it, back when Tripto Labs launched its first commercial plantings on land that had been reclaimed by the feds. Lecker wasn't on it—he knew extreme wealth went best with maximum anonymity. But Helen was, because she really believed in the project—a way to do something with her money that helped people, while generating profits far beyond what the businesses she had inherited were capable of.

The show was propaganda, on one of the channels that pretended to be independent but was owned and controlled by an ally of the President. But it was the kind of propaganda anyone could get behind. Because everyone was hungry in those days. It was easy to get them to go with the program. Especially the way they packaged it, with the happy rainbow families of farmers helping to propagate the new crops that would restore the American breadbasket and clean the air and the soil in the process. As an extra benefit, one of the varietals was optimized for processing into a reasonably clean fuel.

Maybe the backers of the program actually believed that was how it would work. The idea of the independent farmer was the lodestone of the American experiment, even if that species was now as rare as the wild birds that had once inhabited the forests and prairies they plowed under. The problem was, the family farmer model didn't work for the new crops they had engineered to survive in the new conditions. To make them grow, and reproduce, you had to bring back the planta-tion model.

The era when armies of cheap labor would come from the global South were a distant memory, from a more prosper-ous era that played back in your head like a movie that had never been real. Fortunately, the border fortifications they had erected to keep people from leaving meant there was a healthy supply of cheap labor back home—many of them the farmers who had been turned into refugees by the failure of their own business model.

It made perfect sense that Tripto Labs and AMR ended up under common ownership. They had "synergies," as the invest-ment bankers liked to put it. The same synergies as the cotton field had with the whip. The kind of synergies that are so pow-erful in their productive and wealth-generating potential that entire bodies of law are developed to perpetuate them.

And when he finally saw that clearly, Donny realized that he had the theory of his AMR case all wrong. Miles knew, and they killed him for it. The deaths in the camps weren't about politics. They were about labor. About people trying to orga-nize. About who owns the means of production—when the means of production is the very stuff of life.

Too bad he figured it out too late.

WHEN LECKER'S LIMOUSINE ARRIVED AT LOU'S HOUSE, IT WAS AL- ready surrounded by cops and firefighters. Most of the cops were private police—not the ones on Lou's private detail, or the ones on retainer to the gated community where the house was, but the company that had been retained by the breakaway municipality that the wealthy people of the wider neighborhood had formed to protect themselves in the aftermath of the uprising. The backyard mercenaries could not keep the taxman away, but they could keep the refugees and thieves at bay.

They could not prevent a father from welcoming his daughter home, though, no matter what she had done. Or what friends she brought home with her. Or what she had in her luggage.

Donny looked at the house. It was even huger than he had imagined, more compound than house, in the style of an all-American suburban home of your childhood memory that has been crossed with a Spanish castle and then injected with some growth hormone and wrapped in precious stone harvested from faraway mountains. The polished front wall was forbidding, but when the lights of the patrol cars hit the tall thin window over the front door you could get a glimpse at the cavernous hall inside, and even make out the colors of some big contemporary painting on the wall where the lords of yore would have hung a tapestry.

"What are their demands?" asked Lecker, speaking to the officer in charge.

The cop read off the list. It was about what Donny expected. Lawyers, guns, and money, not in that order. Transfer of all of the trust funds, release of prisoners whose convictions for crimes in the uprising had been outside the Compact, amnesty for the kids inside who had taken Lou hostage.

Lecker and the cops were debating how to respond when the first bomb went off, and the top floor erupted in flames. You could hear the gasp of the air around the building being suddenly consumed by the heat, and the gasp of the grizzled old brain busters who thought they had seen it all. It took a moment before the firefighters mobilized, and the officer in charge told Lecker it was time to move in.

"Let me try," said Donny, not really asking. But they let him do it. Walk right up to the front door, ring the doorbell, and walk right in.

Have you heard the one about the lawyer in hell? said the fireman.

58

THAT FRIDAY, *HARRISON V. AMR* WAS THE FIRST THING ON THE docket in Judge Larriva's court.

Karen Keller had just the one junior associate with her, and she could have handled it alone. Her clients stayed home.

Donny's client wasn't there either. His grandma was, however, in one of her vintage People's Lawyer outfits. And after Judge Larriva got done welcoming Carol, whose career she knew of, the current status of Donny's client was the first thing the judge asked.

The second thing she asked was whether it was true Donny had walked into a burning building to save that client.

"Not really save, Your Honor," he said. "Persuade. And it wasn't just my client there. Ms. Keller's client was there too."

"So you negotiated this *ex parte*, without telling Ms. Keller?" said the judge. Ex parte was lawyer code for talking to the other lawyer's client without the other lawyer present, unless you had their permission—a big no-no in a system that took for granted every lawyer's ability to perform necromantic mind tricks on anyone untutored in their dark arts.

"Well, it wasn't until after we left the building that she, Ms. Hamilton-Green, became Ms. Keller's client. And technically she still isn't. She just became the controlling stockholder of the corporation, and that indirectly, through a series of investments."

"Are you okay with this, Ms. Keller?" asked the judge.

"Mr. Kimoe has walked up to the edge of the rules, but not crossed it," said Karen. "And we now have new instructions from our client. A settlement."

"What are the terms?" said the judge.

Donny told her.

The judge only blinked a few times.

59

THE NEWS OF THE ESCAPED EX-PRESIDENT'S CAPTURE AND DELIV-
ery into the hands of international war-crimes investigators
was all over the news when Donny stepped into the private club
that had taken over the viewing area of the Reunion Tower.
The images of the President were the old ones, from before,
because the international authorities didn't do perp walks. The
new footage they had was from the airfield in Metairie, of a
bright-blue United Nations C-130 sitting on the tarmac preparing to leave the country with its precious cargo already loaded.
They had kept it quiet for a few days as they debriefed him and
the others who were involved, but now it was all anyone would
be talking about for weeks.

Donny stood and watched for a minute while the host
checked his name against the guest list, trying to look at the
windows of the plane, thinking maybe he would see Marianne.
Then the guy led him to a booth in the back, where Thelen was
already waiting.

"Thanks for the wire, sport," he said, standing to greet
Donny. "Looks like I owe you a small refund."

"You can make it a prepayment against the next one," said
Donny.

"Doesn't sound like you're going to need any loans for a
while," said Thelen. "I know it's not public, but this is a small
town, and word gets around."

"Don't believe everything you hear," said Donny. "Especially not about money. And especially not in Dallas."

"I heard you're behind this too," said Thelen, pointing at the TV.

"I tricked a lot of clients at the same time," said Donny.

"So they had him in New Orleans the whole time?"

"I can't say. I signed a confidentiality agreement with the Interpol people. And there are others to protect. I'm sure it will all come out in time, though."

"Well, cheers," said Thelen as the server poured the Champagne he had already ordered.

Donny took his glass and joined in the toast. The late-afternoon light made the bubbles look like a thousand tiny suns. Donny wondered if it was the residue of Dallas acid or New Orleans mushrooms that made him think about the other worlds that must be floating in there too. And then he drank them down, with a gulp that felt like pleasure and regret all at the same time.

Thelen was staring at him, with the enthusiastic smile of a deal guy who wants to know the war story.

"Don't tell me you gave it all away, Donny."

Donny looked back at him. "No wonder you're such a good outlaw underwriter, Terry. You read people better than most cops."

"I just know what an idiot you are with dough. What are you thinking? That's some serious fuck-you money you tricked your way into, pal."

"Well, I kept enough to pay you back. And a little more as walking-around money."

"Right, but the rest—"

"We all have our price to pay. And I wasn't the only one

who's giving money away. We worked out a deal that will fund a lot more future than we had before."

"How do you mean?"

"I ensured the outcome I was hired to make sure didn't happen. See those fields out there?"

"That's why I like this view. I was an early investor, you know."

"Well, you may want to sell. Because they agreed to give it away."

"The farms?"

"The seeds. More accurately, the genomes. No more patents. All open-source. They can still sell the actual seeds, and the actual crops. But so can anyone. And people can make their own versions. Better versions, like the ones they already developed in New Orleans."

"They're going to give up the most valuable asset of the company?"

Donny nodded. "That, and a lot of cash. All the parties are. Even the Popular Front, though mostly what they're contributing is expertise and ideas."

"Contributing to what?"

"A new fund, for restoration and conservation, education, land reform. To kick-start a new ecology, or that's the idea. And with the rights to the seeds opened up, we might even figure out ways to get it all to pay for itself, under a new business model that's about a different kind of free market than the economists had in mind."

"Can I keep my BMW?"

"The idea is that you won't want it anymore."

"Fat chance of that."

"Then they'll work on your kids."

"I don't have any kids."

"Even better. Spread it around among your friends and business associates."

Thelen laughed.

"This sounds big. Will they roll it into the new Constitution?"

"I wish. We talked about it. Even about getting a new bill of rights for plants and animals. But it's not happening."

"Why not?"

"Didn't you hear? Negotiations have broken down. They got stuck."

"Wouldn't be the first time."

"No, but this really does sound like the last. The major players walked. Maybe next year. And it's not totally dead. I mean, people are still showing up for work at the Pentagon. But we're basically on our own."

"Jesus," said Thelen.

"It'll be okay," said Donny. "We need to take care of each other. Rethink our whole setup. That's kind of what this deal is about. There's even a mutual defense component."

"Sounds like a train wreck to me," said Thelen. "Is that why you had to give up your fee?"

"I had to do that to get them to all agree to the deal. To get them all to agree to get along."

"What do you mean?"

"I had AMR nailed for their crimes, Terry. Them and Tripto Labs, as it turned out. The whole enchilada. The camps. The extermination program, how they disappeared all those people—for money, not politics like I thought. And how they hid the evidence. Lecker was running a program to help all the guys who were involved disappear themselves. DIY witness protection, but better than anything the government did."

"Where are they?"

"All over. Some overseas, but most still here. And now they are all going to get turned in."

"No way."

"Way. Lou's daughter took over the company that has to write the check for what happened. She owned it all along, and pretty much knew what was going down, even when she was a kid, so no surprise how eager she was to try to fix that. And how quickly she grabbed the reins and grew the heck up when it was real. Even managed to corral her overly enthusiastic boy-friend, my client, whose parents were among the victims of her family business."

"Sounds like my family."

"Not funny, Terry."

He tipped an apologetic glass. "And so your fee?"

"To get Lecker to sign, I agreed to put my fee, which was just a tip over a million bucks, into a legal-defense fund for all those murdering bastards to get a fair trial."

"Why the fuck would you do something as stupid as that? Even I think those guys should all rot."

"Maybe I want to try to fund a future I would actually want to live in. One based on cooperation more than competition. One that's not run by guys meeting for drinks in private clubs."

Thelen nodded. "That's fair."

"The only thing I know for sure is I have lost enough peo-ple to the fighting," said Donny. "Haven't you?"

Thelen didn't need to answer. You could see it in his eyes.

"What about Joyce?" he asked.

"I lost her too," said Donny. "I lost her eight years ago, re-ally, but it just took me a while to figure it out."

"I could have told you that when you came to borrow the money to spring her."

"I wouldn't have listened. That was the right thing to do, even if it was too late. But even she agreed to stop fighting, and focus on building."

"Maybe you'll meet someone new."

"I did," said Donny. "She was trying to arrest me."

Thelen laughed.

"No kidding. She arrested that guy instead." Donny pointed at the TV.

"Oh," said Thelen.

"She offered me a job. Said I was pretty good at hunting down war criminals for a guy who looked like such a loser."

"Did you take it?"

"No, Terry. I would have had to move. To Switzerland, or India."

"Sounds pretty good to me."

"I've had so many chances to leave. But this is home. I have a future to build here. And some trees to plant. And I wanted to talk to you about whether you'd be willing to donate that money I just gave you to the cause. Because no one is going to fix the future for us. No government, no NGO, no beneficent tycoon. We each need to pick up the spade, and use it to help put it all back the way it was when our ancestors found it. Or whatever wacked-out new version of that we can manage."

Thelen looked at him, and then he looked out the window. Donny looked, too, and they could see the river, and the city, and the suburbs going back to green. And then they heard the tap-tap-tap, and saw a big fat bumblebee at the glass, legs loaded with pollen, trying to find its way through the world we made our slave.

Acknowledgments

THIS BOOK IS IN LARGE PART A CONTINUATION OF THE STORIES related in *Rule of Capture* and *Tropic of Kansas*. And while this text should stand on its own, it would not have been possible without the advice and support of the people I acknowledged in those books. These include my family, innumerable friends and colleagues (especially those who brought me to Dallas over the years to get a feel for the city I put a fun-house mirror up to here), my literary agent Mark Gottlieb, and David Pomerico, cover designer Owen Corrigan, and the rest of the amazing team at Harper Voyager. I owe particular thanks to "human webcrawler"* Bruce Sterling for his helpful and timely research on early utopias, Craig Campbell for invaluable anthropological wayfinding, L. Timmel Duchamp for her annual prompts to think about my reading through a different prism, and the librarians at the University of Texas Law School who helped me research the legal systems imagined in this book. Notable texts that were indispensable include James C. Scott's *Against the Grain*, Christopher Stone's *Should Trees Have Standing?*, Simon Roberts's *Order and Dispute*, *Njal's Saga*, and *Laxdaela Saga*.

While I was working on this book, I acquired two new daughters, one by birth, and one by marriage. This book was inspired by the idea of trying to imagine a future I would want

---

* Full credit to another generous colleague, Rudy Rucker, for this spot-on handle for every science-fiction writer's dream research correspondent.

them to be able to live in, and trying to imagine the more hopeful world the protagonists of *Rule of Capture* and *Tropic of Kansas* fought to realize. I don't know if I entirely succeeded in finding it, but I like to think the characters in this book have started to map some of the unexplored territory where that lies. And I don't know if the future in this book is as female as the one I expect the real world to bring us. But I hope it will provide some inspiration to Octavia and Ajin and their peers to help us get there, and it is to them that this book is dedicated.

For more of the story of the dark years between the events of *Rule of Capture* and *Failed State*, check out *Tropic of Kansas*, which tells the story from the perspective of people much further from the sources of power.

Excerpt from *Tropic of Kansas*

EAGLE ONE **FLEW IN FAST FROM THE WEST, THEN YAWED BACK**
over the East Lawn, engines whining overthrottle, blasting air
onto the ground.

Eagle One was the flagship of a new line of Anglo-American
tactical aircraft the President had promoted as superior to the
helicopter. It could fly faster and higher, with even better vertical takeoff and landing capabilities. All jet, no wings—just
stabilizers at the tail. Manufactured by a company he still had
stock in.

Tania tried to see through the cockpit window, to see if he
really was the pilot, but the glass was as opaque as the midnight blue fuselage.

It was a beautiful and scary thing, with its Luftwaffe '46
lines guided by twenty-first-century electrorobotics. Visitor
from a different tomorrow. She'd seen it on the big screens for
the last inaugural, when it flew in from Camp David, but seeing it in person was a whole different deal. Pure wonder. Like
some cross between a royal yacht, an experimental supercar,
and a unicorn.

Piloted by God.

"Dark Apollo has landed," joked Odile, barely audible
through the noise.

Tania had been close enough to see him once before—
two years earlier, on the day they swore him in for his third
term, wearing his medals. Tania had watched the parade, just

down the road, on an office balcony with Odile and a bunch of other silk suits cheering on their sugar daddy in chief. Tania remembered the snowflakes melting on the military robots as they rumbled down the street. The big land drones with their black beret Engineer escorts walking alongside. The double-wide floats with their maudlin pageants of the martyrs of Tehran, Seoul, Panama City. She'd seen a guy in the crowd throw a snowball at the Vice President's limo, then watched the silver helmets swarm him.

"Which one's your boyfriend?" she teased Odile now, as they watched the soldiers mark out a landing pad with their regimented bodies, so close Tania could almost reach them through the fence.

They felt the thrust as the turbine turned down, like a hot hard wind. The craft dropped fast, then slowed just above the flickering turf, gently moving through the final phase into a soft landing.

There were no tourists on this side of the checkpoint, but everyone around turned to watch. The President, even just the idea of his imminent presence, compelled your gaze.

The Secret Service detail assembled around the rear of the aircraft, waiting for the door to drop. The sanctioned cameras were right behind them.

Tania's view was occluded, but she could see the colored light leak out from inside when they opened the hatch.

The personal guard emerged first. A detail of three. All tall, handpicked from the best corporate security firms. One of them, a blond woman with a white scarf instead of a necktie, looked right at Tania, through lenses that clearly read her face.

"Don't forget to smile," said Odile.

"You're the one she should be checking out," said Tania.

"Look," said Odile. "The dogs!"

Sure enough, the presidential pets trotted out on cue. The wolfhound, then the ridgeback. Everyone knew their names. Ulysses and Lee.

The man who followed looked like the President, but wasn't.

Odile squealed.

"Newton!" she yelled.

Others joined in with shouts and whistles. Tania gasped.

The man turned, flashing a white porcelain smile. Newton Towns. The actor who played the President in the movies. The one that popularized Mack's narrative before he first ran for office, dramatizing his escape from the North Koreans after his fighter jet went down in the DMZ. Then the sequel, a miniseries about the Panamanian crisis of his first term. They were working on a third one now, about the retaking of New Orleans.

"He's fucking glowing," said Odile, and Tania laughed with her.

He wasn't, really, but he had that aura. Opposite of what Tania expected, he was even better-looking in person. Beautiful, in an unreal way, yet there he was, magazine cover model of a good-looking, friendly white man, the archetype they wanted you to believe in. He wore a suit, but no tie. One of those suits built to your scan, that draped elegantly and suggested superhero bulges all at the same time.

One of the cameras came in close for the star, then moved toward the crowd. Not that you could tell what it was filming. There was more than one eye behind the black glass of those rotored orbs.

As she thought of it scanning them, Tania got anxious for a second, then remembered how that inspector sucked up to Odile. If they were watching them, it was probably to protect her.

Two women walked out. The girlfriends. Newton's date, the country singer Ashley Lionel, and the presidential companion, triathlete Patricia Wood. They looked rich, unnaturally young, and happy.

Then *He* emerged.

The Commander in Chief, wearing an old-school bomber jacket with flight patches and the left sleeve pinned up over his stump. He didn't look back. All business, the busy boss headed back to the office. His hair was going white. It looked like some of his skin was, too, scar tissue you could see on the back of his neck. He was shorter than they made him look on TV. And something about seeing him in the flesh, feeling him that close, made all your deep down feelings about him come right up to the surface.

Tania wished she could see his eyes.

"Yo, Tommy!" she yelled, insanely, uncontrollably, as if momentarily possessed by the rabble-rousing spirit of her mom. "Look at your people, tyrant!"

Odile gasped.

And as soon as the words left her mouth, Tania could feel she had breached the terms of their unofficial permission to be here.

Shit.

Tania was right at the fence now, fingers through the chain link, eyes on, like some crazy starfucker. Or assassin. She suddenly realized how very close they were to the most protected man in the world.

She glanced at Odile's freaked-out face, and the uniformed dudes gaping behind her, all staring at Tania.

But she got what she wanted.

She got the President of the United States to look right

at her. They locked gazes. No more than a second, but long enough to register the judgment of those cold blue eyes.

It was not a safe feeling.

"Let's go," said Odile.

The President turned. Barked something at his guard. One of his dogs actually barked.

The blond lady bodyguard was really watching Tania then. So were half the people around her.

Tania felt the shudder of fear come up through her body.

She looked up and around, at the cameras you could see, and the ones you couldn't. One of the news cameras was on her now.

OMFG.

"Come on!" said Odile, grabbing Tania, pulling her hard.

"Yeah, okay," said Tania. They turned and headed back the way they came.

"What the fuck!" said Odile, glaring, as they walked as fast as they could without running.

"Sorry!" said Tania. "I think you just got me all riled up with all that crazy talk at lunch and hollering at Newton."

"That was all you," said Odile. "I say what I think sometimes, but in the right time and place. I thought you knew how this town works!"

"Same way the whole country works," said Tania. "I didn't do anything wrong."

She knew that was a lie, even if it was true.

When they got to Lafayette Square, they were waiting for them. Of course they were. The soldiers surrounded them, separated them, frisked them. Tania saw Odile crying as that same inspector, Nichols, escorted her back behind the checkpoint. Then four Secret Service agents took Tania away in a car with windows tinted so dark she couldn't see where they were.

She asked what cause they had to detain her, but they didn't say anything. As she knew, they didn't have to.

It was an emergency.

It had been an emergency for as long as Tania could remember.

About the Author

Christopher Brown is the Campbell and World Fantasy Award–nominated author of *Rule of Capture* and *Tropic of Kansas*. He lives in Austin, Texas, where he also practices law.

THE DYSTOPIAN FUTURE OF CHRISTOPHER BROWN

TROPIC OF KANSAS

"Timely, dark, and ultimately hopeful: it might not 'make America great again,' but then again, it just might."
—Cory Doctorow, *New York Times* bestselling and award winning author of *Homeland*

Acclaimed short story writer and editor of the World Fantasy Award–nominee *Three Messages and a Warning* eerily envisions an American society unraveling and our borders closed off—from the other side—in this haunting and provocative novel.

RULE OF CAPTURE

Better Call Saul meets Ben Winter's *The Last Policeman* in this first volume in an explosive legal thriller series set in the world of *Tropic of Kansas*—a finalist for the 2018 Campbell Award for best science fiction novel of the year.

Defeated in a devastating war with China and ravaged by climate change, America is on the brink of a bloody civil war. Seizing power after a controversial election, the ruling regime has begun cracking down on dissidents fighting the nation's slide toward dictatorship. For Donny Kimoe, chaos is good for business. He's a lawyer who makes his living defending enemies of the state.

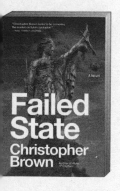

FAILED STATE

In this second dystopian legal thriller from the author of the acclaimed *Rule of Capture* and *Tropic of Kansas*, lawyer Donny Kimoe juggles two intertwined cases whose outcomes will determine the course of America's future—and his own.

In the aftermath of a second American revolution, peace rests on a fragile truce. The old regime has been deposed, but the ex-president has vanished, escaping justice for his crimes. Some believe he is dead. Others fear he is in hiding, gathering forces. As the factions in Washington work to restore order, Donny Kimoe is in court to settle old scores—and pay his own debts come due.

Praise for Tami Hoag

'Her books are cleverly plotted, feature strong female protagonists and are extremely – often emetically – violent . . . Hoag
has the bestselling writer's way with a punchy sentence and
keeps the surprises coming right up to the very last page'
The Times

'First-rate procedural detail with credible crew of homicide
cops, spectacularly foul-mouthed and fending off the horrors
with dirty jokes. Some ornate plotting . . . Worth your while,
though, if not for the faint-hearted' *Literary Review*

'Grisly tension is not the only commodity on offer here – the
internal politics of the police investigations are handled with
genuine panache . . . Hoag has demonstrated . . . an effortless
command of the thriller technique, adroitly juggling the twin
demands of character and plot. The set-piece confrontations
will ensure that it will take quite a lot to distract the reader
from Hoag's narrative' *Crime Time*

'Tragedy, sexual tension and high-level politics – a fair diet to
feast upon! Along with Patricia Cornwell and Barbara Taylor
Bradford, Tami Hoag adorns the bestseller list with the
fashionable prose of the day' *Focus*

'Lock all the doors and windows and turn on all the lights –
Hoag has crafted a knuckle-whitening, spine-chilling thriller'
New Woman

'Accomplished and scary' *Cosmopolitan*

With thirteen consecutive *New York Times* bestsellers to her credit, including *The Alibi Man, Kill the Messenger* and *Dust to Dust*, Tami Hoag has over twenty-two million books in print in more than twenty languages worldwide. Tami divides her time between Los Angeles and Palm Beach Country, Florida. Visit her website at www.tamihoag.com.

TAMI HOAG
Night Sins

An Orion paperback

First published in Great Britain in 1995
by Orion
This paperback edition published in 1996
by Orion Books Ltd,
Orion House, 5 Upper St Martin's Lane,
London WC2H 9EA

An Hachette UK company

15 17 19 20 18 16 14

Reissued 2010

A CIP catalogue record for this book
is available from the British Library.

ISBN 978-1-4091-2145-9

Printed and bound in Great Britain by
Clays Ltd, St Ives plc

The Orion Publishing Group's policy is to use papers
that are natural, renewable and recyclable products and
made from wood grown in sustainable forests. The logging
and manufacturing processes are expected to conform to
the environmental regulations of the country of origin.

www.orionbooks.co.uk

*To Andrea for opening doors. To Nita for
pushing me through them. I owe you both so much.*

To Irwyn for your support and your genius.

*To Beth for another fine job, and to Kate Miciak
for going above and beyond the call of duty.*

*And to Dan, who is patient enough and understanding enough to
put up with all my characters—real and imagined—and with my
artistic temperament, which is all too real. You are my anchor, my
support, and the one who lifts me up to help me reach for stars. I
love you.*

Acknowledgments

My sincere thanks to Special Agent in Charge Don Peterson of the Minnesota Bureau of Criminal Apprehension for graciously taking time out of your busy schedule to answer my endless questions and give me the grand tour. Your generosity in sharing your expertise was greatly appreciated. I followed procedure as closely as fiction allows and hope that any dramatic license taken will not be held against me. (And for those who will inevitably ask, no, Don was not the model for SAC Bruce DePalma. Don is far more charming and bears no resemblance whatsoever to Richard Nixon.)

Additional thanks go to Amy Muelhbauer for serving as research assistant, and Elizabeth Eagle for sharing your experience and knowledge of migraine and medications. Also to Dr. Karen Björnigaard for answering what had to be the weirdest questions ever put to you in your professional life.

To Trisha Yearwood and Jude Johnstone—your words and music made me see what had been missing. You touch the most tender of hidden-heart secrets simply and beautifully. I stand in awe.

And last, but certainly not least, thanks to my sister-in-crime, drinking buddy, and pub singer extraordinaire, the notorious suspense diva Eileen Dreyer, for tutoring me in trauma lingo and gizmos, and for sharing all the weird stuff. May all your royalty checks have commas.

And much of Madness, and more of Sin,
And Horror the soul of the plot.

Edgar Allan Poe,
The Conqueror Worm

PROLOGUE

JOURNAL ENTRY
AUGUST 27, 1968

They found the body today. Not nearly as soon as we expected. Obviously, we gave them too much credit. The police are not as smart as we are. No one is.

We stood on the sidewalk and watched. What a pitiful scene. Grown men in tears throwing up in the bushes. They wandered around and around that corner of the park, trampling the grass, and breaking off bits of branches. They called to God, but God didn't answer. Nothing changed. No lightning bolts came down. No one was given knowledge of who or why. Ricky Meyers remained dead, his arms outflung, his sneakers toes-up.

We stood on the sidewalk as the ambulance came with its lights flashing, and more police cars came, and the cars of people from around town. We stood in the crowd, but no one saw us, no one looked at us. They thought we were beneath their notice, unimportant. But we are really above them and beyond them and invisible to them. They are blind and stupid and trusting. They would never think to look at us.

We are twelve years old.

CHAPTER 1

Josh Kirkwood and his two best buddies burst out of the locker room, flying into the cold, dark late afternoon, hollering at the tops of their lungs. Their breath billowed out in rolling clouds of steam. They flung themselves off the steps like mountain goat kids leaping from ledge to ledge and landed hip-deep in the snow on the side of the hill. Hockey sticks skittered down, gear bags sliding after. Then came the Three Amigos, squealing and giggling, tucked into balls of wild-colored ski jackets and bright stocking caps.

The Three Amigos. That was what Brian's dad called them. Brian's family had moved to Deer Lake, Minnesota, from Denver, Colorado, and his dad was still a big Broncos fan. He said the Broncos used to have some wide receivers called the Three Amigos and they were really good. Josh was a Vikings fan. As far as he was concerned, every other team was just a bunch of wusses, except maybe the Raiders, 'cause their uniforms were cool. He didn't like the Broncos, but he liked the nickname—the Three Amigos.

"We are the Three Amigos!" Matt yelled as they landed in a heap at the bottom of the hill. He threw back his head and howled like a wolf. Brian and Josh joined in, and the racket was so terrible it made Josh's ears ring.

Brian fell into a fit of uncontrollable giggles. Matt flopped onto his back and started making a snow angel, swinging his arms and legs in wide arcs, looking as if he were trying to swim back up the hill. Josh pushed himself to his feet and shook like a dog as Coach Olsen came out of the ice arena.

Coach was old—at least forty-five—kind of fat and mostly bald, but he was a good coach. He yelled a lot, but he laughed a lot, too. He told them at the beginning of hockey season that if he got too cranky they were to remind him they were only eight years old. The team had picked Josh for that job. He was one of the co-captains, a responsibility that pleased him a lot even though he would never say so. Nobody liked a bragger, Mom said. If you did your job well, there wasn't any reason to brag. A good job would speak for itself.

Coach Olsen started down the steps, tugging down the earflaps of his hunting cap. The end of his nose was red from the cold. His breath came out of his mouth and went up around his head like smoke from a chimney. "You guys have rides home tonight?"

They answered all at once, vying for the coach's attention by being loud and silly. He laughed and held his gloved hands up in surrender. "All right, all right! The rink's open if you get cold waiting. Olie's inside if you need to use the phone."

Then Coach jumped into his girlfriend's car, the way he did every Wednesday, and off they went to have dinner at Grandma's Attic downtown. Wednesday was Grandma's famous meat loaf night. All-U-Can-Eat, it said on the menu. Josh imagined Coach Olsen could eat a lot.

Cars rumbled around the circular drive in front of the Gordie Knutson Memorial Arena, a parade of minivans and station wagons, doors banging, exhaust pipes coughing. Kids from the various Squirt League teams chucked their sticks and equipment in trunks and hatches and climbed into the cars with their moms or dads, talking a mile a minute about the plays and drills they had worked on in practice.

Matt's mom pulled up in their new Transport, a wedge-shaped thing that to Josh looked like something from *Star Trek*. Matt scrambled for his gear and dashed across the sidewalk, calling a good-bye over his shoulder. His mother, wearing a bright red stocking cap, buzzed down the passenger window.

"Josh, Brian—you guys have rides?"

"My mom's coming," Josh answered, suddenly feeling eager to see her. She would pick him up on her way home from the hospital and they would stop at the Leaning Tower of Pizza to get supper and she would want to hear all about practice.

Really want to hear. Not like Dad. Lately, Dad just pretended to listen. Sometimes he even snapped at Josh to be quiet. He always apologized later, but it still made Josh feel bad.

"My sister's coming," Brian called. "My sister, Beth Butt-head," he added under his breath as Mrs. Connor drove away.

"You're the butt-head," Josh teased, shoving him.

Brian shoved back, laughing, three big gaps showing in his mouth where teeth had been. "Butt-head!"

"Butt-breath!"

"Butt-face!"

Brian scooped up a mitten full of snow and tossed it in Josh's face, then turned and ran up the snow-packed sidewalk, bounded up the steps, and dashed around the side of the brick building. Josh let out a war whoop and bolted after him. Immediately they were so involved in their game of Attack, the rest of the world ceased to exist. One boy hunted the other to deliver a snowball up close in the face, in the back, down the neck of the jacket. After a successful attack the roles reversed and the hunter became the hunted. If the hunter couldn't find the hunted in a count of a hundred, the hunted scored a point.

Josh was good at hiding. He was small for his age and he was smart, a combination that served him well in games like Attack. He smashed Brian in the back of the head with a snowball, whirled and ran. Before Brian had shaken the snow off his coat, Josh was safely tucked behind the air-conditioning units that squatted beside the building. The cylinders were covered with canvas for the winter months and blocked the wind. They sat well back along the side of the building, where the street-lights didn't quite reach. Josh watched as Brian ventured cautiously around a Dumpster, snowball in hand, pouncing at a shadow, then drawing back. Josh smiled to himself. He had found the all-time best hiding place. He licked the tip of a gloved forefinger and drew himself a point in the air.

Brian homed in on one of the overgrown bushes that lined the edge of the parking lot and separated the ice rink grounds from the fairgrounds. Tongue sticking out the side of his mouth, he crept toward it. He hoped Josh hadn't gone farther than the hedges. The fairgrounds was the creepiest place in the world this time of year, when all the old buildings stood dark and empty and the wind howled around them.

A car horn blared and Brian swung around, heart pounding. He groaned in disappointment as his sister's Rabbit pulled up around the curve.

"Come on, hurry up, Brian! I've got pageant practice tonight!"

"But—"

"But nothing, twerp!" Beth Hiatt snapped. The wind whipped a strand of long blond hair across her face and she snagged it back behind her ear with a bare hand white with cold. "Get your little butt in the car!"

Brian heaved a sigh and dropped his snowball, then trudged toward his gear bag and hockey stick. Beth the Bitch raced the Rabbit's motor, put the car in gear, and let it lurch ahead on the drive, as if she might just leave him behind. She had done that once before and they had both gotten hollered at, but Brian had gotten the worst of it because Beth blamed him for getting her in trouble and spent four days tormenting him for it. Instantly forgetting his game and the remaining amigo, he grabbed his stuff and ran for the car, already plotting ways to get his sister back for being such a snot.

Behind the air-conditioning units, Josh heard Beth Hiatt's voice. He heard the car doors slam and he heard the Rabbit roar around the circle drive. So much for the game.

He crawled out of his hiding spot and went back around the front of the building. The parking lot was empty except for Olie's old rusted-out Chevy van. The next practice didn't start for an hour. The circular drive was empty. Packed over the asphalt by countless tires, the snow gleamed in the glow of the streetlights, as hard and shiny as milky-white marble. Josh tugged off his left glove and shoved up the sleeve of his ski jacket to peer at the watch Uncle Tim had sent him for Christmas. Big and black with lots of dials and buttons, it looked like something a scuba diver might wear—or a commando. Sometimes Josh pretended that he was a commando, a man on a mission, waiting to meet with the world's most dangerous spy. The numbers on the watch face glowed green in the dark: 5:45.

Josh looked down the street, expecting to see headlights, expecting to see the minivan with his mom at the wheel. But the street was dark. The only lights glowed dimly out the windows of houses that lined the block. Inside those houses, people were having supper and watching the news and talking about their day. Outside, the only sound was the buzz of the street lamps and the cold wind rattling the dry, bare branches of winter-dead trees. The sky was black.

He was alone.

5:17 P.M.   22°

She nearly escaped. She had her coat halfway on, purse slung over her shoulder, gloves and car keys clutched in one hand. She hurried down the hall toward the west side door of the hospital, staring straight ahead, telling herself if she didn't make eye contact, she wouldn't be caught, she would be invisible, she would escape.

I sound like Josh. That's the kind of game he likes—what if we could make ourselves invisible?

A smile curved Hannah's lips. Josh and his imagination. Last night she'd found him in Lily's room, telling his sister an adventure story about Zeek the Meek and Super Duper, characters Hannah had made up in stories for Josh when he was a toddler. He was passing on the tradition, telling the tale with great enthusiasm while Lily sat in her crib and sucked her thumb, her blue eyes wide with astonishment, hanging on her brother's every word.

I've got two great kids. Two for the plus column. I'll take what I can get these days.

The smile faded and tension tightened in Hannah's stomach. She blinked hard and realized she was just standing there at the end of the hall with her coat half on. Rand Bekker, head of maintenance, shouldered his way through the door, letting in a blast of crisp air. A burly man with a full red beard, he pulled off a flame-orange hunting cap and shook himself like a big wet ox, as if he could shake off the chill.

"Hiya, Dr. Garrison. Decent night out there."

"Is it?" She smiled automatically, blankly, as if she were

speaking with a stranger. But there were no strangers at Deer Lake Community Hospital. Everyone knew everyone.

"You bet. It's looking good for Snowdaze."

Rand grinned, his anticipation for the festival as plain as a child's eagerness for Christmas morning. Snowdaze was big doings in a town the size of Deer Lake, an excuse for the fifteen thousand residents to break the monotony of Minnesota's long winter. Hannah tried to find some enthusiasm. She knew Josh was looking forward to Snowdaze, especially the torchlight parade. But it was difficult for her to feel festive these days.

For the most part, she felt tired, drained, dispirited. And stretched over it all was a thin film of desperation, like plastic wrap, because she couldn't let any of those feelings show. People depended on her, looked up to her, thought of her as a model for working women. Hannah Garrison: doctor, wife, mother, woman of the year; juggling all the demanding roles with skill and ease and a beauty queen smile. Lately the titles had felt as heavy as bowling balls and her arms were growing weary.

"Rough day?"

"What?" She jerked her attention back to Rand. "I'm sorry, Rand. Yeah, it's been one of those days."

"I better let you go, then. I got a hot date with a boiler."

Hannah murmured good-bye as Bekker pulled open a door marked Maintenance Staff Only and disappeared through it, leaving her alone in the hall. Her inner voice, the voice of the little goblin that kept the cling wrap pulled tight over her emotions, gave a shout.

Go! Go now! Escape while you can! Get away!

She had to pick up Josh. They would stop and get a pizza, then go on to the sitter's for Lily. After supper she had to drive Josh to religion class. . . . But her body refused to bolt in response. Then the great escape was lost.

"Dr. Garrison to ER. Dr. Garrison to ER."

That selfish part of her prodded once more, telling her she could still get away. She wasn't on call tonight, had no patients in the hundred-bed facility who were in critical need of her personal attention. There was no one here to see her escape. She could leave the work to the doctor on duty, Craig Lomax, who believed he had been set on earth to rush to the aid of mere mortals and comfort them with his cover-boy looks. Hannah wasn't even the backup tonight. But guilt came directly on the heels of those thoughts. She had taken an oath to serve. It didn't matter that she'd seen enough sore throats and bruised bodies to last her one day. She had a duty—a bigger one now that the hospital board had named her director of the ER. The people of Deer Lake depended on her.

The page sounded again. Hannah heaved a sigh and felt tears warm the backs of her eyes. She was exhausted—physically, emotionally. She needed this night off, a night with just herself and the kids; with Paul working late, keeping his moods and his sarcasm in his office instead of inflicting them on the family.

A wavy strand of honey-blond hair escaped her loose ponytail and fell limply against her cheek. She sighed and brushed it back behind her ear as she stared out the door to the parking lot that looked sepia-toned beneath the halogen lights.

"Dr. Garrison to ER. Dr. Garrison to ER."

She slipped her coat off and folded it over her arm.

"God, there you are!" Kathleen Casey blurted out as she skidded around the corner and hustled down the hall, the tails of her white lab coat sailing behind her. The thick, cushioned soles of her running shoes made almost no sound on the polished floor. Not a fraction of an inch over five feet, the nurse had a leprechaun's features, a shock of thick red hair, and the tenacity of a pit bull. Her uniform consisted of surgical scrubs and a pin that proclaimed No Whining. She drew a bead on Hannah that had all the power of a tractor beam.

Hannah tried to muster a wry smile. "Sorry. God may be a woman, but she's not *this* woman."

Kathleen gave a snort as she curled a hand around Hannah's upper arm. "You'll do."

"Can't Craig handle it?"

"Maybe, but we'd rather have a higher life form with opposable thumbs."

"I'm not even on call tonight. I have to pick up Josh from hockey. Call Dr. Baskir—"

"We did. He's in bed with your friend and mine, Jurassic Park flu, also known as tracheasaurus phlegmus. That's one butt-kicking virus. Half the staff is down with it, which means I, Kathleen Casey, queen of the ER, may press you into service against your will. It won't take long, I promise."

"Famous last words," Hannah muttered.

Kathleen ignored her and started to turn as if she had every intention of towing all five feet nine inches of Hannah in her wake. Hannah's feet moved of their own accord as the wail of an ambulance sounded in the distance.

"What's coming in?" she asked with resignation.

"Car accident. Some kid hit a patch of ice on Old Cedar Road and spun into a car full of grandmas."

Their pace picked up with each step, the low heels of Hannah's leather boots pounding out a quick staccato rhythm. Her fatigue and its companion emotions slipped under the surface of duty and her "doctor mode," as Paul called it. Power switches flipped on inside her, filling her brain with light and energy, sending a rush of adrenaline shooting through her.

"What's the status?" Hannah asked, her speech taking on a sharper, harder quality.

"They flew two critical to Hennepin County Medical Center. We get the leftovers. Two grandmas with bumps and bruises and the college kid. Sounds like he's banged up pretty good."

"No seat belt?"

"Why bother when you haven't lived long enough to grasp the concept of mortality?" Kathleen said as they reached the area that served as a combination nurses' station and admissions desk.

Hannah leaned over the counter. "Carol? Could you please call the hockey rink and leave word for Josh that I'll be a little bit late? Maybe he can practice his skating."

"Sure thing, Dr. Garrison."

Dr. Craig Lomax arrived on the scene in immaculate surgical greens, looking like a soap opera doctor.

"Jesus," Kathleen muttered half under her breath, "he's been watching *Medical Center* reruns again. Get a load of the Chad Everett hair."

Strands of black hair tumbled across his forehead in a careless look he had probably spent fifteen painstaking minutes in front of a mirror to achieve. Lomax was thirty-two, madly in love with himself, and afflicted with an overabundance of confidence in his own talents. He had come to Deer Lake Community in April, a reject from the better medical centers in the Twin Cities—a hard truth that had not managed to put so much as a dent in his ego. Deer Lake was just far enough outstate that they couldn't afford to be choosy. Most doctors preferred the salaries in the metro area over the chance to serve the needs of a small rural college town.

Lomax had arranged his features in a suitably grave expression that cracked a little when he caught sight of Hannah. "I thought you'd gone home," he said bluntly.

"Kathleen just caught me."

"In the nick of time," the nurse added.

Lomax sucked in a breath to chastise her for her attitude.

"Save it, Craig," Hannah snapped, tossing her things on a waiting area couch and moving forward as the doors to the ER slid open.

A stretcher was rolled in, one paramedic at the rear, one bent over the patient, talking to him in a soothing tone. "Hang in there, Mike. The docs'll have you patched up in no time."

The young man on the stretcher groaned and tried to sit up, but chest and head restraints held him down on the backboard. His face was taut and gray with pain above the cervical collar that immobilized his neck. Blood ran down across his temple from a gash on his forehead.

"What have we got here, Arlis?" Hannah asked, shoving up the sleeves of her sweater.

"Mike Chamberlain. Nineteen. He's a little shocky," the paramedic said. "Pulse one twenty. BP ninety over sixty. Got a bump on the noggin and some broken bones."

"Is he lucid?"

Lomax cut her off on the way to the stretcher with a move as smooth as glass. "I'll handle it, Dr. Garrison. You're off duty. Mavis." He nodded to Mavis Sandstrom. The nurse exchanged a glance with Kathleen, her expression as blank as a cardshark's.

Hannah bit her tongue and stepped back. There was no point in fighting with Lomax in front of staff and the patient. Administration frowned on that kind of thing. She didn't want

to be there anyway. Let Lomax take the patient who would require the most time.

"Treatment room three, guys," Lomax ordered, and ushered them down the hall as a second ambulance pulled into the
drive. "Let's start an IV with lactated ringers . . ."

"Dr. Craig Ego strikes again," Kathleen growled. "He has
yet to grasp the notion that you're his boss now."

"No biggie," Hannah said calmly. "If we ignore him long
enough, maybe he'll stop trying to mark territory and we can
all live happily ever after."

"Or maybe he'll flip out and we'll find him in the parking
lot, peeing on car tires."

There wasn't time to laugh. A heavyset EMT from the second ambulance charged into the reception area.

"We've got a full arrest! Ida Bergen. Sixty-nine. We were
bringing her in with cuts and bruises, and as we pulled into the
drive, *bam!* She grabs her chest and goes—"

The rest of her words were lost as Hannah, Kathleen, and
another nurse bolted into action. The emergency room
erupted into a whirlwind of sound and action. Orders shouted
and relayed. Pages sounding for additional staff. The stretcher
wheeling into the reception area and down the hall. The
trauma cart and crash cart thundering into the treatment
room.

"Standard ACLS procedure, guys," Hannah called out.
"Get me a 6.5 endotracheal tube. Let's get her bagged and
get some air into her lungs. Do we have a pulse without
CPR?"

"No."

"With CPR?"

"Yes."

"BP forty over twenty and fading fast."

"Start an IV. Hang bretylium and dopamine and give her a
bristoject of epinephrine."

"Goddammit, I can't get a vein! Come on, baby, come on,
come to Mama Kathleen."

"Allen, check for lung sounds. Stop CPR. Angie, run a
strip. Is respiratory coming?"

"Wayne's on his way down."

"Gotcha!" Kathleen slipped the line onto the catheter and

secured it with tape, her small hands quick and sure. A tech handed her the epinephrine and she injected it into the line.

"Fine v-fib, Dr. Garrison."

"We need to defibrillate. Chris, continue CPR until my word. Allen, charge me up to 320." Hannah grabbed the paddles, rubbing the heads together to spread the gel. "Stand clear!" *Paddles in position against the woman's bare chest.* "All clear!" *Hit the buttons.* The old woman's body bucked on the gurney.

"Nothing! No pulse."

"Clear!" She hit the buttons again. Her eyes went to the monitor, where a flat green line bisected the screen. "Once more. Clear!"

The woman's body convulsed. The flat line snapped like a cracking whip and the monitor began to bleep out an erratic beat. A cheer went up in the room.

They worked on Ida Bergen for forty minutes, pulling her out of the clutches of death, only to lose her again ten minutes later. They worked the miracle a second time, but not a third.

Hannah delivered the news to Ida's husband. Ed Bergen's chore clothes emanated the warm, sweet scent of cows and fresh milk with a pungent undertone of manure. He had the same stoic face she had seen on many a Nordic farmer, but his eyes were bright and moist with worry, and they brimmed with tears when she told him they had done their best but had been unable to save his wife.

She sat with him and led him through some of the cruel rituals of death. Even in this time of grief, decisions had to be made, etc., etc. She went through the routine in a low monotone, feeling on autopilot, numb with exhaustion, crushed by depression. As a doctor, she had cheated death time and again, but death wouldn't let her win every time and she had never learned to be a gracious loser. The adrenaline that fueled her through the crisis had vaporized. A crash was imminent. Another familiar part of a routine she hated.

After Mr. Bergen had gone, Hannah slipped into her office and sat at the desk with the lights off, her head cradled in her hands. It hurt worse this time. Perhaps because she felt perilously close to loss for the first time in her life. Her marriage was in trouble. Ed Bergen's marriage was over. Forty-eight years of partnership over in the time it took a car to skid out of control on an icy road. Had they been good years? Loving years? Would he mourn his wife or simply go on?

She thought of Paul, his dissatisfaction, his discontent, his quiet hostility. Ten years of marriage was tearing apart like rotted silk, and she felt powerless to stop it. She had no point of reference. She had never lost anything, had never developed the skills to fight against loss. She felt the tears building—tears for Ida and Ed Bergen and for herself. Tears of grief and confusion and exhaustion. She was afraid to let them start falling. She had to be strong. She had to find a solution, smooth over all the rough spots, make everyone happy. But tonight the burdens weighed too heavily on her slender shoulders. She couldn't help thinking the only light at the end of the tunnel was the headlight of a big black train.

Knuckles rapped against her door and Kathleen stuck her head in. "You know she'd been seeing a cardiac specialist at Abbott-Northwestern for years," she said quietly.

Hannah sniffed and flicked on the desk lamp. "How's Craig's patient?"

Kathleen slid into the visitor's chair. She crossed a sneaker over one knee and rubbed absently at an ink mark on the leg of her scrub pants. "He'll be fine. A couple of broken bones, a slight concussion, whiplash. He was lucky. His car was turned sideways at the moment of impact. The other car hit him on the passenger side.

"Poor kid. He feels terrible about the accident. He keeps going on and on about how the road was dry and then suddenly there was this big patch of ice and he was out of control."

"I guess life can be that way sometimes," Hannah murmured, fingering the small cube-shaped clock on her desk. The wood was bird's-eye maple, smooth and satiny beneath her fingertips. An anniversary gift from Paul four years ago. A clock so she would always know how long it would be before they could be together again.

"Yeah, well, you've hit your patch of ice for the night,"

Kathleen said. "Time to pick yourself up, dust yourself off, and get home to the munchkins."

A chill went through Hannah like a dagger of ice. Her fingers tightened on the clock and tilted the face up to the light. Six-fifty.

"Oh, my God. Josh. I forgot about Josh!"

The plan has been perfected.
The players have been chosen.
The game begins today.

CHAPTER 2

Megan O'Malley had never expected to meet a chief of police in his underwear, but then again, it had been that kind of day. She had not allotted enough time for moving into the new apartment. Rather, she had not allowed for as many screwups as she had encountered before, during, and after the move. She kicked herself for that. Should have known.

Of course, there were things that couldn't have been foreseen. She couldn't have foreseen the key breaking off in the ignition of the moving van yesterday, for example. She couldn't have foreseen her new landlord hitting it big on the pull tabs at the American Legion hall and skipping town on a charter trip to Vegas. She couldn't have imagined that tracking down the keys to her apartment would involve a manhunt into the deepest, darkest reaches of the BuckLand cheese factory, or that once she got into the apartment, none of the utilities that were to have been turned on two days before were operational. No phone. No electricity. No gas.

The disasters and delays clustered together in a spot above her right eye. Pain nibbled at the edge of her brain, threatening a full-blown headache. The last thing she needed was to start her new assignment with a migraine. That would establish her all right—as weak. Small and weak—an image she had to fight even when she was in the best of health.

As of today she was a field agent for the Minnesota Bureau of Criminal Apprehension, one of the top law enforcement agencies in the Midwest. As of today she was one of only eleven field agents in the state. The only woman. The first female to crash the testosterone barrier of the BCA field ranks. Someone somewhere was probably proud of her for that, but Megan doubted that sentiment would extend to the male bastions of outstate law enforcement. Feminists would call her a pioneer. Others would use words omitted from standard dictionaries for the sake of propriety.

Megan called herself a cop. She was sick and tired of having gender enter into the discussion. She had taken all required courses, passed all tests—in the classroom and on the streets. She knew how to handle herself, knew how to handle anything that could shoot. She'd done her time on patrol, earned her stripes as a detective. She'd put in the hours at headquarters and had been passed over twice for a field assignment. Then finally her time had come.

Leo Kozlowski, the Deer Lake district agent, dropped dead from a heart attack at the age of fifty-three. Thirty years of doughnuts and cheap cigars had finally caught up with him and landed poor old Leo facedown in a plate of post-Christmas Swedish meatballs at the Scandia House Cafe.

When the news of his demise swept through the warren of offices at headquarters, Megan observed a moment of silence in honor of Leo, then typed yet another memorandum to the assistant superintendent, submitting her name for consideration for the post. When the day for decision-making drew near and she had heard nothing encouraging, she gathered her nerve and her service record and marched to the office of the special agent in charge of the St. Paul regional office.

Bruce DePalma went through the same song-and-dance he'd given her before. There were reasons all the field agents were men. The chiefs and sheriffs they had to work with were all men. The detectives and officers who made up their network were nearly all men. No, that wasn't discrimination, that was reality.

"Well, I've got another dose of reality for you, Bruce," Megan said, plunking her file dead center on his immaculate blotter. "I've got more investigative experience, more class time, and a better arrest record than any other person in line for this assignment. I've passed the agent's course at the FBI academy and I can shoot the dick off a rat at two hundred yards. If I get passed over again for no other reason than the fact that I have breasts, you'll hear me howling all the way to the city desk of the *Pioneer Press*."

DePalma scowled at her. He had a Nixonesque quality that had never endeared him to the press. Megan could see him playing the scene through his mind—reporters calling him evasive and uncooperative while the cameras focused on his deep-set, shifty eyes.

"That's blackmail," he said at last.

"And this is sex discrimination. I want the assignment because I'm a damn good cop and because I deserve it. If I get out there and screw up, then yank me back, but give me the chance to try."

DePalma slumped down in his chair and steepled his fingers, bony shoulders hunched up to his ears, a pose reminiscent of a vulture on a perch. The silence stretched taut between them. Megan held her ground and held his gaze. She hated to stoop to threats; she wanted the job on merit. But she knew that the brass was especially skittish of words like *harassment* and *gender bias,* was still smarting from the sexual harassment charges several female employees had made against the outgoing superintendent months before. It may have been a risk, but the reminder might be just enough to make DePalma pay attention.

He scowled at her, jowls quivering as he ground his teeth. "It's an old-boy network out there. That network is essential to successful police work. How do you expect to get in when everyone else thinks you don't belong?"

"I'll make them see that I do belong."

"You'll hit a stone wall every time you turn around."

"That's what jackhammers are for."

DePalma shook his head. "This job calls for finesse, not jackhammers."

"I'll wear kid gloves."

Or mittens, she thought as she fiddled with the car's heater setting. Frustrated and cold to the bone, she smacked the dashboard with a fist and was rewarded with a cloud of dust from the fan vents. The Chevy Lumina was a nag from the bureau's stable. It ran, had four good tires, and the requisite radio equipment. That was it. No frills. But it was a car and she was a field agent. Damned if she was going to complain.

Field agent for the Bureau of Criminal Apprehension. The BCA had been created by the state legislature in 1927 to provide multijurisdictional investigative, lab, and records services to the other law enforcement agencies in the state, a scaled-down version of the FBI. Megan was now the bureau's representative to a ten-county area. She now served as liaison between the local authorities and headquarters. Consultant, detective, drug czar—she had to wear many hats, and as the first woman on the job, she would have to look damn good in all of them.

Being late for her first meeting with the chief of police in the town that would be her base of operations was not a good beginning.

"Should have made the appointment for tomorrow, O'Malley," she muttered, climbing out of her car, struggling with what seemed to be twenty yards of gray woolen scarf.

The scarf was like a python twisting itself around her neck, around her arm, around the handle of her briefcase. She snatched at it and pulled at it, cursing under her breath as she made her way across the skating rink that passed for a parking lot behind the Deer Lake city hall and law enforcement center. Getting hold of the end of the scarf, she flung it hard over her shoulder—and threw herself off balance. Instantly, her feet went out from under her and she scrambled in a mad tap dance to keep from going down. The heels of the boots she had chosen to give herself the illusion of height acted like skate blades instead of cleats. She danced another five feet toward the building, then fell like a sack of bricks, landing with teeth-rattling impact smack on her fanny. The pain shot up her spine from her butt to her brain and rang there like a bell.

For a moment Megan just sat there with her eyes squeezed shut, then the cold began to penetrate through the seat of her black wool trousers. She looked around the parking lot for witnesses. There were none. The afternoon had been crushed beneath the weight of darkness. Five o'clock had come and gone; most of the office personnel had already left for the day. Chief Holt was probably gone as well, but she wanted it on the log that she *had* shown up for their appointment. Three hours late, but she had shown.

"I hate winter," she snarled, gathering her legs beneath

her, and rose with little grace and confidence, slipping, stumbling, finally grabbing hold of a car door to steady herself. "I *hate* winter."

She would rather have been anywhere south of the snow belt. It didn't matter that she had been born and raised in St. Paul. A love for arctic temperatures was not part of her genetic makeup. She had no affinity for down jackets. Wool sweaters made her break out in a rash.

If it hadn't been for her father, she would have been long gone to friendlier climes. She would have taken the FBI assignment that had been offered when she'd been at the academy in Quantico. Memphis. People in Memphis didn't even know what winter was. Snow was an event in Memphis. Their thermometers probably didn't have numbers below zero. If they'd ever heard the words *Alberta clipper,* they probably thought it was the name of a boat, not a weather system that brought wind-chill factors cold enough to freeze marrow in the bones of polar bears.

I stay here for you, Pop.

As if he cared.

The teeth of the headache bit a little harder.

The Deer Lake City Center was new. A handsome V-shaped two-story brick building, it testified to the growing tax base brought about by professional people moving out from the Cities. The town was just within commuting distance of the south end of the metro area. With crime and crowding on the rise in Minneapolis and St. Paul, those who could afford to and didn't mind the drive sought out the quaint charm of places like Deer Lake, Elk River, Northfield, Lakefield.

The city offices were housed in the south wing of City Center, the police department and the office of the late lamented Leo Kozlowski in the north, with the city jail on the second floor. Additional jail facilities were available across the town square in the old Park County courthouse and law enforcement center, where the county sheriff's offices and the county jail were located.

Once inside the building, Megan hung a left and marched down the wide hall, ignoring the pretty atrium with its skylights and potted palms and pictorial history of Deer Lake. Catching a glimpse of her reflection in the glass of a wall-mounted display case, she winced a little. She looked as if she'd just pulled a gunnysack off her head. That morning— seemed like a month ago—she had swept her dark mane back into a low ponytail and secured it with a small, no-nonsense bow in a dark Black Watch plaid. Neat. Businesslike. Now, strands fell like fine silk thread across her forehead and along her cheeks and jaw. She tried to sweep the stragglers back with an impatient gesture.

The reception desk at the head of the police wing had been abandoned for the day. She marched past it and on to the security doors that kept the city council safe from criminals and cops, and vice versa. She punched the buzzer and waited, looking into the squad room through the bulletproof glass. The room was bright and clean—white walls, slate-gray industrial-grade carpet that had yet to show any signs of wear. A small platoon of black steel desks squatted in two rows. The desks, for the most part, were not neat. They were piled with files and paperwork, crowded with coffee mugs and framed photos. Only three of them were manned, one by a massive uniformed cop talking on the phone, the other two by men in plainclothes, eating sandwiches while they tackled paperwork.

The uniform hung up the phone and rose to a towering height, big, drowsy eyes on Megan as he lumbered to the door, unwrapping a stick of Dentyne. He looked thirty and Samoan. His hair was dark and unruly, his body as thick as the trunk of an oak tree, and probably just as strong. His name tag said NOGA. He popped the gum in his mouth and punched the intercom button.

"Can I help you?"

"Agent O'Malley, BCA." Producing her ID, Megan held it up to the glass for his inspection. "I had an appointment with Chief Holt."

The cop studied the photo with mild interest; he looked half asleep. "Come on in," he said with a casual wave. "Door's open."

Megan gritted her teeth and willed herself not to blush. She didn't care to be made a fool of, especially not at the end of a day like this one or by a man who was a part of her network. Noga pulled one of the doors open and she marched in, fixing him with a steely look.

"Shouldn't this area be secured?" she asked sharply.

Noga appeared unperturbed by her manner. He shrugged his shoulders, a move that looked like an earthquake going through a small mountain range. "Against what?" When she just glared at him, he smiled a crooked half-smile, his thick lips tugging upward on the right side. "You aren't from around here, are you?"

Megan was getting a crick in her neck from looking up at him. Hell of a trick, trying to do imperious on someone a full foot taller than you. "Are you?"

"For long enough. Come on back." He led the way through the rows of desks to a hall with private offices off it. "Natalie's still around. No one sees the chief without seeing Natalie first. She runs the place. We call her the Commandant." He eyed her with mild curiosity. "So what are you here for? Filling in until they find a replacement for Leo?"

"I *am* the replacement for Leo."

Noga arched a thick brow, schooling a look of shock and dismay into something that more resembled indigestion. "No shit?"

"No shit."

"Huh."

"You got a problem working with a woman?" Megan worked to keep the edge out of her voice. But she was tired and her temper was running on a real lean mix. She could feel it simmering just beneath the surface of her control.

Noga played innocent, eyes wide. "Not me."

"Good."

He ducked into an office, drumming his knuckles on the open door as he went. "Hey, Natalie! The BCA guy—er—gal—" Noga cast a self-conscious glance at Megan.

"Agent O'Malley," she said stiffly.

"—is here," he finished.

"Well, it's about damn time."

The churlish line came from an office beyond the one in which they were standing. Stenciled on the frosted glass was MITCHELL HOLT, CHIEF OF POLICE, but it was not Mitchell Holt who came to the door with black eyes blazing.

The infamous Natalie was no taller than Megan's five feet five, but considerably more substantial of body. She had a certain squareness about her that suggested immovability, but she draped that squareness in a rust and purple ensemble that more than suggested taste. Her skin was the color of polished mahogany, her face as round as a pumpkin and crowned with a fine cap of tight black curls that looked like the wool of a newly shorn sheep. One hand propped on a hip, the other braced against the doorjamb, she gave Megan a hard once-over from behind the lenses of huge, red-rimmed glasses.

"Girl, you are *late*."

"I'm well aware of that," Megan replied coolly. "Is Chief Holt still in?"

Natalie made a sour face. "No, he isn't *in*. You think he'd just be sitting here, waitin' on you?"

"I *did* call to say I'd be late."

"You didn't talk to me."

"I didn't know that was necessary."

Natalie snorted. She pushed herself away from the door and bustled around her desk, adding papers to a file, filing the file in one of half a dozen black file cabinets behind her. Every move was efficient and quick. "You *are* new. Who'd you talk to? Melody? That girl would forget her own behind if some man didn't always have his hand on it to remind her."

Noga edged his way toward the door, trying to be unobtrusive. "Noogie, don't you try to sneak out on me," Natalie warned, not bothering to look at him. "Have you finished that report Mitch asked for?"

He made a pained face. "I'll finish it in the morning. I've got patrol."

"You got trouble, that's what you got," Natalie grumbled. "That report is on my desk by noon or I take the electric stapler after your ass. You hear me?"

"Loud and clear."

"And don't forget to drive by Dick Reid's place twice. They've gone to Cozumel."

Megan heaved a sigh and wished she were gone to Cozumel. A faint tic had begun in her right eyelid. She rubbed at it and thought about food for the first time since breakfast. She needed to eat something or the headache would take a stronger hold and she wouldn't be able to keep medication down.

"If Chief Holt is gone for the day, then I'd like to reschedule our appointment."

Natalie pursed her thick lips and fixed Megan with a long, measuring look. "I didn't say he was gone. I said he wasn't *in*," she qualified. "What kind of cop are you, you don't listen to nuances?" She made a sound of disgust and led the way out of the office. "Come on, *Agent* O'Malley. You're here, you might as well meet him."

Megan marched along beside the chief's secretary, careful not to step ahead, well aware the woman was taking her measure.

"So you're here to fill Leo's spot."

"I couldn't hope to fill Leo's spot," Megan said, deadpan. "I don't eat enough fried food."

A muscle ticked at the corner of Natalie's mouth. Not quite a smile. "Leo could pack it away, that's for sure. Now they've packed Leo away. I told him to watch his cholesterol and quit smoking those damn cigars. He wouldn't listen to me, but that's a man for you. Look up *obtuse* in the dictionary—they ought to have a picture of a man beside it.

"Everybody liked Leo, though," she added, her gaze sharpening on Megan once more. "He was a hell of a guy. What are you?"

"I'm a hell of a cop."

Natalie snorted. "We'll see."

When she first heard the music, Megan thought she was imagining it. The sound was faint, the tune something from the Christmas season. Nobody played Christmas music in January. Everybody had OD'd on it by the middle of December. But it grew louder as they went down the hall. "Winter Wonderland."

"The cops and the volunteer firemen put on a show for Snowdaze and give the proceeds to charity," Natalie explained. "Rehearsal goes on till seven."

A roar of male laughter drowned out the music. Natalie tugged open a door marked CONFERENCE 3 and motioned for Megan to precede her. Half a dozen people lounged in chrome-and-plastic chairs that had been set up in two haphazard rows. Another half dozen stood along the paneled walls. All were in various states of hysteria—laughing, slapping thighs, doubled over, tears streaming. At the front of the room a Mutt and Jeff team lumbered through a soft-shoe routine in red longjohns while from the speakers of a boombox a man with an overdone Norwegian accent sang, "Itch a little here. Scratch a little dere. Valkin' in my vinter undervear . . ."

Megan stared openly at the spectacle. The man on the right had a build like the Pillsbury doughboy and wore a red plaid Elmer Fudd cap. The one on the left was a different story altogether. Tall and trim, he had Harrison Ford's looks and an athlete's body. The underwear fit him like a second skin, announcing his gender in no uncertain terms. Megan fought to drag her gaze to less provocative details of his anatomy—his sculpted chest, narrow hips, long legs as muscular as a horseman's. Whoever had meant for the outfit to make him look ridiculous was obviously without hormones.

The headgear was another matter. The Minnesota Vikings stocking cap sported yellow felt horns and long braids made of yellow yarn. The braids bounced as he shuffled and hopped through the steps of the dance. His expression was one of disgruntled indignity, but he was having a hard time maintaining it.

When the routine ended, the performers took exaggerated bows, laughing so hard they couldn't straighten. He had a wonderful laugh, Harrison. Warm, rough, masculine. Not that it affected her, Megan thought, attributing the wave of warmth to being overdressed. She didn't have involuntary physical reactions to men. She didn't allow it. It wasn't smart—especially when the man was a cop.

Harrison straightened, and a wide grin lit up his face; an interesting, lived-in face that was a little bit rough, a little bit lined, not exactly handsome, but utterly compelling. An inchlong scar hooked diagonally across his chin. His nose was substantial, a solid, masculine nose that might have been broken once or twice. His eyes were dark and deep-set, and even though they gleamed with good humor, they looked a hundred years old.

Megan hesitated and Natalie bumped her forward, then stepped past her.

"Have you no pride at all?" she demanded of her boss, tugging hard on one of his yellow braids. She shook her head, and her black eyes sparkled as she fought a smile.

Mitch Holt blew out a big breath. "You're just jealous because I've been asked to model in *Victoria's Secret*." He grinned down at the woman who ran his professional life. *Secretary* was far too lowly a title for Natalie Bryant. He considered her an administrative assistant and had bullied the city council into paying her accordingly, but he thought her nickname suited her best. She was a commandant in pumps.

Natalie made a sound like a horse blowing air through its lips. "*Farmer's Almanac* is more like it. You look like a reject from the rube factory."

"Don't spare my ego," he drawled, giving her a cranky look.

"I never do. You got company. *Agent* O'Malley from the BCA." She swung a hand toward the woman who had come in with her. "*Agent* O'Malley, meet Chief Holt."

Mitch leaned forward to offer his hand, sending a yellow braid swinging. He snatched the stocking cap off his head and tossed it to his dance partner without looking. "Mitch Holt. Sorry you're catching me out of uniform."

"I apologize for being so late," Megan said, stepping forward to shake his hand.

His hand engulfed hers, broad and strong and warm, and she felt a little involuntary jolt of something she would neither name nor acknowledge. She looked up at Mitch Holt, expecting to find something smug in his expression, finding instead confidence and the keen gleam of awareness. The word *dangerous* came to mind, but she dismissed it. She tugged her hand back, trying to break the contact. He held on just a second longer, just long enough to let her know they would do things his way. Or so he thought. Business as usual . . .

"I ran into some unforeseen complications moving in," she said crisply. "I'm ordinarily very punctual."

Mitch nodded. *I'll bet you are, Agent O'Malley.* He kept his gaze steady on hers, searching for a reaction to the physical contact. Her gaze was cool green ice. He could almost feel the shields go up around her.

"It wasn't a problem," he said, absently combing a hand back through his thick tawny hair in an attempt to tame the havoc wreaked by the stocking cap.

"So you're Leo's replacement." He cocked a brow and tried to visualize her without the mega-parka. "Well, God knows you'll be easier to look at."

The remark struck like flint against steel, sparking off Megan's frayed nerves. "I didn't get the job because I look good in panty hose, Chief," she said, cutting him a wry look.

"Neither did Leo, thank Christ. There are some things I can go my whole life without experiencing. Leo Kozlowski in lingerie is right up there on the list. He was a hell of a guy, though, Leo. Knew every good fishing hole for a hundred miles."

Megan had never felt that was one of the more crucial talents a field agent should possess, but she kept her opinion to herself.

Rehearsal had been declared officially over. The participants drifted out the door, Natalie bringing up the rear like a shepherd. A couple of men called good-byes back to Mitch. He raised a hand to acknowledge them, but kept his attention on Agent O'Malley.

He wondered if she realized the tough-cookie act was more intriguing than if she had been skittish. It made him wonder what was behind the shields. A thread to play with just to see how it might unravel. It was his nature to work at puzzles, a compulsion that suited his profession. He let the silence hang, to see how she would react.

She held his gaze and waited him out, her head cocked to one side. Casually she brushed back the wisps of dark hair that had escaped her ponytail. Its color made him think of cherry Coke—nearly black with a hint of red. Exotic in this land of Swedes and Norwegians. Aside from the stubborn set of her chin, she most resembled an escapee from a convent school. Her face had that earnest quality usually reserved for CPAs and novice nuns. A pale oval with skin like fresh cream and eyes as green as the turf in Killarney. Pretty. Young. Mitch suddenly felt about ninety-three.

"Well," Megan started. What she needed was to end this conversation, retreat, regroup, come back tomorrow, when she was feeling stronger and he was dressed in something more than long underwear. "It's late. I can come back tomorrow. We'll have more time. You'll have pants on. . . ."

He grinned the crooked grin. "Are you uncomfortable with this situation, Agent O'Malley?"

Megan scowled at him. Her eyelid ticked, ruining the effect. "I'm not in the habit of doing business with men in their underwear, Chief Holt."

"I'll be happy to take it off," he said, scratching his arm. "It itches. Come on back to my office and I'll climb out of this sausage skin."

He started for the door of the conference room, reaching a hand out as if he meant to sling it around her shoulders. Megan shied sideways. Her temper boiled up, rattling the lid on her control. She was feeling tired and testy, in no mood to deal with yet another come-on or innuendo.

"I am an agent of the Bureau of Criminal Apprehension, Chief," she said, fighting to hang on to her last scrap of humor. "I served two years on the St. Paul police force, seven years on the Minneapolis force—five of them as a detective. I've been a narc. I've worked vice. I have a degree in law enforcement and have passed the agent's course at Quantico. I really don't think the taxpayers would be getting their money's worth if I came here in the capacity of sex toy."

"Sex toy?" Mitch leaned back, brows raised, caught somewhere between amusement and insult. "Perhaps I should rephrase my suggestion," he said. "You may wait in Natalie's office while I change into my clothes. Then I will be glad to escort you—in a strictly businesslike fashion—to one of the finer dining establishments in our fair town, where we might partake of a meal." He held his hands up to ward off potential protest. "Feel free to pay for your own, Agent O'Malley. Far be it from me to threaten your feminist sensibilities. You can accept or decline this offer. I make no attempt at coercion, but, if you'll pardon my candor, you look like you could use a little meat loaf.

"For the record, I have no problem with an agent who happens to be a woman. I'm a reasonably enlightened nineties kind of guy. So you can take the chip off your shoulder and put it in your briefcase, Agent O'Malley. Believe me, there will be plenty of guys in line to knock it off, but I won't be one of them."

Megan felt herself shrinking with each sentence. She

wished fervently for a break from the laws of physics so she could melt down into the tight fibers of the carpet and disappear.

"Way to go, O'Malley," she muttered to herself. Her eyelid ticked furiously. She reached up to rub it, took a deep breath, and swallowed what pride she had left. "I'm sorry. I don't usually jump to insulting conclusions. I don't know what to say other than this hasn't been one of my better days."

Two years in St. Paul, seven in Minneapolis. A detective, a narc. Impressive record, especially for a woman. Mitch knew what a fight it was for a woman to make it in this business. The odds stood against women, shoulder to brawny shoulder, in the form of a fraternity as old as dirt. Equal opportunity quotas notwithstanding, Ms. O'Malley had to be tough and she had to be good. It looked as though the effort was costing her today.

Her efforts would cost him, too, he thought irritably. He ran a department and a life that were equally well ordered and calm. He sure as hell didn't need some woman charging in, waving her bra like a banner, spoiling for trouble where there was none to be had.

"If I need a sex toy, I'll consult a mail-order catalogue," he said darkly. "Don't rock my boat, Agent O'Malley. I don't like troublemakers—whether they look good in panty hose or not."

He drew in a breath as he stepped back from her and wrinkled his nose as he caught an odd scent. "Interesting perfume you're wearing. Cheddar?"

Her cheeks bloomed pink. "I spent half the afternoon in the cheese factory, tracking down my apartment keys."

"You *have* had a rough day. I prescribe meat loaf," he declared. "Maybe a glass of wine. Definitely a piece of carrot cake . . . God, I'm starving," he muttered, rubbing a hand over his flat belly as he headed for the door.

Megan followed hesitantly, trying to decide if dinner with him would be a chance to start fresh or a continuing exercise in conversational combat. She wasn't sure she had the steam left for either, but she wouldn't let Mitch Holt see that. Despite his professions of enlightenment, she knew he would be both colleague and adversary. She had learned long ago to show no weaknesses to either.

CHAPTER 3

He didn't look bad with his clothes on, either. Just a casual observation, Megan told herself as Mitch hung their coats in the cloakroom at Grandma's Attic. He had dressed in dark pleated trousers, an ivory broadcloth shirt, and dark tie with a small print she couldn't make out. He'd combed his hair—or tried to. Tawny brown and thick, it stubbornly defied the stylish cut that was short on the sides and longer on top. He parted it on the left and had a habit of brushing it back with his fingers. Not a vain gesture, but an absent one, as if he were used to having it fall in his eyes.

Megan had made her own repairs, slipping into the ladies' room at the station. The hair got a quick brushing back into its simple ponytail. The lips got a slicking with gloss. She tried to rub the mascara smudges out from under her eyes, but discovered to her dismay the marks were natural, the telltale signs of fatigue. Her face was chalk white, but there was nothing to be done about it. She didn't wear much makeup as a rule and carried nothing with her.

No matter, she told herself as she glanced around the restaurant. This wasn't a date, it was a business dinner. She wasn't out to impress Mitch Holt as a woman, but as a cop.

The restaurant was crowded and noisy, the air thick with conversation and the warm, spicy smell of home cooking. Waitresses in ruffled muslin aprons and high-necked blouses with puffed sleeves wound through the array of mismatched wooden tables with heavy stoneware plates and trays laden with the special of the day. Grandma's was housed in a section of a renovated woolen mill. Its walls were time-worn brick, the floors scarred wood, and the ceiling beams exposed. A row of tall, arched windows had been installed on the street side of the main dining room. Lush ferns in brass pots hung from an old pipe that ran from wall to wall parallel to the windows.

Household antiques decorated every available spot—copper kettles, graniteware coffeepots, china teapots, kitchen utensils, butter churns and wooden butter molds, salt boxes and blue Mason jars. Steamer trunks were strategically located around the dining room to be used by the waitresses as serving tables. In addition to the more mundane items, there was a marvelous collection of ladies' hats that dated back a century. Broad-brimmed hats wound and draped with yards of sheer fabric. Pillbox hats and hats trimmed with ostrich plumes. Driving hats and riding hats and hats with black lace veils.

Megan took it all in with a sense of delight. She loved old things. She enjoyed hunting through flea markets for items that might have been heirlooms, things passed down from one generation of women to another. There were no such things in her family. She had nothing of her mother's. Her father had burned all of Maureen O'Malley's things a month after she had abandoned the family when Megan was six.

The hostess greeted Mitch by name, eyed Megan with interest, and led them back to a booth in a raised section of dining room where things appeared less hectic and the noise level was cut by the high walls of the booths.

"It's the usual madness," she said, smiling warmly at Mitch. She looked mid-forties and attractive, her pale blond hair cut in a pageboy she tucked behind her ears. "And then some, with everybody gearing up for Snowdaze. Denise said she might come for the weekend."

Mitch accepted a menu. "How's she doing at design school?"

"She loves it. She said to tell you thanks again for encouraging her to go back—and to look her up sometime when you're in the Cities. She's dating an architect, but it isn't serious," she hastened to add, her gaze darting Megan's way with a gleam of sly speculation.

"Nnnn," Mitch said through his teeth. "Darlene, this is Megan O'Malley, our new agent from the BCA. She's taking over Leo Kozlowski's job. It's her first night in town, and I thought I'd introduce her to Grandma's. Megan, Darlene Hallstrom."

"Oo-oh!" Darlene cooed, the exclamation spanning an octave as she gave Megan a plastic smile and a once-over that scanned for signs of matrimony. "How nice to have someone new in town. Is your husband working in Deer Lake as well?"

"I'm not married."

"We-ell, isn't that interesting." She ground the words through the smile as she thrust a menu out. "We all sure liked Leo. Have a nice dinner."

Mitch heaved a sigh as Darlene swept away, skirt twitching.

"Who's Denise?" Megan asked.

"Darlene's sister. Her *divorced* sister. Darlene had ideas."

"Really? What did your wife have to say about that?"

"My—?"

Her gaze pointed a straight line to the hands that held the menu. The gold band on his left ring finger gleamed in the soft light. He wore it for a variety of reasons—because it helped to ward off prowling females, because it was habitual, because every time he looked at it he still felt the sting of grief and guilt. He made the excuse that he was a cop and cops were perverse by nature and Catholic in their guilt if not in any other way.

"My wife is dead," he said, his voice a hard, cold whisper, the emotional shields coming up around him like iron bars. Nearly two years had passed and the words still tasted like the glue of postage stamps, bitter and acrid. He hadn't gotten any better at saying them. He fielded sympathy as awkwardly as a shortstop with a catcher's mitt.

"I don't talk about it," he said flatly, mentally drawing a line in the sand and chasing her back to her side.

His pride and sense of privacy shunned the sympathy of virtual strangers. And simmering beneath that boar's nest, feeding on it, was the anger, his constant companion. He contained it, controlled it, ruthlessly. Control was the key. Control was his strength, his salvation.

"Oh, God, I'm sorry," Megan murmured. She could feel his tension across the table. His shoulders were rigid with it, his jaw set at an angle no sane person would challenge. She felt as if she had trespassed on sacred ground.

She propped her elbows on the table and rubbed her hands over her face. "You're batting a thousand, O'Malley. If there's a pile of shit to be found today, you'll step in it with both feet."

"I hope you're not referring to the cheese factory," Mitch said dryly. He forced a wry smile. "I'd hate to have to send the health inspector down there again."

Megan peeked out at him from between her fingers. "Again?"

"Yeah, well, last year there was a minor incident involving a mouse tail and a brick of Monterey Jack . . ."

"Gross!"

"Les Metzler assures me that was a one-time thing, but I don't know. Personally, I make it a policy not to buy cheese from a place where the gift shop also features taxidermy."

"They don't," she challenged.

"They do. I can't believe you didn't see the sign when you were out at the factory. *Metzler's BuckLand Fine Cheese and Taxidermy.* Les's brother Rollie does the taxidermy. He got hit in the head with a rolling pin as a child and became obsessed with roadkill. He's not quite right," he said in an exaggerated whisper, twirling a forefinger beside his temple. Leaning across the table, he glanced around for eavesdroppers and whispered, "I buy my cheese in Minneapolis."

Their gazes locked and Megan felt something she didn't want or need to feel. She jerked her eyes down and studied the pattern in his necktie—a hundred tiny renditions of Mickey Mouse.

"Great tie."

He glanced down as if he'd forgotten what he was wearing. All the cynicism melted out of his smile. The rough edges of his face softened as he ran the strip of burgundy silk between his fingers. "My daughter picked it out. Her tastes run a little off the *GQ* scale, but then, she's only five."

Megan had to bite her lip to keep from sighing. He was the chief of police, a big tough macho guy whose main fashion accessory was probably a nine-millimeter Smith & Wesson, and he let his little girl pick out his neckties. Sweet.

"A lot of cops I know don't have the fashion sense of a five-year-old," she said. "My last partner dressed like a bad parody of a used car salesman. He had more plaid polyester pants than Arnold Palmer."

Mitch chuckled. "You didn't list fashion police in your oral résumé."

"I didn't want to overwhelm you."

They both ordered the meat loaf. Megan declined the suggestion of a glass of wine, knowing it would aggravate her headache. Mitch asked for a bottle of Moosehead beer and made a point of noticing the waitress—a blond girl of eighteen or nineteen—had had her braces removed. The girl smiled shyly for him and went away blushing.

"You seem to know everyone here," Megan said. "Is this one of those hometown boy-makes-good stories?"

Mitch pulled apart a dinner roll, steam billowed up from the center of it. "Me? No, I'm a transplant. I put in fifteen years on the force in Miami."

"No way!" She gripped the edge of the table as if the shock had knocked her loopy. "You moved *here* from *Miami*? You gave up *Florida* to live in this godforsaken tundra?"

Mitch arched a brow. "Am I to assume you don't like our fair state?"

"I like summer—all three weeks of it," she said, her voice crackling with sarcasm. "Fall is pretty, provided it isn't prematurely buried under ten feet of snow. That's as far as my love goes, despite the fact that I'm a native. In my opinion, life is too damn short to have half of it be winter."

"Then why do you stay? With your qualifications, you could probably have your pick of jobs in a warmer climate."

He recognized the defenses the instant they switched on. They were a mirror image of his own—built to protect, to deflect, to keep outsiders from moving in.

"Family complications" was all she said, turning her attention to a dinner roll. She picked a chunk out of it and played with the bread between her fingers. Mitch didn't probe, but he wondered. What family? What kind of complications would make her duck his gaze? Another loose thread for him to worry at. Another puzzle piece to define and fit.

She tossed the conversational ball back in his court. "So what'd you do in Miami?"

"Homicide. Did a stint on the gang task force. My last two

years were on the major case squad. Tourist murders, socialite drug busts—high-profile stuff."

"Isn't life around here a little slow for you?"

"I've had enough excitement to last me."

Another answer with a past, Megan thought, glancing at him through her lashes as he took a long pull on his beer. Another reason to steer clear of him in all ways but the professional. She didn't need anyone else's emotional baggage. She had enough of her own to fill a set of Samsonite luggage. Still, the curiosity itched and tickled, the need to solve riddles and uncover secrets. She attributed the need to her cop instincts and denied that it had anything to do with the guarded shadows in his eyes or with some convoluted desire to comfort a man in pain. If she had a brain in her head, she wouldn't think of Mitch Holt as a man.

Fat chance, O'Malley, she thought as he took another swallow of Moosehead, his eyes narrowed, firm lips glistening with moisture as he set the bottle down. In the subdued light of the booth, his five o'clock shadow seemed darker against the lean planes of his cheeks, the scar on his chin looked silver and wicked.

"So how did you end up in the frozen North?" She ripped another chunk from her roll.

Mitch shrugged, as if it had been a random thing of little consequence, when that was about as far from the truth as any lie. "The job was open. My in-laws live here. It was a chance for my daughter to spend time with her grandparents."

Their salads arrived, along with a member of the Moose Lodge, who wanted to remind Mitch that he was to speak at their Friday luncheon. Mitch introduced Megan. The Moose man looked at her and chuckled as if to say "great joke, Mitch." He shook the hand Megan offered him, giving her a patronizing smile.

"You're Leo's replacement? Well, aren't you cute!"

Megan bit down on a caustic reply, reminding herself she had asked for this assignment.

Mr. Moose departed and was quickly replaced by one of the organizers of the Snowdaze torchlight parade, who went over details regarding the barricading of the streets involved. The introduction ritual was a near replay of the one before it.

"She's Leo's replacement? Easier on the eyes than ol' Leo, eh?"

Megan gritted her teeth. Mitch diplomatically refrained from comment. The meat loaf arrived and parade man took his leave, winking at Megan as he went.

She stared down at her plate. "If one more person calls me cute, I'm going to bite them. Is it 1994 or have I fallen through a time warp?"

Mitch chuckled. "Both. This is small-town Minnesota, Agent O'Malley. You ain't in the big city anymore."

"I realize that, but this is a college town. I expected attitudes to be more progressive."

"Oh, they are," he said, dumping pepper on a mountain of scalloped potatoes. "We no longer require women to hide their faces or walk three steps behind men."

"Very funny." Megan cut into her meat loaf and thought the aroma of herbs and spices might just induce her to fall face-first on her plate and inhale everything on it.

"Seriously, Deer Lake is very progressive as small towns go. But the men you're likely to meet in the line of duty are going to be from the old school. There are still plenty of guys around who believe the little woman should stay home darning holey socks while they're off whooping it up at the NRA meeting. You can't tell me you haven't run up against your share in the departments you've worked."

"Sure I did, but in the city the threat of lawsuits means something," Megan replied. "You seem to have made the adjustment to small-town life without any trouble. What's your secret? Besides having a penis, I mean."

"Gee, honey, I'm flattered you noticed," Mitch drawled.

Poor choice of words there, O'Malley. "It was kind of hard to miss, considering what you were wearing when we met."

"I feel so cheap."

She made the mistake of giving him a look, and her gaze locked onto his again like iron drawn to a magnet. God, of all the rotten luck. Attraction. A rare phenomenon in the life of Megan O'Malley. Naturally, it would strike when she least expected it, least needed it. Naturally, it would be sparked by a man she couldn't touch. Old Murphy and his laws of irony had nothing on her.

Mitch Holt felt it, too. Chemistry. His gaze drifted to her mouth. The moment stretched into two.

"I thought you said you weren't one of them," she murmured, mustering all defenses.

"One of who?"

"The gun-toting, flag-waving, Neanderthal rednecks who consider anything in a bra to be fair game for their I'm-God's-gift-to-women brand of charm."

Mitch sat back and sighed, forcing the tension out of his shoulders. He could have argued, but there didn't seem to be any point in it at the moment.

"You're right," he admitted grudgingly. "I let my testosterone run away with me there for a minute. Temporary hormone psychosis. Really, I'm enlightened enough to pretend I'm not attracted to you, if that's what you want."

"Good. That's what I want." Megan turned back to her meat loaf and discovered her appetite had gone south. "Because that's my number one rule: I don't date cops."

"A wise policy."

A matter of survival was what it was, but Megan kept that information to herself. She couldn't afford to be vulnerable in any way. Not in police work. The ranks were too heavily dominated by men who didn't want her there. Her gender was a strike against her. Her size was a strike against her. If she let her sexuality be used as a strike against her, she'd be out. That would be the end of her career, and her career was all she had.

"Yeah." Mitch recovered his sense of humor as the madness receded. "There's a certain wisdom in not letting the people you work with see you naked."

"The underwear was close enough," Megan said dryly.

"But now you've got me at a disadvantage," Mitch pointed out. "You've seen me in my underwear. It would be only fair for you to return the favor. Then we'd be even."

"Forget it, Chief. I'll take all the advantages I can get."

"Hmmm . . ."

Across the room he caught sight of one of his patrol officers winding his way awkwardly through the maze of tables, struggling to keep from conking some unsuspecting diner in the back of the head with the revolver strapped to his hip. He clomped up the steps, his eyes on Mitch.

"Hey, Chief, sorry to interrupt your dinner." Lonnie Dietz pulled a stray chair up to the end of the booth and straddled it. "I thought you'd want to hear the update on that accident out on Old Cedar Road."

"I'm Leo's replacement," Megan said, offering her hand.

Dietz ignored the hand. His eyebrows disappeared beneath the black Moe Howard wig that crawled down over his forehead. He looked fifty and intolerant, lean everywhere but his beer belly. "I thought all the field agents were men."

"They were," she said sweetly. "Until me."

"So what's the latest?" Mitch asked, forking up a mouthful of potatoes.

Dietz tore his gaze away from Megan and flipped through a notebook he pulled from his shirt pocket. "Two fatalities. Ethel Koontz was DOA at Hennepin County Medical Center—massive trauma to the head and chest. Ida Bergen passed away at Deer Lake Community—heart attack on her way in for treatment of minor injuries. Mrs. Marvel Steffen is critical but stable—she's at HCMC too. Clara Weghorn was treated and released. Mike Chamberlain—the kid who lost control—he's banged up but he's going to be okay. Pat Stevens took his statement and I've been over the scene."

"And?"

"And it's like the kid said. The road was bare until just after that curve by Jeff Lexvold's place. There's a patch of glare ice about ten feet long, goes across both lanes of the road. This is where it gets odd," Dietz confided, looking troubled. "I figure there's no reason for ice there, right? The weather's been good. God knows it hasn't been warm enough for anything to melt and run down the hill from Lexvold's. So I go have a look. You know Jeff and Millicent are gone to Corpus Christi for the winter, like always, so there's no one home. But it looks to me like someone snaked a garden hose down the driveway from the faucet on the front side of their house by the garage there."

Mitch set his fork down and stared hard at his patrolman. "That's crazy. You're saying someone ran water across the road and made that ice slick on purpose?"

"Looks like. Kids playing around, I suppose."

"They got two people killed."

"Could have been worse," Dietz pointed out. "There's some kind of music recital going on at the college tonight. Seems like more people use that back way onto the campus than the front. We could have had a real pileup."

"Have you questioned the neighbors?" Megan asked.

Dietz looked at her as if she were an eavesdropper butting in from the next booth. "There aren't any close by. Besides, Lexvolds, they've got all them overgrown spruce trees along the front of their place. You'd have to be right there to see anyone screwing around."

"Well, Jesus," Mitch muttered in disgust. "I'll have Natalie write up an appeal for the media tomorrow, asking for anyone with information to call in."

Megan trespassed a second time into the conversation. "Was there any sign of a break-in?"

Dietz looked at her sideways, scowling. "No. Everything was locked up tight." He turned back to his chief as he rose from his chair. "We got a DOT crew out to scrape and sand the slick spot. Hauled the cars in—one to Mike Finke's and one to Patterson's. That's it."

"Good. Thanks, Lonnie." Mitch watched the officer weave his way back through the tables, what little he'd eaten of his supper sitting like gravel in his stomach. "What the hell do kids think about, pulling shit like that?"

Megan considered the question rhetorical. The wheels of her brain turning, she stared at the Mickey Mouse figures on Mitch's tie until they started to swim in front of her eyes.

Mitch's gaze drifted to the restaurant entrance, where people were still coming in from the wide hall of the old warehouse-turned-mini-mall. Half a dozen people from the Snowdaze pageant committee were waiting to be seated. Here for after-practice pie and coffee. Hannah Garrison came in and pushed her way past them. Strange.

She looked harried. Her coat was open and hanging back off one shoulder. Her blond hair was a mess, curling ropes of it falling across her face as her eyes scanned the dining room with a wild look. She waded through the sea of chairs and faces, bumping into people, nearly colliding with Darlene Hallstrom. The hostess reached out to steady her, smiling, bemused. Hannah shoved her away and lunged ahead to the table where John Olsen and his girlfriend were lingering over coffee. Damn strange.

Mitch kept his eyes on her like a bird dog on point, pulling his napkin off his lap. He crumpled the heavy green cloth and dropped it blindly on the table.

"So where's the hose?" Megan muttered. She looked up as Mitch started to rise.

"Excuse me," he mumbled, sliding out of the booth.

He couldn't hear the conversation going on at John Olsen's table. The din in the restaurant drowned out individual words. But he could see the expression on Hannah's face, the wild gestures of her long, graceful hands. He could see John's look of shocked surprise, watched him shake his head. Mitch descended the steps and strode toward the table. A fist of instinctive tension curled in his gut.

Hannah was one of the first people he had met when he and Jessie had moved to Deer Lake. Hannah and her husband, Paul Kirkwood, and their son had lived across the street then. Hannah, pregnant with her second child, had dropped by that first day on her way to work to welcome them to the neighborhood with a pan of brownies. She was one of the most capable, unflappable people he knew. Grace under fire personified. She ran the emergency room at Deer Lake Community Hospital with skill, volunteered for community causes, and still managed a house with a husband, son, and baby daughter. All with a dazzling smile and sweet good humor.

But Hannah didn't look cool or unruffled now. She looked on the brink of hysteria.

"What do you mean, you don't know?" she demanded, her voice loud and raw. She slammed a fist down on the table. John's girlfriend squealed and jumped up out of her chair as coffee sloshed out of her cup and splashed across the tabletop.

"Dr. Garrison, calm down!" John Olsen pleaded, coming up out of his chair. He reached out for Hannah's arm. She jerked away from him, her eyes blazing.

"Calm down!" she shrieked. "I won't calm down!"

Everyone in the restaurant had stopped to watch. The air was electric with tension.

"Hannah?" Mitch said, approaching her side. "Is something wrong?"

Hannah wheeled at the sound of his voice. The floor seemed to tilt beneath her feet. Heat pressed in on her like an invisible blanket, burning her skin, choking her. *Is something wrong?* Everything was wrong. She could feel a hundred pair of eyes on her. She could feel the darkness creeping down from the rafters and in through the high, arched windows.

She was caught in a nightmare. Wide awake. Like being buried alive. The thoughts and impressions zoomed across her brain, too many, too fast. *Oh, God. Oh, God. Oh, God!*

"Hannah?" Mitch murmured, gently sliding his fingers over her shoulder. He eased a little closer. "Honey, talk to me. What's wrong?"

Hannah stared at him, at the concern in his eyes. He moved closer. *What's wrong?* Something inside her burst and the words came rushing out, screaming out.

"I can't find my son!"

CHAPTER 4

What do you mean, you can't find Josh?" Mitch asked calmly.

Hannah sat in the manager's chair, shaking uncontrollably, tears leaking from her big blue eyes. Mitch dug a clean handkerchief out of his hip pocket and offered it to her. She took it automatically but made no effort to use it, crumpling it in her hand like a wad of paper.

"I m-mean I c-can't find him," she stammered. She couldn't find Josh and no one seemed to grasp what she was trying to tell them, as if the words coming out of her mouth were nonsense. "Y-you have to help m-me. *Please*, Mitch!"

She started to come up out of the chair, but Mitch pressed her back down. "I'll do everything I can, Hannah, but you have to calm down—"

"Calm down!" she shouted, gripping the arms of the chair. "I can't believe this!"

"Hannah—"

"My God, you've got a daughter, you should understand! You of all people—"

"Hannah!" he barked sharply. She flinched and blinked at him. "You know I'll help, but you have to calm down and start at the beginning."

Megan watched the scene from her position by the door. The office was a claustrophobic cube of dark, cheap paneling. Certificates from the chamber of commerce and various civic groups decorated the walls in plastic frames that hung at slightly drunken angles. Nothing about the filing cabinets or battered old metal desk suggested the success or the quaint charm of the restaurant. The woman—Hannah—slumped down in the chair, squeezing her eyes shut, pressing a hand over her mouth as she fought to compose herself.

Even in her current state—crying, hair disheveled—she was a strikingly attractive woman. Tall, slim, with features that belonged on the pages of a magazine. Mitch positioned himself directly in front of her, back against the desk, but leaning forward, his concentration completely on Hannah, waiting, patient, intent. Without saying anything, he reached out and offered her his hand. She took it and squeezed hard, like someone in extreme pain.

Megan watched him with admiration and a little envy. Dealing with victims had never been her strong suit. For her, reaching out to someone in pain meant taking on some of that pain herself. She had always found it smarter, safer, to keep some emotional distance. Objectivity, she called it. Mitch Holt, however, didn't hesitate to reach out.

"I was supposed to pick him up from hockey practice," Hannah began in little more than a whisper, as if she were about to confess a terrible sin. "I was leaving the hospital, but then we had an emergency come in and I couldn't get away on time. I had someone call the rink to tell him I'd be a little late. Then one of the patients went into cardiac arrest and—"

And I lost the patient and now I've lost my son. The sense of failure and guilt pressed down on her, and she had to stop and wait until it seemed bearable again. She tightened her hold on Mitch's big, warm hand. The sensation only built and intensified until it pushed the dreaded words from her mouth.

"I forgot. I forgot he was waiting."

A fresh wave of tears washed down her cheeks and fell like raindrops onto the lap of her long wool skirt. She doubled over, wanting to curl into a ball while the emotions tore at her. Mitch leaned closer and stroked her hair, trying to offer some comfort. The cop in him remained calm, waiting for facts, reciting the likely explanations. Deeper inside, the parent in him experienced a sharp stab of instinctive fear.

"When I g-got to the rink he w-was g-gone."

"Well, honey, Paul probably picked him up—"

"No. Wednesday is *my* night."

"Did you call Paul to check?"

"I tried, but he wasn't in the office."

"Then Josh probably got a ride with one of the other kids. He's probably at some buddy's house—"

"No. I called everyone I could think of. I checked at the sitter's—Sue Bartz. I thought maybe he would be there waiting for me to come pick up Lily, but Sue hadn't seen him." And Lily was still there waiting for her mother, probably wondering why Mama had come and gone without her. "I checked at home, just in case he decided to walk. I called the other hockey moms. I drove back to the rink. I drove back to the hospital. *I can't find him.*"

"Do you have a picture of your son?" Megan asked.

"His school picture. It's not the best—he needed a haircut, but there wasn't time." Hannah pulled her purse up onto her lap. Her hands shook as she dug through the leather bag for her wallet. "He brought the slip home from school and I made a note, but then time just got away from me and I—forgot."

She whispered the last word as she opened to the photograph of Josh. *I forgot.* Such a simple, harmless excuse. Forgot about his picture. Forgot about his haircut. Forgot him. Her hand trembled so badly, she could barely manage to slip the photograph from the plastic window. She offered it to the dark-haired woman, realizing belatedly that she had no idea who she was.

"I'm sorry," she murmured, dredging up ingrained manners and a fragile smile. "Have we met?"

Mitch sat back against the edge of the desk again. "This is Agent O'Malley with the Bureau of Criminal Apprehension. Megan, this is Dr. Hannah Garrison, head of the emergency room in our community hospital. One of the best doctors ever to wield a stethoscope," he added with a ghost of his grin. "We're very lucky to have her."

Megan studied the photograph, her mind on business, not social niceties. A boy of eight or nine dressed in a Cub Scout uniform stared out at her with a big gap-toothed grin. He had a smattering of freckles across his nose and cheeks. His hair was an unruly mop of sandy brown curls. His blue eyes were brimming with life and mischief.

"Is he normally a pretty responsible boy?" she asked.

"Does he know to call you if he's going to be late or to get permission to go to a friend's house?"

Hannah nodded. "Josh is very levelheaded."

"What did he wear to school today?"

Hannah rubbed a hand across her forehead, struggling to think back to morning. It seemed as much a dream as the last few hours, long ago and foggy. Lily crying at the indignity of being confined to her high chair. Josh skating around the kitchen floor in his stocking feet. Permission slip needed signing for a field trip to the Science Museum. Homework done? Spelling words memorized? A call from the hospital. French toast burning on the stove. Paul storming around the kitchen, snapping at Josh, complaining about the shirts that needed ironing.

"Um—jeans. A blue sweater. Snow boots. A ski jacket—bright blue with bright yellow and bright green trim. Um . . . his Vikings stocking cap—it's yellow with a patch sewn on. Paul wouldn't let him wear a purple one with that wild coat. He said it would look like Josh was dressed by color-blind Gypsies. I couldn't see the harm; he's only eight years old. . . ."

Megan handed the photograph back and looked up at Mitch. "I'll call it in right away." Her mind was already on the possibilities and the steps they should take in accordance with those possibilities. "Get the bulletin to your people, the sheriff's department, the highway patrol—"

Hannah looked stricken. "You don't think—"

"No," Mitch interceded smoothly. "No, honey, of course not. It's just standard procedure. We'll put out a bulletin to all the guys on patrol, so if they see Josh they'll know to pick him up and bring him home.

"Excuse us for just a minute," he said, holding up a finger. He turned his back to Hannah and gave Megan a furious look. "I need to give Agent O'Malley a few instructions."

He clamped a hand on her shoulder and herded her unceremoniously out the door and into the narrow, dimly lit hall. A round-headed man in a tweed blazer and chinos gave them a dirty look and stuck a finger in his free ear as he tried to have a conversation on a pay phone outside the men's room door. Mitch hit the phone's plunger with two fingers, cutting off the conversation and drawing an indignant "Hey!" from the caller.

"Excuse us," Mitch growled, flashing his badge. "Police business."

He shouldered the man away from the phone and sent him hustling down the hall with a scowl that had scattered petty drug pushers and hookers from the meanest streets in Miami. Then he turned the same scowl on Megan.

"What the hell is wrong with you?" she snapped, jumping on the offensive, knowing it was her best defense.

"What the hell is wrong with me?" Mitch barked, keeping his voice low. "What the hell is wrong with you—scaring the poor woman—"

"She has reason to be scared, Chief. Her son is missing."

"That has yet to be established. He's probably playing at a friend's house."

"She says she checked with his friends."

"Yes, but she's panicked. She's probably forgotten to look in an obvious place."

"Or somebody grabbed the kid."

Mitch scowled harder because it took an effort to dismiss her suggestion. "This is Deer Lake, O'Malley, not New York."

Megan arched a brow. "You don't have crime in Deer Lake? You have a police force. You have a jail. Or is that all just window dressing?"

"Of course we have crime," he snarled. "We have college students who shoplift and cheese factory workers who get drunk on Saturday night and try to beat each other up in the American Legion parking lot. We don't have child abductions, for Christ's sake."

"Yeah, well, welcome to the nineties, Chief," she said sarcastically. "It can happen anywhere."

Mitch took a half step back and jammed his hands at his waist. The president of the Sons of Norway lodge went into the men's room, smiling and nodding to Mitch. A cloud of chokingly sweet air freshener escaped the room as the door swung shut. Mitch blocked it out just as he tried to block out what Megan was telling him.

"The people in St. Joseph didn't think it could happen there, either," Megan said quietly. "And while they were all standing around consoling themselves with that lie, someone made off with Jacob Wetterling."

The Wetterling case in St. Joseph had happened before Mitch had moved to Minnesota, but it was still in the hearts and minds of people. A child had been stolen from among them and never returned. That kind of crime was so rare in the area that it affected people as if someone from their own family had been taken. Deer Lake was nearly two hundred miles away from St. Joseph, but Mitch knew several men on his force and in the sheriff's department had worked on the case as volunteers. They spoke of it sparingly, in careful, hushed tones, as if they feared bringing it up might call back whatever demon had committed the crime.

Swearing under her breath, Megan grabbed the telephone receiver. "We're wasting time."

"I'll do it." Mitch reached over her shoulder and snatched the phone from her.

"A little rusty on our telephone etiquette, aren't we?" she said dryly.

"Our dispatcher doesn't know you" was all the apology he offered.

"Doug? Mitch Holt. Listen, I need a bulletin out on Paul Kirkwood's boy, Josh. Yeah. Hannah went to pick him up from hockey and he'd gone off somewhere. He's probably in somebody's basement playing Nintendo, but you know how it is. Hannah's worried. Yeah, that's what women do best."

Megan narrowed her eyes and tipped her head. Mitch ignored her.

"Let the county boys know, too, just in case they spot him. He's eight, a little small for his age. Blue eyes, curly brown hair. Last seen wearing a bright blue ski jacket with green and yellow trim and a bright yellow stocking cap with a Vikings patch on it. And send a unit over to the hockey rink. Tell them I'll meet them there."

He hung up the phone as the Sons of Norway leader emerged from the men's room and sidled past them, murmuring an absent greeting, his curious gaze sliding to Megan. Mitch grunted what he hoped would pass for an acknowledgment. He could feel Megan's steady gaze, heavy, expectant, disapproving. She was new to this job, ambitious, eager to prove herself. She would have called out the cavalry, but the cavalry wasn't warranted yet.

The first priority in a missing persons case was to make certain the person was actually missing. That was why the rule with adults was not to consider them missing until they had been gone twenty-four hours. That rule no longer applied to children, but even so, there were options to consider before jumping to the worst conclusion. Even levelheaded kids did stupid things once in a while. Josh might have gone home with a friend and lost track of time, or he might have been intentionally punishing his mother for forgetting him. There were any number of explanations more probable than kidnapping.

Then why did he have this knot in his gut?

He dug another quarter out of his pants pocket. He dialed the Strausses' number from memory and murmured a prayer of thanks when his daughter answered on the third ring with an exuberant "Hi! This is Jessie!"

"Hi, sweetheart, it's Daddy," he said softly, ducking his head to elude Megan's curiosity.

"Are you coming to get me? I want you to read me some more of that book when it's bedtime."

"I'm sorry, I can't, sweetie," he murmured. "I've got to be a cop for a while longer tonight. You'll have to stay with Grandma and Grandpa."

There was a heavy silence on the other end of the line. Mitch could clearly picture his little daughter making her mad face, an expression she had inherited from her mother and perfected by imitating her grandmother. An eloquent look, it could provoke feelings of guilt in the blink of a big brown eye. "I don't like it when you're a cop," she said.

He wondered if she had any clue how badly it hurt him when she said that. The words were a knife slipped into an old wound that wouldn't heal. "I know you don't, Jess, but I have to go try to find somebody who's lost. Wouldn't you want me to come find you if you were lost?"

"Yeah," she admitted grudgingly. "But you're *my* daddy."

"I'll be home tomorrow night, honey, and we'll read extra pages. I promise."

"You better, 'cause Grandma said she could read with me about Babar, too."

Mitch clenched his jaw. "I promise. Give me a kiss good night, then let me talk to Grandpa."

Jessie made a loud smacking sound over the phone, which Mitch repeated, turning his back to Megan so she couldn't see the color that warmed his cheeks. Then Jessie turned the phone over to her grandfather and Mitch went through the ritual explanation that wasn't an explanation—police business, hung up on a case, nothing major but it might drag on. If he told his in-laws he had to see about a possible kidnapping, Joy Strauss would burn up the phone lines whipping the town into a frenzy.

Jurgen didn't press for details. A born-and-bred Minnesotan, he considered it rude to ask for more information than the caller was willing to give. Aside from that, the routine wasn't unfamiliar to him. Mitch's job dictated a late night from time to time. The standing arrangement was for Jessie to remain with her grandparents, who looked after her every day after school. The routine was convenient and provided stability for Jessie. Mitch might not have been enamored of his mother-in-law, but he trusted her to take good care of her only grandchild.

He hated to miss seeing Jessie, to miss tucking her in and reading to her until her eyes drifted shut. His daughter was the absolute center of his universe. For a second he tried to imagine what it would feel like if he couldn't find her, then he thought of Josh and Hannah.

"He'll turn up in no time," he murmured to himself as he hung up the receiver. The knot in his gut tightened.

Megan's temper dropped from a boil to a simmer. For a second there Mitch Holt had seemed vulnerable, not tough, not intimidating. For a second he was a single father who sent his little girl kisses over the phone. The word *dangerous* floated through her head again and took on new connotations.

Kicking the thought aside, she gave him a no-nonsense look. "I hope you're right, Chief," she said. "For everyone's sake."

CHAPTER 5

The last of the senior league hockey players were limping and shuffling their way out of the Gordie Knutson Memorial Arena when Mitch pulled his Explorer into the drive. Fifty or older, the senior leaguers still displayed an amazing amount of grace on the ice, as if they somehow shed the cumbersome stiffness of age in the locker room as they laced on the magic skates. They skated and passed and checked and laughed and swore. But when the game was over, the skates came off and the realities of age settled in with a vengeance. They inched their way down the steps, faces contorted in grimaces of varying degrees.

Noogie watched them with a grin as he stood leaning against his patrol car parked in the fire lane in front of the building. He gave them a thumbs-up, then laughed when Al Jackson told him to go to hell.

"Why do you keep playing when it does this to you, Al?"

"What kind of stupid question is that?" Jackson shot back. "Oh, yeah, I forget—you used to play football; too many knocks in the head."

"At least we had sense enough to wear helmets," Noogie goaded.

"You mean there's no excuse for that face?"

Noga growled and waved them past.

"What's going on, Noogie?" Bill Lennox asked, hiking up the strap on his duffel bag. "Caught Olie speeding on the Zamboni machine?"

They all laughed, but their gazes slid past Noogie to Mitch and Megan as they came up the sidewalk.

"Evening, Mitch," Jackson called, raising the end of his hockey stick in salute. "Crime wave at the ice rink?"

"Yeah. We've had another complaint that your slap shot is criminal."

The group roared. Mitch kept an eye on them until they were well out of earshot, then turned to his officer.

"Officer Noga, this is Agent O'Malley—"

"We've met," Megan said impatiently, tapping a foot against the snowpack on the sidewalk for the dual purpose of releasing energy and trying to keep the feeling in her toes.

Her gaze scanned the area. The ice rink was at the end of a street, set well back from the residences. Located at the southeast edge of Deer Lake, it was half a mile off the interstate highway. Beyond the island of artificial light that was the parking lot, the night was black, vaguely ominous, certainly unwelcoming. On the other side of a wall of overgrown leafless shrubbery, the Park County fairgrounds stretched out across a field, an array of old vacant buildings and a looming grandstand. It looked abandoned and somehow sinister, as if the shadows were inhabited by dark spirits that could be chased away only by carnival lights and crowds of people. Even looking in the other direction, toward the town, Megan felt a sense of isolation.

"Is this about the missing kid?" Noga asked.

Mitch nodded. "Hannah Garrison's boy. Josh. She was supposed to pick him up here. I figured we'd take a look around, talk to Olie—"

"We should have uniforms canvassing the residential area," Megan interrupted, drawing a narrow look from Mitch and owl eyes from Noga. "Find out if the neighbors might have seen the boy or anything out of the ordinary. The fairgrounds will be the likely place to start the search once we've secured this area."

Mitch had tried to stick her with baby-sitting detail, suggesting she stay with Hannah and offer moral support while they waited for word of Josh. She had informed him that moral support was not part of her job description, then suggested they call a friend to come stay with Hannah and help make another round of phone calls looking for Josh among his friends. In the end Mitch called Natalie, who lived in Hannah's neighborhood.

His gaze hard and steady on her, he took a deep breath and spoke to his officer in a tone too even to be believed. "Go on inside and round up Olie. I'll be there in a minute."

"Gotcha." Noga hustled off, clearly relieved to be out of the line of fire.

Megan braced herself for a skirmish. Mitch stared at her, his jaw set, his eyes dark and deep beneath his brows. She could feel the tension coming off him in waves.

"Agent O'Malley," he said, his voice as cold as the air and deceptively, dangerously soft, "whose investigation is this?"

"Yours," she answered without hesitation. "And you're screwing it up."

"How diplomatically put."

"I don't get paid for diplomacy," she said, knowing damn well that she did. "I get paid to consult, advise, and investigate. I advise that *you* investigate, Chief, instead of dragging your butt around, pretending nothing's happened."

"I didn't ask for your consultation or your advice, *Ms.* O'Malley." Mitch didn't like this situation. He didn't like the possibilities and what they could mean to Deer Lake. And at the moment he was nursing a strong dislike for Megan O'Malley just because she was there and witnessing everything and poking at his authority and his ego. "You know, old Leo wasn't much to look at, but he knew his place. He wouldn't stick his nose into this until I asked him to."

"Then he would have been dragging his butt, too," Megan said, refusing to back down. If she backed away from him now, God knew she would probably end up sitting around the squad room monitoring the coffeepot. It wasn't just a question of turf, it was a matter of establishing herself in the pecking order. "If you don't call in uniforms to question the neighbors, I'll question them myself as soon as I've had a look around."

The muscles in his jaw flexed. His nostrils flared, emitting twin jet streams of steam. Megan held her place, gloved hands jammed on her hips, the muscles in the back of her neck knotting from looking up at him. She had ceased to feel her smaller toes as the cold leeched up through the thin soles of her boots.

Mitch ground his teeth as that fist tightened a little more in his belly and a voice whispered in the back of his mind. *What if she's right? What if you're wrong, Holt? What if you blow this?* The self-doubt made him furious, and he readily transferred that fury to the woman before him.

"I'll call for two more units. Noga can start looking around out here," he said tightly. "You can come with me, Agent O'Malley. I don't want you running unchecked in my town, spooking everyone into a panic."

"I'm not yours to keep on a leash, Chief."

His lips curled in a smile that was feral and nasty. "No, but it's a great fantasy."

He stalked off down the sidewalk and up the steps, denying her the chance for rebuttal. She hurried after him, cursing the slippery footing with every breath she didn't use to curse Mitch Holt.

"Maybe we ought to set some ground rules here," she said, coming up alongside him. "Decide when you'll be enlightened versus when you'll be an asshole. Is that a matter of convenience or a territorial thing, or what? I'd like to know now, because if this is going to degrade into a fence-pissing contest, I'm going to have to learn how to lift my leg."

He shot her a glare. "They didn't teach you that at the FBI academy?"

"No. They taught me how to subdue aggressive males by ramming their balls up to their tonsils."

"You must be a fun date."

"You'll never know."

He pulled open one of the doors that led into the ice arena and held it. Megan deliberately stepped to the side and opened another for herself.

"I don't expect special treatment," she said, stepping into the foyer. "I expect equal treatment."

"Fine." Mitch pulled his gloves off and stuffed them into his coat pockets. "You try to go over my head and I will be as equally pissed off with you as I would be with anyone else. Make me mad enough and I'll punch you out."

"That's assault."

"Call a cop," he tossed over his shoulder as he jerked open a door into the arena and strode through it.

Megan cast a glance toward heaven. "I asked for this, didn't I?"

Olie Swain had done most of the grunt work at the Gordie Knutson Memorial Arena for the better part of five years. He worked from three till eleven six days a week, keeping the locker rooms in order, sweeping trash from the seating areas, resurfacing the ice with the Zamboni machine, and doing whatever odd jobs needed doing. His real name was not Olie, but the nickname stuck with him and he made no effort to lose it. He figured the less anyone knew about the real him, the better—an attitude he had developed in childhood. Anonymity was a comfortable cloak, truth a neon light that directed unwanted attention on the unhappy story of his life.

Mind your own business, Leslie. Don't be proud, Leslie. Pride and arrogance are the sins of man.

The lines that had been hammered into him in childhood with iron fists and pointed tongues rang dully in the back of his head. The mystery had always been what he could possibly have to be proud of. He was small and ugly with a port wine birthmark spreading over a quarter of his face like a stain. His talents were small and of no interest to anyone. His experiences were the stuff of shame and secrets, and he kept them to himself. He always had, shrugging off what few concerns were expressed on his behalf, denying bruises and scars, excusing the glass eye as the result of a fall from a tree.

He had a clever mind, a head for books and studies. He had a natural aptitude for computers. This fact he kept mostly to himself as well, cherishing it as the one bright spot in an otherwise bleak existence.

Olie didn't like cops. He especially didn't like men. Their size, their strength, their aggressive sexuality, all triggered bad feelings in him, which was why he had no real friends his own age. The closest he came to having friends at all were the hockey boys. He envied their exuberance and coveted their innocence. They liked him because he could skate well and do acrobatics. Some were cruel about his looks, but mostly they accepted him, and that was the best Olie could ever hope for.

He stood in the corner of the cramped storage room he had converted into an office of sorts, his nerve endings wiggling like worms beneath his skin as Chief Holt's tall frame filled the doorway.

"Hey, Olie," the chief said. His smile was fake and tired. "How's it going?"

"Fine." Olie snapped the word off like a twig and tugged on the sleeve of the quilted flight jacket he'd bought at an army-navy store in the Cities. Inside his heavy wool sweater, perspiration trickled down his sides from his armpits, spicy and sour.

A woman peeked in around the chief's right arm. Bright green eyes in a pixie's face, dark hair slicked back.

"This is Agent O'Malley." Holt moved no more than a fraction of an inch to his left. The woman glanced up at him, her jaw set as she wedged herself through the narrow opening and into the little room. "Agent O'Malley, Olie Swain. Olie's the night man here."

Olie nodded politely. Agent of what? he wondered, but he didn't ask. *Mind your own business, Leslie.* Good advice, he'd found, regardless of the source. Early in life he had learned to channel his curiosity away from people and into his books and his fantasies.

"We'd just like to ask you a couple of questions, Mr. Swain, if that's all right with you," Megan said, loosening the noose of her scarf in deference to the heat of the room.

She took in everything about Olie Swain in a glance. He was jockey-size with pug features and mismatched eyes that seemed too round. The left one was glass and stared straight ahead while the other darted around, his glance seeming to bounce off every surface it touched. The glass eye was a lighter shade of brown than the good eye and ringed in brighter white. The unnatural white was accentuated by the scald-red skin of the birthmark that leeched down out of his hair and across the upper left quadrant of his face. His hair was a patchwork of brown and gray and stood up on his head like the bristles of a scrub brush. He was probably in his late thirties, she guessed, and he didn't like cops.

That was, of course, a hazard of the job. Even the most innocent of people became edgy when the cops invaded their territory. And then again, sometimes it turned out to be more than routine jitters. She wondered which explanation applied to Olie.

"We're trying to find Josh Kirkwood," Mitch said, his tone very matter-of-fact. "He plays on John Olsen's Squirts team. You know him?"

Olie shrugged. "Sure."

He offered nothing else. He asked no questions. He glanced down at his Ragg wool half-gloves and smoothed his right hand over his left. Typical Olie, Mitch thought. The guy possessed no social graces to speak of, never had much to say, and never said anything without prompting. An odd duck, but there was no law against that. All he seemed to want in life was to do his job and be left alone with his books.

From his position in the doorway Mitch could see Olie and the whole room without moving his eyes. An old green card table with a ripped top and a paint-splattered wooden straight chair took up most of the floor space. On top of and beneath the table were piles of outdated used textbooks. Computer science, psychology, English literature—the books ran the gamut.

"Josh's mom was late coming to get him," Mitch went on. "When she got here he was gone. Did you see him leave with anyone?"

"No." Olie ducked his head. "I was busy. Had to run the Zamboni before Figure Skating Club." His speech was a kind of linguistic shorthand, pared down to the bare essentials, just enough to make his point, not enough to encourage conversation. He stuck his hands in his coat pockets and waited and sweat some more.

"Did you take a call around five-fifteen, five-thirty from someone at the hospital saying Dr. Garrison would be late?" Megan asked.

"No."

"Do you know if anyone else did?"

"No."

Megan nodded and ran the zipper of her parka down. The little room was located next door to the furnace room and apparently absorbed heat in through the walls. It was like a sauna. Mitch had unzipped his parka and shrugged it back on his shoulders. Olie kept his hands in his jacket pockets. He rolled his right foot over onto the side of his battered Nike running shoe and jiggled his leg.

"Did you notice if Josh came back in the building after the other boys had gone?"

"No."

"You didn't happen to go outside, see any strange cars?"

"No."

Mitch pressed his lips together and sighed through his nose.

"Sorry," Olie said softly. "Wish I could help. Nice kid. Don't think something happened to him, do you?"

"Like what?" Megan's gaze didn't waver from Olie's mismatched eyes.

He shrugged again. "World's a rotten place."

"He probably went home with a buddy," Mitch said. The words sounded threadbare, he'd said them so often in the past two hours. His pager hung like a lead weight on his belt, silent. In the back of his mind he kept thinking it would beep any minute and he'd call in to hear the news that Josh had been found eating pizza and watching the Timberwolves game in a family room across town. The waiting was eating at his nerve endings like termites.

Megan, on the other hand, appeared to be enjoying this, he thought. The idea irritated him.

"Mr. Swain, have you been here all evening?" she asked.

"That's my job."

"Can anyone verify that for you?"

A bead of sweat rolled down Olie's forehead into his good eye. He blinked like a deer caught in a hunter's crosshairs. "Why? I haven't done anything."

She offered him a smile. He didn't buy it, but it didn't matter. "It's just routine, Mr. Swain. Have you—"

Mitch caught hold of a belt loop on the back of her parka and gave it a discreet tug. She snapped her head around and glared at him.

"Thanks, Olie," he said, ignoring her. "If you think of anything at all that might help, would you please call?"

"Sure. Hope it works out," Olie said.

The feeling of claustrophobia lifted from his chest as Holt and the woman backed away from the door. As their footsteps faded away, Olie's sense of solitude began to return. He moved around the room, running his fingertips over the block walls, marking his territory, erasing the intrusion of strangers. He slid into the chair and ran his hands over his books, stroking them as if they were beloved pets.

He didn't like cops. He didn't like questions. He wanted only to be left alone. *Mind your own business, Leslie.* Olie wished other people would take that advice.

I didn't appreciate the little gaff hook gag," Megan snapped. Walking beside Mitch, she nearly broke into a jog to keep up with him. Their footfalls against the concrete floor echoed through the cavernous building. Lights shined down on the sheet of smooth white ice. The bleachers that climbed the walls were cloaked in heavy, silent shadows, a cold, empty theater.

"Pardon me," Mitch said sardonically, gladly picking up the hostilities where they had left off. "I'm used to working alone. My manners may need a little polish."

"This doesn't have anything to do with manners. It has to do with professional courtesy."

"Professional courtesy?" He arched a brow. "Seems a foreign concept to you, Agent O'Malley. I don't think you'd recognize it if it bit your tight little behind."

"You cut me off—"

"Cut you off? I should have thrown you out."

"You undermined my authority—"

Something hot and red burst behind Mitch's eyes. The flames burned through his control for the first time in a very long time. He wheeled on Megan without warning, grabbed her by the shoulders, and pinned her up against the Plexiglas that rose above the hockey boards.

"This is *my* town, *Agent* O'Malley," he snarled, his face an inch from hers. "You don't have any authority. You are here to *assist upon request.* You may have degrees out the wazoo, but apparently you were in the ladies' room when they gave that particular lecture at the bureau."

She stared up at him, her eyes impossibly huge, her mouth a soft, round O. He had meant to frighten her, shock her. Mission accomplished. Her heavy coat hung open, and Mitch could almost see her heart racing beneath her evergreen turtleneck.

Fascinated, he let his gaze slide downward. With her shoulders pinned back, her chest was thrust forward and her breasts commanded his attention. They were small round globes, and even as he stared at them, the nipples budded faintly beneath the fabric of the sweater. The heat within him altered states, from flames of indignation to something less civilized, something primal. His intent had been to establish professional dominance, but in the heat the motivation melted and shifted, sliding down from the logical corners of his mind to a part of him that had no use for logic.

Slowly he dragged his gaze up to the small chin that jutted out defiantly. Up to the mouth that quivered slightly, betraying her show of bravado. Up to the eyes as deep and rich a green as velvet, with lashes short and thick, as black as night.

"I never had this kind of trouble with Leo," he muttered. "But then, I never wanted to kiss Leo."

Megan knew better than to let him. She knew every argument against it by heart—had repeated them over and over in her mind tonight like chants to ward off evil spirits. *It's stupid. It's dangerous. It's bad business.* . . . Even as they trailed across her brain she was lifting her chin, snatching a breath. . . .

She flattened her hands and shoved at him, succeeding only in breaking Mitch's concentration. He pulled his head back an inch and blinked, his head clearing slowly. He had lost control. The thought was like a bell ringing between his ears. He didn't lose control. *Contain the rage. Control the mind. Control the needs.* Those dictates had gotten him through two long years, and in the time it took to draw a breath Megan O'Malley had driven him to the verge of breaking them.

They stared at each other, wary, waiting, breath held in the cool of the dark arena.

"I'm going to pretend that didn't happen," Megan announced without any of the authority or righteous indignation she had intended. The announcement came out sounding like a promise she knew she couldn't keep.

Mitch said nothing. The heat abruptly died to a glow. He lifted his hands from her shoulders and stepped back. She wanted to usurp his authority, then rob him of his sanity, then pretend it hadn't happened. A part of him bridled at the thought. But that wasn't an intelligent part of him.

It wasn't smart to want Megan O'Malley. Therefore, he

would not want Megan O'Malley. Simple. She wasn't even his type. Pint-size and abrasive had never done anything for him. He liked his women tall and elegant, warm and sweet. Like Allison had been. Not at all like this little package of Irish temper and feminist outrage.

"Yeah," he muttered, digging deep for sarcasm. "Good move, O'Malley. Forget about it. Wouldn't want to get caught with your femininity showing."

The words stung, as he had intended them to, but the hit brought no satisfaction. All that stirred within him was guilt and a hint of regret that he had no desire to examine more closely.

An entrance door banged open, the sound bounced around the quiet like a rubber ball.

"Chief!" Noga bellowed. "Chief!"

Mitch bolted, that knot in his stomach doubling, tripling, as he ran along the back side of the boards. *Please, God, let him say they found Josh. And let him be alive.* But even as he made the wish, cold dread pebbled his skin and closed bony fingers around his throat.

"What is it?" he demanded, rushing up to his officer.

The look Noga gave him was pale and bleak, the face of fear. "You'd better come see."

"Jesus Christ," Mitch whispered desperately. "Is it Josh?"

"No. Just come."

Megan brought up the rear as they ran from the building. The cold hit her with physical force. She zipped her jacket, dug her gloves out of her pockets, and pulled them on. Her scarf trailed off one shoulder, fluttering like a banner behind her and finally falling off as she dashed across the parking lot.

Mitch sprinted ahead, running across the rutted ice in dress shoes, as surefooted as a track star. Midway down the lot, along the far edge, three more uniformed officers stood huddled together by a row of overgrown leafless hedges.

"What?" he barked. "What'd you find?"

None of them spoke. Each looked to another, mute and stunned.

"Well, fuck!" he yelled. "Somebody fucking say something!"

Lonnie Dietz took a step to the side, and a ray of artificial light fell on a nylon duffel bag. Someone had written across the side of it in big block letters: JOSH KIRKWOOD.

Mitch dropped to his knees in the snow, the duffel sitting before him with all the potential of a live bomb. It was partially unzipped and a slip of paper stuck up through the opening, fluttering in the breeze. He took hold of the very edge of the paper and eased it slowly from the bag.

"What is it?" Megan asked breathlessly, dropping down beside him. "Ransom note?"

Mitch unfolded the paper and read it—quickly first, then again, slowly, his blood growing colder with each typed word.

a child has vanished
ignorance is not innocence but SIN

CHAPTER 6

Kids do the damnedest things," Natalie said. She worked at the kitchen counter, building turkey sandwiches while the coffeemaker hissed and spit. "I remember Troy pulling a stunt like this once. He was ten or eleven. Decided he was going to go door to door, selling newspaper subscriptions so he could win himself a remote-control race car. He was so caught up in winning that prize, he couldn't think of anything so minor as calling from school to tell *us* what he was doing. *Call my mother? Why should I call her when I see her every day?*"

She shook her head in disgust and bisected a sandwich corner to corner with a bread knife the size of a cross-cut saw. "This was when we lived in the Cities and there was starting to be a lot of gang activity going on in Minneapolis. You can't imagine the things that went through my head when Troy hadn't come home yet at five-thirty."

Yes, I can. The same thoughts were trailing through Hannah's mind in an endless loop, a litany of horrors. She paced back and forth on the other side of the breakfast bar, too wired to sit. She hadn't been able to bring herself to change out of the clothes she'd worn to work. The bulky sweater held the faint tang of sweat from the exertion and stress of working on Ida Bergen. Her black hose bit into her waist, and her long wool skirt was limp and creased. She had taken her boots off at the door only out of habit.

She walked back and forth along the length of the counter, her arms crossed in a symbolic attempt to keep herself together, her eyes never straying from the phone that sat silent beneath a wall chart of phone numbers. *Mom at the hospital. Dad at his office. 911 for emergency.* All printed by Josh with colorful markers. A home project for safety week.

The panic rushed up inside her again.

"I tell you, I was a wild woman," Natalie went on, pouring the coffee. She added a drop of skim milk to each and set them on the bar next to the plate of sandwiches. "We called the police. James and I went out looking for him. Then we damn near ran over him. That's how we found him. He was riding around in the dark on his bike, so obsessed with winning that damned toy, he couldn't be bothered to look out for traffic."

Hannah glanced at her friend as the silence stretched and she realized this was where she was expected to interject. "What did you do?"

"I went tearing out that car before James could put it in park, screaming at the top of my lungs. We were right outside a synagogue. I screamed so loud, the rabbi came running outside, and what does he see? He sees some crazy black woman screaming and shaking this poor child like a rag doll. So he goes back inside and calls the cops. They came flying with the lights and sirens and the whole nine yards. 'Course by then I had my arms around that boy and I was crying and carrying on—*My baby! My baby boy!*" She shrieked at the ceiling in a hoarse falsetto, waving her arms.

Rolling her eyes, she pursed her lips and shook her head. "Looking back on it, we probably didn't have to punish Troy. The embarrassment was probably enough."

Hannah had zoned out again. She stared at the phone as if she were willing it to ring. Natalie sighed, knowing there was really nothing she could do that she wasn't already doing. She made coffee and sandwiches, not because anyone was hungry but because it was a sane, normal thing to do. She talked incessantly in an attempt to distract Hannah and to fill the ominous silence.

She went around the end of the counter, put her hands on Hannah's shoulders, and steered her to a stool at the breakfast bar. "Sit down and eat something, girl. Your blood sugar has to be in the negative digits by now. It's a wonder you can even stand up."

Hannah perched a hip on one corner of the stool and

stared at the plate of sandwiches. Even though she hadn't had a bite since lunch, she couldn't work up any desire to eat. She knew she should try—for her own sake and because Natalie had gone to all the trouble to make them. She didn't want to hurt Natalie's feelings. She didn't want to let anyone down.

You've already managed to do that today.

She'd lost a patient. She'd lost Josh.

The phone sat silent.

In the family room, where the television mumbled to itself, Lily woke up and climbed down off the couch. She toddled toward the kitchen, rubbing one eye with a fist, the other arm clutching a stuffed dalmatian in a headlock. A fist squeezed Hannah's heart as she watched her daughter. At eighteen months Lily was still her baby, the embodiment of sweetness and innocence. She had her mother's blond curls and blue eyes. She didn't resemble Paul in any way, a fact Paul did not care to have pointed out to him. After all the indignities he'd had to suffer in the long effort to conceive Lily, he seemed to think he deserved to have his daughter look like him.

Thoughts of Paul only made Hannah more aware of the mute telephone. He hadn't called, even though she had left several frantic messages on his machine.

"Mama?" Lily said, reaching up with her free hand in a silent command to be picked up.

Hannah complied readily, hugging her daughter tight, burying her nose against the little body that smelled of powder and sleep. She wanted Lily as close as possible, hadn't let her out of her sight since bringing her home from the sitter's.

"Hi, sweetie pie," she whispered, rocking back and forth, taking comfort in the feel of the warm, squirming body clad in a purple fleece sleeper. "You're supposed to be sleeping."

Lily deflected the remark with a beguiling, dimpled smile. "Where Josh?"

Hannah's smile froze. Her arms tightened unconsciously. "Josh isn't here, sweetheart."

The panic hit her like a battering ram, smashing the last of her resistance. She was tired and terrified. She wanted someone to hold her, to tell her everything would be all right—and mean it. She wanted her son back and the fear gone. She clutched Lily to her and shut her eyes tight against the onslaught of tears. As scalding as acid, they squeezed out and ran down her cheeks. A low, tortured moan tore free of her aching throat. Lily, frightened and unhappy at being held so tightly, began to cry, too.

"Hannah, honey, please sit down," Natalie said softly, leading her to the camelback love seat. "Sit. I'll bring you something to drink."

Outside the house, the dog barked and a car came up the driveway. Hannah swallowed back the rest of the tears, though Lily made no similar attempt. The suspense was as thick as smoke in the air. Would Josh come bursting in the kitchen door? Would it be Mitch Holt with news she couldn't bear to think about?

"Why isn't Gizmo in the backyard, where he belongs?"

Paul stepped into the kitchen, a petulant frown turning his mouth. He didn't look across the room to Hannah, but went about his nightly ritual as if nothing were wrong. He went into his small office off the kitchen to put his briefcase on the desk and hang up his coat. Hannah watched him disappear into the room that was his sanctuary of perfect order. Fury boiled up inside her. He cared more about hanging his coat perfectly in line with his other coats—arranged left to right from lightest weight to heaviest, casual to dress—than he cared about his son.

"Where's Josh?" Paul snapped, striding back into the kitchen, tugging loose the knot in his striped tie. "That dog is his responsibility. He can damn well go out and put him away."

"Josh isn't here," Hannah answered sharply. "If you would bother to return my phone calls, you would have known that hours ago."

At the tone of her voice, he glanced up, his hazel eyes wary beneath the heavy line of his brow. "What—?"

"Where the hell have you been?" she demanded, unconsciously squeezing Lily harder. The baby made a fist and hit her shoulder, wailing. "I've been frantic trying to get you!"

"Jesus, I've been at work!" he shot back, trying to take in the scene and make some sense of it. "I had a hell of a lot more important things to do than answer the damn phone."

"Really? Your son is missing. Do you have a client more important than Josh?"

"What do you mean, he's missing?"

Natalie stepped between them and reached up to rescue Lily. The baby went gratefully into her arms. "Let me put her to bed while you and Paul sit down and discuss this *calmly* and *rationally*," she said firmly, her eyes hard on Hannah's.

"Missing?" Paul repeated, hands jammed at the waist of his fashionable brown trousers. "What the hell is going on here?"

Natalie wheeled on him. "Sit, Paul," she ordered, swinging an arm in the direction of the kitchen table. His eyes widened, his frown deepened, but he obeyed. She turned back to Hannah, her fierce expression softening. "You sit, too. Start at the beginning. I'll be right back."

Cooing to Lily, she headed across the plush carpet of the family room for the short flight of steps that led up to the bedrooms. Hannah watched her go, guilt rising at the way Lily laid her head on Natalie's shoulder and blubbered a watery, "No, no, Mama," her big eyes full of accusation as she stared at Hannah.

God, what kind of mother am I? Goose bumps turned her skin the texture of sandpaper, and she pressed a hand over her mouth, afraid an answer might come out that she didn't want to hear.

"Hannah, what's going on? You look like hell."

She turned back toward her husband, wondering bitterly why the effects of stress seemed to lend character to a man's appearance. Paul had just put in better than twelve hours at the accounting firm he was partners in with his old college friend Steve Christianson. He looked tired, the lines that fanned out from the corners of his eyes and bracketed his mouth were a little deeper than usual, but none of that detracted from his attractiveness. Just an inch taller than she, Paul was trim and athletic, with a lean face and a strong chin. His pinstripe shirt had lost its starch, but with the tie hanging loose at his throat, he looked sexy instead of rumpled. She glanced down at herself as she sank onto a chair and felt like something that had crawled out of the depths of the clothes hamper.

"We had an emergency at the hospital," she said softly, her eyes on her husband's. "I was late picking up Josh. I had Carol call the rink to leave word, but when I got there he was gone. I looked everywhere but I couldn't find him. The police are out looking now."

Paul's face hardened. He sat up, shoulders squared. "You *forgot* our son?" he said, his voice as sharp as a blade.

"No—"

"Christ," he swore, pushing to his feet. "That damn job is more important to you—"

"I'm a doctor! A woman was dying!"

"And now some lunatic has made off with our son!"

"You don't know that!" Hannah cried, hating him for voicing her fears.

"Then where is he?" Paul shouted, bracing his hands on the tabletop and leaning across into her face.

"I don't know!"

"Stop it!" Natalie barked, storming into the kitchen. "Stop it, both of you!" She gave them both the ferocious glower that had cowed more than one cop on the Deer Lake force. "You have a little girl upstairs crying herself to sleep because her parents are fighting. This is no time for the two of you to be sniping at each other."

Paul glared at her but said nothing. Hannah started to speak, then turned her back on them both when the front doorbell rang. She ran across the family room, stumbled into the hall, and flung herself at the door, her heart hammering wildly in her chest.

Mitch Holt stood on the front step, his face grave, his eyes deep wells of pain.

"No," she whispered. "No!"

Mitch stepped inside and took her arm. "Honey, we'll do everything we can to find him."

"No," she whispered again, shaking her head, unable to stop even as dizziness swirled through her brain. "No. Don't tell me. Please don't tell me."

No amount of training could prepare a cop for this, Mitch thought. There was no protocol for shattering a parent's life. There were no platitudes adequate, no apology that could suffice. Nothing could stem the pain. Nothing. He couldn't be a cop for this, couldn't detach himself even if it would have lessened his own pain. He was a father first, a friend second, and memories and guilt assaulted whatever professional reserve he might have had left. Behind Hannah, he could see Paul and Natalie standing in the hall, waiting, their faces bleak, stricken.

"No," Hannah whispered, her lips barely moving, her tear-filled eyes brimming with desperation. "Please, Mitch."

"Josh has been abducted," he said, the words tearing his voice into a low, hoarse rumble.

Hannah crumpled like a broken doll. Mitch wrapped his arms around her and held her tight. "I'm sorry, honey," he murmured. "I'm so sorry."

"Dear God," Natalie murmured. She stepped past them and shut the front door against the bitter chill of the night, but the cold that had come into the house had little to do with the weather. It cut to the bone and could not be shaken off.

Paul stepped forward and pried loose one of Mitch's hands from around Hannah's shoulders. "She's *my* wife," he said. The bitterness in his tone caused Mitch to lift his head.

Paul pulled Hannah away as Mitch dropped his arms. But he made no real effort to offer her the same kind of comfort or support. Or perhaps it was just that Hannah drifted away from him when he would have tried. Either way, it seemed odd, but then, what about this night hadn't been surreal? Children weren't abducted in Deer Lake. The BCA didn't have any female field agents. Mitch Holt never lost control.

Christ, what a lie.

The anger flared inside him, saved him, as ironic as that seemed. It gave him something to focus on, something familiar to hold on to. He pulled in a deep breath, pulled himself together. He rubbed a hand across the stubble on his jaw and looked to his assistant. Behind the big lenses of her glasses Natalie's eyes were swimming with tears. She looked nearly as lost as Hannah, who stood hugging the archway into the living room, her face pressed hard against the wall.

"Natalie," he said, touching her shoulder. "Is there any coffee made? We could probably all use some."

She nodded and hustled off to the kitchen, glad for the task.

Mitch herded Hannah and Paul into the family room. "We need to sit down and talk."

"Talk?" Paul snapped. "Why the hell aren't you out trying to find my son? My God, you're the chief of police!"

Mitch gave him an even look and the benefit of the doubt. "Every officer I have available is on the case. We've called the sheriff's department, the state patrol, and the BCA is here. We're organizing search parties at the ice rink. Helicopters are coming with infrared sensors that will pick up anything that gives off heat. In the meantime, Josh's description is being sent out to all surrounding law enforcement agencies and it's being entered into the system at the National Crime Information Center. He'll be registered as a missing child all across the country. I'll be coordinating efforts on the search myself, but first I've got to ask the two of you some questions. You might be able to give us a starting point, something to work with."

"We're supposed to know what madman grabbed our son? Jesus, this is unbelievable!"

"Stop it," Hannah snapped.

Paul gaped at her, feigning shock. "Or maybe Hannah can shed some light on the situation. She's the one who left Josh there—"

Hannah gasped, reeling as if he'd struck her across the face.

Mitch hit Paul Kirkwood hard with the heel of his hand, knocking him backward and dumping him unceremoniously into a wing chair. "Knock it off, Paul," he ordered. "You aren't helping anyone."

Paul slumped in the chair and scowled. "I'm sorry," he murmured grudgingly, leaning heavily against one arm of the chair, his head in his hand. "I just got home. I can't believe any of this is happening."

"How do you know—?" Hannah couldn't bring herself to finish the sentence. She wedged herself into one corner of the love seat as Mitch shrugged off his parka and sat on the other end.

"We found his duffel bag. There was a note inside."

"What kind of note?" Paul demanded. "For ransom or something? We're hardly rich. I mean, I make a good living, but nothing extravagant. And Hannah, well, I know everyone thinks doctors are rolling in it, but it's not like she's working at the Mayo Clinic . . ."

He let the thought trail off. Mitch frowned at him, wondering just how careless the remark had been. It tilted the blame in Hannah's direction again. She began to cry silently, tears rolling down her cheeks, her hand pressed over her mouth.

"It wasn't a ransom note, but it made it clear Josh had been taken," Mitch said. The words were branded in acid on his brain, an eerie message that pointed to a twisted mind. He wished he could give them the confidential evidence line, tell them it might be crucial to keep the information secret, knowledge only the guilty party would have, et cetera, but he couldn't. They were Josh's parents and they had a right to know. "It said, 'ignorance is not innocence but SIN.' "

A chill shot through Hannah. "What does it mean? What—"

"It means he's nuts," Paul declared. He raked his fingers back through his hair again and again. "Oh, Jesus . . ."

"It doesn't ring any bells with either of you?" Mitch asked. They shook their heads, both looking too stunned to think at all. Mitch let out a measured sigh. "What we need to concentrate on now is coming up with possible suspects."

Natalie brought the coffee in on a tray and set it on the cherrywood trunk, where remote controls lay like abandoned toys. She handed Mitch a cup, took another, and pressed it into Hannah's hands, leaving Paul to fend for himself while she coaxed her friend to take a sip. Paul didn't miss the slight. He shot the woman a glare as he leaned forward to add sweetener to his.

"You can't honestly think anyone we know would do this?" he said.

"No," Mitch lied. The statistics scrolled through the back of his head like a news bulletin crawling along the bottom of a television screen. The vast majority of child abductions were not perpetrated by strangers. "But I want you both to think. Have any clients or patients gotten mad at either of you? Have you noticed any strangers in the neighborhood lately, any strange cars driving by slowly? Anything at all out of the ordinary?"

Paul stared into his coffee and heaved a sigh. "When are we supposed to notice strangers hanging around? I'm at the office all day. Hannah's hours are even worse than mine now that she's been named head of the emergency room."

Hannah flinched as another small barb struck its target. It

occurred to Mitch to ask them how long they'd been having problems, but he held his tongue. For all he knew, the stress of the situation was bringing out Paul's cruel streak.

"Has Josh said anything about someone hanging around the school or approaching him on the street?"

Hannah shook her head. Her hand trembled violently as she set her mug back on the tray, sloshing coffee over the rim. Ignoring the mess, she folded herself in two, hugging her knees, dry sobs racking her body. Someone had stolen her son. In the blink of an eye Josh was gone from their lives, taken by a faceless stranger to a nameless place for a purpose no mother ever wanted to consider. She wondered if he was cold, if he was frightened, if he was thinking of her and wondering why she hadn't come for him. She wondered if he was alive.

Paul pushed himself up out of the wing chair and paced the room. His face was drawn and pale.

"Things like this don't happen here," he muttered. "That's why we moved out of the Cities—to live in a small town where we could raise our kids without worrying about some pervert—" He slammed a fist against the fireplace mantel. "How could this happen? How could this happen?"

"There's no way to make sense of it, no matter where it happens," Mitch said. "The best thing we can do is focus on trying to get Josh back. We'll get a tap and a tracer on your phone in case a call comes in."

"Are we just supposed to sit here and wait?" Paul asked.

"Someone has to be on hand if the phone rings."

"Hannah can stay by the phone." He'd volunteered his wife without consulting her or even considering her mental state, Mitch thought, his patience wearing thin. "I want to help with the search. I have to do something to help."

"Yeah, fine," Mitch murmured, watching as Natalie knelt at Hannah's feet and tried to offer her some words of comfort. "Paul, why don't we go out in the kitchen and discuss this, all right?"

"What can I bring to the search?" he asked, trailing after Mitch, his mind completely absorbed with planning a course of action. "Lanterns? Flashlights? We've got some good camping gear—"

"That's fine," Mitch said curtly. He looked Paul Kirkwood

in the eye, giving him a moment to realize this conference wasn't about the search. "Paul, I know this is a tough situation for anyone," he said softly, "but could you show your wife a little compassion here? Hannah needs your support."

Paul stared at him, incredulous and offended. "I'm a little angry with her at the moment," he said tightly. "She left our son to be abducted."

"Josh is a victim of circumstance. So is Hannah, for that matter. She couldn't foresee an emergency coming into the hospital the exact time she was supposed to be picking up Josh."

"No?" He gave a derisive snort. "How much you want to bet she was late leaving as it was? She has regular hours, you know, but she doesn't keep them. She hangs around the place just waiting for something to go wrong so she can have an excuse to stay later. God forbid she should spend any time in our home, with our kids—"

"Put a cork in it, Paul," Mitch snapped. "Whatever problems you and Hannah are having in your marriage go on the shelf this minute. You got me? The two of you need to be together—for Josh's sake—not taking potshots at each other. You need to be angry with someone, be angry with God or with me or with lenient courts. Hannah has enough on her conscience without you climbing on top of the pile."

Paul jerked away from him. Mitch was right—he wanted to lash out at someone. Hannah. His golden girl. His trophy bride. The woman who didn't have a clue about how to make him happy. She was too busy basking in the glow of everyone's adoration to be there for him or for their children. This was Hannah's fault. All of it.

"Bring whatever equipment you have," Mitch said wearily. "Meet me at the ice arena." He started for the hall and brought himself up short. "Bring some clothing of Josh's," he added quietly, his eyes on Hannah, curled into a ball of misery on the love seat. "We'll need something for the dogs to scent."

Natalie followed him to the front hall. "That man needs more than a talking-to. He needs a good swift kick in the pants—right where his brain is."

"That's assault," Mitch said. "But if you want to go in there and get him, tiger, I'll swear in court I didn't see a thing."

"I can't believe that little number-twiddling twerp," she grumbled. "Let that poor girl sit there and cry. Stick pins in her from across the room like she was a voodoo doll. God almighty!"

"Did you know they were having trouble?"

She made one of her faces. "Hannah doesn't talk about personal things. She could be living with the Marquis de Sade and she wouldn't say a word against him. I'm the wrong person to ask, anyway," she admitted ruefully. "I always thought Paul was a stuck-up little prick."

Mitch rubbed at the knots of tension in the back of his neck. "We should cut him a little slack, Nat. No one's at their best in a situation like this. Everyone reacts differently and not always admirably."

"I'd like to react all over his head," she muttered.

"Can you stay with Hannah? Is James home with the kids?"

Natalie nodded. "I'll call some other friends. We can pull shifts here. And I'll get the tuna casserole brigade rolling."

"Use my cellular phone. That way you won't tie up the line here. Someone will be coming over to get the phones wired. If anything happens, I'm on the beeper." He gave her a long look as he shrugged into his parka. "You're worth your weight in gold, Miz Bryant."

"Tell it to the town council," she quipped, struggling for a scrap of humor in this nightmare. "They can start cleaning out Fort Knox."

He slipped the small portable phone from his coat pocket and handed it over. "Call the priest while you're at it. We're going to need all the help we can get."

CHAPTER 7

From a distance, the parking lot of the Gordie Knutson Memorial Arena resembled a giant tailgate party—cars and trucks in makeshift rows, men milling around portable heaters, their voices carrying on the cold night air. But there was no party atmosphere. Tension and anger and fear hovered like a cloud, like a drift of noxious fog.

If there had been any hope of picking up a trace of evidence from the lot itself, it was gone now. That was the risk of working crime scenes with large groups. The attention to small detail was lost in the hunt for larger clues. The sense of urgency fed on itself and grew, making the mob difficult to control.

Control. A prized word in Megan's vocabulary. She had been left in charge, but at the moment she had no control. The men turned to one another for guidance and instruction. They looked for their chief. They paid no attention whatsoever to Megan. She tried twice to raise her voice above the din. No one listened and she turned to Noga.

He gave her a rueful look and shrugged. "Maybe we should just wait for the chief."

"Noga, a child has been abducted. We don't have time to piss around with this male pecking-order bullshit."

Scowling, she went around to the trunk of the Lumina and rummaged through the dusty junk heap for a bullhorn, then went around to the front of the car and scrambled up on the hood, the heels of her boots denting it like hailstones.

"Listen up!" she bellowed.

The sound echoed off across the fairgrounds. As if a switch had been flipped off, the men fell silent and turned to stare at her.

"I'm Agent O'Malley with the BCA. Chief Holt has gone to speak with the parents of the missing boy. In his absence, I'm going to organize you into teams and get you started on the search. Deer Lake cops: I want three teams of two doing house-to-house on this block, asking if anyone saw anything going on between five-fifteen and seven-fifteen. We don't have a photo of the boy to give you at this point, but he was last seen wearing a bright blue ski jacket with green and yellow trim and a yellow stocking cap with a Vikings patch on it. If anyone saw Josh Kirkwood or saw anything odd or suspicious going on, we want to hear about it. The rest of you cops and county boys divide into—"

"I'll direct my own men, if you don't mind, Miss O'Malley."

Megan's gaze dropped like an anvil onto the head of the Park County sheriff. He stood with his hands on his lean hips, a half-smile twisting his nonexistent lips. Somewhere in the vicinity of fifty, he was tall with a lean, bony face and an aquiline nose. The lights of the parking lot gleamed off dark hair that he wore slicked straight back à la basketball coach Pat Riley. His voice boomed, carrying farther than hers did with the bullhorn.

"I want my deputies on the fairgrounds. We'll do a complete sweep—every plowed road, every building. If you find something, call it in to me. Art Goble's coming with his dogs. As soon as Mitch gets back with something for them to scent off, they'll be in business. Let's go!"

Half a dozen deputies started toward the fairgrounds, flashlights bobbing in their hands. The Deer Lake cops shuffled around, uncertain who to send where or if they should do anything at all on the orders of a woman they had never seen before. Megan shot a look at Noga, and he hustled off to get them moving. She hopped down off the hood of the Lumina, landing squarely in front of the sheriff.

"It's *Agent* O'Malley," she said, sticking a gloved hand out in front of her.

Russ Steiger gave her a patronizing once-over with his big

dark eyes, blatantly ignoring her token gesture of courtesy. "What'd they do? Run out of men in St. Paul?"

"No." Her smile was as sharp as a scimitar. "They decided on a novel idea and sent the most qualified person instead of the one with the biggest dick."

The sheriff blinked as if she'd hit him in the forehead with a mallet. Christ, DePalma would have her head on a pike if he heard her talk that way to a county sheriff. Never mind that she knew male agents who had vocabularies that could singe the hair in a sailor's ears. That was guy stuff, locker-room bravado. She had been given explicit instructions to make a good impression, not to offend, not to step on toes. But she knew too well what would happen if she kept her mouth shut and bowed to the local potentates. She'd end up sitting in her office, filling out forms and trimming her cuticles. It didn't take a genius in human behavior to see that this particular potentate was like a big bull moose—a polite tap on the shoulder would not get his attention; he needed something more along the lines of a sharp whack between the ears with a Louisville Slugger.

The sheriff snorted. "Russ Steiger, Park County sheriff. Leo was a hell of a guy."

"Yeah, well, he's dead now and we've got a job to do," she said, fed up to her back teeth with Leo accolades. "Let's get to it before the press shows up." She deliberately turned her back on him, then turned around in calculated afterthought. "Your men find something on the fairgrounds, Sheriff, you call it in to me. I'll be coordinating the effort at the command post."

She blew out a long breath. Fatigue pressed down on her like a millstone. These were hardly the ideal circumstances for her to establish a rapport with the local boys. She would have to be on the offensive every second or get trampled beneath a herd of size-twelve boots—a distraction she didn't need. Every time she closed her eyes, she could see Josh Kirkwood grinning out at her from his third-grade photo. She could see his mother, the elegant beauty of her face twisted with guilt and a terrible fear Megan could only imagine.

Pain stabbed as sharp as an ice pick above her right eye. She had a bad feeling about this one. Abductions seldom ended happily. The message they had found in Josh's duffel bag rang like a bell of doom in her head: *ignorance is not innocence but SIN.*

That the note was typed suggested premeditation, and the whole idea of abduction reeked of a seriously disturbed mind. She wondered if they were dealing with a local or a drifter, someone already familiar with the community or someone who had hung around just long enough to get down the town routines. Or maybe the perp was someone who prowled the interstate highway systems, pulling off when the mood or opportunity hit to grab a kid and go. Maybe he had a whole glove compartment full of typed notes composed to strike terror into the hearts of those left behind. The possibilities were multifarious, the probabilities chilling.

Every step of the way a cop was taught not to become emotionally involved in a case. Good advice, but damn hard to follow when the victim was a child. Megan's heart wrenched at the idea of a small boy dragged into God knew what terror. She knew what it was to be small and alone and afraid, to feel abandoned. Those memories of her own childhood swirled like oil on water down in the pit of her soul.

A shout went up off to Megan's right, snapping her back to the moment just in time to see a pair of coon hounds bearing down on her with bright eyes and long pink tongues lolling out the sides of their mouths. At the last second one darted right and one left, their big, muscular bodies glancing off her legs, knocking her flat in the driveway.

"Aw, damn, they're after a rabbit!" A man who looked like one of the Keebler elves in a snowmobile suit looked down at Megan in disgust, then offered his hand. "Sorry, miss."

"Agent O'Malley, BCA," she said automatically, grimacing as she let him help her up.

"Art Goble. Excuse me, miss, while I round up Heckle and Jeckle."

"Heckle and Jeckle?" She watched him trundle off after the dogs, her heart sinking as she stepped up onto the sidewalk. "Jesus, Mary, and Joseph."

"They're the best we can do on short notice," Mitch said. He had parked his Explorer in the fire zone in front of the arena. "I called the volunteer canine search and rescue club, and the canine unit in Minneapolis. They'll have dogs here inside two hours."

The challenges of law enforcement in the hinterlands. Megan sighed. "The mobile lab is on its way and the choppers should be here within the hour. How are the parents?"

He shook his head, his expression bleak. "Hannah is despondent. Paul is angry. They're both scared. I left Natalie in charge at the house to deal with your techs."

"Good. It'll go more smoothly that way."

"Paul is coming down to help with the search."

Megan squeezed her eyes shut and groaned.

"I know, I know," Mitch muttered. "But I couldn't stop him. He needs to feel like he's taking some kind of action."

"Yeah, well, if we knew where *not* to look for Josh, we could send him thataway." She could sympathize with a parent's need to do something proactive in a situation like this, but no one wanted a father to discover his child's body or a civilian to unwittingly miss or destroy evidence.

"I'll let him bring up the rear with the county boys. They've started?"

"Oh, yeah. Me and Wyatt Earp got them all whipped into a frenzy," she replied sarcastically.

"So you met Russ?"

"A charming fellow. Were I a fish, he would have thrown me back in disgust."

"Don't say I didn't warn you."

"I'll be hearing that in my sleep," she muttered. "If I ever get any. This is liable to be a long night."

"Yeah, and it's about to get longer," Mitch snarled as a *TV 7* news van rolled up to the curb in front of them. "Here comes the sideshow. There ought to be a law against civilians owning scanners."

"Would that apply to the media? They only appear to be humanoid."

The newspeople piled out of the van like the troops landing at Normandy. Technicians grabbed equipment, flipped on blinding portable strobes, tossed coils of electrical cord out onto the sidewalk. The passenger door opened and the star emerged, glamour-girl looks and too-blue contact lenses, thick sandy hair spray-starched into a helmet impervious to weather.

She wore a stylish blue ski jacket open over an equally stylish sweater, and navy leggings tucked into tall leather boots. The latest outfit for reporters on the go tracking down misery and tragedy in the dead of winter.

"Oh, shit," Mitch growled through his teeth. "Paige Price."

While he had no great love for any reporter, he knew only too well this one was hungry, ambitious, and ruthless in her pursuit of a story. She would do anything for a scoop, for a fresh angle, for an edge against the competition.

"Chief Holt!" The smile that graced Paige Price's mouth was small, appropriate, businesslike. The gleam of excitement in her eyes was not. "Can we get a few words from you about the abduction?"

"We'll hold a press conference in the morning if necessary," he said curtly. "We're very busy right now."

"Of course. This will take only a moment," she said smoothly. "Just a sound bite."

She turned toward Megan, her reporter's eyes glinting with shrewd speculation, but she quickly arranged her features into perfect concern touched with sympathy. "Are you the boy's mother?"

"No. I'm Agent O'Malley with the Bureau of Criminal Apprehension."

"You must be new," she said, the speculation sharpening.

"To the bureau, no. To the Deer Lake area, yes. This is my first day here."

"Really? What a terrible way to start a new job." Paige mouthed the platitudes automatically while she scanned the files of her brain, ferreting out pertinent kernels of information. "I don't recall ever hearing of a female agent in the field. Isn't that unusual?"

"You might say that," Megan said dryly. "If you'll excuse me, Ms. Price, I have work to do. This is Chief Holt's investigation, at any rate," she added, tossing the ball into Mitch's court and not missing the narrow look he shot her. She kept her focus on the reporter, however, knowing better than to turn her back on a viper poised to strike. "Any help we can get from the media in achieving the safe return of Josh Kirkwood will be greatly appreciated."

On that note, she abandoned Mitch, heading for the relative warmth of the ice arena to await the arrival of the crime scene unit. Relief flooded through her for escaping Paige Price's manicured claws. Bureau policy was to remain in the background of investigations, leaving the publicity and the credit to fall on the shoulders of the local chief or sheriff, where it belonged. The BCA was a workhorse at the disposal of local authorities, not an organization of grandstanders looking to bask in the limelight.

The policy suited Megan fine. She wanted to be a cop, not a celebrity. She could imagine the minor strokes touched off in the bureau hierarchy if Paige Price latched on to her for an exclusive. *BCA's First Female Field Agent Fields Sensational Child Abduction Case.* She had no desire to be held up by Paige Price or anyone else as a curiosity or an icon for the women's movement. All she ever wanted was to do her job.

She climbed the stairs into the darkened bleachers and settled in an aisle seat two-thirds of the way up, grateful for the silence. It wouldn't last long. The mobile lab would arrive to collect what pitifully meager evidence they had—the duffel bag, the note. She would send the techs to the Kirkwood house to wire the phones. Then she would work with Mitch to establish a command post where searchers would report any findings, where a telephone hotline would be set up to receive tips from the public. A million details flew around inside her head like a swarm of fireflies, threatening to overwhelm her.

This was the kind of responsibility she had asked for. This was as close as she would come to FBI work as long as her father was alive. *Careful what you wish for, O'Malley.*

Punchy with exhaustion, she tried to imagine what Neil O'Malley would have done if she had been abducted as a child. Pretend paternal outrage and hoist a bottle of Pabst in private, glad to be rid of the daughter he never wanted.

"There's a million stories in the Naked City," she mumbled absently, dismissing her own as she glimpsed movement down in the shadows near the doors to the locker rooms. Olie Swain? Uneasiness danced across her nerve endings as she pictured his ugly face and remembered the sour smell of sweat in his little cubbyhole next to the furnace room. "A million stories in the Naked City. What's yours, Olie?"

Mitch stood scowling into the glare of the *TV 7* portable lights and gave a terse, much-abridged version of the abduction of Josh Kirkwood, assuring the ten o'clock news audience that everything possible was being done to find the boy, asking them to come forward with any information they might have.

A lot of people in Deer Lake watched KTVS, channel seven out of Minneapolis. If there was any chance that one of them had even a scrap of information, Mitch was more than willing to beg for it. It galled him to give Paige Price the exclusive, but he couldn't let personal feelings enter into the picture. He would use whom he could, however he could. If it meant getting Josh back, he would deal with the devil himself—or the devil's sister.

Paige stood beside him, looking grave and glamorous. The scent of her perfume seemed intensified by the heat of the lights—something thick and expensive. Choking. Or was that his own temper rising up in his throat and pounding between his ears? When he finished his statement, she was right there with a question, deftly heading off his escape.

"Chief Holt, you're calling this an abduction. Does that mean you have proof that Josh Kirkwood was kidnapped? And if so, what kind of proof?"

"I'm not at liberty to divulge that kind of information, Ms. Price."

"But it's safe to say you fear for Josh Kirkwood's life?"

Mitch gave her a cold look. "Someone has taken Josh Kirkwood. Any rational person would be concerned for Josh's safety. We're doing everything we can to find him and bring him home to his family, unharmed."

"Is that a realistic hope, considering the outcome of such cases as the Wetterling abduction or the Erstad disappearance? Or the cases gaining national prominence at the moment—Polly Klaas in California and Sara Wood in upstate New York? Isn't it true that with every moment that passes, the chances of a child's safe return diminish?"

"Cases are individual, Ms. Price." He mentally cursed her for trying to sensationalize an already terrible situation. Unprincipled bitch. But then, he knew that firsthand, didn't he? "There's no reason to frighten people by connecting either the crimes themselves or their outcomes to this incident."

Paige didn't bat an eyelash at the reprimand. She forged onward—straight for the jugular. "Does this case hold a special significance for you, Chief Holt, considering your own personal—"

Mitch didn't wait for a conclusion to the question. He ended the interview for her, turning on his heel and stalking off toward the arena, shrugging off the hand that reached for his arm. The rage seethed inside him, hissed like steam in a pressure cooker. Behind him he could hear Paige saving herself gracefully, tying up the story with a neat, touching bow of words.

". . . first on the scene as a big-city horror strikes at the heart of this quiet small town, this is Paige Price, *TV 7 News.*"

Someone called out, "And . . . we're clear! That's it for the moment, folks."

He heard the technicians bitching about the cold, then the sharp clack of boot heels on the sidewalk, rushing up behind him.

"Mitch, wait!"

He jammed his hands in his coat pockets and continued up the steps without sparing her so much as a glance. Not that she was the least daunted by his ignoring her. Paige Price didn't dignify subtle hints.

"Mitch!"

"Nice save, Paige," he said flatly. "A touch of sensationalism, a touch of sympathy, let the viewers know you're the first vulture to roost. Very professional."

"It's my job." Somehow she managed to sound both apologetic and proud of herself.

"Yeah, I know all about it."

"You're still angry with me."

Mitch jerked open a door with more force than was necessary and stepped into the dimly lit foyer. His temper surged at the false note of hurt in her voice. She had a hell of a nerve playing the part of the wounded party. He was the one who had been sliced and diced in public, dissected by the cold metaphorical scalpels of Paige Price's shrewd mind and sharp tongue.

She had told him she wanted to do a piece on the native Floridian relocating to Minnesota, the big-city cop adjusting to small-town life. A harmless public interest story. What had aired was an exposé of his life. She had callously exhumed the past he had buried and broadcast it all over the state, the crowning jewel for her first prime time special for *TV 7 News*. The tragic tale of Mitchell Holt, soldier for justice, his life shattered by a random act of violence.

"Score another point for the investigative reporter." His sarcasm echoed harshly. The smile that twisted his mouth was mocking and bitter. He turned it on her like a spotlight. "Congratulations on once again discerning the obvious."

Her mouth tightened. She stared up at him, her eyes luminous. "What I reported was a matter of public record."

Just doing my job. Common knowledge. The public has a right to know. The excuses throbbed in his brain like hammers hitting at his sense of decency. The pressure hit the red line and his control snapped like brittle old metal.

"No!" Mitch bellowed, charging her a step. She backpedaled, eyes wide, and he pursued, leading with a finger that pointed at her like the lance of justice. "What you reported was *my life*. Not *background*. Not *color*. *My life*. I prefer *my life* to remain *my own*. If I wanted everyone in the state of Minnesota to know *my* life story, I'd be writing a fucking autobiography!"

She was against the wall now, the top of her head just below the photograph of Gordie Knutson shaking hands with Wayne Gretzky. No amount of professional polish could hide the fact that she was trembling. Even so, her gaze was steady on his, reading everything, soaking it all in and storing it away in that calculating brain. Mitch could all but see her searching for a way to use this, to gain something, to add a shade of "close personal knowledge" to her angle on the story. It made him sick. He'd known plenty of reporters over the years. All of them were a nuisance, but most of them played by a set of rules everyone understood. Paige Price disregarded rules as casually as most people disregarded the speed limit. Nothing was out of bounds.

She gathered her cool expertly, bent her perfect mouth into an arc of contrition. "I'm sorry if the story upset you, Mitch," she said quietly. "That wasn't my intent."

Mitch pulled himself back, his face twisting at the acrid

taste of disgust. He wanted to wrap his hands around her slender, lovely throat and shake her like a rag doll. He envisioned banging her beautiful head against the block wall until Gordie's picture fell down, in an attempt to physically knock some sense of propriety into her. But he couldn't do that and he knew it.

With an extreme effort he carefully packed the rage into that little room in his chest and slammed the door.

"I know your intent, Ms. Price," he said tightly. "Touch some hearts and win yourself the local news pissant version of an Emmy. I hope it looks good on your trophy shelf. I could suggest several more creative places for you to put it, but I'll leave them to your imagination."

She put her hand on his arm. "Mitch, I'd like us to be friends."

"Christ." He laughed. "I'd hate to see how you treat your enemies!"

"Okay," she admitted, her voice soft, her sapphire gaze steady and earnest, "I should have been more up front with you about the background for the story. I can see that now."

"Twenty-twenty hindsight."

She ignored his sarcasm. "Don't I get a second chance? We could have dinner. Sit down together and clear the air—when this case is over, of course."

"Of course," Mitch sneered. "And as you dangle that promise out in front of me like a carrot on a stick, I'm supposed to give you little scoops on the case, right? Isn't that how it works?" His eyes narrowed with revulsion. "I had dinner with you once, Paige. Once was enough."

She blinked as if he'd hurt her. As if I could, Mitch thought.

"It could have been more than dinner," she whispered, her expression softening, the hand on his arm moving in a subtle caress. "It still could be. I like you, Mitch. I know I made a mistake. Let me make it up to you."

She didn't seem to feel it necessary to point out her own appeal. Her ego probably let her believe any man with feeling below the waist would want her, regardless of the less attractive aspects of her personality.

Mitch shook his head. "Amazing. You'd literally do anything, wouldn't you?" Turning a pointed look on her hand, he lifted it from his arm and dropped it. "Frankly, Ms. Price, I'd sooner stick my dick in a meat grinder. Now, if you'll excuse me, I have a stolen child to find. Impossible as it may be for you to comprehend, he's a hell of a lot more important than you."

CHAPTER 8

"Old girlfriend?" Megan asked carefully as Mitch stormed up the steps.

He automatically shot a look in the direction of the lobby. From her vantage point she had probably witnessed the entire scene. For that matter, the *TV 7* camera and sound people looking in from the outside had probably seen it as well. Great.

He dropped into the seat beside her, glowering. "Not in this lifetime."

"What happened? She burn you on a case?"

"Dismembered might be a better description," he muttered to himself, his gaze shifting to the ice below.

He had no desire to talk about the story, no desire to satisfy Megan O'Malley's curiosity about his past. His eyes landed on the spot along the boards where he had pinned her. It seemed a year ago, and yet he could still taste the desire to kiss her, still smell the faint aroma of cheese that clung tenaciously to her coat. He wished they could have been suspended in that moment indefinitely. Dangerous thinking for a man who wasn't looking for a relationship and a woman who didn't date cops. They were going to have problems enough with the matter of who was in charge without adding sex to the equation.

"Let's just say Paige Price should have her promo photo taken with an ax in one hand and a butcher knife in the other," he grumbled.

While wearing black lace underwear and stiletto heels. Megan kept the thought to herself. A catty remark might be misconstrued. *And just how would you mean for it to be construed, O'Malley?* She didn't care to answer that question. She didn't care to think how Paige Price—so tall and elegant and model-perfect—made her feel short and plain and unkempt. Glamour looks were not a prerequisite of her job. And the job was all that mattered here.

"So where do you want to set up the command post?" she asked.

"The old fire hall. It's on Oslo Street, half a block from the station and half a block from the sheriff's department. The garages are being used for parade floats, but there are a couple of large meeting rooms that will serve the purpose, and a bunk room upstairs. I've already called the phone company, and Becker's Office Supply is hauling in copy and fax machines. CopyCats are working on the fliers."

"Good. What information we have is already going out on the bureau teletype. I've been in touch with the National Center for Missing and Exploited Children. They're sending a support person down from the Cities. So is Missing Children Minnesota. They'll be a big help with getting the fliers distributed regionally and nationally. They'll also offer support for the family."

Mitch thought of Hannah sitting on the love seat, alone, in misery, and his heart ached. "They'll need it."

"I've got Records compiling a list of all known child molesters in a hundred-mile radius and a list of all reports of attempted abductions and suspected child predator situations in that same radius."

"That's like building a haystack in which to find our needle," Mitch said glumly.

"It's a starting place, Chief. We've got to start somewhere."

"Yeah. If only we knew where we were going."

They sat in silence for a moment. Mitch leaned ahead in his seat, his elbows on his knees, shoulders sagging beneath the weight of it all. No crime of any note had taken place in Deer Lake since he'd come on the job. Burglaries, fights, domestic disputes—those were the stock crimes of a small town. Drug deals were as heavy-duty as it got, and what they had here didn't hold a candle to what he'd seen on a daily basis in Florida.

He'd grown complacent, maybe even a little lazy. He'd let

down his guard. A far cry from his days on the force in Miami. He'd been like a racehorse then—all taut muscles and nerves strung as tight as violin strings, instincts and reflexes like lightning, running on adrenaline and caffeine. Every day had brought a crisis of magnitude, dulling his sensitivity until murder and rape and robbery and kidnapping seemed normal. But those days were long behind him. He felt rusty now, slow and clumsy.

"Have you done an abduction before?" he asked.

"I've been in on a couple of searches. But I know the procedure," she added defensively. She sat up a little straighter in her seat. "This is all SOP. If you want to waste our time checking—"

"Whoa, Fury!" Mitch held up a hand to check her tirade. "Innocent question. I wasn't impugning your abilities."

"Oh. Sorry." She shrunk down, heat rising into her cheeks.

Mitch dismissed her embarrassment, looking back out onto the ice. His eyes were bleak, the lines of strain beside them etching deeper into his skin.

"I've done four."

"Did you find the kids?" She wished instantly she hadn't asked. Her sixth sense—her cop sense—twisted uneasily inside her.

"Twice." A simple one-word response, but his face spoke volumes about tragedy and disappointment and the hard life lessons cops had to suffer again and again with the families of victims.

"They don't all end that way," Megan asserted, pushing herself to her feet. "This one won't. We damn well won't let it."

They would have damn little say in the matter, Mitch thought as he rose. That was the bald, ugly truth. They could launch an exhaustive search, utilize incredible manpower, use every tool modern technology had to offer, and it still came down to luck and mercy. Someone in the right place at the right time. The whim of a warped mind and a twisted conscience.

She knew it, too, he thought, but she wouldn't say so. She wouldn't jinx them and she wouldn't give in to the fear. Her jaw was set at a stubborn angle, her brows pulled tight and low over her jewel-green eyes. He could feel the determination rolling off her in waves and he wanted to pull her close and absorb some of it because all he was feeling at the moment was tired and disillusioned. Not a smart idea. Still, he reached out and brushed a thumb across a streak of dirt on her cheek, picked up no doubt in the close encounter with Art Goble's hounds.

"Let's hit the bricks, O'Malley," he said. "See if we can't make good on that promise."

The mobile lab and technicians from Special Operations arrived almost simultaneously with the BCA helicopter. The chopper set down in a parking lot on the fairgrounds and Mitch hustled to meet them. Megan led the other agents into the ice arena to brief them.

"What have you got for us, Irish?"

Dave Larkin was an evidence tech, thirty, cute in a beach-boy sort of way. He loved his job, if not the crimes that made it necessary, and always came to the scene eager to dig in. He was a good guy and a good cop, one of Megan's first friends when she had joined the bureau. If it hadn't been for his badge and his string of amiable ex-girlfriends, she might have taken him up on one of his many offers for a date.

"Not much," she admitted. "We assume the boy was taken off the sidewalk out front, but we have no witnesses at the moment to substantiate this, therefore, no true crime scene. In any event, there's been a parade of cars over the drive and in the parking lot, so we're screwed there. In the way of evidence, we've got Josh Kirkwood's duffel bag—which we left where we found it—and we have this note, which was sticking up out of the bag."

She handed Dave a glassine bag with the note inside. He read it and frowned. "Christ, a head case."

"Anyone who grabs a little boy off the street is a head case, whether he leaves a note or not," said Hank Welsh, a still photographer for Special Operations. The others nodded gravely.

Dave went on studying the note, looking displeased. "This ain't much, kiddo. Looks like a laser printer on ordinary copy paper. We'll run Ninhydrin and argon-ion laser tests, but our chances of getting a decent fingerprint off this . . . ? You'd get better odds on the Mets winning the next World Series."

"Do what you can," Megan said. "Our priorities now are to get the Kirkwoods' phones wired and to get the command post up and running. You graphics guys—I know it might seem pointless at the moment, since we haven't been able to preserve a scene, but I'd like you to shoot stills and video outside. It might come in handy later on."

"You're the boss," Hank replied archly, coming to his feet.

Megan's gaze sharpened on him. Welsh was heavyset with a ruddy face left pitted by a long-over adolescent battle with acne. He was closer to fifty than forty and he looked none too pleased to be there. Megan wondered if it was the case or her that gave him that look of a man with chronic heartburn.

The techs moved toward the doors, but Dave Larkin hung back, planting a hand on Megan's shoulder. "Rumor has it Marty Wilhelm was up for Leo's job," he said in a low voice. "Do you know him? He's a Spec Op guy."

Megan shook her head.

"Marty is engaged to Hank's daughter, et cetera, et cetera . . ."

"Oh, swell."

"Don't sweat it. Hank knows his job and he'll do it." He flashed her one of his beach-bum grins. "For what it's worth, I'm glad you got the assignment. You deserve it."

"At the moment, I'm not sure if that's a compliment or a curse."

"It's a compliment—and I'm not making it for the sole purpose of getting you to go out with me. That will just be a bonus."

"In your dreams, Larkin."

Impervious to put-downs, he went on as if she hadn't spoken. "I'm not the only one rooting for you, either, Irish. A lot of people think it's great you got the nod. You're a pioneer."

"I don't want to be a pioneer; I want to be a cop. Sometimes I think life would be so much easier if we were all gender neutral."

"Yeah, but then how would we decide who leads when we dance?"

"We'd take turns," she said, pushing open a door. "I have no desire to spend my whole life dancing backward."

As they stepped out into the cold, his grin faded. "How

many guys will they spare you from Regional for the investigation?"

"Maybe fifteen."

"You'll get at least another ten volunteers. This kind of thing rings a lot of bells. You know, if kids aren't safe on the streets of a town like this . . . And if we can't catch the scumbags who pull this kind of shit, what kind of cops are we?"

Desperate cops. Scared cops. Megan kept the answer to herself as she looked around. Down the block, porch lights burned bright. She could see a couple of Mitch's uniforms tramping from one house to another. In the other direction, the beams from flashlights bobbed and darted like fireflies across the dark fairgrounds. Overhead, the eerie thump of helicopter rotors broke the calm of the night. And somewhere out there a faceless person held the fate of Josh Kirkwood in his hand.

Desperate and scared barely began to cover the feelings that thought inspired.

DAY 2
4:34 A.M. 12°

Paul pulled his Celica into the garage, killed the engine, and just sat there, numb, staring straight ahead at the bicycles he had hung up on the wall for winter. Two mountain bikes and the new dirt bike Josh had gotten for his birthday. The dirt bike was black with splashes of neon-bright purple and yellow. The wheels were like big blank eyes staring back at him.

Josh. Josh. Josh.

They had called the ground search at four A.M. and told everyone to regroup at the old fire hall at eight o'clock. Cold to the bone, exhausted, disheartened, the deputies and patrolmen and volunteers had trooped back to the ice arena parking lot.

Paul could see himself as if he were watching a movie—arms gesturing angrily, his face contorted as he'd railed at Mitch Holt.

"What the hell is going on? Why are you calling this off? Josh is still out there!"

"Paul, we can't push people beyond human endurance." They stood beside Holt's Explorer and Holt tried to put himself between Paul and any onlookers lingering around the lot. "They've been at it all night. Everybody is frozen and tired. It's best if we call it now, get some rest, and regroup when we have daylight to work with."

"You want to sleep?" Paul shouted, incredulous, wanting the whole world to hear him. Heads turned their way. "You're leaving my son out there with some madman so people can go home and sleep? This is incredible!"

Those lines had struck the ears of the press people who hadn't left for warm motel rooms, and they had descended like a swarm of mosquitoes smelling blood. Holt had been furious with the impromptu mini press conference that transpired, but Paul didn't give a shit what Mitch Holt liked. He wanted his outrage on the record. He wanted his grief and desperation on videotape for all the world to see.

Now he felt drained, empty. His hands were trembling on the leather-wrapped steering wheel. His heart beat a little faster, seeming to rise up to the base of his throat until he felt as if he couldn't breathe. Somewhere in the distance a helicopter passed over the rooftops.

Josh. Josh. Josh.

He bolted from the car, walked around the hood of Hannah's van, up the steps, and into the mud room. The kitchen lights were on. A stranger sat at the table in the breakfast alcove, bleary-eyed, paging through a magazine and drinking coffee out of a giant stoneware mug from the Renaissance Festival. He came to attention as Paul stepped into the room, shrugging out of his down coat.

"Curt McCaskill, BCA." Stifling a yawn, he held up an ID.

Paul leaned across the table and studied it, then gave the agent a suspicious look, as if he didn't quite trust the man to be who he said he was. McCaskill endured the examination with stoic patience. His bloodshot eyes were primarily blue, his hair a thick shock of ginger red. He wore a multicolored ski sweater that looked like a television test pattern.

"And you are . . . ?" the agent prompted.

"Paul Kirkwood. I live here. That's my table you're sitting at, my coffee you're drinking, my son your colleagues would be out looking for if they weren't too lazy to bother."

McCaskill frowned as he came around the table and offered Paul his handshake. "Sorry about your son, Mr. Kirkwood. They've called the search for the night?"

Paul went to a cupboard, pulled down a mug, and filled it with coffee from the pot on the warmer. It was bitter and strong and swirled in his stomach like discarded crankcase drippings.

"Left my son out there to God knows what fate," he mumbled.

"Sometimes it's better if they can regroup and start fresh," McCaskill said.

Paul stared at the pattern in the vinyl floor. "And sometimes they're too late."

In the silence, the refrigerator began to hum and the ice maker chattered.

Josh. Josh. Josh.

"Ah . . . I'm here to monitor the phones," McCaskill explained, avoiding the topic of outcomes. "All calls will be taped, in the event the kidnapper makes a ransom demand. And we'll be able to trace them."

Kirkwood didn't seem to have any interest in the technology. He went on staring at the floor for another minute, then brought his head up. He looked like a junkie in need of a fix. His eyes were red-rimmed, his face drawn, skin ashen. His hand was shaking as he set his cup down on the counter. Poor guy.

"Why don't you go take a hot shower, Mr. Kirkwood. Then get some rest. I'll call you and the missus if anything comes in."

Without a word Paul turned and went into the family room, where a single ginger-jar lamp burned low. He started past the couch and jumped when Karen Wright sat up, blinking and disheveled. A bloodred afghan dropped into her lap as she braced her arm against the back of the couch and looked up at him. Her other hand automatically combed back through her fine ash-blond hair. It fell into place like a silk curtain, a classic bob cut that fell just short of her slender shoulders.

"Hi, Paul," she murmured. "Natalie Bryant called me to come sit with Hannah. I'm so sorry about Josh."

He stared at her, still trying to adjust to her sudden appearance in his living room. Nausea swirled through him like water sucking down a drain.

"All the neighborhood women are taking turns."

"Oh. Fine," he mumbled.

She frowned prettily, her lips a feminine bow set in a fine-featured oval face. From the corner of his eye he could see McCaskill sliding back down into his chair at the kitchen table, his attention already on his magazine.

"Are you all right?" she asked. "You should probably go lie down."

"Yes," Paul murmured. His heartbeat stuttered and pumped as his brain swam dizzily. *Josh. Josh. Josh.* "Yes, I'm going."

He was turning as the words came out of his mouth, struggling to keep himself from running out of the room. He was sweating like a horse, even as chills raced through him. He peeled his sweater off over his head and dropped it on the floor in the hall. His fingers fumbled over the buttons of his Pendleton shirt. The shakes went through him like the tremors before an earthquake. His heart raced. His head pounded. *Josh. Josh. Josh.*

The shirt was hanging from one arm as he stumbled into the bathroom. He fell to his knees in front of the toilet and retched, his whole body convulsing with the effort to vomit. On the third attempt the coffee came up, but there was nothing else in his stomach to be discarded. Clutching the bowl, he dropped his head on his forearm and closed his eyes. The image of his son pulsed behind his eyelids.

Josh. Josh. Josh.

"Oh, God, Josh," he whimpered.

The tears came, scalding and scarce, squeezing out of him. When they were spent, he pushed himself up off the floor and finished undressing, folding his clothes neatly and dropping them into the hamper on top of half a dozen tangled wet towels. Shaking like a palsy victim, he climbed into the tub and turned the shower on full blast, letting the hot water pound the cold out of his bones. It pelted his skin like hailstones, washed away the sweat and tears and the faint tang of sex that clung to him.

After he had dried himself off and hung the towel on the bar, he slipped into the thick black terry robe that hung on the back of the door and went out into the hall. The door to Lily's room was ajar, letting a sliver of the hall light fall across the rose-pink carpet. Farther down the hall, the door to Josh's room stood open.

Everything about the room said *boy*. A friend of Hannah's had painted murals on each wall, each mural depicting a different sport. A poster of Twins outfielder Kirby Puckett held a place of honor on the baseball wall. A miniature desk sat between two windows, piled with books and toy action figures. Bunk beds were stacked along another wall.

Hannah sat on the bottom bed, her long legs curled beneath her, her arms wrapped tight around a fat stuffed dinosaur. She watched Paul as he turned on the small lamp on the bedside table. She wanted him to grin at her and hold his arms out as he told her they had found Josh safe and sound, but she knew that wouldn't happen. Paul looked old and drawn, a preview of how he would look in twenty years. With his wet hair slicked back, the bones of his face stood out prominently.

"They called off the ground search until morning."

Hannah said nothing. She didn't have the energy or the heart to ask if they had found any clues. Paul would say if they had. He just looked at her. The silence spoke for itself.

"Have you slept?"

"No."

She looked as if she hadn't slept in days, he thought. Her hair frizzed around her head; mascara and fatigue had left dark smudges beneath her eyes. She had changed out of her clothes into another of his bathrobes, a cheap, garish blue velour job his mother had given him for Christmas years before. Paul refused to wear it. He had worked hard to be able to afford better than the junk Kmart had to offer. But Hannah refused to throw it out. She kept it in her closet and wore it from time to time. To irk him, he thought, but tonight he ignored it.

She looked vulnerable. *Vulnerable* was a word Paul seldom used to describe his wife. Hannah was a nineties woman—intelligent, capable, strong, equal. She didn't need. She could have lived just as well without him as with him. She was exactly the kind of woman he had dreamed of marrying. A wife he could be proud of instead of embarrassed by. A woman who was someone other than her husband's shadow, slave, and doormat.

Be careful what you wish for, Paul . . . His mother's mousy voice whispered in the back of his mind. He shut it out as successfully as he had always managed to shut her out.

"I've just been sitting here," Hannah murmured. "I wanted to feel close to him."

Her chin quivered and she squeezed her eyes shut. Paul sat down on the edge of the bed, reached over, and touched her hand. Her fingers were as cold as ice. He covered them with his, thinking that it used to be easy to touch her. There had been a time when they couldn't get enough of each other. That seemed ages ago.

"About— When you told me—" He broke off and sighed, then tried again. "I'm sorry I jumped on you. I wanted to blame somebody."

"I try," she whispered almost to herself, tears squeezing out between her lashes. "I try *so hard*."

To be a good wife. To be a good mother. To be a good doctor. To be a good person. To be everything to everyone. She tried so hard and thought she succeeded most of the time. But she must have done something wrong to be made to pay this way.

"Shh . . ." Paul pried the dinosaur from her grasp and pulled her into his arms, letting her cry on his shoulder, letting her lean on him. He rubbed her back through the cheap velour robe and felt needed. "Hush . . ."

He kissed her hair and breathed in its scent. He listened to her soft weeping, absorbed the feel of her clinging to him, and desire drifted through him like smoke. Hannah needed him now. Superwoman. Dr. Garrison. She didn't need his income or his friends or his social position. God, she didn't even need his name. He was chronically superfluous to her life. He was the shadow, the nobody. But she needed him now. She wrapped her arms around him and hung on tight.

"Let's go to bed," he whispered.

Hannah let him help her up from Josh's bed and walk her down the hall to their own room. She made no protest as he slipped the robe from her shoulders and kissed the side of her neck. Breath shuddered out of her lungs as his hands cupped her breasts. She had felt so alone all night. Emotionally abandoned. Exiled. She needed so badly to feel loved, comforted, forgiven.

She turned her head and brushed her mouth across his, inviting his kiss, rising into his kiss, her breasts pressing into his chest, her back arching as his hand settled low along the valley of her spine. The need burned out the fear for a few moments. It suspended time and offered a refuge. Hannah took it gladly, greedily, desperately. She pulled Paul down to the bed with her, wanting his weight on top of her. She opened herself to him as he pressed his erection between her legs, needing to feel him inside her. She held him while he arched into her again and again, wanting nothing more than the contact, the illusion of intimacy. And when it was over, she closed her eyes and lay her head on his shoulder, wishing against the hollow ache in her chest that the sense of closeness could last. But it wouldn't. Not even on this night, when she longed so desperately for something to cling to.

What happened to us, Paul?

She didn't know how to ask. She still couldn't believe it was real, this distance and anger that hung between them. It seemed all a bad dream. They had been so happy. The perfect couple. The perfect family. The perfect life of Hannah Garrison. Now her marriage was falling apart like a cheap tapestry and her son had been stolen. *Stolen . . . taken . . . abducted. God, what a nightmare.*

Her eyes drifted shut on that terrible thought, the exhaustion winning out at last, and she slid from the nightmare into blessed blackness.

Paul knew the instant she fell asleep. The tension went out of the arm she had banded across his chest. Her breathing deepened. He lay there, staring up at the skylight, feeling caught in the middle of some surreal play. His son was gone. By this time tomorrow Josh Kirkwood would be a household word all over the state. Newspapers would splash his picture all over their front pages, along with the impassioned plea Paul had made in the parking lot of the ice arena at four A.M. *Please bring my son back!*

Josh. Josh. Josh.

His eyes burned as he stared up at the starless sky. And the play went on. Act Two. His wife lay naked in his arms hours after his mistress had done the same. Overhead, helicopter blades beat the night air.

5:43 A.M. 12°

Mitch climbed out of his truck, his gaze automatically scanning the alley behind his house for signs of reporters, skittish after the debacle in the ice arena parking lot. He wouldn't have put it past any of them to follow him. *Get a shot of the failure of a police chief as he drags his sorry ass home. Lets child predators snatch kids off the streets of his town. No big surprise. Look what happened in Miami.*

It settled on his aching shoulders like a cloak—the guilt, edged in anger, dyed black by his mood. He threw it off with a violent swing of his arm, snarling in self-contempt.

What a jerk you are, Holt. This isn't about you. It isn't about Miami. Hold the old rage inside where it belongs, and rage anew for Josh.

Easier said than done. The anger, the sense of impotence and loss and betrayal, were echoes from his past. And as much as every cop knew better than to personalize a case, he couldn't stop himself from feeling as if this crime had been perpetrated in part against him. This was his town, his haven, the safe little world he could control. These were his people, his responsibility. He represented safety to them, and they were his extended family.

Family. The word hung with him as he went up the path to the back door, the snow squeaking beneath his feet in the icy stillness of the early morning. He let himself into the house and toed off his heavy Sorel boots in the back hall.

In the kitchen Scotch, the old yellow Labrador who was

his only roommate in Jessie's absence, cracked open one eye and looked at him without raising his head from his cushioned dog bed. At twelve, Scotch had officially retired from guard duty. He filled his time sleeping or wandering around the house, carrying in his mouth whatever object struck his fancy en route on his travels—a shoe, a glove, a throw pillow from the couch, a paperback book. One of Jessie's Minnie Mouse dolls was wedged between his head and his paws for a pillow.

Mitch let him keep it. The old scoundrel might have stolen it out of her bedroom, but it was just as likely Jessie had put him to bed with it. The Strausses lived across the alley, and every day after school Jessie came over with her grandfather to let Scotch outside and to play with him. She adored the old dog. Scotch patiently suffered through dress-up games and tea parties with her, faithful, gentle, returning the little girl's love unconditionally.

The images striking on tender feelings, Mitch padded into the kitchen in his stocking feet. The light above the sink cast the room in amber and shadow. His gaze wandered aimlessly. The house dated back to the thirties. A nice, solid story-and-a-half with hardwood floors and a fireplace in the living room and big maple and oak trees in the yard. A house with character that remained mostly repressed because of his lack of decorating skills.

That had been Allison's forte. She was a nest builder with an eye for style and a love of small detail. She would have converted this kitchen into a place of warmth and charm with framed prints and strings of peppers and old Mason jars filled with cinnamon-scented potpourri. Mitch had left the room exactly as it was when he moved in—the walls mostly bare, the curtain at the window above the sink an old rummage sale reject left by the last owners. The only things Mitch had added were drawings Jessie had done for him. Those he mounted on the refrigerator with magnets and stuck up on the wall with tape. Somehow, the bright, childish images in the otherwise vacant room served only to point out how bleak and empty the house was.

He felt hollow as he stared at the pictures. Alone. Lonely. God, sometimes the loneliness ached so badly he would have given anything to escape it—including his life. He would have died as penance, but then, living was a harsher punishment.

Crazy thoughts. Irrational thoughts, the department psychiatrist had told him. Logically, he knew it wasn't his fault. Logically, he knew hc could not have prevented what happened. But logic had little to do with feeling.

Leaning back against the sink, he squeezed his eyes shut and saw his son. Kyle was six. Bright. Quiet. Wanted a two-wheeler for Christmas. Took his dad to school during job week and beamed while Mitch told the first grade about being a policeman.

"Policemen help people and protect them from the bad guys."

He could hear the words, could look out on the small sea of little faces, his gaze homing in on Kyle's expression of shy pride. So small, so full of innocence and trust and all those things the world had ground out of his father.

"Policemen help people and protect them from the bad guys."

A hoarse, tortured sound wrenched out of Mitch's throat. The feelings ripped loose, the bars of their cage weakened by fatigue and memory and fear. He clamped a hand over his mouth and tried to swallow them back. His whole body shook with the effort. He couldn't let them loose; he would drown in them. He had to be strong. He had to focus. He had a job to do. His daughter needed him. The excuses came one after another. Deny the feelings. Ignore them. Put them off. His town needed him. Josh Kirkwood needed him.

He forced his eyes to open. He stared out the kitchen window at the velvet gray of the day before dawn, and still in his memory he could see Kyle. His vision doubled, the image splitting, the face of the second body going out of focus and coming back as Josh.

God, please no. Don't do that to him. Don't do that to his parents.

Don't do that to me.

Shame washed through him like cold water.

Across the alley a light came on in the Strauss kitchen. Six A.M. Jurgen was up. He had been retired from the railroad for three years, but kept his schedule as regular as if he were still going down to the Great Northern switching yard every day. Up at six, start the coffee. Drive down to the Big Steer truck stop on the interstate to pick up the *StarTribune* because paperboys were unreliable. Home for coffee and a bowl of hot cereal while he read the paper. His quiet time before Joy emerged from their bed to begin the recitation of her daily litany—a deceptively soft, deceptively mild running commentary on all that was wrong with the world, the town, the neighbors, her home, her health, her son-in-law.

As badly as Mitch wanted to avoid his in-laws, the sudden need to see Jessie was stronger. To look at her and hold her and see that she was real and alive and warm and sweet and safe. He stepped back into his boots and trudged outside without bothering to lace them.

Jurgen came to the back door of the neat Cape Cod house in his daily uniform of jeans and a flannel shirt, neatly tucked in. He was a stocky man of medium height with piercing Paul-Newman-blue eyes and military-cropped gray hair.

"Mitch! I was just making the coffee. Come on in," he said, his expression a mix of surprise and annoyance at having his regimen interrupted. "Any word on the Kirkwood boy? Cripes, that's a terrible business."

"No," Mitch replied softly. "Nothing yet."

Jurgen swung the basket out on the coffeemaker and dumped in a scoop of Folger's. Too much, as usual. Joy would comment on it being too strong, as always, then drink it anyway so she could later complain about the heartburn it gave her.

"Have a seat. You look like hell. What brings you over at this time of day?"

Mitch ignored the chairs arranged neatly around the kitchen table. "I came to see Jessie."

"Jess? It's six o'clock in the morning!" The older man glowered at him.

"I know. I've only got a little time," Mitch mumbled. Going into the dining room and up the stairs, he left Jurgen to think what he wanted.

Jessie had the room her mother had grown up in. The same bed, same dresser, same ivory wallpaper strewn with mauve tea roses. Jessie, being Jessie, had, of course, added her own touches—stickers of the Little Mermaid and Princess Jasmine from *Aladdin*. Joy had scolded her, but the stickers were the variety that did not peel off without a fight, and so they had remained. Because she spent so much time there, the dresser drawers were filled with her clothes. On the toy shelves, the place of honor was given over to figurines of Disney characters—Mickey and Minnie, Donald Duck and nephews, a broken alarm clock with Jiminy Cricket perched on top with his cricket hands clamped over his ears.

The clock had been Kyle's. Seeing it never failed to bring Mitch a stab of pain.

He crept into the room, closed the door softly behind him, and leaned back against it. His daughter slept in the middle of the old double bed, her arms curled around her teddy bear. She was the picture of childhood lying there asleep, dreaming sweet dreams. Her long brown hair was plaited in a thick loose braid that disappeared beneath the covers. The frilly collar of her flannel nightgown framed her face and her dark lashes curled against her cheek. Her plump little mouth was pursed in a perfect O as she breathed deeply and regularly.

He couldn't look at her like this—when she seemed most precious, most vulnerable—without having emotion kick him in the belly with all the strength of a mule. She was everything to him. She was the reason he had never given in to the desperate wish to end his pain after Allison and Kyle had been taken from him. His love for her was so deep, so fierce, it sometimes scared him. Scared him to think what he would do if he ever lost her, too.

Carefully he lifted the layer of blankets and quilt and eased himself down, resting his back against the carved oak headboard. Jessie's eyes blinked open and she looked up at him, smiling a sleepy smile.

"Hi, Daddy," she murmured. She wriggled herself and her bear onto his lap and snuggled against him.

Mitch tugged the covers up beneath her chin and kissed the top of her head. "Hi, cuddlebug."

"Whatcha doing here?"

"Loving you up. Is that okay?"

She nodded, burrowing her face into the thick cotton sweater that spanned his chest. Mitch just wrapped his arms around her and held her, listening to her breathe, breathing deep the scents of warm child and Mr. Bubble.

"Did you find the lost boy, Daddy?" she asked in a drowsy voice.

"No, honey," he whispered around the ache in his throat. "We didn't."

"That's okay, Daddy," she assured him, hugging him tight. "Peter Pan will bring him home."

Act I: Chaos and panic. Predictable and pathetic. We watched, amused by their pointless sense of urgency. Going nowhere at a breakneck pace. Grasping at the dark. Finding nothing but their own fear.

But is there any comfort to be found?
Man . . . loves what vanishes;
What more is there to say?

CHAPTER 9

The old fire hall in downtown Deer Lake was overflowing with law enforcement officers, volunteers, media people, and locals who had come out of fear and morbid curiosity. Mitch arrived, freshly showered and shaved and running on a giant mug of coffee grabbed at Tom Thumb and drunk en route.

He had expected the place to be in a state of chaos, had wondered where he was going to find the patience to deal with it, but there seemed to be a sense of order to the madness. The command post had been set up in one of the two community rooms used mainly for the senior citizens card club and 4-H meetings since the fire department had been moved into snazzier quarters on Ramsey Drive. The hotline telephones had been set up—six of them spaced apart on a long bank of tables. Two of the phones were already manned and busy. Copy and fax machines sat along the opposite wall. At another long table volunteers were stacking up the fliers that had been run off during the night with Josh's picture and vital statistics.

Mitch moved on to the room down the hall where those who would be resuming or joining the search milled around, drinking coffee and eating doughnuts. This room would serve as meeting place and makeshift media center. The walls were painted a moldy shade of green—a clearance color from Hardware Hank in 1986. The sickly hue went well with the musty smell of old linoleum and dust. Two dozen dismembered construction-paper hands decorated the wall behind the podium at the front of the room, the 4-H pledge scrawled on them in crayon. Each macabre masterpiece was signed by the artist and marked with his or her age.

Already the room was crowded with reporters and photographers and cameramen from newspapers, radio and television stations all around the state. A photographer stood three feet back from the wall, killing time taking artsy shots of the hands. A television reporter stood along another wall, beside the wall plaque of Boy Scout knots, staring gravely into the lens of a video camera as he oozed platitudes about Norman Rockwell towns and all-American families.

The ranks of those who had come to document the tragedy would only grow as the search continued. At least for the next week—if it lasted that long. While the search was at its most intense, they would be constantly underfoot, looking for a scoop, an exclusive, an angle no one else had.

Damn bunch of parasites, Mitch thought as he shouldered his way through the throng of reporters, scowling and snarling in answer to their shouted questions.

At the front of the room Megan was overseeing the setup for the press conference, directing the placement of the podium, a screen and overhead projector. Her small mouth set in a tight line, she wheeled on a reporter who ventured too near.

"For the sixty-ninth time, Mr. Forster, the press conference will not begin until nine," she said sharply. "Our first concern is to find Josh Kirkwood. If he is still in the vicinity, that means we have to get these people organized and resume the search."

A reporter for the *StarTribune* since the days of Linotype, Henry Forster had the face of a bulldog, a balding head adorned with liver spots, and long, weedy strands of gray hair he wore in a classic horizontal comb-over. His trademark dirty horn-rimmed bifocals sat crooked beneath a pair of bushy eyebrows that should have had their own zip code. He was a big old warhorse with hips that had splayed out in his later years to provide a good base for his medicine-ball belly. Megan would have guessed he had slept in his brown trousers and cheap white dress shirt, but she knew from past acquaintance Henry always looked that unkempt.

The eyebrows crawled up his forehead. "Does that mean you think the boy has been taken out of this area?"

Two of his cohorts perked up and inched forward away from the wall, like rats venturing forth to sniff at some promising crumb.

Megan stopped them in their tracks with a look that had incinerated humans. She turned the look on Henry, who stood close enough that the fumes of his Old Spice burned her nasal linings. He didn't retreat. He kept staring at her as if he fully expected an answer.

No doubt he did, Megan thought. Forster had seniority and a track record that had littered his office with awards, which he allegedly used as paperweights and ashtrays. Politicians cowered at the mention of his name. The BCA brass cursed the day he was born—one of the original seven. Henry Forster had been the man who'd blown the lid off the sexual harassment charges in the bureau the previous fall. He was the last man Megan wanted sniffing after her heels. The pressure of this case would be enough without Henry Forster's grimy bifocals magnifying her every move.

Show no fear, O'Malley. He can smell fear—even through that aftershave.

"That means Officer Noga is going to escort you out of this room if you don't get out of the way," she told him without flinching.

She turned her back on Forster as he snorted his affront. One of the other reporters who had been standing in his considerable shadow hoping for a scrap muttered, "Little bitch." Megan wondered if they would dare make slurs behind Noga's broad back. She caught hold of the patrolman's sleeve and he looked down at her, his dark eyes bloodshot and bleary.

"Officer Noga, would you please herd these press weasels out of the way before I rip out their windpipes and have them for breakfast?"

He scowled at the reporters. "You got it, Miss—Agent."

"No offense," Mitch muttered, easing into the spot Noga vacated, "but I don't think you have much of a shot at Miss Congeniality today."

"Miss Congeniality is a wimp," Megan returned. "Besides, neither one of us is beauty pageant material. You look like I feel."

Mitch made a face. "Gender confusion. Don't let the boys from the *Pioneer Press* hear that."

"I think they already have their theories."

"Did you get any sleep?"

The question seemed perfunctory. It looked to Mitch like she had gone through the same minimal morning routine as he had. She had changed into a pair of snug black ski pants and a heavy Irish fisherman's sweater over a turtleneck. Her dark hair was clean and brushed back into a utilitarian ponytail. Her makeup was scant and did nothing to hide the violet smudges beneath her eyes.

She shot him a look. "Who needs sleep when you can take an ice cold shower? I have an apartment with no utilities. I shaved my legs by lantern light, fed my cats, and came back here. How about you?"

"I have a dog and hot water," he said, moving around the end of the table. "And I'll keep my legs hairy, thanks. Has anything come in from your people?"

"Besides ten pages of known pedophiles? No."

Mitch shook his head, his stomach turning at the idea that there were so many scumballs preying on children within a hundred miles of his town—and his daughter. Christ, the world was turning into a cesspool. Even out in rural Minnesota he could feel the muck seeping up around his shoes. It was as if overnight someone had opened the floodgates on the sewer.

He looked out over the crowd as he stepped behind the podium—men from his own office and the sheriff's department, volunteer firemen, concerned citizens, Harris College students who had stayed in town for their winter break. What he saw in their faces was determination and fear. One of their own had been taken and they were there to get him back. Mitch wanted to believe they would do it, but in his experience hope didn't get the job done.

Still, he drew himself up and put on the game face. He addressed the troops and issued orders and sounded like a leader. He narrowed his eyes against the glare of the television sun-guns and thought he probably looked determined and purposeful instead of blind.

The cameras rolled film, not willing to wait for the official press conference, not wanting to miss out on any of the drama.

Flash strobes went off at irregular intervals as the newspaper photographers shot stills of the cops and the crowd. The reporters scribbled. In one of the front row chairs Paige Price sat with her long legs crossed and a notebook on her lap. She gazed up at Mitch with an earnest expression while her cameraman knelt at her feet and got a reaction shot of her. Business as usual.

A map of Park County went up on the projection screen, the area cut into sections by red lines Mitch and Russ Steiger had drawn at five A.M. Teams of searchers were numbered and assigned areas. Instructions were given as to technique, what to look for, what to call to the team leader's attention. Mitch gave the mike over to Steiger, who added orders and details for the SO deputies, the mounted posse volunteers and snowmobile club members who would be searching the fields and densely wooded areas outside of town.

As fliers were passed out to all those present, media people included, Josh's photograph went up on the projection screen. The room went still. The murmured conversations died. The rustle of paper faded away. The silence was as heavy as an anvil, the soft whir of video cameras underscoring and somehow amplifying it. Every eye, every thought, every prayer, every heartbeat, was focused on the screen. Josh stared out at them with his sunny, gap-toothed smile, his hair a tangle of soft brown curls; every freckle was a mark of innocence, as much a symbol of boyhood as the Cub Scout uniform he wore so proudly. His eyes were bright with excitement for all life had to offer him.

"This is Josh," Mitch said quietly. "He's a nice boy. A lot of you have little boys just like him. Friendly, helpful, a good student. A happy, innocent little kid. He likes sports and playing with his dog. He has a baby sister who's wondering where he is. His parents are good people. Most of you know his mother, Dr. Garrison. A lot of you know his dad, Paul Kirkwood. They want their son back. Let's do everything we can to make that happen."

For a moment the silence hung, then in a gruff voice Russ Steiger ordered his men out and the search parties began filing from the room. Mitch wanted to go with them. The burden of rank prevented him. It was his job to deal with the press and the mayor and the city council. The position of chief often had less to do with the kind of in-the-trenches police work he had once thrived on and more to do with politics than he had ever cared for. He was a cop at heart. A damn good one once upon a time.

His gaze cut involuntarily to Paige Price. She caught the action as quickly as a trout snagging a fly, and rose gracefully, coming toward him while her colleagues remained seated, furiously jotting notes and mumbling into microcassette recorders.

"Mitch." She reached across the podium, deftly flicking off the switch of the microphone. Her expression was perfect—contrition and regret with just the right touch of caring. "About last night . . . I don't want cross words between us."

"I'm sure you don't," Mitch said coldly. "Keeps you from getting an edge."

Paige gave him the wounded look she had used to melt more than one wall of male resistance. But Mitch Holt wasn't buying and she called him a son of a bitch in her mind. Her exclusive of the night before had won her words of praise from the news director and station manager. Her agent had two words for the scoop—dollar signs. If she could keep ahead of the pack on this story, it would mean serious money, maybe even an offer from one of the larger network affiliates. She was shooting for L.A. Warm, sunny L.A. Regardless of where she went, it would beat this godforsaken icebox. But Mitch Holt stood in her way, a tarnished, battered knight upholding antiquated ideals.

"I'm sorry you think that's my only motivation," she murmured. "I'm not a barracuda, Mitch. Yes, I want a story out of this, like every other reporter in this room. But my first concern is this poor little boy."

Mitch didn't blink. "Save it for the Nielsen families."

Paige bit down on the tip of her tongue. From the corner of her eye she could see Henry Forster from the *StarTribune* shoving past people to reach them. She could feel his angry stare burning into her. Forster hated nothing more than being scooped by someone in television, unless it was being scooped by a woman in television. But before Forster could intrude on her moment, Agent O'Malley stepped into the picture.

"The press conference will begin shortly, Ms. Price," she said, steering Paige away from the podium. "Why don't you help yourself to a cup of coffee and a nice fat doughnut?"

The suggestion came with a smile etched in steel. Paige looked down at Megan O'Malley, amused that this slip of a woman was coming to the aid of a man who dwarfed her. She flicked a glance between them, speculating. Neither face gave anything away, which, to Paige's way of thinking, gave away much. She backed off toward the coffeepot, a hand raised in a false gesture of surrender.

"And may it all go straight to your hips," Megan muttered under her breath, moving back to her position behind the front table. She caught the wry look Mitch sent her and scowled at him. "Lack of sleep makes me uncharitable."

He raised an eyebrow, shuffled his papers, and flicked the microphone back on.

The press conference was woefully short on information. They had no suspects. They had no witnesses. They had no leads but the note the kidnapper had left behind and Mitch would not divulge the contents on the excuse that to do so might compromise the investigation later on. His official statement was that the Deer Lake Police Department, along with the other agencies involved, was taking every possible step to find Josh and apprehend his abductor.

Russ Steiger added that the sheriff's department would work around the clock. He would be overseeing the search himself in the field—a statement made with a bravado borne of self-importance. Park County attorney Rudy Stovich made the requisite statement about prosecuting to the full extent of the law. Megan gave the usual bureau line, offering investigative support, lab and records assistance at the request of the police and sheriff's departments.

Then began the feeding frenzy. The reporters clamored for attention, blurting out questions, each trying to shout the next one down.

"Is it true you're looking for a known pedophile?"

"Will the parents be giving statements?"

"Has the FBI been called in?"

"They're aware of the situation," Mitch said, fielding the last of the barrage. "We already have three agencies working on the case. We have all the resources of the BCA at our disposal. At the moment we don't believe Josh has been taken out of the immediate area. If the prospect of interstate flight arises, then by all means the FBI will be called in. In the meantime, I believe the agencies involved are best equipped to deal with the situation."

"Is it common practice for eight-year-olds to be left unsupervised at the ice arena?"

"Have there been any previous incidents of child molestation in Deer Lake?"

"Is it true the boy's mother simply forgot him at the ice rink?"

His face tight with anger, Mitch drew a bead on the *Pioneer Press* reporter. "There's nothing *simple* about this. Dr. Garrison was trying to save a life in the emergency room. She did *not simply* forget her son and should in no way be made to feel responsible for his abduction."

"What about the father's statement that rink management and the hockey coach should be held responsible?"

"What about you, Chief Holt?" Paige stood. "Do *you* hold yourself responsible?"

He met her eyes without blinking. "In a manner of speaking, yes. As chief of police, it is ultimately my responsibility to keep the citizens of this town safe."

"Is that strictly your professional philosophy or are your feelings tainted by the guilt related to your personal—"

"*Ms.* Price," he ground out her name between his teeth. "I believe I made it perfectly clear last night that this case should in no way be tied to any other. We're here to talk about Josh Kirkwood and the efforts being made to find Josh Kirkwood. Period."

Megan watched the exchange, her attention focused on Mitch. She thought she could feel the anger vibrating in the air around him. Something about the defensive set of his shoulders, the taut line of his mouth, made her feel as if Paige Price had hit below the belt. Megan told herself it was just her sense of justice that responded, nothing more than the loyalty she would feel toward any other cop. She pushed to her feet to draw the fire away from him.

"On behalf of the BCA I would like to put extra emphasis

on what Chief Holt is saying. It is essential that we keep the focus here on Josh Kirkwood. It is essential that we keep the focus of your readers, listeners, and viewers on Josh. We need
him in the hearts and minds of everyone we can reach. We ask
especially that his photograph receive maximum exposure. For
you radio people—detailed descriptions of Josh and what he
was last seen wearing. If there's a chance that anyone has seen
him, we need to do everything possible to make certain those
people recognize Josh as the victim of an abduction."

"Agent O'Malley, is it true yesterday was your first day on
the job in Deer Lake?"

She gave Henry Forster a cool look and cursed herself for
volunteering that information to Paige Price the night before.
"I fail to see how that pertains to what I've just said."

He shrugged without apology. "That's news, too."

A number of heads nodded agreement. Not to be outdone
by her rival, Paige rose again.

"Miss O'Malley, can you tell us how many women hold positions as field agents with the BCA?"

"*Agent* O'Malley," Megan corrected her firmly. This was all
she needed—a bitch with nightly airtime on her case. She
could already imagine Bruce DePalma's blood pressure sky-
rocketing. She drew in a slow breath and struggled to find a
diplomatic way of saying fuck off.

"There are a good number of female agents with the bureau."

"At headquarters, in office jobs. What about in the field?"

Mitch nudged Megan away from the mike. "If none of you
have any more questions in direct reference to the abduction
of Josh Kirkwood, we'll have to end this now. I'm sure you all
can appreciate the fact that we have a great many more important duties to attend to. We've got a child missing, and
every second we waste could make a difference. Thank you."

He switched off the mike and nodded Megan toward a side
door that would get them out of the room without having to
pass through the swarm. Megan went readily, noticing that
both Steiger and the county attorney remained behind to catch
any leftover attention. The reporters rushed forward to snatch
one more statement, one more sound bite. Paige snagged the
sheriff, beating Forster to the punch. She turned her big phony

blue eyes up at Steiger with an expression of interest-touched-with-awe, and the sheriff's chest puffed up a notch.

"She didn't waste any time catching herself a consolation prize," Megan muttered as Mitch opened the door.

"Better him than me."

"Ditto."

They both heaved a sigh. Megan leaned back against the wall, grabbing a moment's peace. They had escaped into the garage that had once housed Deer Lake's entire fleet of fire trucks, all three of them. One remained, a round-fendered antique. Taking up most of the floor space now were a pair of hay wagons tricked out as parade floats. The near one featured a gigantic fiberglass trout leaping from a puddle of blue fiberglass water. Chicken wire had been stapled around the sides of the wagon and stuffed with blue and white paper napkins to form a decorative border. The glittering sign that rose at the back of the wagon invited one and all to CATCH SOME FUN at Trout Days, May 6, 7, 8.

The creation of the Deer Lake Trout Unlimited club was a far cry from the professionally designed floats of St. Paul's Winter Carnival. It was quaint and tacky and the club members who had put it together in their spare time were probably enormously proud of it. The thought struck Megan unexpectedly, hitting a vulnerable spot, reminding her of the innocence and naïveté of small towns. Things that had been shattered in a single ruthless act.

ignorance is not innocence but SIN

Josh's image floated up in her memory, and she blinked it away before it could undermine her focus on the job.

"Steiger isn't going to be a problem, is he?" she asked, glancing at Mitch.

He mimicked her pose—shoulders back against the wall, arms crossed. He looked weary and dangerous despite the fact that he had obviously showered and shaved before coming back in. The rugged lines of his face were set like stone, deeply etched, weathered and tough. He looked at her sideways, his dark eyes narrowed.

"How do you mean?"

"That I-am-the-field-general shit. He isn't going to go territorial on us, is he? We don't need a loose cannon on a case like this."

He shook his head a little, pulled a roll of Maalox tablets from his pants pocket, and thumbed one off. "Russ is okay. He has to worry about the next election, that's all. He'll grab press time and I'll be glad to let him. I thank God daily my job isn't decided in a voting booth."

But his reins were held by the town council, and Mitch had the sinking feeling that he would have to answer to each and every member before the day was out.

He rolled onto his left shoulder and gave Megan a wry look. "I thought you were the loose cannon."

Green eyes blinking innocence, she touched a hand to her chest. "Who, me? Not me. I'm just doing my job."

Mitch frowned at the reminder. "Yeah. And I should have listened. Maybe if I'd moved as fast as you wanted to—"

"Don't," Megan ordered, reaching out as if she meant to lay her hand on his arm.

The gesture was out of character and she caught it and pulled it back quickly. She wasn't a touchy-feely person. Even if she had been, the job would have cured her of it. She couldn't afford to make overtures that might somehow be misinterpreted. Image was everything to a woman in this business—her edge, her armor, her command for respect. Still, she couldn't simply dismiss the guilt in Mitch's face. In the back of her mind she could hear Paige Price's honey-smooth voice— *are your feelings tainted by the guilt related to your personal . . .* What? she wondered, and told herself it didn't matter. She couldn't let another cop second-guess himself when it wouldn't matter, that was all. Really.

"We were too late before we even knew," she said. "Besides, it's your town. You know it better than I do. You reacted accordingly. You did your best."

Their voices had softened to whispers. Their gazes held fast. She looked so earnest, so sure that what she said was the absolute truth. Her green eyes glowed with it, and with the determination to make him see it. Mitch wanted to laugh—not with humor, but with the cynicism of someone who was too intimate with life's more twisted ironies. Apparently Megan hadn't seen enough to be jaded, hadn't failed enough to quit trusting herself. She would believe that good was good and bad was bad with no gray zone in between. He had believed that, too, once. Live by the rules. Do the job right. Fight the good fight. Toe the line and reap the rewards of a righteous man.

His mouth twisted in a sad parody of a smile. One of life's crueler jokes—there were no rewards, only random acts of good and madness. A truth he had tried to run from, but it had found him here, found his town, reached out and struck at Josh Kirkwood and his parents.

He touched Megan's cheek and wished he could lean down and kiss her. It would have been nice to taste some of that sweet certainty, to believe he could drink it in and heal the old wounds. But at the moment he felt he was tainting her enough as it was, so he tried to content himself with the feel of her skin warming beneath his palm.

"My best wasn't good enough," he murmured. "Again."

Megan stared after him as he walked away, her fingertips brushing the side of her face, her heart beating a little too hard. Just a show of support for a fellow officer. Nothing personal. The covers slipped off to show those lies for what they were. Somewhere in that moment the lines of distinction had blurred. That was a dangerous thing for someone who needed to maintain a clear vision of the world and her place in it.

"Just so it doesn't happen again, O'Malley," she whispered, refusing to acknowledge her lack of hope as she started for the door.

The office of the late lamented Leo Kozlowski resembled Leo as much as a room can resemble a person. Square and plain, it was an unkempt mess of rumpled papers and coffee stains, ripe with the aromas of stale cigars and Hai Karate.

"Jesus, Mary, and Joseph," Megan muttered. She ventured slowly into the room, wrinkling her nose at the state of the place and at the vicious-looking dust-covered northern pike mounted on the wall with a cigar stuck in the corner of its toothy mouth. A monument to Leo's fishing skills and Rollie Metzler's taxidermy talents, she guessed.

Natalie scrunched her entire face into a look of utter disgust as she pulled the key from the lock. "Leo was a hell of a guy," she reiterated. "Didn't know shit about housekeeping, but he was a hell of a guy."

Megan reached into an abandoned doughnut box with a pencil and stabbed a cruller that was well on its way to petrification. She lifted it out and dropped it into the wastebasket. It sounded like a shotput landing in an oil drum. "Good thing he didn't die in here. No one would have noticed."

"I would have sent the cleaning people in after Leo passed on," Natalie said. "But we didn't want anyone touching anything until the new agent was assigned."

"Lucky me."

Megan pulled a brass nameplate out of her briefcase and set it along the front edge of the desk, staking her territory with the present she had bought herself to celebrate her new assignment. Her name was engraved in bold Roman type on the front: AGENT MEGAN O'MALLEY, BCA. On the back side was the motto TAKE NO SHIT, MAKE NO EXCUSES.

Natalie eyeballed both sides. She gave a crack of laughter as loud and abrupt as an air horn. "You might just be all right, *Agent* O'Malley."

"If the fumes don't get me first," Megan said dryly.

She started sifting through the debris on the desk, shoving the paperwork into haphazard piles; discarding candy wrappers, enough empty foam coffee cups to put a hole in the ozone the size of Iowa, two glass ashtrays overflowing with cigar stubs, and a half-finished Slim Jim. She unearthed the telephone just as it began to ring.

Natalie laid the key on a square inch of bare space on the corner of the desk and backed out the door, promising to send someone from maintenance with a Dumpster and a case of air freshener. Megan waved her thanks and snatched up the receiver.

"Agent O'Malley, BCA."

"The ink hasn't even dried on your transfer and already we've had no less than a dozen calls from reporters asking about you."

At the sound of DePalma's voice, she closed her eyes and thought uncharitable thoughts about reporters and what they should do with their laminated press passes.

"The issue is the abduction, Bruce," she said, sinking down

into the old snot-green desk chair. The seat had been beaten into a sorry state by Leo's big behind, and listed sharply to the left. The upholstery was worn smooth in some spots, nubby in others, and spotted all over with stains of dubious origin that made Megan grimace. "I'm doing everything I can to keep the reporters focused on the case instead of on me."

"You had damn well better be. The superintendent doesn't want a spotlight put on the bureau. He sure as hell doesn't want you making headlines. Is that understood?"

"Yes, sir," she answered with no small amount of resignation. The ghost of her headache was coming back to haunt her. She reached up and rubbed at it with two fingers.

"How's the search coming?"

"Nothing yet. We're praying for a lead. I don't expect the note to get us anywhere."

"It's a tough deal—a child abduction," DePalma said quietly, the professional concern melting into something personal. DePalma had three boys, one of them not much older than Josh. Megan had seen the family photograph on his desk many times. They all looked like Bruce, poor kids, miniature Nixon masks on gangly bodies of varying heights. "I worked the Wetterling case," he continued. "It's tough on all concerned."

"Yeah, it is."

"Do your best and keep your head down."

Mitch's words echoed in her mind as she hung up the phone and sank down into Leo's battered chair—*my best wasn't good enough . . . again.* She couldn't allow herself to wonder what he had meant by *again.* Their collective best had to be good enough for Josh.

The line from the note came back to her. She found a clear spot on the blotter between the coffee stains and phone numbers for local takeout restaurants and printed the message out in ink: *ignorance is not innocence but SIN.* Ignorance of what? Of whom? The quote was from Robert Browning. Was that significant? Her mind shuffled possibilities like a deck of cards. Ignorance, innocence, sin, poetry, literature— Books. She stopped on that card as the memory came and a dozen other questions rapidly branched off from it.

Her brain buzzing, she grabbed the phone and punched out the number for BCA records division. Sandwiching the receiver between her shoulder and her ear, she dug through her briefcase for the printout of known offenders and began scanning the list of names and addresses.

"Records. This is Annette speaking, how may I help you?"

"Annette, it's Megan O'Malley. Can you run one for me yesterday?"

"Anything for our conquering heroine. What's the grease spot's name?"

"Swain. Olie Swain."

The morning was an endless barrage of phone calls and impromptu appointments. As predicted, Mitch had the town council members calling and Don Gillen, the mayor, in his office, all of them expressing their horror, their outrage, and their blind faith in Mitch's ability as chief of police to make it all better.

With the start of Snowdaze just a day away, there was much discussion over whether the event should be cancelled or postponed. On the one hand, it seemed ghoulish to proceed with the festivities. On the other were economic considerations, courtesies to the high school bands bussing into Deer Lake and the tourists who had already booked the hotels and B&Bs full. If they cancelled the event, would they be surrendering to violence? If they went on, would it be possible to use the event to the benefit of the case by amassing fresh volunteers and holding rallies to show support and raise money?

After twenty minutes with the mayor, Mitch washed his hands of those decisions. Don was a good man, capable, concerned. Mitch appreciated his problems but made it clear that his time had to be spent on the case.

In addition to Josh's disappearance, there were daily duties that couldn't be ignored—rounds of the jail, logs to review, paperwork to be dealt with, an ongoing investigation into a series of burglaries, a bulletin from the regional drug task force, a call from the administrator at Harris College about the criminology course Mitch was to help teach this semester. The tasks were the ordinary daily course of life for a small-town police chief. Today each one felt like a stone in an avalanche, all coming down on him at once.

Natalie stormed in and out of his office, relieving him of as much of the menial stuff as she could. He could hear her phone ringing almost without cease and silently blessed her for passing through only the most pressing of the calls to him. At twelve-fifteen she delivered a takeout bag from Subway. At two-fifteen she scolded him for not having opened it.

"You think the calories are going to jump out that bag and be absorbed into your body through the air?" she demanded, snapping a pen against the bag. "You and my Troy ought to get together. He thinks just being in the same room with his advanced algebra book will be enough to make him into a mathematical genius. You all could start a club—the Osmosis Gang."

"Sorry, Nat." Mitch rubbed a hand across his eyes as he paged through six months' worth of reports of prowlers and Peeping Toms, looking for anything that might connect to Hannah or Paul or Josh or children in general. "I just haven't had two seconds."

"Well, take two now," she ordered. "You won't get through this day running on empty."

"Yes, Mother."

"And share some of those potato chips with *Agent* O'Malley," she said, pulling the door open. Megan stood waiting on the other side. "She looks like a stiff wind would blow her to Wisconsin."

"I brought my own, thanks," Megan said, holding up a banana.

Natalie rolled her eyes. "A whole banana? How will you ever finish it?"

"I'll be lucky if I get to peel it, let alone take a bite," she muttered, slumping down into the visitor's chair. She dropped a sheaf of computer paper onto the desk and deposited the banana on top of the pile.

"A little light reading?" Mitch asked, digging a turkey sandwich out of the Subway bag. He took a big bite and chewed aggressively, his eyes on Megan.

Her gaze fixed on his mouth, and a strange heat crept through her, which she put down to being overdressed. He ate like he didn't want to waste calories chewing, devouring the sandwich in huge bites. A small comma of mayonnaise punctuated his chin, shadowing his scar. He wiped it away impatiently and licked it off the pad of his thumb, an action that seemed to have too much influence over her pulse.

Disgusted with herself, she jerked her gaze away and did a quick survey of the office. Neat and tidy, it was devoid of mounted fish and bowling trophies. More curious, there was no ego wall of certificates and commendations. A cop of Mitch's stature and longevity would have accumulated a boxful by now. But the only frames that hung on the walls contained photographs of a little girl with long dark hair and a big yellow dog with an in-line skate in its mouth.

"Earth to O'Malley," he said, waving a hand. "What's the printout?"

"The known offenders," she replied, kick-starting her brain. "I've been trying to cross-reference with reports of recent incidents in the vicinity and DMV records when there was a vehicle sighted or involved on the off chance that something might eventually match up. Narrow down the possibilities, then if we get a break . . ."

"Find anything?"

"Not yet. I also called Records and ran a check on your boy Olie Swain—or tried to. They don't have anything on him. The guy doesn't have so much as a traffic ticket."

Mitch took another bite out of the sandwich and wolfed it down. "Olie? He's harmless."

"You're that close, you and Olie?" she asked, holding up crossed fingers.

"No, but he's been here longer than me and we've never had a serious complaint against him." He washed the turkey down with warm, flat Coke and grimaced.

Megan sat up straighter. "Does that mean you've had complaints that *weren't* serious?"

He shrugged. "One of the hockey moms got a little bitchy about him hanging around the kids at the rink, but it was nothing. I mean, hell, his job is at the rink. What's he supposed to do—hide out in his cubbyhole all day and night?"

"Did she allege anything specific?"

"That Olie gave her the creeps."

"Gee, imagine that."

"She also accused the Cub Scout leader of the same thing, told me I ought to send someone undercover into St. Elysius because everyone knows priests are homosexual pedophiles and accused her son's second-grade teacher of subverting the minds of children by reading Shel Silverstein books aloud to the class and displaying the illustrations—which any Christian person can see are filthy with phallic symbols."

"Oh." She sank back down in her chair, chagrined.

"Right. The kids have never complained about Olie. The coaches have never complained about Olie. What set you off?"

"He gave me the creeps," she said sheepishly, scowling at her banana as she peeled back the skin. She took a bite and chewed, regrouping mentally. Olie Swain still gave her the creeps. Unfortunately, that was not considered probable cause for running someone in and taking their fingerprints. "He seemed evasive last night. Nervous. I got the impression he didn't like cops."

"Olie's always nervous and evasive. It's part of his charm," Mitch said, practicing a few evasive maneuvers of his own, shuffling papers as an excuse to keep from watching her wrap her lips around that banana. "Besides, I ran a check on him myself when Mrs. Favre made her complaint. Olie keeps his nose clean."

"If no other part of his anatomy." Megan wrinkled her nose at the remembered aroma of ripe body odor. "You don't think he had anything to do with Josh disappearing?"

"He'd never have the balls to steal a kid, then stand there and look me in the eye and tell me he didn't know anything about it."

"He looked you in the eye? With his real eye or the fake one?"

He shook his head at her as he leaned over to hit the button on the buzzing intercom. "Yes?"

"Christopher Priest to see you, Chief," Natalie announced. "Says he might be able to help with the investigation."

"Send him in."

Mitch dumped the remnants of his lunch in the trash and scrubbed his hands with a napkin as he came around the desk. Megan stood, too, and tossed the last of her banana. Adrenaline shot through her at the possibility of a lead.

The man who let himself into the office didn't look like anyone's savior. He was small, slight, his body swallowed up by a blue and white varsity jacket from Harris College. Even with the jacket, no one would ever have mistaken him for a jock. Nothing short of a truckload of steroids could have delivered the professor from his computer-geek looks. Christopher Priest had the pale, fragile look of a man whose most dangerous sport was chess. Megan put him in his late thirties, five feet nine, mousy brown hair, dirt brown eyes behind a pair of glasses too big for his face. Unremarkable.

"Professor," Mitch said, shaking hands. "This is Agent O'Malley with the BCA. Agent O'Malley, Christopher Priest, head of the computer science department at Harris."

They shook hands—Megan's firm and strong, a hand that could hold a Glock 9-mil semiautomatic without wavering; Priest's a thin, collapsible sack of bones that seemed to fold in on itself. She had to fight the urge to look down and make certain she hadn't hurt him. "Your name seems familiar to me," she said, scanning her brain for filed information. "You do some work with juvenile offenders, right?"

Priest smiled, a mix of shyness and pride. "My claim to fame—the Sci-Fi Cowboys."

"It's a great program." Mitch motioned Priest into a vacant chair as he went back around behind his desk. "You should be proud of it. Taking kids off the wrong track and giving them a shot at getting an education and having a future is more than commendable."

"Well, thanks, but I can't take all the credit. Phil Pickard and Garrett Wright put in a lot of time with the kids as well." He settled into the chair, his oversize jacket creeping up around his earlobes, making him look like a cartoon turtle ready to pull his head into his shell. "I heard about Josh Kirkwood. I feel so terrible for Hannah and Paul."

"Do you know them well?" Megan asked.

"We're neighbors of a sort. Their house is the last one on Lakeshore Drive. Mine is behind them, in a manner of speaking, a quarter of a mile or so to the north through Quarry Hills Park. Of course, I know Hannah. Everyone in town knows Hannah. We've been on several charity committees together. Has there been any word?"

Mitch shook his head. "You thought you might be able to help—in what way?"

"I heard you had set up a command post. That serves as a clearinghouse for leads and information, right?"

"Yes."

"Well, I remember reading the newspaper reports during the search for that young girl in Inver Grove Heights. The police talked about the volume of information they had to deal with and how cumbersome it was. Things got left out, some jobs were repeated several times due to lack of communication, it was time-consuming to cross-reference facts and so on."

"Amen to that," Megan said, fanning the pages of her known-offenders printout.

"I'd like to offer a solution," Priest said. "My department has plenty of personal computers available. With winter break, I'm short on students at the moment, but I know those who are still in town would be more than willing to help out. We can put everything you want on our computers, give you the ability to pull specific information, cross-reference, whatever you need. We can also scan in Josh's photo and send it across the United States and Canada on electronic bulletin boards. It would be a good project for my students and save you guys a lot of headaches."

Mitch sat back and swiveled his chair as he thought. One of the things he missed most about being on a big-city police force was the access to equipment. The Deer Lake town fathers had seen a need for a pretty new building to house their jail and police department, but they were having a harder time seeing a need for up-to-date computer equipment. At present the department had half a dozen PCs from the Stone Age. Natalie brought in her own personal laptop to do her work.

"I don't know," he said, scratching a hand back through his hair. "The students might be privy to confidential information. They're not sworn personnel. That could be a problem."

"Couldn't you deputize them or something?" Priest asked.

"Maybe. Let me check with the county attorney and I'll get back to you."

The professor nodded and pushed himself up out of his chair. "Just give me a call. Moving the equipment is no problem; we have access to a van. We'd be set up in no time."

"Thanks."

They shook hands again and Priest moved toward the door. He hesitated with his hand on the doorknob and shook his head sadly. "This has been a bad week all the way around. Josh Kirkwood abducted. Now I'm off to the hospital to visit a student who was involved in that terrible car accident yesterday. My mother always said trouble comes in threes. Let's hope she was wrong."

"Let's hope," Mitch murmured as the professor went out, closing the door behind him.

"It would be great to have those computers," Megan mused. "It'd be even better if we had a lead or two to put in them."

"Yeah. I haven't heard anything but lame excuses all day," Mitch grumbled. "I wish I were out there myself. Sitting around here is getting old in a hurry."

"So let's go," Megan said impulsively. She kicked herself mentally the instant the words came out. There was plenty of work to be done in the office, and it made no sense to pair herself with a man who could distract her by doing something so innocuous as chewing his lunch.

"I mean, I thought I'd go over to the command post and then join one of the teams for a couple of hours," she backpedaled smoothly. "You could do that, too. Not *with* me, necessarily. In fact, it would probably be better if we split up."

Mitch watched the color rise in her cheeks. His sense of humor was running low, but a smile of wry amusement curled up a corner of his mouth. It was a relief to think of something besides the case for a minute. The cool and collected Agent O'Malley blushing seemed as good a diversion as any.

He rose and strolled around the desk with his hands in his trouser pockets, his gaze pinning Megan to her chair. "You're blushing, Agent O'Malley."

"No. I'm just hot." She winced mentally at the implications. "It's warm in here."

He prowled a little closer. "You're hot?"

He looked into her eyes, his gaze shrewd and predatory. It seemed a prudent time to snap off a sharp retort and get her ass away from this fire. But no retort formed, no words came out of her dry mouth. Her muscles tightened, but she didn't move quickly enough. He read her thoughts and in a heartbeat was leaning down over her, his big hands gripping the arms of the chair as she jerked her own hands back.

"What's making you hot?" he whispered, forgetting his pledge to not want her. He liked the little rush of excitement. It made him feel alive instead of weary, made him feel anticipation instead of dread. "Are you afraid to ride in the same car with me, Agent O'Malley?"

"I'm not afraid of you," Megan whispered, grabbing ahold of her pride and wielding it like a sword. She didn't like this insidious desire that drifted in and out of their relationship like smoke. Elusive and intangible, it obscured boundaries, altered expectations. She didn't trust it, and she didn't trust herself when it came over her like a boiling tide. "I'm not afraid of anything."

Mitch watched her resolve harden in the deep green of her eyes. She would let him pursue the attraction just so far and then she started pushing back. Just as well, he told himself. Just as well for both of them. Wrong time, wrong place, wrong people. She had a chip on her shoulder the size of Gibraltar.

"Don't sell yourself short," he murmured as the old weariness came washing back through him, dousing the spark. "We're all afraid of something."

CHAPTER 10

Through the long hours of the day Hannah gained a new sympathy for the family members who sat in the hospital lounge waiting while their loved one underwent surgery. She could do nothing but wait and pray. There was no control. There was no participation. There was no energy to distract herself with menial chores—not that anyone would have allowed her to attend to menial chores. All she could do was wait and listen to the unearthly sound of helicopter blades beating the air as the search choppers passed slowly back and forth over the town. Giant vultures hovering over the rooftops, scanning the ground with electric eyes for any sign of her son . . . or his body.

Her house was full of interlopers. Strangers from the BCA, watching her telephone as if waiting for a vision. Friends from the neighborhood and from around town, watching *her* as if they all had money riding on the exact time she would have a nervous breakdown. They attended her tag-team fashion, one person hovering and fussing, denying her even the small comfort of tending to Lily's needs, while another did her laundry or scrubbed the soap scum out of her bathtub. Every hour or so they would switch jobs, and Hannah caught herself wondering which was considered the worst duty.

She knew which *she* hated most. She would rather have been cleaning her tile grout than sitting in the family room with watcher number two, a truth that clearly demonstrated how desperate she was feeling.

Paul would have readily testified that she had no affinity for housework. She managed the basics, but took no enjoyment in them. They were nothing but chores that seemed to need doing again the moment she had finished them. They took away time she would rather have spent with her children. She cursed every second she had spent vacuuming the carpet instead of playing with Josh. She cursed Paul for guilting her into continuing the thankless jobs. She would have long ago hired someone to come in and do the cleaning and the laundry and bake fresh cookies once a week if it hadn't been for Paul and his little digs about her lack of domesticity.

His mother's house always smelled of lemon oil and wax from polishing the furniture. His mother always spent Saturday baking bread and sweet rolls and cookies. Hannah had pointed out to him once that he hated his mother, never went to see his mother, had married his mother's opposite and therefore had no right to complain.

"At least I knew she was my mother. At least my father knew she was a woman—"

"You'd know I was a woman, too, if I weren't so exhausted from trying to keep this house up to your lofty standards—"

"The house? You're never in the damn house! You're at the hospital day and night—"

"I happen to think saving lives is a little more important than dusting and baking coffee cakes!"

It was a wonder she remembered the angry words so well; there had been so many of late.

Sighing, she rose and crossed the family room to the big picture window that looked out over the lake. A crooked arm of ice, Deer Lake was seven miles long and a mile across with half a dozen small fingers reaching into the wooded banks. Normally the view brought her a sense of peace. Today it only made her feel more restless and alone.

Cars hung precariously on the snow-packed shoulder of Lakeshore Drive. Reporters camped like hyenas on the fringe of a lion's fresh kill. Waiting for any scrap of news. Waiting for her to emerge so they could pounce on her and tear at her with their questions. A green and white patrol car sat parked in the driveway, a guardian sent by Mitch, God bless him. A mile to the north, ice-fishing huts dotted the public access area of the lake like multicolored mushrooms. No one had come to fish today. What little light the day had offered was fading away. Lights winked on in the houses that ringed the banks. School was out. There should have been children out on the ice, on the end of the lake that had been cleared of snow for skating. There were no children tonight. Because of Josh.

Because of me.

Like ripples in a pond, the effects reached out and touched the lives of people she didn't even know. Everyone was paying for her sin. It seemed such a small thing, a moment's slip, a forgivable lapse. But no one would forgive her, least of all Hannah herself. Josh was gone and she was sentenced to this punishment—to stand and do nothing while her neighbors cleaned her house and a cop sat at her kitchen table reading a paperback novel.

"The waiting is the worst."

Hannah turned and stared at the woman from the missing children's group. Another of the unwanted entourage. She didn't know which was worse—pity from friends or from strangers. She hated the woman's I've-been-where-you-are-and-emerged-a-better-woman-for-it look. The woman stood beside her, the picture of upscale suburbia in a knit ensemble of hunter and rust, accessorized in brass, her deep red hair cut in a smooth shoulder-length bob.

"I went through this two years ago," the woman confided. "My ex-husband stole our son."

"Were you frightened for his life?" Hannah asked bluntly.

The woman frowned a little. "Well, no, but—"

"Then I'm sorry, but I don't think you can possibly know what I'm feeling."

Ignoring the woman's expression of shock, Hannah walked past her and into the kitchen.

"It was still a trauma!" the woman exclaimed, outrage ringing in her voice.

The cop glanced up from his book, looking as if he wanted no part of this scene. Hannah didn't blame him. She wanted no part of it, either.

"I have to get some air," she said. "I'll be just outside if the phone rings."

In the mud room she pulled on the old black parka Paul used for weekend dirty work. As she grabbed mittens off the shelf she visualized the sniping match that would go on if he came home and caught her wearing his coat.

"You have coats of your own."

"What's the difference? You weren't wearing this one."

She wouldn't try to explain to him that it somehow made her feel safer, protected, loved to wear something of his. It made no sense—would certainly make no sense to Paul—that she could draw more comfort from his clothing than she could from him. She could never explain to him that the clothes were like memories of what they had once shared, of who he had once been. They were the shrouds of ghosts, and she wrapped herself in them and ached for what had died in their marriage.

She pulled open the door to the garage and gasped at the dark figure of a man standing on the stoop with his fist raised.

"Hannah!"

"Oh, my God! Father Tom! You nearly gave me a heart attack!"

The priest offered a sheepish smile. He was young—midthirties—tall with an athletic build. Her nurse and friend from the ER, Kathleen Casey, always teased him that he was too good-looking to have taken himself out of the eligible bachelor pool—a joke that never failed to bring a little blush to Tom McCoy's cheeks. Hannah didn't think of him as handsome. The word that came to her when she looked at Father Tom was *kind.* He had a strong, kind face, kind blue eyes. Eyes that offered understanding and sympathy and forgiveness from behind a pair of round wire-framed glasses.

He had been the priest at St. Elysius for two years and was enormously popular with the younger parishioners. Hardliners found him a little too unconventional for their tastes. Albert Fletcher, St. Elysius's only deacon, was a vocal opponent to what he called "this New Age Catholicism," but then, Albert was also against women wearing slacks and often hinted that Vatican II was the work of the Antichrist. Paul derisively called Father Tom's off-the-cuff homilies his "lounge act," but Hannah found them refreshing and insightful. Tom McCoy was a bright, articulate man with a degree in philosophy from Notre Dame and a heart as big as his home state of Montana. On a day as black as this one, she couldn't think of anyone she would rather have as a friend.

"I thought it would be better if I came in this way." A hint of the West accented his warm voice. "There are an awful lot of people watching your front door."

"Yes, it's Eyes-on-Hannah-Garrison Day," she said without humor. "I was just trying to escape for a few minutes."

"Would you rather I left?" He stepped down to the garage floor, showing his sincerity, giving her the chance to answer honestly. "If you need to be alone—"

"No. No, don't go." Hannah walked out onto the stoop and listened to the soft hiss of the storm door as it closed behind her. "Alone isn't really what I want, either."

As her eyes adjusted to the faint gray light, her gaze wandered the cavernous garage, hitting on Josh's bike. Hanging on the wall. Abandoned. Forgotten. A fist of emotion slammed into her diaphragm. She had managed to cocoon herself in numbness all day, as the watchers and well-wishers and sympathizers came and went. But the sight of the dirt bike punched a hole in the gauze, punched a hole in her heart, and the pain came pouring out.

"I just want my son back."

She sank down on the cold concrete step, her legs buckling as her strength drained away. She might have fallen to the floor if not for Father Tom. He was on the step beside her in an instant, catching her. He slid an arm around her shoulders and held her gently. She turned her face into his shoulder and wept, the tears soaking into the heavy wool of his topcoat.

"I want him back. . . . Why can't I have him back? Why did this have to happen? He's just a little boy. How could God do this? How could God let this happen?"

Tom said nothing. He let Hannah cry, let her ask the questions. He thought she didn't really expect answers, which was just as well, because he didn't have any answers to give. He himself had asked all the same questions of a higher power, and his ears still rang with the silence. He didn't know a better person than Hannah. So gracious, so caring, dedicated to her children and to helping others. Her soul was as good as they came. In a just world, bad things wouldn't happen to people like Hannah or innocent children like Josh. But the world was not a just place. It was a hard place full of random cruelty, a truth that always brought him to question God. *If the world is an unjust world, then is God therefore an unjust God?* The guilt that accompanied the question was heavy and cold inside him. Blind faith remained beyond his reach. Doubt was his cross to bear.

He couldn't offer Hannah answers, only comfort. He couldn't take away her pain, but he could share it with her. So he sat on the hard, cold step with his arms around her and let her cry, his heart aching for her, his own tears rolling down into the thick tangle of her honey-blond hair. When she had cried herself out he pulled a handkerchief from his pocket and pressed it into her hand.

"I'm sorry," she whispered, edging away from him, lifting her face from his shoulder and turning it away. "I don't cry on people. I don't fall apart and make other people pick up the pieces."

"I'll never tell," he promised, gently stroking the back of her head. "I'm a priest, remember?"

Hannah tried to laugh, but the sound caught in her throat. She stared down at the handkerchief, her brows drawing together.

"It's clean," he teased, giving her shoulders a squeeze. "I promise."

She sniffed and tried to smile. "I was looking at the monogram. F?"

"Christmas gift from a parishioner. F for Father Tom."

The naïveté of the gesture struck her as sad and sweet and squeezed another pair of tears from her eyes. She wiped them away with the linen and blew her nose as delicately as she could manage. They sat in silence for a while. Night had fallen. The temperature was noticeably dropping. The front security light outside had come on automatically and burned brightly against the dark, warding off danger. What a joke.

"You're entitled to fall apart, Hannah," Tom said softly. "The rest of us are supposed to lift you up and hold you together. That's the way it works."

He didn't understand, she thought. The lifting and the holding had always been her jobs. Now that she was the one in pieces, everyone just stared at her and didn't know what to do.

"Has there been any word?"

Hannah shook her head. "I feel so helpless, so useless. At

least Paul can go out with the search party. All I can do is wait . . . and wonder . . . This must be what hell is like. I can't imagine anything worse than what's gone through my mind in the last twenty-two hours."

She rose slowly, went down the steps to the door that opened to the backyard, and stared out the window into the dark. Weak yellow light seeped out the kitchen window, staining the snow. Gizmo lay in the amber rectangle, a huge immobile lump of shaggy hair. Beyond the dog, the shadow of the swing set stood out, black on white, then the yard melted into the thick woods that wrapped around the north end of the lake, giving the neighborhood a sense of seclusion.

"I did my residency at Hennepin County Medical Center," she said, her voice a flat monotone. "That's a tough ER, a tough part of town, you know. I've seen things . . . the things people can do to one another . . . the things people can do to a child. . . ."

The words faded. She stared out through the window, but Tom could tell she was seeing another place, another time. Her face was strained and pale. He stood beside her and waited quietly, patiently.

". . . Unspeakable things," she whispered. Even with the oversize coat, he could tell she was breathing hard, trembling. "And I think of Josh—"

"Don't," he ordered.

She looked at him sideways and waited. There was no expectation in her eyes, no hope that he would say something that could brighten her perspective. Seldom in his years as a priest had he felt so impotent, so ill equipped to give anything of worth to someone who was suffering. She stared at him and waited, her eyes big and fathomless in the absence of light, her lovely face cast in shadows.

"It won't help," he said at last. "You're only torturing yourself."

"I deserve it."

"Don't say that."

"Why not? It's true. If I'd been there to pick him up, he would be with us now."

"You were trying to save a life, Hannah."

"Kathleen told you that, didn't she?" He didn't answer. He

didn't have to; she knew Kathleen too well. "Did she tell you I went 0 for two last night? Ida Bergen died and I lost Josh in the bargain."

"They'll find him. You have to believe that, Hannah. You have to have faith."

"I had faith that this would never happen," she said bitterly. "I'm all out of faith."

He couldn't blame her. He supposed he should have tried to prod her into retracting the statement. He could have wielded that favorite old Catholic club of guilt, but he didn't have the heart for it. In times like these he had enough trouble hanging on to his own faith. He wasn't hypocrite enough to castigate someone else.

The fire went out of Hannah abruptly. She heaved a sigh and rubbed her mittened hands over her face and back through her hair. "I'm sorry, Father," she whispered. "I shouldn't—"

"Don't apologize for how you feel, Hannah. You're entitled to react."

"And rail at God?" Her mouth twisted up at one corner as a new sheen of tears glazed across her eyes.

"Don't worry about God. He can take it."

He reached out and tenderly brushed a tear from her cheek with the pad of his thumb. For the first time Hannah noticed he wasn't wearing gloves. His thumb was cold against her skin. Father Tom, the absentminded. He routinely forgot little things like wearing gloves in freezing weather, eating meals, and getting his hair cut. The trait brought out the maternal qualities in all the women of St. Elysius Parish.

"You forgot your gloves again," she said, drawing his hand down and holding it between hers to warm it. "You'll end up with frostbite."

He shook off her concern. "More important things on my mind. I wanted to let you know I'm here for you—for you and Paul."

"Thank you."

"I've organized a prayer vigil for Josh. Tonight at eight. I'm praying we won't need it by then," he added, squeezing her hand tight.

"Me, too," Hannah whispered. She couldn't tell him that

she had the sick, hollow feeling her prayers weren't going anywhere, that the pleas did nothing but bounce around inside her head. She clung to his hand a second longer, desperate to absorb some of his strength and faith.

"Would you like to stay for supper?" she asked, scraping together her manners again, and again need and honesty cut through them. "I have a house full of women who don't know what to do except stare at me and thank their lucky stars they aren't in my shoes," she confided. "It would be nice to break that up. On the menu we have a variation on the miracle of the loaves and fishes—the miracle of the tuna casseroles. I can't imagine there's a can of tuna left in town."

"Did Ann Mueller bring the kind with the fried onions on top?" he asked, giving her a gentle comic look of speculation, giving her something other than pity.

"And a pan of crème de menthe brownies."

He grinned and draped an arm around her shoulders, steering her toward the kitchen door. "Then I'm all yours, Dr. Garrison."

5:28 P.M.   17°

Mitch walked alone down the hall of Deer Lake Elementary School. Immune to his teasing, Megan had gone off with two of his officers for round two of questioning Josh's hockey buddies and the youth team coaches. Had they seen anything at all? Had Josh talked to them about being afraid of somebody? Had Josh been acting differently? The questions would be asked again and again by this cop, that cop, the next cop, all of them hoping to shake loose a memory. All of them hoping to find some small piece of information that might seem insignificant in itself but fit together with another piece to form a lead. It may have seemed tedious to the people being questioned, and it certainly created mountains of paperwork, but it was necessary.

Mitch had chosen to meet with the schoolteachers and

other school personnel for the same purpose. One of his men had already questioned Josh's teacher, Sara Richman. Mitch addressed the entire staff in the cafeteria, conducting the meeting as an informal question-and-answer session. He told them what little he knew, tried to stem the flow of wild rumors, asked them for any information they had. Had anyone been hanging around the school? Had any of the children reported being approached by a stranger?

Mitch studied the faces in the room—the teachers, the cooks, the janitors, the office help—wondering, as a cop, if any one of them could have done this; wondering, as a father, if any of the people who came into contact with his daughter every day could have been a danger to her.

After nearly two hours, he left them to their own discussion of plans for a schoolwide safety assembly, and headed down the long hall for the side door. His head felt like a walnut in a vise. Questions chased each other around and around his brain. Questions with no answers. He had his own staff meeting at six, to talk with his men about what the day had yielded in terms of information, and to brainstorm for ideas. With no real leads and no real suspects, it was difficult to focus the investigation.

As he walked, Mitch couldn't help but notice the miniature lockers that made him feel like a giant, the artwork taped to the walls at his hip level. He caught glimpses of classrooms with pint-size desks. All of it served only to make him more painfully aware of the vulnerability of children.

He had asked to look inside Josh's locker. One of O'Malley's evidence techs had beat him to it, cleaning out Josh's desk and locker of notebooks and textbooks, leaving behind a stash of Gummi Bears and Super Balls and a glow-in-the-dark yo-yo. The detritus of boyhood. Evidence of nothing more than Josh's normalcy and innocence.

Every day this hall was filled with little kids just like Josh, just like his Jessie. It pissed him off to think that all of them would be touched by this crime. Their innocence would be marred like a clean white page streaked by dirty fingers.

Mitch didn't bother to zip his coat as he stepped outside, but he dug his gloves out of his pockets and pulled them on. Day had yielded to night. Security lights shone against the brick walls of the school and illuminated the parking lot at intervals.

The school had been built in 1985 to educate the children of baby boomers and the influx of new families into Deer Lake. The site was on Ramsey Drive, in a newer part of town, just two blocks from the even newer fire station, ensuring disruptions of class every time a fire truck rolled out for duty. The parking lot stretched out before Mitch, edged on two sides by thick rows of spruce trees. The playground sprawled across three acres just to the west. A handy arrangement for parents picking up their kids—or for anyone looking to steal a kid.

Now everywhere Mitch looked he saw hazards, potential for danger, where before he had seen only a nice, neat, quiet town. The knowledge served only to darken his mood. Fishing his keys out of his pocket, he headed for the Explorer.

The truck sat alone in the second row, just out of reach of a light. Mitch stuck the key in the lock of the door, his mind already on the meeting to come and the night beyond that. He wanted to make it to his in-laws before eight o'clock, before Joy could get Jessie into pajamas. He wanted his daughter home with him tonight. A brief oasis of normalcy before another day of madness and frustration.

As he moved to open the truck's door, something caught his eye, something out of place, something on the hood.

Even as he turned, the reaction began—the rush of adrenaline, the tightening of nerves, the instincts coming to attention. Even as he reached for the spiral notebook, his heart was pounding.

He picked it up gingerly, pinching the wire spine between left thumb and forefinger, lifting the opposite edge with the tip of his right forefinger. The cover was dark green, decorated with the image of Snoopy as Joe Cool. Printed in Magic Marker across the top was "Josh Kirkwood 3B."

Mitch swore. His hands were shaking as he eased the book back down on the hood. He went into the truck and returned with a flashlight and a slim gold pen. Using the pen, he opened the notebook and turned the pages.

Nothing remarkable, just a little boy's doodling. Drawings of race cars and rocket ships and sports heroes. Notes about kids in his class. A boy named Ethan who puked during music—*He herled chunks all over Amy Masons shoes!* A girl named Kate who tried to kiss him at his locker—*gross! gross! gross!* On one page he had carefully traced the Minnesota Vikings' logo and drawn a jersey with the number twelve and the name KIRKWOOD in block letters.

A little boy's dreams and secrets. And tucked in before the final page, a madman's message.

i had a little sorrow, born of a little SIN

CHAPTER 11

DAY 2
8:41 P.M. 16°

Hannah took one look at the notebook, turned chalk white, and sank into the nearest chair. It was Josh's, no question. She knew it well. He called it his "think pad." He carried it everywhere—or had.

"He lost it," she murmured, rubbing her fingers over the plastic evidence bag, wanting to touch the book. Something of Josh. Something his kidnapper had tossed back at them. A taunt. A cruel flaunting of power.

"What do you mean, he lost it?" Mitch asked, kneeling beside her, trying to get her to look at him instead of the notebook. "When?"

"The day before Thanksgiving. He was frantic. I told him he must have left it at school," she said. "But he swore he hadn't. We tore the house apart looking for it."

She remembered that all too well. Paul had come home from racquetball and blown up at the sight of the mess. His family was coming for Thanksgiving. He wanted the house to be perfect, to rub it in to his relatives how well he had done. He hadn't wanted to waste time looking for a stupid notebook he thought could be easily replaced.

Hannah looked down at that "stupid notebook" now and wanted to hug it to her chest and rock it as if it were Josh himself. She wanted to turn to Paul and ask him how he felt about Josh's stupid notebook now, but Paul had yet to come home. She imagined he had gone straight from the search to the prayer vigil—something she couldn't think of facing. Father Tom had understood. Somehow she knew Paul would not.

"He was upset for days," she murmured. "It was like losing a diary."

Megan exchanged looks with Mitch. "He must have found it again, though," she said. "He must have had it with him last night."

Hannah shook her head, never taking her gaze off the book lying in her lap. "I never saw it again. I can't believe he wouldn't have told me if he found it."

Lily peeked around the side of the chair, turning an impish smile up at her mother, her blue eyes wide, her golden curls tousled around her head. The notebook caught her eye and she gave a little squeal of delight, pointing a finger at the figure of Snoopy on the cover.

"Mama! Josh!" she declared. Giggling, she reached for the notebook.

Mitch caught the end of the plastic bag and lifted it away from her. Megan took the bag from him. "I'll give this to my guy," she murmured. "It'll be in the lab first thing in the morning."

Mitch remained behind to offer empty words of little comfort and less hope. Hannah seemed dazed. A blessing, he supposed. He left her sitting in the wing chair with Lily on her lap and a cop in her kitchen.

Megan waited for him in the Explorer. She had come to the elementary school in a squad car with Joe Peters, the officer who had been helping her interview the youth hockey crowd. They had yet to return to City Center, where her Lumina was parked.

The search of the school grounds had been an exercise in futility and frustration. The notebook could have appeared by magic for all anyone could discern. The school staff had all been in the cafeteria with Mitch—no witnesses. It would have been simple enough to drive up alongside the Explorer and place the book on the hood. The perpetrator wouldn't have even had to get out of his car. Slick, simple, diabolical.

Fury curdling like sour milk in his stomach, Mitch climbed into the truck and slammed the door shut.

"Mother-fucking son of a bitch!" he snarled, pounding a hand against the steering wheel. "I can't believe he just plunked it down on the hood of my truck. *Here, chump, get a clue!* Fuck!"

Like throwing down the gauntlet, he thought, and the thought sickened him. It turned a crime into a game. *Catch me if you can.* A mind that worked that way had to be black with rot and soaked with arrogance. So sure of himself he believed he could drop evidence in their laps and calmly slip away—which was exactly what he had done.

"I want this bastard," he growled, twisting the key in the ignition.

Megan took his temper and his language in stride. Neither were anything new to her. In his position she imagined she would have been saying the same things. The kidnapper had shown him up, made him feel like a fool. It was difficult not to take that personally, but personal couldn't enter into the picture. There was too much potential for distorting perceptions.

The notebook was the only lead they'd picked up since the night before. Nothing had been turned up by the teams in the field. The volunteer ground search had been called for the day. Teams of Deer Lake police, the county boys, and Megan's agents-on-loan from the St. Paul regional district continued on, checking vacant and abandoned buildings, warehouses, the railroad yard; patrolling the streets and side roads for signs of anything remotely suspicious; following up on anything promising picked up by the flyboys in the search choppers, scrambling from point to point like participants in a macabre scavenger hunt.

The BCA and State Patrol helicopters would continue through the night, creeping over every inch of Park County again, their rotors breaking the quiet peace of the winter night. But unless they found something to go on, they would not be coming back the following day. They had covered a territory of two hundred square miles with nothing to show for it and no clue as to which direction to expand the search.

At the command post the hotline phones had been ringing off the hooks—mostly calls from concerned citizens wanting to check up on the progress of the search or express their fears and anger about the abduction. No one had seen a thing. No one had seen Josh. It was as if an unseen hand had reached out of another dimension and plucked him off the earth.

And the clock was ticking. Twenty-six hours had passed, the sense of urgency and desperation increasing with every one of them. Twenty-four was the magic number. If the missing person wasn't found in the first twenty-four hours, the odds against finding the victim went up with every passing minute.

Night had fallen around them like a black steel curtain. The wind was starting to pick up, whipping mare's tails of snow along the white-blanketed ground. The temperature kept dropping, aiming for a nighttime low of ten degrees. Cold, but January nights could get colder. Ten below zero, twenty below, thirty below. Brutal cold. Deadly cold. In the back of everyone's mind was the fear that Josh's abductor might have left him somewhere, alive only to die of exposure before anyone could get to him.

"We need to go over these pages," Megan said, looking down at the stack of photocopies on her lap, copies of every page in Josh's think pad. "I can't imagine the kidnapper would have left anything truly incriminating in it, but who's to say."

Mitch turned toward her. In the glow of the dashboard lights, his lean face was all rough angles and shadowed planes, the deep-set eyes hard and unblinking.

"What about the big question?" he asked. "Where and when did our bad guy get the book? It's been missing nearly two months. If he's had it all that time, we're looking at a crime with a lot of premeditation."

"And where did he get it from? Josh's locker? That could implicate a school employee—"

"Anybody can walk into that school at any time of the day. The halls aren't monitored. There are no locks on the lockers."

"Josh might have dropped the notebook walking home," Megan offered. "Anybody walking down the street could have picked it up. Anybody coming into the Kirkwood house might have taken it, for that matter."

Mitch said nothing as he backed the Explorer out of the drive and headed it south on Lakeshore, then east on Ninth Avenue. He ran through the mental list of new complications created by the notebook.

"We'll have to find out if any school employees were missing from that meeting tonight, find out if anybody's been fired in the last six months, get a list of everyone who has been through Hannah and Paul's house since mid-November—friends, neighbors, service people . . ."

The idea of the manpower, the tedium, the paperwork, was daunting. The irony made him see red—that their perpetrator had handed them a clue and in doing so had built a bigger haystack to hide the needle in.

Mitch swore. "I need some food and a bed."

"I can offer the first," Megan said cautiously. "You're on your own for the bed."

It wasn't that she wanted his company, she told herself. It had nothing to do with the hollow feeling that came with the thought of sitting alone in her apartment that night. She had spent most of her life alone. Alone was no big deal.

Josh's image floated through her mind like a specter as the glowing green numbers of the dashboard clock marked another passing minute. Alone was a very big deal. Like most of the cops on the case, she would have worked around the clock if she could have forgone food and rest, but the body needed refueling. So she would pull herself off the streets for a few hours and lay in bed staring at the dark, brooding about Josh while the clock ticked. And Mitch would do the same.

"We can go over these pages without any distractions," she said.

"Do you have utilities?" Mitch asked, his thoughts following the same line.

"I'm hopeful, but as a born cynic I took the precaution of calling for a pizza on your cellular phone while you were talking to Hannah."

He arched a brow. "Using police equipment for personal business, Agent O'Malley? I'm shocked."

"I consider the need for pizza a police emergency. And so will the delivery boy if he knows what's good for him."

"Where are you living?"

"Eight sixty-seven Ivy Street. Drop me off at my car and I'll lead the way."

"We go back to the station now, we've got reporters to face," Mitch said. "My temper is too short for one more asinine question."

"Then I guess I won't ask you if you're a mushroom man or strictly a pepperoni guy."

"My only requirement tonight is that it isn't alive and it doesn't have hair. We'll eat, take a look at these pages. With any luck, by the time we get back to the station the press people will have given up for the night."

They rolled past the turn for downtown and City Center. Mitch hit the blinker when they reached Ivy Street and eased the Explorer in along the curb. The three-story house on the corner was a huge old Victorian that had been cut up into apartments. The wraparound porch was lit up invitingly, the lack of natural light hiding the fact that the house was in need of a coat of paint. A Christmas wreath still hung on the front door.

They climbed the creaking old staircase to the second floor and wound their way down a hall. The sounds of television sets and voices drifted out of apartments. Someone had fried onions for supper. A mountain bike was propped in the hall with a sign taped to the handlebars—RIGGED TO BLOW. THIEVES, TAKE YOUR CHANCES. Then they turned onto another flight of stairs and left the neighbors behind.

"I've got the third floor to myself," Megan explained, digging her keys out of her coat pocket. "It's big enough for only one apartment."

"What made you pick this place instead of one of the apartment complexes?"

She shrugged off the question a little too easily. "I just like old houses. They have character."

A blast of heat hit them as she opened the door. Light banished the darkness as she hit the switch.

"Behold utilities!"

"God, it must be eighty degrees in here!" Mitch declared, peeling his coat off and tossing it over the back of a chair.

"Eighty-two." Megan gasped for breath and gave the thermostat a twist. "Guess there's a trick to this. I had it set for seventy-two." She sent Mitch a wry look as she shrugged out of her parka. "You ought to like this, you're from Florida."

"I've acclimated. I own snowshoes. I go ice fishing."

"Masochist."

She tossed the stack of photocopies on the table and disappeared down the hall and into what Mitch guessed was a bedroom. He stood in the center of the living room and surveyed the apartment, trying to find clues to Megan O'Malley as he rolled up his shirtsleeves.

The kitchen and living area flowed together, divided only by an old round oak table surrounded by mismatched antique chairs. The kitchen cupboards were painted white and looked as though they had been salvaged out of another old house. The walls were a soft rose pink and, while he knew Megan couldn't have had time to paint them herself, he thought they suited her. He also thought she would deny it if he said so. The color was too feminine. That was a side she didn't show to the public. But he had caught glimpses of it.

The furniture in the living room was all old, and what he could see of it was lovingly well kept. Boxes were piled on every available surface. Books, dishes, quilts, more books. It looked as if nothing but the bare essentials had been unpacked.

"Just move the boxes anywhere if you want to sit down," she called.

She emerged from the bedroom rolling up the sleeves of a flannel shirt three sizes too big for her. The heavy sweater and turtleneck were gone. The black leggings remained, hugging her slim legs like a second skin. A pair of shorthaired cats wound themselves around her ankles, begging for attention. The larger one was black with a white bib, white paws, a crooked tail, and a complaining voice. The smaller one, a gray tabby, flung himself on the rug in front of her and rolled on his back, purring loudly.

"Beware the watchcats," she said dryly. "If they mistake you for a giant hunk of Little Friskies, you're a goner." She turned for the kitchen and they trotted after her with their tails straight up. "The black one is Friday," she said, popping open a can of food. "The gray one is Gannon."

Mitch smiled to himself. She would name her cats after the characters on *Dragnet*. Nothing soft and fuzzy, no Puff, no Fluff. Cop names.

"My daughter would love them," he said. Guilt nipping him, he checked his watch and realized he'd missed Jessie's bedtime for the second night in a row. "We've got a dog and that's enough animal life for our house. She's been begging her grandparents to get a kitten, but her grandfather is allergic."

Or at least that was Joy's excuse. Dump the blame on Jurgen. Mitch suspected it was more a matter of Joy being allergic to changing litter boxes and brushing hair off her furniture.

"You're lucky to have someone to look after her," Megan said. She tossed the empty can in the trash and bent to dig through a brown Coleman cooler on the floor next to the refrigerator.

"Yeah, I guess," Mitch said, taking the bottle of Harp she handed out to him. "I'd rather be with her myself."

"Really?"

"Yeah, really," he answered defensively, trying to decipher the expression in her eyes. Surprise? Vulnerability? Wariness? "Why wouldn't I? She's my daughter."

She lifted a shoulder but dodged his eyes, dropping her gaze to her hands as she twisted the cap off her beer. "Raising a child alone is a burden a lot of men wouldn't want."

"Then there are a lot of men who shouldn't be fathers."

"Well . . . that's a fact."

Mitch stood with the beer bottle dangling from his fingers, his attention sharp on Megan as she tossed the cap in the wastebasket and took a long drink. The offhand remark had a sting of truth in it, an old thread of experience.

"You said your dad was a cop."

"Forty-two years in the blue." She leaned back against the counter, crossing her ankles, crossing her arms. "Got his sergeant's stripes and never went any higher. Never wanted to. As he says to anyone who will listen, all the *real* cop work is done in the trenches."

The touch of humor didn't quite cover the bitterness. She heard it, too. He saw the flash of caution in her eyes. Setting her beer aside, she turned to the window above the sink, opened it a crack, then stood back and stared out at nothing. Mitch moved to the end of the counter, just close enough to read her, just close enough to feel her tension.

"Got any brothers?"

"One."

"He a cop, too?"

"Mick?" She laughed. "God, no. He's an investment broker in L.A."

"So you followed in Dad's footsteps instead?"

He didn't know how true that was, Megan thought, staring out at the night as its cool breath whispered in through the open window. It had begun to snow lightly, fine, dry flakes sifting down from the clouds, shimmering like sequins under the streetlight. She had spent much of her life dogging her father like a shadow, unknown, unseen. What a sad, stupid cycle of life.

In the corner of her eye she could see Mitch standing there, tie loose around his neck, top two buttons of his shirt undone, sleeves rolled up neatly, exposing muscular forearms dusted with dark hair. The pose was nonchalant, but there was a certain tension in the broad shoulders. His expression was pensive, expectant, the dark, deep-set eyes locked on her, studying, waiting.

"I like the job," she said flatly. "It suits me."

It suited the image she presented the world, Mitch thought. Terrier-tough, tenacious, all business. It suited the image she was trying to present to him. He should have taken it at face value. God knew, she was trouble enough as the first female field agent the bureau had ever inflicted upon the unsuspecting county cops of rural Minnesota. He didn't need to look deeper. He didn't need to understand her.

Still, he caught himself moving toward her, close enough so he could feel the electrical field come to life between them, close enough that she narrowed her eyes in subtle warning. But she didn't back away. She wouldn't. He was probably a fool to let that please him, but he didn't seem to have any say in the matter. His response to her was elemental, instinctive. She was a challenge. He wanted to crack the tough-cookie façade. He wanted . . . and that surprised him. He hadn't wanted a woman since Allison. He had *needed* and he had succumbed to that need, but he hadn't *wanted*. It amazed him to want now, to want her.

"Yeah, the job suits you," he murmured. "You're a tough cookie, O'Malley."

Megan lifted her chin a proud notch, not taking her eyes off him. "Don't you forget it, Chief."

He was standing too close. Again. Close enough that she could see the shadow of his evening beard on his hard jaw. Close enough that some reckless part of her wanted to lift a hand and touch it . . . and touch the scar that hooked across his chin . . . and touch the corner of his mouth, where it pulled into a frown of concentration. Close enough that she could see into the depths of the whiskey-brown eyes that looked as though they had seen far too much, none of it good.

Her heart beat a little harder.

"We have a case to discuss," she reminded him. He raised a hand and pressed a finger against her lips.

"Ten minutes," he whispered, lifting her chin with his thumb. "No case." He leaned down and touched his lips to hers. "Just this."

He parted her lips and slid his tongue between them, into her, as if he had every right; plunging deep and retreating slowly in a rhythm that was primal and unmistakable, blatantly carnal. She rose in his arms, into the kiss, answering with a hunger of her own.

His hands slid over her back and he pressed closer, trapping her between the cupboards and his body. For just this sliver of time there was nothing but need between them. Simple. Strong. Burning. His body was hot and hard, muscle and desire, undeniably male. And she was melting against him, on fire.

With his hands at her waist, Mitch lifted her easily and set her on the counter. She let her knees part, let her stocking feet hook around behind his thighs as he stepped in close. As he found her mouth again, she speared her fingers back through his thick hair and ran them down the muscles of his neck to his big, hard shoulders. He cradled her face in his hands as the kiss grew wilder, more urgent. Her barrette clattered into the sink and her hair spilled around her shoulders, mahogany silk he sifted through his fingers and combed back from her face.

Even as the cool night air streamed in through the window, the heat around them and between them intensified. The back of his shirt was damp with it. It burned the breath from her lungs. A bead of perspiration pooled in the hollow at the base of her throat and trickled down. He chased it with his lips. Her head fell back. Her eyes drifted shut. She could feel his knuckles against her chest as he thumbed the buttons of her shirt free. Then the flannel dropped back off her shoulders and his mouth was on her breast.

She gasped as he took her nipple between his lips and caressed it with his tongue. The need exploded. Tore through her. Shocked her back to sanity.

Mitch knew the instant it happened. He heard her sharp intake of breath, felt the muscles of her back go rigid beneath his hands. And he thanked God she had a better warning system than he did, or in another five minutes he would have taken her right there without benefit of a bed or any other consideration. He wanted her too badly and for reasons he couldn't quite fathom. Need pounded through his body, throbbing relentlessly in his groin.

Slowly he raised his head, raised his heavy-lidded gaze to meet hers. Just as slowly he pulled the halves of her shirt together over her small, plump breasts and held them there.

"You're sure you won't reconsider on the offer of the bed?" he asked, his voice a low, husky rasp.

"I'm sure," she murmured.

He let her slide down from the counter but held her there, trapped her there with his legs on either side of hers. Leaning down, he feathered slow, soft kisses along her hairline and drew her up against him, pressing his erection against her belly, letting her know just what he wanted, just what she did to him.

Megan trembled at the feel of him hard against her, at the mental image of the two of them together, naked in the bed in the next room. She trembled at the ache of desire and at the consequences that desire could bring. He could ruin her, ruin the career she had worked so hard to build. And even knowing that, she wanted him. The wind blew in through the open window behind her and chilled the sweat on her skin.

"Not that it isn't tempting," she admitted with as much cool as she could scrape together as a fist hammered against the apartment door and the smell of pizza crept in through the wood. "But our ten minutes are up."

9:16 P.M. 15°

Paul sat in the leather executive's chair behind his desk. Beyond the puddle of light from the brass gooseneck lamp, his office was dark. The accounting firm of Christianson and Kirkwood rented a suite in the Omni Complex, an overnamed two-story brick building that also housed a real estate agency, an insurance agency, and a brace of small law firms. Every other office in the building was empty at this time of night. All the lawyers and agents and secretaries had gone home.

The idea cut into Paul like a dull blade.

His family was broken, torn. Even before last night it had been skewed, fractured. Because of Hannah. The great Dr. Garrison, savior of the unwashed masses. The town darling. The model of modern womanhood. Because she was selfish, because she valued her job more than her marriage, the whole structure of their family life had cracked and eroded. Because of her he didn't want to go home. Because of her he was having an affair. Because of her Josh was gone.

Hours after coming in from the search, his hands and feet were still cold. Adrenaline continued to race through him, pushing him up out of his chair to pace. Scenes ran through his mind on fast forward. The volunteers, hundreds of them, tramping through the knee-high snow; the air fogged with their breath, electric with their tension. The pounding of helicopter blades. The baying of bloodhounds and barks of police dogs. The motor drives of cameras and the whine of audio equipment. The glare of lights. The urgency of reporters' questions.

"Mr. Kirkwood, do you have a comment?"

"Mr. Kirkwood, would you like to make a statement?"

"I just want my son back. I'll do anything—I'll give anything to get my son back."

It seemed unreal. As if life had fallen out of sync. As if this existence were the mirror image of reality, cast in shadows and sharp relief. It made him uneasy, uncomfortable, made him feel as if his skin didn't fit. He was a man who needed order, craved order. Order had gone out the window.

"Paul, sit down. You need to rest."

The voice came from the shadows. He had almost forgotten her. She had followed him from the prayer vigil, careful not to come into the building right behind him. That was one of the things he liked most about her—her sense of discretion, her sensitivity to his needs. She did part-time secretarial work in the State Farm office. Not a career, just a small job for pin money. Her husband taught at Harris College. He had lost interest in her and in her desire for a family, totally immersing himself in his work in the psychology department. His work was important. His work was essential. Like Hannah's.

Paul lowered himself on the upholstered couch and sat leaning forward, elbows braced on his thighs. She was beside him instantly, her legs curled beneath her, her hands on his shoulders, kneading the knotted muscles through his L. L. Bean wool shirt.

"There were volunteers from all over in the command post," she said softly. She always spoke softly, the way he believed a woman should. He closed his eyes and thought of how feminine she was, what a fool her husband was to turn his back on her. "Just at my table there was a woman from Pine City and two from Monticello. They came all that way just to help label fliers."

"Can we not talk about it?" Paul said tersely.

Images whirled in his brain faster and faster. The volunteers, the cops, the reporters; fliers, bulletins, police reports; lights, camera, action. Faster and faster, out of control. He pressed his thumbs against his eyes until colors burst behind the lids.

He shrugged off her touch, standing once again. "Maybe you should just go. I need to be alone."

"I only want to help, Paul." She lay her head against his hip. Sliding her arms around his legs, she stroked her hands lightly up and down the fronts of his thighs. "I only want to give you some kind of comfort." Her touch grew firmer, bolder, sliding upward. "Last night I wanted so badly to come to you, to lie down with you and just hold you."

While he had been lying naked with Hannah . . . He closed his eyes again and pictured her coming to him, pictured himself making love to her in his own bed while Hannah watched from the corner. Shame and desire twisted inside him, a potent, bitter mix as he turned to face her and she undid his pants.

As he always did, he began the petition of excuses. He deserved this. He deserved comfort. He was entitled to a few moments' release. Closing his eyes, he gave himself over to it. He tangled his hands in her silken hair and moved his hips in rhythm with her. He lost himself in the pleasure for a few brief moments. Then the end came in a rush and it was over, and the feeling of vindication faded into something dirty.

He didn't see her to the door. He didn't tell her he loved her. He let her assume the grief had swamped him again and went to stand at the narrow window behind his desk, looking down on the parking lot. He listened to his office door close, then the door to the hall. Automatically, he checked his watch so he would know when ten minutes had passed and he would be free to go.

Free.

Somehow, he didn't think he would feel free tonight. In a dim corner of his mind, where primitive fears stirred, he wondered if he would ever feel free again. He watched Karen Wright get into her Honda two stories below, pull out onto Omni Parkway, and drive off into the dark, taillights glowing like a pair of demon-red eyes.

Slowly he turned and went back to his desk, staring down at the answering machine that took all calls to his personal line. A cold, clammy sweat broke over his body. The images of the day whirled and spun crazily in his head, making him dizzy. His stomach cramped and his finger shook as he reached down and punched the message button. His legs buckled. He sank down into his chair, cradling his head in his hands as the tape played.

"Dad, can you come and get me from hockey? Mom's late and I wanna go home."

CHAPTER 12

They paged through Josh's private thoughts with Phil Collins singing something melancholy in the background. Here were Josh's personal drawings and doodlings, not something meant for strangers to paw over and pick apart. Megan let that fact run off her like rain against glass, concentrating instead on anything that seemed to indicate unhappiness or fear or dislike for an adult.

There were careful drawings of race cars and notes bemoaning the tenacity of a little girl named Kate Murphy who had set her sights on making Josh her boyfriend. He had a crush on his teacher. Brian Hiatt and Matt Connor were his best buddies—Three Amigos. There was mention of hockey and one page with a cartoonish image of Olie Swain, recognizable by the dark smudge of his birthmark, doing a flip on skates. Beside the picture Josh had written *Kids tease Olie but that's mean. He can't help how he looks.*

He knew his parents were having problems. There was a drawing of his mother facing one way, a stethoscope hanging around her neck, and his father facing the other way, his eyebrows dark, angry slashes of black. A big storm cloud hung over their heads, spitting down raindrops the size of bullets. At the bottom of the page he had printed: *Dad is mad. Mom is sad. I feel bad.*

Megan turned the page over and rubbed her hands over her face.

Mitch stared at the note the kidnapper had slipped into the back of the book. It looked just like the one that had been left behind in the duffel bag. Laser print on cheap office paper.

i had a little sorrow, born of a little SIN
ignorance is not innocence but SIN

SIN. This was the second reference to sin. Josh had been an altar boy at St. Elysius. He would have gone to religion class Wednesday night if he hadn't vanished. Someone had already interviewed his instructor, asking if there had been any call saying Josh would be late or absent, asking all the same questions that had been asked of all the adults who came into contact with Josh on a regular basis. But there were other people connected with the church, a few hundred parishioners, for instance. Or it could be that the kidnapper had nothing to do with St. Elysius at all; he could have been a member of any one of the eight churches in Deer Lake—or none of them.

Mitch's beeper went off. He dropped a half-eaten slice of pepperoni and mushroom back into the cardboard box as he rose from the table. Heedless of the grease on his fingers, he dug a hand into his coat pocket, fished out his portable phone, and punched out the number.

"Andy, what's up?" he asked, his eyes on Megan. She rose from her chair slowly, as if a sudden move might ruin their chances of good news.

"We've got a witness!" The excitement in the sergeant's voice sang over the airwaves. "She lives over by the ice arena. She thinks she saw Josh last night. Says she saw him get in a car."

"Well, Christ, what took her so long to call?" Mitch barked. "Why didn't anyone talk to her last night?"

"I dunno, Chief. She's coming into the station. I figured you'd want to be there."

"I'll be right in." He snapped the phone shut, his eyes still on Megan. "If there's a God in heaven, we've got a break."

9:54 P.M. 14°

I feel so terrible about this, Mitch."

The fluorescent lights of the conference room washed down on Helen Black, giving her a haunted look that seemed appropriate to the circumstances. Helen was forty-three and divorced, preserved—in her own words—by treadmill torture, Elizabeth Arden, and SlimFast. In kinder lighting she was not unattractive, but tonight the lines of strain and time were too evident beside her eyes and mouth; the shade of blond she had chosen at the Rocco Altobelli Salon had taken on a brittle, brassy cast that only accentuated her pallor.

Helen ran her own portrait photography studio on the second floor of a renovated building downtown. She had taken the shot of Mitch and Jessie that sat on his desk in his office. She had a talent for capturing the personalities of her subjects that brought her business from miles around. Successful and single, Helen was one of the many women Mitch's friends had tried to steer him toward in the past two years. He had ducked the fixup, deflecting Helen's attention elsewhere.

"I was getting ready to leave for the Cities. Your friend from the wildlife art gallery in Burnsville, Wes Riker, asked me to *Miss Saigon*. I was rushing around the house like a chicken with its head cut off, and I just happened to look out the front window—"

"What time was this?" Megan asked, pen poised above a legal pad.

She sat across the imitation walnut table from Helen Black. Russ Steiger had pulled out the molded plastic chair to Megan's left and planted his heavy winter boot on it. Melting snow and dirt dripped out of the treads to pool in the deepest part of the seat. Mitch sat next to the witness, his chair turned to face her. He had a pad and pen as well, but they lay on the table untouched. Helen Black had his complete attention.

Helen made a helpless motion with her hands. "I couldn't say exactly. It had to be before seven, and it had to be later than when the boys usually get picked up or I wouldn't have thought anything of it at all. I *didn't* think anything of it. It just stuck in my mind because I thought, Here's someone running as late as I am."

"Can you swear it was the Kirkwood kid?" Steiger asked.

She looked even more distressed, her brows tugging together, digging a deep furrow into her forehead. "No. I wasn't paying that much attention. I know he had on a light-colored stocking cap. I know he was the only boy on the sidewalk." Tears welled up in her eyes. She gripped a tattered tissue in her fist but made no move to use it. "If I'd known— If I'd had any idea— God, that poor kid! And Hannah—she must be going crazy."

She pressed her fist against her mouth and still the tears came. Mitch reached out and covered her other hand on the table.

"Helen, it wasn't your fault—"

"If I'd thought— If I'd paid closer attention— If I could have called someone then—"

Unmoved, Steiger chewed a toothpick. He shot a glance at Megan, but only to check for cleavage. She glared at him, resisting the urge to button her shirt up to her throat.

"It would have been nice to hear this twenty-some hours ago," he muttered.

"I'm so sorry!" Helen cried, apologizing to Mitch. "I just didn't think. I went into Minneapolis for the play, and stayed over to shop. I spent the whole day at the Mall of America. I never heard a word about Josh until I got home tonight. My God, if I'd known!"

As she dropped her head down into her hand and sobbed, Mitch sent the sheriff a scathing glare. "Helen," he said softly, patting her shoulder. "You had no reason to think anything was wrong. What do you remember about the car?"

She sniffed and swiped at her dripping nose with the disintegrating tissue. "It was a van. That's all. You know me—I don't know one end of a car from the other."

"Well, was it full-size?" Steiger asked impatiently. He pulled his foot down off the chair and paced like a Doberman on a short leash. "Was it a panel van, a conversion van? What?"

Helen shook her head.

Megan bit down on a suggestion for the sheriff to go pass

the time attempting the anatomically impossible and leave the interview to her and Mitch. She focused instead on the witness. "Let's try this another way, Ms. Black," she said evenly. "Do you remember if the van was light-colored or dark?"

"Um—it was light. Tan or maybe light gray. It might have been dirty white. You know, the lighting around that parking lot has an amber cast to it. It distorts color."

"All right," Megan said, jotting *color: light* on her notepad. "Did it have windows—like a minivan or a shuttle-type van?"

"No. No big windows. There might have been small ones on the back doors. I'm not sure."

"That's okay. A lot of people couldn't tell you if they had back windows on their own van, let alone the make and model of someone else's."

Helen managed a wry smile. "My ex was a car nut," she confessed with a woman-to-woman look. "He could remember the day the odometer in his four-by-four turned over on 100,000 miles. Couldn't remember our anniversary, but he knew to the minute how long it had been since his precious 'vette had its lube job. All I want to know is can it get me where I want to go."

"And does it have a heater," Megan said, winning another watery smile.

Helen brushed her bangs back out of her eyes, relaxing visibly. "It wasn't the kind of van I'd want to run around town in. It was more the kind of thing a plumber would drive."

Steiger scowled. "What the hell does that mean?"

"I know exactly what you mean," Megan said, and noted *panel van*. "A scuzzy plumber or a good one?"

"Scuzzy. It looked older. Dirty or maybe rusty in spots." She hesitated, considering. "Plumber," she murmured. "You know, I wasn't sure why I said that, but now that I think about it, the shape of it was the same as Dean Eberheardt's van. He came to fix my shower and tracked mud all over the house. I remember watching him drive away, thinking, My God, I wonder what kind of pigsty that van is."

"Are you saying Dean Eberheardt is the kidnapper?" Steiger said, incredulous.

"No!" Helen looked horrified at his conclusion.

Megan gritted her teeth and looked to Mitch.

"Ford Econoline, early eighties," he said, ignoring the sheriff. "Dean snaked out my kitchen sink. It took a whole bottle of Mr. Clean to do the floor."

"Relative of yours, Sheriff?" Megan muttered, rising with notepad in hand. She gave Steiger a pointed look and directed his gaze to the muddy puddle his boot had left in the chair.

"Did you notice anything else, Helen?" Mitch asked. "Anything that struck you as odd or stuck in your mind for any reason."

"The license plate, for instance," Steiger grumbled.

Helen gave him a narrow look. "I would have needed binoculars. I don't know about you, Sheriff, but I don't keep them handy in my living room."

"I'll get this on the wire right away," Megan told Mitch. "Thank you so much, Ms. Black. You've been an enormous help."

Fresh tears glazed across Helen's eyes. "I just wish I could have helped sooner. I hope it's not too late."

That was everyone's hope, Megan thought as she went out into the hall and headed toward her office. The bulletin had to go over the teletype to BCA headquarters. From headquarters the information would go out immediately to every agency in Minnesota and to surrounding states.

"What are you going to put in the bulletin?" Steiger asked, striding up alongside her. "Someone saw a kid get into a van a plumber might drive?"

"It's more than we had an hour ago."

"It's shit."

Megan bristled. "You think so? I've already got a printout of recent incidents involving possible and known child predators in a hundred-mile area. If one of them was driving a light-colored, older, full-size van, we've got a suspect. What have you got, Sheriff?"

Indigestion, if his expression was anything to go by. He scowled down at her, his face a weathered roadmap of lines, his nose so sharply aquiline, it was nearly a vertical blade protruding from his lean face. He caught hold of Megan's shoulder and stopped her. The overhead lighting gleamed against the oil slick in his dark hair.

"You think you're pretty smart, don't you?" he rasped.

"Is that a rhetorical question or would you care to see my diplomas?"

"You can get by on that smart mouth in the Cities, but it won't fly out here, honey. We have our own way of doing things—"

"Yes, I took note of your style in the conference room. Badgering a cooperative witness to tears. What do you do for an encore—take a rubber truncheon to Josh's playmates?"

Heat flared in Steiger's eyes, and he raised a finger in warning. "Now, listen—"

"No. *You* listen, Sheriff," Megan said, stabbing him in the chest with a forefinger, backing him off a step. "We've all been working around the clock and tempers are wearing thin, but that's no excuse for the way you treated Helen Black. She gave us a lead, now you want to blow it off because it doesn't spell out the crook's name in big capital letters—"

"And you're going to crack the case with it," he sneered.

"I'll damn well try, and you'd better, too. This investigation is a cooperative effort. I suggest you go look up *cooperative* in the dictionary, Sheriff. You don't seem to grasp the concept."

"You'll be out of here inside a month," he growled.

"Don't count on it. There are plenty of people who bet against me ever getting this job. I'm planning to feed them the crow myself. I'll be more than happy to add your name to the guest list."

She turned to go, knowing she was making an enemy of Steiger, too angry to care. But she whirled back toward him for a parting shot. "One other thing, Steiger—I'm not your honey."

10:58 P.M. 14°

The image of Olie Swain's ugly pug face hovered at the back of Mitch's mind like a gremlin from a bad dream as he drove out of the parking lot. Olie Swain drove a beat-up, rusted-out 1983 Chevy van that had once been white. Olie, who was strange by anyone's standards. Olie, who had access to nearly every little boy in town. Olie, whom Mitch had sworn was harmless.

"This must be especially hard for you," Helen said softly.

Mitch glanced at her sitting in the passenger seat of his truck, wrapped in a goofy-looking faux leopard jacket. The jacket suited her sense of humor, but there was no trace of that humor in her expression. There was pity, something Mitch had seen enough of to last him a lifetime.

"It's hard on everybody," he said. "You might want to give Hannah a call. She's really hurting. She blames herself."

"Poor kid." Helen called anyone more than a month younger than her "kid," a habit that made her seem world-weary. "Mothers aren't allowed to make mistakes anymore. A generation ago everyone just assumed they would screw up their kids. Now they've got to be Wonder Woman." Her tone hardened and chilled as she said, "I don't suppose Paul is taking any of the burden of guilt."

"He was working. It was Hannah's night to pick up Josh."

"Uh-huh. There but for the grace of God goes Paul."

Mitch glanced at Helen again. Her mouth was pinched tight. "You and Paul don't get along?"

"Paul is a horse's ass."

"For any particular reason?"

Helen didn't answer. Mitch let it drop. "Helen, would you be willing to take a look at a couple of vans, tell me if any of them resemble the one you saw last night? Just so I can get an accurate description?"

"Of course."

They drove out to the car dealerships on the east side of town, where flags and giant inflatable animals enticed people to turn off the interstate and buy a different car. At Dealin' Swede's Helen pointed out a gray Dodge utility van and said "sort of but not quite." On the way back across town, Mitch slowed beside several parked vans, giving her a chance to look at a number of vehicles. On her own block he drove past her house and into the parking lot at the ice arena. He slowed to a stop thirty feet away from Olie's van, saying nothing.

Helen's brows knitted. She nibbled her lower lip. Mitch's stomach twisted.

"More like this one," she said slowly.

"But not *just* like this one?"

She turned her head to one side and then the other as if a memory might shake loose. "I don't think so. Something's different—the color or the shape—but it's close. . . . I don't know." She faced him, shaking her head, her expression apologetic. "I'm sorry, Mitch. I saw it for only a few seconds. I just got an impression, is all. I wish I could say it looked exactly like this one, but I can't."

"It's okay," he murmured, swinging the Explorer around and driving back to Helen's house. "Did you have a good time at the play?" he asked as she picked her purse up off the floor.

"Yeah," she said with a small smile. "Wes is nice. Thanks for the introduction. You're a good guy, Mitch."

"That's me—the last of the good guys."

The tag struck him as ironic. Yeah, he was a great guy—deflecting the interest of women onto his friends so he wouldn't have to deal with them.

You weren't exactly dodging Megan tonight, were you, Holt?

A memory of heat and softness and the cool breath of night air stole into his consciousness. The taste of sweetness. Odd how someone with a tongue as tart as hers could taste sweet. She had been the one to pull back. He would have taken them past the point of no return.

"Your timing stinks, Mitch," he muttered, turning south. At the next corner he turned east and drove down the street that ran behind the ice arena.

The case demanded all their energy. And he would be the one dodging when Megan found out Olie Swain drove a van, that he had been to Olie's house without her. She already had her suspicions about Olie. She would jump on this van connection like a she-wolf on a rabbit—and spook Olie in the process. Mitch knew even the most harmless of women made Olie uncomfortable. Mitch couldn't afford to have Olie bolt if he did have something to do with Josh's disappearance.

Olie's house was a converted single-car garage that sat on the last property on the block. The main house on the lot was owned by old Oscar Rudd, who collected junker Saabs and parked them on every available inch of ground in the yard and on the street, in violation of three city ordinances, leaving no room for Olie to park his van. Olie left the van in the lot at the rink and walked back and forth, tramping through the snow, slush, mud—whatever the season left for him in the vacant lot between his home and the arena.

Like the main house, the garage was covered with brown asphalt-coated tar paper designed to look like brick. It fooled no one. A stovepipe stuck up through the roof at a crooked angle, venting the smoke from the woodstove that was the main source of heat. Light glowed out through the single window in the side of the building. Mitch could hear the chatter of a television as he walked up the shoveled path toward the door. *Letterman*. He wouldn't have given Olie credit for having a sense of humor. He knocked and waited. The television went mute. He knocked again.

"Olie? It's Chief Holt."

"What'd you want?"

"Just to talk. I have a couple of questions you might be able to answer."

The door cracked open and Olie's ugly face filled the space, his eyes round and wary. "Questions about what?"

"Different things. Can I come in? It's freezing out here."

Olie backed away from the door, as much of an invitation as he was willing to give. He didn't like people coming into his place. This was his safe spot, like the old shed he had stumbled across as a kid. The shed sat on an abandoned piece of land, not far from his house out on the edge of town where the trashy people lived. The land backed onto a city park, but the paths in that part of the park were overgrown and so no one came near the shed. Olie had pretended the shed was his own, his place to hide to avoid a beating or to hole up after a bad one. In the shed he was safe.

He had transferred that feeling of safety to this place. The garage was small and dark. A cubbyhole. He filled it with his books and the stuff he bought at junk shops. He invited no one inside, but he couldn't say no to the chief of police. He stepped back to his makeshift desk and absently stroked the top of his computer screen, petting it as if it were a cat.

Mitch had to duck a little to come in the door. He took in the state of Olie's domain with a seemingly casual glance.

There was only one room. One dark, cold room with dirty blue indoor-outdoor carpet covering the concrete floor. The kitchen consisted of an ancient refrigerator and a cast-off olive green electric range. The bathroom was partitioned off by a pair of mismatched curtains hanging from a wire. The curtains gaped, offering a glimpse of a tin shower stall.

"Cozy place you got here, Olie."

Olie said nothing. He wore the same green flight jacket, the same dark wool sweater, the same Ragg wool half-gloves he had worn the night before. Mitch wondered if he bothered to change clothes all winter. For that matter, he wondered if he ever bothered to use that shower stall. The place smelled like dirty feet.

He looked for a place to sit, hoping to put Olie at ease, but settled for leaning against the back of a ratty old recliner. There were books everywhere. Shelves and shelves of books. Piles and piles of books. What furniture there was seemed to serve only as another place to pile books. What room wasn't taken up by books was taken up by computer equipment. Mitch counted five PCs.

"Where'd you get all the computers, Olie?"

"Different places. In the Cities. Businesses throw 'em out 'cause they're out of date. I didn't steal them."

"I didn't think you did. I'm just making conversation here, Olie." Mitch offered him a smile. "Businesses throw them out? That's quite a deal. How'd you find out about that?"

Olie eased down into his chair, his good eye darting from the computer screen to Mitch and back. The glass eye stayed on Mitch. "Professor Priest." His hand darted over the keyboard to hit a button. "He lets me sit in on some classes."

"He's a nice guy."

Olie didn't comment. He hit another button and the screen before him went blank.

"So what do you do with all these machines?"

"Stuff."

Mitch forced another smile and let out a measured sigh between his teeth. That Olie, master of small talk. "So, Olie, did you work tonight?"

"Yeah."

"Anything going on at the rink around five-thirty?"

He shrugged. "Skating club."

"Practicing for the big show Sunday, I suppose."

Olie took it for a rhetorical statement.

"I wanted to ask you a couple of questions about last night," Mitch said.

"You haven't found that boy."

It seemed more a statement than a question. Mitch watched him carefully, his own expression impassive. "Not yet, but we're looking real hard. We've got a couple of leads. Did you think of anything that might help us?"

Olie's good eye looked down at his keyboard. He flicked a lint ball off one of the keys.

"Someone thinks they saw Josh get into a van last night. A van that looked something like yours—older, light-colored. You didn't see a van like that, did you?"

"No."

"You didn't loan your van to someone, did you?"

"No."

"You leave the keys in it?"

"No."

Mitch lifted a book from the pile on the seat of the recliner and studied the cover idly. *Story of the Irish Race*. He wondered if Olie was Irish or just curious. He'd never thought of Olie as being anything but weird.

Olie popped up from his chair. His brows pulled low over his mismatched eyes, seeming to tug at the port wine birthmark on the left side of his face. "It wasn't my van."

"But you were inside the arena," Mitch said. He set the book aside and slid his hands into his coat pockets. "Running the Zamboni, right? Maybe someone used your van without asking."

"No. They couldn't."

"Well . . ." Yawning hugely, Mitch pushed away from the decrepit recliner. "People do strange things, Olie. Just to be safe, we should probably take a look inside. Would you mind showing me?"

"You don't have a warrant." Olie immediately regretted the words. Mitch Holt's gaze sharpened like a gun scope coming into focus.

"Should I get one, Olie?" His soft, silky voice raised the short hairs on the back of Olie's neck.

"I don't know anything!" Olie shouted, shoving at a stack of books on a TV tray. They tumbled to the floor, sounding like bricks as they hit the concrete. "I didn't do anything!"

Mitch watched the outburst stonefaced, his expression giving away nothing of the tension tightening inside him like a watch spring. "Then you don't have anything to hide."

His mind was racing. If Olie consented to a search of the vehicle now and something turned up, would a judge later toss out the evidence on the argument of no warrant, consent given under duress? Without a positive ID on the vehicle, Mitch didn't have enough cause to obtain a warrant, and he doubted he could get Olie to sign a consent form. Goddamn technicalities. What he had was a missing child and a need to find him that far outstripped the needs of the courts.

If Olie let him take a look and he saw something in the van, he could have the vehicle towed in on the grounds that overnight parking was technically not permitted in the Gordie Knutson Memorial Arena lot. Upon impounding the vehicle, they would be able to inventory the contents, and anything suspicious listed on the inventory would give them probable cause to ask for a warrant authorizing seizure of it as evidence of a crime.

Okay. He had a plan. His ass was covered. The next move was Olie's.

Olie glared at him, his small mouth puckered into an angry knot. The birthmark that spilled down his forehead seemed to darken, and the rest of his face paled. His hand was trembling as he raised it and pointed a finger at Mitch.

"I don't have anything to hide," he said.

The eye staring defiantly at Mitch was made of glass. The other one slid away.

Round and round and round they go. Will they find Josh? We don't think so.

CHAPTER 13

Megan overslept, dreaming dark, sensuous dreams about Harrison Ford. As she slowly blinked her eyes open, the feelings lingered—forbidden needs and a lush, heavy sense of pleasure; guilt and gratification; the taste of Mitch Holt's kiss, the feel of his hands on her body, the feel of his mouth on her breast . . .

She stared at the hairline cracks in the ceiling plaster. The predawn light seeped into the room through sheer curtains, casting everything in shades of gray, like a dream. She lay beneath the tangled sheets and quilt, her heart beating slowly, strongly, her body warm, nerve endings humming. She could feel Gannon curled against her, the cat tucked into his favorite spot behind her knees. Friday would be in the kitchen, prowling for breakfast.

Megan's mind wandered into forbidden territory, and she wondered if Mitch might have dreamed about their kiss, wondered if the sensations hung around him like a heavy, sultry cloud as he lay in his bed.

Not a smart thing to wonder. He should have been just another cop, just someone she had to work with. But she had the feeling there was nothing simple about Mitch Holt. The Everyman façade hid a complex core of anger and need and pain. She had glimpsed those things in his eyes, tasted them in his kiss, and the hidden mysteries drew her in. She could have resisted mere sex appeal, but a mystery . . . Her mind was naturally geared to solving mysteries.

There was a more pressing mystery to solve. The reminder

was a poke in the conscience that drove Megan out of bed and into the shower. She let the water beat down on her in an attempt to pound out the numbness of sleep. Her head seemed as heavy and dense as an anvil. Her eyes felt as if they had grown a coat of fur. Five hours of sleep in forty-seven was not enough. She could have slept for a day, but she didn't have that luxury and wouldn't until this case was over. Even then she would be behind in her duties. All appointments with the other chiefs and sheriffs of her territory had been put on hold, but crime in those other counties and towns didn't stop just because Deer Lake had been hit with a big one. There was no balance maintained at the courtesy of lowlifes.

Friday jumped up on the edge of the old clawfoot tub and stuck his head inside the shower curtain. He wore a disgruntled expression on his round black face, golden eyes glowering at Megan, white whiskers twitching in annoyance as water droplets pelted him. He yowled at her in his complaining voice and swiped at his whiskers with his paw.

"Yeah, yeah, you want breakfast. You want, you want—what about what I want, huh?"

As he hopped down from the tub, he made a sound that indicated he was patently disinterested in her needs. A typical male attitude, Megan thought, cranking the faucet off and reaching for a towel.

After pulling on sweats, she fed the cats, then fed herself an English muffin. Sitting at the table, she stared unseeing at the depressing mess in her living room, the unpacked and half-unpacked boxes. She didn't let herself think about the need to build herself a nest and surround herself with the things she had collected—other people's heirlooms and memories, the false sense of belonging and family she had attached to her flea-market finds.

Her mind sorted tasks into a priority list and tumbled bits of information over and over in an attempt to sift out anything useful. Helen Black's statement played in the back of her mind like a videotape, and she strained to see something, hear something that might trigger an idea. She had found nothing encouraging in the reports she had gone through the night before, her share of the reports of recent incidents and known offenders. But then her eyes had given out before she could get through everything. One of her men may have had better luck.

Licking strawberry jam off her fingers, she grabbed her portable phone and punched the speed dial button for the command post.

"Agent Geist. How may I help you?"

"Jim, it's Megan. Any word?"

"Nothing yet, but the news about the van is just hitting the airwaves. I expect the hotline phones to light up like Christmas trees in another hour or so. Every third person in the state probably knows someone with a junker van."

"What about those listings? Anything turn up?"

"Close but no stogie. We've got a couple of aborted attempts to pick up kids in Anoka County in a brown van, a convicted pedophile in New Prague who drives a yellow van—"

"It's worth checking out. Did you call the chief in New Prague?"

"He's not in yet, but he'll call back as soon as he gets there."

"Good. Thanks. I'm going over to talk to the parents. Page me if anything goes down."

She dried her hair and brushed it back into the usual ponytail. Makeup amounted to a touch of blusher and two swipes with the mascara wand. In the bedroom she dug through her suitcase for a pair of burgundy stirrup pants and a bulky charcoal turtleneck. The cats found perches on the boxes in the living room and watched her shrug into her parka and struggle with her scarf.

"You guys feel free to unpack and decorate while I'm out," she told them.

Gannon curled his paws beneath him and closed his eyes. Friday gave her a look and said, "Yow."

"Yeah, well, be that way. You don't have any sense of style anyway."

The Lumina started grudgingly, growling and coughing. A belt somewhere in the inner workings squealed like a stuck pig when she cranked the knob for heat. The air that blasted out of the vents was like a breath from the Arctic.

To distract herself from the fact that her fingertips were going numb and the hair inside her nose was frosting over,

Megan studied the town as she cruised the tree-lined streets from the east side to the west side. The established, older part of Deer Lake was a Beaver Cleaver kind of town—comfortable family homes, dogs peeing on snowmen built by the children being trundled off to school in minivans. She saw no children walking to school. Was it the cold or Josh Kirkwood that kept them off the sidewalks?

Downtown looked like a movie set for the all-American town. The city park square in the center with its quaint old bandshell and statues to long-forgotten men, the old false-front brick shops, the courthouse built of native limestone. The Park Cinema theater with a vintage 1950s marquee jutting out, heralding the showing of *Philadelphia* at 7 & 9:20, and the grand old Fontaine Hotel, five stories of renovated Victorian splendor.

North and west of downtown, the old neighborhoods gave way to sixties ramblers, then seventies split-level homes, then the latest upscale developments—expensive hybrid homes on lots of an acre or more. Pseudo-Tudors and pseudo-Georgians, saltboxes with attachments, and yuppie-rustic homes like the Kirkwoods', sided in split cedar and landscaped with river birch and artfully arranged boulders. The builders had gone to great pains to make it seem as if the houses had been there for decades. Strategic sites, mature trees, and winding lanes gave the impression of seclusion.

The Kirkwood house faced the lake, an expanse of snow-dusted ice dotted with ice-fishing huts. In the early morning gray it looked desolate. Beyond the western bank, the buildings of Harris College squatted like a crop of dark mushrooms among the leafless trees. South of the college lay what had once been a town called Harrisburg. In the last century it had competed with Deer Lake for commerce and population, but Deer Lake had won the railroad and the title of county seat. Harrisburg had faded, had eventually been annexed, and now bore the indignity of the nickname Dinkytown.

Megan parked, cringing as the Lumina's engine knocked and rattled before going silent. Maybe if she solved this case the bureau would give her a better car. Maybe if she solved this case there would be a little boy playing in the half-finished snow fort on the Kirkwoods' front lawn.

Hannah Garrison answered the front door herself, looking drawn and thin. She wore a faded Duke sweatshirt, navy leggings, and baggy wool socks, and still somehow managed to project an air of elegance.

"Agent O'Malley," she said, her eyes widening at the possibilities Megan represented standing there on her front stoop. She gripped the edge of the door so hard, her knuckles turned white. "Have you found Josh?"

"No, I'm sorry, but we may have a lead. Someone may have seen Josh getting into a van Wednesday night. May I come in? I'd like to talk to you and your husband."

"Yes, of course." Hannah backed away from the door. "Let me catch Paul. He was just leaving to go out on the search again."

Megan stepped inside and closed the door behind her. She drifted after Hannah, staying far enough behind to remain unobtrusive, to observe without seeming to take in anything at all.

In the family room a fire crackled in the fieldstone fireplace, closed off from the room by glass doors and a safety screen in deference to the baby, who was curled up dozing on the back of a huge stuffed dog on the floor. The *Today* show was playing on a television set into a cherry armoire. Katie Couric needling Bryant Gumbel, Willard Scott laughing like an imbecile in the background. A petite woman with big brown eyes and an ash-blond bob silenced them with a remote control and looked up at Megan expectantly.

"Can I help you?" she asked in a hushed voice. "I'm Karen Wright, a neighbor. I'm here to help Hannah."

Megan gave her a cursory smile. "No, thank you. I need to speak with Mr. and Mrs.—um, with Mr. Kirkwood and Dr. Garrison."

Karen made a sympathetic face. "Awkward, isn't it? Life was simpler when we were all less liberated."

Megan made a noncommittal sound and moved on toward the kitchen, where Curt McCaskill was pouring himself a cup of coffee and reading the *StarTribune*. The agent glanced up with an exaggerated show of surprise.

"Hey, O'Malley, I was just reading about you. Did you really crack a kiddie porn ring when you were in vice?"

Megan ignored his question, zeroing in on the article

spread out on the kitchen table. *Female Agent Fighting Crime and Gender Bias.* The byline was Henry Forster's, the jerk. "Oh, Jesus, Mary, and Joseph, DePalma will shit a brick when he sees this!"

The piece detailed her service record and her struggle to gain a field post at the bureau. There were no direct quotes from her, but "sources in the bureau" had made several uncharitable remarks about her ambition. The article went on to recount the sexual harassment brouhaha of the previous fall, which had not involved her at all but had made life at headquarters unpleasant for everyone for a month or two. Battle lines had been drawn between the sexes and hard feelings still lingered. Forster's article would poke a stick at that old hornet's nest, but no one would turn on Forster. They would turn on her.

She groaned when she finished reading.

"You want a cup of coffee?" McCaskill asked.

"No, thanks. I need something stiffer than caffeine."

"I could make a joke here, but it might seem inappropriate, all things considered."

Megan laughed. She had always liked Curt. He had a sense of humor, something in increasingly short supply in the world at large.

His blue eyes twinkled. With his thick shock of ginger hair he looked like a leprechaun on steroids. "What brings you to this neck of the woods?"

"We have a witness who may have seen Josh getting into a van. I want to talk to the parents about it. Nothing happening on your end of things?"

The smile faded. He shook his head and lowered his voice to a confidential murmur. "I gotta tell you, thirty-nine hours and no word . . . If we haven't heard anything by now, we're not liable to. What we've got here is an abduction by a predator, not a kidnap for ransom."

Megan didn't answer him, but the weight of truth pressed down on her just the same. Just because she didn't give it voice didn't make it any less real. She pulled in a hard, deep breath, trying like hell to hang on to her determination. "You want to take a break? I'll be here half an hour or better."

He rose from his chair, trying to work the kinks out of his

shoulders. "Thanks. I could use some fresh air." He made a fist and scuffed it against her upper arm. "You're okay—for a chick."

She rolled her eyes at him, but the sound of sharp voices coming from the other side of the kitchen door drew her attention. The door swung open and Hannah stomped in, hugging herself against the cold that drifted in from the garage beyond. Her wide mouth was drawn in a thin, angry line, and her eyes gleamed with tears or temper or both. Paul stalked in behind her, looking irritated.

Megan had taken an instant dislike to Paul Kirkwood and she chided herself for it. The poor man had lost his son, he had every right to behave in any way he wanted. But there was just a certain petulant arrogance about Paul Kirkwood that rubbed her the wrong way.

He looked at her now, his mouth set in an expression that was more pout than frown. "What's this about a van?"

"A witness thinks she may have seen Josh getting into an older, light-colored van Wednesday night. I was wondering if either of you knows anyone with a van that matches that description or if you might have seen one in the neighborhood recently."

"Did they get a license plate?"

"No."

"A make and model on the van?"

"No."

He shook his head, not bothering to hide his impatience with her incompetence. "I told Mitch Holt neither of us is here enough to notice anyone hanging around. And if we knew anyone sick enough to steal our son, don't you think we would have said so?"

Megan bit down on her temper.

Hannah gave her a brittle, sour smile. "Paul is in a hurry," she said sarcastically. "God knows, they can't start the search without him. Heaven forbid he should be held up by something as trivial as a real lead—"

Paul cut her a narrow look. "Someone thinks they *might have* seen a boy who *might have been* our son getting into a van they can barely describe. Big fucking lead, Hannah."

"It's more than anyone else has come up with," she shot

back. "What have you found out there tramping around in the snow? Have you found Josh? Have you found anything at all?"

"At least I'm doing something."

He might as well have slapped her. Hannah pulled back, chin up, mouth quivering as she tightened it against the sobs that ached in her throat. "Implying that I'm not?" she whispered. "I'm not in this house by choice. You want to stay here with Lily and wait for the phone to ring? I will gladly trade places with you."

Paul rubbed a hand over his face. "That's not what I meant," he said softly, knowing it was exactly what he had meant. He had meant to hurt her. This was all her fault in the first place. If it hadn't been for Hannah and her all-important career . . . Hannah this, Hannah that, Hannah, Hannah, Hannah . . .

Megan watched the exchange, uncomfortable with being a spectator to something that should have been private.

"Mr. Kirkwood," she said, drawing his attention away from his wife, trying to diffuse the tension between them and get their focus back on the task at hand. "You're telling me you don't know anyone with a van that fits that general description—eighties model utility van, tan or light-colored?"

He shook his head absently. "No. If I think of anyone, I'll call Mitch."

"Do that." She ignored the slight. It didn't matter as long as the job got done.

Without a word to his wife, Paul turned and left. The tension hung in the air as they listened to his car start and back out of the drive. Hannah closed her eyes and pressed the heels of her hands against them. Karen Wright came in, wide-eyed. Bambi in the headlights, Megan thought. What an ugly little scene to play out in front of the neighbors.

"I know this is hard on both you and Paul," Megan said, her attention on Hannah. "And this lead probably doesn't seem like much, as vague as it is. I can understand he feels more useful physically searching for Josh—"

"I'm sure it makes Paul feel useful," Hannah snapped. "Just as I'm sure nothing could make anyone feel more use*less* than sitting around this house all day with people staring at them."

Karen blinked her big doe eyes, her brows knitting into an expression of hurt. "If I'm not being a help, maybe I should just leave."

"Maybe you should."

Hannah regretted the words the instant they were out of her mouth. Karen meant well. Everyone who had come to the house had meant well. Josh's disappearance had touched all their lives to a certain degree. They were only trying to cope, only thought they were trying to help *her* cope. The problem was, there was no coping. She could handle a city ER, deal with the stress of juggling that career with her family life, but there were no coping skills for this. She couldn't handle it and she couldn't see beyond it. The well-meaning hands reaching out to her seemed only to trap her in this nightmare.

Karen had her coat in hand and was halfway to the hall. Hannah blew out a breath and rushed after her, the need to smooth over bad feelings overruling deeper needs.

Megan watched her go, turning all these new puzzle pieces over in her head—the tension between Hannah and Paul chief among them. The situation was acting like a pressure cooker. Megan supposed even a good relationship would be strained under the circumstances, but she would have expected the husband and wife to turn to each other for support. That wasn't happening here. The pressure was crushing down on Hannah and Paul, and their relationship seemed to be cracking like an eggshell. The page from Josh's notebook rose in her memory—angry storm clouds and scowling people. *Dad is mad. Mom is sad. I feel bad.* . . .

Her instinct was to blame Paul Kirkwood entirely. He had an aura that left a bad taste in her mouth. Selfish, self-important—like her brother Mick, she realized. But it wasn't just that similarity she disliked. She had come here to tell him they had their first real lead and he hadn't wanted to take the time to listen. He wanted to be out in the field, where the television cameras could capture the grieving father in action.

A tug on the leg of her slacks pulled Megan's mind back to the present. She looked down in surprise to see Lily Kirkwood staring up at her with huge deep blue eyes and a shy smile.

"Hi!" Lily chirped.

"Hi there." Megan smiled, at a complete loss what to do.

She knew nothing about babies. Or children, for that matter. She had once been a child, of course, but she hadn't been very good at it. Always shy, feeling out of place, in the way, unwanted; the daughter of a woman who had been a dismal failure at mothering.

Megan's own awkwardness around children never failed to make her wonder just how much of her mother's lack of skill had been passed on to her. Not that it would matter. When she looked to the future, she saw her career, not a family. That was what she wanted. That was what she was good at.

Her heart gave a traitorous thump as Josh Kirkwood's baby sister stretched her arms up. "Lily up!"

"Lily, sweetheart, come to Mama."

Hannah scooped the baby up and pressed a fierce kiss against her cheek, hugging her tight, then turned to Megan. "I'm sorry about . . ." She shook her head. "I'm sorry, I'm sorry. The first words out of everyone's mouth these days."

"Sorry, Mama," Lily murmured, tucking her head beneath her mother's chin.

"Why don't I pour us both a cup of coffee?" Megan offered. The pot was still on the table, along with an assortment of clean mugs sitting in a cluster, waiting for the endless parade of cops and friends and neighbors.

"That sounds great." Hannah sank down on the chair McCaskill had vacated earlier, her cheek pressed against the top of Lily's head. Lily traced a miniature forefinger around the D of Duke on her mother's sweatshirt.

"Would you like something to eat? We have every kind of sweet roll and doughnut and muffin known to man." She gestured to the countertops that were lined with pans and plates and baskets heaped with baked goods. "All of them homemade except the Danish from Myrna Tolefsrud, who has sciatica on account of Mr. Tolefsrud's wild polka dancing at the Sons of Norway lodge." She repeated the stories she had taken in by rote. "Of course, according to Myrna's sister-in-law, LaMae Gilquist, Myrna has always been a poor cook and lazy to boot."

Megan smiled as she chose a tray of cinnamon rolls with thick creamy frosting and brought it to the table. "There's a lot to be said for small-town life, isn't there?"

"Usually," Hannah murmured.

"Chief Holt and I are encouraged about the lead. We're pursuing it very enthusiastically." Megan dug a roll out of the pan, plopped it on a paper plate, and set the plate in front of Hannah—directly on top of the newspaper article about herself.

Lily twisted around on her mother's lap and attacked the treat with both hands, ripping off a chunk and plucking out the raisins to be set aside in a little pile.

"I know," Hannah said. "I'm sure Paul knows, too. He's just—" *What?* Ten years of marriage and he was more a stranger to her now than he had ever been. She didn't know what or who Paul was anymore. "You're not exactly catching us at our best."

"In this line of work, I seldom catch anyone at their best."

"Me, neither," Hannah admitted quietly, her mouth twisting at the irony. "I'm not used to being on the other side of it. The victim. This might sound stupid, but I don't know how to behave. I don't know what's expected of me."

Megan licked frosting off her finger, her eyes on Hannah's. "No, that's not stupid. I know exactly what you mean."

"I've always been the one people turned to. The strong one. The one who knew how to get things done. Now I don't know what to do. I don't know how to let people take care of me. And I don't think they know what to do, either. They come here out of duty and then they sit around and look at me out the corner of their eye like they've just figured out I'm human and they don't like it."

"Don't worry about them," Megan said. "It doesn't matter what they think or what they want. Concentrate on getting through this any way you can. Make yourself eat; you need what strength you can get. Make yourself sleep. Prescribe something for yourself if you need to."

Hannah dutifully put a scrap of the demolished sweet roll in her mouth and chewed without tasting. Lily looked up at her, annoyed. Megan dug another roll out of the pan, put it on another plate, and slid it across the table. Without asking. Like a friend, Hannah thought. What an odd time to make a friend.

"What I need," she said, "is to *do* something. I know I have to be here, but there has to be something I can *do*."

Megan nodded. "Okay. The volunteers at the command

post are labeling fliers to be mailed out across the country. Thousands of them. I'll send someone over with a stack for you to work on. In the meantime, how about thinking on this lead? Do you know anyone with a van that even vaguely matches the description? Have you seen one parked someplace that struck you as strange? Near the school or the hospital or the lake."

"I don't pay attention to cars. The only van I can think of is an old clunker Paul used to have when he was going through his manly-hunter phase."

"When was this?" Megan asked, tensing automatically.

Hannah shrugged. "Four or five years ago. When we first moved out from the Cities. He had an old white van to haul his hunting buddies and their dogs, but he sold it. Hunting was too disorderly for Paul."

"Do you know who he sold it to? Someone you know?"

"I don't remember. It didn't concern me." Her eyes widened as the import struck.

Mitch had steered his questions on Wednesday night in the same direction. And she had pushed aside the possibility then that someone who had been in their home, eaten from their table, been taken into their trust, could turn on them so viciously. But even as her heart rejected the idea, her mind began scanning the names and faces of everyone she knew, everyone she didn't quite like, everyone on the fringe of their circle of acquaintance.

"We can't rule it out," Megan said. "We can't afford to rule out anything at this point."

Hannah pulled her baby close, ignoring the sticky fingers and a face smeared with frosting and cinnamon. She stared unseeing across the room, rocking Lily. Her thoughts were on Josh—where he might be, what he might be going through. Horrors enough at the hands of a stranger, but how unspeakably terrible to suffer at the hands of someone he had known and trusted. It happened all the time. She read it in the paper, saw it on television, had been in a position to try to mend such damage to other people's children.

"My God," she whispered. "What is this world coming to?"

"If we knew that," Megan murmured, "maybe we could stop it before it got there."

They sat in silence. Lily's eyes roamed the kitchen and she

squirmed a little, wrenching her head out from under her mother's chin. She looked up into the beautiful face that had the answers to all of her questions and asked in a small voice, "Mama, where Josh?"

8:22 A.M.   12°

Megan tracked Paul Kirkwood down at a parking area on the edge of Lyon State Park, seven miles west of town. The main search party was gathered—officers from the sheriff's department, officers from the Minneapolis Police Department canine unit with a trio of barking German shepherds, volunteers from all walks of life, so many people that the lot was full and cars were hanging off the shoulder a quarter mile up and down the main road. Four TV station vans had parked where they wanted, blocking in cars. Their satellite dishes telescoped up from their roofs, shooting signals to Minneapolis and St. Paul and Rochester.

Megan parked behind the KTTC van and headed for the crowd. Russ Steiger shouted out instructions, posing for the cameras with his fists propped on his narrow hips and his feet spread wide, mirrored sunglasses hiding his squinty eyes. Paul stood fifteen feet away, looking grave, the cold wind ruffling his brown hair. Megan slipped in beside him, hoping the newspeople would be too enraptured with the sheriff to notice her.

"Mr. Kirkwood, can I have a word?" she asked quietly, turning her back to the cameras.

Paul frowned. "What now?"

"I'd like to ask you a couple of questions about the van you used to have for hunting."

"What about it?"

"For starters, why didn't you mention it to me this morning?"

"I sold it years ago," he said irritably. "What could it possibly have to do with Josh?"

"Maybe nothing, but we want to check every possible avenue."

She caught hold of his coat sleeve and moved away from the crowd and the ears tuned like microphones to catch any squeak of information. Paul reluctantly followed her out of the line of cameras behind a Park Service truck.

"Hannah told me you sold the van several years ago," Megan said. "Who was the buyer? Would he have seen or met Josh at your house?"

"I don't know," Paul snapped. "It was years ago. I put an ad in the paper and someone answered it."

"You don't have any record of who?"

"No. He was just some guy. He paid cash, took the van, and left. It was a piece of junk. I was happy to get rid of it."

"What about the title? You didn't go with him to transfer the title?"

He gave her a look. "Surely, you're not that naïve, Agent O'Malley."

"No," Megan said evenly. "I'm not naïve. But you don't strike me as the kind of man who would ignore the rules."

"Jesus Christ." He stepped back from her and lifted his arms out in a gesture that invited the world to share his disbelief. "I can't believe you!" His raised voice drew the attention of a number of people clustered near Steiger. "*My* son has been kidnapped and you have the gall to stand here and treat *me* like a criminal?"

Megan could see people turning their way. Tension closed bony fingers on the back of her neck. The last thing she needed was to attract more attention from the press. DePalma would yank her off this assignment and bury her so deep in the bowels of headquarters, she wouldn't be able to find her way out to University Avenue.

"Mr. Kirkwood, I'm not accusing you of anything." She used the same low, even tone she would have used with a jumper on a ledge. "I apologize if it sounded that way."

"I'll tell you how it sounds," Paul said, his temper humming in his voice. "It sounds to me like you don't know how to find my son and you're doing whatever you can to cover your ass! That's how it sounds!"

He stormed away from her, away from the hundred or so

people who had gathered to watch the show, away from the cameras and the reporters. They set their sights on Megan and zeroed in.

"Agent O'Malley, do you have any comment on Mr. Kirkwood's accusations?"

"Agent O'Malley, does the BCA consider Mr. Kirkwood a suspect?"

"Agent O'Malley, do you have a comment on the article in the *Tribune*?"

Megan ground her teeth on a hundred nasty retorts. Diplomacy. Low-key, unobtrusive diplomacy. Those were her instructions from DePalma. That was bureau policy. She had sworn she could handle it. She had promised herself she could control her temper and take anything the press or anyone else dished out to her. She pulled in a deep breath and faced the cameras without flinching.

"Mr. Kirkwood is understandably distraught. My only comment is that the BCA is doing all it can in cooperation with the Deer Lake Police Department and the Park County sheriff's office to find Josh Kirkwood and bring his abductor to justice."

Ignoring the volley of questions, she moved through the crowd, headed back to her car.

"Did I say you'd be here a month, O'Malley?" Steiger murmured with a nasty smile as she strode past him. "That might have been optimistic."

CHAPTER 14

"What the hell were you thinking?" Mitch slammed the door shut behind him and Leo's 1993 Women of the Big Ten calendar jumped on its peg, sending Miss Michigan rocking back on her lovely haunches.

Megan didn't bother to play dumb and she refused to play meek. Temper snapping, she shot up out of the decrepit chair she had barely settled her fanny on. "I was thinking of doing my job."

"By going after Paul Kirkwood—"

"By following up on all possible leads," she qualified, rounding the desk.

"Why the hell didn't you check with me first?"

"I don't have to check with you. You're not my boss—"

"Jesus Christ, don't you think the man's going through enough?" he snapped, leaning over her, his dark eyes blazing with fury.

Megan met his glare head-on. "I think he's going through hell and I'm doing everything I can to get him out of it."

"By grilling him in front of the press?"

"That's bullshit! He's the one who made a big scene, not me. I was asking for information he should have given me an hour before. Information that could very well prove pertinent to his son's disappearance. Don't you find it just a little odd that he would be annoyed with me for that?"

Mitch went still, pulling all his anger and energy inward, smoothing his face into a blank mask. He stared down at Megan. "Just what the hell is that supposed to mean?" he asked, his voice a razor-edged whisper. "Are you saying you think Paul Kirkwood kidnapped his own son?"

"No."

She blew out a breath and swept back the tendrils of hair that had escaped her ponytail. Control. If he could have it, she could, too. Besides that, she was running low on adrenaline. As always happened on a big case, it would ebb and flow in an erratic tide, following the radical ups and downs of the investigation. She stepped back from him and leaned a hip against the desk as she dug a prescription bottle of ergotamine out of her briefcase, fished out one tablet, and washed it down with Pepsi to ward off the headache that was sinking its talons into her forehead.

"I'm saying I went to him this morning with a lead and he blew me off," she said. "I'm saying he committed a rather peculiar sin of omission by not telling me he had once owned and sold a van that meets the general description of the one we're looking for, and when I called him on it, he went off. Don't you find that all just a little strange, Chief?"

"You don't know the kind of pressure he's under."

"And you do?"

"Yes," Mitch returned too sharply. The tone revealed too much when his instincts told him to reveal nothing.

He kicked himself mentally for the tactical blunder and turned away. Hands jammed at his waist, he prowled the small office, restless, edgy.

For the first time he noticed all of Leo's certificates and commendations still tacked up on his ego wall, and Wally the Walleye preserved for all eternity on a walnut plaque above the file cabinets, cigar butt sticking out of his ugly fish mouth. Poor old Leo had left no one behind to collect the souvenirs of his life. The malodorous aroma of his cheap cigars lingered in the air, lurking darkly beneath the choking sweet perfume of air freshener. Sitting on the front edge of the desk was the only physical sign of Megan taking over the office, a shiny brass nameplate—AGENT MEGAN O'MALLEY, BCA.

Megan watched him carefully, reading the set of his broad shoulders, the angle of his head. He wanted to dismiss her, but he was on her turf. He wanted to walk out, but he wouldn't.

Even before she asked the question, she knew what his answer would be.

"Would you care to enlighten me, Chief?"

"We aren't here to talk about me," he said, the words short and terse.

"Aren't we?" Megan advanced on him, hands on her hips, unconsciously mimicking his stance. They faced each other like a pair of gunslingers, and the tension in the air was as thick as the smell of old Dutch Masters cigars.

He glared at her, his face a rigid mask of hard planes and sharp angles. Pride and anger and something like panic squeezed into a knot in his chest. He wanted to push it away. He wanted to push *her* away, out of his way, away from the dark territory that was his past. Like a cornered wolf, he wanted to lash out, but the need to control that rage overruled. So he stood there with every muscle as rigid as the walls he had built to protect himself.

"You're on thin ice, O'Malley," he said in a deadly whisper. "I suggest you back off."

"Not if what's going on here is you projecting your feelings onto Paul Kirkwood," Megan said, stubbornly taking another step out onto that proverbial thin ice, knowing that if it cracked, she would be sucked into the vortex of the rage whirling beneath his surface. "If that's what's going on, then we'd damn well better talk about it. An investigation is no place for that kind of involvement, and you know it."

An investigation was no place for the kind of emotions that were stirring inside her now, either. She wanted to break his iron fist of control. She wanted him to let go. She wanted him to confide in her—not for the good of the case, but because in a corner of her heart she seldom acknowledged and never indulged, she wanted to get closer to him. Dangerous stuff all the way around. Dangerous and seductive.

The heat between them intensified by one degree and then another. Then he turned away abruptly, snapping the thread of tension.

As he fought to regulate his breathing and his temper, Mitch found himself staring at a snapshot of Leo at the annual Park County Peace Officers Association barbecue—red-faced, wearing a stained chef's apron over his considerable bulk and a cap with a plastic trout head sticking out one side and its tail sticking out the other. Beer in hand, cigar clamped between his teeth, he stood beside a pig roasting on a spit.

Life had sure as hell been simpler with Leo around. Leo had been a grunt-work old-fashioned cop not interested in new theories of criminology or psychology or personnel dynamics. He had never wanted to spill his guts to Leo. He didn't want to unlock the door to the old pain, didn't want to show any sign of vulnerability, especially not here, on the job. Here, more than anywhere, he needed to keep the emotions closed up tight in their little box in his chest.

"Look," he said in a low voice, "I think you could have been more diplomatic, that's all. If you want to track down Paul's van, fine. Do it through the DMV. I'll handle any questioning."

"I've already called the DMV. They're checking," Megan said, the adrenaline receding sharply, leaving her feeling drained. "Or, rather, they're trying to. Their computer is down.

"I just wanted an explanation from him," she confessed. "I realize people react differently to this kind of stress, but . . . I get the feeling he doesn't want to talk to me—or look me in the eye, for that matter. My gut feeling is he's holding something back, and I want it."

"It may have nothing to do with Josh," Mitch said irritably. "Maybe he doesn't like women cops. Maybe he feels guilty because he wasn't there for Josh that night. That kind of guilt can tear a man up inside. Maybe you look just like the girl who turned him down for the senior prom way back when."

"Where was he that night?" Megan demanded, unwilling to give in. "Why wasn't he there?"

"He was working."

"Hannah called him repeatedly and he didn't answer the phone."

"He was working in a conference room down the hall."

She gave him a look of astounded disbelief. "And he returns to his office and ignores the message light on his machine? Who does that? And while we're at it, who can corroborate it?"

"I don't know," Mitch conceded. "Those are valid questions, but I'll be the one to ask them."

"Because you're the boss?" Megan said archly.

The muscles in his jaw tightened. A sculpture in granite couldn't have looked more forbidding. "I told you not to rock my boat, O'Malley," he said softly. "This is my town and my investigation. We'll do it my way. There's only one top dog around here, and it's me. Is that clear?"

"And I'm supposed to come to heel and sit like a good little bitch?"

"Your analogy, not mine," he said. "This case is giving the press enough fodder as it is. I don't need Paul going off like a rocket in front of them."

"We're agreed on that much. I don't need any more airtime, either, thanks anyway," she said dryly. "DePalma has already left three messages for me to call him so he can chew me out over the StarTribune article."

"And you ignored them?" he mocked. "Who does that?"

Megan narrowed her eyes. "He isn't calling to tell me my child is missing. He's calling to sink his teeth into my throat and shake me like a dead rat—something I'd like to see someone do to that hack Henry Forster, now that I think of it."

"Maybe we can set it up as a media event," Natalie suggested, letting herself into the office. Her face was screwed into an expression of supreme displeasure as she looked up at Mitch. "I like that irony, don't you? We can add Paige Price and her 'inside informant' to the list of headline acts. Someone gave her the scoop on the notes."

"No," Mitch said, as if that would make it so. The bottom dropped out of his stomach as Natalie refused to retract the information.

"TV 7 just did a live report from the steps of the courthouse. Paige Price read the world the messages you've found. She said the notes came from a laser printer and were printed on common twenty-pound bond paper."

"Shit." Mitch rubbed a hand over his face, imagining how Hannah would feel hearing those lines read aloud on television, imagining Paul's rage. Imagining every nut in the state cranking up their laser printers. Imagining wrapping his fingers around Paige Price's throat and squeezing.

"Jesus fucking Christ," he snarled, his temper sparking like a live wire. He turned to Natalie. "Call Hannah and tell her I'm on the way and tell her why. Radio Steiger. Tell him I need Paul ASAP and to get him away from the search with as little hoopla as possible."

He rattled off the orders like a field general, a man who was used to giving orders and having them obeyed without question. The top dog, Megan thought. The alpha wolf.

His assistant nodded, sifting through the sheaf of pink message slips she carried, sorting them by priority. "Just so you know, Professor Priest and his students are setting up in that vacant store next door to the command post—used to be Big D Appliance. It looks like all the volunteers are going to move in there, too. There's too many of them to all fit into the fire hall."

"Go take a look at their setup," Mitch ordered Megan as her phone rang.

She scowled at his back as he left the room. "Bossy son of a bitch," she muttered.

The answering machine spun out its request to leave a message and Bruce DePalma growled out an order to return his call *immediately*. Megan winced and reached for her parka.

10:02 A.M. 16°

With the scanner we're able to create a high-grade computer image of Josh that can be transmitted electronically to computers all over the country and printed off from those computers onto more fliers," Christopher Priest explained, raising his voice to be heard above the din of voices and the clank of chairs and tables being set down and shoved into place. In the background a radio was tuned to a local country station blasting out Wynonna Judd.

The student at the terminal was one of five in down coats and stocking caps clacking away on keyboards. Megan watched as Josh's image came up on the screen in full color. The bright smile, the unruly hair, the Cub Scout uniform—everything about the picture hit her like a fist in the solar plexus every time she saw it. He looked like such a happy little boy. He had so much life ahead of him.

If they could find him. Soon. She felt the seconds ticking by one after another, and resisted the urge to glance at her watch.

She looked away from the screen, taking in the makeshift volunteer center. The room was being transformed before her eyes. Tables and chairs and office equipment were being hauled in through both the front and back doors, creating a wind tunnel of frigid air through the building. The volunteers took positions at the tables the instant the legs hit the floor, piling all available surfaces with fliers and envelopes, staplers and stamps and boxes of rubber bands.

They came from all walks of life, from all over the state. Some men, many women. Middle-aged, elderly, college aged. They had already papered over the big front windows of the store with bright yellow Missing posters and with posters that had been drawn by Josh's third-grade classmates calling for Josh to come home, as if the power of their collective plea might be enough to bring him back. Nearly every storefront in town wore similar window dressing.

"We can also communicate with the National Center for Missing and Exploited Children and with Missing Children Minnesota," the professor went on. He was bundled into a black down parka that seemed to be swallowing him whole. It crept up around his ears, and he jammed his hands in his pockets and jerked it back down. "We can connect with a number of missing children's networks and foundations around the country. It's amazing how many there are. Tragic is the word I ought to use, I suppose. It seems for every child that disappears, a foundation springs up in his name."

"Let's hope we don't need a Josh Kirkwood Foundation," Megan murmured.

"Yes, let's hope," he said on a sigh. He tore his eyes away from the computer screen and blinked at her behind the lenses of his oversize glasses. "Can I offer you a cup of coffee, Agent O'Malley? Hot cider, hot tea? We don't have a shortage of volunteers or food."

"Cider would be great, thanks."

She followed him to a long table at the back of the main room, where all the edible donations had been laid out, and gratefully accepted the cup of steaming spiced cider. The heat radiated out through the cup and through her gloves to fingers that felt brittle with cold. She looked across the room bustling with volunteers, people who were giving their time, their talents, their hearts, and their money to bring Josh home. A fund had already been established for reward money, and donations were pouring in from all over the Upper Midwest, from individuals, civic groups, businesses. At last report they had collected in excess of $50,000.

One table of volunteers was dedicating their time to stamping the latest reward information on reams of fliers. Another table addressed and stuffed envelopes, another sorted the packets by zip code and bagged them for delivery to the post office. The fliers would go to law enforcement organizations, civic organizations, businesses, schools, to be distributed and posted in windows, on bulletin boards, stapled to light poles, tucked under windshield wipers all across the country.

Megan knew too well that their efforts could all be for nothing, that no matter how many people helped, hoped, prayed, Josh's fate was ultimately in the hands of one twisted person, and finding him would make wandering through a maze blindfolded seem simple by comparison. Still, it helped to know people cared.

"Seeing a community rally together this way helps to renew my faith in humanity a little," she confessed.

Priest watched the crowd, his face lacking the animation he had shown while explaining the computer setup. "Deer Lake is a nice town full of nice people. Everyone knows and loves Hannah. She gives so much to the community."

"What about Paul? Does everyone know and love him, too?"

He shrugged. "Everyone goes to the doctor, not that many people seek out accountants. Paul is less visible. But, then, I suppose most people would be less visible next to Hannah."

Paul was the more visible of the two now, Megan thought, missing the hint of color that stained the professor's cheeks when he mentioned Hannah's name. Paul was shoving his face in front of a camera every chance he got, while Hannah was sentenced to house arrest.

"I believe people come together this way as a defense."

Megan sipped her cider and glanced at the man who had joined them. He was a match for the professor in height—no taller than five nine—and in build, being slim almost to the point of slight. There the similarities ended. The newcomer's hair was blond and fashionably cut. His features were attractive. *Pretty* was the word that came to mind. Finely sculpted, almost effeminate with big dark eyes that seemed drowsy. He was dressed in gray wool trousers and an obviously expensive navy wool topcoat over a dark sweater.

"An instinctive herd-mentality response," he said. "Strength and safety in numbers. Band together to fight off a predator."

"You sound like an expert," Megan said.

"I can't say I've had a lot of direct experience with this kind of situation, but psychology is my department, so to speak. Dr. Garrett Wright," he said, offering his hand. "I teach at Harris."

"Megan O'Malley, BCA."

"I'd say it's a pleasure, but that seems inappropriate," he said, sliding his hands into his coat pockets.

Megan conceded the point with a tip of her head. "Are you here to offer your services, Doctor? We could use some ideas about the mind of the person who took Josh."

Wright frowned and rocked back on the heels of his black oxfords. "Actually, I came to ask Chris for the keys to his file cabinets. We've got students working on a joint project together. In fact," he said, turning to Priest, "I should probably get the key to your office if you're going over to Gustavus Adolphus tomorrow."

Setting aside his cider, Priest dug in his jacket pocket for a ring bristling with keys and set about the task of freeing the ones his colleague needed.

"I wish I could be of some help," Wright said to Megan. "Hannah and Paul are neighbors of mine. I hate to see them go through something like this. My wife has been helping Hannah out. I guess she's the official delegate from our household." He shook his head. "I've studied socially deviant behavior, but I don't have any degree in criminology. My area of expertise is learning and perception. Although, I suppose it's safe to assume you're dealing with a loner, a sociopath. If what they're reporting on the news about the notes he left behind is true, you may be looking at someone delusional—delusions of grandeur, delusions specifically regarding religion."

"Everyone is buzzing about the notes," Priest said, handing over a pair of small silver keys. His jacket crept up around his ears again. He tugged it down and took a sip of his drink, the steam from the cider fogging his glasses. "A lot of the volunteers saw Paige Price's report on the television in the fire hall. Dramatic stuff. What do you make of it, Agent O'Malley?"

"It's not my job to speculate," Megan said, congratulating herself for being a lady and not taking the opportunity to trash Paige Price. She would have given her last nickel to get her hands on the reporter and her inside informant. "I have to deal in facts."

"No intuition?" Wright asked.

Megan regarded him with a cool look, one brow sketching upward. "Is that a sexist remark, Dr. Wright?"

"Not in the least," Priest returned on Wright's behalf. "For all police officers profess to be pragmatic, I've read a lot about 'gut instinct.' What is that if not intuition?"

"You're interested in police work?"

"From a professional standpoint. With more and more law enforcement agencies moving into the computer age, the demand for new and better software increases. When I'm not teaching, I dabble at programming. It pays handsomely to keep abreast of new markets. In fact, we'll be using some of my programs here to sort information."

"I see."

"So, what *are* your gut feelings about the case?" Wright asked. "I've heard theories on everything from radical fundamentalists to satanic cults. You must have an opinion."

"Sure." She tossed back the last drops of cider and set the cup aside, giving them a wry smile. "But I know better than to state it in public. That's something else you should know about cops, Professor—we're a wary bunch."

She wound her scarf around her neck. "Thanks for showing me the setup. If you need anything, please check with Jim Geist next door. Thank you for your time and effort—and your students' as well."

Priest shook off her gratitude. "It's the least we can do."

————

With one eye peeled for stray reporters, Megan slid behind the wheel of the Lumina and coaxed the engine to life. Mitch was off trying to smooth out the wake from the revelation of the note. The BCA agents who had been assigned to Megan were checking out hotline tips on vans; grunt work. Out in Lyon State Park, the ground search continued, but she would be of no real help there, just another pair of eyes, not to mention fair game for the press.

That left the list of Josh's activities. Activities that brought him into contact with any number of adults in the community, from scouting to the summer soccer program to serving as an altar boy at St. Elysius. As she read the list she wondered which of these ordinary boyhood undertakings might have brought Josh to the attention of someone with the potential to hurt him. All of them, sad to say. The news was full of stories about children being abused by priests, coaches, Scout leaders, teachers. While those professions attracted people with a genuine love of children, they also attracted those with a sick obsession for children. There was no way of singling out the bad ones. Pedophiles seldom looked like monsters—quite often just the opposite was true.

Who do you trust? She remembered being taught to trust and obey that same list of people—her teachers, the priest, "nice" people, "good" people. But how could anyone make those distinctions anymore? What were children supposed to be taught today? There seemed to be no one left they could trust absolutely. Not even in Deer Lake, where everyone knew everyone and no one locked their doors at night.

ignorance is not innocence but SIN

Someone who knows the community, she thought. Or someone halfway to Mexico who just enjoyed the idea of screwing with their heads long-distance.

i had a little sorrow, born of a little SIN

Sin. Morality. Religion. Everything from radical fundamentalists to satanic cults. Or maybe a Catholic priest named Tom McCoy.

11:18 A.M. 19°

St. Elysius was the one bastion of Rome in a town overrun with Lutherans. As such, it seemed only fitting that the church be of the grand old style, a mini-cathedral of native limestone and spires thrusting up to heaven, stained glass windows depicting the agony and triumph of Christ. It sat on the Dinkytown side of the lake, nearly out in the country, as if the Norwegians had thought it best to keep the papists out of sight.

Megan climbed the front steps, memories from childhood rushing through her head, old, unwelcome feelings churning in her stomach and bringing sweat to the palms of her hands. She and Mick had gone to parochial school. Mick had participated in every sport he could—as much to avoid having to take care of his little sister after school as out of a love for athletics. And Megan had been left to the care of Frances Clay, the joyless, washed-out woman who cleaned the church. She had spent endless hours in St. Pat's, sitting on a hard, cold pew while Frances chased dust bunnies off the statues of the Holy Mother.

Half a dozen older women were mumbling the rosary as Megan stepped into the nave, the leader rattling through Our Father like an auctioneer. The interior of the church was every bit as lovely as the exterior. The walls were painted slate blue and decorated with intricate stencil and trim work in gilt, white, and rose. The flames of dozens of votive candles flickered patterns of light and shadow against the walls.

At the altar a tall, rail-thin man dressed in black moved around, arranging cloths and candelabra. Megan set her sights on him and marched down the center aisle, fighting the urge to genuflect. She had found neither refuge nor solace in the Church as a child, and so as an adult ignored it 363 days of the year, returning only on Christmas Eve and Easter—just in case.

The priest stood motionless as she drew near, his stare as dark and somber as his clothing. He looked sixty. Silver flecked the temples of his thin brown hair. He stood with his hands braced wide apart on the table, his mouth unsmiling. His face was so thin, he appeared to be anorexic. Hair prickled on the back of Megan's neck, and she said a little prayer for the parishioners of St. Elysius for having the courage to face this grim man every Sunday. He looked like the sort who thought self-flagellation was an acceptable penance for farting in church.

She held up her identification as she mounted the steps. "Agent O'Malley, BCA. I'd like to have a word with you about Josh Kirkwood, Father."

The man frowned at her. "The police have already been here."

"I'm doing follow-up on initial interviews," Megan said smoothly. "I understand Josh had just begun serving as an altar boy here at St. Elysius. We're trying to get a feel for Josh's routines, speak with any adults who might have noticed a change in his behavior recently or made note of anything he might have said regarding someone he was frightened of."

" 'Suffer the little children to come unto me, and do not hinder them; for to such belongs the kingdom of heaven.' " The priest intoned the line from Matthew in a dramatic voice that made the rosary ladies falter in the middle of the Glory Be. The leader shot him a nasty look.

"We've been praying for Josh," he said, lowering his volume to a hushed drone. "I don't remember you being at the service last night." His eyes narrowed just slightly, the perfect hint of censure tinted his words.

Megan bit her tongue on the reflex to beg forgiveness. Four hundred people had crammed into the church for the prayer service. She couldn't imagine he had memorized every face. Still, she said, "No, I wasn't among the faithful in church. I was among the cops out in the cold, searching."

"His fate is in the hands of God. We must have faith that God will bring him home."

"I've been a cop for ten years, Father. I trust God about as far as I can throw him."

He stepped back from her, looking as horrified as if her head had just spun around on her shoulders. Megan fully expected him to point a bony finger at her and scream, "Heretic." He drew in a breath that rattled in his throat ominously. The rosary ladies went silent and stared.

The merry mechanical music of a GameBoy cracked the tension. Heads turned in the direction of the sanctuary as a good-looking man in his thirties emerged, head bent over the game. Big shoulders tested the seams of a Notre Dame sweatshirt. His tan corduroy trousers were rumpled and he was wearing cowboy boots. The game ended with a series of bleeps and he made a fist and whispered, "Yes! Twelve fifty-one!"

Megan thought it was probably the thick quality of the silence that made him bring his head up. He looked at the people assembled, blinking behind a pair of gold-rimmed spectacles. A blush rose in his lean cheeks, and he flicked the switch on the game.

"Am I interrupting something?" he whispered, his mildly confused gaze landing on Megan.

"Agent O'Malley, BCA," she said automatically. "I need a few minutes of Father McCoy's time."

"Oh? Well, fine. I'm Father Tom McCoy."

"But—" Megan shot a look at the thin man.

McCoy frowned. "Albert, thank you for entertaining Ms. O'Malley in my absence." He took hold of Megan's arm gently but firmly and escorted her back whence he had come, his head bent down toward hers. "Albert is very devout," he whispered. "In fact, he will gladly tell you he is more qualified for my job than I am."

"I don't think he'll gladly tell me anything," Megan confessed. "I think he was about to douse me with holy water to see if I'd burn."

McCoy directed her to a chair as he closed the door of his office. "In another time Albert Fletcher would have been called a zealot. In the nineties with a shortage of priests we call him a deacon."

"Is he all there?" she asked, tapping a finger to her temple.

"Oh, yes. He has an MBA from Northwestern. A very intelligent man, Albert." Father Tom sank down into the high-backed chair behind his desk and swiveled it back and forth. "Socially, he's not exactly the life of the party. He lost his wife three years ago. Some kind of mysterious stomach ailment no one could ever quite pin down. After she was gone, he became increasingly involved with the church."

"Obsessed."

McCoy gave her a look and shrugged. "How do we draw the line between devotion and obsession? Albert functions well, keeps his house and yard immaculate, belongs to civic groups. He has a life; he just chooses to spend most of it here."

He tossed his GameBoy onto the blotter and gave her a sheepish look. "This is what keeps *me* sane when the world gets a little too heavy." The smile faded. "The treatment isn't holding up too well these days."

"Josh Kirkwood."

The priest shook his head. "My heart breaks every time I think of him. Who knows what he's going through. And Hannah . . . This is killing her. She's tearing herself up trying to find some logic in it, but there's no understanding why things like this happen."

"I thought you'd have all the answers."

"Me? No. The Lord works in mysterious ways and I'm not privy to His motives. I'm just a shepherd; my job is keeping the flock together and herding them in the right direction."

"Somebody's fallen off the path in a big way."

"And you think that somebody is from St. Elysius?"

"Not necessarily. I'm talking with everyone who had regular contact with Josh, looking for any scrap of information that might be helpful. Something Josh might have said, a change in his attitude, anything. Hannah tells me he had just started training as a server."

The look in McCoy's blue eyes was sad and knowing. "The altar boy and the priest. Is that what this is about, Agent O'Malley?" He shook his head slowly. "I'm always amazed when one victim of stereotyping turns around and pigeonholes someone else."

"I'm just doing my job, Father," Megan replied evenly. "It's not my place to draw conclusions, but it is my place to go on the basis of what evidence I have and pursue any and all leads. I'm sorry if that makes you feel discriminated against, but that's the way it is. If it makes you feel any better, I'll also be talking with Josh's teachers and coaches and his Scout leader. You're not a suspect."

"I'm not? I'll bet I could find plenty of people in this town who have already decided otherwise." He rose from his chair and walked back and forth behind the desk with his hands in his pockets. "Can't really blame them, I guess. I mean, the papers are full of it, aren't they? This priest, that priest, a cardinal. It's deplorable. And the Church covers it up and pretends nothing is wrong, carrying on the fine tradition of corruption that's plagued us since the time of Peter."

"Are you allowed to say that kind of thing?" Megan asked, amazed at his candor.

He flashed her a roguish grin. "I'm a radical. Ask Albert Fletcher. He's spoken with the bishop about me."

He seemed extremely pleased to be the object of controversy. Megan couldn't help but smile. She liked Tom McCoy. He was young and energetic and not afraid to say what he thought—a stark contrast to the priests she had grown up around. A stark contrast to Albert Fletcher. And she caught herself wondering why a man as charming and handsome as McCoy was would become a priest.

He read her thoughts too easily. "It's a calling," he said gently, easing back down into his chair, "not a consolation prize for men who can't do anything else."

"But sometimes it calls the wrong sort of people," Megan said, steering back onto the topic and away from her embarrassment.

Father Tom's boyish face appeared to age before her eyes. "No," he said grimly. "Those people are hearing a different voice."

"The voice of evil? The devil?"

"I believe in it absolutely. You do, too, don't you, Agent O'Malley?"

She didn't answer right away. She sat for a minute, thinking about her Irish Catholic upbringing. Even with that stripped away, her answer would be the same. She had seen too much on the streets to believe anything else. "Yes, I do," she said quietly. "And as far as I'm concerned, child predators are about as evil as it gets. So is there anything you can think of that will help me nail this bastard's ass to a wall?"

He didn't bat an eye at her language. "No. I wish I could. We had a prayer vigil here last night. I spent most of the time scoping out the crowd, thinking maybe I'd see someone who didn't fit in, thinking maybe he would come to see the kind of havoc he's wreaked on this community. Thinking maybe I'd see a sign, you know—glowing red eyes, 666 marked across his forehead—but I guess that happens only in the movies."

"What about regarding Josh himself? Had you noticed any change in his behavior?"

"Well . . ." He took a moment to choose his words carefully. "He'd been quieter lately. I think Hannah and Paul are having some trouble. Not that either of them has said anything; it's just a feeling I get. Josh is a sensitive boy. Kids pick up a lot more than adults realize. But I hadn't noticed anything overt. He takes his duties as a server very seriously."

"You train the boys yourself?"

"We have girls now, too. The Church's effort to join the age of equality. Of course, they'll never consider women as priests, but—" He cut himself off from another radical tangent, giving Megan a sheepish look. He pushed his glasses up on his nose with a forefinger against the bridge. "Anyway, to answer your question, Albert Fletcher and I both work with the kids. We do a kind of a good cop–bad cop routine. Albert drills the rules into them, then I give them a wink and let them know it's okay if they goof up every once in a while just as long as they don't sneeze on the hosts."

Megan smiled at the joke, but her mind had turned toward Albert Fletcher. Albert Fletcher, the religious fanatic, the man who quoted the Bible in answer to her questions. She wondered if he could quote Robert Browning as well: *ignorance is not innocence but SIN.*

"Do you happen to know what kind of car Mr. Fletcher drives?"

"A brown Toyota wagon. Is Albert *not* a suspect, too?" the priest asked dryly.

Megan rose from her chair, her expression sober. "At this time, Father, everyone is *not* a suspect. What about you? What do you drive?"

"A red Ford 4X4 truck." He grinned his rogue's grin and shrugged. "Somebody's got to shake up the status quo. It might as well be me."

She couldn't help but smile. If there had been any priests like Tom McCoy around when she was growing up, she might have actually paid attention in church instead of spending all her time doodling on the back of the missalette.

"Father Tom, can I have a word?"

Megan swung toward the door at the sound of Mitch's voice. He strode into the office, his coat hanging open, his hair windblown. He looked annoyed at finding she had beat him to St. Elysius.

"Ah, Agent O'Malley," he said, "grilling the local clergy now?"

"Just asking Father to help me pray for patience in dealing with arrogant territorialism."

Lacking a good comeback, he gave a snort and turned his attention to the priest. He played golf with Tom McCoy during good weather and liked him. There was always some gossip floating around town that the Father was in trouble with the diocese mucky-mucks for being too liberal, news Father Tom shrugged off with an indifference Mitch respected.

Tom McCoy met his gaze. "You think I'm not a suspect, too?"

"Did Agent O'Malley lead you to believe otherwise?" Mitch asked.

"Father Tom and I were just having a routine chat," Megan said coolly. "Did I need your permission for that, Cujo?"

"Did you discuss the notes?"

"No."

"What notes?" Father Tom asked. "Has there been some kind of ransom demand?"

"I wish it were that simple," Mitch said. "Two notes have been found—one in Josh's duffel bag, one in a notebook of his. Both make a reference to sin."

"And the natural correlation is to the Church," the priest concluded.

"I'm looking for names of anyone in your parish you might think of as being mentally unstable, fanatical—particularly anyone with a connection to the Kirkwoods."

"Our resident fanatic is Albert Fletcher, but Albert would no more commit a crime than he would denounce the Pope," said Father Tom. "And he was teaching Josh's class that night, if he needs an alibi. Mentally unstable—we've got a few of those, but I'm talking about people with problems, not psychotic monsters. Nor can I think of anyone who would have it in for Hannah or Paul."

Mitch did his best to take the disappointment in stride. Cases like this were seldom made in one smooth move. A cop couldn't afford to take every setback and dead end hard; there would be too many of them. There had been too many today already. The search was going nowhere. Hannah and Paul had been predictably upset with the disclosure of the notes on television. The interviews of school employees were netting them nothing but paperwork. He had a leak in his department, every man on his force pulling overtime, and Megan O'Malley challenging his authority. The combination ate at the lock on his temper like a voracious virus.

"We've already discussed Josh's altar-boy training," Megan told him. "That looks like another dead end."

"Then I guess we can let you get back to work, Father," Mitch said. "Give me a call if anything comes to mind."

"I will," Father Tom said, a grave expression tugging at his features. "And in the meantime, we should all pray like hell."

Megan preceded Mitch out the side door of the church and started down the steps to the neatly shoveled sidewalk. Snow was piled on the boulevard between the walk and the parking lot, rising up like a miniature mountain range through which passes had been cut at thirty-foot intervals. She aimed for the one nearest the Lumina.

"Did you expect me to sit in my office and do my nails all day?" she asked without bothering to look back at Mitch. "But that wouldn't make me like Leo, either, would it?"

She paused on the sidewalk to pose with her chin on her mittened fist. "Let's see. What would Leo do? I know," she said brightly. "We'll go on down to the Blue Goose Saloon and slam a few brewskis. Then we can sit around belching and farting and cursing our lack of clues."

"Hey," he barked, "Leo was a good cop. Don't slam Leo. And I never said you shouldn't do your job."

He started for his truck without waiting for a rebuttal. Megan hustled after him, tossing the tail of her scarf back over her shoulder.

"No, you said I shouldn't do it without asking first. So, in the interest of diplomacy, I'm asking where you want me to go next."

His laugh cracked the cold air like a gunshot. He looked back at her over his shoulder. "You're asking for it all right, O'Malley."

"I've been hearing that for years."

"Think it'll ever sink in?"

"I doubt it," Megan said as they turned through the pass into the parking lot. She fished her keys out of her coat pocket while Mitch turned toward his truck. "So where are you going?"

"Oh, I thought I'd stop off at the He-Man Woman Haters Club and then go bowling with the guys from the Moose Lodge." He unlocked his door and pulled it open. "Us guys are like that, you know."

Megan cocked her head.

"I'm going to go hunt for the animal who took Josh Kirkwood," he said. "You, Agent O'Malley, can stay out of my way."

CHAPTER 15

Daylight was fading to black when Megan checked back in at the command center. She had spent the afternoon personally rechecking the other people on the list of adults with whom Josh had regular contact, dispensing sympathy and tissues and getting no answers to the questions that loomed larger with every tick of the clock.

Josh's teacher, Sara Richman, had two sons of her own. Despite the fact that she had been questioned twice already, she still couldn't speak or even think about what had happened without starting to cry. His Scout leader, Rob Phillips, was a clerk in the county attorney's office, a man who had been confined to a wheelchair for the last three years and for the rest of his life, thanks to a drunk driver. Phillips had taken vacation time from work to help at the volunteer center.

People were heading out of the fire hall—some to go home to their families, some to grab dinner and come back. Megan went in search of Jim Geist and found Dave Larkin in his place in the room where some of her agents and several of Mitch's men handled the hotline phones. There seemed to be a phone ringing constantly, punctuating the running underscore of mumbling voices. Cops and volunteers came in and left the room, bringing in fliers and food, taking out scrawled notes and fax messages.

Larkin wore a blue and white aloha shirt that accented his beach-bum image. A phone receiver was sandwiched between his shoulder and ear, and he was scribbling furiously on a legal pad. He glanced up at her and rolled his eyes.

"No, I'm sorry, Mr. DePalma, I haven't seen Agent O'Malley. She's been out in the field all day working on a lead. Yes, sir, I understand it's important. I'll see that she gets the message." He grimaced at Megan. "She should call you at home? I understand. Yes, sir."

He hung up the phone, stuck a finger in his ear, and wiggled it around, giving Megan a comic look of distress. "Irish, you owe me *so big.*"

Megan slid into the chair beside him and leaned an elbow on the table. "I'll promise you anything that isn't sex related."

"Hell," he grumbled. "If I'd known that, I would have made you take the call."

"You're such a pal. DePalma is the last person I want to talk to."

"Rightly so. He sounded in a mood for some grilled agent."

She sniffed. "It's the reporters he ought to want roasted. If someone wants to run a spit through Henry Forster and Paige Price, I'll make the potato salad. So what are you doing here?" she asked. "Did Jim go back to the hotel?"

"Yeah. I'm here on my own time," he said, giving her a little smile. "Told you you'd get volunteers."

"And I appreciate it. Any word from the lab on the notes?"

"Nothing that hasn't already been on TV. We accelerated the reaction on the ninhydrin test with heat and humidification and ran it under the ultraviolet. If there were prints on the paper, they would have gone purple and fluoresced under illumination. We got zip. Sorry, kiddo."

Megan sighed. "Yeah, well, I didn't think we'd get that lucky. We're not dealing with your garden-variety idiot. This one would know enough to wear gloves. So what's the latest on the van?"

"I'd say every third person in the state knows someone weird who drives a light-colored utility van." He pulled Geist's notes in front of him and flipped through the pages. "First of all, the chief in New Prague checked the con with the yellow van. The van is now sporting an airbrushed mural of a desert sunset, and the con bowls Wednesday nights in a league. This week he scored a 220 high and won the beer frame twice."

"Lucky dog," she muttered without enthusiasm. "Anything else turn up?"

"Jim organized the tips geographically. He met with Chief Holt this afternoon. They went over the list of local calls together, sorted a few out, then Jim sent a guy with one of Holt's men to check the rest."

"Let me see the list."

Larkin handed it over and leaned back in his chair, stretching his arms over his head. "So after we nail this piece of dirt, you want to take a weekend and go skiing in Montana? I know a guy who has a friend who has a condo in Whitefish."

Megan scanned the names and addresses of people in Park County whose neighbors had ratted on them. "I don't ski."

"That's even better. We can spend our time in the hot tub."

"Maybe you should spend some time under a cold shower," she suggested.

The name hit her with all the force of a line drive. She sat up straight in the chair as she took in the number of calls that had come in about this particular van and the fat red line drawn through them. "What the hell is this?"

Larkin leaned over and glanced at the list. "Holt said he already checked it out."

"That son of a bitch," Megan growled, shooting to her feet. She could feel her blood pressure climbing into the red zone. It pounded in her ears as her temper boiled. She stepped away from the chair and shoved it hard against the table. The noise cut through the bleating of telephones and low rumble of conversations and drew wide-eyed looks in her direction.

"Where are you going?" Larkin called as she stormed out.

"To kick some ass!"

He cupped his chin in his hand. "I guess this rules out dinner and an evening of wild, unbridled sex."

5:01 P.M. 23°

Mitch sat in his office with only the amber light of the lamp shining down on the reports and statements strewn across the desktop. He had sent Natalie home to help her two teenagers get ready for the torchlight parade. Valerie played flute in the high school band. Troy was riding on the senior class float. The town council had voted to go on with the Snow-daze activities, but every event would in some way now focus on Josh's abduction. The show of community unity would be both tremendous and tragic.

The day had beat Mitch down physically and mentally. The constant pressure, the sense of urgency, wore on nerves and patience. He had personally questioned much of the elementary school staff and walked the grounds again, trying to find something, anything, that would be a connection to or spark an idea as to the identity of the person who had planted Josh's notebook on the hood of his truck. All with reporters swarming after him like gnats. All for nothing. The parking lot was easily accessible and no one had seen anything. Planting the evidence had been a simple matter of driving up alongside the Explorer and reaching out the window. Slick, simple, diabolical. Infuriating. It made him feel like a chump, as if he'd been had in a shell game, played for a fool and beaten.

Somehow, he was going to have to rally in time to take his daughter to the parade. His mother-in-law had called to suggest she and Jurgen take Jessie, saying Jessie was, after all, staying with them for the weekend. Besides, she thought it might upset Jessie to go with him now, what with all this terrible business going on and policemen walking into the classrooms at school, frightening all the children.

Mitch had lost his temper. Joy tried his patience in the best of times, and this was hardly the best of times.

"Are you saying my daughter should be frightened of me?"

"No! Not at all! I'm just saying—"

"You're just saying what, Joy?"

"Well, that Kirkwood boy was taken right off the street."

"Trust me, Joy, someone tries to take Jessie off the street while I'm standing there, I'll blow his fucking head off."

"Well, you don't have to take that tone—"

"I get a little testy when you suggest my daughter isn't safe with me, Joy."

"I never said that!"

But she thought it. She thought it all the time and she slipped those thoughts under his skin like poisoned slivers, so clever, so subtle. She had trusted him with her daughter and her daughter was dead. She had trusted him with her grandson and her grandson was dead. She blamed Mitch entirely and she kept that blame inside her, never saying a word outright, letting that blame grow and metastasize like a malignant tumor.

He knew because he did the same thing.

He rubbed his hands over his face. A part of him wished he could just go to sleep until the nightmare was over, but he got a nightmare either way. Awake, there was the case. Asleep, he dreamed of drowning in a sea of blood.

"Couldn't you just pick up those few things on your way home?"

"Allison, I've been on the job eighteen hours. I've got three hours to come home, sleep, eat, shower, and shave before I've got to be in court. The last thing I want to do is stop at the goddamn 7-Eleven. Can't you stop on the way to T-ball?"

"I hate that store on the way to the park. That's a rotten neighborhood."

"For Christ's sake, you won't be in there five minutes. It's broad daylight. Those places get hit at night, when there's no one around."

"I can't believe we have to have this argument at all. Why do we stay here? Every day it gets worse. I feel like a prisoner in my own home—"

"Jesus, don't start that now. Can we wait until I've slept thirteen or fourteen hours before we have this fight again?"

"All right. Fine. But I want to have a real discussion, Mitch. I mean it. I don't want to live this way."

As his wife's last words echoed in his mind, he fingered the gold band that circled his finger.

There was no justice. No logic. There was no justice in Hannah Garrison losing her son to a faceless phantom whose only explanation was a cruel taunt. The joke was on the people who thought life should make sense.

And while Mitch stole these few moments for the futile exercise of punishing himself and shaking his fist at an unjust world, the clock ticked, each second adding to the sense of desperation inside him.

He needed to clear his mind and center himself, focus. Tightly gripping the arms of his chair, he tried to draw in a deep, calming breath the way the department shrink in Miami had tried to teach him. Focus the mind on a single thought and breathe slowly and deeply. More often than not, Mitch had focused on the idea of beating the ever-loving shit out of the psychologist, the pompous, condescending ass.

"If he's back here, he damn well *will* see me!"

The voice was unmistakably Megan's. Unmistakably furious. Punctuated by Noga's thundering footfalls.

"But Miss O—Agent, he said he didn't want to be disturbed."

"Disturbed? How about dismembered?"

She was through the door before Mitch could do more than stand up. She stopped halfway into the room with her hands on her hips, her oversize coat falling back off her shoulders. The long gray scarf she could never quite seem to manage was slithering down over one shoulder, trailing nearly to the floor.

Noga appeared behind her. "Sorry, Chief, I couldn't stop her."

He had been able to stop Division I defensive linemen in college, but he couldn't stop Megan O'Malley. Somehow that made perfect sense to Mitch. He waved the patrolman off.

"My turn, Chief," Megan snapped as the office door closed behind her. "Why wasn't I told that Olie Swain drives an eighty-three white Chevy van? Why was I not informed that you spoke with Olie Swain about this van last night?"

"I don't answer to you, Agent O'Malley," he said, tossing her own words back at her. "You don't outrank me. You're not my boss."

"No, you don't answer to anyone, do you?" she spat out angrily. "You're Matt fucking Dillon and this is Dodge City. *Your* town. *Your* people. *Your* investigation. Well, it can be on *your* head when someone finds this kid's body in a Dumpster and it turns out Olie Swain did the job."

Megan could almost feel him tense as he took that blow. Good. He needed to be hit over the head—figuratively if not literally.

"At least Steiger is up front. I knew he was an asshole the minute I laid eyes on him. You cooperate when it suits you, and when it doesn't, you pick up your toys and tell me to go home."

"All right," he said in that cutting, deceptively soft tone. "Go home. I'm operating on a real lean mix here, Agent O'Malley. I'm in no mood to listen to you whine that I don't play fair."

"In no mood—" Megan broke off, choking on her fury. For an instant she contemplated launching herself at him across the desk. She wanted to shake him until his teeth rattled. Instead, she glared at him.

"Your mood notwithstanding," she continued sharply, "I think we had better get a few things straight here. This is an investigation and I am a part of this investigation. Therefore I am entitled to know when someone I consider a suspect turns out to have a van matching the witness's description."

"Nothing came of it," Mitch snapped. "Helen Black couldn't identify the van. Olie has an alibi—"

"Which no one has substantiated absolutely—"

"There was nothing inside the van—"

"You looked inside that van *without a warrant?*" Megan exclaimed, incredulous. "God, of all the stupid—"

"I had his verbal consent—"

"Which doesn't mean shit!"

"If I'd seen anything, I could have had the van towed on a parking violation and we would have ended up with a warrant. I saw nothing whatsoever that could link Olie or the van to Josh's disappearance."

"You can see fingerprints, Superman?"

Her sarcasm stung in ways she couldn't know. Anger was his automatic response against the pain. "You couldn't have gotten a warrant on the van, Agent O'Malley," he said, advancing on her. "There's no way in hell you could have dusted it for prints or vacuumed it for fibers or sprayed it down with luminol, looking for traces of blood. We don't have *anything* on Olie Swain."

"The fact remains," she said, "you know I consider the man a suspect. I should have been notified—if not last night, then at least this morning."

"It didn't come up." Mitch knew damn well he should have told her. He had known she would find out. She had hit too close to home with the Matt Dillon line. He wanted control of the game and the players. In a way she couldn't understand,

Deer Lake *was* his town, his haven. He hated having it pointed out to him that his sense of control was just an illusion.

"We're working this investigation together, Chief," Megan said. "I'm not here for window dressing; I'm here to do a job and I don't appreciate being left out of the loop."

That was the source of much of her anger: She had been excluded. Everyone had known about Olie and his van before her. The old-boy network had pulled another end-around and left her feeling like a fool, like an outcast. It wasn't the first time and it wouldn't be the last, but that didn't mean she had to like it or take it lying down.

He backed away from her slowly and turned away. The desk lamp hummed softly. The ringing of the telephones in the squad room barely penetrated the walls, the distant sound only adding to the sense of isolation.

"All right," he conceded. "I should have told you and I didn't. Now you know."

It was as close to an apology as he was likely to give. Megan knew enough to take small victories when she could get them. She let some of her own tension go and looked around the office as if seeing it for the first time since she had come in.

"Why were you sitting here in the dark?"

"I was just . . . railing against fate," he murmured. "I prefer to do that in private, if you don't mind."

"It doesn't do much good, does it?"

A statement of fact. A confession of sorts. Mitch heard the empathy. They were a lot alike, he supposed. As odd as that sounded. As cops, they had been through the same grind, seen too much, cared too deeply. She had his sense of justice, it just wasn't as tarnished as his. That truth made him feel old and battered.

He stared out the window behind his desk, through the open slats of the vertical blinds. The night looked as black as ink, cold, unwelcoming.

"You can't blame yourself, Mitch," Megan said, easing closer to him without realizing they had shifted out of one quadrant of their relationship and into another. She hadn't called him Chief.

"Sure I can. For a lot of things."

She took the final step, closing the distance between them,

and looked up at him. They stood at the edge of the lamplight, near enough that it revealed lines of strain and old memories that etched deep into his face. He looked away, frowning, the scar on his chin shining silver in the pale light.

"For what?" she asked softly. "Your wife?"

"I don't want to talk about it." He turned toward her, his expression hard. "I don't want to talk at all."

He pulled her against him roughly, dropping his head down to touch his face against her cool, dark hair. It smelled faintly of jasmine. "This is what I want from you." He tipped her chin up and found her lips with his.

The heat of the kiss was searing. The kiss was rough and wild, pure raw sex that sparked a hot, elemental response. Megan kissed him back, trembling at the need it unleashed. The need to let go of her control and be swept away on this tide of fundamental need. She focused on the taste of him, the warm male scent of him, the contrast in their size and strength, the feel of the muscles in the small of his back, the erotic sensation of his tongue thrusting against hers.

A small sound of longing escaped her, and he responded to it instantly, hungrily. The arm he banded around her back tightened and lifted her against him. His other hand closed boldly over her breast and Megan gasped at the feel of his fingers kneading the sensitive globe, his thumb brushing across her nipple, teasing it through the fabric of her sweater.

"I want you," he growled, dragging his mouth from hers to plant kisses against her cheekbone, her brow. "I want to be inside you. Now."

Megan shivered at the images his words evoked, at the sensations that rippled along her nerve endings. She could feel him against her belly, hard, ready to make good on his statement. And she wanted him. God, she ached with wanting him. She wanted to feel the full power of this desire unleashed, to know what it was like to let go completely of the control that ordered her life.

But they were in his office. He was the chief of police and she was an agent of the BCA. They would see each other in this office, conduct business in this office. And what happened when this fire between them died and they still came to this office every day?

"I—we can't," she murmured, breathless, her body humming with the need to say yes.

"The hell we can't." Mitch caught her chin in his hand and forced her to look at him. His gaze was hot, glittering with passion and the determination to lose himself in it. That was what he wanted—to sink into her and into some kind of white-hot oblivion where there was no guilt and no burden.

"It's sex." He tightened his hand against her back, letting her feel him against her. "We won't be wearing badges. Or maybe that's what you're afraid of?"

Pushing against his chest, Megan tried without success to back away from him. "I told you, I'm not afraid of you."

"But are you afraid to be a woman with me?"

She didn't answer him. She couldn't, Mitch thought. If she said yes, she admitted a vulnerability. If she said no, she committed herself to sleeping with him. She was too wary to box herself in that way. And not without good reason. He doubted he was the first cop to come on to her in her ten years on the job. He remembered the way it had been in Miami, the locker room bets on who would be the first to score with the new skirt on the squad. And he knew what it meant when it happened. The woman lost any respect she might have had from her fellow officers. Respect was everything to Megan. The job was everything to Megan. It would take more than simple lust to get her to cross that line, and Mitch reminded himself that he didn't want to give more.

Slowly, reluctantly, he let her go. "It's probably just as well," he muttered as he turned away to grab his parka off the coat tree.

Megan stood back, incredulous, as she watched him shrug into the heavy coat. He could kiss her like that, then calmly turn away and dismiss it as if it had been nothing. The idea made her want to kick him, but she didn't. And she swallowed back the scathing words that burned on the tip of her tongue. He had made an overture, she had declined. Simple.

"Where are you going?"

"I promised Jessie I'd take her out to McDonald's and to the torchlight parade."

"Oh."

Mitch glanced at her as he clipped his pager to his belt. Her dark hair had escaped its barrette altogether and fell like a wild horse's mane around her shoulders. Her eyes were wide and showing more than she would have allowed. She looked like the girl who never got asked to dance at the high school sock hop.

"You game for a Big Mac and some frozen Shriner clowns?" he asked, surprising himself.

Megan narrowed her eyes in suspicion. "Why are you being nice to me?"

"Jeez, O'Malley. It's McDonald's, not Lutèce. Come or don't."

"You're so gracious, I can hardly resist," she said dryly, "but I wouldn't want to intrude."

He smiled a little at her rancor. "Aw, tell the truth," he said. "You were on your way to Grace Lutheran Church for the annual Snowdaze lutefisk supper."

Megan wrinkled her nose. "Not in this lifetime. I make it a point never to eat anything that can take the finish off a table. Besides, I think lutefisk is one of those foods people used to have to eat because there wasn't anything else and it somehow became a tradition by mistake."

"Yeah, no wonder Scandinavians are so morose. If I had to eat boiled cod soaked in lye solution, I'd look like Max von Sydow too."

They shared a laugh that eased them back into the friends division of their relationship again.

"Big Mac?" Mitch asked, raising his brows.

She wanted to. But she really should go back to the office . . . call DePalma. A grim evening.

"Come on," he said. "I'll spring for the fries. What do you say, O'Malley?"

"Okay, let's go, Diamond Jim." She twisted her scarf around her neck. "You get the fries, I'll get the Tums."

CHAPTER 16

Jessie was dubious about having an extra dinner partner. She gave Megan a long, hard look as they sat in their booth, waiting for Mitch to return with their supper. Megan said nothing, taking that time to size up Mitch's daughter. Jessie Holt was a darling little girl with big brown eyes and a button nose. Her long brown hair had been carefully combed back and plaited into a single thick braid that fell halfway down her back. Two Princess Jasmine barrettes had been added in odd places at odd angles that suggested they were Jessie's own touch.

"Are you my daddy's girlfriend?" she asked baldly, looking none too pleased with the prospect.

"Your dad and I work together," Megan replied, neatly sidestepping the issue.

"Are you a cop, too?"

"Yep. I sure am."

Jessie mulled this over, sitting back in the seat and crossing her arms. She wore a white turtleneck dotted with tiny colored hearts. Over that was a sweater knit in bright blocks of primary colors. On the front of the sweater was an appliqué of the face of a girl with freckles and braided yarn hair. She took hold of one of the braids and tickled the end of her nose with it.

"I never saw a girl cop."

"There aren't very many of us," Megan confessed, leaning her elbows on the table. "My dad was a cop, too. Do you think you might be a cop when you grow up?"

Jessie shook her head. "I'm gonna be a beterinarian. And a princess."

Megan contained the laugh that threatened. "That sounds like a plan. What does a beterinarian do?"

"She helps aminals when they get sick and makes them better."

"That's a good job. I like animals, too. I have two cats."

Jessie's eyes widened. "Really? I have a toy cat named Whiskers. My grandma says I can't get a real cat 'cause Grampa's 'lergic."

"That's too bad."

"I have a dog, though," she added, scooting ahead on her seat. She laid her arms on the table in an imitation of Megan's pose. "His name is Scotch—like butterscotch. He's older than me, but he's my dog. Daddy says so."

"What Daddy says goes," Mitch said, setting the heavily laden tray down on the table.

Jessie grinned. "Goes where?" She scrambled into his lap as he sat down. She tipped her head back and looked at him upside down.

"Goes to Timbuktu!"

He made a goofy face, wrapped his arms around her, and pretended to tickle her. Jessie giggled and squirmed. They had obviously been through the routine many times before.

Megan felt she didn't belong. Mitch wanted to spend time with his daughter, had asked Megan along only as a courtesy. She kicked herself for accepting, and she kicked herself again for letting old memories sneak up on her. She was a grown woman and she had better things to do with her time than feel sorry for herself because she had a family that defined the word *dysfunctional.*

"Hey, O'Malley? You okay?"

"What?" She glanced back at Mitch, embarrassed to see concern in his eyes. "Yeah, sure," she mumbled, giving her attention over to the paper-wrapped burger in front of her. The smell of fried onions wafted up to tempt her. "I was just . . . thinking about the case. Um . . . I should have gone over the background checks the guys ran on the hospital staff today. You know, maybe I'll pass on the parade."

"Cut yourself some slack," Mitch said. "I realize the clock's ticking, but you can't work twenty-four hours a day. You go at it that hard, you burn up physically and mentally, then you're no good to anyone."

Megan shrugged. "I've put in only ten hours today. I can do a few more and still have a couple to spare." She gave him her best poker face. "I think better at night. There aren't so many distractions."

Mitch frowned but said nothing.

Jessie took a gulp of her milk. "Daddy, do you think—um—in the parade that there'll be those guys dressed up like pieces of cheese like last time? They were funny."

"Probably, sweetheart," he murmured, his eyes still on Megan.

Jessie launched into a detailed account of last year's torch-light parade. And Megan, glad for the distraction from Mitch's probing, concentrated on the little girl, knowing that by the time the story ended, the meal would be over and she would be able to escape. Mitch deserved some time alone with his daughter, and Megan wanted to retreat from this unfamiliar ground to the one thing she knew she could do well—her work.

8:19 P.M. 20°

Megan drove the deserted streets of Deer Lake, cursing the car's heater. It seemed a ridiculous time of year for a parade, and yet that seemed to be where everyone was. Megan wondered how many of the brass players in the high school bands would get their lips frozen to the mouthpieces of their horns.

Jessie's tale of last year's parade brought a smile to her lips. She could picture the floats she'd seen in the garage at the old fire hall. She could envision the clowns and the skiing wedges of cheddar from the BuckLand cheese factory slipping and falling in the street, tangling up with one another, the crowds on the sidewalks doubled over laughing.

How much laughing would there be tonight? Tonight, when

a missing child was on everyone's mind, when every marcher wore a yellow ribbon and every float bore a banner that said BRING JOSH HOME.

Megan wished with all her heart they could bring Josh home. They had so little to go on. The hotline tips hadn't produced anything but dead ends and false hopes. Megan's mind kept going in the direction of Olie Swain. He was the closest thing they had to a suspect. Mitch had to think so, too, or he wouldn't have risked taking a look inside Olie's van.

She wished again he would have confided in her about the van. And about himself. She could have picked up the phone and uncovered his past with a couple of calls. If she had wanted, she could have called *TV 7* and gotten a copy of Paige Price's hatchet job on him. She could have reached out to someone on the force in Miami or tracked down the story through the archives of the *Miami Herald*. But she would do none of those things. It had to come from Mitch himself, and the reason for that scared the hell out of her. Deep inside, where logic meant nothing, she wanted him to trust her.

You're too stupid for words, O'Malley.

He wanted to take her to bed, not give her his heart.

She wanted to go with him. Her third day on the job and she wanted to have sex with the chief of police.

You're too stupid to live, O'Malley.

Lust. Chemistry. Animal attraction. The heightened emotions of a volatile situation. Physical needs too long ignored. The excuses bounced through her head, all of them true, none of them the truth. She wouldn't look for the heart of truth. She was too afraid of what she would find. A need that had never been fulfilled. A longing that had been with her forever. Foolish dreams.

There was no place in her life for a relationship, especially one with Mitch Holt with all the complications that would bring. She couldn't believe she was even toying with the idea. Fantasies of love and family and dark-haired little children had always been relegated to the deepest, darkest, most lonely hours of the night, where they could be dismissed as dreams when daylight and reality dawned. It confounded her that they would surface now, when she had neither the time nor the energy to deal with them. Her focus had to be on the case.

With the single-minded determination that had gotten her through her career, she turned her mind in that direction and pointed the car toward the hockey rink. She sat in the parking lot for a long while, staring at Olie's battered van, what-iffing, something anxious stirring inside her. A hunch, just forming, just out of reach, teased her like an itch she couldn't quite scratch. And in the back of her mind she could almost hear Josh's voice reading the line from his notebook: *Kids tease Olie but that's mean. He can't help how he looks.*

Inside the arena music sang out over the speaker system— Mariah Carey's "Hero." The seats were empty and dark. Lights shone down on the ice, where a single skater was going through a routine, moving and jumping in harmony with the flowing, lovely song. Megan made her way to the team bench, where she took a ringside seat at the red line.

The skater was a young woman, blond, petite but athletic in black leggings, a purple skating skirt, and a loose-fitting ivory sweater. She concentrated on the music, her footwork and arm movements. Every move was held out perfectly until it flowed into the next. Her jumps were graceful, powerful, with landings so smooth they seemed to defy physics. The music swelled and soared, then softened. The skater went into a final layback spin, looking like a ballerina on a music box.

Megan applauded, drawing the young woman's attention her way for the first time. The skater smiled and waved to acknowledge her tribute, then skated over with her hands on her hips.

"That was great!" Megan said.

She managed a shrug as she worked to even out her breathing. "It still needs work, but thanks. Could you hand me that bottle of water?"

Megan picked a plastic bottle of mineral water up from the player's bench and handed it over. "I'm Megan O'Malley with the Bureau of Criminal Apprehension."

"Ciji Swensen." She pulled a towel off the gate and blotted her lips and forehead, her dark blue eyes on Megan. "I read about you in the paper. Are you here about the kidnapping? I feel so bad for Dr. Garrison."

"Do you know Josh?"

"Sure. I know just about everybody in town who can lace on

a pair of skates. I'm an instructor with the Figure Skating Club."

"Working overtime tonight?"

"Practice. The club does a little show every year for Snowdaze. This is one of my pieces. I knew everyone would be at the parade tonight, so I thought I'd take advantage of having the ice all to myself. It's a special number—for Josh, you know? The club voted to give the profits from the show to the volunteer center."

"That's very generous."

"Yeah, well, we had to do something. It makes me sick to think some pervert picked Josh up right outside this rink. For all I know, I could have been standing right here when it happened."

"You were here that night?"

Ciji nodded as she took another swig of water. "I had a class at seven."

A male voice called out from the darkness at the far end of the rink. "You want that music again, Ciji?"

"No, thanks, Olie," she called back. "I'm taking a break."

Megan stared hard, just making out the shape of Olie Swain's head and shoulders as he moved in the shadows. "Did you see Olie that night?"

"Yeah, sure." She shrugged. "Olie's always around here somewhere."

"He resurfaced the ice before your class?"

She nodded. "He did the ice right after the Squirts finished practice."

"What time was that?"

"Five-fifteen, five-thirty." Ciji's delicate brows pulled together in a look of concern. "Look, I know there are people in town who are ready to blame Olie, but he's not a bad person. He's just odd. I mean, he's really kind of sweet, you know? I've never seen him behave inappropriately around the kids."

"Did you see him later that night?"

"Sure. He did the ice again before seniors hockey at eight."

Which left hours in which he could have done anything, including abduct Josh Kirkwood.

Ciji set her water on the ledge along the boards and wound

the towel around her hands. "You don't really think he did it, do you?"

"We're just trying to establish a chronology of the events Wednesday night," Megan said smoothly, neither confirming nor denying. "It's important that we know who was where when. You were here until what time?"

"Eight-fifteen. I always stay until the senior guys warm up." She smiled a little. "They like to flirt. They're a bunch of sweeties."

"And you didn't see anything or anyone unusual?"

The smile disappeared. "No. Like I told the officer who questioned me yesterday—I wish I could say otherwise. I wish I could be a hero for Josh, but I just didn't see anything."

"Thanks anyway," Megan said. "I'll let you get back to work. It was nice meeting you."

"Sure." Ciji tossed her towel over the gate and gracefully skated backward toward center ice. "I hope you can make it to the show Sunday!"

"I'll try," Megan called, already moving out of the box and toward the end of the arena.

Olie saw her coming. That lady cop who looked right at him. He didn't want to talk to her. He didn't want to talk to anybody. He knew what people were saying—that his van was like the one the cops were looking for. Well, Mitch Holt had already looked inside his van and hadn't found anything. So they could all just go hang themselves, those people who stared at him sideways and said things about him behind his back. He didn't care what they thought, anyway. All he wanted was to be left alone.

He grabbed his plastic liter bottle of Coke and his book on chaos theories and started toward the door to the locker rooms.

"Mr. Swain? Can I have a word with you?"

"Talked to the chief," he grumbled. "Nothing else to say."

Watch your manners, Leslie! Don't be rude, Leslie. Never turn your back to me while I'm talking, Leslie.

He winced at the strident voice in his head.

"This will take only a minute."

If he went to his office, she would follow him. He didn't

want that. He didn't like anyone going in there. He couldn't breathe when other people came into his space.

"I just have a couple of questions for you," Megan said, catching up with him.

She could smell him five feet away. The rank onion smell of poor hygiene and overactive sweat glands wafted from him like cologne gone bad. He was wearing the same sweater and jacket he'd had on the first night. He stood facing her, a textbook clutched against his chest, his glass eye staring, his good eye darting all around her.

"Mr. Swain, I know you did the ice here the night Josh disappeared. Right after his team finished practice, right?"

He nodded.

"And again just before the seniors team played?"

His head jerked again.

"Could you tell me where you were during the time in between?"

"Around." He flinched at his own belligerence.

Don't take that tone with me, Leslie. You'll wish you hadn't, Mr. Smartmouth. I'll make you wish you hadn't.

The lady cop was staring at him. He wanted to shove her away. He wanted to hit her in the face to make her stop staring, and hit her again while he screamed at her to leave him alone. But he couldn't do those things, and knowing he couldn't made him feel puny and weak and impotent. A runt. A freak. A mistake of nature. His hand tightened around the Coke bottle and he scowled, frowning so hard, his small mouth bent into the shape of a horseshoe.

"Can anyone back you up on that?" Megan asked. Her gaze flicked down to Olie's right hand covered by the same Ragg wool half-gloves. As he squeezed the bottle until it made a crackling sound, the fingerlets pulled back from his knuckles, revealing a glimpse of thin blue lines traced on each finger. Her heart kicked against her ribs.

"I didn't do anything," Olie said angrily.

"I didn't say you did, Mr. Swain," Megan countered calmly. "But you know, that van of yours looks a lot like the one our witness described. If you weren't driving it, who was? You have a buddy you might have loaned it to? You can tell me. You won't be in any trouble."

"No," he snapped, rocking back and forth on the sides of his ratty Nikes, squeezing the Coke bottle rhythmically.

"And you say you were here that whole evening, but you don't have anyone who can back you up on that?"

"I didn't do anything!" Olie shouted. "Just leave me alone!" He hurled the Coke bottle into the trash barrel beside the door, then turned and ran down the dark hall.

"I don't know if I'll be able to do that, Mr. Swain," Megan murmured. Holding her breath, she leaned down into the trash barrel and came up holding the Coke bottle gingerly by the throat.

8:43 P.M. 20°

The torchlight parade included the usual Snowdaze traditions—King Frost and the Queen of the Snows with thermal underwear beneath her gown, the Happy Hookers ice fisherman drill team twirling their rods like parade rifles, the schnapps-soaked Shriners weaving precariously from curb to curb on their mini-snowmobiles. There were horse-drawn sleighs and dog sleds and a herd of Rotarians dressed as abominable snowmen. But as Mitch had suspected, the atmosphere was anything but festive. The spectators that lined the streets were all too conscious of the banners and posters of Josh and of the television cameras that had come to capture the small town's despair on videotape. When the contingent from the volunteer center silently marched past with candles burning, he could hear people around him crying.

Jessie clung to Mitch throughout, growing quieter and quieter until she put her head on his shoulder and asked to go home.

Mitch kissed the tip of her nose and hugged her. "Sure, honey. We'll go see if Grandma will make us some hot chocolate to warm up our noses and toesies. Right?"

The giggle he had hoped for didn't materialize. She merely nodded and tightened her stranglehold around his neck.

"Mitch, can we have a word from you?"

Mitch wheeled on Paige Price, then herded her away from the crowd. "Jesus Christ, Paige, do you never quit? Do you have any limits at all?"

Paige gave him the wounded look, though knowing he didn't buy it. If Garcia got any good shots of her, they could always use them later on, splice them into another piece. The cameraman backpedaled with her, tape running. "This is hardly out of bounds, Chief Holt."

"No, I guess this doesn't even begin to compare with giving away key evidence. My, you've had a busy day, Ms. Price." His voice sizzled with sarcasm. From the corner of his eye, he could see people looking at them, their attention drifting away from Debbie Dutton's Little Sprites baton twirlers going by in snow-suits, twirling to the tinny sound of "Winter Wonderland" blasting out of a boom box.

"I fail to see how the information on the notes could compromise the case," Paige said.

"I'll enlighten you tomorrow, when we get a hundred and fifty laser-printed notes on twenty-pound bond in the mail claiming responsibility for the kidnapping. Maybe you and your cameraman here could go out on a hundred and fifty calls to check out the crackpots instead of spending time with the search and rescue squads or the few remaining officers who will be left to hunt for real clues."

Jessie lifted her head, her lower lip trembling. "Daddy, don't be ornery!" she whimpered, tears glittering in her eyes.

"It's okay, honey," Mitch whispered. "I'm not mad at you; I'm mad at this lady." He tucked Jessie's head against his shoulder and backed Paige toward the renovated brick front of the Fine Line stationery store. "Who's your source, Paige?"

"You know I can't divulge that information."

"Oh, that's perfect," he sneered. "Your sources are sacrosanct, but confidential police information is fair game? There's something wrong with this picture, Paige."

Giving her no chance to refute the statement, he jerked to the right and nearly hit Jessie's head against the lens of the video camera. He swatted the thing aside and leaned into the face of the cameraman. "Get that fucking thing out of my face or you'll be wearing it for a hat!"

Jessie began to cry. Mitch tried to comfort her and glare at Paige simultaneously. "I find out who leaked that information, I'll kick his ass into the middle of next week," he said through clenched teeth. "And then I'll get mean."

Paige said nothing, feigning calm when everything inside her was trembling at the fury she saw in Mitch Holt's face. As Holt stalked away with his daughter in his arms, Garcia cradled his camera like a baby and leaned toward her conspiratorially.

"Shit, that guy has a temper. Remind me never to resist arrest around here."

9:05 P.M. 19°

Joy Strauss clucked her disapproval as she hung Jessie's coat in the hall closet. "This is just what I was afraid of," she muttered just loud enough for Mitch to hear.

He glared at the back of his mother-in-law's head, in no mood for Joy's pecking. She was a slim, graceful woman who would have been attractive if not for the sour bend to her mouth. Her brown hair was threaded with silver and worn in a shoulder-length style that was ageless. She dressed in social matron wear and wore her pessimism like a strand of accent pearls.

"This kidnapping has just terrified her," she continued. She shook her head as she closed the closet door. "It's a wonder she's been able to sleep. Maniacs roaming loose, snatching children off the curbs."

Mitch held Jessie close and gave Joy a warning look. "It's one incident, Joy, not an epidemic," he whispered. "Jessie's just tired, aren't you, sweetheart?"

Jessie nodded.

Joy held her arms out. "Well, come to Grandma, Jessie. We'll go up to bed."

"I'll take her," Mitch snapped. Joy sniffed, but didn't push her luck. Clucking her tongue, she moved off into the living room where *Washington Week* grumbled along on the television and Jurgen was engrossed in a book.

Mitch took Jessie to her room and helped her change into her nightgown. He rambled on about the Snowdaze activities that would take place over the weekend and how much fun she would have with her grandparents. Maybe Grandpa would take her to see the ice sculptures in the park or the human snow bowling. Maybe they would be able to go for a sleigh ride. Grandma had tickets to the figure skating show. Wouldn't that be fun?

Jessie contributed nothing to the conversation. She dutifully washed her face and brushed her teeth and climbed into the bed Mitch had turned down for her. He sat beside her and brushed a hand tenderly over her hair.

"Say your prayers, munchkin," he murmured, pressing a kiss to her forehead.

Jessie turned her face up to him, her big brown eyes swimming with tears. In a tiny, trembling voice, she said, "Daddy, I'm scared."

Mitch held his breath. "Scared of what, honey?"

"Scared that a maniac will get me, too!"

She crawled into his lap as the tears came in earnest. Mitch wrapped his arms around her and held her tight. "Nobody's going to take you, sweetheart."

"B-but s-somebody t-took J-Josh! G-Grandma s-says i-it h-happens e-every d-day!"

"Not here, it doesn't," Mitch said, rocking her. "Nobody's going to take you, honey. Remember how we talked all about how to be safe? Remember how we talked about stranger danger and how you should run away when you feel afraid of somebody?"

"B-but they t-took Josh and h-he's a b-big kid. I'm just little!"

Mitch's heart ripped. He pulled Jessie's head back against his chest and rocked her harder, blinking furiously at the heat stinging his eyes. "Nobody's going to take you, baby. I won't let that happen."

He would keep her safe.

The way he had kept her brother safe?

The thought was a knife. A stiletto driving deep, piercing

flesh and bone and soul. He bit his lip until he tasted blood, squeezed his eyes shut until they burned. He held his daughter and knew she was his only child because he hadn't been able to keep her brother safe. And he knew that no matter how hard he tried, no matter how strongly he believed he deserved it, there were no guarantees he could keep Jessie safe, either.

Damn you, whoever you are. Damn you for taking Josh, for stealing this town's innocence. Damn you to hell and gone. I'll send you there myself if I ever get the chance.

He rocked Jessie and whispered to her until her tears ran out and she fell asleep. Then he tucked her under the covers with Oatmeal Bear and just sat there, watching her, drinking in the sight of her, loving her so much it was a physical ache. He sat there, unaware of time passing. He heard Jurgen and Joy come upstairs, knew Joy stopped and stood outside Jessie's door. He didn't acknowledge her and she finally turned away, shutting off the hall light as she went.

The house had been silent for a long while when he eased away from Jessie and slipped out of her room. He left the light burning on the bedside table in case she woke up afraid. He wished he could have taken her home with him, but Joy had asked for this weekend a month ago. Then there was the case. He had left standing orders to be called the instant anything happened regarding Josh. He didn't want to further upset Jessie by having his pager wake her.

The clock on the dash of the Explorer read 12:13. Around him the neighborhood was quiet and dark. The bars downtown would still be open, but he didn't want the noise. The Big Steer truck stop out on the interstate was open all night, but he didn't want the questions or the talk that would come from the patrons and the help. Across the alley his house sat empty, but he couldn't stand the idea of being alone.

He thought of Megan and almost laughed at himself. Of all the women . . .

Since Allison's death he had suffered an endless parade of eligible ladies. Nice women, gentle women, women who would have done anything to please him, and women who would have done anything to win his heart. He had turned them all away and sent them in search of worthier men. He had denied himself their company and their sympathy. When physical needs could no longer be ignored, he took himself to the Cities and found release with no strings attached. The one-night stands had become just another part of the cycle into which his life had settled.

It never occurred to him it was a pathetic excuse for a life. It was what he wanted and all he was ready for. It was safe and painless. And empty . . . and lonely . . . and he didn't want to suffer it tonight.

Without allowing himself to question the wisdom of it, he put the truck in gear and drove toward Ivy Street.

CHAPTER 17

Megan dreamed of a world coated in the fine black soot of fingerprinting powder. It hung in the air like smog, and her lungs ached as she tried to breathe, as if she had an elephant standing on her chest. Every surface was covered with fingerprints. They floated in space like cinders in the wind. She woke with a start to find Friday sitting on her chest, staring down at her, his eyes liquid gold in the dim lamplight.

"God, you weigh a ton! Get off!" Megan groused, struggling to sit up.

The cat hopped onto a box of books and shot her a dirty look, then lifted his hind leg up behind his head in a yoga move and calmly began to groom his rear end.

Megan dismissed him and tried to dismiss the disorientation she felt waking up in what was essentially a strange place. She had to unpack her junk soon and make this apartment into a home, she thought, tightening the belt on her old blue plaid flannel robe. She couldn't stand the feeling of transience. Of course, she admitted, transient might well describe her state in Deer Lake if DePalma's fuse got any shorter.

If she could get a lead on the case, it would take some of the heat off, direct the press to something more important than the state's first female field agent. More important, if she could get a lead, they might be able to find Josh and bring him home.

Using her own ident kit, she had lifted Olie Swain's prints from the Coke bottle, transferred them to lift cards, and faxed them to Records at headquarters to be run through the

MAFIN network. The automated system would search through its database for a match. If they got a hit, she would be notified immediately. She had also faxed the prints to the National Crime Information Center at FBI headquarters in Washington, D.C., to be run through their automated fingerprint identification system. They would do a search starting with the Upper Midwest and work their way out to the rest of the country.

Someone somewhere knew Olie Swain. Someone somewhere had sent him to prison.

In her mind's eye she saw again the fine blue lines on the backs of his fingers. A crude tattoo job. The kind cons gave other cons in the joint. She hadn't gotten a good enough look to swear, but it felt right. He smelled like a con in more ways than one.

The knock at the door was like another world crashing into her sphere of silence. Megan shot to her feet, automatically reaching for her gun on the end table. Out of habit she skirted around the door and flattened herself against the wall beside it. The knock sounded again. She waited, breath held deep in her lungs.

"Megan? It's Mitch."

She blew out a breath, then undid the lock. "Did you drop in on Leo after midnight?" she asked, pulling the door open.

"No," he said softly.

He stepped inside, his hands stuffed into his jacket pockets, shoulders still hunched against the chill he had left outside. His gaze strayed to the slim black nine-millimeter pistol she set aside on the kitchen table, but he made no comment about it. Maybe all the women he visited in the dead of the night answered their doors with a fistful of firepower.

"I was driving by," he murmured. "Saw your light."

Megan debated telling him about taking Olie's prints. She had railed against him for keeping information from her, but she didn't want to bring up the subject now. It was late. Besides, maybe nothing would come of it. Beyond that, he didn't look as if he wanted to talk business. He looked exhausted and lost. He wandered through the maze of boxes to the window that looked down on Ivy Street and just stood there, staring out at the night.

She followed the path he had taken, absently brushing her hand over Gannon as she passed the box he had picked for his bed. The gray cat raised his head and blinked at her, then turned his steady gaze on Mitch and made a throaty sound of contentment.

"Why'd you skip out tonight?" he asked as she leaned a shoulder against the window frame.

"You needed to be with Jessie. I didn't want to intrude . . ." She let the thought trail off. "How was the parade?"

"Sad. They're all trying so hard . . . because they want to make a difference, because they're scared. They look to me to save them and they don't realize—" He looked at her, his whiskey-brown eyes bleary and bloodshot, the strain carved like knife lines into his face. "I'm nobody's savior. I'm just a cop. And I'm tired of it." He turned back toward the window but closed his eyes. "I'm tired of it."

Tired of the pain. Tired of the responsibility. Tired of the panic in his gut, the fear that he had no special powers to right all the wrongs, that he wasn't Superman, just Clark Kent with delusions of grandeur. He turned toward Megan, letting her read it all in his face.

The Megan of the slicked-back hair and gender-neutral wardrobe and the rules and regulations was not this woman who stood before him now. Her hair was loose around her shoulders. With nothing on her feet but a pair of baggy wool socks, she was short. Swallowed up inside an old plaid robe, she looked tiny, delicate. St. Joan without her armor. She stood there, waiting, silent, patient.

"I'm not much of a hero," he murmured. "They ought to know that."

"You're doing all you can," Megan said. "We all are."

My best wasn't good enough. Again. The words he had spoken the day before in the garage of the old fire station came back to her, heavy with regret and self-loathing.

He turned his gaze out the window again. "I keep thinking I should have been able to prevent this from happening, that I should have been able to see it coming, do something about it." His mouth twisted with bitter black humor. "A recurring theme in my life."

Megan didn't ask. She wouldn't beg and she wouldn't drag

it out of him. He would tell her because he needed to or wanted to, or they would stand there all night, saying nothing.

"I had a son," he said at last. "Kyle. He was six."

Megan's breath caught on the lump in her throat.

"They were in the wrong place at the wrong time." He shook his head at the irony. "Why do we always say that? They weren't in the wrong place. My wife and son went to the store for milk and bread. The doper with the sawed-off shotgun was in the wrong place. But I sent them there, so what does that make me?"

A victim, Megan thought, though she knew his answer would be "guilty." No court would ever convict him, but he had convicted himself and for the rest of his life he would dole out the punishment. What a screwed-up world that a good man should have to pay again and again for something as small as a word or two, as simple as a decision of who should go to the store, while a killer would have no remorse, never feel a second's pain for the lives he had ruined.

"He just blew them away," he whispered. "Like they were nothing."

He could still see them, bloody, lying on the dirty linoleum floor, their lives drained out of them. Their bodies bent at odd angles, like dolls that had been cast aside, their eyes wide open, staring the bleak, hopeless stares of the dead. Allison with one arm outstretched toward their son. Kyle, just out of reach, his too-big baseball uniform dyed maroon with his blood, a pack of baseball cards clutched in one hand. That bright small life crushed, wasted, discarded as carelessly as an empty can.

"I heard the call on the radio," he said. "Even before I saw Allison's car in the parking lot, I knew. I just knew."

And the recriminations had started, as they started now. Relentless. Brutal. Inescapable. And the questions had started, as they started now, the rage building and building behind them. He worked so hard for right, for justice. He followed the rules. He had principles. He was a good man, a good cop, a straight arrow. He should have been rewarded, and instead, he had the most precious parts of his life torn out and blown apart.

"One hundred sixty-nine dollars," he said, still staring out at the night. "That's what the crook got out of the deal. That's what their lives were worth to him."

He closed his eyes and a single tear slid down his cheek. He was a proud man, a tough man, but the pain and the confusion undid him. He was a cop. He believed in right and wrong, black and white, but his world had turned into a hazy place of smoke and mirrors. Megan could hear it in his voice—the desperation of a man trying to make sense of the senseless.

It must have been unbearable to have loved a partner, to have made a child and loved and hoped for that child, and lost them both. Better to have loved and lost, the saying went, but Megan didn't believe it. Better not to love at all than to have the heart torn out by the roots.

"I think of Hannah and Paul," he murmured. "I wouldn't wish this pain on anyone."

Needing to offer him comfort, Megan slipped her arms inside his open coat, around his lean waist, and pressed her cheek to his chest. "We'll find him. We will."

Wishing he could absorb her certainty, he wrapped his arms around her and hugged her tight. He didn't think about her rule against cops. They weren't cops now. In his mind he pared away all but the basic truth—he was a man and she was a woman, and the electricity between them was hot and compelling, inviting them to shut out the rest of the world. He had no intention of resisting the temptation. Tonight that was all he wanted—to be a man with no past or tomorrow with a woman he could hold and a need he could lose himself in.

He slid a hand through her hair, the glossy strands sifting through his fingers. He lowered his mouth to hers, his kiss smothering any protest she might have made. The taste of her was sweet. The feel of her body in his arms regenerated his strength. Desire burned away the fatigue and the kiss burned hotter, wilder.

Megan hung on, her fingers pressing hard into the small of his back. She couldn't find the words to tell him no. All she could find inside herself was need. He bent her back over his arm, his mouth trailing heat down the side of her neck to the V of flesh exposed by her robe. Then he was sweeping her up into his arms.

He crossed the room in a matter of a few long strides, tumbling boxes en route, sending a cat scurrying for safer ground. His eyes never left hers. The expression he wore was fierce, determined, intense, as if he thought blinking or glancing away would snap the spell. In the bedroom he deposited her in the middle of the unmade bed and stepped back to shrug off his coat, never looking away. He pulled his sweater and T-shirt off over his head and flung them aside.

Megan sat up on her knees, drinking in the sight of him. His hair was tousled. The shadow of his beard darkened his jaw and accented the lean planes and angles of his face. He had the body of a warrior who had seen his share of battles. Trim, lean, ridged with muscle, scarred in places. Dark hair swirled across the planes of his chest and flat belly, arrowing into a line that disappeared beneath the low-riding waist of his jeans.

Her eyes on his, she undid the belt of her robe and let the garment fall open and fall back off her shoulders. There was no right. There was no wrong. There were no rules. There were no words. There was only this incredible sense of expectation and merging, aching souls.

Mitch reached out and ran the fingertips of one hand along her shoulder and down her arm. He traced the angle of her waist, the graceful flare of her hip. Her skin was the color of cream, the texture of silk. He kissed her slowly, erotically, his tongue probing deep into the warm, wet recesses of her mouth as his hand explored her. He wanted to devour her, to absorb the comfort of her soft warmth into his body—or better yet, be taken into hers. Lose himself. Feel the hard knot of loneliness and pain break apart and melt in the heat of their union.

They sank down on the bed, stretching against each other chest to chest, legs tangling. Megan arched into him, loving the feel of his hard body, the heat of his skin, the brush of his chest hair against her nipples. She gave herself over to sensation— touching him, tasting him, breathing in the warm musk of male need. She gave herself over to him, letting him take control. Surrendering . . . The word brought a shiver, but then his mouth was on her breast and thought was gone.

She tangled her hands in his hair, kneaded the muscles in his shoulders, ran the arch of her foot along the back of his leg, frowning at the fact that he still had his jeans on. Twisting beneath him, she reached for the button. Mitch allowed her, rising up on his knees as she tugged the zipper down over his erection.

Her hands were trembling as she pulled down jeans and briefs. Her whole body was trembling with the need to take him inside her. She curled her fingers around his shaft and stroked him gently. He closed his eyes and groaned.

"Come here," he whispered, reaching for her.

Megan went to him, welcoming his kiss, pressing her body into his. She put her arms around his neck and let her head fall back as he trailed his mouth down her throat. His big hands stroked down her back to her buttocks and he lifted her and pulled her onto his lap as he sat back on his haunches. She reached between their bodies and guided him, held him steady as he lowered her.

Her breath left her in a slow hiss as he entered her. Her body tightened around him, on the brink of fulfillment. He lifted her again and slid her back down on him slowly, inch by inch.

Anticipation wound like a spring inside her, tighter and tighter, pounding for release. She began to move on him at her own pace, hands gripping his big shoulders, her head flung back. Faster and faster, until she was breathless, until the heat condensed to a slick gloss of sweat on her skin, until the anticipation exploded into a firestorm of sensation.

They held each other tight as they came back to earth, as their heartbeats slowed, as the real world took form around them. Mitch pulled the quilt up over them. The heat of passion had waned and the January night chilled them.

Gannon jumped up on the bed and curled into his spot behind Megan's knees. As if Mitch didn't exist at all. Megan could hardly remember the last time she'd had a man in her bed. Her relationships could be counted on one hand. All of them dismal failures. The rule of her love life was a catch-22: She didn't date cops, but no one understood cops except other cops, therefore . . . And beneath that excuse lay deeper reasons, intrinsic fears, demons that had followed her like shadows all her life. The fear that no one would ever love her, that she was inherently unlovable, tainted by the stain of her mother's sins. Fears that had no logic. Fears that existed in the darkest corner of her heart like toadstools.

Stupid to even think of them now. Mitch Holt didn't love her, he had needed her. They had needed each other to escape a lonely night, to escape a horrible case. It wasn't love. More like a favor between friends. Cast in that light, the beauty of their lovemaking faded, the comfort of lying there together lost its warmth.

He's not even single, she thought, staring at the ring on his left hand. She had just broken all her own rules for a man who was married to his past. *You sure know how to pick 'em, kiddo.*

Still, she couldn't find it in her to regret what they had just shared. Just as she couldn't stop herself from wanting something more. Just as she couldn't stop that need from scaring the hell out of her.

Mitch felt her shiver against him and pulled the covers up higher around her shoulders. She felt good in his arms. She fit against his side like a puzzle piece. Comfortable. Comforting. The sex had been incredible. Just thinking about it made him want her all over again.

He waited for the stab of guilt, that jagged dagger that had plunged into his heart after every sexual encounter he'd had since Allison's death. But it didn't come. He'd found an oasis for a little while, for a night. Dawn would arrive soon enough and they would be cops again, thrown back into the living nightmare of trying to find a kidnapper but with no real leads and no real suspects and no motive save a madman's. But until dawn, they had the night.

He turned onto his side, bracing himself up on one arm so he could look down at Megan. She stared back at him, her expression slightly wary, slightly defiant.

"If this is where you make the speech about what a big mistake we just made, you can save your breath," she said.

"Because you already know it was a mistake?" he asked carefully.

Mistake was too small a word, too innocent. This was the kind of misstep that could end her career. Getting in too deep with Mitch Holt could leave her with nothing but a broken heart, and she'd had enough of those to last her.

"Are you saying you regret making love with me?" he said.

She stared up at him, at the lived-in, beat-up face and the eyes that looked as old as time. She thought of all the feelings he kept boxed inside—the rage, the pain, the self-doubt—that he allowed out only in small increments. She thought of his tenderness and his passion and the unabashed love he gave to his daughter. It would have been smart to say yes; the best defense was a good offense. She couldn't see a future for them. There was no point in prolonging the inevitable. She could end it now and come away with her pride battered but intact, but . . .

"No," she whispered. "I just don't think we should make a habit of it."

She swung her legs over the side of the bed and grabbed her robe. Mitch leaned across and caught hold of one sleeve before she could slip into it. She met his gaze over her shoulder, her expression wary.

"Why not?" he challenged.

"Because."

"That's not an answer for anyone over the age of seven."

"The answer was implied," Megan said. "You shouldn't have to ask the question."

She tugged her sleeve free of his grasp and walked away, pulling the robe around her and tying the belt tight. She went to her dresser and fingered the few items she had unpacked and set on top of it. The small gray china cat statue that had been a graduation gift from Frances Clay, the church cleaning lady who had looked after her when she was small. The jewelry box she had bought in a secondhand shop with her own money on her twelfth birthday. For a time she had pretended that her mother had given it to her, when in fact no one had given her anything.

"We're working together," she said tightly. "We shouldn't be sleeping together."

She watched him in the mirror as he threw the covers back and climbed out of her bed. The automatic flush of desire frightened her. It frightened her that her body could so quickly become so attuned to his, that she could want him this badly, need him this much. Need. God, she couldn't let herself need him.

Their gazes met in the mirror. His expression was hard, predatory.

"This doesn't have anything to do with work," he said, his voice a low rumble in his throat.

Slowly he turned her around to face him and tugged her belt loose. She sucked in a shallow breath as he slid his hands inside the robe and opened it, exposing her to his gaze, his touch. He cupped her breasts gently, brushing his thumbs across her nipples, and her breath caught again. Satisfaction and arousal flared in his gaze. His fingers skimmed down her sides and his hands scttled on her hips. He lowered his mouth toward hers. "And who said anything about sleeping?"

Take a perfect family. Tear it all apart. We hold the pieces. We hold the power. As simple as nothing. Like pulling the linchpin on this small, stupid place. Like ringing the bell for Pavlov's dogs.

The police chase their tails. They search for evidence they won't find. They wait for signs from above. They bluster and threaten, but nothing will come of it. We watch and laugh. The volunteers pray and pin themselves with ribbons and pass out posters, thinking they can make a difference. Such fools. Only we can make a difference. We hold all the cards.

The game is growing dull. Time to up the ante.

CHAPTER 18

Hannah sat on the window ledge, staring out at the trees as they transformed from shadows to vague shapes. The black of night was fading, shade by subtle shade. Another night gone. The start of another day without Josh. She couldn't imagine how she would live through it. She took no comfort in the knowledge that she would.

The line from the notes whispered through the back of her mind. The words crept over her skin like bony fingers. *ignorance is not innocence but SIN. i had a little sorrow, born of a little SIN.* Cold fear twisted inside her and she trembled with the longing for someone to take it away.

Paul lay sleeping, sprawled facedown in the center of the bed, his arms flung wide, claiming the entire mattress as his own. She wondered if he would go through his same routine when he woke to face the day. She wondered what had happened to the two of them. She closed her eyes and saw them each in separate rowboats on a sea that tossed them farther apart with each pulsing wave. In her mind's eye she reached out toward him mutely, but his back was to her and he didn't turn around.

Loneliness tightened like a fist in her chest, crushing her lungs, crushing her heart.

God, I'm not strong enough to get through this alone. . . .

She pressed a hand to her mouth to hold back the cry of helplessness and need, and ached inside at the thought that she wouldn't even share this with her husband, with the father of her children.

Things had been so different when Josh was a baby. Paul had been different. He had been proud of her. She had never doubted his love. He had looked at life's opportunities with enthusiasm, eager to give his family the things he had missed out on growing up in a blue-collar neighborhood, where paychecks had to be stretched. He had looked at Josh and seen the chance to be the supportive, loving father he'd never had. He had looked at his wife and seen an equal, a partner, someone he could love and respect.

Now Hannah looked at him and saw a selfish, bitter man, jealous of her successes, resentful of his own anonymity. A man consumed by the need to acquire things and baffled that the things didn't give him the happiness he expected. She wondered what had become of the man she had married, wondered if he was as lost to her as Josh.

Oh, God, I didn't mean to think that! I don't believe he's gone. I won't believe it.

ignorance is not innocence but SIN. Loneliness, fear, guilt, hurtled through her. Panic closed her throat. She forced herself to her feet and paced the rectangle of pale light that fell from the window onto the carpet, forcing herself to think, to plan, forcing the wheels of her mind to turn. She was trembling like a drunk in the throes of DTs. It took every molecule of strength she had to keep from crumpling to the floor. Gritting her teeth, she fought against the need to double over. *One foot in front of the other, in front of the other, in front of the other . . . Step, step, step, turn. Step, step, step, turn . . . .*

She paced the floor in an oversize Vikings jersey and wool socks, her legs and forearms bare. The cold seemed to seep through skin and tissue into her bones. It seemed to spill in through the window like moonlight.

So cold . . . Is Josh cold? Cold and alone. Ice cold. Stone cold . . .

"What are you doing?"

Hannah jerked around at the sound of Paul's voice. Her hands were like ice. She could see her palm prints on the window where her breath had steamed the glass around them.

"I couldn't sleep."

Paul swung his legs over the edge of the bed and sat up with the comforter pulled across his lap. He looked thin and gray in the pale light of the room, older, harder, lines of anger and disappointment etched into his face beside his eyes and mouth. A sigh leaked out of his lungs as he flicked on the lamp and looked at the alarm clock on the nightstand.

"I have to do something today," Hannah announced, surprising herself as much as him. The words echoed in her mind and hardened with resolve. She stood a little straighter. She wanted—needed—to get back something of herself. She was accustomed to taking action in the face of a crisis. Action at least provided the illusion of control. "I have to get out of this house. If I have to sit here another day, I'll go crazy."

"You can't leave," Paul said. He tossed the covers back and rose, hitching up a baggy pair of striped pajama bottoms. He grabbed his black terry robe from the foot of the bed and thrust his arms into the sleeves. "You have to be here in case they call."

"You can answer a telephone as well as I can."

"But I have to go out with the search party—"

"No, Paul, *I'm* going out."

He gave a bitter laugh. "What do you think you're going to do? You think you're going to save the day? Dr. Garrison to the rescue. Her husband can't find their son, but she will?"

"Oh, Jesus, Paul!" she snapped, flinging her arms down to her sides. "Why does everything have to be about you? I'm so sick of this jealous act of yours, I could scream. I'm sorry if you feel inadequate—"

"I never said I felt inadequate," he barked, his eyes glowing with temper. "I meant that you don't believe anyone can do anything as well as you."

"That's absurd." She turned her back on him. She pulled clothes out of her dresser drawers and tossed them into a tangled pile on top of her jewelry box, heedless of the bottles of perfume she overturned in the process. "You've been out the last two days looking for Josh. Why can't you see that I need that chance, too? Why can't you—"

The rest of the question died as a wave of emotion surged through her.

"We used to share everything," she whispered, her eyes on his reflection in the mirror. "We used to be partners. As horrible as this is, at least we would have shared the burden. God, Paul, what's happened to us?"

She heard him sigh, but she didn't turn around and she didn't meet his gaze in the mirror, afraid that what she would see on his face would be impatience instead of regret.

"I'm sorry," he murmured, stepping up behind her. "I feel like I'm losing my mind. I feel helpless. You know what that does to me. I need to feel like I can make a difference."

"So do I!" She swung around to face him, her expression a plea for understanding. She looked into his eyes, trying to find the man she had married, the man she had loved. "I need that, too. Why can't you see that?"

Or don't you care? The question hung between them, unspoken, as the moment stretched taut. A dozen scenarios flashed through Hannah's mind—the rift between them healing, the Paul she used to know returning, the nightmare ending abruptly with her waking suddenly, the light going cold in his eyes as he told her he didn't care, the crevasse between them ripping as wide as a canyon. . . .

He looked away as Lily started to cry in her room down the hall. "Yeah . . . Go ahead," he said softly. "I'll stay with Lily for a while."

"She'll ask where Josh is," Hannah murmured. "It's been three days . . ."

She dragged a hand back through her tangled hair as the fears surged up inside her again. "God, the things that go through my mind . . . Is he asking for us, is he cold, is he hurt?" The worst of the questions stuck like peanut butter to the roof of her mouth, gagging her, choking her. She was afraid to give them voice, and yet she needed to. "Paul, what if he's—"

"Don't!" He pulled her roughly into his arms, his eyes still trained on the door, as if looking at her would turn the fears to reality. "I don't want to think about it," he whispered.

He was trembling. She pressed a hand over his heart and felt it race. *ignorance is not innocence but SIN*

"Go take your shower," he murmured. "I'll get Lily up."

11:20 A.M. 20°   ·

Buy a chance! Give a dollar! Help bring Josh home!" Al Jackson's voice boomed across the park from the Senior Hockey League booth. He had found a rhythm and stuck with it, repeating the chant with the regularity of a metronome. The call was too reminiscent of a carnival barker luring the naïve to a rigged shell game.

Hannah's stomach churned. She looked out across the park, seeing a surreal version of the annual Snowdaze fair. Wooden booths draped in colorful festoons ringed and crisscrossed the park. Behind them, portable heaters rumbled, generating billowing clouds of steam in the cold air. Crowds had turned out in full winter regalia to play the games and watch the ice sculptors at work. But in addition to the usual causes—new band uniforms and computers for the public library and funds for the Legion Auxiliary summer beautification project—every game, every booth, was pledging money to the effort to find Josh.

Noble gestures. Overwhelming generosity. A touching show of support and love. Hannah repeated these phrases over and over, and still she couldn't shake her gut-level reaction—that she had escaped one nightmare and run headlong into another. There was something too Kafkaesque about watching people slide one by one down the hill from the courthouse into a stand of giant bowling pins, knowing they had each given a dollar to help bring her son home. It made her feel sick to think this festival had been twisted into so many acts of desperation and that she was queen for the day, the center of attention, the star attraction.

She had been led to the volunteer-center booth to be put on display like some freak. *See the grieving mother hand out posters! Watch the guilty woman pin yellow ribbons on the faithful!*

She could feel the gazes of the reporters on her. The second they spotted her, questions spewed out of them in an endless stream—questions about her feelings, questions of guilt and suspicion, requests for exclusive interviews. She had finally given them a statement and made a plea for Josh's return, but they weren't satisfied. Like a pack of hungry dogs that had been thrown a few meat scraps, they lingered and watched her, hopeful of more. She couldn't move or speak or wipe her nose without feeling their camera lenses zoom in on her.

The faces of some of the television people were familiar. She seldom had time to sit down and watch the news, but at six and ten it was always on in the background regardless of where she was. Minnesotans didn't miss their news; it was something of an inside joke among natives. Aside from the goings-on in the Cities, nothing much of consequence happened in the state as a rule, but everyone insisted on having the nonevents relayed to them at the end of the day.

Hannah could put names to several of the Twin Cities' reporters. Several of the stations themselves had set up booths to help raise money for the cause. Down the row from the volunteer-center booth, the channel eleven weatherman was offering his face as a target for cream pies. The *StarTribune* had teamed up with the policemen's association to fingerprint and photograph children for a dollar donation per child—a safety precaution most parents in Deer Lake had never thought about.

Noble gestures. Overwhelming generosity. A touching show of support and love.

A macabre drama, and she was the focal point.

It's your own fault, Hannah. You want to do something, to take charge like you always do.

But she couldn't find the strength to present herself as a leader. She felt drained, wilted. Dizziness swam through her head and she closed her eyes and leaned against the counter.

"Dr. Garrison, are you all right?"

"I think she's going to faint!"

"Should we call a doctor?"

"She *is* a doctor!"

"Well, she can't treat herself. She'd have a fool for a patient."

"That's lawyers—"

"What about lawyers?"

Fragments of conversation came to Hannah as if from a

great distance down a long tunnel. The world swayed beneath her feet.

"Excuse me, ladies. I think maybe Dr. Garrison needs to take a little break. Isn't that right, Hannah?"

She felt a strong hand close gently on her arm and willed her eyes to open. Father Tom came into focus. Her gaze locked onto the concern in his face.

"You need a little quiet time," he said softly.

"Yes."

The word barely made it out of her mouth when the ground seemed to dip. He caught her against his side and started across the square toward the volunteer center. Hannah did her best to move her feet. Reporters moved in on them, cameramen and photographers closing off the escape route.

"Please, folks." Father Tom spoke sharply. "Show a little decency. Can't you see she's had enough for one day?"

Apparently unwilling to risk the wrath of God, they stepped out of the way, but Hannah could hear the click of shutters and the whir of motor drives until they reached the curb.

"How you doing?" Father Tom asked. "Can you make it across the street?"

Hannah managed a nod, though she wasn't at all sure she wouldn't just collapse. Out of self-preservation she hooked an arm around Tom McCoy's waist and leaned into him, grateful for his solid strength.

"That's right," he murmured. "You just hang on, Hannah. I won't let you fall."

He took her into the volunteer center, where volunteers ignored ringing telephones and blinking cursors on computer screens to stare. Hannah kept her head down, embarrassed to be seen this weak and more than a little uncomfortable being seen snuggled up to the town priest. But Father Tom ignored her feeble effort to put space between them. A determined look on his face, he guided her toward what had once been the stockroom, where chairs and tables had been set up for coffee breaks.

He eased her down onto a chair and shooed out the curious and concerned onlookers with the exception of Christopher Priest, who came bearing gifts of caffeine and sugar. The professor set a paper plate of brownies down on the table. Tom accepted the cup of coffee and pressed it into Hannah's hands.

"Drink up," he ordered. "You look like an ice sculpture. My truck is out back. I'll go warm it up, then I'm taking you home."

Hannah murmured her thanks, trying to smile bravely. The compassion in his eyes let her abandon the effort. Compassion, not pity. An offer of the strength of his friendship. He brushed the back of his knuckles along her cheek absently, as if he did such things every day, but Hannah felt a tingle of electricity. She sat back, beating herself up mentally for her reaction. He was Father Tom, priest, confessor, erstwhile cowboy, absent-minded shepherd of the flock of St. Elysius.

"You forgot your gloves again," she murmured.

He pulled them out of his pockets and waved them at her, then headed for the back door. Hannah turned her attention to the coffee cup warming her hands, to put her mind on something mundane. She sipped the steaming brew, surprised that it had been lightened to her preference.

"I remembered you take milk," the professor said, a twinkle of pride in his eyes. "You sat across the table from me at the chamber of commerce dinner last year."

"And you remembered that I take milk?" Hannah offered him a small smile.

He sat back against the edge of another table, his hands tucked into the pockets of a black down jacket that puffed out around him like an inflatable muscle suit. His head poked up above the collar on a skinny neck.

"I have a head for trivia," he said. "I haven't had a chance to tell you how sorry I am about Josh."

"Thank you," she murmured, glancing away. What an odd ritual, the manners dance of condolences. It seemed so useless for people to apologize over something in which they had no part; it seemed too civilized to thank them for it. This was just another aspect of her role of victim she couldn't reconcile herself to.

She could feel the professor's gaze on her, steady, studying as he studied everything that lived and breathed and couldn't be plugged into an electrical socket—as if he understood machines far better.

"I guess I'm not handling it very well," she confessed.

"How do you think you should handle it?"

"I don't know. Better. Differently."

He put his head on one side in a pose reminiscent of the android Data on *Star Trek: The Next Generation.* One of Josh's favorite TV shows. The reminder stabbed like a needle. "It's curious," he said, "that people have come to a point where they almost feel they should be preprogrammed for everything that happens in their lives. Spontaneous reaction is a rule of nature; people can't control their responses any more than they can control the random events that trigger them. And yet they try. You shouldn't apologize, Hannah. Just let yourself react."

A rueful smile turned her lips as she took another sip of coffee. "Easier said than done. I feel like I've been cast in a play but I don't have a script."

The professor pressed his lips together and hummed a note of consideration. Hannah envisioned his brain clicking and clacking like a computer as he processed the information.

"I should thank you while I have the chance," she said, looking out through the open door into the former appliance showroom where people she didn't know were squinting at computer screens and stuffing envelopes with fliers. "We really appreciate the time and talent you and your students have given. Everyone has tried so hard to be helpful."

A hint of a blush tinted his pale cheeks as he waved off her gratitude. "It's the least we can do."

The back door opened and Father Tom made a dramatic entrance in a cloud of wind-driven exhaust fumes, his glasses completely fogged over. "Come along, Doctor. If we hurry, we can still ditch those reporters."

He tossed her a long, hideous scarf that had been knitted from every unappealing and uncoordinating color in the spectrum, and a black baseball cap with the words THE GOD SQUAD printed in bold white letters on the front.

"What's this?" Hannah asked.

From his coat pocket he pulled a pair of fake glasses with a big plastic nose and mustache attached. He flipped the bows open and shoved the glasses onto her face, then smiled at the effect. "Your disguise."

12:04 P.M. 20°

I'm not much of a cook, but I can microwave leftovers with the best of them."

"It smells wonderful," Hannah said dutifully but without enthusiasm as he set the stoneware plate of beef stew down on the table in front of her. It looked like a cover shot for *Woman's Day*—thick chunks of meat and potatoes, bright orange disks of carrot, peas as green as spring grass, all in a thick, rich gravy. Too bad she couldn't find any desire to eat it.

"Don't even think about pushing it away," Father Tom warned, sliding into the chair across from her. "You'll eat it or I'll feed it to you. You need food, Hannah. You almost passed out."

Reluctantly, she picked up her fork and speared a slice of carrot. Her hand was shaking as she raised it to her mouth. Tom watched her like a hawk while she chewed and swallowed. He twisted the cap off a bottle of Pete's Wicked Ale and slid it across the table to her.

"Improves the appetite," he explained with a wink. "Spoken like a true Irishman, eh?"

Hannah laughed softly. She tried a small bite of beef and washed it down with the ale. They sat in the kitchen of the rectory, a big old Victorian house that occupied the lot behind St. Elysius. In times past, when clergy had been in more abundance, the house had served as home and hotel to a host of priests and ecclesiastics. It had served a stint as a halfway house for alcoholic priests in the fifties. Now the rambling place housed only Father Tom. He had closed off the whole second story to conserve heat.

The kitchen was sunny, with old glass-fronted cabinets and yellow wallpaper featuring teakettles. The small table was tucked into an alcove out of the flow of traffic—not that there was any. The house was empty except for the two of them.

"Thanks for rescuing me," Hannah murmured, eyes downcast.

Tom buttered a chunk of homemade bread and handed it across to her. She was ashamed to need rescuing, he could see that plainly, just as she had been ashamed to cry on his shoulder. She was too brave for her own good. He ached painfully at the thought of her trying to get through this ordeal as the Hannah Garrison everyone in Deer Lake knew and loved—calm, stoic, confident, and wise enough to solve everyone's problems. The calm had been shattered, the confidence destroyed, all in a single blow. She was lost and he saw no sign of Paul helping her navigate.

What kind of man could be so blind that he could look at Hannah and not see a jewel?

"I know everyone is trying to help," she said in a small, strained voice. "They're being so wonderful, it's just that . . . It's all so . . . *wrong.*"

She raised her head and looked at him, pain and confusion swimming in her blue eyes. Her hair was still rumpled from wearing his cap. Curling strands of gold fell across her forehead and trailed down a cheek. She looked like an angel who had taken a long fall from her cloud.

"It's *wrong,*" she whispered. "It's like we're on a train that's jumped the tracks and nobody can stop it. I want to make it stop."

"I don't think we can, Hannah," he confessed sadly. "We can only hang on for the ride."

He reached out to her across the table, offered his hand silently. For good reasons, just reasons, and reasons he wouldn't give voice even in the deepest, most private part of his mind. Reasons she could never know and would probably never suspect. So where was the harm? That question would open the floodgates on a hundred more for which he would find no answers, and so he silenced it. Nothing mattered at that moment but giving Hannah some comfort, some sign that she wasn't alone.

A single tear spilled over her lashes. Slowly she slid her hand across the table and took hold of his. Their palms fit against each other perfectly. Their fingers curled automatically. At the warmth of the contact and the feelings it stirred inside, Hannah's eyes widened slightly in surprise.

"I'd change it for you if I could, Hannah," he whispered. "If I could work a miracle, I'd do it in a heartbeat."

Hannah thought she should thank him, but no words

formed in her mouth. She couldn't seem to do anything but hold on to him and take in the quiet strength and conviction he offered. And she couldn't help but feel the sting of irony that the one man willing to share her burden and help her through this ordeal was not her husband but her priest.

She felt the intrusion seconds before Albert Fletcher cleared his throat. A sense of anger and disapproval tainted the moment like a layer of soot settling on her skin. She jerked her gaze to the basement door, cursing herself and Fletcher as she pulled her hand out of Father Tom's grasp. How long had Fletcher been standing there? He had no business spying on them or frowning at them as if he'd caught them doing something wrong. And she had no business feeling guilty . . . but she did.

"Jeez, Albert," Tom said, pulling back the hand he had offered Hannah and pressing it against his chest. "Give us heart attacks, why don't you? What the devil were you doing in the basement?"

The deacon regarded him with a somber look. He was dressed in his usual black garb—slacks, turtleneck, old quilted jacket—a habit that might have grown out of mourning his dead wife or out of his obsession with the church. He held a good-size cardboard box in his arms, a box with water stains and the white film of mildew. Its musty smell slipped beneath the robust aroma of the stew. "I'm sorting through the storage room."

"Back in the dungeon?" Tom shuddered in distaste. "That stuff's been back there since the Resurrection. What would you want with any of that?"

"It's history. It deserves preservation." The deacon shot a dark glance at Hannah. "I'm sorry if I interrupted something."

Tom pushed his chair back from the table and rose, working at containing his temper. God alone would be his judge. For all of Fletcher's pious posturings, he was not God or even a reasonable substitute.

"Dr. Garrison needed a sanctuary. The last I heard, we were in the business of offering refuge and comfort."

Fletcher looked through him. "Of course, Father," he murmured. "If you'll excuse me . . ."

He nodded to Hannah and slipped out the back door, leav-

ing behind a tension that hung in the air. Hannah dodged
Tom's gaze and got up from the table. She pulled her coat off
the back of her chair.

"I should get home," she said quietly. "Paul will be wondering."

Tom sighed and pushed his glasses up. "You didn't finish
your lunch."

"I'll eat when I get home. I promise. I've got plenty to pick
from; the casseroles are multiplying geometrically." She
zipped her coat, then forced herself to push past her guilt and
embarrassment and raised her eyes to his. "Thanks, though.
For the food . . . for the support . . . for everything."

He started to say it was nothing, but it wasn't nothing. It
was something more complicated than either of them needed
and something so simple, it should have needed no explanation
or apology. He shrugged his jacket on and dug his keys out of
the pocket.

"Come on, Doc, I'll drive you home."

They left her van downtown to avoid alerting the media to her
plans. Hannah didn't ask him in. She didn't want to further
ruin the day by having to listen to Paul snipe at him. But a
heavy sense of loneliness pressed down on her as she climbed
the steps and let herself in the mudroom. A BCA man sat at
the kitchen table drinking Mountain Dew and reading *Guns &
Ammo*. He gave her a nod. In the family room, the television
was showing a figure skating competition to no one. The low
murmur of voices drew her up the stairs and down the hall toward Lily's room.

"Paul? I'm home."

Hannah pushed the door open and stopped. Karen Wright
stood next to the crib with Lily perched on one hip. Karen was
smiling at the baby, tickling her chin and cuddling her close.
Paul stood beside her. Raising his eyes to meet Hannah's, he
took a half step back, his face carefully blank.

Impervious to the sudden unease in the room, Lily beamed
a smile and reached a hand out to Hannah. "Hi, Mama!"

"Hi, sweetie," she responded, her gaze skating past her
daughter. "Karen, I didn't expect you to come over again today. Is the neighbor brigade running low on recruits?"

Color flared across Karen's cheekbones. "Oh, well, I, a— I hadn't planned to, then Garrett told me he had to go somewhere today, so I was alone, and I just thought—"

"Jesus, Hannah," Paul grumbled. "People are trying to be helpful. Do you have to give them the third degree?"

"I wasn't!"

He ignored her protest. "Did you save the world while you were out?"

His sarcasm stung. Down the hall behind her the phone rang. "I think I'll go change clothes."

As she backed out into the hall, the BCA agent caught her attention. "Dr. Garrison? Please take the call in the family room."

"Call?"

The phone chirped again and she hurried to the family room, unable to scrape together much hope. It was probably yet another reporter. Paige Price had been after her to do an in-depth interview. Heartless vampire. Didn't these people realize what it was to hurt, to be afraid? Didn't they realize their morbid curiosity only made things worse?

She snatched up the receiver. "Hannah Garrison."

The static of a bad connection crackled over the line. Then came the voice, small and so soft she had to strain to hear it.

"Mom? I want to come home."

CHAPTER 19

DAY 4
9:55 P.M. 13°

They traced the call to a phone booth outside the Suds Your Duds laundry sixty-five miles away in the small, quiet town of St. Peter, home of Gustavus Adolphus College and the state's maximum security institution for the mentally ill. The phone, its receiver dangling, was on the end of the building—a dreary little strip mall built in the sixties when blond brick and flat metal awnings were considered in good taste. Also occupying the shopping center was a small appliance repair service shop that was closed Saturday afternoons, a Vietnamese grocery where English was not even a second language, and the Fashion-aire Beauty Salon, where the wash-and-set crowd got their beehives teased and their white hair dyed blue.

None of the patrons at the grocery wanted anything to do with cops. All the customers of the beauty salon wanted in on the action. Unfortunately, none of them had seen anything. Aside from being at the opposite end of the strip mall from the Suds Your Duds, the heat from the bonnet hair dryers and the mist from the rinse sinks combined to completely fog over the front windows of the shop. In the laundry two college students and three mothers of sticky-faced, wide-eyed toddlers answered all questions asked. But there were no windows looking out on that end of the building and there was no reason to go out into the cold to use the phone because there were two inside the laundry.

No one had seen Josh. No one had seen a light-colored van. For the cops, the wave of hope crashed and washed back out on yet another tide of disappointment.

"It could be a hoax," Mitch said. "Kids playing around. Hannah said she couldn't swear it was Josh's voice."

He sat across from Megan at the fake woodgrain table in her room at the Super 8 Motel. The remains of a mostly un-eaten Chinese takeout dinner cluttered the tabletop. The smell of congealing broccoli and beef almost masked the acrid stink of age-old cigarette smoke that permeated everything in the room. On the nightstand next to the bed, a cheap clock-radio glowed red: 9:57 P.M. Michael Bolton rasped out a song lamenting the demise of a love affair on the airwaves of the only station that would come in.

Megan flicked a chunk of almond chicken across her paper plate with her fork. "I'd say I can't believe anyone would be that cruel, but then, that would sound stupid, wouldn't it?"

"I don't know," he said quietly. "Is it stupid to wish for small mercies? Crime is one thing, expecting ordinary people to be decent to each other is something else. If we can't even hope for that . . ."

"It gives me the creeps that that call came from here," Megan admitted. "I keep thinking about some of the people in that state hospital and my skin crawls. Sexual psychopaths, the criminally insane . . ."

"But they're *in* the hospital," Mitch said. "Not out. The county sheriff checked with the administration. They had no reports of anyone missing. They had no day passes issued to anyone we would have to worry about. That the call came from here and the hospital is here is just a coincidence. One thing we know for certain," Mitch continued. "Olie Swain didn't make the call. No less than fifty people can swear he was at the ice rink at the time the call came in."

"That doesn't mean he's not involved," Megan said stub-bornly. "It means he might not be in this thing alone. We've considered that option—that he *was* at the rink at the time of the kidnapping and someone else was driving his van."

"Helen didn't ID the van," he reminded her.

"Helen is confused and upset and couldn't tell a Ford from a Volkswagen if the fate of the nation depended upon it."

The heater kicked in with an angry growl and blasted hot, dry air, recirculating the aroma of stale smoke.

"It could have been a tape recording," Megan offered.

They had been over this ground enough to wear a trench into it. All afternoon and half the evening, while the St. Peter cops did a sweep of their city streets and the boys from the BCA mobile lab went over the phone booth with a fine-tooth comb, they had speculated and hoped and muttered threats they would never make good on. And still there was a need to chew that same bone with the hope of getting something out of it.

The choppers had been called out again. The original search area had been widened to include portions of Nicollet, Le Sueur, and Blue Earth counties. Search teams of county and municipal law enforcement agencies and local volunteers began a new ground search. Fliers with Josh's photo went up everywhere, in every store, on every light pole, on every bulletin board in every restaurant and bar.

The press had been there to record it all for the evening news. The frantic rush to grab the new lead. The desperate hope that limned every face of every cop and edged every question asked. A fresh lead brought a fresh rush, like speed in the bloodstream. It sent expectations soaring up from the depths of despair. It deepened the cold, it amplified the ticking of the clock that marked the hours a child had been gone from his family. And in the end it left them lost, struggling and wondering.

"Hannah said it was a bad connection. McCaskill told me it could have been a tape," Megan said. "The boys in the sound lab will be able to tell. They're the best."

"And if it was a tape," Mitch mumbled, "the question is, why?"

They both knew the answer. Neither of them would say it. If the perp used a tape of Josh's voice, it was likely because he couldn't use Josh himself. Mitch dug a roll of Maalox tablets out of his shirt pocket and thumbed off three.

"Why call at all if not to make a ransom demand?" Megan asked.

The threat of a migraine had settled in behind her right eye like a hot coal, stubbornly defying the Cafergot she'd taken half an hour earlier. She needed something stronger, but anything stronger would knock her out, and she needed to think. She rubbed her forehead and stared down at the mess on her plate until it blurred into a mosaic of earth-toned colors.

"If this was the perp calling and all he did was play a tape of Josh asking to come home . . . That's taunting. That's just pure cruelty. And it's personal. He's jerking Hannah and Paul around for kicks. That seems personal."

Mitch shrugged. "Or it's power. Part of his game—like leaving that notebook on the hood of my truck. He's the kind of guy who pulls the wings and legs off flies and thinks it's funny."

"A game," Megan whispered. She didn't want to think that was the mentality of the person they were dealing with, because if it was, things were likely to get worse. "Why would anyone pick on Hannah and Paul? They don't seem to have an enemy in the world."

"What difference does that make?" Mitch snapped, too tired to keep the bitterness from his voice. "You think bad things don't happen to good people?"

Megan winced. "That's not what I meant."

She thought of reaching out to touch his hand. A simple gesture that was against her nature. She never reached out. If she did, she could be pushed away. It was smarter to keep feelings buried deeply. She had let her guard down last night, but last night was over. The new day brought a fresh vow: no cops, no chiefs of police.

"We should call it a night," she said, pushing to her feet.

Mitch watched as she fluttered around the table like a hummingbird, gathering the dirty plates and plastic silverware. The woman who burned like fire in his arms last night had transformed at dawn. All the passion, all the softness, had been zipped back up inside this woman with the slicked-back hair and unsmiling mouth. This woman of the baggy corduroy slacks and baggier sweater, who hid her femininity like a guilty secret.

He watched her as she stuffed the garbage into a wastebasket the size of a shoebox, her movements jerky and quick, her body language snapping that she didn't want his scrutiny. She was the first woman he'd slept with in two years who hadn't wanted to cling to him when it was over. He almost smiled at the irony. He had spent the last two years ducking the attentions of women who wanted more from him than he had to give. Megan wanted nothing from him, and his strongest urge at the moment was to pull her into his arms and make love to her. A curious puzzle, but for once he had no desire to take it apart and figure out the mystery.

". . . and I thought, if nothing goes down tonight," she rattled on, "I'd go up to St. Paul tomorrow. I should look in on my dad and I could stop at headquarters and see if I can't grease some wheels with the sound guys. Ken Kutsatsu likes to work Sundays. If he's in, maybe I can talk him into listening to our tape. And I could see if they've turned anything up on the notebook, though I'm not too hopeful. I also thought I'd try to see Jayne Millard—she does our suspect profiles. Maybe she can give us an edge somewhere."

"You talk about your father," Mitch said casually, rising from his chair, slowly twisting sideways to stretch the tightness out of his back. "You never mention your mother. Is she around?"

Wrong question. Her face closed down defensively. "I wouldn't know. She left when I was six. I never saw her again."

She threw the pronouncement between them like a gauntlet, as if she dared him to make something of it. Mitch frowned. "I didn't mean to pry. I just . . ."

Just what? *Wanted to know more about you. Wanted to know what makes you tick. Wanted to get close to you on a level I have no business thinking about.* Even as he told himself that, another part of his mind was busy fitting this new piece into the Megan O'Malley puzzle. He could picture her too easily—small and alone, too serious, trying not to draw any attention to herself; a little girl with big green eyes and long dark hair, trailing after her father the cop. The way Jessie trailed him.

"You and your dad must be close."

She smiled. Not the warm smile of pride and affection; the brittle smile at a bad joke. "It's late. Let's call it a day."

He caught her arm as she tried to walk past him. "I'm sorry if I said the wrong thing."

"You didn't," she lied, knowing the truth would be far too complicated and too messy to deal with tonight. "I'm tired, that's all." In a cool voice, she added, "I believe your room is across the hall, Chief."

She tried to pull away, but Mitch held on, annoyed with her for trying to give him the brushoff, annoyed with himself for wanting to break down her defenses. If he had any sense, he would take their one night of great sex and let the rest go. He didn't need the headache of a relationship, especially now. And he didn't need a woman with a chip on her shoulder the size of New Zealand.

But he didn't let her go.

"I know where my room is," he murmured. "I'd rather stay here."

"And I'd rather you didn't."

He narrowed his eyes in speculation. "Do you mean that, or is this more of the tough-cookie act?"

"It's not an act," she snapped, glaring at him, praying he wouldn't see the lie through the defiance.

"You can't pretend we haven't already crossed the line, Megan," he said softly.

"Maybe it would be best if we did."

"Why? What are you so afraid of?"

The answer came readily, but she refused to give it to him. She was too good at protecting herself to make that mistake.

This time he let her go when she stepped back from him, though she felt his narrow gaze on her as tangibly as his touch.

"Look . . ." Glancing down at her sweater, she scraped at a spot of dried garlic sauce with her thumb. "It just complicates things, that's all. I mean, I can't be effective at my job if you don't respect me—"

"I respect your authority on the job—"

She strolled around behind the table with her hands on her hips, casually putting distance and furniture between them. "Really? You've had a funny way of showing it."

"I don't treat you any differently than I treat any of my men," he said, stalking her.

"You try to get Noogie to go to bed with you? That's an . . . *adventuresome* lifestyle for a small-town cop."

"Goddammit, don't be flip," he growled, rounding the table. "You know what I mean."

Megan stepped away from him. "Sure I do. Just like I know that if I have an affair with you, when it's over, everything will be awkward and there'll be resentment to deal with and my reputation will be damaged—"

"You're making some pretty ugly assumptions about my character."

She stopped and held her ground, looking him in the eye, jaded and tough because that was how she had survived. "I can't afford not to."

"And why is that?" he asked, his mouth twisting with derision. "Is the job that important to you—that you don't trust anyone, that you give your whole life to it? Jesus, what kind of life is that?"

"It's all I have."

The instant the words were out, she wanted them back. She bit her tongue, but it was too late. They were out there, hanging in the air to be absorbed and digested by Mitch Holt. She felt as if she had torn a chunk out of her soul and tossed it to him, and she knew she could never get it back.

God, how stupid. How could you be so careless, O'Malley?

Appalled at her blunder, she turned her back to him and hoped he would have the good grace to simply leave. She didn't want his pity or his ridicule. She wanted him gone. She wanted to turn the world around and start this damned week over. Pain cut through her head like the blade of an ax, sharp enough to bring tears to her eyes. The last thing she would do was cry in front of him. And so she held her breath against the need to cry and held her muscles stiff against the aching weariness that pulled at her.

Mitch stared at the back of her head, at the uncompromising, rigid set of her slender shoulders. He called himself a bastard for picking a fight with her. The job came with its own kit for building walls of isolationism. He knew. He had walls of his own and he'd seen plenty of other cops put them up brick by brick. He understood the protection they afforded. He of all people should have respected them, but he didn't want walls between him and Megan. He wanted what they had found last night—mind-numbing passion . . . the comfort of holding each other.

She tensed even more as he settled his hands on her shoulders. He stood close behind her, bent his head down close to hers, close enough that he could catch just the faintest hint of perfume on her skin. The scent was so soft, so thin, it seemed almost imagined, as if she put on just enough that only she would know, as if it were only for that secret self she kept so carefully locked inside—the soft Megan, the feminine Megan, the Megan who liked pink walls and flowered sheets and little china statues of cats.

He let his hands slide down from her shoulders and slipped his arms around her. She held herself as straight as a post, unforgiving, unyielding, unwilling to surrender any more of her pride.

"The job is the job," he murmured, his lips brushing the side of her neck. "What goes on between us in bed has nothing to do with it. It's a rotten night, a rotten case, a rotten motel— why can't we at least have this? Hmm? Why can't we give each other a little pleasure?" He flattened his hands against her belly, his fingertips massaging subtly, awakening the fire inside her.

"Just go," Megan said. She didn't want his tenderness. Anything else she could have fought off, but she had no defense against tenderness. God help her, she couldn't defend against something she'd craved all her life.

"Go," she said on a trembling breath.

"No," he murmured, tracing the tip of his tongue behind her ear.

She called on anger to save her. "Go!" she shouted. "Get out!"

"No." He pulled her so close against him she couldn't hurt him and she couldn't escape him. "Not now. Not like this."

"Damn you," she mumbled against his chest, her voice breaking as the tears fought for release and the frustration choked her. She struggled against him, tried to kick him, but her heart wasn't in it.

He tipped her chin up so she had no real choice but to look at him. "Look me in the eye and tell me you don't want this," he said darkly, his breath coming harder as desire pooled warm and heavy in his groin.

Megan glared at him, hating the way her body was heating and humming with awareness pressed to his. "I don't want this," she said defiantly.

His nostrils flared. Amber fire flashed in his eyes. "Liar," he said, but he let her go.

Megan stood at the foot of the bed for a long while after

the door clicked shut, knowing what he'd said was too true for comfort.

DAY 5
12:11 P.M. 16°

"Mick says he'll make a hundred thou this year."

"Good for Mick." *And did you ask your loving son why he never sends you a dime of it when he knows you eat beans and wieners twice a week because your pension check doesn't stretch and your daughter—who pays half your bills—is just a cop and doesn't get paid shit compared to a hotshot investment broker from L.A.?*

Megan didn't ask the question. She knew better. They had played out that scenario more than once. It didn't ease her own resentment. It only got Neil's blood pressure up. Yet it never ceased to amaze her that the child her father still doted on and bragged about could care so little, while she, the unwanted reminder of the faithless Maureen, the child who could have grown up alone in an alley somewhere for all Neil O'Malley cared, was the one who remained behind, chained to memories she hated by a man who had never loved her.

As if it would take her mind away from the memories, she looked around the tiny kitchen with the garish turquoise walls and the checked curtain that was stiff with the starch of age and airborne grease. She hated this room with its cheap, chipped white tin cupboards and enormous old dingy cast-iron sink. She hated the smell of lard and cigarettes, hated the gray linoleum and the chrome-legged table and chairs where her father sat. It was an ugly place, stripped bare of life and warmth—not unlike her father himself in some ways.

Not that Neil O'Malley was physically ugly. His features were sharp—had once been handsome—and his eyes were a brilliant blue. But time and bitterness had stolen their sheen as they had stolen the color from his hair and the vigor from his body. The man she remembered as a small block of muscle in a cop's blue uniform had shrunk and sagged. His right hand quaked as he raised his drink to his lips.

Megan stirred the thick roux in the Dutch oven on the old gas stove. Lamb stew. The same thing she always made when she came to visit on Sundays—not because she liked it, but because Neil would grouse about anything else. God forbid she should do something to displease him. She sniffed at that. She had never in her life done anything that *pleased* him.

"Have you talked to Mick lately?" she asked. *Of course not. Mick doesn't call you, even though he knows what it would mean to you. He hasn't visited since the year the NCAA basketball tournament finals were held in the Metrodome and he managed to weasel a ticket out of a wealthy client from L.A.*

"Aw, no." Neil waved it off as if her question were nothing more than a cloud of bad gas. "He's busy, you know. He damn near runs that outfit he works for. Probably would if it weren't for the goddamn Jews—"

"You want a refill on that beer, Pop?" She had no desire to hear for the millionth time his anti-Semitic diatribe or his anti-Black diatribe or his anti-English diatribe.

He lifted the bottle of nonalcoholic brew and grimaced at it while he hacked up a rattling glob of phlegm. "Christ, no. This stuff tastes like shit. Why don't you bring me something decent to drink?"

"Because your doctor doesn't want you drinking at all."

"Fuck him. He's a fucking fascist. He's not even American, y'know." He pulled a cigarette from the pack of Kents on the table and shook it at her. "That's half of what's wrong with this country. They let in too many goddamn foreigners."

"And where did *your* father come from?" The sarcasm slipped out against her better judgment, but she couldn't help herself. If she held it all in, she figured she would die of something akin to uremic poisoning.

"Don't get smart with me," Neil warned. "My da was Irish and proud of it. He'd'a stayed in Connemara if it weren't for the goddamn Brits."

He lit the cigarette, sucked in a lungful of smoke, and went through the ritual choking and hacking. Megan shook her head in disgust. His arteries were in worse shape than the seventy-year-old water pipes in the house—clogged with the crud of sixty-some years of fat, cholesterol, tar, and nicotine. It was a pure wonder a drop of blood made it to his brain—which, she supposed, could explain a lot. He had already suffered one small stroke, and his doctor warned that the big one was imminent if Neil didn't change his lifestyle. The doctor could have saved his breath on the antismoking speech as well. Despite the warning signs of lung disease, Neil went on with his habit as if he thought the congestion and shortness of breath were merely incidental to his smoking.

"You shouldn't smoke, either," Megan grumbled, hefting the stew pot off the stove and carrying it to the table.

"And you, girlie, should mind your own goddamn business."

She made a rude noise. "Don't I wish."

She stared down at the stew she had dished herself and pushed the plate away. She hated lamb. Her father chewed vigorously and sopped up a puddle of gravy with a chunk of butter-coated bread.

"So, have you heard about the big case I'm working, Pop? That child abduction down in Deer Lake?"

"World's full of perverts."

"It's a tough one. Hardly any leads at all. We've been working practically around the clock—my guys from the bureau, the sheriff's department, the police department. The chief is an ex-detective from the Miami PD. We've even got a team of computer experts from Harris College working on it."

"Worthless boxes of wire," he grumbled, forking up another cube of lamb. "They can't match good old-fashioned police work. Footwork—that's how cases get solved. And not by a bunch of college-boy pricks-up-their-butts detectives, either."

"I'm the agent in charge, you know," she went on doggedly. "There was an article in the *Tribune*. You might have read it."

Good for you, honey. I'm so proud of you. . . . Yeah, right.

Neil looked down at his plate, spit out a piece of gristle, gave a muffled snort, and shook his head. "Worthless rag. I take the *Pioneer Press*. Always have."

"God, would it kill you to say something nice to me just once?" she snapped, knowing it wasn't worth the effort. "Would it be so hard? I'd settle for anything, you know—'congratulations,' 'good stew,' 'nice shoes.' Even a noncommittal hum would do," she said sarcastically. "Anything to keep me from wondering why in hell I bother to come here. Do you think you could manage that just once, Pop?"

Neil's face flushed an unhealthy shade of maroon. He shook his fork at her, flinging little specks of gravy onto the table. "You watch that smart mouth, girlie. You're just like—"

She cut him off with a violent wave of her hand. "Don't you dare. Don't you *dare*! I'm *nothing* like her. She had the good sense to leave you twenty-six years ago!"

Her father's mouth tightened into a knot as he stared at his plate.

With angry tears stinging her eyes, Megan shoved her chair back from the table and went to stare out the window at Mrs. Gristman's backyard, where her ancient poodle, Claude, had dotted the snow with little piles of shit. The neighborhood was drab and ugly, like everything about this house was drab and ugly. She wished she could stop coming back here, but she wouldn't. Because he was her father, her responsibility. She wouldn't shirk her duty to him the way he had done to her.

Unbidden, unwanted, an image of Mitch came to her. Mitch and Jessie, teasing and tickling over a Happy Meal at McDonald's.

She sniffed and wiped her nose on the back of her hand. She said nothing as she pulled her coat off the hook by the back door, giving Neil a chance to redeem himself. He didn't. He never would.

"Don't forget to take your medication," she said tightly. "I'll get back when I can . . . for all you care."

CHAPTER 20

DAY 6

7:00 A.M. -18° WINDCHILL FACTOR: -55°

Monday morning dawned rudely with a blast of air sweeping down from the Arctic and bringing a temperature of eighteen degrees below zero. A howling wind out of the northwest chased the windchill factor to a brutal minus fifty-five. Megan's spirits dropped in direct correlation. She lay in her bed at the Sheraton, dreading her meeting with DePalma, listening to the radio disc jockeys delight in telling Twin Citians that exposed skin could freeze in as little as sixty seconds.

Sunday had been a bust all the way around. Preliminary tests on the tape of the phone call had been inconclusive. No usable prints had been lifted from the notebook. Dinner with Jayne Millard, the agent who worked up suspect profiles, had netted Megan nothing but commiseration for having so little to go on and congratulations for breaking the glass ceiling that had heretofore kept women out of the field.

She lay in bed, staring at her reflection in the mirror above the dresser, thinking about the way some people perceived her as a heroine and others as a troublemaker. She felt curiously removed from the issue, as if the Megan O'Malley those people were looking at were nothing more than a hologram. She didn't want to be their champion or their demon. She wanted to do her job. She wanted to find Josh.

Hung over from fatigue and muscle relaxants, she dragged herself out of bed and into the shower. She dressed for her meeting with DePalma in the one change of clothes she'd thrown into the car—a pair of slim charcoal trousers and a soft black turtleneck that emphasized her pallor and the dark circles under her eyes. She thought she looked like a zombie or a coffeehouse refugee, but there was no hope for better.

She fantasized about an FBI assignment in Tampa as she zipped her parka, clamped on earmuffs, and wound her scarf around her head and neck. Florida shimmered in her mind like a distant mirage that was swept away the instant she stepped outdoors and the wind hit her like a brick in the forehead. No less than a dozen cars in the parking lot had their hoods open—the northland symbol of surrender—waiting for service trucks to show up and jump dead batteries. Two minutes later, Megan popped the hood on the Lumina and stomped back inside the hotel, muttering her cold weather mantra. "I *hate* winter."

9:00 A.M. -18° WINDCHILL FACTOR: -55°

DePalma paced behind his desk with his hands on his hips and his head ducked down between his shoulders. He looked like Nixon doing Ed Sullivan.

"We've never had so many calls from the press," he said, wagging his head.

"I'm a curiosity," Megan pointed out. She stood on the opposite side of the desk. He hadn't asked her to sit. Bad sign. "They'll get over it. Pretend I'm no big deal. *I* shouldn't be a big deal. Their focus should be Josh, not me."

"You made it difficult for them to ignore you, interrogating the father in front of them."

"I asked him a few questions. He lost his temper, that's all—"

DePalma wheeled on her, incredulous. "That's all? Megan, the man has lost his son—"

"He deliberately withheld information from me! The man is holding something back. What am I supposed to do—act like a lady and shut my mouth or act like a cop and do my job?"

"You don't do that kind of a job with the press within shouting distance, and you damn well know it!"

Megan clamped her mouth shut. There was no weaseling out of this. She'd blown it with Paul Kirkwood. She wanted to say Paul Kirkwood had blown it for her, but life didn't work that way. Take no shit, make no excuses. She should have seen the potential for trouble, but she'd let her temper get the better of her. A good agent didn't do that.

"Yes, sir," she murmured.

DePalma sighed as he slid into his high-backed chair. "Whether you like it or not, you've got a great big magnifying glass on you and this case, Agent O'Malley. Watch your step and watch your mouth. You're a good cop, but no one's ever accused you of being overly diplomatic."

"Yes, sir."

"And for God's sake, don't bring up that sexual harassment business from last fall. The superintendent about had a stroke—"

"That's unfair," Megan charged. "I did *not* bring that up. It had nothing to do with me. Henry Forster opened that can of worms on his own—"

DePalma waved off her protest. "It doesn't matter. We're all under scrutiny. If you can't handle the pressure or your own temper, I won't have a choice; I'll yank you in."

He let that hang for a moment as he slipped on a pair of half glasses and glanced at the top page of a mountain of paperwork neatly stacked beside the spotless blotter. Megan drew a breath to ask permission to leave, and he looked up at her, the expression on his bloodhound face softening.

"Do you have anything at all?"

"Puzzle pieces. Nothing fits yet."

His dark eyes strayed to the photograph of his sons. "Make them fit. Make this case, Megan. Make it stick."

11:13 A.M. -20° WINDCHILL FACTOR: -48°

The weight of DePalma's ultimatums pressed down on Megan as she slipped into the law enforcement center via a little-used side door. The press were starved for any scrap of news on the phone call and she had none to give them. After her dressing-down, she wished fervently she could become invisible to media people, but she knew the only successful vanishing act around here was Josh Kirkwood's and it was her job to make him reappear.

The lingering aroma of cigars and air freshener hit her like an invisible wall when she let herself into her office. She made a mental note to buy an air-filtering gizmo.

The message light on her answering machine was flashing like a strobe. She hit the playback button, then unwound the scarf from her head. Paige Price wanted to do an interview.

"When pigs fly," Megan muttered, prying off her earmuffs.

Henry Forster wanted a comment on the recorded phone call.

"Yeah, I'll give you a comment, you myopic old sack of shit," she growled, unzipping her parka.

"Agent O'Malley, this is Stuart Fielding at NCIC. Please call me back ASAP. I've got a hit on your fingerprints."

Olie Swain's prints.

"Jesus, Mary, and Joseph," she whispered, her heart kicking into high gear.

She flung the parka in the general direction of the coat rack as she dove into her broken chair and grabbed the telephone receiver. Her whole body trembling, she punched in the number for FBI headquarters in Washington. Even her voice shook as she went through the usual rigmarole with receptionists. Finally, Stuart Fielding himself came on the line.

"Sorry it took so long for the search, but we couldn't get a match on the name or the prints in your geographical region. We had to enlarge the parameters of the search repeatedly. Finally got a hit in Washington State. Are you ready?"

"You can't know how ready. Shoot."

"According to AFIS and the criminal history database, your guy is Leslie Olin Sewek. Born October 31, 1956. Served five years out of ten in the state facility at Walla Walla and was paroled on his birthday in 1989."

"What was he in for?" Megan held her breath.

"He was convicted on two counts of child molestation. I'll fax you his rap sheet."

Megan was vaguely aware of thanking Fielding and hanging up the phone. Her eyes burned as she stared at the notes she'd taken.

> *Olie Swain: AKA—Leslie Olin Sewek*
> *5 of 10—Walla Walla*
> *Child molest*

Olie Swain had a light-colored van.

Olie Swain had access to Josh.

Olie Swain was a convicted pedophile.

"Gotcha, you son of a bitch."

After receiving the fax she bolted out of her office and charged down the hall, weaving around officers and secretaries and citizens who had come in for reasons unknown. Heads snapped her way as she cut through the squad room and down the hall to Mitch's office. Natalie whirled around from her file cabinets, clearly affronted that anyone would have the temerity to barge into her stronghold.

"I have to see the chief."

"He's with the sheriff—"

Megan didn't even slow down. She burst into the inner office, eyes bright, color high on her cheekbones. Not sparing Russ Steiger a glance, she marched up to Mitch's desk, tossed down the curled tube of thermal paper that was the faxed pages of Olie's rap sheet, and slammed a small hand down beside it.

"Your harmless Mr. Swain is a convicted pedophile from the state of Washington."

Mitch stared at her, stunned, dread coiling in his gut. "What?"

"Leslie Olin Sewek, a.k.a. Lonnie O. Swain, a.k.a. Olie Swain, was sentenced to a state penitentiary in 1984 for forced sex with a nine-year-old boy."

"Jesus, no."

Mitch sat perfectly still in his chair. He'd had no way of knowing Olie Swain was anything other than a strange little man who worked at the ice rink. And still he felt responsible. This was his town. It was his job to protect the people of Deer Lake. And all this time a child predator had been living right under his nose and he hadn't suspected a thing. A pedophile had been working in proximity with children, and he had allowed it.

"How the hell did you get his prints?"

Megan had the grace to look sheepish, though she turned her back on Steiger's scrutiny. "An opportunity presented itself," she fudged. "I had to run him as a nonsuspect, but at least we got him.

"We can't arrest him for our case on the basis of his record alone," she went on, "but there is a bench warrant outstanding in the state of Washington for parole violation. I've already called Judge Witt about a search warrant for the house and vehicle. The rap sheet combined with the witness description of the van and the opportunity Olie had to take Josh gives us probable cause for a search. When we bring him in this time, we can let him have it with both barrels."

She paced in front of his desk, her focus on her plan. "But I was thinking we might want to hold off," she said.

"What the hell for?" Steiger demanded, pushing to his feet from the visitor's chair. "Let's go in and rattle the little shit's cage."

" 'Let's'? As in 'let *us*'?" Megan sneered. "Olie Swain lives within the city limits of Deer Lake. This is a police matter; it's out of your jurisdiction, Steiger."

"Forget that." Steiger glared at her. "This is a multijurisdictional investigation. I'm in on nailing this creep—"

"Well, then, how about *we* prove he did it?" Megan interrupted. "We can set up a surveillance and see if he leads us to Josh. We know Josh isn't at his place. He must have him stashed somewhere. And then there's the question of whether or not he acted alone. We know he didn't make that call from St. Peter or leave the notebook on Mitch's truck. He might lead us to the person who did."

Steiger looked at her as if she'd proposed they all put lampshades on their heads and dance the hokey-pokey. "How the hell are we supposed to do a surveillance on somebody in a town this size? I take a dump at seven o'clock, everybody in Deer Lake knows it by five after."

"That probably doesn't have anything to do with the size of the town," Megan said derisively.

"The house across the street from Olie's place is vacant," Mitch said as he rose from his chair to pace. "Arlan and Ramona Neiderhauser spend the winter in a trailer park in Brownsville, Texas. I can get us into the house."

"And what happens when Olie leaves his place?" Steiger challenged. "There's no way in hell you can tail somebody through Deer Lake without getting made."

"We do the surveillance at night. Use unmarked cars. Stay well back, leave the lights off. If he makes us, we're screwed, but if he doesn't, he might lead us to Josh."

Steiger snorted. "He's a little worm. I say if we roust him, he'll turn over and give us what we want."

"And what if he doesn't?" Mitch demanded. "What if he's got an accomplice? We drag Olie in, the partner panics, and Josh is dead."

He punched his intercom button. "Natalie? Will you please get me Arlan Neiderhauser on the line?" Turning back to the sheriff, he said, "We have to give this a shot, Russ. If it doesn't work, we'll still have the warrants."

"Damn waste of time, that's what it is," Steiger grumbled.

"It's a shot at getting Josh back alive and nailing his abductors red-handed." Mitch checked his watch and did some quick figuring in his head. "Olie's at work from three until eleven. I'll put a man outside the rink right now, just in case. Let's pick our teams and meet in the war room at eight."

Steiger left the office snarling. Megan blew out a breath as he slammed the door shut behind him. "The loose cannon rumbles."

"Fuck him."

"I'll pass, thanks," Megan drawled.

Mitch dismissed Steiger and the remark as he came around the desk. "Good police work, Agent O'Malley. I'm in town two years and I don't get Olie Swain for anything; you're here five days and you prove he's a child molester. Hell, I even ran a check on him. Nothing. Nada. Zippo."

Megan frowned at the self-recrimination in his voice. "He had a valid driver's license in his assumed name and no record. You did your job. I just went a step further—and I may not have except that I saw Olie Friday night and I caught a glimpse of what I thought was maybe a crude tattoo job across his knuckles. I played a hunch that he got it in the joint. It paid off. I got lucky."

"Luck had nothing to do with it," Mitch murmured. "You're a good cop."

The sentiment was hardly intimate, but Megan felt a warm rush of pleasure just the same. The fact that he said it almost grudgingly, that he clearly didn't like being one-upped, made the compliment sweeter.

"Thanks, Chief," she said, trying to sound unaffected.

Mitch didn't miss her embarrassment. The fact that she tried to mask her pride with indifference touched him.

"Why didn't you tell me you had his prints?" he asked.

Megan shrugged, not meeting his eyes. "It didn't come up," she said, unwittingly using the same line he had given her about Olie's van. "I was just playing a hunch. I didn't know anything would come of it." She lifted the glass Mickey Mouse paperweight from his desk and rolled it between her hands like a snowball. "Technically, I suppose I went over your head. Does that mean you get to punch me out now?"

He sat back against the edge of the desk. "I can't be too pissed off since the hunch paid out big-time," he said. "That doesn't mean I have to be happy about it."

She set the paperweight back down with Mickey standing on his head. A frown curved her mouth. "Happy's got nothing to do with this case, Chief."

They hadn't spoken since Sunday evening, when she had called to let him know the lab had nothing for them yet. Neither of them had said a word about Saturday night. It was in his eyes as he looked at her now—remembered hunger and heat. She could feel it just beneath her skin. An unnecessary complication, but there was no going back, and she knew she wouldn't have changed it if she had the chance. Not smart, but there it was.

"How'd it go with DePalma?" he asked.

Megan held her arms out at her sides. "I still have all my limbs."

"And your job?"

She gave him a wry smile. "For the moment. Let's just say if this stakeout pays off, Josh won't be the only one getting saved. So, I'd better get back at it. I thought I'd run by the hospital and talk to the receptionist who called the rink the night Josh disappeared. See if she might be able to do a voice ID of the man she spoke with. If she could ID Olie's voice, then we'd know he took the call and that he knew Hannah would be late. Makes a stronger case for opportunity."

"Good. I'll reach out to the authorities in his old stomping grounds, see if they can give us anything to go on. And I'll call the county attorney and apprise him of the situation."

"Great."

"Megan." He said her name just to say it, then kicked himself for being a sap. The job was the job, he'd said. What went on between them in bed couldn't enter into it—nor should he have wanted it to. "I'm glad DePalma didn't do any damage."

"Nothing wounded but my pride," she murmured. "I'm out of here, Chief. Catch you later."

1:07 P.M. -21° WINDCHILL FACTOR: -48°

I'm sorry. I just couldn't—s-s-s-ah-ah-ah-chew!" Carol Hiatt buried her nose in a handful of tissues and closed her eyes for a moment of weary surrender to the virus that was sweeping through the hospital staff.

"Bless you," Megan said.

The receptionist blew her nose loudly and tossed the tissues into a brimming wastebasket. "This bug is the worst," she confided in a raspy voice. The virus had rendered her hair a wilted mop of dyed-black waves atop a long, oval face. Her ski-slope nose was an angry shade of red. She sniffed and groaned. "I wouldn't be here myself, but the rest of the staff is sicker than I am."

Megan nodded, trying to impart sympathy. Behind her, in the waiting area, a baby and a toddler were crying a discordant duet while a third child pounded out an atonal piece on a Fisher-Price xylophone. *Geraldo* was on the television—adult children of cross-dressing clergymen.

"I'm sorry," Carol said again. "I went through all this with that other officer on Friday. I know I made the call, but it was just nuts here that night. I can't tell you who answered the phone at the rink."

"He didn't identify himself?"

"I don't know any men who identify themselves over the phone. They all just start talking like they think you ought to know who they are, like they think you were just sitting around waiting for them to call," she said with weary disgust. She swiped a fresh tissue under her nose and crunched it into the shape of a carnation.

Megan drew a fat black line through the word *receptionist* in her notebook. "You don't think it might come back to you if you heard his voice?"

"I wish I could say yes," Carol said. She pulled another fist-ful of tissues out of the box beside the phone as her eyes filled and emotional distress tightened her features. "I think the world of Hannah. She's the best person I know. And to think that anyone would just take a little boy and do God knows what to him—"

Carol Hiatt raised a face twisted with anguish. "I'm sorry. I have a little boy of my own—Brian. He's best friends with Josh. They play on the same hockey team. He was there that night at the rink. It could have been him— It's so hard—"

Megan reached across the counter and touched the woman's shoulder. "It's okay," she said softly. "I know you'd help if you could. This was a long shot; don't worry about it."

"*Please* find Josh," the woman whispered. Her plea struck Megan as the voice of every person in Deer Lake. They were all hurting, all stunned. They left their porch lights burning at night with signs on their front doors that said LIGHTS ON FOR JOSH. Because it wasn't only Josh who had been stolen, it was a part of their small-town innocence and trust.

Leslie Olin Sewek had a hell of a lot to answer for.

"We're doing all we can," Megan said.

Walking away from the desk, she spotted the arrow on the wall pointing the way to the cafeteria. She followed it. Maybe caffeine would chase away her headache.

The cafeteria proved to be nothing more than a room with tables and chairs and a row of vending machines. A couple of maintenance guys sat at a far corner table throwing dice and drinking coffee. They didn't even look up when she came in.

Megan fed two quarters into the pop machine and punched the Mountain Dew button. Christopher Priest wandered in as the can rumbled down out of the belly of the machine. The black turtleneck clung to his narrow chest and crept up his forearms. His thin, bony hands looked a foot long sticking out of the too-short sleeves.

"Agent O'Malley." His eyes brightened with surprise behind the big lenses of his glasses. The corners of his wide, lipless mouth flicked upward. "What brings you here? Not that virus going around, I hope."

"No. I'm fine. What about yourself, Professor?"

"I have a student here." He fed change into the coffee machine and ordered himself a cup of sludge with cream and sugar.

Megan popped the top of her Mountain Dew, fished a Cafergot out of her purse, and washed it down with a long swallow, all the while absently watching Priest's attention to neatness and detail as he retrieved his cup and took it to a table. He gingerly wiped the overflow off the side of the cup with a paper napkin, which he folded neatly and placed squarely on the table just to the left of the cup.

"Oh, yeah," she said, sliding down sideways onto the chair to the professor's left. "The kid who was in that car accident the same night Josh was abducted."

"Yes." He sipped his coffee, his eyes straight ahead as the steam fogged over his glasses. "Precisely."

"How's he doing?"

"Not very well, actually. He seems to have developed some complications. They may have to transfer him to a larger hospital in the Cities."

"That's too bad."

"Mmm . . ." He stared off across the room at a particularly colorful poster for the Heimlich maneuver. "Mike was running an errand for me," he said so softly he might have been talking to himself. "For the project concerning perceptions and learning."

"The one Dr. Wright mentioned the other day."

"Yes. Mike keeps saying the road was completely bare and then he hit that curve." He took another sip of coffee, blotted his lips with the napkin. "Life is funny, isn't it?"

"Yeah, it's a laugh riot from where I stand."

He ignored her sarcasm. His curiosity seemed wholly analytical; the question he posed was posed to the world at large. "Is it fate or is it random? What brought Mike Chamberlain to that corner at that moment? What put Josh Kirkwood on that curb alone that night? What put you and me here at the same time?"

"Sounds like questions for the philosophy department."

"Not necessarily. Computer science deals in logic, cause and effect, patterns of thinking."

"Well, Professor," Megan announced as she finished her soda and tossed the can into the recycling bin, "if you and your computer come up with a logical explanation for the shit that happens in this world, I'd like to be the first to know."

CHAPTER 21

Arlan and Ramona Neiderhauser's home smelled strongly of mothballs. The smell wafted up Mitch's nostrils and burned his sinus linings. Sitting in a straight chair he had hauled up from the dining room, he stared through binoculars out the bedroom window at Olie's dark hovel across the street. Lights were on in Oscar Rudd's house, the illumination spilling out onto the junker Saabs parked in his side yard.

Megan stood beside the window, leaning a shoulder against the wall, peeking out from behind the curtain. They both wore their coats—to be ready to run out and to ward off the stale, cold air of the house. The Neiderhausers left their thermostat turned up just enough to keep the pipes from freezing. Outside, the temperature was inching downward, threatening to shatter a record low that hadn't been broken in thirty years. The cold was so extreme that ice crystals had begun to form in the air, creating a phenomenon called snow fog, a weird, thin fog that hung above the ground like a special effect from a horror movie.

Despite the cold, Steiger had opted to remain on the street in an unmarked car. BCA, police, and sheriff's department personnel had been dispatched to strategic locations around town so that no matter which way Olie went, he would be followed. The mobile lab waited at the old fire hall, ready to roll out at a moment's notice to execute the search warrants.

"God, I hate this weather," Megan said, her voice lowered to the hushed tone darkened bedrooms seemed to require.

"Do you know it's going to be warmer at the North Pole tonight than it will be here?"

"You want to move to the North Pole?"

"I want to move to Grand Cayman."

"The steel-drum music would drive you to suicide inside a month."

"At least I'd die warm."

Mitch switched hands on the binoculars and stuck his right one in his jacket pocket to snuggle up to a chemical hand-warmer packet. "You know Olie's got something like five computers in there?"

"Where'd he get the money for five computers?"

"He told me they were castoffs from businesses upgrading their systems. The warden at Walla Walla told me Olie tested high for intelligence. He's always studying something."

"Little boys, for instance."

"Yeah, but Olie's parole officer seemed surprised when I told him what was going down here. He didn't think Olie would get violent."

Megan dropped the curtain and gave Mitch a look. "He was behind bars for forced sex with a child. That's not violent?"

"Force can be coercion. Violence has varying degrees."

"Yeah, well, I read the sheet on this guy. It looked to me like he showed classic signs of escalation—window-peeping, then exposing himself, then fondling, then rape. What'd the boys in Washington have to say for their parole follow-up?"

Mitch shrugged. "Olie's not the first con who skipped."

Megan checked her watch. Nine o'clock. Olie wasn't supposed to get off at the rink until eleven, but they needed to be in place just in case. Her gaze swept the small, cluttered bedroom, lingering on the bed, where they had tossed their two-way radios on the white chenille spread. Walkie-talkies, cops loitering with guns strapped under their armpits and binoculars trained on the house across the street. If this wasn't the most excitement this room had ever seen, Arlan and Ramona were one fun couple.

Mitch's cellular phone bleeped. He set the binoculars down and snapped the phone open. "Chief Holt."

"Daddy?"

The tremulous little voice swept Mitch from one tension to another. "Jessie? Honey, what are you doing up this late?"

There was a sniffle and a hitched breath. "Are y-you gonna c-come and g-get me tonight?"

Mitch's heart crashed. Jessie. He'd forgotten her. There had been calls to make and a meeting with the county attorney. He'd had to pick his team and organize equipment and set up the surveillance points. And in the midst of all that he had forgotten his daughter.

"I'm sorry, honey," he murmured. "No, I can't make it tonight. You'll have to stay with Grandpa and Grandma. It's really important that I work tonight."

"Y-you always s-say that!" Jessie wailed. "I don't like you when you're a cop!"

"Please don't say that, sweetheart." Did the plea sound as plaintive to Megan's ears as it did to his? He hated letting Jessie down. He hated it even more when she blamed his job, because that brought back memories of Allison and the arguments they'd had, the appeals she'd made that had fallen on deaf ears. Guilt wadded into a sour lump in his throat. "I promise we'll have a night together soon, honey. This is just so important. I'm trying to find Josh so he can be with his mom and dad. You know, he hasn't seen them in almost a week."

The line was silent while Jessie mulled this over. "He must miss them," she said softly. "He must be sad. I miss you, too, Daddy." She sounded too old to be five, too disillusioned to be a little girl.

"I miss you, too, baby," he whispered.

Joy came on the line, her voice like a razor in his ear. "I'm sorry we bothered you, Mitch," she said with more rancor than contrition. "Jessie was just so upset, we couldn't get her to settle down. I've told her she shouldn't count on you—"

"Look, Joy." Mitch struggled hard to hold on to his temper. This wasn't the time or place. "I'm in the middle of something here and I have to keep this line open. I'm sorry I forgot to call you. I hope it isn't an inconvenience for Jessie to stay tonight. We'll discuss whether or not Jessie can count on me at a later time."

He broke the connection before she had a chance to cluck her tongue at him. He could see her pacing back and forth in front of their picture window—*I wonder where your daddy is . . . Funny he hasn't called . . .* —working Jessie into a state. Why the hell had he come here of all places after Allison and Kyle had been killed?

To punish himself for life.

Megan stood in silence along the wall, watching him through her lashes. The moment should have been private, but she couldn't just ignore his pain.

"My old man worked second shift so he wouldn't have to spend time with me," she said. "He never once said he missed me."

Mitch looked up at her. Moonlight filtered in through the lace curtain and illuminated her face. The vulnerability she usually guarded so zealously with her pride was the most intimate thing she'd given him yet.

"Jessie's very lucky to have you," she murmured.

Noga's voice came over the two-way and the moment shattered like glass. "Chief! I got him going out a side door. He's headed your way on foot. Out."

Mitch grabbed the radio. "Roger, Noogie. All units—he's moving on foot toward home. Be ready."

Megan crouched at the window. It was impossible to see the path Olie had tramped down between the ice arena and his converted garage home, but he had to round the side of the building to get in. She stared at the corner of the little asphalt-shingled building until her eyes burned and her lungs ached from holding her breath. Finally, Olie Swain appeared with a backpack dangling by one strap from his left hand. He fumbled with his keys, dropped them on the sidewalk, and bent to pick them up. As he straightened, the *TV 7 News* van pulled up in the street.

"No!" Megan shouted, springing to her feet.

"Shit!" Mitch overturned his chair as he grabbed his two-way and bolted for the stairs.

They burst out the front door and into the bitter cold night, one behind the other. Mitch ran ahead, the two-way jammed against his face.

"We're screwed!" he barked into the unit. "And the son of a bitch who tipped the press had better eat his gun before I get my hands on him!"

Olie stood, frozen, horrified. The book bag dropped from his fingers and fell with a muffled thud at his feet. The side door of the *TV 7* van rolled open like the belly of the Trojan horse, and a mob spilled out. A man with a big video camera on his shoulder. Another with a brilliant white light on a long pole. Leading the charge was a woman he had seen on the news and around the ice arena in the past week. She was probably beautiful, he thought, but bearing down on him, she looked like one of his worst nightmares.

They found you, Leslie. You thought you could hide, but they found you. You're so stupid, Leslie.

Cold sweat ran down his body like rain.

The woman thrust a microphone in his face. The light on the pole blinded him. Questions came at him like a hail of bullets.

"Mr. Swain, do you have any comment on the abduction of Josh Kirkwood? Is it true you were convicted of child molestation in Washington? Are you cooperating with the police in this investigation? Was the chief of police here aware of your history of crimes against children?"

They know. They know. They know. The voice chanted inside his head, louder and louder and louder. Until it was screaming. Until he thought his skull would split wide open and his brain would boil out of it.

Mitch Holt came running and put a shoulder into the back of the cameraman, sending him sprawling. The video camera crashed against the side of the house and fell into a snowbank.

Olie's bladder let go and warm urine gushed into his pants, freezing almost immediately on the fabric. He turned and bolted, running nowhere, running because instinct dictated it. His feet churned in the snow of the vacant lot. Beneath the drifts, dead weeds pulled at his boots like fingers reaching up from hell. The cold air sliced at his lungs, each ragged breath like a thousand knives. He flailed his arms like a struggling swimmer, trying to plunge onward. The world seemed to jerk up and down around him, a blur of stars and sky and snow and naked trees. He could hear nothing but the voice in his mind and the pounding of his pulse in his ears.

They know. They know. They know.

Then something hit him hard in the back and he went down with a strangled cry.

Mitch came down on Olie with a knee in the small of his back. He yanked the handcuffs off his belt and snapped one around Olie's right hand.

"Leslie Olin Sewek," he said between gulps of frigid air. "You're under arrest. You have the right to remain silent. Anything you say may be used against you in court. You have the right to an attorney. If you can't afford an attorney, the state will provide one free of charge."

He twisted Olie's left arm up behind his back with enough force to make him cry out and slapped on the other cuff. "Do you understand what I just told you?"

Coughing hard against the ache of cold in his lungs, he pushed himself to his feet and yanked Olie up with him.

"It wasn't me," Olie whimpered. Tears ran down his face. Blood dribbled from a cut on his lip and froze on his quivering chin. "I didn't do anything."

Mitch jerked him around and leaned down into his ugly pug face. "You've done plenty, Olie, but, by God, if you've done anything to Josh Kirkwood, you'll wish you'd never been born."

Olie hung his head and sobbed. A mob had gathered behind his house at the edge of the vacant lot—cops, TV people. They all knew. They knew all about him. They knew his past and they would crush his future with the weight of it.

You'll wish you'd never been born, Leslie.

What none of them knew was that he had wished that already. Every day of his life.

Steiger pulled up in an unmarked Crown Victoria with a blue beacon held on the roof by a seventeen-pound magnet. Cops and *TV 7* personnel scattered as the car roared up the walk alongside Olie's house, narrowly missing the fenders of two of Oscar Rudd's decrepit Saabs. Steiger climbed out, shouting orders.

"Get him in the car! I'll take him downtown." He flashed a stern look at the small crowd, unaware that the video camera had been dispensed with. "Move back, folks. This is police business."

Paige stepped forward, microphone in hand. If they got the audio, they could run it with still shots they had on file and claim technical difficulties on the video. She already had the scoop; that was all that really mattered. "Sheriff, do you believe this is the man who abducted Josh Kirkwood?"

"We'll be questioning Mr. Swain in connection with this case as well as on charges pending in the state of Washington. That's all I can say at the moment."

"How did you zero in on this suspect?"

He looked at her down his aquiline nose. His hair gleamed like a fresh oil slick in the moonlight. "Good old-fashioned police work."

Mitch steered Olie to the passenger side of the Crown Vic and handed him over to Noga. "Put him in your car."

Noogie looked from his chief to Steiger and back. "But, Chief—"

"Put him in the goddamn car and drive him to the station," Mitch ordered. "If Steiger gives you any lip, shoot him."

Noga's brows rose. "Yessir."

"I'll follow you downtown," Megan told the patrolman. She put a hand on Mitch's arm. "Nice collar, Chief. You nailed his ass."

"Yeah?" he muttered, cutting a glance at Paige on the other side of the car. "Well, you ain't seen nothin' yet."

Megan refrained from comment and turned back to Noga. The patrolman clamped a huge gloved hand on the back of Olie's neck and ushered him past Steiger's car and toward the street where green and white cruisers sat in a haphazard cluster with lights flashing like carnival rides. Catching sight of Noga and Swain, Steiger abandoned Paige and hustled after his erstwhile prisoner.

"Hey, Noga! Load him into this car!"

"That's okay, Sheriff," Noogie called. "We can take him. Thanks anyway!"

Down the street, neighbors were peering out their front windows. Oscar Rudd came out of his kitchen door wearing trousers with red suspenders hanging down in big loops, and dress shoes with no socks. Only a grungy thermal undershirt covered his chest and enormous belly. More white hair sprouted out of his ears than covered his head.

"Hey!" he shouted at Steiger. "Get that car off the lawn! And don't you back into my Saabs! They're collector's items!"

Mitch ignored the small circus and went straight for Paige. She held her microphone up in front of her like a cross to ward off vampires.

"Chief Holt, do you have any comment?"

He snatched the mike out of her hand and hurled it twenty feet into a snowdrift, then grabbed the zipper tab of her ski jacket and yanked it down.

"Is that it, Ms. Price?" he snarled. "No body mike? No tape recorder stuck in your bra?"

"N-no," she stammered, stumbling back.

He stayed in her face, matching her step for step. The cameraman attempted to come to her rescue. "Hey, pal, that was an expensive piece of equipment you trashed back there. You'll be lucky if the station doesn't sue."

Mitch turned to him. His voice was eerily soft. "*I'll* be lucky? *I'll* be lucky." He leaned down toward the cameraman until they were nose to nose. "Let *me* tell *you* something, *pal*. I don't care about your fucking camera. You and the ice bitch here have interfered with a police investigation. That's a crime, junior. And if Josh Kirkwood dies because you blew this for us, you're an accessory to murder in my book."

He wheeled back around on Paige. "How would you like to report on that, Paige?" He swung an arm in her direction and bellowed out a cutting imitation of an emcee. "Live from the women's correctional facility in Shakopee—it's Pai-ai-ge Price!"

Paige was shaking with fear and anger. She hated him for scaring her and she hated him for making her feel responsible. "I'm just doing my job," she said defensively. "I didn't make Leslie Sewek into a child molester. I didn't abduct Josh Kirkwood and I won't be responsible for anything that happens to him."

Mitch shook his head in disgust and amazement. His lungs hurt from sucking in too much subzero oxygen during his sprint after Olie. His bare hands suddenly ached with cold, but he made no move to dig his gloves out of his pockets or to zip his coat. For the most part, he felt numb, stunned by the lost opportunity. Olie might have led them to Josh. The woman before him had stolen that chance and didn't even have the grace to apologize.

"You just don't get it, do you, Paige?" he murmured. "This isn't about you. You're nobody. You're nothing. Your job, your ratings, your station—don't mean shit. This is about a little boy who should be home listening to a bedtime story. It's about a mother whose child has been torn away from her and a father who has lost his son. It's real life . . . and it could be real death, thanks to you."

He turned and headed for the lone green-and-white that waited for him with the motor running, exhaust billowing in white clouds from the tailpipe. Paige watched him go, feeling a twinge of conscience for the first time in a long time. She thought she had eradicated it years before, removed it like an unsightly mole from her perfect chin. A conscience was excess weight. While she knew she had colleagues who carried it without complaint, she had always felt the run to the top would be easier without it. Now . . .

She shook the sensation off as she turned to Garcia. "Did you get all that?" Paige asked.

The cameraman pulled a microcassette recorder from the breast pocket of his parka and clicked it off.

Paige glanced at the illuminated dial of her watch. "Let's go. If I hurry, I can still have a story ready by ten."

10:27 P.M. -30° WINDCHILL FACTOR: -62°

Would you like to have a lawyer present at this questioning, Mr. Sewek?"

Olie flinched at the name as if it were a hand reaching out of his past to slap him. The voice in his head shrieked *Leslie! Leslie! Leslie!* like a record with a needle stuck in the groove. He didn't look up at the woman cop who sat across from him.

He could feel her eyes on him, burning with accusation. He could feel it pouring over his skin like acid.

"Mr. Sewek? Are you aware of what I'm asking you?"

"It wasn't me," he mumbled.

His vision blurred as he stared at his hands on the table. He picked at the ratty edges of his fingerless gloves, keeping them carefully pulled over the reminder of his stay in Walla Walla. He could still remember the crushing weight of the biker who had sat on him while a man called Needles dug the letters into the backs of his fingers. He could still remember the harsh laughter as he begged them to stop. The tattoo was the least of what they'd done to him during his five years. Not once had his pleas been answered with mercy, only sadism.

". . . there is a warrant outstanding for your arrest for violation of parole . . ."

They could send him back. The thought sent agony rushing through him like an arrow.

"We know what you did to that boy back in Washington, Olie," Mitch Holt said. He paced back and forth behind the woman, his hands on his hips. "What we want to know is what you've done with Josh Kirkwood."

"Nothing."

"Come on, Olie, don't jerk us around. You've got the record, you had opportunity, you have the van—"

"It wasn't me!" Olie shouted, raising his face to glare at Mitch Holt.

Cops never believed him. They always looked at him like something they had to scrape off their shoe. A piece of dog shit. An ugly bug, squashed and oozing. In Mitch Holt's face Olie saw the same combination of disbelief and disgust he had seen so many times before. Even though he had seen it again and again over the course of his miserable life, he still felt a little piece of him break inside.

He had never meant to hurt anyone.

His lips curled back, quivering, and a strange whine crept up the back of his throat as he gritted his teeth against the urge to cry. He clamped a hand on top of his head and wiped it across his brush-bristle hair, down the port wine stain and over his glass eye. He felt as if his body were being steamed inside his heavy winter clothes. His pants and long underwear clung to him where he'd wet himself. The smell of urine burned his nose.

"Did you have an accomplice?"

"Is Josh all right?"

"Cooperation will make all the difference when it comes to indictments."

"Is he safe?"

"Did you molest him?"

"Is he alive?"

The questions came in a relentless barrage. And between each one the voice shrieked, *Answer me, Leslie! Answer me! Answer me!*

"Stop it!" he cried, slapping his hands over his ears. "Stop it! Stop it!"

Mitch banged his fists down on the table and leaned across it. "You think this is bad, Olie? You want us to stop asking you questions? How do you think Josh's parents are feeling? They haven't seen their little boy in a week. They don't know whether he's alive or dead. Can you even imagine how much they hurt? How bad do you think they want this to stop?"

Olie didn't answer. He stared down at the imitation walnut grain of the table, his head and shoulders shaking. Mitch fought the impulse to grab him by the throat and shake him until his eyes popped out.

"Mr. Sewek," Megan said in a voice like polished marble, "you are aware of the fact that even as we speak, a team of crime-scene experts is conducting a thorough search of your house and vehicle."

"You're going down for the kidnap, Olie," Mitch said tightly. "And if we don't find Josh alive—if we don't find Josh at all—you'll go down for murder. You'll never ever see the light of day again."

"You can only help your situation by cooperating, Mr. Sewek."

Olie put his head in his hands. "I didn't hurt him."

There was a knock at the door and Dave Larkin stuck his head in. His trademark beach-bum smile was nowhere in sight. "Agent O'Malley?"

The formality was almost as alarming as his bland expression. Megan rose and slipped out the door into a narrow hall bleached by harsh fluorescent lights. Phones rang incessantly in the squad room down the hall, where the level of activity belied the hour. Paige Price might have scooped the competition, but everybody wanted a piece of the action before the end of the ten o'clock reports.

"Is he talking?" Larkin asked.

"No. What's going on at the house?"

"Jeez, that place is unbelievable. You wouldn't believe the stuff he's got crammed in there. He must have a thousand books and five or six computers—"

"Laser printer?"

"Dot matrix. But we came across something else I knew you'd want to see right away."

He reached into an inside pocket of his thick down coat and pulled out a plastic bag of snapshots. Megan felt the color drain out of her face as she pulled the photographs from the bag and went through them one by one. There was no way of telling when or where they had been taken. She couldn't identify any of the subjects—all of them little boys in various stages of undress.

Her hands were trembling as she slipped the evidence back into the bag.

"They were in a manila envelope under his mattress," Larkin said. "Flash those and let's hear what tune he sings."

Megan nodded and turned back toward the door.

"Hey, Irish?"

She glanced at him over her shoulder.

"Nail his ass good."

Olie still had his head in his hands when she strode into the interview room. Mitch looked at her expectantly. Without a word she tossed the bag of photographs down on the table.

Olie peered down at them through his fingers and felt the bottom fall out of his stomach.

"What the hell have you got to say for yourself now, Mr. Sewek?"

Olie squeezed his eyes shut. He whispered, "I want a lawyer."

————

Steiger had a ringside seat of the interrogation. The trouble was, he wanted to be *in* the ring, not sitting on the other side of a two-way mirror. Holt and O'Malley had shut him out. It wasn't his case. It wasn't his collar. It was fine for him to spend the last week tramping around in the snow, freezing his balls off for the cause, but they didn't want him in the room for the questioning.

Mr. Hotshot Miami Detective Holt would grab all the glory for himself—what he could wrest away from that pissy little BCA bitch. First female field agent. Big fucking deal. She was nothing but a publicity stunt, the bureau trying to get equal rights advocates off their backs. Holt treated her as if she was a real cop, but he was probably drilling her after hours. Steiger smiled to himself as he thought of how the shit would fly if that kind of news hit the airwaves.

Propping his boots up on the window ledge, he checked his watch and sighed. Twelve-fifteen. The interrogation was fruitless. Swain, or Sewek, or whatever the little turd's name was didn't have anything to say without a lawyer or with one. Ken Carey, the public defender, advised him unnecessarily to keep his mouth shut. Finally, Holt threw up his hands and called the thing to a halt. Olie would be held pending charges on the possession of child pornography, suspicion of the abduction, and on the Washington State warrant. Noga was called in to usher Olie to a cell. The room was vacated, the lights flipped off, end of show.

Steiger stood and stretched, switching on the lights in his theater. He wondered if any reporters were left out in the cold, waiting for a word from someone important.

The door swung open and Holt stepped inside, closing it quietly behind him.

"I thought he would have rolled," Steiger said. "I thought the pictures would have kicked him over. How bad were they? I couldn't see them from here. Were they just naked kids or was there sex involved?"

Mitch narrowed his eyes. "Yeah, that would be a juicy little detail for Paige, wouldn't it? What would she give you for a tidbit like that, Russ?"

"I don't know what the hell you're talking about." Steiger reached for the coat he had tossed over the back of a chair.

"Leslie Olin Sewek," Mitch said carefully. "Only three people knew that name. Only one of us gave it to Paige Price."

"Well, it wasn't me."

"Would you care to look me in the eye when you say that?"

"Are you calling me a liar?" The sheriff didn't wait long enough for an answer. "I don't have to take this from you," he snapped, and started for the door.

Mitch caught him by the shoulder. "You were against the surveillance so you called Paige and gave it to her." He shook his head, his expression sour with disgust. "Jesus, you're worse than she is. You're sworn to uphold the law, not break it. You're supposed to protect and serve the people of this county, not sell them to the highest bidder."

The rage pushed harder, squeezed into his veins. He hit Steiger in the chest with the heel of his hand. "You jeopardized the investigation. You jeopardized Josh—"

Steiger gave a hard laugh. "You don't believe he's alive any more than I do. The kid is dead and—"

The kid is dead.

Instantly Mitch saw the convenience store, the bodies, the blood, the baseball cards in his son's limp hand. He heard the voices of the paramedics.

"Hey, Estefan, let's get 'em bagged and downtown."

"What's the hurry? The kid is dead."

In a heartbeat the walls shattered. The rage poured out. Blinding, wild, burning. His vision misting red, Mitch lowered a shoulder and slammed it into the sheriff's sternum, running him backward like a blocking dummy. Steiger's breath left him with a *whoosh* as his back hit the wall.

"His name is Kyle!" Mitch yelled point-blank into Steiger's face. The sound of his own voice rang in his ears—the fury, the volume, the name. *Kyle . . . oh, sweet heaven.*

Weakness washed through him and he fell back a step, shaking his head, as if the realization had hit him physically and dazed him. Steiger was staring at him, waiting, wary.

"Josh," Mitch said quietly. "His name is Josh, and you'd better believe he's alive, because we're all the hope he's got."

CHAPTER 22

News of Olie Swain's arrest and his secret life swept through Deer Lake like the howling northwest wind. With the help of every television station, radio station, and major newspaper in the state, there was scarcely a person in town who wasn't able to shake their head and bemoan the state of affairs over breakfast. The stories emphasized Olie's past history—"The Making of a Child Predator"—and sensationalized his flight from Washington and the subsequent years spent hiding out in Deer Lake. Much was made of his chameleon ability to hide his true self and live an outwardly quiet life. More was made of the shock and horror of the citizenry at discovering that not only had they had a monster living in their midst, they had let him into close contact with their children.

Mitch and the county attorney held a press conference in a vain attempt to stem the flow of wild gossip. By afternoon there were stories all over town about Olie Swain molesting boys in the furnace room at the hockey rink and exposing himself to children in the city parks and peering in people's windows in the dead of night. There were rumors that horrific stuff had been discovered in the search of his house and van, and rumors that Josh Kirkwood had been found alive, half dead, dead, decapitated, mutilated, cannibalized.

By evening most of the townspeople had been whipped into a frenzy by a tangled mix of truth and fiction. The only thing that kept them from marching to the city jail to demand the head of Leslie Olin Sewek was an inbred Minnesotan aversion to creating a spectacle and a windchill factor of sixty-two degrees below zero.

The brutal cold had virtually brought the state to a standstill. The governor himself had ordered all schools and state offices closed. In Deer Lake, as in most towns around the state, every function, meeting, class, and gathering that could be canceled was canceled due to the dangerous conditions. Still, a group of nearly a hundred people made it to the volunteer center, where Paige Price and the crew from *TV 7 News* were doing a live special report on the case.

7:00 P.M. -29° WINDCHILL FACTOR: -62°

Tonight no police, no one from the sheriff's department." Because Mitch Holt had forbidden any of his people to talk to her and Steiger had thought it best to lay low for a day or two. "Tonight we talk with the citizens of Deer Lake, the small town rocked by the abduction of eight-year-old Josh Kirkwood and by the discovery of a monster in its midst."

She moved between a computer desk and a long table stacked with bright yellow fliers. The people seated at the table in the Josh Kirkwood Volunteer Center gazed up at her. She had chosen slim dark slacks and a cashmere sweater set in a muted shade of violet that brought out her too-blue eyes. A look that was dressy enough to show respect, casual enough to make her seem almost one of the crowd. Her blond hair had been deliberately mussed and carefully sprayed into place, her makeup downplayed.

"Tonight we will listen to the people of Deer Lake, to the volunteers who have given their time, their money, their hearts to the effort to find Josh Kirkwood and bring his kidnapper to justice. We'll speak with a psychologist about the impact this crime has had on the community and about the minds of men who prey on children. And we'll talk with Josh's father, Paul Kirkwood, and get his reaction to the arrest of Leslie Olin Sewek."

7:04 P.M. -29° WINDCHILL FACTOR: -62°

It isn't bad enough that she blew the surveillance," Megan said in disgust when the show broke for a lottery commercial featuring a hibernating cartoon bear. "By the time Paige and her cohorts are finished, there won't be an impartial juror left in the state."

They watched the broadcast on the small color TV that perched on an old oak credenza in the office of assistant county attorney Ellen North. Mitch sat with his back to the set, refusing to look at Paige in her hour of glory. The show was on at Ellen's request. Her boss, Rudy Stovich, may have been the one telling the press they would prosecute the case to the full extent of the law, but most of the work of that task would fall on Ellen's shoulders.

Stovich was more politician than prosecutor. In Mitch's opinion, he was a bumbling idiot in the courtroom, something he could get away with in a rural county, where there wasn't much crime to speak of and not that many attorneys to pick from. The good ones were drawn to the Twin Cities, where there was more action, more money, and more courtrooms. The people of Park County were damn lucky to have Ellen North.

She sat behind her desk, eating a turkey sandwich. Her blond hair was swept back neatly into a tortoiseshell clip. She was thirty-five, a transplant from the judicial system of Hennepin County—or, as Ellen sometimes referred to it, the Magnificent Minneapolis Maze of Justice—where she had a reputation as a tough prosecutor. Tired of the workload, the bureaucracy, the game-playing, and the increasing sense of futility as crime rates in the Cities soared, she had sought the relative peace and sanity of Deer Lake.

"You can bet Sewek will ask for a change of venue," she said, wiping her fingertips on a paper napkin. "And you can bet he'll get it—provided we come up with enough evidence to charge him. Has anything turned up in the search? Possessions of Josh's? Anything in the van—hair, fibers, blood?"

"They sprayed the interior of the van with luminol and

found some bloodstains in the carpet in the back," Megan said. "But at this point we don't even know if the blood is human, let alone Josh Kirkwood's. Trace evidence findings won't be in for a couple of days. We found nothing in the house that can link Olie directly to this crime.

"Early word on the photographs dug up last night is that they're more than five years old. They came from a Kodak instant camera Kodak had to stop making film for in the mid-eighties due to the verdict of a lawsuit brought against them by Polaroid. Which would mean Olie probably brought them with him when he moved here. So far no one has found anything in his books. No one has been able to access the files in his computers; he has all kinds of traps set up in the programming to prevent it."

"And he's not talking." Ellen looked to Mitch. "Can your witness ID the van?"

He shook his head. "Not absolutely."

"Which is as good as nothing." She sipped a can of raspberry-flavored seltzer and shook her head. "We have to hope the lab boys come up with something fast. The public may be ready to convict him, but we don't even have enough to charge him. Unless Paige Price is the judge, we're nowhere with this."

At the mention of Paige's name, Mitch scowled. "Where do we stand in bringing obstruction charges for that stunt she pulled last night?"

Ellen made a face that discouraged hope. "It's been tried once or twice in recent years, but it would be almost impossible to make it stick in this case. We would have to prove absolutely that harm came to Josh as a result of the interference. Media people can wrap themselves in the First Amendment and get away with almost anything. If you could prove collusion between Paige and Steiger, you'd have something, but that's almost impossible unless one of them was stupid enough to tape the conversation or hold it in front of a witness."

"So we've got nothing," Mitch said. The injustice ate at him.

"And Paige Price has the scoop of the week. Again."

Paige slid into a chair beside a heavyset woman with an unsmiling, unpainted mouth and brown hair that had been smashed flat by a stocking cap.

"Mrs. Favre, you told me you had suspicions about the man you knew as Olie Swain long ago. How did you feel when this information about his prior record surfaced?"

"I was furious," the woman said loudly, grabbing hold of the mike and pulling it toward her as if she meant to devour it. "You bet I was. I told the police there was something wrong with him. My boy come home from hockey more than once and told me how Olie was weird and all and acted strange around them boys. And the police didn't do nothing. I talked to Mitch Holt myself and he didn't do nothing. He wouldn't listen to me and now look what's happened. It makes me sick."

Paige took the microphone back and turned to face the camera. "Deer Lake police deny having any prior knowledge of Olie Swain's past life as pedophile Leslie Olin Sewek. City personnel in charge of the Gordie Knutson Memorial Arena also deny any knowledge of Mr. Swain's past. They did not check into Olie Swain's background for a criminal record before hiring him to work as a maintenance man at the ice rink where Deer Lake's children play hockey and practice figure skating."

She rose and walked away from the table, past a computer desk where a Harris College student sat before a color terminal filled with Josh's image. The camera zoomed in on the computer screen, then backed off and swung back to Paige.

"It is important that we make it clear Leslie Olin Sewek has not been formally charged with the abduction of Josh Kirkwood. He is being held in the Deer Lake community jail because of a warrant issued on parole violations in the state of Washington. As of late this afternoon the only evidence gathered implicating Sewek in any crime at all was a packet of sexually explicit photographs involving young boys. Photographs he allegedly brought with him when he came to Minnesota after leaving a Washington State correctional facility.

"Authorities in Columbia County, Washington, are all too familiar with Leslie Sewek. As is the case with the majority of child molesters, Leslie Sewek's record is a long one that began when he himself was little more than a boy. Here with us tonight to talk about the mind of the child predator is Dr. Garrett Wright, head of the psychology department at Harris College." She slid into the vacant chair beside Wright and regarded him with grave interest. "Dr. Wright, what can you tell us about the pattern of behavior in men like Leslie Sewek?"

Garrett Wright didn't look convinced this was a good idea. "First of all, Ms. Price, I want to make it clear that criminal behavior is not my area of expertise. I have, however, studied deviant behavior, and if I can shed some light on the situation and in any way help people deal with it, I will."

"You're a resident of Deer Lake, aren't you, Doctor?"

"Yes. In fact, Hannah and Paul are neighbors of mine. Like most of the people in town, my wife and I are eager to help any way we can. Community support and involvement are very important to all concerned. . . ."

Paige listened with one ear, impatient to get to the juicier stuff, the questions that would keep viewers glued to their sets. Wright might be visually interesting—almost as pretty as she was, and very scholarly in a button-down shirt and blue blazer—but talk of community support was not what she'd had in mind when she had personally coerced him into appearing on the show. She could almost hear the viewing public yawning.

Worse, she could picture the network people yawning. When the news of Leslie Sewek's past record had hit the wires, the networks and tabloid shows had scrambled to get people to Deer Lake. Josh Kirkwood's case was made for television news. And if Paige could pull it off, it was a case that would catapult her to bigger and better things.

"Obviously," Garrett Wright went on, "it helps the victims to cope, but it also helps the rest of us to cope, to feel as if we're taking proactive measures against what is essentially an alien threat to our community—crime."

"And about the crime," Paige interjected smoothly. "There is a fairly consistent story behind men who become child molesters, like Leslie Sewek, isn't there, Doctor?"

"Yes, there seems to be. First of all, pedophiles tend to come from abusive home situations themselves and have strong unmet needs for personal warmth."

"Are you saying we should feel sorry for someone like Leslie Sewek?" Paige asked with perfect indignity. Inwardly, she smiled as the crowd behind her grumbled angrily.

Garrett Wright held up a hand to ward off rebuttal. "I'm merely stating facts, Ms. Price. This is the common background among child molesters; it isn't an excuse to break the laws of society. Nor am I saying this is Leslie Sewek's background. I know nothing about the man. And as you pointed out, we don't know that Leslie Sewek has broken any laws here. We can't say with any certainty that the person who kidnapped Josh Kirkwood is a pedophile. We could be dealing with a very different sort of mind altogether, and frankly, one far more dangerous than the quote *average* unquote pedophile," he argued. The camera zoomed in on his expression of profound concern.

Paige's inward smile stretched wider. "Such as, Dr. Wright?"

Garrett Wright's disapproval was almost a tangible thing. He gave her a long, cool look. "You're playing a dangerous game, Ms. Price. I didn't come here to play Name That Psycho. That kind of conjecture on my part would be inappropriate, to say nothing of ghoulish—"

"I didn't mean to suggest such a thing," Paige interrupted, the internal smile going brittle. *Damn.* "Perhaps you could give us a better understanding of that quote average unquote pedophile?"

Wright relaxed marginally. "Pedophiles often relate better to children than to adults and in most cases they seek to control the child rather than to harm the child," he went on before Paige could jump in with another inflammatory question. "They may truly believe they love children and will often seek employment that will put them in contact with or proximity to children."

"A fact that brings us directly back to Deer Lake and the case of Leslie Olin Sewek," Paige said, abandoning Garrett Wright for her special guest star. "With the shadow of Josh Kirkwood's abduction hanging over this town, the discovery of a convicted child predator at the very ice arena from which Josh disappeared has frightened and outraged the citizens of this quiet community. Certainly no one in Deer Lake has more reason to feel anger at this revelation than Paul Kirkwood, Josh Kirkwood's father."

Paul sat in one of two director's chairs at the front of the room. His brown hair was perfectly combed, the knot of a silk tie perfectly centered above the crew neck of a navy wool sweater he wore over his pinpoint oxford shirt. His deep-set eyes had naturally dark sockets that were emphasized by the camera, intensifying his haunted, angry expression. A great face for television.

Paige slid into the other director's chair. "Paul," she said softly, reaching out to touch his arm. "Again, all our hearts go out to you and your wife, Dr. Hannah Garrison. I understand Hannah is too distraught to join us tonight."

Paul frowned. Hannah had refused to come to the center despite her repeated complaints of not being able to help in the search effort. She found the idea of this program repulsive, exploitative, and mercenary, in no way useful in finding Josh.

The Sunday papers had been splashed with color photographs of her collapsing in the volunteer-center booth and being escorted away by Father Tom McCoy. They painted her a heroine—valiant and courageous, trying to be strong in the face of incredible adversity. The brave, compassionate Dr. Garrison, who had helped so many people. They made little mention of the fact that this whole situation was her fault, that her career had destroyed their marriage, torn their family apart, and driven him into the arms of another woman. Instead, they said that Josh had been abducted while Dr. Garrison was fighting to save the life of an accident victim, turning it all around to make her the object of admiration and pity.

"She's home with our daughter," he said flatly.

Paige looked directly into the camera. "Dr. Garrison, our prayers are with you."

7:30 P.M. -29° WINDCHILL FACTOR: -62°

The television in the family room was on. Hannah could hear it—mumbled voices, changes in pitch, tone, and volume—but she couldn't make out what anyone was saying. She didn't want to. She hated that *TV 7 News* was running the interview, hated that her neighbors and friends would watch it, hated that people she didn't even know would be asked to voice their feelings about the terrible act that was tearing her life apart. She hated that Paul had agreed to be a part of it. That he could so callously discount her feelings was further evidence of the widening rift between them.

There had been a time when he would have found the program as invasive and self-serving as she did. Tonight he had fussed over what to wear and spent an hour in the bathroom getting ready. The thought that she didn't know him anymore whispered through her mind at regular intervals.

She stood in the center of Josh's room because she was too wired to sit. Olie Swain had been arrested but not charged. No official word had come of a confession or clues to Josh's fate. Nothing. Silence. She felt poised on the brink of a high precipice, every muscle, every fiber of her being held taut as she waited to fall one way or the other. The anticipation had built and built until she was certain she would explode from the pressure. But there was no explosion, there was no relief.

She paced the room, her arms wrapped around herself. Even with the thick sweater and turtleneck she wore she felt thin. She was losing weight and, as a doctor, she knew that wasn't good. That professional, practical, intelligent part of her mind told her to eat, to sleep, to get some exercise, but that part seemed to be disconnected from the rest. Emotion ruled. Erratic, irrational emotion.

She tried to think of what it had been like—what *she* had been like—when she had been the calm, rational head of the ER. Cool under fire. A leader. The person everyone looked to in a time of crisis. She tried to remember the afternoon before Josh had been taken. The patients she had treated. The people she had offered comfort and explanations. The precision of the trauma team as she had orchestrated the attempt to save the life of Ida Bergen.

A week had passed. It seemed a lifetime ago.

Squeals of delight came from the living room, where Lily had charmed the BCA agent on duty into playing with her. Hannah swung the bedroom door shut. Here, in Josh's room, she wanted to hear nothing but the silence that waited for his voice. She breathed in the waxy scent of crayons and felt as if one had been driven through her heart. On the small desk lay the photo album she had brought in one of the first days, as if having Josh's picture in there might help conjure him up. She stood over it and looked down at the photographs, each one raising a memory.

The three of them at the beach on the Carolina shore the summer they had gone to visit her parents. The year before Lily was born. Josh riding on his father's shoulders, his arms banded across Paul's forehead, Paul's baseball cap drooping sideways on Josh's head. Josh standing beside a sand castle in a white T-shirt and baggy shorts, his arms spread wide, a bright grin displaying gaps where baby teeth had fallen out. His hair was a tangle of sandy-brown curls, tossed by the same wind that bent the slender stems of spartina and panic grass on the dunes. The ocean was a belt of blue trimmed in lacy white.

The three of them standing together on a jetty. All of them laughing. Hannah wore a filmy summer dress in blue and white. The long skirt whirled around her legs like a matador's cape. Josh was standing on a piling. Paul was hugging him tightly from behind with one arm; his other arm was draped around Hannah's shoulders. Holding them all together. A family. So close, so happy. So distant from here. So far removed from what they had become.

The last picture on the page was of herself and Josh. On a sailboat at sunset. Him sleeping on her lap, her arms cradling him against her. Her eyes were closed as she bent over him. Her hair was blowing over her shoulder. She held him safe while the sea rolled and the wind snapped the sails. Safe and loved.

She could close her eyes and feel the weight of him in her arms. His small body warm against hers. His hair smelled of salt water. His eyelashes curled against his cheek, impossibly long and thick. And she could feel her love for him swell in her chest. Her child. A beautiful little person created and nurtured in love. And she could feel, as she had at that moment, all the hope she had held for him, all the dreams she had dreamed. Perfect dreams. Wonderful dreams.

Dreams that had been snatched away. Josh was gone. Her arms were empty. All she had left were photographs and memories.

A soft knock sounded against the door, startling her. She jerked around as yet another volunteer from the missing children group poked her head into the room. Another stranger from another town she'd never heard of.

"I brought you some hot chocolate," the woman said softly, using the excuse to let herself into the room.

Hannah put her around forty, medium height with curvy hips and no breasts. Her hair was a mop of chestnut curls, and rumpled bangs tumbled over the tops of rimless glasses. Terry something. The names went in one ear and out the other. Hannah made no effort to remember them. They came to offer support, sympathy or empathy, and friendship, but she didn't want to have anything in common with them. Theirs was a club she had no desire to join.

"Your husband is on television," Terry Whoever said as she set the mug of cocoa down on the nightstand. "I thought you might want to know."

Hannah shook her head. Terry made no comment. She stood with her back against the wall beside the door, her hands tucked into the pockets of tan corduroy slacks. Waiting. Hannah told herself again that she didn't want to reach out to this woman, but the warning couldn't penetrate the need to fill the silence.

"They asked me to go on," she said, staring out the window at the cold black night. "I don't want anything to do with it. I won't put what I feel on display for an audience."

The woman didn't chastise her. She didn't say anything, as if she somehow knew there was more. The words tumbled out like a guilty secret.

"People expect me to. I know they do. They expect me to be at the rallies and the prayer vigils and on television. But I don't want to be weak in front of them, and I know I can't be strong. I can't be who they want me to be. Not now." And the guilt from that was another weight added to the burden already crushing her.

"That's all right," Terry said in an unflappable tone. "Don't worry about what anyone else wants from you. You don't have to go on television if it feels wrong for you. We each do what we have to to get through the nightmare. Maybe it helps your husband to go on television."

"I wouldn't know."

Again the silence.

"We're not communicating very well these days."

"It's hard. You do the best you can. Hang on to the pieces of your relationship and worry about putting them back together later. What's important now is just getting through it."

Hannah's gaze strayed to the photo album on the desk, the smiling images of her son. She would have done anything, given anything, to have him back safe. She thought of Olie Swain sitting in a jail cell, thought of the secrets he had yet to reveal, and the unbearable sense of anticipation filled her again. What did he know? What would he tell? And when he told his secrets, would it be over?

"It's not knowing," she whispered. She pressed the heels of her hands against her eyes to hold back the tears, but they came anyway. "God, I can't stand not knowing! I can't stand it!"

Sobbing, she threw herself against the wall and slammed her fist against it again and again, oblivious to the pain. And when the burst of adrenaline was spent, she just stood there pressed against the carefully painted mural of boys playing baseball, and cried. She didn't move when she felt a hand rest on her shoulder.

"I know," Terry murmured. "My son was abducted when he was twelve, on his way home from the movies. We lived in Idaho then, in a town a lot like this one, a quiet, safe place. Not so safe, it turned out. I thought the not knowing would kill me. And there were times I wished it had," she confessed softly.

Gently, she pulled Hannah away from the wall and led her to the bunk beds, where they sat down side by side. Hannah wiped her face on the sleeve of her sweater and struggled to pull herself together, embarrassed that she had come apart in front of this stranger. But Terry acted as if this were the most normal of scenes, as if she hadn't even noticed the outburst.

"He would have been sixteen this year," she said. "He would have been learning to drive, going on dates, playing on the basketball team at school. But the man who took him away from us took him away forever. They found his body in a land-fill, thrown away like so much garbage." Her voice strained and she went silent for a moment, waiting for the pain to ease.

"After they found him there was . . . relief. At least it was over. But when we didn't know at least we had some hope that he was alive and that we might get him back." She turned to Hannah, her eyes bright with tears that wouldn't fall. "Hold on to that hope with both hands, Hannah. It's better than noth-ing."

She's gone through this, Hannah thought. *She knows what I'm feeling, what I'm thinking, what I'm fearing.* The bond was there. That she didn't want it didn't matter; it was there. They shared a common nightmare and this woman was offering what wisdom she had won from the ordeal. It didn't matter that Hannah didn't want to join this club; she was already a mem-ber.

She reached across the bedspread, took Terry Whoever's hand in hers and squeezed it tight.

7:42 P.M. -30° WINDCHILL FACTOR: -62°

". . . and I'm outraged that this sick, perverted animal was not only let out of his cage, but was allowed to work in the same building with my son and the sons and daughters of everyone in this community!"

Applause from the people in the volunteer center made Paul Kirkwood pause. He stared directly at the camera, head up, chin jutting forward, the light in his eyes fanatical. The look seemed to pierce the television screen and travel through the bars of the cell right into Olie's chest. He knew that look, that tone of voice. *You make me sick! You're nothing but a little freak!*

Spawn of the devil, that's what you are! I'll beat some good into you! And the other, shriller voice joined in harmony. *I told you, Leslie! You're good for nothing! Don't you cry or we'll give you something to cry about!*

He huddled into the corner of his bunk, curling up like a frightened animal as the voices ranted on. He had been locked in his own cell in the city jail, a luxurious place as jails went. Mainly empty. The newness of the facility lingered. The walls were white, the hard gray floors polished. Only the vaguest aroma of urine cut through the strong scent of pine cleaners. No smoking was allowed.

In the next cell was the proud owner of the small portable television. A stringy, narrow-eyed character named Boog Newton who was doing three months for repeatedly drinking himself into a stupor and climbing behind the wheel of his four-by-four. In his latest escapade, he had backed into the plate glass display window of the Loon's Call Book and Gift Shop. As the only semipermanent resident in the place, he was allowed amenities.

Boog sat on his bunk with his elbows on his knees, picking his nose, absorbed by Paul Kirkwood's passionate sermon on the failings of the system and the injustices against decent people.

"... I'm sick of turning on the evening news and having to listen to how another child has been raped or murdered or abducted. We have to *do something*. We have to put a stop to this madness!"

The broadcast broke for a commercial on a wave of applause. Boog rose and swaggered over to the wall of iron bars that separated the cells. His face was pitted with acne scars, his mouth twisted into a perpetual sneer.

"Hey, dumbshit, they're talking about you," he said, leaning against the bars.

Olie stood and began to pace back and forth along the far side of his cage, back and forth, back and forth, head down, counting the steps in an attempt to shut the man out. He didn't like men. Had never liked men. Men only ever wanted to hurt him.

"Hey, you know what I'd do if I was a judge? I'd put a bag over your ugly head, give the father of that kid a steel pipe, and lock you in a room together. Let him beat the shit out of you. Let him bash your head in. Let him ream you a new asshole with that pipe."

Olie paced, his hands in his pockets, his breath coming faster and faster.

"Hey, you know what I think they oughta do with freaks like you? I think they oughta cut your pecker off and shove it up your ass. No. They oughta put you in a cell with some nine-hundred-pound no-neck biker and let him put it to you all night every night for the rest of your life. See how you like it."

Olie already knew. He knew what they did to child molesters in the joint. He remembered every excruciating moment, every pain, the sickening fear. He knew what it was to be tortured. Sweat burst out of his pores, sour with the knowledge that it would all happen again. Whether they kept him there or sent him back to Washington, it would all happen again.

"Hey, you're sick, you know that? That's sick, touching little boys and shit like that. What'd you do to that Kirkwood kid? Kill him? They oughta kill you—"

"It wasn't me!" Olie screamed. His whole face was flushed. His good eye bugged out, rolling wildly. He launched himself across the small space and slammed into the bars, pinching Boog's fingers. "It wasn't me! It wasn't me!"

Boog jerked back, stumbling, shaking his stinging fingers. "Hey, you're nuts! You're fucking crazy!"

A shout rang from the end of the hall as the jailer came running.

Olie sank to the floor like a marionette whose strings had been cut, sobbing, "It wasn't me."

CHAPTER 23

Grandma says you put the bad guy in jail and now it'll be easier to breathe," Jessie said as she worked at tying a long, bedraggled red ribbon around Scotch's throat.

The old dog suffered the indignity with good grace, groaning a little and rolling his eyes up at Mitch, who sat on the couch studying the photocopied pages of Josh's notebook, looking for some mention of Olie beyond the one page—*Kids tease Olie but that's mean. He can't help how he looks.* The living room floor was littered with Barbie dolls and their paraphernalia. The television in the oak entertainment center across the room was tuned to a news magazine. As Jane Pauley dished out the headlines, images of the latest L.A. earthquake and a scandal-embroiled figure skater flashed across the screen.

Jessie looked up at Mitch from her seat on the floor. "Why did Grandma say that?"

The first few answers that came to mind were not flattering to Joy Strauss. Mitch bit his tongue and counted to ten. "She meant she feels safer now," he said, turning over a page of carefully drawn spaceships and laying it facedown with the other pages on the coffee table.

And it meant Joy had been given a new needle to stick him with.

"I can't believe someone like him can just be allowed to walk the streets of Deer Lake."

"He wasn't exactly wearing a sign, Joy. He didn't have a big P

for pedophile branded on his forehead. How was I supposed to know?"

"Well, Alice Marshton says police departments have networks that keep track of this kind of person. Alice reads a lot of mysteries and she says—"

"This is real life, Joy, not an Agatha Christie novel."

"You don't have to be so huffy. I was just saying what Alice told me."

She was just saying what more than a few people in town were saying—that they blamed him for Josh Kirkwood's disappearance. He understood that they felt the need to blame somebody. Pointing the finger at a real live person was less frightening than believing they had no defense against what had happened. But that didn't make it any easier to take the abuse. Natalie had fielded angry phone calls all day; the tape on his home answering machine was full of messages from irate citizens.

He continued to let the machine take the brunt of the fury. He had no desire to play whipping boy tonight. He wanted some quiet time with Jessie—even if he had to divide his attention between his daughter and the stack of paperwork he had brought home with him. Joy had clucked about him taking Jessie home on such a cold night, insisting she would catch a virus. Mitch had reminded her they were only going across the alley and told her it was too cold for germs, refraining from yet another futile attempt at explaining how viruses are actually spread. Since he had never worked in the kitchen of the hospital like her friend Ione, Joy had no faith in his medical knowledge.

Finished with the bow, Jessie picked up a brush and began to groom Scotch's back. The Labrador made a sound of contentment and rolled onto his side, offering his belly for this treatment. "Grandma said that man did all kinds of bad things to little kids that only God knows about," Jessie said. "But if God's the only one that knows, then how does Grandma know?"

"She doesn't. She only thinks she knows. No one has proven that man did anything." Mitch felt amazed and vaguely ashamed of himself for defending Olie Swain just to take sides against his mother-in-law.

He turned to another page, this one full of Josh's thoughts about being made co-captain of his hockey team. *Its real cool. I'm real proud, but my Mom says not to brag. Just do a good job. No body likes a bragger.* The next page expressed his displeasure with having to go to religion class in the form of mad faces and thumbs-down signs, God with a long beard and halo, and a devil's scowling face.

"Then how come that man's in jail?"

"Jessie . . ." he said, trying not to grit his teeth. He leaned ahead to brush a hand over his daughter's head. "Honey, Daddy's really tired from this case. Can we talk about something else?"

Guilt nipped him immediately. He had always made a point of being as honest and up front with Jessie as he could. It seemed to him that deflecting a child's questions caused more problems than it cured, but he didn't have the energy for answers tonight. Now that Olie was behind bars, the stress and long hours were hitting with a vengeance. And the worry for Josh's well-being had intensified with the discovery of the bloodstains in the van. They could do nothing but wait for the lab results. Unfortunately, Jessie's idea of changing the subject was not quite what Mitch had in mind.

A page of Josh's drawings caught her eye, and she abandoned Scotch to scoot over to the coffee table on her knees. "Who made these pictures for you?"

"These are pictures Josh made." He ran a fingertip along the crooked line of a forgotten game of tic-tac-toe.

"Can I color them for you?"

"No, honey, this is evidence. Why don't you make me a picture from one of your coloring books?"

Jessie ignored the suggestion. She picked up one of the pages Mitch had already set aside and studied it.

"Did you find Josh?"

Mitch sighed and speared his fingers back through his hair, lifting it into thick spikes. "Not yet, sweetheart."

"He must be sad," she said quietly, carefully laying the drawing down. It showed a boy with freckles and a big hairy dog. *Me and Gizmo.*

"Come here, sweetie," Mitch whispered, opening his arms in invitation. Jessie scrambled around the end of the table and climbed up on his lap. Mitch wrapped his arms around her and pulled her close. "Are you still worried about someone taking you away?"

"A little bit," she mumbled against his chest.

He wanted to tell her not to worry, that he wouldn't let anything happen to her, that nothing bad would happen to her if she followed all the rules. But he couldn't make any of those promises and he hated the sense of impotence and inadequacy that reality gave him. He wished the world were a place where little girls had nothing to worry about except playing with their dolls and dressing their dogs up in red satin bows, but that wasn't the case. Not even in Deer Lake.

He rocked his daughter slowly. "You know, it's not your job to worry, Jess. Worrying is *my* job."

She tipped her head back and looked up at him. "What about Grandma? She worries about everything."

"Yeah, well, Grandma is in a league of her own. But when it comes to you and me, I get to do all the worrying, okay?"

"Okay," she said, trying to smile.

Mitch held a hand out in front of her, palm up. "Here. You crunch up your worry like a piece of paper and give it to me."

Jessie giggled and made a show of pretending to squish her worries into a ball. She plopped the invisible burden in Mitch's hand. He closed a fist over it and stuffed it into the breast pocket of his denim shirt. Scotch watched the proceedings with his head cocked and his ears up.

The doorbell rang and the dog lurched to his feet with a booming bark, tail wagging.

"That'll be Megan," Mitch said, rising with Jessie in his arms.

Jessie stuck her lower lip out. "How come she's coming over? You said I could stay up late 'cause there's no school tomorrow and we'd have fun."

"We've had lots of fun, haven't we?" Mitch said. "But you can't stay up as late as me, so who will keep me company when you go to bed?"

"Scotch."

Mitch growled and tickled her, then sent her into a fit of squealing giggles by swinging her up over his shoulder legs first. He opened the door with a smile and backed into the living room, calling, "Welcome to the monkey house!"

Megan's reluctance couldn't withstand the windchill factor of minus sixty-something. She stepped into the foyer of Mitch's house, closing the door behind her, instantly feeling like an intruder. Mitch was giving Jessie a wild ride around the living room on his shoulders while a big yellow dog gave chase with a Barbie doll in his mouth. No one seemed to notice her standing there swaddled in wool and goose down with a quart of chocolate chip ice cream clutched between her mittens. She wondered if they would notice if she simply backed out the door and went home.

Before she could take a step, however, Mitch came to a halt in front of her and nailed her to the spot with a knowing gaze. With one finger he tugged the scarf down from her face.

"Take your coat off and stay awhile, O'Malley," he said softly.

She gave him a wry smile as she unwound her scarf and draped it over a coat tree. She looked up at the little girl perched on his shoulder. "Hi, Jessie, how are you?"

"I don't have kindergarten tomorrow 'cause it's too cold for brass monkeys. That's what my grandpa says."

"That's pretty cold," Megan agreed, amusement tugging hard at the corners of her mouth.

"So I get to stay up past my bedtime and have fun," Jessie said in a cautionary tone, as if it just might be too much for Megan to deal with.

Mitch rolled his eyes. "Yeah, you get to stay up long enough to have some of this ice cream Megan brought us. Wasn't that nice of her?"

"I like cookies better."

"Jessie . . ." Mitch gave her a stern look as he set her down.

Across the room the phone on the end table rang, the answering machine picked up.

"Mitch? Mitch, can you hear me?" The woman's voice was nearly frantic. "It's Joy. I can see your lights on." She turned away from the receiver and spoke to her husband somewhere in the background. "Jurgen, he's not answering! Maybe you should go over. They could have carbon monoxide poisoning!"

Forcing a weary smile, Mitch heaved a sigh. "I'd better take this." He looked to his daughter. "Jessie, please take Megan into the kitchen and help her get out bowls for the ice cream."

Resigning herself to her fate with a much-put-upon look, Jessie headed for the kitchen. Megan followed dutifully. The dog trotted past them both, the doll in his mouth smiling with one arm raised, as if waving.

"That's my dog, Scotch," Jessie said. "I put that bow on him. I can tie my own shoes and ribbons and stuff. Kimberly Johnson in my class can't tie anything. She has to wear shoes with Velcro and she picks her nose, too."

"Yuck."

"And she eats it," Jessie went on, digging the ice cream scoop out of a drawer crammed with spatulas and plastic spoons. "And she's mean. She bit my friend Ashley once and had to have time-out in the corner all through recess and didn't get to have any of Kevin Neilsen's birthday treats at milk break. And she said she didn't care 'cause they weren't really Tootsie Rolls, they were cat poop." She gave Megan a look. "That wasn't true."

"Sounds like a tough customer."

Jessie shrugged, dismissing the subject. She pulled a chair across the linoleum and climbed up on it to get bowls out of a cupboard. Megan set about the task of opening the carton and dishing out the treat.

"I can eat two scoops," Jessie said, peering over the edge of the tile-topped kitchen table. "Daddy can eat about ten. Scotch can't have any 'cause he's too fat."

Megan's gaze skated around the kitchen, taking in the crayon and fingerpaint masterpieces taped on the wall and refrigerator. They tugged at a vulnerable corner of her heart—their naïveté, their unabashed enthusiasm and attention to odd detail. And the fact that Mitch displayed them so proudly. She could almost picture him, the hard-ass cop fumbling with Scotch tape, cursing under his breath as he tried for the third time to get the latest work of art straight on the wall. She couldn't help but compare this kitchen to the one on Butler Street in St. Paul that smelled of grease and cigarettes and bitter memories. A cardboard box under her bed had acted as treasure chest for the things she and no one else had taken pride in.

"You're quite the artist," she said to Jessie. "You made all these pictures for your dad to put up?"

Jessie went to one that was taped at her eye level. "This is my daddy and this is me and this is Scotch," she explained. Mitch was depicted in an abstract arrangement of geometric shapes like a man made out of building blocks. There was a badge as big as a dinner plate on his chest. Scotch was roughly the size of a Shetland pony with teeth like a bear trap. A long pink tongue hung out of his mouth.

"I used to have a mommy," Jessie said as she came back to the table and rested her arms on top of it. "But she went to heaven."

The statement was matter-of-fact, but it struck a chord in Megan. She slid down onto a chair and leaned against the table, her gaze steady on Mitch's pretty dark-eyed daughter with her crooked barrettes and purple sweatshirt.

"I know," she said quietly. "That's hard. I lost my mom when I was little, too."

Jessie's eyes widened a little at this unexpected common ground. "Did she go to heaven?"

"No," Megan murmured. "She just went away."

"Because you were naughty?" Jessie ventured timidly.

"I used to think that sometimes," Megan admitted. "But I think she just didn't love my dad anymore and I think she didn't want to be a mom, and so she just left."

The moment stretched between them. The refrigerator hummed. Mitch's daughter regarded her with somber brown eyes.

"That's like diborce," Jessie said. "My friend Janet's mom and dad got a diborce, but he still wants to be her dad on Saturdays. It's hard to be a little kid."

"Sometimes," Megan said, amazed with herself. She didn't talk about her past, ever, with anyone. It was over, long gone, didn't matter anymore. Yet here she was having a heart-to-heart with a five-year-old and it felt . . . *right*, which scared the hell out of her. What was she doing? What was she thinking?

You've been working too hard, O'Malley.

Mitch stood in the dining room with his feet rooted to the floor. He hadn't intended to eavesdrop, had meant only to take a peek in through the door to see how Megan and Jessie were getting along. Jessie was very protective of him and jealous of their time together. He wanted to see if she behaved herself without him right there to enforce her manners. He sure as hell hadn't counted on overhearing a confession from Megan about her well-guarded past.

He remembered the way she had told him about her mother. Defiantly. Resentfully. Sticking out that chip on her shoulder as if it were a shield. The woman confiding in his daughter over bowls of chocolate chip ice cream was none of those things. She was a woman who had once been a little girl afraid she had done something to drive her own mother away. That truth struck a tender spot inside him.

Damn. He had decided he could manage the passion that sparked between them. He could understand it, control it to a certain extent. But he hadn't bargained for anything more. Didn't want anything deeper.

Keep it light, Holt. It's just sex, not marriage. She's married to the badge. Lucky you.

He leaned in the kitchen doorway, smiling a pained smile.

"Joy wanted to be certain I was aware Channel Four is doing a special segment on Deer Lake and our 'troubles' on the ten o'clock news. They're going to give safety tips. I guess she thought maybe I could learn something."

Megan bit her lip against a threatening smile.

"Yeah," he drawled, picking up a bowl and spooning up a small mountain of ice cream. "That anchorman Shelby might know something about law enforcement I failed to pick up in fifteen years on the job."

"She's just trying to help," Megan offered.

He swallowed hard and bared his teeth. "If only."

They ate their ice cream and played an exciting round of Candy Land, Mitch and Megan putting off their plan to go over statements until Jessie was in bed. Jessie struggled valiantly to remain awake until the news came on and protested when Mitch declared it time for her to go to bed. Tired and out of sorts, she cried a little as he carried her up to her room, but was asleep almost the instant her head hit the pillow.

When Mitch came back downstairs, Megan was prowling

around his living room restlessly. Scotch lay on his back in the middle of the floor, waiting for a belly-scratching, wagging his tail hopefully every time she stepped past him.

"You've got a nice house," she said, leaning a hip against his leather recliner.

"Thanks."

Mitch looked around the room, seeing it as a stranger would. The walls were blank sheets of eggshell white that blended with a Berber carpet the color of oatmeal. Bland and lifeless, rescued from complete dreariness by a brick fireplace and flanking glass-doored bookcases. The furniture was stuff he had picked out himself. He hadn't been able to bring himself to keep anything he had shared with Allison. Those pieces evoked memories that brought him pain. He had replaced them with uninteresting, overstuffed pieces in neutral colors that evoked nothing. His one indulgence had been the caramel-colored leather chair.

"I guess I should hang up pictures or something," he mumbled awkwardly. "I'm not good at that kind of thing."

Megan refrained from offering to help with his decorating. The idea was too domestic. Domestic and presumptuous. Like she wanted to stake a claim. They would have what they would have until it was over. That was all. They were colleagues first, lovers second. A long way from picking out wallpaper patterns.

"Jessie's asleep?"

"Like a rock. She was worn out, poor kid."

Mitch went to the fire and tossed another log on the blaze. He poked at the glowing embers in the grate, then stood there with one hand braced against the thick mantelpiece, gazing down into the flames. "Her grandmother, the panic queen, has her all wound up over Josh's abduction. And God knows I haven't been paying much attention to her since all this started."

"You've been a little busy."

"The story of my life."

"Well, now we've got Olie . . ."

"But we don't have Josh."

"Maybe we'll get something from the lab we can use as leverage against him."

Mitch didn't want to think about the bloodstains found in

the van. More than anything about this case, he dreaded the thought of having to tell Hannah and Paul their son was dead. He didn't want them to know that pain, and truth to tell, he didn't want it reawakened within himself. And he didn't want to think that he had failed Hannah and Paul as he had failed Allison and Kyle. The chain went on and on, around and around in an endless loop, like a wheel in a hamster cage.

"Have you talked to Hannah about taking blood samples from her and Paul?"

Mitch pushed himself away from the fireplace. Across the room, Scotch was in an armchair watching *Letterman*. "I'll do it tomorrow."

"The lab needs them to make comparisons."

"I know. I'll do it."

"If you don't want to—"

"I said I'll do it." He wheeled around with his hands raised in surrender.

"Fine." Megan mimicked his gesture, backing away from him. She stared down at the stacks of papers strewn over the oak coffee table. Statements from people associated with the ice rink, statements from neighbors of the ice rink, neighbors of Olie's, curling tubes of fax paper with information provided by the authorities in Washington State and NCIC in Washington, D.C. And amid the standard forms with their standard questions, the pages from Josh's think pad.

"Have you found any more references to Olie?" she asked. She already knew the answer, had already been over her own copy of the notebook half a dozen times. There were plenty of drawings of creatures from outer space, only one of Olie, and beside it the note that wrenched her heart when she thought of Olie Swain betraying Josh. *Kids tease Olie but that's mean. He can't help how he looks.*

"No."

"And I've gone over these statements until my brain went dyslexic, and I still can't see anything we can give to the county attorney. Nothing but suspicion and conjecture and downright ugly meanness. Some of Olie's neighbors could stand a lesson in charity."

They could have learned a thing or two from Josh. The irony was too bitter to contemplate.

"I don't like the way it feels," Mitch said, prowling the room with his hands in his pockets, his head down, brow furrowed. "If the kidnapper took Josh's notebook two months ago and planned out this whole deal like a mastermind . . . that just doesn't feel like Olie. It feels . . . sinister. Olie's pathetic, not sinister."

"So his partner is sinister," Megan offered.

"That's the other thing that doesn't feel right. Olie is a loner. Always has been. Suddenly he's got a partner?" He shook his head.

"He's a convicted pedophile with means and a van that has bloodstains in the carpet," Megan argued. "If you've got a better suspect than that, I'd like to hear about it."

"I don't," Mitch admitted. "I'm not saying he's innocent. I'm saying it doesn't feel right."

"What part of this case feels right? The whole thing stinks like a slaughterhouse in a heat wave. His house was full of computer equipment—"

"But not the printer—"

"I've got a couple of guys checking print shops that offer the use of laser printers, all you have to do is take in your diskette."

"Christ, you think he just walked into Insty Prints and ran off a bunch of psycho notes?"

Megan shrugged. "It's a long shot, but I'll take any odds I can get."

Mitch said nothing. He stopped in front of the fireplace again and stared into the flames, turning the questions and facts and theories over and over in his head.

Megan watched him. His doubts irritated already sore spots. "Is it Olie you object to, or the fact that I made him?"

He shot her a narrow look over his shoulder. "Don't be a bitch. I already congratulated you, Agent O'Malley. I'd just feel better if we could turn up some hard evidence—or better yet, if he'd give us Josh."

"Well," Megan said on a long sigh, "that makes two of us."

The phone rang yet again and the answering machine picked up. Mitch glared at it from across the room. "That makes fifteen thousand of us—fourteen thousand nine hundred ninety-eight of whom have called here tonight."

Bone-weary, he shuffled toward the couch, stopping when he came toe to toe with Megan. She was giving him that skeptical what-do-you-think-you're-doing look that had probably backed off more aggressive males than he could shake a stick at. It didn't faze Mitch. It was part of the act, like the tough talk, like the tomboy clothes. He wasn't scared off by an act.

"What do you say we drop this for tonight?" he suggested. "I don't know about you, but my brain feels like fried eggplant. Let's just be people for a while."

Megan glanced away and blew out a breath, shoving her hands into the hip pockets of her jeans. "Yeah, sure, fine." Of course, that would pretty much kill their conversation, since she didn't have anything to talk about except work. *Now is when you show off your amazing social skills, O'Malley. You're such a well-rounded individual.*

Mitch watched her shoulders sag and her gaze drop to her wool socks. She was so sure of herself as a cop, so unsure of herself as a woman. Everything male in him wanted to confirm her femininity for her. The impulse brought a welcome rush of energy, and he let it carry him.

"Come here." He towed her around the end of the coffee table to the couch. He sank down into the cushions, pulling her down with him. "We need to do something mindless."

Megan struggled unsuccessfully to push herself back to her feet, unable to break his hold around her waist. "Sleep is mindless," she said. "I should go home and get some."

Mitch ignored her logic, nuzzling her braid aside to kiss the back of her neck. "Let's make out," he whispered, his voice low and silky. "Like when we were in high school. You know how you'd come home with a date after the basketball game and your folks were asleep and you'd sit out on the couch and make out and hope nobody caught you."

Megan stiffened a little against him. "I didn't date much in high school."

Didn't date at all was more like it. She had been painfully shy with boys, too aware that she had no breasts to speak of and too aware of the blood that ran in her veins. She didn't want to be her mother's daughter, didn't want to give her father any more reason to dislike her than he already had. There had been one boy in her honors English class, studious and serious as she was. Cute behind his thick glasses. They had traded a few kisses, done a little groping. Then he got contact lenses and suddenly became sought after by popular girls, and Megan was forgotten.

Mitch kissed her neck again, nibbled at her earlobe, his tongue caressing the tender bud of flesh. "Ah, well then, let me teach you. Learn from the master makeout artist."

Leaning back without letting her go, he switched off the lamp on the end table, leaving the room illuminated by the fire and the television. He turned her to face him and kissed her lightly on the mouth. "See, the idea," he murmured between kisses, "is for you to pretend you shouldn't let me do anything, even though what we both really want is to get naked and screw our brains out."

Megan laughed softly, twisting out of reach as he tried to brush a hand against her breast. "So, did you ever get lucky?"

"I don't kiss and tell. Maybe I'll get lucky tonight."

"I don't think so." She gave him a teasing look from beneath her lashes as she scooted back toward the opposite end of the couch. "You'll ruin my reputation."

She didn't let herself think about the truth in that statement. They both needed this time together, away from the burdens of the case. Time to be people instead of cops. Time to feel something good, something life-affirming.

Mitch followed her, moving over the cushions on his knees. A wicked grin curved his mouth.

"Oh, come on, Megan," he whispered, trailing a fingertip down the short slope of her nose to the perfect bow of her mouth. "Just a kiss, that's all. I promise."

Megan smiled, surprised at the way her body was responding to the game. Her heart was beating a little too fast. Her skin was warm and tingling with anticipation. Silly. They had already been to bed together. There were few secrets left between them physically. Still she felt excited at the prospect of a little heavy petting.

Their lips met tentatively, experimentally, as if this experience were new. Nothing to be rushed. Something to be savored. Breaths mingling. Mouths softly touching. The slightest increase of pressure. The angle shifting by small degrees. The anticipation warming and thickening. He slid his arms around her shoulders and drew her closer. The kiss deepened just a shade, and then another. The tip of his tongue skimmed the seam of her lips, asking for a little more, probed gently at the corner of her mouth, asking again. She opened her mouth and moaned softly as he took full possession.

Megan caught hold of his hand as he raised it but didn't try to stop him as he filled his palm with the weight of her breast. His fingers kneaded her gently, her fingers closed over his, and he made a low sound of arousal in his throat as she increased the pressure. He found her nipple with his thumb and rubbed it slowly through the soft layers of her clothing. Then the buttons surrendered one by one.

"God, you're pretty," he whispered, exposing her, touching her reverently.

Megan let herself drift on the sea of sensation . . . until she felt his hand on the button of her jeans. And again they went through the game of mock protest and persuasion.

The button gave way. The zipper inched down. She raised her hips. He eased her jeans down, expecting to see a pair of lacy underpants to tease him. What he found was black silk that seemed to go on and on. Brows tugging together in confusion, he looked up at her.

"Long underwear," Megan whispered, embarrassed. "It's thirty below outside!"

Mitch chuckled wickedly, peeling the black silk down. "Yeah, well, it's a hell of a lot warmer in here. Especially down here," he said, sliding his fingers into the thatch of dark curls. "Especially in here," he murmured, easing two fingers deep between her legs.

"Oh—Mitch—" Megan reached for him, tried to pull him down to her.

She wanted him close, wanted him losing his control, finding fulfillment at the same time, not watching her at her most vulnerable.

"Trust me," he whispered.

Trust me. Trust wasn't something she offered easily. There were good reasons not to trust. Logical, practical reasons. But she didn't feel logical or practical. When he touched her, she felt like a woman, not a cop. It frightened her to let go of that identity, but there was Mitch, whispering, coaxing . . . *Trust me* . . . touching the heart of her need . . . stroking the most feminine part of her . . . caressing . . . loving . . . *Trust me* . . .

Megan's eyes drifted shut. Her breath caught. She lay back as the last of her restraint slipped from her mental grasp. Overpowered by sensation and passion and need. Her hips moved in perfect rhythm with his hand. Her breath came in short, shallow puffs. The excitement swelled and burst inside her, hot, dizzying, intoxicating.

"I love to watch your face when you come," Mitch murmured. "You concentrate so hard."

Megan felt a blush spread across her cheeks and tried to deflect his attention from her embarrassment by rolling on top of him. "Your turn, Chief," she said.

The smile that teased her lips as she rose over him was sparkling with wicked mischief. Slowly she unbuttoned his denim shirt and bared his chest. Her small hands massaged the muscles, traced the ridges, brushed across the mat of dark hair. Mitch watched her intently, pleasure and tortured need twisting together inside him like vines. He sucked in a breath as she bent her head and took his nipple into her mouth. The feel of her lips, her tongue, her teeth, fueled the fire burning in his groin.

"Megan—"

She pressed a finger against his lips. "Shh . . . Let me do this for you, Mitch."

She trailed her kisses across his belly. Long, hot, openmouthed kisses. Kisses that followed the descent of his jeans.

"Megan—"

"Shh . . . Trust me."

He groaned as she took him into the silky heat of her mouth. Thought and control burned away, leaving nothing but feeling so intense, he couldn't breathe. Feeling—the stroke of her tongue, the caress of her lips, the touch of her hand, the slight abrasion of her teeth. Feeling—a fire burning hotter and hotter, rushing toward explosion.

He pulled her up into his arms and rolled her beneath him, driving into her, filling her in one powerful thrust. She was hot and tight around him, as wet as her mouth. Her thighs tightened against his sides. Her fingertips dug into the muscles of his back. He moved in and out of her faster, harder, reaching, straining. She gasped his name as her climax gripped her, gripped him, and he came in a hot rush.

Feeling—trust, excitement, a bond that went beyond the physical. Feelings he hadn't known, hadn't allowed himself in two years of one-night stands.

He didn't want to think or talk or ponder the implications. He wanted to pull the cotton throw down from the back of the couch and cover their cooling bodies, capture the heat in a cocoon and hold it around them. Preserve the moment and put off deciphering the meaning.

Still, the doubts were there, as inescapable as ghosts. He shuffled through the excuses and the rationalizations like a deck of dog-eared playing cards. This was just sex. An affair and nothing more. He wasn't ready for more. She didn't want more. He liked his life the way it was—simple, ordered, controllable. He didn't want to commit himself to taking responsibility for another person.

Not that Megan needed anyone to take responsibility for her. Not that she would allow it. Christ, she was the most independent woman he knew. On the outside . . . On the inside she was an abandoned little girl, a woman uncertain of her own appeal and wary of everyone.

Tenderly, he brushed a hand over her hair, brushed a kiss against her forehead.

Megan shifted sideways, wedging herself between Mitch and the back of the couch. She lay her hand on his chest, over his heart, wishing fleetingly she could have access to what was *in* his heart. A pointless wish—a fact that was only emphasized when he covered her hand with his and the gold of his wedding band caught the dying light of the fire.

The hurt was sharp and surprising, and foolish. He wasn't ready to let go of his past. That wasn't any of her business. She hadn't asked him for a future. She wouldn't. She hadn't asked for this affair; it had just happened. He was attracted to her, not enchanted by her. She had never enchanted anyone that she knew of. So what. Big deal. She had better things to do with her time.

"I should go," she whispered. "It's late."

"Five more minutes," he murmured, tightening his arm

around her shoulders. "I just want to hold you. Five more minutes."

She should have said no. But then, she should have said no all along, she thought wearily.

Five more minutes . . .

DAY 8 3:00 A.M. -35° WINDCHILL FACTOR: -69°

The phone on the end table rang, jolting Megan awake. Disoriented, her brain scrambled to sort the facts into place. Mitch. Mitch's house. Mitch's dog lying on his back on the living room rug, watching an infomercial for spray-on hair.

Mitch sat up, groggy, running a hand over his face. The phone rang again and the answering machine kicked on and gave the usual song and dance. At the tone, instead of a voice came a long silence, then whispered words. "Blind and naked ignorance. Blind and naked ignorance. Blind—"

Mitch grabbed the receiver. "Who the hell is this?"

Silence. Then the line went dead.

"Damn crank," he muttered without conviction, turning back toward Megan.

Her fingers fumbled at the task of buttoning her blouse. "Yeah, right. Just a crank."

"He didn't really say anything."

"And Olie Swain is in jail."

"Right."

So why were they both spooked? Mitch had a feeling in his gut that usually came from lingering nightmares. The hair on the back of his neck prickled. Instinctive responses he tried to rationalize away.

When the phone rang again, he jerked as if a hundred volts had gone through him. Megan grabbed his shoulder.

"Let the machine get it."

"Yeah, I know."

The voice that came over the line was breathless with panic, the words tripping over each other on the way out of the speaker's mouth. "Chief, it's Dennis Harding—Sergeant Harding. We need you down to the jail right away. Something's happened— Jesus, it's awful—"

Mitch grabbed the receiver. "Harding, it's me. What's going on?"

"It's—it's Olie Swain. Oh, my God. Oh, sweet Jesus. He's dead."

Blind and naked ignorance
Delivers brawling judgments, unashamed

The police are fools. They stepped on a slug and called him a villain, and the desperate rushed blindly to embrace their ignorance. And the doctor is no god. Just another helpless woman. The illusion of power gone. We are the kings.

CHAPTER 24

The corpse of Olie Swain, a.k.a. Leslie Sewek, lay crumpled on the floor near the back wall of the cell, an empty husk drained of life. Blood pooled on the gray linoleum, as thick and dark as oil. The stench of violent death was thick and cloying, a rancid perfume that invaded the nostrils and crawled down the throat. Blood and bowel content. The sharp scent of vomit from witnesses unaccustomed to horror.

Only sheer stubbornness and an iron will kept the contents of Megan's stomach in place. The smell always got to her; the rest she had hardened herself to long ago. Mitch's face was unreadable, nearly expressionless. She imagined he had seen worse. He had been a detective in a town notorious for drug wars and violent street crime. He had seen his own wife and son lying dead. Nothing could be worse than that.

"Hey! I want outta here!" Boog Newton called, his voice strained with a fear he was trying unsuccessfully to cover with bravado. "I don't have to stay next to no dead guy. That's cruel and unusual."

Mitch shot him a dangerous look. "Shut up."

Boog scuttled to the far side of his bunk and sat with one foot up on the thin mattress. One skinny arm hugged his knee as he rocked nervously. His other hand inched up the side of his face like a crab, making for his right nostril.

Mitch gave Olie one last long look.

Blind and naked ignorance . . . blind and naked ignorance . . . blind and naked ignorance . . . Blind . . . Blind . . . Blind . . .

"What do we do?" Harding asked weakly. He remained outside the cell, hands gripping the bars, his face the color of old paste.

"Call the coroner," Mitch ordered, stepping out of the cell. "Get somebody up here with a camera. We process it like a crime scene."

"But, Chief, nobody could have—"

"Just do it!" he bellowed.

Harding bolted backward, tripping over his own feet, then turned and hustled out of the cell area. Mitch let himself into Boog Newton's cell. Newton's small eyes darted from Mitch to Megan to Olie to Mitch.

"What happened, Boog?" Mitch's voice was silky and low as he moved toward the cot.

"How should I know?" Boog blurted, jerking his finger out of his nose. "It was dark. I didn't see nothin'."

He arched a brow. "A man in the cell next to yours just killed himself and you don't know anything? You must be a sound sleeper."

Boog scratched nervously at a scab on his chin, his eyes on his blank television. His pallor was waxy, shiny with the kind of sweat that comes with nausea. "He maybe made some sounds," he offered weakly. "I didn't know what he was doin'. Pervert child molester. I didn't wanna know what he was doin'. I thought he was gettin' off or somethin.'"

"He was getting dead, Einstein!" Mitch exploded, suddenly looming over Newton like an avenging god or the devil himself. "Our only lead in this fucking case and now he's dead!"

"Jesus, it's not my fault!" Boog whined, covering his head with his arms, cowering like a whipped dog.

"No, nothing's ever anybody's fault," Mitch sneered. "I am so fucking tired of that excuse!"

The fury rolled through him like a storm, clouding his vision and his judgment. He made no attempt to stop it. He kicked the foot of Newton's cot hard, again and again, the clang and rattle of boot connecting with metal reverberating off the block walls. "Goddammit, goddammit, GODDAMMIT!!"

"Mitch!" Megan snapped, rushing into the cell. He wheeled on her as she grabbed hold of his arm, his expression fierce, wild with rage. "Mitch, come on," she said, her gaze steady on his. "Chill out. We've got work to do."

He could see Boog Newton tucked into a ball on his cot, frightened eyes peering at him over his bony knees. *You lost it, Holt. You lost it.*

He'd lost it with good reason. His gaze tracked slowly away from Newton through the bars into the next cell, where Olie Swain lay on the floor in a pool of blood. Their only lead. Their only suspect. He might have led them to Josh, but Paige had blown the stakeout. He might have cut a deal and handed them Josh or cut a deal and handed them his accomplice, but now there would be no deals. Everything he knew was gone, like a slate wiped clean.

Mitch told himself none of this would have happened in the old days, when his instincts were as sharp as razors. He had lost his edge. In the last two years he had purposely let the instincts rust. He had lulled himself into thinking he wouldn't need them here. A chief didn't need instincts; he needed diplomacy. Nothing ever happened in Deer Lake. Nothing at all . . .

The harsh fluorescent light glared down on Olie Swain, on the birthmark dark against his ashen skin, on the empty socket that had held his glass eye. A fragment of the eye lay in the puddle of blood near his left hand—a sharp wedge of brown iris and black pupil staring up at the ceiling. He had smashed the porcelain ellipse and used one of the shards to dig open the veins in his wrists, draining his life's blood onto the floor of the Deer Lake city jail. On the wall above his corpse, smeared in red, were the words NOT ME.

4:32 A.M. -32° WINDCHILL FACTOR: -64°

The Park County coroner was a balding, pear-shaped man named Stuart Oglethorpe, director of the Olgethorpe Funeral Home. He was in his fifties and wore thick black horn-rimmed glasses and a sour frown that made Mitch suspect he could never get the smell of embalming fluid out of his nose.

He examined Olie briefly, touching his body gingerly with gloved hands, grumbling about the empty eye socket and the bloody mess.

It was common knowledge that the only reason Stuart Oglethorpe had run for the job of county coroner was so his funeral home could get first crack at the corpses. If the body was already in his embalming room, the grieving family was likely to leave it there and purchase a casket and order a memorial service. Stuart could then route the flower orders to his cousin Wilmer at the Blooming Bud greenhouse.

No one was going to order flowers for Olie Swain. Unless some long-lost relative from Washington claimed him, he would be buried at the county's expense. No Cadillac casket, no frills, no memorial service. Stuart had been roused from his warm bed to go out into thirty-two-below-zero cold with no hope of big profit. Stuart was not a happy man.

"Well, he killed himself. Any fool can plainly see that."

"Yeah, but we need *your* signature on the report, Stuart," Mitch said. "And he'll have to be transported to Hennepin County for an autopsy ASAP. "

"Autopsy! What the heck for?" Oglethorpe groused. Once the body hit the slab at Hennepin County Medical Center, he had no hope in hell of getting it back. Park County would give it to the cut-rate Qvaam brothers in Tatonka.

"It's standard procedure when a prisoner takes his own life, Mr. Oglethorpe," Megan explained. "It leaves no room for doubt or speculation as to the circumstances of the death."

Oglethorpe scowled at her. "Who's she?"

"Agent O'Malley, BCA."

He snorted in response.

"Charmed, I'm sure," Megan muttered under her breath. She turned to the officers preparing to load Olie into a body bag and cart him away. "Watch the blood, guys. He was low man on the totem pole in prison for five years; he's a definite AIDS risk."

"Oh, jeez," Harding groaned. "And I didn't think this could get any worse."

She gave him a wry look. "Welcome to the club."

10:00 A.M. -27° WINDCHILL FACTOR: -55°

The press room at the old fire hall had been jammed since nine forty-five.

There was no question that missing children and child predators had become the hot topic. But Megan saw the intense coverage as a medium for creating an unwarranted panic that crimes of this nature were increasing at epidemic rates. According to statistics from the National Center for Missing and Exploited Children, the rate of stranger abductions of children remained remarkably constant from year to year—not a statistic to be regarded lightly, but not an epidemic. Many more children were killed with handguns every week.

She watched the camera and sound people jockey for position as reporters did the same. The pecking order had changed dramatically with the local press pushed back by the Cities press, pushed back by the tabloid people, pushed back by the network people. Any space left over at the very back of the room was taken by people from the volunteer center. She caught a glimpse of the disgruntled Mrs. Favre from Paige Price's prime time special. Almost hidden behind her was Christopher Priest. Rob Phillips, head of the volunteer center, had been granted a ringside seat because of his wheelchair.

At ten on the dot Mitch stepped behind the podium. He had showered and shaved and dressed in a dark brown suit, a conservative white shirt, and a tie without cartoon characters. What color the wind had whipped into his cheeks was leeched out by the blinding sun-guns.

"At approximately three A.M. Leslie Olin Sewek, a.k.a. Olie Swain, was found in his cell at the city jail, dead due to self-inflicted injuries," he announced without preamble.

The shock wave that went through the crowd had all the power of a sonic boom. There were gasps and exclamations. Camera shutters clicked at a furious rate, motor drives whined. Then came the questions in a gust that rivaled the wind outside.

"How do you know the wounds were self-inflicted?"
"Wasn't he being watched?"

"What kind of weapon did he use?"

"Did he leave any notes admitting his guilt in the kidnapping?"

"Did he give any indication to the whereabouts of Josh?"

"Mr. Sewek was not considered a suicide risk," Mitch went on. "He exhibited no signs that would have led us to believe he was a danger to himself. I'm not at liberty to divulge the exact details of his death other than to say he did not have access to anything that would be deemed a conventional weapon. His body has been transferred to Hennepin County Medical Center for a routine autopsy. We are confident the medical examiner's findings will support those of my office and of the Park County coroner."

"Did he leave a note, Chief?" called a reporter from *20/20*.

Mitch thought of the two words scrawled in blood on the wall above Olie's body. NOT ME. "He left no note explaining his actions or his state of mind. He left no message about Josh."

"Have you established that he was indeed the kidnapper?"

"We're still waiting for lab reports from the BCA."

"And when will those be in?"

At Mitch's invitation, Megan stepped up to the podium. She had dressed carefully and conservatively in charcoal wool slacks and turtleneck with an unstructured tweed blazer. The antique cameo pin on the lapel was her only ornamentation. She looked out on the crowd with cool professionalism.

"The tests on Mr. Sewek's van have been given priority status. I expect to hear back on several of them today."

"What kind of tests?"

"What was found? Blood?"

"Articles of clothing?"

"It would be premature for me to reveal the nature of the tests without being able to elaborate on the findings or their significance to the case."

Paige Price, who had somehow managed to procure a seat directly behind the *48 Hours* people, rose with pen and pad in hand, as if she might actually take notes. "Agent O'Malley," she said coolly. "Can you tell us your whereabouts when you received word of Leslie Sewek's demise?"

A cold finger of dread traced down Megan's back. Her hands tightened on the podium. "I fail to see the relevance of that question, Ms. Price," she replied coldly, then dismissed the woman by turning her attention toward a reporter for the *NBC Nightly News.*

"Agent O'Malley—" he began.

"I believe your answer may be relevant to the people of Deer Lake," Paige interrupted with just the perfect hint of drama. Inside she was grinning like the Cheshire cat. She had the attention of the other reporters—the network people and those from the syndicated shows, people who could smell a story the way sharks smell blood in the water. She could see the wheels turning in their minds—*How does she know something we don't?* The anticipation was as delicious as fine chocolate on her tongue. God bless Russ Steiger.

"Isn't it true that when the call came at three A.M. announcing Leslie Sewek's death you were at the home of Chief Holt?"

Somewhere beyond the pounding of Megan's pulse in her ears, the crowd's reaction sounded like bees swarming. Her fingers were white. Her knees felt like Jell-O. She didn't dare chance a look at Mitch or solicit support from him. She was on her own, as she had always been. The phrase *swinging in the breeze* came to mind. God, if DePalma got wind of this . . . *When* DePalma got wind of this . . .

She stared hard at Paige. Mercenary bitch. Ms. Blond Ambition, digging for any scrap that could set her apart from the pack. The idea made Megan sick and furious. She had worked damned hard to get where she was. Too damned hard to have her dreams punctured by Paige Price's spike heels.

"Ms. Price," she said evenly, "don't you believe you've done enough damage to this investigation as it is without now trying to divert the focus of this press conference away from the case and the fate of Josh Kirkwood and onto yourself?"

"I'm not diverting the focus onto myself, Agent O'Malley, I'm diverting it onto you."

"That's not how I see it," Megan challenged. "I see you drawing the attention of your peers by implying some imagined impropriety to which only you are privy. Maybe you think this will get you a big job on *Hard Copy,* but I'll tell you, it doesn't cut much ice with me." She dismissed the reporter again. "Does anyone have a question *germane* to the case?"

"Why won't you answer my question, Agent O'Malley?" Paige pressed. "What are you afraid of?"

Eyes blazing, Megan turned back to her adversary. "I'm afraid I'm going to lose my temper, Ms. Price, because your line of questioning is not only irrelevant but the answer is none of your damn business."

She regretted the words the instant they were out of her mouth. She had just as much as admitted her guilt. It didn't matter that what she said was true, that it was nobody's business. She had given just enough answer to pique imaginations. God, what a nightmare. She felt as if she had stepped into a tar pit and was being sucked in deeper with every move she made in an attempt to extricate herself. Now there would be no graceful way out. She couldn't tell the truth and she doubted anyone would swallow an edited version. *We were discussing the case and we just fell asleep. Honest.* Right. She felt like a teenager who had been caught coming home after curfew. The analogy nearly made her laugh out loud as she recalled Mitch's words of the night before—*Let's make out. Like when we were in high school . . .*

Paige put on her righteous-crusader-for-the-First-Amendment face, internally vowing to wring Garcia's neck if he didn't get a long shot of it. "At three A.M., while your prime suspect in an unsolved child abduction was committing suicide, you were reportedly in the home of Chief Holt with all the lights off. If your priority is not with the case, the public has a right to know, Agent O'Malley."

"No, Ms. Price," Megan retorted, her voice trembling with cold rage. "The public has a right to know that I and all the other cops on this case have been working virtually around the clock in the attempt to find Josh, to get just one good lead on the piece of human garbage who stole him. They have a right to know that no one could have known what Olie Swain had done before he came here, that what happened to Josh was an isolated act of senseless violence and not the first sign of anarchy. They have a right to know that your job hinges on your ratings and your ratings hinge on sensationalism and exploitation. They do not have a right to follow me after I've spent eighteen hours on the job. They do not have a right to know what flavor of ice cream I like or what brand of tampons I use.

"Am I making myself clear, Ms. Price? Or do we need to discuss how you came to find out about the stakeout on Olie Swain's house the other night? Perhaps you, in your patriotic, open-minded spirit, can see that the public has a right to know how it came to pass that you and your news crew interfered with an investigation and ultimately ruined our chances of possibly finding Josh Kirkwood that night."

Momentum, fickle bitch that she is, swung heavily away from Paige. She felt it go. She felt the jealous admiration of her fellow journalists cool like a hot iron in the snow. She felt the eyes of volunteers bore into her back, felt their sense of betrayal and their anger. She would lose their trust, which meant she might lose potential sources. Worse than that, she would lose viewers, which meant she would lose leverage in her contract negotiations. She took her seat, her gaze on Megan O'Malley, burning with hate.

DePalma is going to skin me alive and make a desk set out of my hide," Megan muttered. She paced the length of an antique fire truck, shaking, not from the biting cold of the old garage, but from shock.

The press conference was over, but the trouble had just begun. The match had just been touched to the fuse—and the fuse was attached to the dynamite that would blow her out of Deer Lake. "Dammit, I knew something like this would happen! I knew better!"

"Megan, you didn't do anything wrong," Mitch said. He sat on the running board of the old truck, freezing his balls. He was too drained to care. "You said so yourself in there. You made your point very sharply."

Megan stared at him in disbelief. "You think that's going to make a difference? You think that pack of jackals in there is going to say 'Oh, yeah, she's right, it's none of our business who she sleeps with'? What turnip truck did you fall off?"

"I'm saying there are more important things to focus on here. For them and for you."

"What the hell is that supposed to mean? You think I care more about my career than I care about finding Josh?"

Mitch rose. "I don't hear you ranting about the fact that our only suspect is dead. You took that in stride. But somebody takes a poke at you and it's the end of life as we know it."

Beyond words, Megan could only gape at him. Then she looked away, rubbing a hand across her forehead, muttering to herself. "I guess I should have expected this. A man is a man is a man."

"What do you mean by that?"

"I mean, you don't get it," she snapped, wheeling back around on him. Every muscle in her body was rigid with anger, her hands balled into white-knuckled fists at her sides. "My authority and integrity have been compromised. Once this hits the airwaves, my credibility is suspect and my effectiveness on the job suffers. Provided I still have a job. The Vatican likes scandalous publicity more than the BCA does." Phantom images of DePalma's angry face floated through her head. Nixon as the grim reaper, the face of doom.

"Do you know how I got this job, Mitch?" she demanded. "I got this job by working twice as hard and being three times better than any man in line for it. I fought tooth and nail for it, because I believe in what we do.

"There is *nothing* I want more than to find Josh Kirkwood. I have given over all that I am, all that I know, every ounce of will and determination I have to find Josh and stick his abductor's head on a pike. And now I'm very probably going to be denied the satisfaction and this investigation is very probably going to lose one damn good cop because I was stupid, because I broke my own cardinal rule and slept with a cop."

"Stupid?" he said in a deadly quiet voice. "That's what you think about us?"

"What *us*?" Megan asked sharply. She would have liked to believe they had something special, but she had no faith in that being true. She wanted to think he was holding out the chance to her now, but she wouldn't trust him. Love didn't happen this fast. Love didn't happen at all for her. Life had taught her that lesson a long time ago.

"There is no us," she said bitterly. "We had sex. You never made any promises to me. My God, you never even bothered to take off your wedding ring when you took me to bed!"

Instantly, Mitch's gaze dropped to his left hand and to the thick gold band he wore out of habit. He wore it to punish himself. He wore it to protect himself from women who might want more than he was willing to give. And it worked like a charm, didn't it?

Megan stood there in front of him with her feet braced apart, shoulders squared, ready to take a blow—physical or metaphorical. So tough on the outside, so alone on the inside. She had more than made her priorities clear: the job, the job, and then the job. But there was still hurt in her eyes and behind the pride that kept her chin up. He had coerced her into breaking her rules, gave her sex, offered her nothing, and now she would pay the price.

What does that make you, Holt? King of the shitheels.

He blew out a long breath. "Megan, I'm s—"

"Save it." She didn't want to hear the word. Bad enough to see it written all over his face. "We both should have known better." She told herself it wasn't Mitch who was hurting her, that it was the injustice of a double standard that would punish her for attempting to have a private life.

"You won't have to worry, of course." She forced a sharp, unpleasant smile. "Everybody knows boys will be boys. And I'm used to going through my professional life with an ax hanging over my head. So, hey, this is nothing new."

"Megan . . ."

He reached a hand out to touch her cheek. She slapped it away.

"Goddamn you, Mitch Holt, don't you dare pity me!" she said through her teeth. She had no defense against tenderness. She backed away from him, jaw set, her mouth pressed into an uncompromising line. "I'm a big girl. I can take care of myself. Hell, I've been doing it my whole life. Why stop now?"

Chin up, she walked past him, wondering if there was any hope of getting her coat from the press room without being seen.

"Where are you going?"

Megan stopped a foot from the door, but she didn't turn around. She didn't need a man in her life. She didn't need anyone. To be a good cop—that was all she had ever really wanted. She ignored the hollow ring of those words inside her.

"I'm going to work," she told him. "While I still have a job."

CHAPTER 25

Olie Swain had no known associates. He had no friends. He was, as they were so fond of saying on the nightly news, a loner. He did his job and kept to himself. According to the ink stamp on the inside covers, he bought most of his books at The Pack Rat, a secondhand shop near Harris College.

The store was empty except for a clerk who would have looked perfect selling love beads out of the back of a Volkswagen van with a psychedelic paint job. Tall and lean as a stick of beef jerky, he parted his rusty blond hair in the middle and pulled it back into a bushy ponytail. What passed for a beard on his chin more resembled the thin wad of loose hair Megan periodically cleaned out of her hairbrush. He wore a tie-dyed T-shirt with a rumpled plaid flannel shirt open over it. Baggy jeans clung precariously to his skinny hips, held in place by a length of clothesline cord. His name was Todd Childs and he was a psych major at Harris who had been spending some of his free time working in the volunteer center.

Megan let her gaze roam around the store as they chatted about the case. Housed in an old creamery building, the place was jam-packed to the rafters, a treasure trove of outdated textbooks and clothes, "decorative" pieces that cycled between trendy kitsch and unwanted junk, pennants and pompoms and other assorted memorabilia from Harris. Behind the counter, an ancient electric heater that looked like a fire hazard groaned in its effort to supplement the clanking furnace.

Todd tapped a forefinger to the thin gold rim of his glasses. "Observation is the key to insight," he said slowly. He propped his bony elbows on the counter and leaned across it to stare into Megan's eyes. His pupils were dilated to the size of dimes and the scent of burning hemp clung to his clothes. "For instance, I'd have to say you're very tense."

"Comes with the territory," Megan said.

"Yeah . . ." He nodded in slow motion. "Seeking justice in an unjust world. Trying to plug the dam with chewing gum. Most cops are control freaks, you know. That's not meant to be an insult; it's just an observation."

"And what did you observe about Olie?"

"He was weird. He never wanted to talk to anybody. Came in, bought books, left." Todd stood back and sucked down half a Marlboro Light 100. "We were in the same class a couple of times," he said on a cloud of smoke. "He never spoke to the other students. Never."

"He was actually taking courses at Harris?"

"Just auditing. I don't think he could spring for tuition. He was way into computers, you know. I think he felt more comfortable with machines than people. Some folks do. He sure didn't strike me as the kind of guy who likes to fuck with people's heads. You know, with that note business and that phone call and everything." He shook his head, inhaled a quarter of the cigarette, and blew the smoke out through his nostrils. "I don't see it, unless he had a multiple personality disorder, and that's pretty unlikely."

"I guess he was leading a secret life," Megan said, pulling her mittens on.

Todd gave her a dreamy look. "Don't we all? Isn't that what everyone does—build camouflage walls around our inner selves?"

"I guess," she conceded, clamping on her earmuffs. "But most of us don't have inner selves who molest children." She tapped the business card she had left on the counter. "If you think of anything that might help, please give me a call."

"Sure thing."

"Oh, and Todd?" She gave him a look as she tossed the end of her scarf over her shoulder. "Don't smoke dope on the job. You never know when a cop might come in."

From The Pack Rat, Megan hurried next door to a small turquoise clapboard house that had been converted into a coffee place called The Leaf and Bean. The tiny front porch was crowded with snow-crusted bicycles apparently waiting out the winter. Inside, she took a seat at a tiny white-draped table near the front window and ordered latte and a chocolate chip cookie from a girl dressed like Morticia Addams. What few other customers there were sat back by the old wooden counter in what had probably once been a dining room, perusing the newspaper and chatting quietly. An alternative rock station was playing on the radio behind the counter, filling the emptiness with Shawn Colvin's spare, evocative lyrics to "Steady On."

The walls of the place were chalk white and hung with old black-and-white photographs in plain black frames. The windows were curtainless, allowing cold bright sunlight to pour in. Megan left her sunglasses on, to discourage eye contact and to block the light. She sipped her latte and nibbled absently on her cookie as she stared down at her notebook.

She needed to find a thread that would tie the random bits of information together, but there didn't seem to be one. All she had were theories. Olie had acted alone. Olie had an accomplice. Who? He had no friends. Olie had computers no one could get into, but his printer was dot matrix and the note found in Josh's gear bag and in the back of his notebook had come from a laser printer. Olie had photographs of naked boys, but they were years old, from his life in another place.

For someone who knew so much, she knew very little.

> ignorance is not innocence but SIN
> i had a little sorrow, born of a little SIN
> Blind and naked ignorance . . . blind
> and naked ignorance . . .

Mind games. Mitch had said Olie didn't seem the type for mind games. Olie had been lying in his own blood when the call had come to Mitch's house.

Blind and naked ignorance

She had looked up the quotation in *Bartlett's*. It was from Tennyson's *Idylls of the King. Blind and naked ignorance delivers brawling judgments unashamed.*

Someone's way of telling them they had the wrong man? Or was it Olie's partner, unaware that at the very moment he

called to torment them his cohort was slitting his wrists with
the shards of his porcelain eye?

The theories swirled through her mind, making her head
ache. And in a separate swarm were the fears for what would
happen to her career if someone decided to make an issue of
her involvement with Mitch. At best, she would lose face with
the men she worked with. Worst ranged from losing her field
post to ending up as a security guard at a shopping mall someplace. No. Worst would be not being able to close this case, she
decided as she looked down at her copy of Josh's photograph.

He smiled up at her, so full of life and enthusiasm and
bright-eyed innocence. For just a second she let her guard
down and wondered how he was, what he must be thinking,
how frightened he must be . . . provided he was still alive. She
had to think he was. Believing kept everyone going.

And beneath all the other thoughts was the acute awareness of every passing second.

"We're doing the best we can, Josh," she whispered. "Hang
in there, scout."

Tucking the photograph back into her folder, she forced
her gaze to focus again on the notes she had made. *Olie—computers. Olie—audit courses—Harris College. Instructors?*

Christopher Priest was head of the department. Maybe he
would have an idea what Olie kept locked away inside his machines. Maybe he would have an idea of how to get at it.

She paid her tab and went back out into the deep freeze
with her file folder and notebook clutched against her as if they
might afford some protection from the wind. The Lumina
started grudgingly and the fan belt shrieked like a banshee all
the way back to the station.

The only good thing about the extreme cold was that it discouraged the press from hanging around outside the station
doors. Having been banned from the hallways of the law enforcement center, they congregated in the main entry to the
City Center building or sat in their cars in the parking lot with
the motors running. Megan pulled into the slot designated for
Agent L. Kozlowski behind the building and ducked in the
door before any of the vultures could alight from their perches.

Her message light was blinking when she let herself into
her office, but the call was from Dave Larkin, not DePalma.

She hoped the silence meant the dirt from the press conference had yet to hit headquarters. She debated the wisdom of beating them to the punch, calling DePalma herself and giving him the laundered version of what had gone on—she and Mitch had been discussing the case; exhausted from the hours they had been putting in, they fell asleep sitting in front of his fireplace; then came the call . . .

Calls. Plural. *Blind and naked ignorance.* The voice played through her mind as she hung up her coat. Whispery. Low. Eerie. In her mind's eye she saw the message scrawled in blood on the white wall of Olie's cell—NOT ME. What if he were innocent? What if they had wasted all this time chasing down a red herring while the real kidnapper sat back and watched them, laughing?

The what-ifs spun around and around in her head. She needed to put her thoughts back on track methodically, one by one. They had followed their leads. Olie had the record, he had the opportunity. His van matched the witness description. His van had traces of blood in the carpet.

"Larkin," she murmured.

Snatching up the receiver, she punched in the number and prayed he would be at his desk. He picked up on the sixth ring.

"Larkin."

"Dave, it's Megan. What have you got for me?"

"Condolences on the passing of your suspect. Man, Irish, talk about bad breaks."

"Yeah, if it weren't for bad luck, we'd have no luck at all," she said. "Have you heard anything else from this end?" she fished.

"Like what?"

"Nothing. Never mind. Did you get the reports on the blood?"

"Yeah. I personally went over there and hounded them. I figured I'd get back to you quicker than they would."

"Thanks. You're a pal, Dave. What'd they find?"

"It wasn't human."

Megan let out the breath she'd been holding. "God, I don't know if I should be relieved or disappointed."

"I know. I'm sorry, kiddo. I wish I could give you something to go on, but this blood ain't it. It probably came from some poor Bambi and it was probably in that rug for years. There were no sporting rifles or shotguns, no guns of any sort found in your guy's house. I'll fax you the report, and the minute I hear anything on the trace evidence, I'll call you."

"Thanks, Dave. I appreciate it."

"Don't mention it. And chin up, Irish. When you crack this thing, dinner's on me."

Megan didn't bother to tell him he would be dining alone. No cops. Never again.

She wondered what would happen to the easy camaraderie she shared with Dave Larkin when Paige Price's story hit the grapevine. She had kept his amorous advances at bay with her rule of not dating cops. He enjoyed kidding around about the subject, but he had always respected her boundaries. How would he feel when he found out she'd been sleeping with Mitch? Would he try to understand or would his ego inflate between them like an air bag?

She cursed herself for the hundredth time. She had compromised so much, and for what? A few hours of intimacy with a man she barely knew.

Other reasons whispered through her mind. Excuses and half-formed wishes. The physical attraction was stronger than anything she had ever known; she hadn't known how to fight it. He had been persistent, persuasive. She had felt a connection with him that awakened within her the desire for things she had never had—closeness, companionship . . . love.

She closed her eyes and shook her head. She was tough enough to break the testosterone barrier and make detective on the Minneapolis force. She was strong enough to fight for her right to this field post with the BCA. She had taken down characters as bad as any cop ever had to face. And all of that was forgotten in a heartbeat for a little scrap of tenderness and the chance to feel that she mattered to a man as a woman.

The fax machine behind her beeped. Megan swung around on her desk chair, expecting to see the lab report on the bloodstains. Instead, the cover sheet was from the DMV regarding the routine trace on Olie's van. Using the manufacturer's vehicle identification number, they had traced the van's life history in the state of Minnesota from first owner to last. According to the report, the title had been transferred in September 1991 to

Lonnie O. Swain. The previous recorded change of ownership had occurred in April 1989. The lucky owner: Paul Kirkwood.

Goose bumps rippled down Megan's body. The van Paul Kirkwood hadn't wanted to tell her about was Olie Swain's van.

2:14 P.M.

The council members are really upset here, Mitch. They can't understand how something like this could happen. I mean, how did he get hold of a knife? You don't give those guys table knives with their suppers, do you?"

Mitch stared across his desk at Mayor Don Gillen, trying to manufacture patience from stress and stomach acid. "He didn't have a knife, Don. He didn't have a weapon of any kind. He cracked his glass eye and slit his wrists with the pieces, and if you can find me anyone on the town council who could have foreseen that happening, I will gladly pin my badge to their chest and retire from law enforcement."

"Jeez," Gillen muttered, horrified. His blue eyes blinked behind his gold retro spectacles. In addition to his position as mayor, he held an administrative position with the Deer Lake Community Schools. Pushing fifty, he still tended to dress like a yuppie on the cutting edge of fashion, flashy ties and suspenders being his trademarks. "Jeez, Mitch, that's ghoulish."

Mitch spread his hands. "I'd rather you didn't tell anyone but the council members."

"Yeah, sure." Gillen shook his head as he rose from the visitor's chair. "So, you think it's nearly over?" he asked hopefully. "That Olie did it and killed himself because he felt guilty or couldn't face going back to prison?"

"Honestly, I don't know, Don," Mitch said, rising. "I just don't know."

Gillen started to say something, but cut himself off as a sharp knock sounded against the door. Megan stuck her head in the office without waiting for an invitation.

"Excuse me, Chief," she said, glancing quickly past the mayor. "I'm sorry to interrupt, but I have something here that's extremely urgent. I need to speak with you immediately."

She let herself in, a tube of fax paper clutched in one hand, her face taut and pale except for the brightness in her eyes. Mitch's instincts came up like radar. She had something concrete. He could feel it.

"Yes, come in, Agent O'Malley," he said, moving out from behind his desk. "You've met our mayor, Don Gillen?"

Megan offered the mayor a cursory nod, too aware of the cautious look Gillen passed from her to Mitch. The word about the two of them was apparently out around town, but at the moment she didn't give a damn.

"Please keep me up to date, Mitch," Gillen said. "I'll do what I can with the council."

"Thanks, Don."

Gillen slipped out, pulling the door shut behind him. Megan waited a full ten seconds, her heart pounding in her chest, her breath coming as hard as if she had sprinted down the hall from her office. Mitch stood in front of his desk with his hands on his hips, his expression inscrutable, careful.

"Last Friday I requested a report from the DMV on the van Paul Kirkwood used to own—the one that conveniently slipped his mind," she began. "Their computers were down. They didn't get back to me; turns out they lost my request. In the meantime, we requested a check on Olie Swain's van—the results of which I am holding in my hand. Three guesses as to where he got it."

"Not Paul," Mitch said, nerves coiling like snakes in his belly.

Megan handed him the fax as if presenting him with a diploma. "Give the man a cigar. Nailed it in one."

Mitch uncurled the paper and stared at it. "I can't believe he wouldn't remember selling his van to Olie."

"There are a number of things I find difficult to believe about Kirkwood. He's at the volunteer center. I called and asked him to come over for a little chat. I thought you might like to be present."

Paul sold his van to Olie, tried to conceal that fact even before Olie was officially considered a suspect. The implications were too ugly. Mitch didn't want to even consider it, let alone broach the subject with Paul. But he held the proof in his hand, as damning as a smoking gun.

"I think it would be better if I spoke with him," he muttered.

"You thought that last week," Megan said tightly. "I don't remember it happening."

His head snapped up and he stared at her, his eyes as hard and bright as amber beneath the ledge of his brows. "Other things took precedence. Are you suggesting I deliberately avoided talking to him?"

"I'm not suggesting anything," she said, poker-faced. "All I'm saying is: It didn't happen. Now I've called him over here and I fully intend to make sure the questions get asked."

The silence stretched between them as they stood there, squaring off, combatants in a turf war. Mitch felt as if she had taken her toe and drawn a line on the carpet between them. And he felt a vague sense of loss, whether it was smart or not.

He stepped across the line, knowing Megan never would. Neither would she back away. She held her ground defiantly, raising her chin, her gaze steady on his.

"Megan," he said, lifting a hand to brush his knuckles against her cheek.

She turned her face away. "Don't make this any harder than it has to be, Mitch," she murmured. "Please."

"We don't have to be enemies."

"We're not," Megan insisted. She forced herself to take a step sideways. His tenderness was always her undoing. That had to stop if she was to salvage anything from this situation.

"Look," she said on a sigh. "I'm feeling cornered and put upon. I'm not blaming you for what happened. I'm just not being a good sport, that's all."

"I'll talk to DePalma if you want, tell him nothing happened. It's none of their damn business, anyway."

She smiled sadly. "Thanks, but it won't make any difference. He isn't going to be interested in what did or didn't happen between us if they've decided I've become a public relations problem. If that happens, they'll call me in to headquarters and I'll be relieved of my field post, the official reason being I'm not making progress on the case, even though everyone will understand it was my lack of circumspection."

"But you're a hell of a cop," Mitch said, handing her the DMV fax. "Circumspection never sent a crook to jail."

Megan shrugged, trying not to let his compliment mean too much. "Swap you," she said, handing him the second tube of thermal paper.

"What's this?"

"The blood analysis from the van. It's not human. We struck out."

"Thank God . . . I guess."

"Yeah."

Natalie buzzed through on the intercom. "Chief, Paul Kirkwood is here to see you."

Megan arched a brow. "He must have misunderstood my request," she said sardonically.

Mitch went around behind his desk and punched the button. "Send him in, Natalie."

Paul stormed into the office, ready to go off on a diatribe about "that BCA bitch," but he stopped dead in his tracks as his gaze landed on Megan O'Malley. She stood beside Mitch Holt's desk with her arms crossed over her chest. The look she wore was one he recognized from his childhood back in the old St. Paul neighborhood—a touch of defiance, a hint of temper, a hefty dose of plain old toughness. Had they been kids, she might have been telling him she could kick his butt all the way down the block.

He drew himself up and passed his gaze on to Holt, who sat behind his desk with his shirtsleeves rolled up and his elbows on the blotter, relaxed, a little rumpled.

"I thought you were alone," Paul said.

"Anything you have to say about the case, you can say in front of Agent O'Malley," Mitch said. "Take off your coat and have a seat, Paul."

Ignoring the offer, Paul began to pace along the front of the desk. "Yes, I hear the two of you are like this." He held up crossed fingers. "It's nice to know something is being accomplished with all your overtime."

"I think you have some more important things to think

about here besides idle gossip, Mr. Kirkwood," Megan said pointedly. "Your failing memory, for instance."

"My what?"

"Paul, have a seat," Mitch suggested again, the buddy, the pal. "We need to clear up a little something about that van you used to have."

"That again?" He flopped his arms against the loose sides of his black wool topcoat. "I don't believe this. You people manage to kill the one suspect we had—"

"Olie killed himself," Mitch corrected him calmly.

"Or we'd be able to ask *him* these questions," Megan added.

Paul came to an abrupt halt and stared at her. He looked a little thinner—his nose seemed sharper, his eyes set deeper—but instead of looking haggard, he seemed energized, as if he were drawing on the tension of the situation for adrenaline. She couldn't help but think of Hannah, who was looking more like a death camp prisoner every day.

"Just what is that supposed to mean?" he asked.

"Paul, why didn't you tell us you sold that van to Olie Swain?" Mitch asked in a tone that was almost matter-of-fact.

Incredulous, Paul jerked around to stare at him. "I didn't! I said I don't remember who bought it, but it wasn't *him*. Christ, I think I'd remember if I sold it to *him*."

"Funny," Megan muttered, "that's just what I said—'You think he'd remember selling it to Olie'—"

"I didn't!"

Mitch held the fax up and uncurled it like a scroll. "That's not what the DMV says, Paul."

"I don't give a shit what the DMV says! I did *not* sell that van to Olie Swain!" Unable to restrain his agitation, he resumed his pacing. "And what would it matter if I had? That was what—four or five years ago—"

"September 1991," Megan supplied helpfully.

"Of course it wouldn't matter," Mitch said. "What matters is that it appears you lied to us about it, Paul. *That* matters a lot."

Paul slammed his fists down on the desktop, fury forcing a vein to bulge out in his neck. "I did *not* lie to you! How dare you accuse *me*! My son is still missing—"

"And we're examining every lead, every single scrap of anything remotely resembling evidence, Paul," Mitch said quietly. "We're doing our jobs."

"And what were you doing last night when your only suspect was slitting his wrists?" Paul snapped, his face red and twisted.

Mitch rose slowly, his expression stony. He came around the desk, clamped a hand on Paul's shoulder, and assisted him into the visitor's chair. "Have a seat, Paul."

He leaned back against the desk then, half sitting, the pose deceptively casual. "Let's get a few things straight here, Paul. First of all, we're doing everything we can do to get Josh back. *No one* is exempt from scrutiny. Do you understand what I'm saying here, Paul? *No one*. That's the rule. That's the way these investigations are done. Absolutely no stone is left unturned. If that hurts your feelings, I'm sorry, but you have to understand that everything we do, we do for Josh."

"We're not saying you're a suspect, Mr. Kirkwood," Megan interjected. "We ran a routine trace on Olie Swain's vehicle. Believe me when I say I was not expecting to see your name as the last owner listed before Olie."

"If you can set your emotions aside for a second here, Paul, imagine how this looks to us," Mitch said. "You claim you can't remember who bought your van, then it turns up in the hands of the man suspected of kidnapping your son. You'd better be glad I know you, Paul"—he leaned ahead to point a finger in Paul's face—"because, I'm telling you, if I were just another cop, we would be having this conversation down the hall with a lawyer present."

Paul shifted in his chair, his expression half scowl, half pout, like a petulant student trying to act tough in the principal's office. "I didn't sell the van to Olie Swain." His voice trembled slightly. "The guy who bought it from me must have resold it without changing the title."

Mitch sat back with a sigh and picked up the DMV fax. "Do you remember what time of year it was when you sold it?"

"I don't know. Spring, I think. April or May."

"Title was changed in September," Mitch said, handing the document to Megan. She gave him a look that did not go unnoticed by Paul.

"Ask Hannah," he said belligerently. "Hannah remembers everything."

"You wouldn't have any paperwork on the sale in your tax records?" she asked. "You being an accountant and all . . ."

"Probably. I would have looked by now, but I've been busy with the search and, frankly, I couldn't—can't—see what bearing this has on anything."

"Look it up," Mitch suggested, the good guy again. "It'll tie up the loose end."

"Fine." Paul crossed his legs and shifted his body so that his focal point was away from Mitch and Megan.

Wise to that ploy, Megan strolled behind him directly into his line of vision. "Mr. Kirkwood, I still have a couple of questions about the night Josh disappeared."

"I was working," Paul said wearily, rubbing his forehead.

"In the conference room at your office," Megan finished. "And you never checked your answering machine?"

"No," he whispered as Josh's voice played inside his head— *Dad, can you come and get me from hockey? Mom's late and I wanna go home.* A tremor went through him. "Not until . . . after . . ."

"After what?"

Dad, can you come and get me from hockey? Mom's late and I wanna go home.

He sniffed and ducked his head, shielding his eyes with his hand. "The next day."

"Do you still have the tape?"

Dad, can you come and get me from hockey? Mom's late and I wanna go home.

"A—no," he lied. "I . . . I couldn't keep it. I couldn't listen—"

Dad, can you come and get me from hockey? Mom's late and I wanna go home.

He shuddered. "I just want him back," he whispered through the tears. "I just want him back."

Megan blew out a long breath as Mitch sent her a warning look. "I'm sorry to put you through this, Mr. Kirkwood," she said quietly. "I don't enjoy it."

Mitch offered Paul a box of Kleenex and a pat on the shoulder. "I know it's hell, Paul. We wouldn't ask if we didn't have to."

"Chief?" Natalie's voice came over the intercom. "Noogie's on line one and I think you're going to want to hear what he has to say."

He went around the desk again, picked up the receiver, and punched the blinking light. "Noogie, what's up?"

"I'm at St. Elysius, Chief. I think you better come out. I picked up a radio call to the sheriff's department. A woman out here on Ryan's Bay is reporting her dog found a kid's jacket. They think it might be Josh Kirkwood's."

CHAPTER 26

Ryan's Bay was the rather grandiose name for what was essentially a big wet spot in an area of sloughs west of Dinky-town, windswept and bleak in winter's grip. The land had been annexed into the Deer Lake municipality in the seventies, but there was no city sewer or water service and the residents of the Ryan's Bay area thought of themselves as being independent from the town, which explained why Ruth Cooper had called the sheriff's department when her Labrador came charging out of a stand of cattail stalks with a child's jacket in his mouth. Steiger himself was on the scene wearing a shearling coat with the collar turned up, a big fur trapper's hat warming his greasy head. He appeared to be the star attraction in what was already a media circus.

"So much for preserving the scene," Megan muttered as Mitch pulled his Explorer in alongside the KSTP news van, blocking the van in.

Newspeople, civilians, sheriff's deputies, and loose dogs trampled the snow as they milled around. Mitch cut the engine and started to turn toward Paul in the back seat, but Paul was already out the door and hustling toward the center of the storm. Reporters turned and stepped back for him. Cameras swung in his direction. Mitch jumped out of the truck and sprinted after him, hoping in vain that he might be able to prevent the very scene into which Paul Kirkwood plunged himself.

Steiger was holding up the bright-colored ski jacket like a trophy. A strangled cry wrenching from his throat, Paul launched himself at the sheriff, grabbing the jacket and sending Steiger staggering backward. Paul fell to his knees in the trampled snow. Clutching the coat in both hands, he buried his face in it, sobbing.

"Oh my God, Josh! Josh! Oh God! No!"

Mitch shoved his way through the ranks of press that had closed in, his temper spiking. As he broke into the center of the circle, he turned on them, shouting, "Get out of here!" He batted down the lens of a video camera zooming in on Paul. "Jesus, don't you people have any compassion at all? Get out of here!"

Behind him he could hear the awful sound of Paul Kirkwood crying. There was nothing in the human experience with which to compare a parent's grief. It was a dismemberment of a living soul, so excruciating it went beyond all known adjectives. That wasn't a thing for people to witness on the six o'clock news.

Father McCoy was on one knee beside Paul, a hand on Paul's shoulder, his head bent as he tried to keep his words of comfort from being swept away by the cutting wind. Steiger stood six feet in front of them, looking disgruntled and at a loss, spiritual matters beyond him.

Mitch flashed the sheriff a twisted smile. "Thanks for alerting my office, Russ."

Steiger sniffed and spit a glob of mucus in the snow.

"Move it back, people!" Megan called, flashing her ID as Noogie and two other officers herded the crowd back up onto Old Cedar Road. "You're on a possible crime scene! We've got to ask you to move back!"

"Leave me alone!" Paul shouted suddenly. He shoved at Father Tom as he pushed himself to his feet, sending the priest sprawling in the snow. "I don't want anything from you! Get the hell away from me!"

"Hey, Paul." Mitch took hold of his arm and steered him toward the sloughs, away from the watchful eyes of the press. "Come on. We need to take a minute and think about what this means."

"He's dead," Paul said thickly. He held the jacket out in front of him, staring at it as if his son had just vanished from inside of it. "He's dead. He's dead—"

Mitch pushed the coat down. "We don't know that. We've

got his jacket, not him. This jacket is described on every poster and report about Josh. The kidnapper would have been smart to dump it right off the bat."

Beyond reason, Paul had started to cry again, a soft, eerie keening. "He's dead. He's dead. He's dead."

"Houston!" Mitch called, motioning one of his officers over from the crowd-control detail.

The burly, bearded cop shambled over, snow screeching beneath his heavy-duty Arctic boots. The moisture from his breath had frozen white in his thick facial hair. What was visible of his face was red from the cold and the wind.

"I need you to take Mr. Kirkwood home," Mitch said. "Explain what happened to Dr. Garrison and stay with them until I get there."

"You bet." Houston draped a beefy arm across Paul's shoulders. "Come on, Mr. Kirkwood. Let's get you home. It's too darn cold to stand around out here."

Before they could take a step, Mitch took hold of Josh's jacket and tried to extricate it gently from Paul's grip. "Come on, Paul," he said quietly. "This is evidence now. We need to send it up to the crime lab."

Reluctantly, Paul let go. Hands over his face, he walked away with Houston.

"He's in a lot of pain," Father Tom said, dusting the snow off the seat of his parka.

"How about you, Father?" Megan asked. "Are you all right?"

His glasses were askew. He straightened them and tugged down on the earflaps of his hunting cap. "I'm all right. I should have known better. Paul isn't one of my bigger fans. But when Noogie came into St. E's to use the phone and told us what was going on, I felt it was my duty to be here."

"Us?" Mitch said, looking off toward the church. It was perhaps a quarter mile away to the southeast, its spires thrusting up above the naked trees.

"Albert and I were going over some church accounts," the priest said. "If you're concerned about discretion, I think the cat's already out of the bag."

Mitch said nothing. He took a good long look at the area. The "bay" itself was frozen and adrift with snow that piled up against the thick stands of skeletal blond cattail stalks. A winter-white desert with dunes that shifted beneath the frigid breath of the wind. It had to be a haven for mosquitoes in the warmer months, but people had still chosen to build homes around the edge of it. The half-dozen houses that ringed the northwest side of the bay ranged from a winterized cottage to a pricey custom cedar shake job with elaborate decks that would have looked at home on Nantucket. They sat back from the shore on large, well-spaced lots of three to five acres that were thick with evergreen and hardwood trees.

Beyond them to the west, beyond the rolling open farmland and copses of trees, the horizon was milky with airborne snow. The sky was awash with brilliant paintbox shades of fuchsia and tangerine as the sun began its descent. There were no houses on the southeast shore, only a huge thicket of scrubby brush and thin young trees like a stand of giant toothpicks. The nearest homes in that direction ran south on the block behind St. Elysius, small, neat boxes with ribbons of smoke curling up from their chimneys.

Mitch completed the circle, drawing his gaze up to Old Cedar Road, lined with cars and vans and people stamping their feet to keep the feeling in them. Albert Fletcher stood at the end of the line, a tall figure in a somber black coat, a black hood drawn tight around his thin face.

"Did the two of you ride over with Noogie?" Mitch asked.

"I did." Father Tom raised his brows as he, too, spotted the deacon. "Albert must have come on his own. I didn't think he was interested in coming out. He told me he wasn't feeling well, thought he had a cold coming on. . . ."

"Apparently he's feeling better," Megan said, hunching her back against a gust of wind.

"Hmm . . . I'd better get going," the priest said. "I'm sure Paul won't be happy to see me, but I think Hannah is going to need a shoulder to cry on."

He trudged off across the snow and climbed the bank to where Albert Fletcher was standing. The two men left together.

Mitch turned his attention to the small jacket he held and the name that was written inside the collar with indelible laundry marker. He held it out for Megan's inspection and she took it from him, sighing heavily. "This doesn't leave any room for doubt, does it?"

Steiger came over with a woman who held a big black Lab on a leash. The dog danced along beside her, barely able to contain his excitement. "Mitch, this is Ruth Cooper. Her dog found the jacket."

Mitch nodded. "Mrs. Cooper."

Megan shot the sheriff a look, then introduced herself. "Mrs. Cooper, I'm Agent O'Malley with the BCA."

"Oh, yes. How do you do? Caleb, sit," the woman said, tugging on the leash. Caleb had the lean, muscular body of a young dog, and he wiggled and shivered from his head to the tip of his tail as he cast a hopeful look up at his mistress.

Beneath her thick cream knit stocking cap and inside a puffy cream and mauve ski jacket, Ruth Cooper was a small, rounded woman in her sixties. Her pert nose was showing the effects of too much time out in the extreme cold by turning the shade of red worn by deer hunters in the fall. She shifted her weight back and forth from one snowmobile boot to the other as she told her story.

"I was walking with Caleb," she began, and the dog wagged his tail enthusiastically at the sound of his name. "He can go off his leash, but we don't trust him not to run off on an adventure, so either Stan or me goes out with him—even in this weather. And Stan, he can't go out in this now, you know; he's got that awful flu bug going around. I told him to get the shot this fall, but he's so stubborn. Anyway, we were walking around the bay, and Caleb, he likes to go out into the reeds and scare up birds, so off he goes, and he comes running back with this." She grabbed one sleeve of Josh's coat and held it up. "I knew right away. I just knew. That poor little tyke."

"Mrs. Cooper," Mitch said. "You walk Caleb out here every day?"

"Oh, yes. He needs to get out and Stan and me don't care for kennels—not with a big dog like Caleb. We're out here every day. That's our place over there—the tan Cape Cod house. Would you like to come in for coffee? It's awfully cold out here."

"Maybe in a few minutes, Mrs. Cooper," Mitch said. "I'm

sorry to keep you out in the cold like this, but we'll need to see exactly where Caleb dug this up."

Ruth and Caleb led the way with Steiger right beside them.

Noogie walked beside Mitch, talking in a low voice. "Chief, I was on the search team out here Friday. We were all over this ground and no one found so much as a gum wrapper. We had a dog from Search and Rescue, too. That jacket wasn't out here."

Mitch frowned. "When was the last time you saw Caleb go out into this general area, Mrs. Cooper?"

"We were in this same spot yesterday afternoon." She stopped along the edge of the slough and pointed.

"Did you see anyone here between then and this afternoon?" Megan asked, idly unzipping a pocket on the jacket to check the contents—a wad of tissue, a Bubble Yum wrapper.

"I see people out here from time to time. We got this nice path, you know, for snowmobiles or walkers or cross-country skiing. Some of these fitness people are just crazy. They'll go out in all weather for their jogging or whatever," she said. "There was a man out here early this morning. I was in my kitchen heating up water for Stan's Theraflu, and I looked out and saw him walking on the path."

"Did you get a good look at him?" Mitch asked.

"He came right up to the house, but he was all bundled up, you know," she said. "He'd lost his dog. Wanted to know had I seen him. A big hairy thing—the dog, not the man. I told him no and he asked would I keep an eye out. I said sure. You know, I just love dogs. I'd sure look out for one lost in this awful cold." Caleb wagged his tail and bowed at her feet.

"My men searched this area already," Steiger said to Mitch. He had his hands rammed into his coat pockets and looked as stiff as a carved totem pole from the cold. "There's nothing else here to see. I say we take Ruth up on that coffee."

"I just want to have a quick look," Mitch said, and started down the bank.

"His son's dog, he said," Ruth went on. "The dog's name was something kind of odd. Grimsby? Gatsby? Gizmo. That was it. Gizmo."

A cold blade of dread went through Mitch. He froze halfway down the bank. Gizmo. In his mind's eye he could see the drawing from Josh's notebook—a boy and his dog. A hairy mutt named Gizmo.

"Mitch."

Megan's tone turned his head in her direction. He looked up at her. Her eyes were wide, her face as colorless as the snow. In her gloved hand she held a strip of paper. The wind made it flutter like a ribbon.

He charged up the bank and caught the end of it between his fingers. He realized he hadn't known what cold was until he read the words and his blood ran like ice water in his veins.

> *my specter around me night and day*
> *like a wild beast guards my way*
> *my emanation far within*
> *weeps incessantly for my SIN*

4:55 P.M.   -27°   WINDCHILL FACTOR: -45°

What the hell does it mean?" Steiger stalked around the table, his hands on his lean hips.

Megan sat on the table with her feet on the seat of a chair and her elbows on her knees. This was the conference room where she had first seen Mitch, dancing in long red underwear, one week ago to the day. He leaned back against the wall directly in front of her now, his arms crossed, his expression hard and worn. His face was carved with lines of strain and shadowed with fatigue, lean and tough.

The room had changed as well. They called it the war room now. A map of Park County and one of the state of Minnesota covered the cork bulletin board, red pins poked into them marking search territories. The long wall held a time line of the investigation on a sheet of white paper three feet wide and twelve feet long. Everything that had happened since Josh's last sighting was noted on the time line, scribbled tributaries branching out from the main red artery, notes in red ink and blue ink and black ink. On the white message board at the end of the room, Mitch had added the verse from the latest note in his bold, slanted handwriting.

This was where they came to brainstorm. Away from the noise and activity of the command post. The war room had no phone, no volunteers underfoot, no press peering in. In this room they could sit and stare at the latest of the messages and listen to the clock tick as they struggled to decipher the meaning. All they knew with certainty was that the quote was from William Blake's "My Specter."

"He could be saying he has a split personality," Megan offered, earning a derisive snort from the sheriff. "Or an accomplice."

"Olie Swain," he grunted. "He was guilty as sin. You saw those pictures he had—"

"They were old," Mitch argued. "He had a clean record here—"

The sheriff rolled his eyes as they crossed paths in their pacing. "Once a chicken hawk, always a chicken hawk. You think he lived here all that time without putting it to some kid?"

"We never had a report—"

"Big deal. Shit like that goes on and nobody hears about it. Kids are greedy. Olie offers some kid ten bucks for a little touchy-feely, maybe the kid thinks it's no big deal—he takes the cash and keeps his mouth shut. Olie did it."

"Then swore in his life's blood it wasn't him," Megan pointed out, more to needle Steiger than because she believed it.

He scowled at her. "You fell for that?" He shook his head, malicious glee tightening the corners of his mouth. "Well, I guess we all know how you made detective."

"What the hell is that supposed to mean?" Mitch growled, straightening away from the wall.

"It means he's a jerk," Megan said smoothly. She steered the conversation back on track before Steiger could offer a rebuttal. "He could be saying he feels guilty for what he's done, but I don't believe it. He hasn't done anything remorseful; all he's done is taunt us. I think he's standing back, laughing his head off, while we run around like the Keystone Kops."

"Goddamn head games," Mitch muttered. Head games from a mind as twisted as a corkscrew. Warped enough to plant a piece of evidence, then calmly walk up to a house and strike up a conversation with the woman inside, casually dropping clues into the conversation, then walking away.

"I agree. We know Olie didn't have anything to do with the call made Saturday from St. Peter. He didn't plant the notebook. He couldn't have planted the jacket. That call last night didn't come from Olie, either."

"What call?" Steiger demanded.

Megan ignored him. "It might have been a crank, but it fits too well."

The sheriff stepped into her line of vision, a scowl pulling his features into a sour mask. "What call?"

"I got a call last night," Mitch said, pointing to the message board. "He just said the same thing over and over—'blind and naked ignorance.' I wrote it off as a crank."

"Blind and naked?" Steiger sniffed. "Maybe someone was looking in your windows."

"And maybe you should keep your mind on the case and your comments to yourself, Russ."

Megan slipped down off the table as her beeper went off. Unclipping the pager from her belt, she hit the display button and frowned. "I have to make a call," she mumbled, meeting Mitch's eyes with her best poker face. "Chief, are you about ready to go have that chat with the Kirkwoods?"

Mitch nodded. He didn't like the look of strain on her face. The call would be to DePalma. As much as he kept telling himself she was blowing things out of proportion, he still couldn't help but tense. He didn't want her off the case. He didn't want her punished for something he had been as much a part of as she—more, if you got right down to it. Megan had her rule against cops; he was the one who had coerced her into breaking it.

"Five minutes," he said. "I'll stop by your office."

He watched her slip out the door, forgetting Steiger's presence for a moment. A moment was all the sheriff allowed.

"So, how is she?" Steiger asked, swaggering across the room, his arms crossed over his chest, a smirk twisting his thin lips. "She doesn't look like she'd be much of a fuck, but then, maybe she can do better things with that mouth than shoot it off."

Mitch's response was pure reaction. He swung a hard right that caught Steiger square in the nose. The resounding *crack!* of breaking bone went through the room like a gunshot. Steiger's head snapped around and he went down on one knee, blood gushing through the hands he pressed to his face.

"Jethus! Chou bloke my nothe!" he exclaimed. The blood ran thick and red between his fingers, dripping in rivulets down the backs of his hands and falling in droplets to stain the carpet.

Shaking his hand to relieve the stinging, Mitch leaned down over him, his eyes glittering and feral. "You got by easy, Russ," he snarled. "That was for siccing Paige Price on Megan, leaking information, and being a son of a bitch in general. One lousy broken nose for all of that? Hell, you weren't that good-looking to begin with.

"But let me give you a little advance warning here, Russ," he continued, lifting a finger to emphasize his point. "If I turn on the ten o'clock news tonight and hear Paige reciting William Blake, I'm going to come out to that tin can you live in, stick a gun up your ass, and blow your brains out. Do you understand what I'm saying here, Russ?"

"Fluck chou," Steiger blubbered, fumbling in his hip pocket for a handkerchief.

"Well said, Sheriff," Mitch drawled as he straightened and started for the door. "A master of articulation, as usual. Too bad you're not half as good a cop."

She twisted the facts," Megan said into the receiver. Elbows on her blotter, she leaned her forehead heavily against one hand. "What am I saying? She didn't even *have* the facts! Bruce—"

"Don't call me Bruce when I'm angry with you," DePalma snapped.

"Yes, sir," she said on a sigh. She felt as if some unseen hands were stabbing darning needles into her eyes. "She fabricated that story out of thin air—"

"You weren't at Chief Holt's house at three in the morning?"

"There is a very simple, innocent explanation—which, I might add, Paige Price did not bother to try to get from me before jumping me at the press conference."

"So you're saying this is all a misunderstanding that has been blown out of proportion?"

"Yes."

"That's become a recurring theme in your life, Agent O'Malley." The tone was sharp enough to make her wince. "We've already had this discussion about the gender issue. The last thing this bureau needs is to be dragged into a sex scandal."

"Yes, sir."

"Do you have any idea the kind of feeding frenzy that could go on here? We finally give a woman a field post and the first thing she does is seduce the chief of police?"

She nearly came out of her chair. "I did *not* seduce—"

"I'm not saying you did, but that doesn't mean the press will be as kind. What *did* go on?"

Megan swallowed hard and crossed her fingers. "Chief Holt and I were discussing the case over coffee—"

"In the dark?"

"He had a fire going and the television was on. The two combined provided more than adequate light."

"Go on."

"As you know, we've been putting in hellish hours on this case. We were both exhausted. We simply fell asleep."

During the lengthy silence that ensued, Megan felt beads of sweat pop out on her forehead like bullets. She wasn't a liar by nature and she detested the need for it now. What she did after hours should have been nobody's business. Had she been a man, she doubted anyone would have cared enough to follow her around. Had she been a man, she thought sourly, she probably would have been *expected* to have seduced someone by now.

Seduced. The word left a bad taste in her mouth. It sounded so cheap. Regardless of what became of her relationship with Mitch, she didn't want to think of what they had shared in those terms.

"My sixteen-year-old comes up with better stories than that," DePalma said at last.

"It's the truth." *Part of it, anyway.*

DePalma heaved a sigh that sounded like gale-force winds over the telephone. "Megan, I like you. You're a good cop. I want this job to work for you, but you're putting the bureau in an untenable position. We name you our first woman in the field and we get accused of tokenism. Every time you turn around you stick your foot in something new—fighting with Kirkwood, sleeping with Holt—"

"I *told* you—"

"Save your breath. It doesn't matter if you did or you didn't. People will believe what they want."

"Including you."

"And now your only suspect turns up dead in jail—"

"Are you accusing me of murdering him, too?"

"It looks bad."

"God forbid crime should be anything but tidy—"

"That kind of smart remark is exactly what gets you in trouble, Megan. You've got to learn to curb that Irish tongue of yours before it gets you fired."

Which meant she wasn't fired yet. She would have breathed a sigh of relief, but she knew damn well she was still on a high wire juggling bowling balls. One more misstep and it was all over.

"I don't want it to come to that, Megan. God knows what kind of mess we'll have on our hands if we have to pull you in. But we've got a mess already, so don't think that will stop it from happening."

"No, sir."

"Where are you with the case?"

Down a rabbit hole with a madman. She kept that thought to herself and explained without embellishment or false hope where they stood. In police work it didn't pay to promise more than you could deliver.

DePalma asked questions at intervals.

"Can this Cooper woman identify the man who came to her house?"

"She's not sure. He was bundled up pretty well against the cold. I've got her with the composite artist right now."

"Was there blood on the jacket?"

"Not that I could see. It's gone to the lab."

"What do you think about the note? Do you think he's saying he killed the boy?"

"I don't know."

"Have you considered the possibility that Swain's accomplice might have been someone from his past in Washington?"

"According to everything we've got on him," Megan said, "he was a loner there as well. The closest thing he had to a friend was the cousin whose identity he was carrying around, and the nicest thing he has to say is that Olie was a freak. Of course, I'd be a little cranky too if my cousin stole my driver's license and assumed my identity in another state, then committed a heinous crime that garnered national attention."

DePalma ignored her sarcasm. "Maybe you need some help," he suggested.

Megan felt the fine hair on the back of her neck rise. "What do you mean?"

"You're not getting anywhere. Maybe you need someone to come in with a fresh perspective."

"I can handle the case, Bruce," she said tightly.

"Of course you can. I just believe that when things are at a standstill, a person coming in fresh can shake something loose."

Like me, Megan thought sourly. The game plan was painfully clear. DePalma would send out another agent to quietly usurp her authority, and when the reins had changed hands, she would be called back quietly to headquarters. No muss, no fuss, all neat and tidy, just the way the brass liked things.

"I think it would be a mistake." She struggled to hang on to some semblance of cool. "Anyone coming in cold would have to wade through all the statements, reinterview witnesses, get to know the family—and frankly, they don't need any more upheaval in their lives."

"I'll bear that in mind. In the meantime, Megan, you need to make something good happen. Do you understand what I'm saying?"

"Perfectly."

They said their good-byes and she hung up the phone, making a nasty face at it. "And don't call me Megan when I'm angry with you," she jeered.

"Yes, ma'am,": Mitch replied as he stuck his head in the door.

Megan looked up at him, too weary and too worried to even try to smile. "I'm not angry with you."

He ambled into her office with his coat thrown over his shoulder.

"What'd you do to your hand?"

A frown curved his mouth as he glanced at the swollen knuckles. "I felt a need to hit something."

"Like what—a brick wall?"

"Steiger's face."

She raised her brows in amazement. "Damn, Chief, I would have paid money to see that."

He shrugged. "Better not to have witnesses," he said. "Steiger's been leaking information to Paige Price. I expressed my displeasure."

The rage of injustice only made her temples pound harder. "She's screwing Steiger for information and she has the gall to stand up at a press conference and point a finger at me. I wouldn't mind hitting something myself."

"Lay a finger on her and she'll have more than your job," Mitch pointed out, running a finger along the ridge of her brass nameplate. He picked it up and read the inscription on the back: TAKE NO SHIT, MAKE NO EXCUSES. "What did DePalma have to say?"

"What did he say or what did he mean? Officially, they won't comment on hearsay about an agent. They will express their full confidence in me in the most lukewarm terms they can think of. Officially, they may send in another agent 'to assist me with the investigation.' If that happens, he'll end up with my job and I'll end up at a desk in the bowels of head-quarters doing paperwork on petty fraud schemes."

Scowling, Mitch stalked her around the end of the desk as she turned for the coat rack. "I wish you'd let me talk to him."

She shook her head. "I don't want you fighting my battles for me."

"It's called supporting a friend, Megan."

She turned and tipped her head back to meet his gaze. He was standing too close again, trying to intimidate her, calling her attention to the fact that he was bigger and stronger and capable of dominating her—or protecting her. A part of her found the idea tempting, but she wouldn't give in to that part.

"It's called giving false information, which I already did," she said. "I won't have you lie on my account, and that's that."

Her answer brooked no disagreement. Mitch said nothing as he watched her shrug into her monstrous down-filled coat. So damned stubborn. So damned independent. He wanted her to lean on him, he realized with no small amount of wonder. He wanted to help her. He wanted to defend her honor. Old-fashioned notions, and she was no old-fashioned woman. Notions that hinted at commitment—something they both claimed not to want.

"We'll work it out," he murmured, not certain what aspect of this tangled mess he meant.

What? Megan wanted to ask. The job situation? Their personal situation? She chose the former, knowing that was where their focus needed to be, knowing that damn clock would not stop ticking.

"That means one thing," she said, her expression grim. "We find Josh."

CHAPTER 27

Hannah stood at the window, staring out at the lake. The final rays of sunlight streaked the far horizon like angry red lines of infection radiating from a wound. Funny how such a hot color was an indication of such a cold sky. As she stood there, she could feel the cold seeping in through the glass, seeping into her body. She wished it would numb her, but it didn't; it simply made her shiver.

Across the lake, lights winked on. The helicopters had been called in again. She could see one in the distance, hanging over Dinkytown like a vulture. In her memory she recalled the thumping of the rotors and how she had lain awake listening to their eerie passing back and forth over the town. Beyond Dinkytown, out toward the flaming horizon, lay Ryan's Bay. On Ryan's Bay a dog had discovered Josh's jacket, discarded like a piece of litter.

She could see the jacket in her mind's eye—bright blue with splashes of green and yellow. She knew the size and the brand name. She knew the pockets where he stashed small treasures and Kleenex and mittens. She knew the smell of it and the feel of it, and all those memories hovered in her mind, intangible and untouchable. Only the second sign of Josh to surface in a week, and she had not been allowed to see it or touch it. The jacket had been whisked off to St. Paul to be studied and analyzed.

"I would have liked to just hold it," she said quietly. She tried to imagine it in her hands, raising it to her face, brushing it against her cheek.

"I'm sorry, Hannah," Megan said gently. "We felt it was essential to get it to the lab as soon as possible."

"Of course. I understand," she murmured. But she didn't, not outside that logical, practical square of brain that answered by rote.

"You'll get fingerprints off it?" Paul said. He sat by the fireplace in faded black sweatpants and a heavy gray sweatshirt with a University of Minnesota logo. His hair was still damp from the shower he had taken to warm himself. Lily sat on his lap, trying unsuccessfully to interest him in her stuffed Barney.

Megan and Mitch exchanged a look.

"No," Mitch said. "It's virtually impossible for nylon to hold fingerprints."

"What then?"

"Do you really want to make them say it?" Hannah said sharply. "What do you think they'll be looking for, Paul? Blood. Blood and semen and any other grisly leftover from whatever this animal has done to Josh. Isn't that right, Agent O'Malley?"

Megan said nothing. The question was rhetorical. Hannah neither needed nor wanted an answer. She stood with her back to the window, defiance and anger a thin mask over the raw terror that consumed her.

"The woman whose dog found the jacket may have seen the man who planted it," Mitch said. "In fact, she may have had a conversation with him."

"May have?" Hannah said, puzzled.

Mitch told them the story of Ruth Cooper and the man who had come to her door after she'd seen him through her kitchen window. When he came to the part about the dog's name, Hannah turned ashen and took hold of the wing chair for support.

Paul came to attention. He rose slowly, setting Lily down on the floor. She toddled over to Mitch and offered him her dinosaur. Father Tom rose from the couch and scooped her up, tickling her into giggles as he carried her to the bedroom upstairs.

"So, she can identify this man," Paul said.

"She's working with a composite artist," Megan explained. "It's not as easy as we'd like it to be. The man was bundled up to be out in the weather. But she thinks she might be able to pick him out if she sees him again."

"Might? Maybe?" Pulling a poker from the stand of brass tools, Paul turned his attention to the fire, stabbing at the glowing logs, sending a shower of sparks up the chimney.

"It's better than nothing."

"It *is* nothing!" He wheeled around, poker in hand, his lean face twisted with bitter rage. "You've got *nothing*! My son is lying dead someplace and you've got nothing! You can't even manage to keep the one suspect you had alive!"

Hannah glared at him. "Stop it!"

He paid no attention to her, his anger directed for the moment at Mitch and Megan. "You're too busy fucking each other to worry about my son—"

"Paul, for God's sake!"

"What's the matter, Hannah?" he demanded, rounding on her, his fingers tightening on the grip of the poker. "Did I offend your sensibilities?"

"You offended everyone."

"I don't care. They screwed up and my son has to pay the price—"

"He's my son, too—"

"Really? Is that why you left him on the street to be kidnapped and murdered?" he shouted, flinging the poker sideways. It hit the wall with a resounding crack and fell to the floor.

Hannah could barely draw the breath to respond. He could have run the poker through her and not hurt her as badly. "You bastard!" she said, her voice a trembling whisper.

"Paul!" Mitch barked, clamping a hand down on his shoulder, his anger making the grip punishing. "Let's go into your study," he said through his teeth.

Grimacing, Paul twisted away from him. "So you can lecture me again on how I should give my wife my support?" he sneered. "I don't think so. I'm not interested in anything you have to say."

"Tough." Mitch grabbed him again and steered him off in the direction of his office.

Hannah didn't watch them go. Struggling to keep hold of her control, she crossed the room, picked up the fireplace poker, and put it back in its stand. Her hands were shaking so badly, she couldn't remember them ever having been steady enough to hold a scalpel.

"Well," she said, wiping her palms on her jeans, "that was ugly."

"Hannah—" Megan started to say.

"The worst part of it is, it's true. It's my fault."

"No. You were late. That shouldn't have cost you Josh."

"But it did."

"Because of the man who chose to take him. You had no control over his decision."

"No," she murmured. "And now I have control of nothing. Because of that one moment in time, my life is flying apart. If I had made it out of the hospital before Kathleen rounded that corner to call me back in, Josh would be here. I would be picking him up from hockey today. Josh would be complaining about having to go to religion class at seven.

"One moment. A handful of seconds. A heartbeat." Staring at the fire, she snapped her fingers. "That much time and that car accident would never have happened. I wouldn't have been called back into the ER, and Josh wouldn't have been left all alone, and we wouldn't be standing here now, feeling awkward because my husband blames me . . ."

She let the thoughts trail off. There was no going back in time, only forward into uncertainty. Drained, she sank down into a chair and curled her legs beneath her. The muffled sound of angry voices came from behind the closed door of Paul's study.

Hannah picked at a dried scab of blue paint on the knee of her jeans. "I'd like to go back and find that moment when Paul changed, too," she whispered. "He used to be so different. We used to be so happy."

Megan didn't know how to respond. She had never been much for sharing confidences with other women. Her lack of skill with relationships gave her no expertise to draw upon for sage wisdom. She turned to the one thing she knew. "When did you start to notice a change in him?"

"Oh, I don't know." Hannah shrugged. "It was so subtle. In little ways, years ago, I suppose. A year or so after we moved here."

After she had begun to establish herself at the hospital and in the community. Moving here had been Paul's idea, and she often wondered what he had imagined in his heart of hearts. She wondered if he had seen himself as becoming the fixture in the community she had become, becoming someone well known and well liked and well respected. In their early days together he had confided he wanted to be somebody, somebody other than the bookworm son of a blue-collar family. Had he thought he would become someone different here, someone outgoing and gregarious, when he didn't have those qualities in him? She hated to think it was jealousy that had driven this wedge between them and poisoned the love they had shared. It seemed such a pointless emotion, nothing that belonged between people who had pledged to respect and support each other.

"And he's been withdrawing more recently?" Megan asked.

"He resents the time I spend at the hospital since I was promoted to head of the ER."

"What about his schedule? He was working that night."

"It's nearly tax season. He'll be putting in a lot of nights."

"Does he normally ignore his answering machine when you call him at the office at night?"

Hannah sat up a little straighter, her eyes narrowing, something in her chest tightening. "Why are you asking me these questions?"

Megan gave her what she hoped was a convincing sheepish look. "I'm a cop; it's what I do best."

"You can't possibly think Paul had something to do with this."

"No, no, of course not. It's just routine," Megan lied. "We need to know where everyone was—you know, before the lawyers get ahold of the case. They're fanatics for detail. Mother Teresa would need an alibi if she were here. When we catch this guy, his lawyer will probably try to pin it on someone else. He'll try to prove his client was somewhere else at six o'clock this morning. If he's sleazy enough, he'll ask where you were at six o'clock this morning, and where Paul was."

Hannah blinked at her, her face carefully blank. "I don't know where Paul was. He was gone when I woke up. He said

he went out on his own, just driving around town, looking . . .
I'm sure that's what he did," she said, sounding as if she were
trying to convince herself as much as Megan.

"I'm sure you're right," Megan agreed. She was filing
everything about this scene in her memory—the facts, Hannah's tone of voice, her expression, the tension that hovered
around her like static electricity. "I didn't mean to imply otherwise. I just want you to understand how this works, why we
have to ask some of these questions. What I really wanted to
ask was if any names had come to you—people who might have
a grudge against you or Paul. A dissatisfied patient, a disgruntled client, that sort of person."

"You've already interviewed everyone we know," Hannah
said. "I honestly can't think of any patients who would have felt
driven to such horrible lengths. Most of what we see in a small
hospital like ours are cases that are either easily curable or instantly fatal. Most critical cases—accident victims and so on—
are flown directly to HCMC. Patients with serious illnesses are
referred to larger hospitals as well."

"But you must lose a few here."

"A few." Her mouth curved in sad memory. "I remember
when I worked in the Cities we used to call little rural hospitals
like Deer Lake tag 'em and bag 'em joints. We do the best we
can, but we don't have the equipment or the staff of a large
hospital. People here understand that."

"Maybe," Megan murmured, making a mental note to stop
by Deer Lake Community Hospital to feel out the staff in the
ER herself.

"As far as Paul's clients go, there are a few who squawk
every year about what they have to pay in taxes, but that's
hardly his fault."

"No big catastrophic audits, people sent to prison, that
kind of thing?"

"No." Hannah pushed herself up out of the chair, the nervous restlessness never allowing her more than a few minutes
of stillness, regardless of fatigue. "I'm going to make some tea.
Would you like some? It's so cold—"

And Josh was out there somewhere without his coat.

Outside the big picture window, night had fallen, cold and
black as an anvil.

"Do you think he's alive?" she whispered, staring out at the darkness into which Josh had disappeared eight long days before.

Megan rose to stand beside her. A little over a week ago everyone in town would have said Hannah had it all—the career, the family, the house on the lake. Half the town had looked on her as an icon of modern womanhood. Now she was just a woman, shattered and vulnerable, clinging to a thread of hope as thin as a hair.

"He's alive until someone proves to me he isn't," Megan said. "That's what I believe. That's what you need to believe, too."

The door to Paul's office swung open. He stormed out and left the house through the door that led to the garage. Mitch emerged from the study, his face grim and drawn with lines of fatigue.

"I don't know how to get through to him," he muttered as he walked into the family room.

"Neither do I," Hannah confessed. "Should we start a support group?"

Mitch mustered half a smile for her stab at humor. He took her hands in his and gave them a squeeze. Her fingers were as cold as death. "I'm sorry, Hannah. I'm so sorry for all of this. I wish there were something more I could do."

"I know you guys are doing all you can. It's not your fault."

"It's not yours, either." He pulled her into his arms and gave her a hug. "Hang in there, honey."

Hannah walked them to the door and saw them out into the frigid night. On her way back through the family room she stopped for a moment and listened to the silence. Their "watcher," as she referred to the agent assigned to the house, had gone for dinner when Mitch and Megan had arrived, and had yet to return. She had asked for and received a reprieve from the tag team companions sent from the neighborhood and the far-flung reaches of the missing children's organization. The house was quiet, calm, the tension gone.

She wondered where Paul was, wondered how long she would have until he returned and the hostilities resumed. She wondered how long the rift between them would take to heal. A week, a month, a year. She wondered if they would have

Josh back before it happened. She wondered if she really wanted it to heal.

In her mind she saw his jacket lying tangled in the reeds at Ryan's Bay.

As the fear and dread and guilt began another cycle inside her, she went up the stairs and down the hall to Lily's room. Lily would give her comfort and love, unconditional, nonjudgmental, no questions asked.

The sound of a low, soft voice inside the room brought Hannah up short in the hall. The door was ajar, soft light spilling out onto the carpet like a moonbeam. She peered in through the crack and saw Father Tom sitting in the old white wicker rocking chair, Lily on his lap, his arms looped around her to hold the storybook he was reading.

Any stranger would have imagined they were father and daughter. Tom in his sweatshirt and rumpled corduroy trousers, the lamplight striking a starburst off the gold frames of his glasses. Lily in a purple fleece sleeper, her cheeks pink, her big eyes heavy-lidded; drowsy and content to listen to the adventures of Winnie-the-Pooh and his pals.

Something stirred inside Hannah, something she didn't dare name, something that came with an aftertaste of disappointment and shame.

She slipped into the room before the feeling could drive her back. Tom was a friend and she needed a friend, that was all there was to it—no complications, nothing to engender regret. He finished the story and closed the book, and both he and Lily looked up at her expectantly.

"Hi, Mama," Lily said sweetly, tilting her head and waving.

"Hi, Lily-bug. Everyone's gone." She bent down to take her daughter into her arms. Lily snuggled into her mother's embrace, laying her head on Hannah's shoulder.

"Paul, too?" Tom said, raising his brows. He stood up and made a halfhearted attempt to brush the wrinkles out of his pants.

"I don't know where he went." Hannah turned away, not wanting to see the sympathy in his eyes, tired of people feeling sorry for her.

"I heard the fight," he said softly. "I'm sure he didn't mean it. He's just lashing out. Of course, that doesn't make it hurt any less, I know—"

She shook her head. "It doesn't matter."

"It *does*," Tom insisted. "He should be able to see this isn't your fault, or if not that, forgive you at least."

"Why should Paul forgive me when I can't forgive myself?"

"Hannah . . ."

"It's true," she said, restlessly walking around the cozy bedroom with its soft pink walls and Beatrix Potter details. "I've relived that night a thousand times. If only I'd done this. If only I hadn't done that. It always comes down to the same thing: I'm Josh's mother. He relied on me and I let him down. I don't know if anyone should pardon me from that sin."

"God forgives you."

The statement was so guileless, it struck Hannah as being almost childlike in its faith. She turned to him, wishing he could answer her questions, knowing he couldn't.

"Then why does He keep punishing me this way?" she asked, pain swelling inside her. "What have I done to deserve this? What has Josh done or Paul? I don't understand."

"I don't know," he whispered hoarsely. He didn't understand it any better than she did, and that was his sin, he supposed—one of many—not trusting that God knew best. How could this be best for anyone? Why should Hannah suffer when she gave so much to so many people? He couldn't understand or accept it or keep himself from feeling anger toward the God to whom he had devoted his own life. He felt betrayed as Hannah felt betrayed. And he felt guilty because of it, and angry because of the guilt, and rebellious because of the limitations put on him by his station, and frightened by what he thought that might drive him to. The emotions spiraled down and down.

"It hurts *so much*!" Hannah said in a tortured whisper. She squeezed her eyes closed and hugged Lily tight, rocking her back and forth.

Without hesitation, Tom put his arms around her and drew her close. She was in pain; he would comfort her. If there were consequences to pay later, he would pay them. He coaxed Hannah's head to his shoulder and stroked her hair and shushed her.

"I know it hurts, honey," he whispered. "I wish there was something I could do to stop it. I'd do anything to help you. I'd give anything to take this all away."

Hannah let herself cry on his shoulder. She took the comfort he offered. It felt so good to be held. He was solid and strong and warm. Tender. Feeling what she felt. Wanting to take her pain away. All the things her husband should have been and wasn't.

She slipped one arm around his waist and squeezed him tight as another flood of tears came—not for Josh, but for herself and for the torn fabric of the life that had once seemed so perfect. A dream, shattered and swept away. She wondered if it had ever been real.

Tom murmured to her. He touched her hair, her cheek, as careful as if she were made of spun sugar. His lips brushed against her temple. She raised her face and felt the warmth of his breath. She opened her eyes and met his gaze and saw the reflection of the tumult of her own emotions—need, longing, pain, guilt.

The moment caught and held, stretched between what they wanted and who they were, between what was right and what was required. Revelation and fear held them breathless.

It was Lily who broke the spell. Protesting being sandwiched between adults, she pushed at her mother's shoulder in irritation and said, "Mama, down!"

Tom stepped back, Hannah dropped her gaze to the floor.

"It's bedtime, Lily," she said softly, turning around to place her daughter in her crib.

Lily frowned at her. "No."

"Yes."

"Where Josh?" she demanded, standing up at the railing. "Me want Josh."

Hannah brushed Lily's fine gold hair back and bent to kiss her forehead. "Me, too, sweetheart."

Tom stepped around to the end of the crib, curling his hands around the corner posts, too aware that he preferred the feel of Hannah in his arms. He couldn't bring himself to admit that was a mistake. Instead of trying, he changed the subject.

"Can I make a suggestion?" he said. "Do an interview."

Hannah looked up at him, puzzled. "What?"

"I know everyone is clamoring for an exclusive with you, and I know you don't want to do it, but I think it would be good for you. Pick the show with the biggest ratings and go on. Tell America what you told me—how you feel, how difficult it is to deal with the guilt, what you believe you did wrong, what you would change if you could have that night back."

Hannah shot him a look. "I thought confession was sacrosanct."

"Think of it as penance if you want. The point is that maybe by doing this you'll make someone else think twice. You can't have that night back, but you might be able to prevent someone else from having to go through this hell."

Hannah looked down at her daughter, who now lay curled on her side on flannel sheets printed with images of Peter Rabbit and Jemima Puddle-Duck. She would give her own life to protect this precious little one. Such was the bond between mother and child. If she could help another mother, save another child, would that serve as payment for the mistakes she had made?

"I'll think about it." She looked up at Father Tom, at his strong, handsome face and his kind blue eyes. Her heart beat a little too hard. "Thank you. I—a—"

The words didn't form, which was probably just as well. Better for him not to know what she was feeling; it would only make things difficult, and she didn't want to lose his friendship. "Thanks."

He nodded and moved away from the crib, sliding his hands into his pockets. "I should go. And you should try to rest."

"I'll try."

"Promise?" he asked, raising his brows at her as she walked him to the bedroom door.

Her mouth curved. "I promise to try."

"I'll take what I can get. You stay here with Lily; I can find my own way out. You know where to find me if you need me."

She nodded and he turned away before he could say something they would both regret. She didn't have to know the depth of his feelings; only that he cared and was there for her. The rest couldn't matter.

Outside, the night was so cold it seemed that anything

touched would shatter. Like a heart. He dismissed the analogy as foolhardy and tried to concentrate on something priestly as he coaxed his truck to start. Lines from the Lord's Prayer scrolled through his head. *Lead us not into temptation . . . deliver us from evil . . .*

"I'm in love with Hannah Garrison," he murmured. "A madman stole her child."

He looked up through the windshield. Heaven was black and silver with the light of a broken moon. A sea of stars so far away. A feeling of abandonment yawned inside him.

"Someone up there's not doing their job."

6:24 P.M.   -28°   WINDCHILL FACTOR: -50°

Paul's lungs hurt from the cold. His legs ached from struggling through the deep snow and his toes hurt as if each one had been struck with a hammer. The only part of him that was warm was the glowing coal of his anger in his chest. He stepped over a fallen limb and leaned against the trunk of a cedar tree at the edge of the woods that ran behind the houses of Lakeside. To the east and north lay Quarry Hills Park, wooded and pretty with its groomed cross-country ski trails. One of his badges of honor, one of his deserved rewards: living with the lake out his front door and the park out his back door. One of the signs that he had made something of himself.

And Mitch Holt and Megan O'Malley wanted to treat him like a criminal.

How could they look at him as if he were a suspect when he had thrown himself into the effort to get Josh back? He had gone on the searches, made appeals on television. What more could he do?

This was all the fault of that little bitch from the BCA. She was the one who was so hung up on that damned old van. She was the one who kept trying to poke holes in his explanation of why he hadn't checked his messages that night and called Hannah back. And they both, of course, felt sorry for Hannah. Poor

Hannah, who gives so much of herself. Poor Hannah, the mother who lost her son.

The stinging in his fingers brought Paul's attention back to the here and now. He had trudged through the woods because the street in front of his house was lined with the cars and vans of reporters. He had plenty to say to them, but not just then. Now he had other needs. A need to be held by a real woman, someone who understood him and would do anything to please him.

He crossed the Wrights' backyard and went in the back door of the garage. Garrett's Saab was gone. Karen's Honda sat alone, as it did most evenings. Garrett Wright was married to his work, not his wife. Home was the place he came to shower and change clothes. Karen's place in his life was largely ornamental—someone to take to faculty dinners. Any other interest he had once had in her as a woman had dwindled away. According to Karen, they rarely had sex, and when they did, it was more duty than desire on Garrett's part.

They had no children. Karen wasn't able to conceive by the usual means and Garrett wasn't willing to go through the endless marathon of tests and procedures involved with the in vitro process. Having children wasn't important to him. Karen talked of adoption, but that process was daunting as well and she didn't know if she had the strength or endurance to tackle it alone. And so they went on, just the two of them, in a shell of a marriage with which Garrett seemed perfectly content and to which Karen clung because she didn't have the courage to break free.

Paul seldom thought of Garrett Wright in anything but abstract terms. Even though they were neighbors, they barely knew each other. To Paul, Garrett Wright lived in an alternate universe. He was a shadowy figure who buried himself in his psychology texts and his research at Harris and gave what free time he had to a bunch of juvenile delinquents called the Sci-Fi Cowboys. He and Garrett Wright existed on two different planes that intersected in only one place—Karen.

Using the spare key that was always left under an old coffee can full of nails on the workbench, he let himself into the laundry room. He took off his heavy boots and brushed the snow from the legs of his sweatpants.

"Garrett?"

Karen opened the door to the kitchen, her dark eyes going wide at the sight of him. She stood there in her stocking feet, a green checked dish towel in one hand, purple leggings clinging to her legs. A shapeless ivory V-neck sweater reached down to her knees. Her ash-blond hair hung as limp as silk, the bangs soft above her doe eyes. Small and soft and feminine, full of comfort and concern for him. The first rustlings of desire whispered through him.

"Are you expecting him?" he asked.

"No. He just left to go back to work. I thought he might have forgotten something." Self-conscious, she tucked a strand of hair behind her ear and brushed her fingers through her bangs. "I thought you'd be with Hannah tonight. I heard about the jacket. I'm so sorry, Paul."

He slipped off his old black parka and tossed it on the dryer, his eyes on hers. "I don't want to talk about it."

"All right."

He took the towel from her hand and looped it around the back of her neck, pulling her closer with it. "I'm sick of it," he said, winding the checked cloth into his fists. The anger burned in his chest. "I'm sick of the questions and the accusations and the waiting and everyone looking at Hannah and saying 'Poor brave Hannah.' It's all her fault. And that little bitch is trying to blame me."

"Hannah blames you?" Karen asked, puzzled. She had to strain back against the towel to look up at him.

"Agent O'Malley," he sneered. "She's too busy screwing Holt to do her job right."

"How could anyone blame *you*?"

Dad, can you come and get me from hockey? Mom's late and I wanna go home.

"I don't know," he whispered as his throat tightened and tears burned his eyes. "It wasn't my fault."

"Of course it wasn't."

"It wasn't my fault," he murmured, squeezing his eyes shut and dropping his head. He wound the towel tighter. "It wasn't my fault."

Karen flattened herself against him to escape the pain. She slipped her small hands beneath his sweatshirt and stroked the lean muscles of his back. "It wasn't your fault, sweetheart."

Dad, can you come and get me from hockey? Mom's late and I wanna go home.

The voice haunted his mind. It overlaid images of the afternoon: O'Malley questioning him—*you never checked your answering machine?* The jacket in his hands—*He's dead. He's dead. He's dead. . . .*

The towel fell from his hands to the floor.

". . . not my fault," he whimpered, trembling.

Karen pressed a finger to his lips. "Shh. Come with me."

She led him through the kitchen and down the dark hall to the guest bedroom. They never made love in the bed she shared with Garrett. They seldom met there in her house; the risk of discovery was too great. But he made no move to stop her as she undressed him like a child, and he made no move to stop her as she undressed herself. This was what he had come for, but he made no advances. It wasn't his fault. He deserved to be comforted.

He lay on the clean peach sheets in the soft glow of the bedside lamp and allowed her to arouse him with her lips and her hands and her body. She teased with her mouth, caressed with her fingers, rubbed her small breasts against him, opened herself, and took him inside her. She moved on him slowly, murmuring to him, stroking his chest, stoking a fire of physical need that gradually burned through the haze of numbness.

Grabbing her by the shoulders, he pulled her to him and rolled her beneath him. He deserved this. He needed it. Release for his body and for the anger smoldering inside him—anger with Hannah, with O'Malley, anger at the injustices that had been heaped on his life. He let it all pour out as he pumped himself in and out of another man's wife. Deeper, harder, until the thrusts were more punishment than passion.

And then in a burst it was over. The strength was gone. The power drained away. He collapsed beside Karen and stared at the ceiling, oblivious to her curling against him, oblivious to her tears, oblivious to time passing. Oblivious to everything but the insidious weakness that crawled through him.

"I wish you could stay," Karen whispered.

"I can't."

"I know. But I wish you could." She raised her head and gazed at him. "I wish I could give you all the love and support you need. I wish I could give you a son."

"Karen . . ."

"I do," she insisted, rubbing the palm of her hand over his heart. "I'd have your baby, Paul. I think about it all the time. I think about it when I'm in your house, when I'm holding Lily. I pretend she's mine—ours. I think about it every time we're together, every time you climax inside me. I'd have your baby, Paul. I'd do anything for you."

This was just another of life's cruel ironies, he thought as he watched her bend her head and press kisses to his chest. He had the wife he had always thought he wanted—the independent, capable Dr. Garrison—and now he wanted the kind of woman he had grown up loathing—Karen, born to serve, subjugating her needs to his, willing to be anything he wanted just to please him.

He checked the clock on the nightstand and sighed. "I have to go."

He washed up in the guest bath while she changed the sheets. As always, there would be no evidence of their stolen time together, not so much as a scent of sex in the linens. They dressed in silence and walked in silence back down the dark hall to the kitchen, where a single light burned over the sink.

"I heard they're going to resume the ground search tomorrow," Karen said, leaning a hip against the oak cupboards. "Will you go out?"

Paul took a glass from the drainer beside the sink and filled it. "I guess," he said, staring at his reflection in the window.

He took a sip from the glass and dumped the rest of the water. He rinsed the glass and put it back in the drainer; blotted his mouth with the green checked towel, refolded it, and laid it back on the counter.

From beyond the laundry room came the sound of the door to the garage opening and closing. Paul's nerves jangled. Guilt gripped its fist inside of him. The kitchen door swung open and Garrett Wright walked in, tucking his gloves into the pockets of his navy wool topcoat.

"Paul!" he said, his dark eyes widening. "This is a surprise." He set his briefcase on the oak kitchen table and unbuttoned his coat. Karen took up her rightful place beside him, leaning up to brush a passionless kiss to his cheek. They made a pretty couple, both blond and fair with dark eyes and carefully sculpted features. The kind of couple that could have passed for brother and sister.

"I stopped by to ask Karen if she would be willing to do some extra duty at the volunteer center tomorrow," he said. "We're resuming the ground search, regardless of the cold."

"Yes, I heard. I didn't see your car out front."

"I walked."

Garrett's pale brows rose in unison. "Cold night for a walk."

"I thought it might clear my head."

"Yes, well," he said, making a good show of being concerned, "you've got a lot on your mind these days. How are you holding up?"

"I'm getting by," Paul said, trying not to sound grudging. On the occasions of his conversations with Garrett Wright he had always felt like a bug under a microscope. As if he were a potential candidate for psychoanalysis, as if Wright was, even as they spoke, analyzing his words and gestures and expressions or lack of them.

"I know you've been very active in the search," Garrett said, slipping off his coat. The dutiful wife, Karen took it from him without a word and went to hang it in the front hall closet. "That's a healthy way of dealing with the situation, even if there are a lot of frustrations. How's Hannah doing?"

"As well as she can," Paul said stiffly.

"I haven't seen her on the news—except in the paper last Sunday. She collapsed, didn't she?" Garrett shook his head. Frowning gravely, he slipped his hands into the pockets of his dark pleated pants and rocked back on his heels. "The loss of a child is a terrible strain on the parents."

"I'm well aware of that," Paul said tightly.

Garrett gave a little jolt of realization, his dark eyes widening with contrition. "I'm sorry. I didn't mean to sound patronizing, Paul. I just wanted to say if either of you feel a need to talk to someone, I can recommend a friend of mine in Edina. He specializes in family therapy."

"I've got better things to do," Paul said, his jaw rigid.

"Please don't take offense, Paul." Wright reached a hand out toward him. "I only meant to help."

"If you want to help, then show up at Ryan's Bay tomorrow morning. That's the kind of help we need, not some overpriced shrink in Edina." He turned his attention to Karen. "I'll see you tomorrow at the center."

Karen nodded, her gaze on the floor. "I'll be there."

She stood there, holding her breath until she heard the door to the garage open and close.

"That wasn't very sensitive of you, Garrett," she admonished her husband softly.

"Really? I think it was extremely generous of me, all things considered."

He went to the sink and ran a finger down the side of the water-dotted glass in the drainer. He picked up the neatly folded green checked towel, dried the glass, and refolded the towel.

"You should be more careful where you leave things," he said, holding up the towel.

The towel Paul had taken from her. The towel with which he had drawn her to him, his fists wrapping tighter and tighter into the cloth.

The towel he had dropped on the floor in the laundry room.

Karen said nothing. Garrett set the towel aside on the counter and walked away.

CHAPTER 28

Mitch stared at the message board on the war room wall until the messages from the kidnapper began to swirl together. Elbows on the table, he put his face in his hands and tried to rub the weariness from his eyes. A futile effort. The fatigue went far deeper. It beat at him relentlessly, a cold, black club that struck again and again to loosen his hold on his logic, his objectivity. It stung his temper, made him feel mean and dangerous. It cracked the hard protective shell of control and allowed guilt and uncertainty to seep in like a toxic ooze.

Guilt. He'd seen the look on Hannah's face when Paul had hurled his accusation at her with the same violence that had sent the fireplace poker hurtling into the wall. A burst of pain, but beneath it guilt. She blamed herself as much as Paul blamed her. He knew exactly how that felt—the constant, pointless self-punishment, the pain that became so familiar that in a perverse way you almost didn't want to let it go.

"You should probably put something on those knuckles," Megan said quietly. "God knows what kind of cooties might be running around in Steiger's bodily fluids. I'm on my way to the hospital. Wanna ride along?"

Mitch jerked his hands from his face and slapped them palms-down on the tabletop. He didn't know how long she had been standing there, leaning against the door frame, while he wrestled with his inner demons. She came into the conference room with her eyelids at half mast as she rubbed at the tension in the back of her neck.

"I'm fine," he said, glancing at the hand he had skinned breaking Steiger's nose. "I've had my tetanus shot."

"I was thinking more along the lines of rabies or maybe hoof-and-mouth disease," she said dryly, perching a hip on the tabletop across from him.

"Why are you going to the hospital?"

"Trolling for suspects. I know we've questioned everyone down there, but I want to dig a little more. Hannah doesn't think any of her patients or their families could have been driven to something like stealing Josh, but I think it's worth checking out again. Hannah might not be aware of any animosity toward her, but I'm willing to bet the nursing staff will come up with a name or two. Everybody is hated by somebody."

"Cynic."

"Realist," Megan corrected him. "I've been on the job long enough to know that people are basically selfish, bitter, and vindictive, if not out and out nuts."

"And then there's our guy." Mitch rose from his chair, his eyes on the message board. His gaze passed over each line, the hair on the back of his neck prickling. "Evil."

Evil. The thing all of them had feared from the beginning. A kidnapping for ransom was about greed; greed could be dealt with, greed could be tricked. Mental illness was dangerous and unpredictable, but sickos usually screwed up somewhere along the line. Evil was cold and calculating. Evil played games with unknown rules and hidden agendas. Evil planted evidence, then calmly walked to a neighbor's house and asked for help finding his victim's dog.

The composite drawing of Ruth Cooper's early morning visitor was pinned to the cork bulletin board. A man of indeterminate age with a lean face that seemed almost devoid of features. The eyes were hidden behind a pair of high-tech sport sunglasses. The hair might have been any color beneath the dark cap. Not even his ears were visible. The hood of a black parka created a tunnel around his face, making him seem like a specter from another dimension.

"It's not exactly a photograph, is it?" Megan said dejectedly.

"No, but at least Mrs. Cooper thinks she might be able to

ID him if she sees him again. She thinks she'll remember his voice."

The rage rose inside him at the thought of the overconfidence, the contempt, the cruelty of the act this man had played out to flaunt his power and his cunning mind. Mitch's hands curled into fists at his sides. "Arrogant son of a bitch," he muttered. "You'll take a wrong step somewhere, and when you do, I will take you down hard."

"If we're lucky, his partner might trip him up for us," Megan said, slipping down off the table. "I'm arranging to have Christopher Priest take a look at Olie's computers and see if he can get into the files. Olie was auditing computer courses at Harris. I figure if anyone has a chance at getting past his booby traps it's Priest. In the meantime, there's still Paul to deal with."

Before Mitch could react, she hurried on. "You can't deny his connection to the van," she said, ticking her points off one by one on her fingers. "You can't deny that he tried to hide it from us. His alibi for the night Josh disappeared holds as much water as a two-dollar sieve. No one knows where he was at six o'clock this morning while Ruth Cooper was meeting our mystery man. He told the agent on duty he was going out to drive around, looking for Josh. The timing seems a little coincidental, don't you think?"

"What's his motive?" Mitch demanded. "Why would he do something to his own son?"

"It happens," Megan insisted. "You know it does. What about that case up on the Iron Range last year? What that man had done to his own daughter was unspeakable, and he showed up for the search every day, made pleas through the media, took a second mortgage on his house to put up reward money. It happened there and it could happen here.

"This is not Utopia, Chief," she continued, her patience wearing thin with his resistance, with the situation. "It's just a town like any other town. The people are just like people everywhere—some are good and some are rotten. Even the Garden of Eden had a snake in it. Deal with it."

The look he cut her way was dark and dangerous. "You think I'm not dealing with it?" His voice was whisper-soft and stiletto-sharp.

"I think you don't want to."

"Well, we know you do, don't we?" he said sardonically. "All you care about is pulling your fanny out of the fire and getting a nice gold star on your evaluation sheet. Even if you have to tear up a few people on the way. The end justifies the means."

"You can save that bullshit speech for Paige Price," Megan snapped, jamming her hands at her waist. "You know damn well I want to get Josh back. Don't you snipe at me for telling the truth. I think it's too easy for you to put yourself in Paul Kirkwood's place, and that could cost us."

Mitch was in no mood to have his conscience or his cop instincts poked at. Tired and frustrated, he lashed out at her.

"In other words, Agent O'Malley, I should forget this man has lost his son and go straight for the jugular. I should get my priorities straight, like you. The job comes first. The job, the job, the fucking job!" he shouted in her face.

"The job is who I am," Megan said, fierce pride sparking in her eyes. "If you don't like it, tough shit."

"It's who you are because it's all you'll allow," Mitch snarled. "God forbid you should take off the badge and be a woman for a while. You wouldn't know what to do."

Megan jerked back as the blow landed with almost physical force. She *had* taken off the badge. She *had* been a woman. For him. Apparently, she hadn't done a very good job of it. The idea cut her to the quick.

"Oh, like you'd give me so much more?" she struck back, her tone dripping sarcasm. "What will you give me, Chief? A roll on your sofa? Yeah, that's worth throwing my career away."

His mouth twisted in a sneer. "I don't recall you complaining when you had your legs wrapped around me."

"Oh, no," Megan admitted without flinching, holding the hurt deep inside a fist of control. "It was great while it lasted. Now it's over. A big relief to you, I'm sure. Those relationships that drag on for more than three or four days can put a real crimp in your martyrdom."

"Don't!" Mitch shouted, holding up a hand in warning. His left hand. The hand that bore his wedding ring. The gold band caught the light, gleaming, giving the lie to the denial that hadn't even made it out of his mouth.

He turned away from her and blew out a long breath. Jesus, how had they gotten on to this? What did he care what Megan O'Malley would and would not allow in her life? They'd had sex. Big deal. He didn't want anything more from her and his reasons had nothing to do with penance for past sins. *This* was why he didn't want anything more from Megan O'Malley. She was bullheaded and opinionated and she provoked him and antagonized him. He couldn't control himself when he was around her, and he sure as hell couldn't control *her*.

Megan pulled the emotions back and locked them up where they belonged. *This* was why she couldn't fall for Mitch Holt. He had just proven the very rule he had coaxed her to break: no cops. Now that it was over between them, everything she had given him, every private aspect of herself she had shared, would be used against her. Now there would be this awkwardness between them. Every time they had to be in the same room together, every time they had to work together.

Work should have been her only focus all along. *You knew better, O'Malley. Whatever made you think you could have something more?* She swallowed down the knot of emotion in her throat and forced her mind back on track.

"We have to get Paul's fingerprints," she said. "He owned that van; he might still have a key. If his prints are in it now, after all this time, he'll have some explaining to do. You get him in here, Chief, or I will."

Mitch marveled at the way she slid into her cop skin so easily and ignored the emotional blood they had just drawn. He could almost feel the cold from the walls of ice that went up around her to close him off, to protect herself and the feelings he had just raked his claws through. It irked him that she had that kind of control when he felt wild inside, when he wanted to scream at her and shake her. It irritated him that he felt the slightest twinge of remorse and regret, that he felt something when she seemed to have turned her feelings off.

"Don't boss me around, O'Malley," he warned.

Megan arched a brow. "What are you going to do about it? Tell the press you've seen me naked?" She walked away from him with her head up. "Do your job, Chief, or I'll do it for you."

Mitch said nothing as she walked out of the war room and closed the door. He paced the room, trying to hang on to his control, trying to put his focus where it belonged.

Snarling, he wheeled around and glared at the message board. He couldn't see Paul typing out those twisted missives. He knew parents lost their tempers or their minds and committed sins that could never be atoned for. Then he thought of Kyle and what it had felt like to see his son lying dead, to live every day with the thought of how old Kyle would have been and what he would have been doing had he lived. He thought of the way it hurt every time he saw little boys playing ball, chasing up and down the street on bikes with dogs in hot pursuit. He couldn't reconcile the idea of willfully harming a child, because he still hurt so badly from having his taken from him.

I think it's too easy for you to put yourself in Paul Kirkwood's place, and that could cost us.

Easy? No. *Easy* wasn't the right word at all.

He walked back to the table, where Josh's think pad lay. He needed a suspect. Someone who knew the Kirkwoods, knew the area, knew Josh.

He turned through the pages of doodling and games of hangman, his pride at being made co-captain of his hockey team, his sadness at the trouble between his parents. *Dad is mad. Mom is sad. I feel bad. . . .* Marital problems didn't make Paul Kirkwood the kind of monster who could steal his own son and leave behind quotes on sin and ignorance.

Sin.

Mitch turned another page and stared hard at the drawings. Josh's interpretation of God and the devil, his opinions of religion class—mad faces and thumbs-down signs. *Sin.* In his mind's eye he could see Albert Fletcher, the St. Elysius deacon, standing on the verge of Old Cedar Road with the hood of a black parka framing his lean face.

9:57 P.M. -30° WINDCHILL FACTOR: -55°

"In a perfect world, Hannah would be a candidate for saint-hood," Kathleen Casey pronounced. She sat on the sagging couch in the nurses' lounge, running shoes propped up on a blond oak Scandinavian coffee table. Dressed in green surgical scrubs and a white lab coat with the business end of a stetho-scope tucked into the breast pocket, she chewed thoughtfully on a plastic needle cap as she stared unseeing at the television across the room. "All those in favor of making this a perfect world, say aye."

Megan sank deeper into what had once been an over-stuffed leather armchair. Barely stuffed was a more appropri-ate description. They were the only people in the lounge. Beyond the open door, the small hospital was quiet. The occa-sional telephone ringing. The occasional page. A far cry from the city hospitals with their codes and crises. Megan enter-tained thoughts of finding an empty bed and crashing. Maybe one nice shot of Demerol and then eight or ten hours of obliv-ion. She rubbed at her forehead and sighed.

"How do her co-workers feel toward her?" she asked, un-derlining the word *co-workers* on her notepad.

"Like I told the last nine cops, she's a nurse's dream. I reg-ularly pinch myself when we're working together." Her small bright hazel eyes showed her years of a different experience. "Sixteen years in this business. I cut my teeth on arrogant res-idents and chiefs of staff who swore they couldn't have a God complex because they *were* God. If those guys are in heaven when I get there, I want my visa revoked at the gate."

"How does she get along with the other doctors?"

"Great—with the exception of our Chad Everett wannabe. Dr. Craig Lomax. He was miffed when Hannah was named head of ER. It has somehow escaped his attention that he's a lousy doctor."

"How miffed?"

"Enough to punish us all with his sulking. Enough to chal-lenge Hannah's authority." She took a sip of her caffeine-free Pepsi, then replaced the needle cap between her teeth and bit down. "If you're asking me was he pissed enough to take Josh, the answer is no. He's obnoxious, not insane. Besides, he was on duty that night."

"What about patients?" Megan asked. "Anyone you can think of who didn't handle the outcome of a case well? Someone who would have blamed her."

Kathleen ran a hand back through her thick hedge of red hair as she thought. "This isn't like the city, you know. People in small towns don't sue for malpractice. They trust their doctors and have enough common sense to know everything doesn't always work out for the best and it isn't always somebody's fault."

Megan persisted. "What about relatives of people who didn't make it? A parent who lost a child, maybe."

"Let's see. . . . The Muellers lost a baby to SIDS last fall. Brought him in DOA. Hannah worked on him forever, but there was nothing she could do."

"Were they angry?"

"Not with Hannah. She went above and beyond the call." She thought some more, scanning a mental list and discarding names. "I can't think of anyone who would do this kind of thing. Hannah is an excellent doctor. She can calm people down faster than a handful of Valium. And she knows the limitations of our hospital. She doesn't hesitate to send a patient on to a better-equipped facility if she thinks it's warranted." She pulled her feet off the coffee table and tucked them beneath her on the couch. Tugging the needle cap from between her teeth, she used it like a pointer. "I remember the time she personally drove Doris Fletcher to the Mayo Clinic for tests because her husband refused to take her."

"Fletcher?" Megan sat up straight. "Any relation to Albert Fletcher?"

Kathleen rolled her eyes. "Deer Lake's own Deacon of Doom. The world's going to hell on a sled. Women are the root of all evil. Sackcloth and ashes as a fashion statement. *That* Albert Fletcher? Yes. Poor Doris had the misfortune to marry him before he became a zealot."

"And he wouldn't take her to a hospital for tests?" Megan asked, incredulous.

The nurse rolled her eyes. "He thought they should have

waited for the Lord to heal her. Meanwhile the Lord is throwing His hands up in heaven, saying 'I gave you the Mayo Clinic, for crying out loud! What more do you want!' Poor Doris."

"How did Fletcher react to Dr. Garrison taking his wife for those tests against his will?"

"He was pissed. Albert isn't big on women asserting themselves. He thinks we should all still be paying because Eve screwed up."

"What did his wife die of?" Megan asked.

"Her whole gastrointestinal system went haywire, then her kidneys failed," she explained. "It was sad. No one ever came up with a concrete diagnosis. I said Albert was feeding her arsenic, but nobody listens to nurses."

When Megan didn't laugh, Kathleen gave her a look. "I was joking. About the arsenic. That was a joke."

"Could he have killed her?" Megan asked, straight-faced.

The nurse's eyes widened. Her pale brows shot up toward her hairline. "The deacon break a commandment? The sky would turn black and the earth would shake."

"Was there an autopsy?"

Kathleen sobered. She turned the needle cap over and over in her small hands. "No," she said softly. "Mayo pressed for it. They couldn't stand the idea of a disease they had no research funding for. But Albert refused on religious grounds."

Megan stared at her notes. Messages about sin. A personal vendetta. If Fletcher had somehow managed to poison his wife and get away with it, he might still be inclined to punish Hannah for interfering. If he were crazy enough, twisted enough. He had been teaching religion classes the night Josh disappeared, but if they were looking at tag-team lunatics, then all alibis were irrelevant.

"You don't really think he took Josh, do you?" Kathleen asked in a quiet voice. "I'd rather believe Olie did it and now he's roasting in hell."

Megan heaved herself up out of the armchair. "I imagine he's roasting, but I think he's probably saving a spot for somebody. It's my job to find out who."

The question that nagged her as she drove across town was whether or not it would still be her job by the end of the week.

She cursed office politics to hell and gone. She had come

here to do a job, plain and simple. But there was nothing plain or simple about the situation into which they had all been thrust—herself, Mitch, Hannah, Paul, everyone in Deer Lake, all the people from outside the community who had come to help. One act of evil had changed all their lives. The taking of Josh had set into motion a chain of actions and reactions. Their lives had been wrested from their control and now hinged on a madman's next move.

She wondered if he knew that, whoever he was. As she stared out the windshield into the bleak shadows of the cold night, she wondered if he was thinking even now about his next move and how it would affect the unwilling players of his sick game.

Power. That was what this was all about. The power to play God. The power to break people until they begged for mercy. The rush of showing how much smarter he was than everyone else.

"It's easy to win the game when you're the only one who knows the rules," Megan muttered. "Give us a clue, jerk. Just one lousy clue. Then we'll see what's what."

Soon. It had to happen soon. She could feel her time running out. DePalma's ultimatum hung over her head like an anvil—*make something good happen.*

She turned onto Simley Street a block west of St. E's, killed the headlights, and let the Lumina roll for half a block before pulling in along the curb. There was no life on Simley Street at ten o'clock. Residents of the neat, boxy houses were all glued to the news—with the notable exception of Albert Fletcher. There was no light in the living room window of 606 Simley. There was no light in any window of the story-and-a-half house.

Where would a sixty-year-old Catholic deacon be at ten-fifteen on a Wednesday night? Out tripping the light fantastic with some hot widow? The image made Megan grimace.

She crossed the street and made her way down the sidewalk with a purposeful stride, as if she had every reason to be there. The trick of fitting in where you don't belong—pretend you do. She headed up the driveway of 606 and slipped around the side of the garage, taking herself out of sight of any neighbors who happened to glance out their front windows.

The snow screeched like Styrofoam beneath her boots. Even the fabric shell of her parka was stiff from the cold. Every move she made sounded like someone crumpling newspaper. She cursed herself for staying in this godforsaken deep-freeze as she fumbled in her coat pocket for a small flashlight. Mittens did not lend themselves to skills involving dexterity—one reason the number of burglaries always fell off dramatically during cold spells.

The side door of the garage was locked. Shielding the light with one hand, Megan held it up to the window and peered in, holding her breath so as not to fog the glass in the window. The only car in the garage was a sedan of indeterminate make encased in canvas sheeting, like an old couch hiding beneath a slipcover. The near stall was empty. The place was immaculate. Not so much as a grease spot on the floor.

She turned and followed the walk toward the back porch steps. She wanted to peek in the windows, but all shades were drawn. Even the basement windows were covered. The foundation of the house had been wrapped with thick, cloudy plastic, then banked with snow for insulation.

Swearing, Megan knelt down directly beneath a first-floor window and dug the snow away with her hand. She pulled off one mitten, dipped in her coat pocket for a penknife, and used it to pry loose a few of the staples from the lathe that held the plastic in place. Tugging the plastic down, she shined the flashlight into the basement. What she could see of it was swept as clean as a dance floor. No stacks of old paint cans. No piles of newspapers. No boxes of discarded clothing. No dungeon. No chamber of horrors in evidence. No little boy.

Half disappointed, half relieved, Megan sat back on her haunches and shut off the flashlight. At the same instant, headlights beamed up the driveway.

"Shit!"

She scrambled to stuff the flashlight and penknife back into her pocket, managing to stick herself in the palm with the blade in the process. Biting down on the desire to yelp, she used her good hand to scoop the snow back up against the window. The garage door began its automatic ascent. She packed the snow as best she could, slapping at it with both hands. Her eyes kept darting to the garage. Fletcher drove in without seeing her, but if he came out the side and headed for his back door, her ass was fried.

The car engine rumbled, then quit. Crouching, Megan ran up the back steps, jumped down off the stoop, and ducked around the far side of the house, running headlong into a man.

Her scream was smothered by a big gloved hand. An arm banded around her with punishing strength, pulling her hard against a man's body. Twisting around, he pinned her between himself and the side of the house. Megan lashed out with the toe of her boot, connecting with his shin. He grunted in pain, but only leaned into her harder.

"Be still!" he ordered in a harsh whisper.

A familiar whisper.

Megan stared up inside the tunnel of his hood. Even in the shadows it was impossible not to recognize Mitch's face. He slid his hand away from her mouth.

Megan didn't say a word, but struggled instead to breathe in soundless pants. The cold air felt like fists pounding her lungs, and she brought a hand up to cup around her mouth as a filter. Fletcher's car door slammed. His footsteps crunched up the packed snow toward the back door. Chances were good that he would walk up his steps and into his house as he had done a million times without noticing anything out of the ordinary, like a footprint in the snow where there should not have been one. People were creatures of habit and routine, for the most part unobservant—unless they felt they had to be on guard.

He hesitated. She could picture him standing in the spot where she had dug the snow away from the basement window. *Come on, Albert. Move. Move. Please.* He moved on slowly. Up the steps slowly. Megan held her breath. Was he wondering? Was he looking off the south side of the stoop? Could he make out footprints in the shadows?

The rattle of keys. The turn of a lock. The heavy door thumped shut and the storm door sighed as it settled back against the frame.

Megan let out an echoing sigh. The adrenaline rush passed, leaving her trembling. She looked up at Mitch and whispered, "What the hell are you doing here?"

"What the hell are *you* doing here?" he demanded.

"Do you think we could have this argument inside a building?" she muttered. "I'm freezing my butt off."

10:55 P.M. -30° WINDCHILL FACTOR: -55°

There wasn't much action at the Blue Goose Saloon, a hole-in-the-wall bar with blessedly poor lighting to keep the patrons from noticing the moth-eaten condition of the dead animals mounted on the walls. The bartender, a portly woman with mouse-brown curls that fit her head like a stocking cap, stood behind the bar, smoking a cigarette, and drying beer mugs with a dingy towel. She stared up at a *Cheers* rerun on the portable television, small dark eyes tucked into the fleshy folds of her face like raisins in bread dough. Her only customer at the bar was an old man with bad teeth who drank schnapps and carried on an animated conversation with himself about the sorry state of politics in Minnesota now that Hubert Humphrey was gone.

Mitch had chosen the last booth in the line before the poolroom and sat so he could see the entrance and the front window that looked out on the street. Old habits. He ordered coffee and a shot of Jack Daniel's on the side. The Jack went down in a single gulp. He sipped at the coffee while Megan told him about her conversation with Kathleen Casey, the mysterious demise of Doris Fletcher, and her husband's enmity toward Hannah Garrison for interfering.

Megan dumped her whiskey into the coffee and added fake cream. The drink was hot and potent and warmed her from the inside out, taking the edge off her shivering. She checked her hand, squinting in the dim light. The penknife had lanced her palm with a short cut now decorated with drying blood and mitten fuzz. It would need a Band-Aid but nothing more.

"Why wait three years to get revenge?" Mitch asked.

"I don't know. Maybe it took that long for the plan to ferment—or for his mind to snap."

"He was teaching class at St. E's the night Josh disappeared."

"Enter the ever-popular accomplice."

On the television above the bar Cliff Claven did a manic dance as someone zapped him with jolts of electricity. The bartender's cigarette bobbed on her lip as she chuckled with malicious glee. Another shiver went through Megan and she took a long sip of her drink.

"You were at Fletcher's, too, Chief," she pointed out. "Why are you playing devil's advocate with me?"

"Because I like it."

"Your natural perverse tendencies aside, I have to assume you had a reason for being there."

He gave a lazy shrug. "Just sniffing around. Fletcher's obsessed with the church. Three of the notes mention sin. Josh didn't like religion class."

"Who could blame him with Fletcher for an instructor?" Megan said, shuddering. "Albert Fletcher would have given Vincent Price the creeps."

"I went back over the statement he gave Noogie the night Josh disappeared," Mitch said. He chose a peanut from the basket that sat on the table, cracked it with one hand, and tossed the nuts into his mouth. "There's nothing in it to draw suspicion."

On the surface there was nothing about Albert Fletcher that would have drawn notice. He was a retired professional, a respected member of the community. Not what most people would consider the profile of a child predator, but there were just as many pieces that fit. Fletcher's duties with the church put him in proximity with children. His authority at St. E's translated into trust in the eyes of children and adults alike. He would hardly have been the first to abuse that trust.

"Did he know Olie?"

"I can't imagine they ran in the same circles, but we'll check it out. I'll talk to him myself in the morning." He wished he could have run Fletcher in to the station that night, but that wasn't how things were done. He couldn't go after the man with nothing more than a hunch and some three-year-old rumors. No one had mentioned him in connection with Josh other than in his position with the church. No one had reported anything suspicious going on at Fletcher's house. Mitch had assigned a man to keep an eye on the residence through the night, just the same.

He dug out his wallet and tossed some ones on the table. Megan followed suit. The bartender waddled out from behind her post to scoop up her booty as they headed for the door.

"You folks come again," she called in a voice that sounded like Louie Armstrong with a bad head cold.

As they stepped out onto the sidewalk, the cold nearly took Megan's breath away. Not even the warmth of the whiskey in her belly could keep her teeth from chattering.

"Jesus, Mary, and J-Joseph," she stuttered, digging her car keys out of her pocket. "If it weren't for Josh, I think I'd be *hoping* to get fired. Humans weren't meant to live like this."

"Get tough or die, O'Malley," Mitch drawled without sympathy.

"If I get any tougher, bullets will bounce off me," she tossed back as she slid behind the wheel of the Lumina.

She began the ritual of coaxing the car to start, her gaze on Mitch as he climbed into the Explorer. The streets of Deer Lake were deserted, the Blue Goose the only business open. Watching him drive away gave her an empty feeling inside, as if she were the only human left on the planet.

There were worse things than being alone. But as she sat there alone in the cold, dark night with a child missing and her future hanging by a thread, she had a hard time thinking what they were.

They found the jacket today. They don't know what to think. They don't know which way to turn. We can smell their panic. Taste it. It makes us laugh. They are as predictable as rats in a maze. They don't know which way to turn, so they turn on each other and they grasp at anything, hoping for a clue. They deserve whatever fate befalls them. The wrath of God. The wrath of colleagues, of neighbors, of strangers. Wrath rains down on the heads of the guilty and the fools.

Should we give them something and see where it leads them? All scenarios have been mapped out, far beyond the immediate moment. If we give them A, will it lead them to B? If it leads them to C, what then? On to D or E? We can't be surprised. We have planned for all contingencies, all possibilities. Ultimately, we are invincible and they will know that. The game is ours. The suffering is theirs. Deserving victims of the perfect crime.

CHAPTER 29

The ground search resumed in the gray light of a sunless morning. The governor had volunteered cold-weather gear from the National Guard, and a pair of military trucks sat in the alley behind the old fire hall to dispense Arctic mittens and thermal ski masks to any volunteer in need.

With the discovery of Josh's jacket, the panic level around town had soared. More volunteers than ever crowded the briefing room in the fire hall, anxious, desperate to help. They flocked to the focal point of the search with the zeal of the mob storming Dr. Frankenstein's gates. They were angry and terrified and tired of the waiting. They wanted their town and their lives back, and they wanted to believe determination alone could win the day.

Mitch sat in his Explorer and watched the search teams and search dogs disperse. Most cases had a feel to them, a rhythm that picked up as things progressed and clues came in and leads were followed and evidence built. This one had no rhythm, and the only feeling he got was bad. The deeper they went into this maze the more lost and disoriented they became.

Maybe there were two kidnappers. Maybe Olie had been one of them. Maybe not. Maybe Paul was involved, but how and why? Maybe Albert Fletcher was a suspect. Maybe he was insane. Had he known Olie, or was the accomplice someone they hadn't even considered? Was there an accomplice at all?

A stocky sergeant from the Minneapolis K-9 squad directed his German shepherd into the stand of cattails. The dog loped up onto the bank, tail wagging, nose to the snow. Uniformed officers herded volunteers out of the dog's path. Mitch's heart picked up a beat. The dog seemed to have a scent. He trotted south, away from the houses, along the snowmobile trail and up onto Mill Road, which ran east into town and west to farm country. He stood there, looking toward town, looking toward the field across the road where ash-blond cornstalks stood un-harvested, row upon row, in testament to the wet fall and early winter.

The scent was gone. Like every other scrap of hope they had been given, this one was snatched away. Mitch put the truck in gear and headed for Albert Fletcher's house, less than a half-mile away.

By daylight the Fletcher home was an uninspired square, one-and-a-half stories high, painted a somber shade of gray. No remnants of the Christmas season decorated the door or the eaves. Albert apparently refrained from garish displays. Mitch recalled hearing something about a brouhaha in St. E's over decorating during Advent. The ladies' guilds were for it, the deacon was against it. Mitch hadn't paid much attention. His Sunday mornings were spent beside his daughter and his in-laws at Cross of Christ Lutheran, where he spent every ser-mon doing math in his head as an act of rebellion.

He rang the doorbell and waited for the sound of footsteps. None came. No light escaped through the drawn shades. He hit the bell again and bounced on the balls of his feet in an at-tempt to shake off the cold. Earmuffs clamped his head like a vise. The hood of his parka stemmed the flow of body heat out the top of his head.

No one came to the door. Of course, Albert was the only known resident of the house. Mrs. Fletcher was dead and the deacon had never been linked romantically with anyone. De-spite the fact that he had had a successful career as comptrol-ler of BuckLand Cheese and was probably comfortably well off, the ladies apparently did not consider him a catch.

Doris wasting away might have had something to do with that, Mitch thought as he made his way along the neatly shov-eled path to the garage. As far as he had been able to discern, no one had suspected Albert at the time of his wife's illness and subsequent death.

The garage was immaculate from what he could see

through the window. The doors were locked. The only car in residence sat beneath a dust-laden canvas cover. It looked as if it hadn't been moved or touched in years. Garden tools were lined up neatly along the wall. Peg-Board above the workbench displayed a neat array of Joe Handyman stuff—wrenches, screwdrivers, hammers.

Clutching the chemical hand-warmer packets in his coat pockets, Mitch headed around the back of the house to check the basement window.

His temper boiled at the memory of how close Megan had come to getting caught snooping around here the night before. What if Fletcher was insane? What if he had found her there alone?

Mitch looked down at the foundation of the house, at the thick plastic sheeting that obscured the basement windows.

The staples had been replaced.

At the church Mitch found Father Tom kneeling with two dozen women, chanting the decades of the rosary. A wall of votives flickered and saturated the air with the thick vanilla scent of melting wax. On the wall beside the tiers of candles, the catechism classes had taped handmade posters. Carefully printed messages in colored marker on newsprint paper—*Jesus, please keep Josh safe. Lord, please bring Josh home.* Crayon drawings of angels and children and policemen.

All eyes turned to Mitch as he hesitated beside the priest's pew. They looked to Mitch for some kind of deliverance, for some news he couldn't give. Father Tom rose and slipped out the end of the pew. The leader of the prayer dragged the rest of them on with her droning monotone.

"Hail Mary, full of grace. The Lord is with thee . . ."

"Is there some news?" Father Tom whispered, his voice as taut as a guy wire. He let out a breath as Mitch shook his head.

"I need to ask you a couple of questions."

"Let's go in my office."

Father Tom led the way, genuflecting hastily at the foot of the altar before moving on. In the office he motioned Mitch to a chair and shut the door. He looked as priestly as Mitch had ever seen him, with a clerical collar standing up stiffly above the crew neck of his black sweater. Comb tracks suggested he had even made an attempt to style his unruly hair into submission, though sandy sprigs sprung up defiantly at the crown of his head like wheat stubble. The pope gazed down on him from an oil painting on the wall behind him, looking more skeptical than benevolent, as if the collar didn't fool him in the least.

"What's the occasion?" Mitch needled, pointing at his throat. "Is the bishop coming to town?"

Tom McCoy gave him a sheepish look. "One of those little deals we make with God. I'll try to be a better priest if He'll give Josh back to us."

Mitch sensed an underlying motive but didn't press. He knew Father Tom well enough to golf with him, not well enough to act as confessor to a man rungs above him on the spiritual ladder.

"Unfortunately for all concerned, I don't think God kidnapped him," he said. "How was Hannah when you left last night?"

The priest frowned down at the Game Boy on his blotter. "She's doing the best she can. She feels helpless; that's unfamiliar territory for her."

"Paul isn't exactly helping."

Father Tom's jaw tightened. "No. He isn't," he said shortly. He drew in a slow breath and raised his head, his gaze glancing off Mitch's left shoulder. "I suggested she take up one of the news magazines on their request for an interview. I think it might help her if she can present her story in a way that could benefit other mothers, help prevent this kind of thing from happening to someone else. That's the role she's most familiar with—helping others."

"Maybe," Mitch murmured, thinking of his own role as helper/protector and how he had retreated from it after his crisis.

"You said you had some questions?"

"Is Albert Fletcher around?"

Father Tom's brows pulled together. He tucked his chin and sat back in his swivel chair. "Not at the moment. I think he's at the rectory. Why?"

Mitch gave him his deadpan detective face. "I need to talk to him about a couple of things."

"Is this about Josh?"

"Why would you ask that?"

Father Tom gave a laugh that held no amusement. I believe we already had this little chat. Albert had Josh for server instruction and religion class. Doesn't that automatically make him a suspect?"

Mitch let the defensive tone slide. "Fletcher was teaching classes the night Josh disappeared. Why? Do you think he could have done it?"

"Albert is the most devout man I know," Tom said. "I'm sure he secretly thinks I'm doomed to perdition because I had cable installed at the rectory. No." He shook his head. "Albert would never blatantly break the law—secular or holy."

"How long have you known him?"

"About three years."

"Were you around during his wife's illness?"

"No. She died, I believe it was January ninety-one. I came here that March. I got the impression he must have been close to her by the way he turned to the church for solace afterward. The way he immersed himself, he must have had a big void to fill."

Or he had already been in love with the church and wanted Doris out of the way so he could pursue his obsession with full zeal. Mitch kept that theory to himself.

"He had a funny way of showing his affection for her," he said. "It seems to be fairly common knowledge that he didn't want her to seek treatment for her illness. He claimed he wanted to heal her through prayer, and he wasn't too pleased when Hannah intervened."

A frown curved Father Tom's mouth. "Mitch, you're not suggesting—"

"I'm not suggesting anything," Mitch said, getting out of his chair, hands raised in denial. "I'm fishing, that's all. I'll throw back a lot of chubs before I catch anything for the frying pan. Thanks for your time, Father."

He started for the door, then turned back. "Would Fletcher have made a good priest?"

"No," Father Tom answered without hesitation. "There's more to this job than memorizing scripture and church dogma."

"What's he lacking?"

The priest thought about that for a moment. "Compassion," he said softly.

Mitch had never been a fan of old Victorian houses with their heavy dark woodwork and cavernous rooms. The St. Elysius rectory was no exception. It was big enough to house the entire University of Notre Dame football team, whose photograph hung prominently on the wall of the den above the evil cable box.

He wandered through the rooms of the first floor, calling for Albert Fletcher and receiving no answer. The smell of coffee and toast lingered in the kitchen. A box of Frosted Flakes sat on the table. Beside it squatted a half-empty coffee mug, a souvenir from Cheyenne, Wyoming. The *StarTribune* had been left open to a story about the plight of the Los Angeles quake victims and the reprise of the old fake-priest scam—con men impersonating clergy and collecting cash donations intended for those left homeless.

"Mr. Fletcher?" Mitch called.

The basement door opened and Albert Fletcher emerged from the gloom. Gaunt and pale, he looked as if he had been held captive down there. His black shirt hung on shoulders as thin and sharp as a wire hanger. A black turtleneck showed above the button-down collar—a reverse image of Father Tom's clerical collar. The dark eyes that met Mitch's were bright with something like fever, but opaque, hiding the source of their glow. They were set in a face that was long and sober, the skin like ash-white tissue paper stretched taut over prominent bones, the mouth an unyielding line that seemed incapable of bending upward. Mitch tried to superimpose this face over the featureless composite drawing of Ruth Cooper's visitor. Maybe. With a hood . . . with sunglasses.

"Mr. Fletcher?" Mitch held out his hand. "Mitch Holt, chief of police. How are you today?"

Fletcher turned away to close the basement door behind him, ignoring the pleasantry as if pleasantry were against his personal beliefs.

"I need to ask you a couple of questions, if you don't mind," Mitch continued, sliding his hands into his pants pockets.

"I've already spoken with several policemen."

"It's standard procedure to follow up interviews," Mitch explained. "New questions come up. People remember things after the first cop is gone. We don't want to miss anything."

He leaned back against the work island and crossed his ankles. "You can have a seat, if you'd be more comfortable."

Apparently comfort was also a sin. Fletcher made no move to find himself a chair. He folded his long, bony hands in front of him, displaying the evidence of his trip to the basement. The deacon looked down at the dirt-streaked backs of his hands, and frowned. "I've been going through some church artifacts in the storage room. They've been down there a long time."

Mitch called up a phony smile as he straightened. "Must be quite a basement under a big old place like this. Mind if I take a look? These old Victorian houses fascinate me."

Fletcher hesitated just a second before opening the door. Then he descended once more into the bowels of the St. Elysius rectory. Mitch followed, quelling a grimace at the scent of mold.

The basement was exactly what he'd expected—a chambered cave of old brick and cracked cement. Rafters hung with festoons of cobwebs. Bare bulbs gave off inadequate light. The chamber beneath the kitchen held the water heater, the furnace, the electrical circuit box, and an ancient chest-type freezer. In the next section was junk—old bicycles, a hundred battered folding chairs, a stack of collapsible tables, row upon row of green-painted window screens, a squadron of rusty little wire carts loaded with croquet equipment, a forest of bamboo fishing rods.

The room Fletcher led him to was crammed with statuary from the days when church icons came complete with human hair and everyone in the Holy Family looked amazingly Anglo-Saxon. The moldering relics stared unseeing into the gloom, their limbs and faces chipped and cracked. An old altar and baptismal font gave testimony to the rise and fall in popularity of cheap blond wood veneer. A jerry-rigged rack hung down from an exposed water pipe and displayed the fashion in clerical vestments through the years, the damp rotting the garments on their hangers. Floor-to-ceiling shelves lined three walls of the room. The shelves and all available flat surfaces were

stacked with boxes of old church records and curling photographs. Decaying books gave off a musty sweet aroma.

Albert Fletcher looked oddly at home among the forgotten
castoffs of the faithful of generations past. "I've been making
an inventory," he explained, "and moving the old books and
records out to properly preserve them."

Mitch arched a brow. "That on top of your duties as deacon and teacher? I know you were Josh Kirkwood's instructor
for religion class, as well as being in charge of the altar boys.
You're very generous with your time."

"My life belongs to the church." Fletcher folded his hands
in front of him again, as if he wanted to be ready at any moment to fall to his knees in prayer. "Everything else is sec-
ondary."

"That's admirable, I'm sure," Mitch murmured. "I was
wondering, Mr. Fletcher, if, as his instructor, you might have
noticed any changes in Josh's behavior over the last few
weeks?"

Fletcher blinked, the glow went dark, like a light switching
off inside him. "No," he said, his thin mouth pinching closed
into a tight hyphen.

"Had he been unusually quiet or had he mentioned any
problem, anyone who might have been bothering him?"

"The children come to me for instruction, Chief Holt. They
go to Father McCoy for confession."

Mitch nodded. Pretending interest, he touched a tarnished
chalice, brushed a finger over an old brass collection plate.
"Well, do you have any personal observations about Josh? Do
you think he's a nice kid, a troublemaker, what?"

"He is generally well behaved," Fletcher said grudgingly.
"Although children these days seem to have no grasp of respect
or discipline."

"He's Dr. Garrison's son, you know." Mitch fingered the
dusty brass plate on the old baptismal font that read GIVEN IN
MEMORY OF NORMAN PATTERSON 1962. "You know Dr. Garrison, don't you?"

"I'm aware of who she is."

"Wasn't she your wife's doctor?" Mitch asked, watching
Fletcher's reaction through his lashes.

The eyes narrowed slightly. "Doris saw her on occasion."

"I was of the understanding Dr. Garrison actually drove your wife to the Mayo Clinic once to see that she had tests run. Above and beyond the call of duty, don't you think?"

Fletcher offered no reply. Mitch could feel anger vibrating out from the rigid body.

"Dr. Garrison is a remarkable woman," he continued. "She's dedicated her life to saving lives and helping people. It's a tragedy that someone so good has to go through something like this."

The mouth tightened into a sour knot. "It's not our place to question God."

"We're looking for a madman, Mr. Fletcher. I'd hate to think he's doing God's work."

Albert Fletcher made no comment. He didn't even bother to feign sympathy or offer the platitudes people unaffected by a tragedy mouth out of a sense of decency. He stood rigid before a statue of Mary, the Holy Mother reaching a hand out over his head as if she couldn't decide whether to give him her blessing or a karate chop. Mitch would have rooted for the latter. For a man so devout, Albert Fletcher seemed awfully short on the more popular Christian virtues. Father Tom had said he lacked compassion. Mitch wondered if he lacked a soul as well.

"Terrible what happened with Olie Swain, isn't it?" Mitch said. "He might have been able to end this whole nightmare for us if he hadn't killed himself. Did you know Olie?"

"No."

"Well, I guess we have to hope he finds some peace in the next world, huh?"

"Suicide is a mortal sin," Fletcher informed him piously, the knuckles of his clasped hands bone-white from the tension of his grip. "He damned his own soul to hell."

"Let's hope he deserved it, then," Mitch said tightly. "Thank you for the tour. It's been . . . enlightening."

He made his way out of the storage room and back to the stairs. Fletcher followed like the shadow of doom. Mitch turned back toward him, one hand on the stair railing.

"One last thing," he said. "We had a report of a prowler in your neighborhood last night. I was wondering if you had seen anything suspicious."

"No," Fletcher said flatly. "I was out until after ten, and when I got home, I went straight to bed."

"After ten, huh?" Mitch forced a conspiratorial smile. "Kind of late for such a cold night. Seeing someone special?"

"The Holy Mother," Fletcher said, deadpan. "I was praying."

As he walked back to his truck, Mitch wondered why Fletcher's admission left him feeling queasy instead of comforted.

11:00 A.M. -20° WINDCHILL FACTOR: -46°

> *ignorance is not innocence but SIN*
> *i had a little sorrow, born of a little SIN*
> *my emanation far within*
> *weeps incessantly for my SIN*

The messages burned in the back of Megan's mind as she walked up and down the time line Mitch had taped to the long wall of the war room. At the end of the room the messages from the original notes had been copied in red ink against the white board. Urgent red. Bloodred.

She stared at the time line, looking for a key, looking for something they had missed the first few hundred times they had looked at it. Looking for anything that should have given them a name. It was there somewhere. She wanted to believe they were close, they weren't just seeing something they needed to see, something just around the corner, teasing them, taunting them, waiting for them to pick up the one key piece of information that would unlock all the doors and lead them to Josh.

Ignorance and *sin*. The words suggested feelings of superiority and piety. Albert Fletcher had a grudge against Hannah. A grudge three years old. *Revenge is a dish best served cold.* That was not among the quotes on the message board, but it could have applied.

There was Paul Kirkwood with his violent temper and his

secrets. He hadn't told them about the van. What else might he be hiding? He played the martyr for the television cameras, then turned on his own wife in rage and contempt. Could he have turned on his own son? Why? What could possibly have driven him to do such a thing? To have taken Josh and then put on the elaborate show of the grieving father would take a soul as black and cold as obsidian. But Megan knew it happened. She had read files of other cases, cases with details that had made her physically ill, where parents had harmed their own offspring in the most hideous ways, then covered their tracks with grief.

Kirkwood would have to come in today to give them his fingerprints so they could check them against prints found in the van. Megan's stomach rolled at the thought of the stink he would make. If he chose to play the persecuted innocent for the press, the heat from the resulting furor would be enough to melt badges and fry careers—namely hers.

Ignorance and *sin*. The words throbbing in her mind, she walked slowly backward along the time line, from that day's date back, reading the notations, the most significant details in red, the peripheral events in blue. The discovery of the jacket. Olie's suicide. Olie's arrest and interrogation. The phone call to Hannah. The discovery of the duffel bag. The first report of Josh missing.

She stood at the far end of the line. Day one. Ground zero.

5:30—Josh leaves GKM Arena after hockey practice.

5:45—Hospital calls GKM to notify Hannah will be late.

5:45—Beth Hiatt picks up Brian Hiatt at GKM. Brian last to see Josh.

6:00–7:00—During this time period Helen Black sees boy getting into light-colored van in front of GKM Arena.

7:00—Josh no-show at St. E's religion class taught by A. Fletcher.

7:00—Hannah calls Paul at work. NA. Leaves message.

7:45—Hannah reports Josh missing.

8:30—Olie Swain questioned at GKM. Did not *take call from hospital regarding Hannah being late.*

8:45—Josh's duffel bag found on grounds of GKM with note: a child vanishes, ignorance is not innocence but SIN.

They had reduced the crime down to a timetable. What

they didn't have was the itinerary of the criminal. What time, what day was it when he first decided to take Josh Kirkwood? What did he do that day? Whom did he see, talk to? Who could have stopped him? If the guy ahead of him at the convenience store had decided to buy fifty lottery tickets and held up the line for another ten minutes, would Josh still be with them today?

Timing is everything.

And ignorance is not innocence but sin.

Tension gripped Megan by the temples like a pair of ice tongs. Tighter and tighter.

"I'll see it," she muttered. "I'll see it and I'll nail your ass."

A sharp rap on the door preceded Natalie's appearance. She stepped into the room with a sheaf of files and papers in her left arm and a steaming coffee mug in her right hand. Behind her big red-framed glasses, her dark eyes were bleary and bloodshot, reminding Megan she wasn't the only one losing sleep over this case.

"Girl, you need coffee," Natalie announced, plunking the mug down on the table.

Megan lifted it and breathed in the aroma as if it were smelling salts. "I'd take it intravenously if I could. Thanks, Nat."

Natalie waved off the gratitude with a cranky snort, a trio of colorful wooden bead bracelets clacking together on her arm. A matching necklace that looked like Tinkertoys on a rope rode the slope of her bosom. She looked like a fashion ad for larger women in a rich mocha tunic over a matching calf-length broomstick skirt. Megan felt like the Before photo. She had dozed off at dawn, overslept, and jumped into the first clothes that had come to hand as she stumbled out of bed—a pair of gold corduroy pants with diagonal wrinkles from having been thrown haphazardly over the back of a chair and a hunter green sweater Gannon had used for a bed. She picked off a cat hair and flicked it away.

"The way my phone's been ringing off the hook, I figure you need all the friends you can get," Natalie said, sitting in one of the chrome-and-plastic chairs. "The tabloid shows have offered me big bucks if I could give them evidence you and the chief been doing the wild thing in his office."

Megan closed her eyes and groaned, sinking down onto the next chair.

"I told them they could take their dirty money and give it to the volunteer center. It's none of my business what goes on with folks behind their own closed doors and it's none of theirs, either."

"Amen."

"Personally, I'd like to see Mitch find someone who could make him happy. God knows, we've all been trying to find that someone for him ever since he moved here. Poor man's had more blind dates than Stevie Wonder."

She gave another snort as Megan managed a weary chuckle.

"I appreciate the support," Megan said, "but I don't think I'm that someone. We're at each other's throats half the time."

"And the other half you're at something else altogether. Sounds like love to me," she said as matter-of-factly as if she'd been diagnosing a common cold.

Megan didn't want to think the situation was so transparent. It wasn't that simple. It was never as simple as loving someone. They had to love you back.

"Well," she said, "the way things are going with the case, I won't be here long enough to unpack my bags."

Natalie shook her head. "I pray to God and then I swear at Him and then I pray some more. I want a miracle and I want it now," she said, thumping her fist on the table.

"I'd settle for a clue," Megan admitted. "Is Mitch in yet?"

"No, but Professor Priest is here looking for you. Should I send him this way?"

Megan glanced around the war room with the time line and the messages written out and the chalkboard for brainstorming with names and motives and question marks. It wasn't the place to bring a citizen, but the urge was strong. Maybe what they needed was someone with a computer brain like Christopher Priest's to walk in cold and analyze the whole mess. Someone to walk in cold . . . like a new agent.

"No," she said, shrugging off the thought and pushing herself to her feet. "I'll see him in my office. Thanks, Natalie."

"Anything for the cause. And don't you scratch Mitch off your dance card yet, girl. He's a good man . . . and you're okay," she said, the twinkle in her eyes betraying her grudging admission. "You'll do."

The professor listened, wide-eyed and attentive, as Megan laid out the situation with Olie's computer booby traps. He had shrugged off his black down jacket to reveal a blue Shetland wool sweater he must have inadvertently tossed in the dryer. The sleeves hit two-thirds of the way down his forearms, showing too much of the white oxford shirt beneath it.

Megan felt a certain amount of frustration at the thought that the case might not be solved by sweat and grunt police work, but by a pencil-necked computer nerd. But solved was solved, and Megan would take Josh back any way she could get him. If she had to resort to psychics and séances, she would pay for the crystal balls out of her own pocket.

"I understand Olie was auditing computer courses at Harris," she said. "We're hoping you might be able to get past these traps he'd set up. If we can find out what information he kept on those computers, we might find a clue as to his involvement in Josh's kidnapping."

"I'll be glad to help in any way I can, Agent O'Malley," the professor said, his eyebrows lifting into a little tent of concern. "I have to say, I have a hard time believing Olie was involved. He certainly never gave me any indication . . . I mean, he worked hard in class, never bothered anyone . . . I never would have imagined . . ."

"Yeah, well, John Wayne Gacy dressed up as a clown and visited sick kids in hospitals."

" 'Who knows what evil lurks in the hearts of men?' " the professor quoted, murmuring the words almost to himself.

"If we knew by looking, the prisons would be overflowing and the streets would be safe," Megan said. "Do you have any idea what Olie was doing with all those machines?"

"He liked to tinker with them. Upgrade the boards, augment the memories, then write his own programs to perform various functions. He had an old Tandy model when he first approached me about auditing classes. It wasn't good for much besides word processing. I told him where he might be able to get a better machine for little or nothing. I guess he turned that into his hobby."

"If we're lucky, his hobby might lead us to Josh. We might even find out if he had an accomplice, but we have to get into the computers first."

"As I said, I'll help any way I can, Agent O'Malley," Priest reiterated, rising from his chair, tugging on the bottom of his too-small sweater that had crept up to his waistband. "I can't make any promises, but I'll do the best I can."

"Thank you, Professor. We'll set you up in a room here. A computer expert from the BCA will be working with you. That's standard procedure when someone from outside the agency is called in."

"I understand. I don't have a problem with that."

"Good."

Megan reached out to shake his hand, but the contact was never made. Her office door swung open and Mitch leaned in.

"Paul's coming in," he announced in a voice as hard as rock. "And he's bringing an entourage."

CHAPTER 30

DAY 9 ·
11:57 A.M. -20° WINDCHILL FACTOR: -46°

The circus set up in the City Center lobby. A ring made of television lights and cameras. An audience of shocked and angry people from the volunteer center, print media reporters, reporters from competing television stations, their eyes glowing with jealousy. As ringmaster: Paige Price, resplendent in a cardinal-red hacking jacket over a short black shift and black hose.

The main attraction at the City Center circus was, of course, Paul Kirkwood. He had been livid when Mitch had cornered him at Ryan's Bay and informed him he had to come in to be fingerprinted. He was still livid. This was all the fault of that bitch O'Malley. By God, he would make her pay. She and Mitch could both pay as far as Paul was concerned—for the humiliation, for the suspicion. He should have been the object of sympathy and concern and compassion. Instead, he was being fingerprinted.

He put on his best martyr's expression and gave it the perfect hint of indignation and outrage. He had considered going home first to shower and change into better clothes, but Paige had pointed out the potential for impact if he came in straight from the search in his jeans and Sorels and heavy sweater. His hair was mussed from his cap, his nose still red from the cold.

A *TV 7* technician did a light check on Paige's face. Another minion sidled up to her with a compact mirror so she could check her makeup. She nodded her readiness. The countdown came from a disembodied voice just beyond the ring of light.

"Three . . . two . . . you're live."

"This is Paige Price coming to you live from the Deer Lake City Center with Paul Kirkwood, whose son Josh was abducted outside an ice arena here in Deer Lake eight days ago. As the search for Josh and his abductor drags on, law enforcement authorities working on the case have suddenly turned their focus on Josh's father. Today Paul Kirkwood was ordered by Deer Lake Chief of Police Mitchell Holt to submit to having his fingerprints taken." She turned to Paul, microphone in hand, grave expression in place. "Mr. Kirkwood, can we get a reaction from you on this latest development?"

"It's an outrage," Paul replied, his voice shaking with the strength of his fury. "The BCA and the police have botched this case from the beginning. The only real suspect they had committed suicide while in their custody. They're desperate to appear as though they're making progress on the case when all they're doing is grasping at straws. But to turn the focus on me is absolutely unconscionable."

Tears welled up in his eyes, sparkling like diamonds under the lights. "Josh is my son. I love him. I would never, *never* do anything to harm him. We did everything together. Camping, sports. He used to come to my office sometimes and I'd give him a calculator and he would pretend h-he was j-just like m-me."

Giving Paul a chance to compose himself or make a spectacle of himself, whichever way he wanted to play it, Paige turned once again to face the camera. She let a single tear slide down her cheek, her big too-blue eyes like a pair of shimmering lakes. "This is certainly an unexpected and, if I might editorialize for a moment, a most callous turn taken by the BCA-led investigation into the disappearance of Josh Kirkwood. From the first terrible moments of this investigation we've seen Paul Kirkwood at the forefront of the search to find his missing child."

She turned back to Paul, who was managing to look noble and long-suffering at once. "Mr. Kirkwood, do you have any explanation for their interest in you as a suspect?"

He shook his head sadly, wearily. "I once owned the van that belonged to Olie Swain. Years ago. Agent O'Malley has decided those intervening years mean nothing."

"Agent Megan O'Malley with the BCA?"

"Yes."

"And Chief Holt is going along with her theory that you are somehow involved in Josh's kidnapping because of this vague past connection to the van?"

"I don't understand it. I've done everything I can to aid in the investigation. How they can turn on me like this, I—I just don't understand. I've known Mitch Holt since he moved here. I can't believe he could think I was involved."

Mitch and Megan and Sergeant Noga stood on the periphery of the mob at the mouth of the hall to the law enforcement center, unnoticed at first with all the jockeying for position by rival camera crews, their attention on Paul and Paige. Then at the mention of Mitch's name, one person turned and glared at him, then another. Then a camera swung around in his face and a microphone was thrust out in front of him.

"Chief Holt, do you have any comment on the situation with Paul Kirkwood?"

Before Mitch could do more than think of an obscenity he couldn't voice, the whole media tide swung toward them, babbling questions, thumbing their noses at Paige Price. Mitch made no attempt to answer or to placate them. A ferocious scowl tightening his features, he waded through them, his eyes on Paul. Megan tailed him. Noogie fell in behind her, guarding them from the rear.

Paige's face lit up. She couldn't have written a more perfect scenario. She stepped in front of Paul to intercept Mitch.

"Chief Holt, do you have anything to say about this apparent lack of compassion for this poor grieving father?"

He wanted to smack the poor grieving Paul upside the head for pulling this stunt. The play for sympathy had nothing to do with Paul's grief and everything to do with his petty vindictiveness. Mitch turned his glare on Paige, then looked over her shoulder at the mayor and half the town council standing in the hallway to the city offices.

"As I explained to Mr. Kirkwood quite thoroughly this morning," he answered, "this procedure is necessary for the purpose of identifying all prints found in the van. He once owned the van, therefore, we're taking his fingerprints for comparison. Mr. Kirkwood is under neither arrest nor suspicion."

He turned back to Paul, his face ruddy with anger. "If you'll come with me, Paul, we can have this over in a matter of minutes with a minimum amount of fuss."

Paul's expression would have looked more fitting on a pouting ten-year-old. Noogie turned around to clear the path, and they started for the law enforcement center. The shouted questions of reporters echoed and amplified, filling up the atrium with a tower of sound.

Megan wasn't quick enough in her attempt to fall in line. Paige cut her off, clearly annoyed at having her exclusive interview disappear down the hall with a police escort.

"Agent O'Malley, what do you have to say about the BCA's role in this drama?" she asked, a gleam of vengeance in her eyes. "Do you consider Paul Kirkwood a suspect?"

Megan frowned as a spotlight hit her in the face. "No comment."

"Is it true you're responsible for focusing this attention on Paul Kirkwood?"

Megan's stomach churned as she imagined DePalma watching this, his blood pressure hopping higher into the danger zone with every second. "A connection was found between Mr. Kirkwood and the van owned by Olie Swain," Megan replied, measuring her words carefully. "What we're doing now is simply standard procedure and is in no way an indictment or a persecution of Mr. Kirkwood. We're simply doing our jobs."

Paige moved in a little closer. Her eyes narrowed with what looked to Megan like malicious glee, though viewers would probably mistake it for sharp journalistic instincts. "Your job is pulling the focus of your investigation off legitimate leads and placing it on Josh's father?"

"We're following *all* leads, Ms. Price."

"By 'we,' you mean yourself and Chief Holt, with whom you've been linked—"

"By 'we,' I mean the agencies involved—"

"And this attention on Paul Kirkwood is not in retaliation for his criticism of your handling of the case?"

"I'm with the BCA," Megan snapped. "Not the Gestapo."

"Mr. Kirkwood has been openly critical of your conduct—"

"*My* conduct?"

A red haze filmed Megan's vision. How dare Paige Price prostitute herself for inside information, then turn around and point a pious finger at someone else?

"We're doing everything we can to find Josh. Perhaps you could ask Sheriff Steiger to elaborate on the details the next time you're in bed with him."

Paige fell back a step, gasping, her face flushing as red as her jacket. Megan gave her a *gotcha, bitch* smile, then turned on her heel to push her way through the mob.

She ignored the hands that grabbed at her. The shouted questions ran together in a cacophony of babble. She had nothing to say to any of them. These parasites offered little in the search for Josh or the effort to capture the predator who had taken him. As far as she was concerned, they were nothing but carrion feeders, getting in the way and clouding the focus of the case with their endless dust storms of manufactured controversy.

Let them feed on each other, she thought, striding purposefully down the hall of the law enforcement center. Her gaze was focused straight ahead, her mind moving beyond, to the booking room where Paul Kirkwood was grudgingly giving up his fingerprints.

9:23 P.M. -23° WINDCHILL FACTOR: -50°

The reaction to Paul's theatrics was immediate and overwhelming. Phones in the police department and city hall offices rang off the hook all afternoon. Paul would have been dismayed, however, to learn that not all of the callers were expressing their displeasure with "this disgraceful turn of events," as one of his supporters called it. While some sympathies ran in Paul's favor, there were those who thought he'd done it all along. And on the gossip grapevine, which thrived even in these frigid temperatures, the rumor that his arrest was imminent quickly gained momentum and strength.

On the more visible pro-Paul front, outraged citizens called their council members, council members called the mayor, the mayor called on Mitch in person. Mitch, still furious with Paul, offered no apology. He got paid to do a job and he did it. If people wanted control of who fell under suspicion, they would have to find someone else to wear the badge.

At the moment, that didn't seem like such a bad idea, he thought.

To get away from ringing telephones, Mitch sat in the war room, but reminders of the case shouted at him from the walls and the tables that were piled with copies of reports and statements and files on hopeful tips that had hit dead ends. Where the clock on the wall ticked the seconds away loudly: 9:23.

He had spent the past four hours personally checking out a possible sighting of Josh in the small town of Jordan, seventy-five miles away. Another dead end. Another adrenaline rush and crash. He had returned to a desk stacked with statements from Deer Lake citizens pointing the finger of blame at neighbors, at cops, at teachers, at Father Tom, at Paul. He returned to a telephone that refused to stop ringing with calls from more people casting more blame.

This was an ugly case full of ugly possibilities, the ugliest being that Paul was indeed somehow involved.

Logic made a case against Paul that he had not been able to argue away without leaving behind the metallic aftertaste of lies. Logic dictated they take Paul's fingerprints, and Paul had protested too much.

Logic also made a case against Albert Fletcher. The man also made the hair on the back of Mitch's neck stand up. He didn't like the deacon, got that old corkscrew feeling in his gut when he thought of Fletcher. He would have bet his badge Fletcher was guilty of something. Trouble was, he didn't know what and couldn't prove anything. So far the most suspicious thing his men had to report on the deacon was a trip to a dry cleaner's in Tatonka even though there were two in Deer Lake. Not exactly a smoking gun.

Mitch stared at the blackboard. Chalk circles wreathed names and questions—scattered clouds from various brainstorming sessions. Suspicions and conjecture. Theories about the darker minds and motives in Deer Lake. His haven. His purgatory. He felt as if he had been living in a fog of bland niceness for the past two years, oblivious to the abscesses beneath the placid surface of the town. Willingly blind to it. Willfully shutting off his cop instincts.

He resented Megan for going after him every time he turned around, pushing him to see things he didn't want to see, to consider things he didn't want to consider. But she was right in doing it. He might have come here with the idea of hiding to lick his wounds, but he couldn't hide from this. He couldn't look at Deer Lake and see a haven. He had to think like a cop.

He stared hard at the chalkboard, at the thick white circle around Albert Fletcher's name.

Fletcher had been teaching class at the time of the kidnapping. If he was involved, he had to have had an accomplice. No connection had been made between him and Olie Swain.

No solid connection had been made between Olie and the crime. Olie's van was a near-perfect fit to the one Helen Black had seen the night of the abduction, but the lab had turned up nothing useful in the van Olie had purchased from Paul. . . .

The message board mocked him.

> *ignorance is not innocence but SIN*
> *i had a little sorrow, born of a little SIN*
> *my emanation far within*
> *weeps incessantly for my SIN*

"Give me something to go on, you son of a bitch," Mitch muttered. "Then we'll see who's ignorant."

"I keep thinking maybe he's already given us something and we're just not seeing it."

Megan stood just inside the door, looking rumpled and ragged. Of course, her day had been the equal of his. Possibly worse. She looked in need of someone to lean on, but she wasn't likely to accept an offer from him. He could all but see the chip on her shoulder, and he knew he'd put it there.

"Hear anything from DePalma?" he asked after she sat two chairs down from him.

Megan shook her head. "I would like to think no news is good news, but I'm not that naïve. Aside from fingering Paul, I revealed Paige's secret life as a mercenary slut on live TV. I'll hear something. No good deed goes unpunished."

Mitch gave her a crooked smile. "As a diplomat, you make a great street cop."

Her mouth tugged up on one corner. "Thanks." She drew an aimless pattern on the tabletop with her thumb. "There seem to be more than a few people around town willing to believe Paul could have done it."

"They want to believe someone did it," Mitch said. "They would rather believe it was one of their own than some faceless evil. They would rather believe it was Paul, because then the evil would all be contained nice and neat within one family. Then they can go back to thinking they're all safe because the rotten apple was in someone else's barrel."

"That or they really believe he did it."

Mitch sighed. As badly as she felt pressured, Megan knew the pressure was, in many different respects, worse for him. He had family and friends taking sides in the case, looking for him to tie it all up in a nice neat yellow bow like the ones the residents of Deer Lake had tied around tree trunks and light poles in a show of hope. He had the past she had thrown in his face last night.

"We'll see what the lab has to say about his prints," he mumbled, staring once more at the time line taped to the wall.

"The lack of his prints in the van won't clear him," she reminded him, winning herself a scowl. "Logic dictates he would have been wearing gloves."

"Logic dictates," Mitch repeated. Logic dictated many things. It seemed few people took heed—including him. Logic dictated he steer clear of Megan, yet he made no real effort to do so. "I think logic clocked out a while ago. We should do the same. How about a pizza?"

The easy camaraderie in his offer surprised her. Mitch made a face at the wary look she was giving him. "Truce, okay? It's late. It's been another pisser of a day."

"Do I have to take off my badge?" she said, her voice cool.

He winced. "Okay, I was a jerk last night," he admitted, sliding into the chair between them. "This case hasn't done much for my temper. We both said some things we wouldn't have if the world were a sane place." He gave her his shrewd, hard-bargain look. "I'll spring for extra cheese."

"See each other after hours?" Megan made her eyes wide with false shock. "What will the public think?"

"Screw 'em," Mitch growled. "If we don't crack this case, they'll throw us both out in the street anyway."

"No," she said. "You'll survive failure; people forgive that all the time. But heaven help you if the bad guy turns out to be someone they really like. That kind of truth pisses them off every time."

She stared at the door that seemed a mile away. The idea of a cold apartment full of boxes served as no incentive.

"Come on, Megan," he cajoled. "It's just a pizza."

Temptation curled its tentacles around Megan and pulled. It was just a pizza. And then it would be just a touch, just a kiss, just a night, just sex.

"Thanks anyway," she murmured. "I think I'll just go home and lose consciousness."

But she just stood there. Wanting.

"Megan . . ."

He said her name in a low voice, a quiet, intimate tone that struck a chord of longing inside her. The beam of his whiskey-amber gaze caught her and held her in place as he rose from his chair. Then his arms were around her.

Mistake. Weakness. The words stabbed her hard, but her lips parted and met his. Her lashes fluttered down and heat enveloped her, enveloped them both. The kiss was long, yet impatient; gentle and urgent; aggressive and questioning and comforting. She wanted to touch him, to feel his need for her, to imagine it was the kind of need that transcended the physical. But it wasn't.

"What are you doing?" she asked as she pulled back, the demand lacking the sting she had intended.

"Changing your mind," Mitch told her. "If I'm lucky."

Megan stepped out of his arms. She pressed her hands together and brought her fingertips to her lips as if in prayer. She tried to focus on the granite-gray carpet, but her gaze strayed back to Mitch, standing now with his hands on his hips and one leg cocked—not in any attempt to disguise his state of arousal, but daring her to look. The aura of the dangerous male glowed around him—rough, slightly rumpled, impatient, big, and masculine—as if the day had rubbed away the polish of manners and civilization.

"No," she whispered, everything inside her protesting the denial. "My job is hanging by a thread."

"And the people with the ax will cut it regardless of what we do."

"Oh, thanks for the vote of confidence," Megan said, her voice sharp with sarcasm and hurt.

"It's got nothing to do with what I want or what I think, or what you want or what you think," he argued. "They'll do whatever is best for them. You know that as well as I do."

"So if they're going to punish me, I might as well be guilty of something?" she said bitterly.

He gave a shrug, as if to say "why not?" his face hard, impassive.

"I don't think so," she said softly. As foolish as it was to want to love him, she couldn't think of loving him as an act of spite or a consolation prize.

She turned slowly and went to the door, holding her breath against a hope she wouldn't name. Mitch said nothing. She forced her chin up and gave him a last look as she gripped the doorknob. "I won't go to bed with you just because it's convenient. I've got my faults, but a lack of self-respect isn't one of them."

DAY 10 1:02 A.M. -24° WINDCHILL FACTOR: -41°

Hannah sat in the wing chair in a corner of her bedroom. She was wide awake. Again. In the nine long nights that had passed since Josh had disappeared, she had forgotten what it was like to sleep deeply and peacefully. She had written herself a prescription for Valium but hadn't been able to bring herself to have it filled. Maybe she didn't want the sympathy of the pharmacist, or maybe it was symbolic of a weakness she didn't want to display. Maybe she didn't want—didn't deserve—the relief of sleep. Or maybe she was afraid she would give in to the pressure and the despair and succumb to the temptation to take too many.

Paul had been asked to submit to fingerprinting.

He had come home from the police station outraged, his temper out of control. Hannah had witnessed the *TV 7* live report, by turns shocked, angered, sickened, and frightened. Shocked because she'd had no warning; Paul had told her nothing. Angered that he would be so thoughtless. Sickened by the possibilities that pried open in her mind. Frightened because she couldn't make them go away.

She stared at their empty bed, while in the theater of her mind she replayed the scene. She could see herself standing in the family room, arms crossed, jaw clenched, gaze hard on Paul as he stormed in. She could see the agent of the day at the kitchen table, fielding yet another of the calls that had come without cease since the *TV 7* broadcast. Friends and relatives expressing their concern, offering their support, probing for oily secrets. She could see Paul's mouth moving and realized she wasn't hearing him above the roar of her blood in her ears.

". . . that little bitch," he snapped, jerking off his coat. He threw it on the love seat and toed off the heavy boots he should have left at the door. The laces were matted with snow that melted and ran like beads of sweat down into the carpet. "The only part of her job she can handle is fucking Mitch Holt."

Hannah ignored the remark. "I'd like to speak with you privately," she said tightly.

Paul stared at her, perturbed that she had interrupted his tirade. "I suppose you like her," he accused. "You progressive women have to stick together."

"I don't even know who you're talking about," she snapped.

"Thanks for paying attention, Hannah," he sneered. "It's so nice to have the support of my wife."

"If you want my support, you might consider letting me know what's going on." Her gaze darted to the agent at the table and back to Paul, who seemed oblivious to the third party. The phone rang yet again, the sound piercing her brain like a skewer. "You were asked to give your fingerprints and you didn't bother to let me know. How do you think that made me feel?"

"*You?*" Paul said, incredulous. "How do you think it made *me* feel?"

"I'm sure I wouldn't know. You certainly didn't share it

with me. It was just a fluke that I saw that sideshow at City Center. Did you think it was more important to get Paige Price on your side than me?"

"I shouldn't have to *get you* on my side. You should *be* on my side!"

His raised voice drew a look from the agent.

"If you want to continue this conversation," Hannah said, "I'll be in our room."

She strode across the room and up the steps. She felt as if they were living in a fishbowl; she didn't need a live audience for the disintegration of her marriage.

Paul caught hold of her arm from behind and jerked her to a stop. "Don't you walk away from me!" he snarled. "I've about had it with your attitude."

"*My* attitude!" Hannah gaped at him. "*I'm* not the one who was fingerprinted today!"

"You think I wanted that?"

She stared at him, at the hand that gripped her arm so hard his knuckles had gone white, at the lean face that was red and twisted with rage. She didn't know this man, didn't trust him, didn't know what to believe about him.

She pulled away from his grasp and rubbed at the soreness in her arm. "I don't know what to think," she whispered, shivering.

He blinked at her, color draining from his face. "Jesus, Hannah. You can't think I had anything to do with it."

Guilt came on a tide of exhaustion. It wasn't that she believed he had, it was that she wasn't sure he hadn't. The technicality would be lost on Paul. Truthfully, it was all but lost on her. How could she think Paul would hurt their son, take their son away, put her through this hell? How could she think it? What kind of wife was she? What kind of person?

"No," she said in a small voice. "I just don't know what to think, Paul. We used to share everything. Now we can't even talk without going for each other's throats. You can't imagine how I felt seeing you on television, hearing about the van and the fingerprints. All of it was like a scene from a bad soap opera. Why didn't you tell me?"

He dodged her plaintive look by staring into Lily's empty room. Karen Wright had offered to take the baby for the evening. Hannah had been too much in shock after seeing Paul on television to protest.

"There wasn't time," he explained. "I was out on the search and Mitch Holt came and . . ."

He was lying. The thought was instantaneous. Hannah felt ashamed for thinking it, but she couldn't push it aside. It was written all over her face.

"And you wonder why I didn't confide in you?" He shook his head. "I'm out of here."

"Paul—"

"I'll be at my office," he snapped, turning away. "You might want to alert the police so they can set up a surveillance."

He hadn't returned. He hadn't called. She hadn't tried to call him for fear he wouldn't answer. The way he hadn't answered the night Josh disappeared.

A tremor shook her and she curled herself more tightly into the chair, wrapping her arms around her knees. She didn't want the doubts and questions that ate away at the corners of her mind like mice. She didn't want to think about the interview she would do tonight with Katie Couric. All she wanted was to close her eyes and make it all go away.

Instead, she closed her eyes and saw Josh.

He was alive. Expressionless. Standing in a gray, formless void. He didn't speak. He showed no sign of recognizing or even seeing her. He simply stood there as her perspective shifted around him, circling slowly, taking in everything about him. There was a bruise on his right cheek. He wore striped pajamas she had never seen before. Even though she couldn't see through the sleeves, she knew he wore a gauze bandage on his left arm at the inner elbow. Just as she knew his mind was filled with the same gray fog that surrounded him, with the exception of one thought—*Mom.*

Hannah's heart raced out of control. She wanted to touch him, but couldn't move her arms from her sides. She tried to call out to him, but no sound came out of her mouth. She willed him to look at her, but he looked through her, as if she were not there. Frustration built and built inside her like steam in a kettle until she screamed, and screamed and screamed.

She jerked in the chair, her eyes snapping open, her heart galloping. The nightshirt and leggings she wore were soaked

with sweat. She thought she'd slept a matter of minutes. The
clock on Paul's nightstand told her she had dozed more than
an hour. It was two-forty.

The bed was still empty.

The phone rang and she dove for it, knocking the base to
the floor. "Paul? Paul?"

Silence answered her, heavy and dark.

She sank down to sit on the floor, leaning back against the
bed.

"Paul?" she tried again.

The voice came, low and eerie, a whisper like smoke. "A lie
is the handle which fits them all. A lie is the handle which fits
them all. A lie is the handle which fits them all."

CHAPTER 31

S in has many tools, but a lie is the handle which fits them all
came from Oliver Wendell Holmes, they found out.
They had looked the phrase up in an old dog-eared book of
quotations in Paul's home office, an immaculate room that
should have been featured in a home decorating magazine.
Megan's gaze had roamed. Not a book, not a pen out of place.
Not a speck of dust. Not a picture hanging crooked on the wall.
Compulsively, fanatically neat. Not Hannah's doing; Hannah
wasn't certain Paul had a book of quotations. Anyone keeping
a room that clean had to know every title on the shelves.

Serial killers were often compulsively neat. Megan knew
that from her behavioral science courses at the FBI academy.
No one considered Paul Kirkwood a potential serial killer; still,
she filed his compulsive tendencies away in the back of her
mind. That and the fact that he had been out of the house
when the call had come. The watch commander had sent a unit
to the Omni Complex, and the officers had awakened Paul
from what he claimed was a sound sleep on the sofa in his office and escorted him back home.

Megan saw the apprehension in Hannah's eyes when Paul
came into the kitchen. She felt the tension that lay between
them like a sheet of ice. God, wasn't the loss of Josh enough?
Did they have to lose their marriage, too? On the other hand,
didn't Hannah deserve better than Paul? Weak and petulant
and self-absorbed, he got Megan's back up, and had almost
from the moment she'd met him. But had he called his wife in
the dead of night and taunted her with hints of lies?

If he had, he was a damn good actor. News of the call had shaken him. With fear or abject guilt?

The call had come from somewhere in Deer Lake. There hadn't been sufficient time to trap it to get more than the exchange. It could have come from anywhere—a house across the street or across town or across the lake where Albert Fletcher lived in the shadow of St. Elysius. It could have come from Paul's office. It could have come from any pay phone in town.

The possibilities buzzed like flies in Megan's brain. She hadn't been sleeping long or well when the call had come. Thoughts of the curt message DePalma had left on her answering machine for her to call him ASAP had kept her mind from winding down. And now that she was back home from the Kirkwoods' house, it was too late to go back to bed and too early to go in to the office.

She sat at the round oak table she had rescued from a flea market and stripped herself, another of her faux heirlooms. A tremor rattled through her body. Caffeine overload. Between the coffee and the drugs to stave off a monster migraine, she felt as if her body were running on rocket fuel. Her heart was pumping too fast and she felt dizzy. She had been abusing her body and abusing her medications, taking too much of some and ignoring others because they knocked her out and she couldn't afford to be groggy or unconscious.

She would be paying for her sins soon. She just had to hang in there a while longer. Just until they could make the pieces fit. Just until they saw the one thing they had been missing.

Sin has many tools, but a lie is the handle which fits them all.

Whose lie? Whose sin? What was there that they couldn't see?

Pain squeezed her temples like a giant forceps. Trying to will it away, she pushed herself to her feet and went into the bathroom. She fumbled with the cap on the prescription bottle of Propranolol, finally tipping a pill into her trembling hand. She washed it down with water and stood there for a moment after, scowling at herself in the mirror.

"One more strike and you're out, O'Malley," she mumbled.

The pain dug into her temples like a pair of spurs.

A little voice in the back of her head whispered she was out already.

7:15 A.M. -19° WINDCHILL FACTOR: -38°

She avoided her office, having no burning desire to return De-Palma's call of the night before. She stopped first at the command center to see if anything useful had come in over the hotline. Lots of calls pro- and con-Paul. One call from a woman who claimed Josh had been abducted by aliens. A dozen or more from people who wanted to chastise Megan personally for picking on Paige Price. A whole lot of nothing. She left the center with a promise to return at eight to brief her people on the latest developments and make assignments for the day.

At the station her first stop was the war room. Mitch had been there ahead of her. The Oliver Wendell Holmes line had been added to the list on the message board. The call to Hannah had been noted on the line, and Paul's noticeable absence had been starred.

Megan walked backward along the line, looking for a sign that Paul was at the heart of the mystery. Paul had lied to them. Paul had been evasive. He had a secret, of that she was certain, but was his secret dark enough, evil enough to drive him to harm his own son?

Albert Fletcher appeared on the time line only once—on the night of Josh's abduction, when he had been teaching the class Josh should have attended. The line was for facts only, no conjecture, no suspicions, which served only to magnify their lack of solid leads. Their crook might be any one of fifteen thousand people in Deer Lake—if he was from Deer Lake at all. He might be someone she had passed on the street. He might be sitting at the coffee shop down the block. All they knew with any certainty was that someone had happened upon Josh at a moment when he was absolutely vulnerable. That truth pointed to Olie Swain, and Olie Swain was gone forever.

Her next stop was to see that Olie's computers had been set up for Christopher Priest. Not only had they already been set up, Priest was already inspecting them. The machines had been lined up on a long table in a small gray room that held nothing else but a pair of chrome-and-plastic chairs. The disk drives hummed quietly. The monitors glowed in varying shades and combinations of black and white and green. Priest was bent over one, frowning at the message on the screen. He looked up as Megan entered the room and pushed his oversize glasses up on his nose.

"You're early, Professor. I wasn't expecting you until eight-thirty."

"I just stopped in to see if we're set up." The sleeves of his blue turtleneck crept halfway to his elbows. "I'd like to get an early start if possible."

"I'll see if the computer guy from headquarters is around," Megan said. "He must be here somewhere if the machines are on. You didn't turn them on, did you?"

"No." The professor crossed his arms like a little boy who had been told not to touch anything in the toy store.

"Good. Actually, you shouldn't even be in here without him," she pointed out, her gaze scanning the screens in the fruitless hope of detecting whether or not they had been tampered with. What she knew about computers was limited to writing reports and calling up information from headquarters. "Procedure," she added as a diplomatic afterthought.

Priest looked at her blankly.

"Why don't you have a seat in the break room, help yourself to a cup of coffee while I see if I can find him?" Megan suggested, holding the door open.

"I hope he's here," he said, reluctantly backing away from the table. "I have a faculty meeting at one. I would like to be finished . . ."

He let the thought hang, sliding the computers a longing glance.

"He's probably waiting in my office," Megan said, standing firm, doorknob in hand. They couldn't afford a kink in the chain of evidence. If Olie's machines yielded some relevant link to an accomplice, their means of obtaining that tidbit had to be squeaky clean in order to stand up to a judge's scrutiny.

If that connection ended up getting thrown out because a judge decided they hadn't played by the rules, everything they found as a direct result of that link would go as well. Fruit of the poisoned tree, the lawyers called it. Cops called it bullshit nitpicking, for all the good it did them.

Priest slipped past her into the hall. "I *am* trustworthy, Agent O'Malley," he said, giving her a hurt look. "I've worked with the police before."

"Then you know it's nothing personal." She gave him a pained smile as she locked the door behind him. "I'm just covering my backside."

And she felt a little bit of a draft. Christopher Priest might have been a model of virtue, teacher, volunteer, role model for rehabilitating juvenile delinquents; but he had known Olie Swain. A defense attorney would gnaw on that bone all day long if he found out Priest had been in the room with the computers all by his lonesome.

She made her way through the labyrinth of halls, oblivious to the people she passed. Her vision was changing subtly, blurring a bit at the edges, her perception of light and dark becoming sharper. Warning signs. If she could just hold it off until afternoon, until this, until that. The bargains were old and timeworn. She would leave early and sleep all night. She would eat regular meals and avoid stress. Lies she told herself every time the talons of pain began to dig in.

Her hand was trembling so badly, she could barely insert the key in the lock of her office door. As it turned out, she didn't need to. The door was open, the office occupied.

A man rose from her visitor's chair with a copy of *Law and Order* in one hand and a half-eaten glazed doughnut in the other. He looked about thirty, though he had the kind of face that would appear boyish long after thirty had passed him by. His eyes were wide, bright, and brown, and his nose was too short. His hair—a mop of brown curls—put Megan in mind of a cocker spaniel. She scowled at him for invading her territory.

"Megan O'Malley," she said, tossing her briefcase on her desk. She went on glaring at him as she hung her coat on the rack. "In case you were wondering whose office you'd barged into."

Spaniel Boy gave her a look of exaggerated sheepishness,

fumbling with the magazine and the half-eaten doughnut, dumping them on her desk. He brushed his hand off on the leg of his navy chinos, leaving behind flakes of sugar glazing, then offered the hand to Megan.

"Marty Wilhelm."

Megan ignored the show of manners. The message light on her phone was blinking like an angry red eye. "I assume you know you're all set up in the small room down by Evidence. The professor is chomping at the bit to get started."

"Ah . . . huh?"

"The professor. The computers," Megan said flatly. "Out the door. Hang a left. I'd say you need a key, but that didn't stop you from coming in here."

A crooked, embarrassed smile quirked his lips. "I think you have me confused with someone else."

"That depends on who you are."

"*Agent* Marty Wilhelm. Headquarters was supposed to notify you. Actually"—he lifted a finger to emphasize the point, still grinning—"Bruce DePalma said he would speak to you personally."

Megan's gaze shot to the blinking message light. A chill swept over her. She forced her eyes back to Marty with his puppy-dog enthusiasm and regimental-striped tie.

"I'm sorry," she said, amazed that she sounded perfectly normal when all internal systems were going haywire. "I'm afraid you have me at a loss. I haven't spoken with Bruce today."

"Oh, gee. This is awkward." He cleared his throat and patted his chest, then raised both hands with fingers spread. ' I'm your replacement. You've been temporarily suspended from active duty. You're off the case."

The internal alarm went off, too late to do any good. Marty Wilhelm. The Marty Wilhelm who had reportedly been in the running for this field post before affirmative action bumped him out. The Marty Wilhelm who was engaged to the daughter of Hank Welsh from Special Operations. The Marty Wilhelm who had evidently been standing in the wings, waiting for her to screw up.

Megan's first impulse was to pull her Glock 9-mil and blow that silly fucking smirk off his face. Smarmy little weasel, play-

ing dumb, stringing her along. She could imagine the only thing
that would have made him happier was to have had an audience. It was a wonder he hadn't waited for her in the squad
room so he could have made a fool of her in front of other cops.

"I'll need to see some ID," she said, biting down hard on
her temper.

Marty's brows shot up. But he dug his ID out and handed
it over. Megan glanced at it, then dropped it like a hot rock on
her desk—*Spaniel Boy's* desk. Her knees shook a little and she
sat down on Leo Kozlowski's broken chair.

"I'll need to make a couple of phone calls," she announced.

Marty eased back down into the visitor's chair and made a
magnanimous gesture toward the phone.

"And you will kindly get the hell out of this office while I do
so," she said through her teeth.

"Now, Megan," he began in a practiced patronizing tone.
"You're really not in any position to order me around."

"No," she said, "but I am in a position to generate headlines the likes of 'Disgruntled Agent Goes on Shooting Spree.'
You wouldn't want to be listed first in a story like that, would
you, Marty?"

His chuckle was forced and more than a little tense. He
stood again and backed toward the door. "I'll just see if I can't
straighten out this confusion about the computers and the professor."

"You do that."

"I'll stop back."

"Take your time."

He slipped out the door and closed it quietly. The sound
was magnified in Megan's mind. The door slamming on her career, shutting her out.

*You blew it, O'Malley. You're screwed. They were waiting like
wolves for you to stumble and now they're going to chew you up
and spit you out. Way to go.*

The self-recriminations were like lashes from a whip. What
was the matter with her? This was the job she'd been waiting
for, and she'd ruined it—by compromising herself with Mitch
Holt. And how many times had she warned herself to curb her
tongue, to restrain her temper, just to turn around and blow up
on live TV.

Stupid. Careless.

She tried to gather her composure. She wouldn't give up without a fight. She wouldn't be reduced to the kind of bawling, begging woman she despised.

She reached for the telephone, her hand shaking like a palsy victim's as the migraine expanded in her head like a balloon. As she pressed the receiver to her ear, the dial tone sliced through her brain. Groaning, head swimming, she dropped the receiver and threw up in the wastebasket.

7:42 A.M. -19° WINCHILL FACTOR: -38°

I saw Josh."

Father Tom slid into the pew beside Hannah. She had called him at the crack of dawn and asked to see him before morning Mass. The sun had been up barely an hour, sending pale fingers of light through the stained glass windows. Cubes and ovals of soft color flickered shyly on the drab flat carpet that ran down the center aisle. Tom had rolled out of bed and pulled on pants and a T-shirt and sweater. He hadn't bothered to shave. Absently, he combed his hair with his fingers, as unconcerned with his own appearance as he was concerned with Hannah's.

She was pale and wan, her eyes fever-bright. He wondered when she had last eaten a meal or slept for more than an hour or two. Her golden hair was dull and she had swept it back into a careless ponytail. A bulky black cotton sweater disguised her thinness, but he could see the bones of her wrists and hands as she gripped them together in her lap, as delicate as ivory carvings, the skin almost translucent over them. He offered her his hand and she immediately took hold with both of hers.

"What do you mean, you saw him?" he asked carefully.

"Last night. It was like a dream, but not. Like a—a—vision. I know that sounds crazy," she added hastily, "but that's what it was. It was so real, so three-dimensional. He was wearing pajamas I'd never seen before and he had a bandage—" She broke off, frustrated, impatient with herself. "I sound like a lunatic, but it happened and it was so *real*. You don't believe me, do you?"

"Of course I believe you, Hannah," he whispered. "I don't know what to make of it, but I believe you saw something. What do you think it was?"

A vision. An out-of-body experience. A psychic something-or-other. No matter what she called it, it sounded like the desperate ravings of a desperate woman. "I don't know," she said, sighing, shoulders slumping.

Father Tom measured his words carefully, knowing he was treading a fine line through sensitive territory. "You're under tremendous stress, Hannah. You want to see Josh more than you want to breathe. It wouldn't be unusual for you to dream about him, for the dream to seem real—"

"It wasn't a dream," she said stubbornly.

"What does Paul think?"

"I didn't tell him."

She pulled her hands back and rested them on her thighs, staring at the rings Paul had placed on her finger to symbolize their love and their union. Was she betraying him with her doubt? Had he betrayed them all? The questions twisted in her stomach like battling snakes, venomous, hideous, creatures over which she had no control. She turned her gaze to the soaring arched ceiling of the church, to the intricate and towering glass mosaic window of Jesus with a lamb in his arms. She stared at the ornately carved crucifix, Christ looking down at the high altar from his place on the cross. Empty, the church seemed a cavernous, cold place, and she felt small and powerless.

"The police asked him to give his fingerprints yesterday," she murmured in the hushed tone of confession.

"I know."

"They're not saying it, but they think he's involved."

"What do you think?" Father Tom asked gently.

She was silent as the snakes wrestled inside her. "I don't know."

She closed her eyes and let out a shuddering breath. "I shouldn't doubt him. He's my husband. He's the one person I should trust. I used to think we were the luckiest people on earth," she murmured. "We used to love each other. Trust. Respect. We made a family. We had priorities. Now I wonder if any of that was real or was it just a passing moment. I feel like maybe our lives were set to run on the same plane for just that time and now we've gone in such different directions, we can't even communicate. And I feel so cheated and so stupid. And I don't know what to do."

She sounded so lost. As capable and intelligent as she was, Hannah was ill-prepared to face this kind of catastrophe in her life. She had lived the kind of life most people dreamed of. She came from a loving family, had been given advantages, had achieved and excelled, married a handsome man and started a nice family. She had never developed the tools to deal with pain and adversity. To him now, she looked stunned and defenseless, and he caught himself cursing God for being so cruel.

"Oh, Hannah," he murmured. He didn't try to stop himself from brushing a lock of hair back from her cheek. He was well-schooled in the art of compassion, but if he had ever held any wisdom, it deserted him with this woman. There was nothing he could offer her that was more than empty words . . . except himself.

She turned to him, put her head on his shoulder. Her tears soaked into his sweater. Her muffled words tore at him.

"I just don't understand! I'm trying so hard!"

To deal with something that should never have touched her life.

Tom folded his arms around her and held her protectively, tenderly. He looked around his empty church at the votives—small tongues of flame in cobalt glass, symbols of hope that flickered out and died unanswered. The fear that yawned inside him made him tighten his arms around Hannah, and Hannah's arms stole around him, her fingers curling into the soft wool of his sweater. He rubbed a hand up and down her back, up into the fine hair at the base of her skull. He breathed in the clean, sweet scent of her, and ached with a longing he had never known. A longing to connect with the kind of love men and women had shared since the dawn of time.

He didn't ask why. Why Hannah. Why now. The questions and recriminations could wait. The need could not. He held her tight, held his breath, prayed for time to stand still for just a moment, because he knew this couldn't last. He brushed a kiss to her temple, and tasted her tears, salty and warm.

"Sinners!"

The charge came like thunder from heaven. But the bellow was not from God; it was from Albert Fletcher. The deacon descended on them from behind the screen that hid the door to the sacristy. He flew down the steps, a wraith in black, his eyes wild, his mouth tearing open, a large stoneware bowl in his hands. At the same time, the doors of the narthex at the back of the church were pulled open. The morning faithful wandered in to be struck dumb by the bizarre tableau in front of them.

Father Tom surged to his feet. Hannah twisted around to face Fletcher. He bore down on her, a madman shrieking like something from a nightmare.

"Sinners burn!" he screamed as he flung the contents of the bowl.

The holy water hit Hannah like a wall and splashed Father Tom. An elderly woman at the back of the church let out a shriek.

"Albert!" Tom yelled.

"The wages of sin is death!"

He was beyond hearing, certainly beyond listening to anything Father Tom had to say.

"Wicked daughter of Eve!"

Fletcher hurled the stoneware bowl at Hannah. She screamed, trying to dive out of the way and ward off the blow at the same time. Tom lunged in front of her, grunting as the missile glanced off his right hip. It clattered down onto the seat of the pew in front of him and bounced onto the floor, shattering with a loud *crack!* Ignoring the pain, Tom launched himself into the aisle, grabbing for Fletcher. The deacon jumped back, just out of reach.

"The wages of sin is death!" he screamed again, backing up the steps toward the altar.

"Albert, stop it!" Tom demanded, moving toward him aggressively. "Listen to me! You're out of control. You don't know what you're doing. You don't know what you saw. Now, calm down and we'll discuss it."

Fletcher moved continually backward, up another step, onto the level of the altar. His narrowed eyes never left Father Tom.

" 'Beware of false prophets who come in sheep's clothing but inwardly are ravening wolves,' " he quoted in a low monotone. He backed into the altar, his hands behind him, fingers searching. His face was waxy white and filmed with sweat, the muscles drawn against the bone as tight as a drumhead, twitching spasmodically.

Father Tom eased up onto the last step, reaching out slowly. Should he have seen this coming? Should he have done something sooner to prevent it? He had always thought of Albert Fletcher as obsessive, not insane. There were worse obsessions than God. But madness was madness. He reached out with the intention of pulling his parishioner back across that line.

"You don't understand, Albert," he said quietly. "Come with me and give me a chance to explain."

"False prophet! Son of Satan!" He swung his arm and caught Father Tom hard in the side of the head with the heavy base end of a fat brass candlestick.

Stunned, Tom fell to his knees on the steps and couldn't stop himself from veering backward, sideways, down. He had no control of arms or legs. What senses hadn't been knocked out entirely were a hopeless jumble in his pounding head. He tried to speak but couldn't, tried to point as people rushed up to surround him, gaping at him in astonishment. Albert Fletcher fled out a side door.

CHAPTER 32

L onnie, Pat, check the garage. Noogie, you're with me; we'll take the house."

They stood beside a pair of squad cars in front of Albert Fletcher's house, the cold pressing in on them, penetrating the layers of Thinsulate and Thermax and goose down and wool as if they were gossamer chiffon. None of the neighbors seemed curious enough about the presence of police to step outside into the cold. Mitch caught the flick of a drape in the rambler across the street. A wrinkled face peered out at them from the window of the Cape Cod next door to Fletcher's house.

"Don't look like he's home," Dietz said, rubbing his gloved hands against each other. The black fake-fur hat perched on his head looked like some synthetic creature trying to mate with his wig.

"He just assaulted a priest," Mitch drawled. "I don't think he'd be inclined to roll out the welcome mat."

Assault with what intent? he wondered. With what motive? Father Tom had explained as much as he could in the Deer Lake Community Hospital ER while Dr. Lomax poked at the gash in the side of his head and made grave doctor faces. Fletcher had seen him with his arms around Hannah and misunderstood the embrace.

An innocent hug hardly seemed enough to catapult a man over the edge of sanity.

Mitch had looked to Hannah for confirmation as she paced the width of the small white room. She was shaking—with cold or with shock or both. Shaking hard.

"I don't know what he was thinking," she muttered, eyes downcast. "The whole world has gone insane."

Amen, Mitch thought as he started up the walk to Fletcher's front door. Noogie went around to the back in case Fletcher was home and would try to make a break for it. Wherever the deacon had gone, he had gone on foot. His Toyota sat in the parking lot beside St. E's.

Mitch had assigned half a dozen officers to search the neighborhood on foot and in cruisers. Every other cop in town and the county was on the lookout. He doubted Fletcher had come home, but that might depend on just how far Albert had gone off the deep end. In any event, they had a search warrant. If they didn't get Fletcher, they would at least get a look around.

He pulled open the storm door and knocked hard on the inner door.

"Mr. Fletcher?" he called. "Police! We have a search warrant!"

He waited a slow ten count. Megan would have his hide for doing this without her, but she hadn't been in her office when the call came in, and he couldn't wait. He raised the two-way radio and buzzed Noga.

"Do your thing, Noogie."

"Ten-four, Chief."

Mitch figured he was too damn old to be busting exterior doors in with any part of his anatomy. They had a battering ram in the trunk of Dietz's cruiser, but they had something bigger and better in Noga. After the demise of his college football career due to a bum knee, Noga was always happy to crash into something or someone.

The sharp *crack!* of splintering wood cut through the crisp morning air. Seconds later, Noga pulled the front door open from the inside. "Whatever you're selling, I don't want any."

Mitch stepped into the small foyer. "Really? I'm running a two-for-one special on excessive force this month. Anyone giving me shit gets his ass busted twice."

Noga's thick eyebrows reared up like a pair of woolly caterpillars. He stepped back into the living room, waving Mitch inside. "You want the upstairs or the downstairs?"

"Up. Be sure to check the basement."

Mitch took the stairs slowly, knowing he was vulnerable if Fletcher was perched up there waiting for him with a candlestick or an Uzi. There was no predicting what Fletcher might feel driven to do. There was no telling what he might already have done. He may have lost his marbles years ago, but managed to keep a lid on his madness until now. Until he had seen Hannah in the arms of his priest.

The wages of sin is death. Wicked daughter of Eve.

Had he hated her all this time for interfering with his wife's treatment, for trying to cure the illness that had eventually killed Doris Fletcher? Had he killed Doris himself?

"Mr. Fletcher? Police! We have a search warrant!"

There was an arrest warrant as well, though Mitch doubted Father Tom would press charges. It gave them access to him for the time being. The fact that Fletcher had run off with the weapon had been enough for Judge Witt to issue the search warrant.

A floorboard creaked a protest as Mitch stepped up into the narrow hall. A window straight ahead let in butter-yellow morning light through a double layer of sheer white curtains that obscured the view to and from the street. On either side of the hall, matching white six-panel doors led into what would be architecturally matching bedrooms.

He tried the door on the left first, letting himself into the room cautiously, but the room was vacant in more ways than one. It had been stripped of whatever life it might have held when Doris Fletcher was alive. Mitch felt instinctively the stark monastic quality of the furnishing and decoration was post-wife. The bed was a narrow bunk covered with an army surplus wool blanket made up so tight, he could have bounced dimes off it. The nightstand held a lamp and a worn black Bible. The only other piece of furniture was a chest of drawers, the top bare of the usual personal debris. The only decorations on the stark white walls were a crucifix and a sepia-toned print of Jesus festooned with old palm fronds.

The room across the hall was locked, a situation that was dealt with with the bottom of Mitch's boot. The door swung back on its hinges, banging against the wall. Downstairs, Noogie responded to the sound with a shout, but Mitch was too stunned to answer him.

Blackout shades blocked all light and all vision from the outside world, but the room was aglow with the flames of candles, their waxy scent thick in the air. A single row of sconces lined the walls, the shadows of their flames dancing. Candles in glass holders—some clear, some red, some blue—sat in clusters on side tables. Their light was sufficient to show the room for what it was—Albert Fletcher's personal chapel.

The walls of the room were painted the same shade of slate as the walls of St. E's, and someone had gone to great pains to imitate the intricate stencil patterns that adorned the church. Even the ceiling was painted to simulate the arches and frescoes. Crude renderings of angels and saints looked down from gray clouds, their faces weirdly distorted, grotesque.

At one end of the room stood an altar draped with a white brocade antependium and rich lace runners. On it were arranged all the accoutrements of a Catholic Mass—the thick cloth-bound missal, the golden chalice, a pair of candelabra mounted with more fat white candles. On the wall above the altar hung a huge old crucifix with a painted effigy of Christ as gaunt as a greyhound, dying in agony, blood running from the gory wounds in his hands and the gash in his side.

Artifacts. The word struck Mitch as he took it all in. These were not homemade imitations, they were the genuine articles. He could envision Albert Fletcher sneaking them up here from the basement of the St. Elysius rectory in the dark of night; cleaning them, his long, bony fingers stroking over them lovingly as he stared at them with the light of fanaticism in his eyes. The candlesticks, the crucifixes, the plaques of the stations of the cross, the statuary.

Perched on mismatched pedestals around the perimeter of the room were old statues of the Holy Mother and various saints whose names he could only guess at. Their sightless eyes stared out from faces that were chipped and cracked. Their human hair was ratty and thin, looking chewed off in places and plucked out in others. They stared over a congregation that was equally unanimated—four small pews of mannequins.

Mitch's skin crawled as he looked at them. Heads and torsos, some with arms, some without. None with legs. The males were dressed in shirts and ties and old castoff suit coats. The females were swaddled in black cloth, sheer black draped over their heads. They all sat at perpetual attention, staring blankly at the altar, the light from the candles flickering over their plastic faces.

And to the side of the altar stood yet another of their silent rank. The mannequin of a boy dressed in a black cassock and dingy white surplice. An altar boy.

A rumble of thunder announced Noogie's ascent up the stairs. He pounded down the hall and came to a dead stop in the doorway of the room, his service revolver pointed at the ceiling.

"Holy sh—shoot." He stared, wide-eyed, his jaw hanging halfway to his chest. "Man," he whispered. "I've never seen anything like this. This is creepy."

"Did you find anything downstairs?" Mitch asked as he bent and ran a hand over the well-worn velvet padded kneeler before the altar.

"Nothing." Noga remained in the doorway, his gaze skating nervously over the faces of the mannequins.

Mitch rose. "It's not a real church, Noogie. You don't have to whisper."

The big officer's gaze fixed on the statue of the Virgin Mary with half its face missing. He swallowed hard and a shudder rippled down him. "It's weird," he said, his tone still hushed. "Downstairs it's like no one lives here. I mean, there's no stuff—no newspapers lying around, no mail, no knickknacks, no pictures on the wall, no mirrors." His eyes went wide again. "You know, vampires don't keep mirrors."

"I don't think he's a vampire, Noogie," Mitch said, opening the closet door at the back of the chapel. "Crosses ward them off."

"Oh, yeah."

In the closet hung a row of priest's vestments, old and frayed but clean and pressed. Some were still in the plastic bags from Mueller's Dry Cleaning in Tatonka. Black cassocks and red ones, white surplices and mantles in royal purple and cardinal red and rich ivory with elaborate embroidery.

"Mitch!" Lonnie Dietz hollered below. "Mitch!"

"Up here!" Mitch bellowed.

The run up the stairs winded Dietz. His face was ashen, setting off the bright red of his nose. His hat had tumbled off and his wig was askew, looking like a small, frightened animal clinging to his head. He stopped on the landing as Mitch wedged himself past Noogie into the hall.

"I think you better come out here," Dietz said. "We think we just found Mrs. Fletcher."

Pat Stevens lifted the dust cover on the mummified remains of Doris Fletcher sitting behind the wheel of her 1982 Chevy Caprice. She was dressed in an old cotton house shift that had rotted away in places where fluids had leaked from the body during one phase of decomposition. Mitch had no idea what she had looked like in life, whether she had been thin or heavy, pretty or homely. In death she looked like something that had been freeze-dried until all fluid evaporated and the tissue and skin shrunk down tight against bone like leather—which was precisely what had happened. Hideous didn't begin to describe her sitting there shriveled inside her dress.

That she had died in the winter had saved her from being ravaged by insects and rot. By the time warm weather had arrived, she had already been partially petrified. Timing had also prevented the neighbors from detecting her fate with their noses. Had Albert Fletcher locked his wife's dead body in a Chevy Caprice in July in Minnesota, he would not have been able to keep the secret three days, let alone three years. But Doris Fletcher had been obliging in death, if not in life.

"How do you suppose he got her here?" Lonnie pondered nervously as he paced back and forth alongside the car. Noogie stood back against the wall of the garage, mouth hanging open in a trance, his winter-white breath the only indication he had survived the shock.

"Religious nut like him, why wouldn't he give her a decent Christian burial?" Pat Stevens asked.

"Apparently, he didn't believe she deserved one," Mitch said.

He read the note pinned to the front of Doris Fletcher's dress.

Wicked daughter of Eve: Be sure
your sin will find you out.

9:41 A.M. -19° WINDCHILL FACTOR: -38°

The press buzzards, circling town with their ears tuned to their police scanners, picked up the radio calls and made it to Albert Fletcher's house ahead of the coroner. They clustered in the driveway, moving like a school of fish—drifting in unison, then scattering as their ranks were broken by cops, quickly drawing back into their group.

Mitch swore at them under his breath as he tried to direct his men and the BCA evidence techs between the garage and the house. The photographers and video people were the worst, trying to blend in with the official personnel in order to sneak shots of the body and the chapel.

The scene was trouble enough without gawkers. A three-year-old mummified corpse presented a whole array of logistical problems. The BCA people argued among themselves as to how to handle the situation. Noticeably absent from the discussion was Megan.

Mitch couldn't believe she hadn't beaten a path to the scene the second the call had gone out. She should have been right there in the thick of it as the crime scene unit took Fletcher's house apart board by board; taking notes, making a mental picture, processing the information through her cop's brain to formulate fresh theories.

He turned away from the bickering agents and headed for the side door of the garage. He jerked the door open and nearly ran head-on into a puppy-faced reporter with bright eyes and a stupid-looking grin on his face.

"You'll have to wait outside," Mitch snarled. "Law enforcement personnel only in here."

"Chief Holt!" The grin stretched wider and he offered Mitch his gloved hand. "I've had a call in to you since nine o'clock. That secretary of yours is a real guard dog."

"Natalie is my administrative assistant," Mitch said coldly, ignoring the proffered hand. "She runs my office, and if she hears you call her a guard dog, she'll rip your head off and shout down the hole. Now, if you'll excuse me, I have work to do."

Puppy Boy didn't seem to know whether he should be

amused or contrite. Mitch scowled at him and backed him into the driveway. Whatever else this guy might have been, he was tenacious. He hustled alongside Mitch as he headed to the house.

"You'll have to wait for the press conference like everyone else," Mitch snapped.

"But, Chief, you don't seem to understand. I'm not with the press. I'm with the BCA." He dug an ID out of his coat pocket and held it up. "Agent Marty Wilhelm, BCA."

Mitch stopped in his tracks, unease creeping along his nerve endings. "I haven't seen you on this case before."

Puppy Boy gave him a lopsided grin that seemed wholly inappropriate considering the circumstances. "I was just assigned."

Mitch kept his expression carefully blank. *Agent?* Megan had told him DePalma was considering sending another field agent to assist her. She said she would take it as a sign of her imminent demise.

"Well, *Agent* Wilhelm," he said softly, tightly. "Where is Agent O'Malley? She's the one you should be dogging, not me."

Marty Wilhelm stuffed his ID back in his coat pocket. "I wouldn't know. She's been relieved of this assignment."

2:20 P.M.   -16° WINDCHILL FACTOR: -32°

You get yanked off the job. You get sued for slander. You get kicked in the head with a migraine. You've just about topped your day of days here, O'Malley. And the night is young.

Megan supposed it was still afternoon, but time had ceased to mean anything to her and the living room shades were down, making the room dark. But not dark enough. Death wouldn't be dark enough to ease the pain in her eyes, or quiet enough to keep sound from piercing her brain. The refrigerator kicked on with a thump and a whine, and she whimpered and tried to curl into a tighter ball.

She still had her coat on, though her boots had come off—one by the door and one somewhere along the path between the still-unpacked boxes. The confounded gray scarf tried to choke her as she changed positions. She jerked at it with a trembling hand and wrestled it off to fling it on the floor. Her hair was still tied back. She could feel each individual strand as if some unseen hand were pulling relentlessly on her ponytail, but she couldn't concentrate hard enough to get the rubber band undone.

The pain was unrelenting, a constant high-pitched drill boring into her head, an ax splitting her skull. God, she *wished* someone would split her skull with an ax and put her out of her misery.

She should have been injecting herself with Imitrex, but she couldn't move from the couch. If she had been able to get herself upright, she didn't think she would even know where the bathroom was. She had pulled one of the few empty boxes in the apartment within puking range. Any port in a storm.

Gannon and Friday had taken up their posts on a stereo speaker box across the room, and watched her intently. They were old hands at the vigil. They never came too close or made a sound. As if they were perfectly attuned to her suffering, they lay across the room and watched her, ever diligent. Friday's white-tipped tail hung down the side of the box, the last inch twitching slowly back and forth, back and forth, like a pendulum.

Megan stared at it for a while, then closed her eyes and saw it still. Back and forth, back and forth. The rhythm made her dizzy, nauseated, but she couldn't erase it from her mind. Right, left, right left. Then it picked up words: *Paige Price, Paige Price, right left, right left, Paige Price, Paige Price.*

DePalma's voice came in, crackling with anger. "How could you be so stupid? How could you say that in front of twenty goddamn news cameras?"

Paige Price, Paige Price, Paige Price . . .

". . . five-million-dollar slander suit . . ."

Paige Price, Paige Price . . .

". . . against you and the bureau . . ."

Paige Price, Paige Price . . .

". . . I don't care if she's the whore of Babylon . . ."

Paige Price.

". . . you're off the case . . ."

Off the case.

Oh, God, she couldn't believe it. Couldn't stand it. Off the case. The words brought a wash of shame. Worse than that— far worse—was the fist of panic that tightened in her chest. She couldn't be off the case. She wanted it so badly. To find Josh. To catch the monster who had taken him and tormented them all. She wanted to be there to slap the cuffs on him and look him in the eye and say, "I got you, you son of a bitch." She wanted it for herself and for Josh and for Hannah. But she was off the case and the truth of that shook her to the core.

The pain burst inside her head like a brilliant white light bulb, and she pressed her face into the couch cushion and cried.

Another wave of pain obliterated all thought. Helpless to do anything else, Megan gave herself over to it. Somewhere in the distance she could hear the beat of helicopter rotors, the sound like bird's wings thumping against her eardrums. The search went on without her. The case went on without her.

The phone rang and the machine picked up. Henry Forster wanted to talk to her about Paige. *When hell freezes over.* Which may be imminent, she thought, shivering, pulling her coat tighter around her.

The phone chirped again, making her whimper, and again the machine picked up. "Megan? It's Mitch. I just heard you got yanked. Um—I thought you might be home, but I guess not. I'll try to get you on the radio. If you get this message first, call me. We've got a situation with Fletcher." There was a beat of silence. "I'm sorry. I know how much the job means to you."

The apology sounded awkward and sincere, as if he didn't make many, but the ones he made counted. He was sorry. He was giving his condolences, one cop to another. *Tough luck, you're off the case. It's been nice knowing you, O'Malley.* She would become a memory, someone who had barged into his life for a week, shared a bed with him for a couple of nights, and moved on.

She couldn't expect him to feel anything deeper than physical attraction to her. She knew nothing of love or relationships, or being a woman—as Mitch had pointed out so bluntly.

He had been in love enough to marry, enough to have a family, enough to still mourn the loss of that woman. She'd never had anything that came close. She only had the job and it was going down in flames.

How could she have been so stupid?

The phone seemed to ring incessantly. The press had gotten wind of the debacle. Paige, the bitch, had probably broken the news herself in a live exclusive from the steps of City Center.

Megan wondered about the "situation" with Albert Fletcher. What situation? She couldn't remember. It hurt to try. A dozen different half-remembered conversations tumbled together in her mind, all the voices talking at once in a dissonant chorus that made her ears ring and her head swim.

Please stop. Please stop.

The telephone shrilled again.

Please stop.

Tears ran down her face. Dizzy, wishing she would pass out, she slid down off the couch and crawled on her hands and knees to unplug the phone. She made it back to her barf box in time to be sick, but she couldn't muster the strength or coordination to get herself back on the couch. Beyond caring, she curled into a ball on the floor and lay there, waiting for the pain to end.

4:27 P.M. -20° WINDCHILL FACTOR: -38°

No one had seen a sign of Fletcher. He had vanished. As Josh had vanished. As Megan had vanished.

She didn't answer her telephone. She didn't answer her car radio. It seemed she had walked out of the station and disappeared off the face of the earth.

Mitch prowled the streets of town looking for any glimpse of Albert Fletcher, directing the search for their fugitive from the radio of the Explorer. The radio crackled. Positions of units. Complaints about the cold. Frustration at another dead end. A chopper passed by overhead, sweeping slowly over the rooftops of Deer Lake for a glimpse of the demented deacon.

Wicked daughter of Eve: Be sure your sin will find you out.

Megan had run into Fletcher at St. E's. He had been less than charmed by her. If Fletcher knew where Megan lived . . . She wouldn't have thought twice about taking him on.

He caught sight of her white Lumina parked at a cockeyed angle to the curb in front of her apartment house. The driver's door was ajar. Visions of her being pulled from the car pushed him into a trot up the sidewalk to the big Victorian house. He took the stairs two at a time to the third floor. No sound came from her apartment. No light leaked out under the door.

"Megan?" he called, pounding on the heavy old door. "Megan, it's Mitch! Let me in!"

Nothing.

If her car is here and she isn't, then where the hell is she?

"Megan?" He knocked again, tried the knob, found it locked. "Shit," he muttered, stepping back. "You're too damn old for this, Holt."

He took a deep breath and did it anyway. Thank God she hadn't thrown the deadbolt. The door gave up on the third kick and swung inward.

"Megan?" Mitch called, his gaze scanning the dark apartment.

The shades were drawn. What sun they had had in the morning had retreated behind a thick shroud of gray in the afternoon, leaving the apartment dimmer than twilight. The room was cold, as if the heat had been off for some time. His heart thumping, Mitch eased his Smith & Wesson out of his parka and pointed it at the ceiling. He moved slowly, silently, through the maze of boxes, walking on the balls of his feet, ready to jump.

His toe kicked a boot that had been abandoned. "Megan?"

Megan thought it was a hallucination. The banging, the voice. She was fading in and out of consciousness, in and out of reality. She wasn't certain the pounding wasn't inside her head— the pain. The pain took on dimensions beyond physical feeling. It became sound and light, an entity unlike any other, beyond description.

"Megan?"

But it never called her name. She was sure of that. The word ripped through her brain and she whimpered and tried to press her hands over her ears.

"Megan? Jesus!"

Mitch dodged a stack of boxes and dropped to his knees on the floor beside her. His hands shook violently as he reached for her.

"Honey, what happened? Who hurt you? Was it Fletcher?"

Megan tried to turn away from him. But he grabbed her shoulder and pulled her onto her back. The lamp at the end of the couch went on and she cried out.

"What is it?" Mitch demanded, leaning over her, pulling her hands aside as she tried to cover her eyes. "Where are you hurt, honey?"

"Migraine," she whispered. She squeezed her eyes shut tight. "Turn off the fucking light and go away."

The light went out, allowing her to breathe again. Weakness trembling through her, she turned onto her side again and pulled her knees up to her chest.

Mitch had never seen anyone in this much agony who wasn't bleeding profusely from a bullet hole or knife wound. He would never have imagined a headache severe enough to knock someone to the ground.

"Should I take you to the hospital?"

"No."

"What can I do, honey?" he murmured, bending close.

"Stop calling me honey and go away." Her pride didn't want him to see her like this—weak, vulnerable.

"The hell I'll leave," Mitch growled.

He scooped her up in his arms and stood. Megan curled against his chest, clenching a handful of his parka, willing herself to not throw up as he carried her out of the living room and down the hall.

He eased her down onto the bed and she sat there shaking, doubled over. He took off her coat, her cardigan and her shoulder holster, her turtleneck and her bra. Then he dressed her in an oversize flannel shirt that lay across the foot of the bed. She lay down and he set about stripping off her slacks and the .380 A.M.T. Back-Up she wore in a custom-made holster around her right ankle.

"Do you have medication to take?" he asked.

"In the medicine cabinet," she whispered, trying to burrow into her pillow. "Imitrex. Don't talk so loud."

He left and returned with the needle cartridge, then argued that he should take her to the hospital when she coached him on how to administer the injection.

"Megan, I can't give you a shot; I'm a cop, not a doctor."

"You're a wimp. Shut up and do it."

"What if I screw up?"

"It's subcutaneous; you can't screw up," she said, swallowing back the nausea. "I'd do it myself, but my hands are shaking."

Scowling ferociously, he pressed the cartridge against her bare arm, depressed the trigger button and counted to ten. Megan looked up at him from beneath half-lowered lids. He tossed the used cartridge in the wastebasket and gazed down at her.

"You're being nice to me again," she muttered.

"Yeah, well, don't get used to it." The words held no sting and the only thing in his touch as he brushed her hair back from her face was tenderness.

"Don't worry, I know better," she whispered.

Mitch didn't know whether she was referring to her job or their relationship. He wasn't certain what they had could be called a relationship, but now was not the time to discuss it.

"You scared the hell out of me," he said softly. "I thought our nut case *du jour* had gotten ahold of you."

"Who?" Megan asked, thoughts tipping and tumbling in her mind again.

"Fletcher flipped out and cracked Father Tom's head open with a candlestick. But then, you probably know how that feels."

"Piece o' cake," she mumbled. "Did you get him?"

"We will." Mitch decided to save the rest of the Fletcher story for later. She was in no condition to hear about the case, especially when she had been taken off it. "Don't worry about it, O'Malley. You'll give yourself a headache."

Megan thought she smiled a little, but she wasn't sure. Her brain kept shorting out as pain flashed like fire behind her eyes.

"You need to rest," Mitch told her. "Is there anything more I can do?"

Strange that she should be stricken with shyness, she thought. What she wanted to ask wasn't intimate in the least. Just a service. But she felt so vulnerable. . . .

"Let my hair down?" She turned her face away from him, giving him access to her ponytail, at the same time avoiding his eyes.

Funny it should seem such a personal thing, Mitch thought as he slipped the bedraggled velvet bow from her dark hair and undid the rubber band. He had done the same for Jessie more times than he could count. Maybe that was part of it—that she seemed as defenseless as a child. That he was taking the role of protector. She had to hate it. She was so fiercely independent, so proud, and pain had reduced her to asking for help with something as simple as taking her hair down. An ironic cycle— that her vulnerability brought out a strength in him that ultimately made him vulnerable as well.

He sifted his fingers through the mahogany silk, spreading it out on the flower-sprigged pillow. His touch as light as a whisper, he massaged the back of her head and the tightly corded muscles in the back of her neck. Tears seeped between her lashes and she cried softly, but she didn't tell him to stop.

"You know, I never did this for Leo," he said quietly, bending to kiss her cheek. "Try to get some sleep, sweetheart—can I call you sweetheart?"

"No."

"Okay, hard case. I'll be in the next room if you need me."

If you need me . . . Megan said nothing as he pulled the covers up around her shoulders, straightened, and turned to go. To leave her alone. Just her and her pain alone in a room that would never be home because she had blown her chance. Already it seemed colder, emptier, as if the place somehow knew she would be leaving.

. . . if you need me . . .

"Mitch?" She hated the weakness in her voice, the echoes from a long, lonely past, but God help her, she didn't want to be alone with those ghosts tonight.

He hunkered down beside the bed and squinted at her in

the dusky light. She closed her eyes against the tears, ashamed to have him see them. "Hold me. Please."

Mitch tightened his lips against the sudden wave of emotion. He touched a fingertip to the tip of her nose and forced words around the rock in his throat.

"Jeez, O'Malley," he said teasingly. "I thought you'd never ask."

He toed off his boots and settled in behind her, the old bed creaking and groaning beneath their combined weight. He tucked her back against him spoon-style. He slipped her hand into his, and kissed her hair so softly she might not have felt it. And he listened to her breathing as she surrendered at last to sleep.

CHAPTER 33

Hannah, beyond fear, what are you feeling throughout this ordeal?"

Hannah breathed deeply, thought carefully, the same steps she had taken for each of the previous questions. She tried to block out the presence of the cameras and lights and focus completely on the concerned face of the woman seated across from her. That was how she thought of Katie Couric—as a woman, as a mother, not as a celebrity or a reporter.

"Confusion. Frustration," she said. "I can't understand why this happened to us. I can't begin to comprehend it, and that's frustrating."

"Do you feel this is some kind of personal attack or vendetta?"

Hannah looked down at her hands in her lap and the handkerchief she had twisted into a knot. "I don't want to think anyone I know could be capable of this kind of cruelty."

Couric leaned ahead slightly in the small rose damask armchair. The NBC news crew had taken over the better part of the top floor of the Fontaine. An elegantly restored Victorian hotel in downtown Deer Lake, the Fontaine was furnished with antiques and reproductions. The crew had chosen the Rose Suite for the interview, partly for its size, partly for its beauty.

"Hannah, you were involved in an incident this morning at St. Elysius Catholic Church," Katie Couric said carefully. "Father Tom McCoy was attacked by Albert Fletcher, the man who taught Josh in catechism and supervised him as an altar boy. Later this morning the police made a bizarre discovery at Mr. Fletcher's home—finding what they believe to be the body of his wife, who passed away several years ago. The authorities are now conducting an extensive manhunt for Albert Fletcher. Do you think he could have been involved with Josh's disappearance?"

"I was so stunned when it happened—the attack," Hannah replied. "I'm still stunned. I would never have thought he could be violent, or we would never have trusted him with our son. That's part of the frustration. I saw this town as being safe. I saw the people in our lives as good people. Now all of that is shattered and it makes me angry and it makes me feel like I was naïve."

"Does it make you more angry that you've been singled out when, as a physician, you've done so much for the people in Deer Lake?"

Deep breath, deep thought. She had been raised to do service for and give to people with no expectations for personal gain. The answer that came automatically brought guilt, but it was the honest answer and she gave it in a strained whisper. "Yes."

Paul watched the interview on a portable television in his office and seethed with a jealousy he would never admit. Local stations weren't good enough for Hannah. She had to hold out for a network interview. She was probably breaking hearts across America with her tear-filled blue eyes and quiet voice. The camera loved her. She looked like an actress with her wavy golden hair pulled back loosely. Darryl Hannah as Hannah Garrison, devastated mother.

He poured himself a shot of scotch from the bottle he had taken out of his partner's office and sipped at it, grimacing. They said scotch was an acquired taste. Paul had every intention of acquiring it as quickly as possible. The burden of his life these days was just too much to deal with. Hannah was certainly no help. Christ, she had all but accused him of taking Josh! After everything he had done to aid in the search. So much for faith. So much for trust. So much for undying love.

So much for undying love.

He had called Karen to come and console him and she had

told him no. Paul had gotten the impression Garrett had been within earshot, but the rejection still stung. He took another face-twisting swallow of scotch and scowled at the television screen.

Katie Couric was managing to look grave and perky at once. She tilted her head and squinted. "Different people react differently to this kind of trauma. Some find strength they never knew they had. Some find that while someone vital is gone from their lives, their relationships with the people around them deepen. Others find it difficult and painful to maintain those relationships. How would you say Josh's abduction has affected your personal relationships, Hannah? How has it affected your marriage?"

Hannah was silent for a moment. Her mouth pulled down at the corners. "It's been a terrible strain."

"Do you think your husband blames you for that night?"

The blue eyes filled with glittering tears. "Yes."

Couric's eyes glistened as well. Her voice softened. "You blame yourself, don't you?"

"Yes." The camera held the close-up as Hannah fought for control. "I made a mistake that seemed so small—"

"But did you make a mistake at all, Hannah? You had someone call the rink to let them know you'd be late. What could you have done differently?"

"I could have had a back-up plan in place, an arrangement with someone I know and trust to pick Josh up if I couldn't. I could have coached Josh more on how to be safe. I could have helped the youth hockey program organize a formal plan to make sure all the children got home safely. I didn't do any of those things and now my son is gone. It never occurred to me I would need to take any of those measures. I was naïve. I could never have imagined the price I would have to pay for that.

"That's what I want other people to get out of this interview: that it took only one mistake at the wrong moment to change our lives forever. I don't want anyone else to have to go through what we're going through. If something I say can prevent that from happening, then I'll say it."

"And yesterday, when your husband was asked to submit to being fingerprinted by the Deer Lake police, what did you think about that? Is there any question in your mind about your husband's involvement?"

Hannah lowered her eyes. "I can't believe Paul would do anything to harm our son."

She said it stiffly, as if it were a rule she had been forced to adopt whether she believed it or not. The bitch. Paul took another hit of scotch and fought the urge to belch it back up.

"Hannah, your husband has charged the law enforcement agencies involved with mishandling the case. Do you share his point of view?"

"No. I know they've done everything in their power. Some of the questions they've had to ask have been difficult, sometimes painful, but I've known Mitch Holt since the day he moved here with his daughter, and I know everything he's done on this case has been with one objective: to find Josh and bring his kidnapper to justice."

Thank you, Hannah," Mitch murmured.

He sat on Megan's couch, watching the nineteen-inch color set with rabbit ears that sat on a box across the living room. Beside him, the black and white cat lay like a lion, watching the television, too. The little gray cat was curled in his lap, asleep.

He had been on the phone every fifteen minutes, keeping in contact with his men. There was still no sign of Fletcher, and with the exception of patrol cars, the ground search was being pulled in because of the extreme cold. If the deacon was hiding where searchers could find him without a warrant, they wouldn't need to worry about his going anywhere—he would be as stiff and cold as old Doris by morning. Hourly calls to the state patrol kept Mitch informed of the lack of progress on their end of things. If Fletcher had somehow managed to escape Deer Lake in a car, no one had seen him on the Minnesota highways.

Not being out in the field beating the bushes for Fletcher himself ate at him. He knew he wouldn't be able to do anything more than what was already being done. But the inactivity went against his street-cop nature. And now that the old instincts had been reawakened, he could feel that old restless edginess coming back to life.

He had left Megan sleeping deeply, and he hoped for her sake she would sleep through the night. It still shook him to think of the pain she had been in . . . and the way it had affected him. He had wanted to care for her, to soothe her, to protect her. He wanted to fight for her, for her job—the thing that meant so much to her, more than him, more than anything. Those individual components added up to something he didn't feel prepared for.

He stared down at his hand on the back of the gray cat, at the ring. He could still hear the bitter hurt in Megan's voice— *"My God, you didn't even bother to take off your wedding ring when you took me to bed!"* And he could still feel the guilt, and knew that in a twisted way he had welcomed it.

God, was that really what he had reduced himself to? Emotional purgatory. And he had dragged Megan there with him. Whatever she wanted out of their relationship, she didn't deserve that.

Allison was gone. Forever. He might have prevented her death, but he couldn't resurrect her from it. How long did he go on paying? How long did he *want* to pay?

Life could change so quickly. In a snap. In the blink of an eye. In a heartbeat.

. . . it took only one mistake at the wrong moment to change our lives forever. Hannah's words echoed what he had known since that day in Miami, when he had been too tired to stop for milk on his way home. One second, one offhand decision, and the world spun off its axis like a top gone berserk.

So was it better to live a half-life and never again run the risk of that kind of pain, or better to grab what came along and live it to its fullest for as long as the fates allowed? He knew which was safer, which hurt less yet punished him more.

He looked at Hannah on the television screen, doing her best to be strong, to atone in her own way for the imagined mistake that had cost her so much. The pain had painted dark circles beneath her eyes and carved hollows beneath her elegant cheekbones. The stress had fractured her marriage. If she could, would she choose to avoid it all by never having had Josh in her life? Mitch thought he knew what her answer would be. He knew *he* wouldn't have traded his time with Allison and Kyle for anything. Not even peace.

"How's she doing?"

Still pale, Megan stood in the doorway, rubbing her eyes, her hair a mess. The flannel shirt hung to her knees.

"She's doing okay, considering," he said. He dumped Gannon on the floor as he rose from the couch. "How about *you*? How are you feeling?"

She gave a small shrug. "A little woozy. I'll be okay. It's nothing new."

Mitch tipped her face up, staring down at her with intense scrutiny. "It's new to me. How often does this happen?"

Megan turned her face away. Now that the worst had passed, she wanted to forget how helpless she had felt and how badly she had wanted his compassion. If she could have suffered through the migraine alone, it would have been easier to slip out of town and out of his life. Now there was the sticky aftermath of compassion and embarrassment to deal with. Emotional loose ends that would not be easily tied off.

"It depends," she said. She sank down into a corner of the couch, her eyes on the television, where an ad genius had somehow managed to connect pizza with an old lady putting on lipstick in the rest room of an airplane. "Every time I lose my job or get sued for five million dollars."

She winced inwardly at his expression. He squatted down beside the arm of the couch, his gaze that same one that had looked too deep inside her before. She refused to meet it. The feelings were far too close to the surface and she was too tired to be anything other than transparent.

"Megan, I wish—"

"Don't bother; it doesn't do any good."

He leaned toward her. "Why won't you let me help or at least sympathize?"

"Because you can't fix it," she said wearily. "There's nothing you can do to change DePalma's mind. You can't change the fact that Paige Price is a mercenary whore, or that I said so on television. You can't fix it and I don't want sympathy."

His temper simmering, Mitch rose. "No, you wouldn't. You don't need sympathy. You don't need anyone—isn't that right?"

Megan stubbornly stared past him at the television. He wanted to shake her. He wanted her to need him and say so.

She had asked him to hold her when she was in so much pain she couldn't see straight, but that Megan and this one were two different people—a pair of nesting dolls, one hiding inside the other, rarely coming out into plain sight.

He could have kicked himself for caring. Hadn't he told himself he liked his life just the way it was—simple, controllable, safe . . . empty?

On the television Hannah's interview was about to resume. Mitch dropped down on the couch a foot to Megan's right, forcing Friday to vacate his spot. The cat gave him a dirty look and stalked away to leap onto a box marked STUFF I DON'T USE.

Katie Couric leaned forward in her chair, eyes luminous with sympathy. "Hannah," she said very softly. "Do you think Josh is alive?"

The camera zoomed in on Hannah's face. "I know he is."

"How do you know?"

She took her time answering, obviously considering both the question and the implication of her answer. When she spoke, her voice was clear and sure. "Because he's my son."

"She wasn't that certain the other night," Megan commented, nibbling at her cuticles. "She asked me twice if I believe Josh is alive. Asked as if she needed my reassurance. What's this about?"

"It's a coping mechanism," Mitch murmured. "She'll believe what she has to believe."

Megan felt there was something more to it, but she couldn't say what. Not that her opinion would have mattered. Marty the Spaniel Boy was in charge now. He wouldn't listen to her if she told him the world was round. It couldn't make any difference in the case, anyway. Hannah could believe or not. Neither sentiment would help them find Josh or his abductor.

"If you knew Josh was listening right now, what would you say to him?" Katie Couric asked Hannah.

The screen was a tight shot of Hannah's face, the camera allowing no nuance of expression to go unrecorded. America saw everything—the anger, the confusion, the pain. Cornflower-blue eyes shimmering with tears. Mouth trembling against the need to cry. "I love you. I want you to know that, Josh, and believe it. I love you so much. . . ."

The close-up of Hannah faded into a shot of Josh. The

school picture. Josh in his Cub Scout uniform. The gap-toothed grin. The bright eyes and unruly hair. The photo faded away and suddenly Josh was alive on the screen, thanks to videotape. Playing the part of a shepherd in a Christmas pageant, posing with Lily in front of the family tree. Linda Ronstadt's clear, sweet soprano voice sang out as the images shifted and changed. "Somewhere Out There," the words poignant with longing, bright with hope.

Megan bit her lip hard. Damn, damn, damn. She could have made it through the interview—she had interviewed Hannah herself—but this was dirty pool. The song could just as well have been Josh himself calling out from the twilight into which he had disappeared ten days before. The video transformed him into a living boy, full of energy and idiosyncrasies and tenderness for his baby sister. His innocent face coupled with the childlike trust in the lyrics of the song swept the case far out of the realm of work and made it achingly, painfully personal.

The case that had been snatched away from her.

Never, never let it get personal, O'Malley.

Too late. The tough dictate couldn't override the emotions. Pandora's box had been pried open. She could only fight to keep all the feelings from flooding out of it. She blinked hard and clenched a fistful of the shirttail that covered her thighs. Maybe if she squeezed hard enough, she could keep from crying.

Then Mitch's hand settled on top of hers, enfolded it within his, tightened with a silent message of understanding and empathy.

Damn you, O'Malley. How can you be so stupid? Why do you have to give in? You ought to be tougher than this by now.

She took a shaky breath, her jaw rigid as she fought to keep her lower lip from trembling. "Dammit," she said between her teeth. "I wanted to get that son of a bitch."

"I know," Mitch murmured.

"He's close. I can feel it. I want him so bad it hurts."

But it didn't matter how badly she wanted it or how deeply Mitch sympathized. She was off the case. DePalma expected her to drop the ball and run back to headquarters so the superintendent could chew her out in person and then she could sit in a room with a pack of lawyers and endure their company while they made plans to do battle with Paige Price and her legal Dobermans. Just like that she was supposed to drop the life she had begun in Deer Lake. Forget about the people; they were only names on reports. Forget about the apartment; she hadn't been in it long enough to call it home. Forget about Mitch Holt; he was just another cop, and she knew better than to get involved with a cop. Forget about Josh; he was Spaniel Boy's responsibility now.

Josh looked out at her from the television screen, wide eyes and freckles, a gap in his grin where a tooth had been. What little control Megan had left snapped in the face of the frustration and fury. She shot up off the couch. Swearing, crying, she swung at a stack of paperbacks perched on top of a box, sending the books hurtling across the room. The cats scrambled down from their perches and streaked down the hall to hide. Megan turned and swung at another target. She turned again and swung her fist, connecting solidly with Mitch's chest.

"Dammit! Goddammit!" she shouted.

Mitch caught her by the upper arms and she fell against him. Her shoulders shook with the effort to hold back the tears.

"Cry, dammit," Mitch ordered, wrapping his arms around her. "You're entitled. Let go and cry. I won't tell anybody."

When the tears came, Mitch pressed his cheek against the top of her head and whispered to her and apologized for things that were beyond his control.

Everything was beyond their control. And all of it had been put in motion by a madman. In one moment, with one action, so many lives had been changed, and none of them could do a damn thing about it. She would lose her job, her home, her chance to belong . . . but she had this moment, and she didn't want to let it go.

She looked at Mitch, at the lines time and pain had etched into his face, at the eyes that had seen too much. She couldn't have him forever, but they could have this night. She could lose herself in his embrace, block out the ugly world with the haze of passion.

He slid his fingers into her hair, his thumb rubbing the tender spot on her forehead where the pain had been centered.

"You should go back to bed," he whispered.

Megan felt her heart beat against him, felt the tempered strength and gentleness in his hands, saw the longing and regret in his eyes. She loved him. As pointless as that might have been. She had to leave. He hadn't asked her not to. He hadn't asked for anything, had promised nothing, had loved someone else so deeply . . . and no one had ever loved her. But she could keep those secrets in her heart, keep her love held tight and safe. This might be the last night they had.

"Will you take me?" she said softly, her eyes locked on his.

"Megan—"

She pressed two fingers against his lips, silencing his concern. Mitch looked down at her, so fragile, so pale, her incredible strength bowing beneath the weight of the world. He was falling in love with her. For all the future there was in that. In a day or two she would be gone to try to salvage the career that meant everything to her. He would be left to the life he had built here—orderly, empty, carefully blank. The life he wanted, safe and plain.

But they could have this night together.

He took her hand and kissed it softly. She turned and led him down the hall to her room, leaving the television on to mumble to itself.

She had left the bedside lamp on to cast a shadowy amber glow over the tangled sheets. It lit her from behind as she unbuttoned the flannel shirt and let it fall back off her shoulders and drop to the floor. It cast an aura around her dark hair and gave her skin an alabaster glow. She stood before him willing to bare herself if not her soul, willing to take as much of him as he would give her. She deserved more than a night. She deserved more than life had given her, more than *he* had given her.

His hands shook as he slipped the wedding band off and set it aside on the dresser.

Megan's heart caught and stumbled. The possibilities raced through her mind, foolish thoughts and hopeless wishes. She pushed them all aside to grasp the one truth she could manage: They would have the night with no shadows of past loves or past sins.

Taking his hand, she raised it to her trembling lips and

kissed the band of pale skin the ring had covered. Then she was in his arms and his lips were on hers.

Megan pushed Mitch's shirt back off his shoulders and he flung it aside, impatient for the feel of her naked against him. He lowered her to the bed, dragging his mouth down her neck to her breasts. She arched beneath him, inviting him, begging him to take the tight bud of her nipple between his lips, crying out as he sucked strongly at the tender point. He swept a hand down her side, over her hip, pulling her leg around him, bringing the moist heat of her womanhood against the quivering muscles of his belly.

A deep animal groan rumbled at the base of his throat as she reached down and took his erection into her hands. He closed his hand over hers and tightened her grip, bent his head down and caught her earlobe between his teeth.

"That's how tight you are when I'm inside you," he said, sending arousal singing through her.

Mitch watched her face as he entered her. Panic seized him at the knowledge that in a handful of days and nights he had fallen in love; at the knowledge that this would all be gone in a day, in a heartbeat.

Then the need overran the fear. He thrust into her fully, deeply, the tight wet heat of her gripping him, squeezing all thought from his mind. They moved together, straining together toward a fulfillment that obliterated the bounds between the physical and the emotional and the spiritual. They reached it, one and then the other. Breathless, shaking, holding tight.

I love you . . . The words were on her lips. She held them back.

I love you . . . He held the thought within his heart, afraid to give it away.

Then it was over and they were silent and still, and old doubts crept back from the corners of their banishment. The boundaries settled back in place, the guards went up again. Hearts in armor, beating separate and lonely into the night.

8:55 P.M. -25° WINDCHILL FACTOR: -47°

Hannah sat in the dark in her room. *Her* room. How quickly the mind made those little alterations. Paul hadn't slept in this bed for two nights and already her brain had omitted plural references. She didn't want to think about what that meant for their future. She didn't want to deal with the feelings of guilt and loss and failure associated with the marriage she would once have called perfect. She had all she could do to shoulder the weight of the guilt and loss and sense of failure associated with Josh.

It would have been so nice to walk off the set of the interview and have the man she had married put his arms around her and reassure her and take her home. To know that she had his love and support. Instead, she had driven herself home. Kathleen Casey, who had volunteered to sit with Lily, was on the couch in the family room with McCaskill, the BCA agent, watching *The X Files* and eating popcorn. Paul was gone.

Paul is gone. The Paul she had loved and married. She didn't know the man who had lied to her, hidden things from her, blamed her for the act of a madman. She didn't know the man who had all but courted the media, the man who had been asked to submit his fingerprints to the police. She didn't know who he was or what he might be capable of doing.

Unwilling to consider the possibilities, she forced herself out of the chair and began to undress. She concentrated on each menial task, unbuttoning buttons, folding, putting away. She chose her well-worn Duke sweatshirt and pulled it on over her head, shaking her hair back out of her eyes. The telephone on the nightstand rang as she reached for her sweatpants.

Hannah stared at it. Memories of the last call she had taken in this room rushed through her, pebbling her skin and filming it with perspiration. She couldn't just let it ring. She didn't want to pick it up. McCaskill and Kathleen would be wondering why she didn't answer it.

With a trembling hand she lifted the receiver.

"Hello?"

"Hannah? This is Garrett Wright. I saw the interview. I just wanted to tell you I thought you were very brave."

"Uh—well—," she stammered. It wasn't a faceless stranger tormenting her or Albert Fletcher spouting lunacy. It wasn't Josh. Just a neighbor. Karen's husband. He taught at Harris. "It was just something I had to do."

"I understand. Still . . . Well, for what it's worth, I think you did the right thing. Listen, if you need any help getting through this, I have a friend in Edina who specializes in family therapy. I mentioned him to Paul when he was here the other night, but I'm afraid he didn't want to hear it. I thought I'd let you know. You can take his name and call him or not, but I thought you should have the option."

"Thank you," Hannah murmured absently, sinking down on the bed.

She copied the name and number down on the notepad automatically, her mind busy wondering what Paul had been doing at the Wrights' house and why he wouldn't have mentioned it to her. But then, a visit to a neighbor's house was the least of his secrets. She didn't want to know what the worst might be.

The thought lingered and echoed in her mind as she hung up the phone, and a terrible sense of loneliness and fear yawned wide inside her, threatening to swallow her whole. That was the hardest part of all of this—the feeling that no matter how the people around her wanted to help, on the most fundamental level she was alone. The one person who should have been closest was drifting farther and farther away.

She stared at nothing. When the phone rang again, she picked it up without hesitation and murmured a flat greeting. The voice that answered her was a low and gentle drawl, as welcome to her raw nerves as the kiss of silk on a sunburn.

"Hannah? It's Tom—Father Tom. I thought you might need to talk."

"Yeah," she whispered with a trembling smile. "I'd like that."

As Shakespeare said:
All the world's a stage,
And all the men and women merely players:
They have their exits and their entrances . . .

And we are the directors, the puppet masters pulling their hidden strings.

And so, from hour to hour we ripe and ripe,
And then from hour to hour we rot and rot,
And thereby hangs a tale.

Time for a new act and another fine twist in the plot.

We are brilliant.

CHAPTER 34

On Saturday the temperature rose and the sky fell. A ceiling of fat clouds the color of lead hung low above the rolling wooded countryside, sifting down a fine powder of snow. In the wake of the deep freeze and the dark moods it had inspired, the radio weathermen had fled the state, leaving the storm predictions to the weekend deejays.

Megan listened with one ear. Blizzard? Maybe if it hit fast enough it could prevent her from driving to St. Paul. If she spent enough time driving around town looking for Albert Fletcher . . . If this old piece-of-shit car would conk out . . . A dozen different scenarios flashed through her mind, like a kid desperate to cut school. If she could just have today . . . But DePalma wanted her out of Deer Lake. He would never have called her in on a Saturday unless he was desperate himself. The lawyers wouldn't be there; the hell if the bureau would pay them time and a half. This was a simple case of snatching her out of town before she could do any more damage.

She would have to go if she was to salvage anything of her career. Go and kiss ass and repent and do penance. The idea stuck in her throat like a fur ball. She was a damn good cop. That should have counted for something, but it wouldn't.

She rubbed her mitten at the sore spot above her right eye. The headache lingered, threatening, then retreating in an exhausting fencing match with her tattered stamina. She should have stayed in bed, but she didn't want to be there alone. She had been driving around since dawn, her brain chewing on the mess she had made of her life. *Should have taken that FBI post,*

O'Malley. She could have been in Memphis now, a thousand miles away from the cold and snow, a thousand miles away from a broken heart.

That heart still wished things could have worked out. Her head knew better. What could she offer Mitch? She wasn't wife material, didn't know anything about raising a five-year-old girl. All she really knew was being a cop. Thanks to her own reckless temper, that would be taken from her, too. Panic tightened in her chest.

Thinking she was asleep, Mitch had slipped out early. He had a manhunt to oversee. According to the snatches of information Megan was picking up on the police radio, there had still been no solid sign of Albert Fletcher. Citizens had been calling in sightings, but none had turned into anything. Deer Lake was crawling with police cruisers and county cruisers and state patrol cruisers. The choppers circled overhead like buzzards.

Megan shook her head in amazement. She had pegged Fletcher as weird right off, but she hadn't envisioned anything like what Mitch had finally described to her last night. No doubt about it, the deacon was a few beads short of a rosary. Crazy enough to kidnap Josh to be his own private altar boy? Yes, but he had to have had help. He'd been lecturing on sin and damnation at St. E's that night. She tried to picture him and Olie as compadres, but couldn't manage it. Fletcher was a loner. He never would have been able to hide his ghoulish secrets otherwise.

She drove slowly through the campus of Harris College, keeping her eyes open for the deacon. She wondered if Mitch had sent any men there. With classes resuming Monday, the buildings had probably been opened but would still be largely unoccupied. Fletcher could have found himself a nice hiding spot out of the elements.

Harris was the kind of college they didn't build anymore. Many of the classroom and administrative buildings were of native limestone and looked as if they dated back to the origin of the school in the late 1800s. Handsome and substantial, they sat back from the winding drive, the grounds around them studded with ancient oak and maple and pine.

The road wound past dormitories, their parking lots a third

full, students tracking back and forth to the buildings to carry in the laundry they had done over the break and the books they had probably neglected. Goalposts sticking up out of the snow marked an athletic field that backed onto a vacant pasture, and suddenly Megan found herself in the farm country that ran on and on to the west.

She turned onto Old Cedar Road and headed south. If she remembered correctly, this eventually ran past Ryan's Bay and served as a back way into Dinkytown. She pulled over to the side of the road and put the car in park, letting the engine rumble on as she stared out the window at the bleak landscape. The naked hardwood trees like blackened matchsticks in the distance; the snow robbing the contours from the land, making everything look flat and one-dimensional; the sky hanging low above it all like slabs of slate. In a field beside the road, a pair of shaggy paint horses pawed listlessly at the dirty blond stubble of cornstalks. Up ahead, at a bend in the road, a rooster pheasant cautiously made his way out from under the low branches of a spruce tree to peck for gravel on the verge. A brown house sat back from the road on a rise, shades pulled, garage closed, looking vacant. The name on the mailbox at the end of the drive was Lexvold.

Lexvold. It rang a dim bell. Maybe she had seen it on a report. The paperwork on the Kirkwood case would put any blizzard to shame. They had interviewed dozens of people, taken countless statements of non-clues from citizens who wanted to be helpful or at least involved. Like ripples in a pond, the crime had touched them all.

Megan put the car in drive and eased back onto the road. The temperature might have climbed to twenty-two degrees, but the Lumina's heater was good to only about twenty-five, if it was any good at all. She needed something hot to drink, which would delay her even more in leaving for St. Paul. Then, if she drank enough, she would have to stop to go to the bathroom, stalling a little longer.

She was thinking of hot chocolate at The Leaf and Bean, when her gaze caught on the angry black skid marks that crisscrossed on the road ahead. Checking the rearview mirror, she pulled off on the shoulder again and sat with her foot on the brake.

Skid marks. Lexvold. Old Cedar Road. Car accident.

The scene blurred as her mind tried to shake loose what she needed.

The college kid. A patch of ice. A patch of ice the officer at the scene had felt was manufactured.

She slammed the transmission into park and climbed out of the car. She trudged back up to the curve and stood there with her hands tucked into the pockets of her parka, her shoulders hunched against the wind. To the north and east lay the Harris campus. To the south, farmland gave way to the sloughs of Ryan's Bay. Old Cedar Road intersected with Mill Road. To the east on Mill the spires of St. E's punctuated the sky above the treetops. She turned and looked up the hill at the brown house and attached garage.

She remembered Dietz in his Moe Howard wig sitting at the end of their booth in Grandma's Attic. . . . *looks to me like someone snaked a garden hose down the driveway* . . .

"So where's the hose?" Megan murmured.

That kind of prank was usually borne of opportunity. If the Lexvolds didn't have a hose out, there was no opportunity. If there was no opportunity, that meant someone brought a hose to the party, which meant premeditation. Premeditation meant motive. What motive?

She turned back toward the road, an empty ribbon of asphalt. The only sounds were the wind and the hoarse cluck of the rooster pheasant, hiding now beneath the spruce trees, annoyed with Megan for interrupting his snack. Up at the drive into Harris, a red Dodge Shadow pulled onto the road and roared toward her, whizzing past with a pair of young men with wispy grunge-look goatees. Students taking the back way off campus. Like that kid the night of the accident.

The accident that had kept Hannah Garrison late at the hospital.

Megan pictured the time line taped to the wall of the war room. Everything started with Josh's disappearance. But what if the thing they had missed, the thing that had been there all along that they hadn't been able to see, had happened earlier? What if the accident hadn't been an accident at all?

Adrenaline surged through her as the possibilities clicked fast-forward through her brain. Students used the back road to the college. Anyone living around there would know that. Albert Fletcher, whose house was no more than a mile away. Olie Swain, who had audited courses at Harris. Christopher Priest, who had sent his student on an errand that night.

Priest. Megan tried to shake off the idea. The funny little professor with the bad fashion sense and limp-fish handshake? He was as unlikely a suspect as Elvis. He had no motive. He openly admired Hannah, had gone out of his way to help with the case. . . . Had installed himself in a position where he would be privy to all incoming news of the case, maybe even have access to confidential police information. He had known Olie Swain, had taught him. He was probably at this very moment communing with Olie's computers down at the station, ostensibly searching for clues. And she had put him there. *ignorance is not innocence but SIN.*

Sin. Religion. Priest. *Christopher Priest.*

"Oh, Jesus," she muttered.

In her mind's eye she could see him bending over the glowing screen of a terminal in the room where Olie's equipment had been set up. She couldn't have put a possible suspect in a position to tamper with evidence. Her stomach rolled and twisted at the thought. She had wanted so badly to crack this case. It was the one that could make or break her career, but the stakes were so much higher than that and she knew it. She would have sold her soul for a nickel to nail the bastard who had taken Josh. If Christopher Priest was dirty and she had put him in that office with those machines . . .

The sound of a car rolling up snapped her back to the moment. A gunmetal-blue Saab had come to a halt in front of her. The passenger's window buzzed down. As the driver hunched down to see her, the fur collar of his navy wool topcoat crept up around his ears.

"Agent O'Malley! Are you having car trouble?" Garrett Wright asked.

"Uh—no. No, I'm fine."

"Kind of a cold day to be standing out in the wind. Are you sure you don't need some help? I've got a cellular phone—"

"No, thanks." Megan forced a polite smile as she leaned down into the window of the car. "I'm just checking something out. Thanks for stopping, though."

"Still looking for Albert Fletcher?" He shook his head, frowning. "Who would have guessed . . ."

"No one."

In the beat of silence his dark eyes went bright with the kind of embarrassed curiosity that fueled the fires of coffee-shop gossip everywhere. "So . . . is Paige Price really sleeping with the sheriff?"

"No comment," Megan replied, forcing a wan smile, straightening away from the Saab. "You'd better move it along, Dr. Wright. We wouldn't want you to cause an accident."

"No, we wouldn't want that. Good luck finding Fletcher."

He gave her a salute as the window hissed upward, and the Saab rolled on. The purr of the motor faded into the distance, leaving her standing there listening to the wind in the pines, staring at the only visible evidence of the accident that had claimed two lives outright and possibly altered the lives of an entire community.

ignorance is not innocence but SIN.

10:28 A.M. 22° WINDCHILL FACTOR: 10°

Where's Mitch?"

Megan burst into Natalie's office. Mitch's assistant stood behind her desk, the telephone receiver pressed to her ear. She gave Megan a scowl and picked up a copy of the *Star-Tribune* from her desk, holding it up to display Henry Forster's headline—*O'Malley Strikes Out: BCA's First Female Field Agent Told to Hit the Road.*

"I'm sorry, *Mr. DePalma*," she said pointedly into the receiver. "I've got to put you on hold."

She punched the hold button and arched a thinly plucked brow. "Well, if it isn't the elusive Agent O'Malley. People in high places are looking for you, girl."

"Screw 'em," Megan snapped. "I've got more important things to do."

Natalie gave her a long, measuring look, pursing her lips. "He's in the war room."

"Thanks." Megan pointed to the blinking red light on the telephone console. "I'm not here."

"I never heard of you," Natalie said, shaking her head.

Megan blew out a breath and turned for the door. "Natalie, you're the best."

"Damn straight."

He has to be somewhere." Marty Wilhelm stated the obvious. He strolled up and down the time line with his hands in the pockets of his teal blue Dockers. "He hasn't been outside all this time. I'm guessing he's holed up wherever he has Josh stashed. We should check at the courthouse and see if he owns any other property in the area—a cabin or something."

Mitch gave the agent an irritated look. "Been there. Done that. He doesn't."

Puppy Boy went on, undaunted. "They haven't found anything useful in Olie Swain's computers—no mention of Josh or Fletcher. We should get Fletcher's phone records—"

"At the command post," Mitch snapped. "Stevens and Gedney are going over them."

He'd been on the manhunt himself since the crack of dawn, had come in to the station only at Wilhelm's request for a brainstorming session. So far the storm had been more of a light drizzle.

"Look, Marty, I've got to tell you, having you jump in here midstream is a real pain in the ass."

Marty grinned that innocent-boy grin Mitch was growing to hate. "I'm doing all I can to get up to speed, Chief. By rights, this case should have been mine from the start. It isn't my fault that didn't happen. I guess I just don't look as fetching in a short skirt."

The veneer of tolerance peeled away like dead skin. A dangerous look tightening his features, Mitch rose from his chair and advanced on Marty Wilhelm one slow step at a time until they were close enough to dance. Wilhelm's bright eyes widened.

"Agent O'Malley is a damn good cop," Mitch said softly. "Now, Marty, for all I know, you can't find your dick in a dark room. But I'll find it for you if I hear you make another remark like that one. Are we clear on that, Marty?"

His face pale, he held his hands up in surrender as he backed away. The trademark grin quivered and twisted. "Hey, Chief, I'm sorry. I didn't know this was a serious thing with you and Megan. I thought it was just—"

The words strangled in his throat at Mitch's glare. This *thing* between him and Megan was nobody's damned business, whatever it was. God knew, he'd bent his brain into a knot thinking about it in the predawn while she lay beside him. It seemed so much simpler in the night, when she wasn't afraid to need him and he couldn't think beyond the next caress. Then morning came, and the world and their lives were just as screwed up as ever.

A knock at the door brought Mitch back to the moment. Megan made her entrance, parka hanging off one shoulder, dark hair escaping her ponytail. The bright color along her cheekbones might have come from the great outdoors, but he suspected it had more to do with the energy radiating around her. He could sense her tension across the room and knew the source of it. He had felt that same rush himself more than once when he'd been onto something.

"What have you got?" he asked, moving toward her.

"I need to talk to you." She made a beeline toward him, not so much as glancing in the direction of her replacement.

"Agent O'Malley," Marty Wilhelm said sardonically, "aren't you supposed to be in St. Paul right now?"

Megan cut him a nasty glare and looked back up at Mitch. "I had an idea about that accident out on Old Cedar Road the night Josh disappeared."

"Bruce DePalma called me looking for you," Wilhelm went on.

Megan turned her shoulder to him. "What if it wasn't an accident at all? What if it was set to happen as a means of keeping Hannah at the hospital?"

Mitch frowned. "It wouldn't change anything, except to make the crime even more diabolical. We already know it wasn't a random act."

"I realize that, but think about it—think about the location. It's a mile or so to Fletcher's and St. Elysius."

Marty perked up at Fletcher's name. "What? How does Fletcher tie in?"

"He could have slipped out of the church, made the icy patch on the road, and gotten back in time for his classes," Mitch speculated. "Causing the accident that kept Hannah at the hospital and still providing himself with an alibi. It works, but he still had to have an accomplice."

"It's probably a long shot," Megan said, "but I was thinking if we could find a witness who saw someone hanging around the Lexvold place that day, we might get a link we don't have now."

"We?" Wilhelm's voice made her cringe as sure as fingernails on a chalkboard. "Agent O'Malley, might I remind you, you're *off* this case."

"I don't need reminding," Megan said, still refusing to look at him.

He gave an incredulous half-laugh. "I beg to differ."

He snatched a copy of the *StarTribune* off the table and displayed it in front of him. "You're on temporary suspension from active duty. That takes you off this case, out of this room, and all the way to St. Paul."

She tilted her chin up, glaring at him. "I'm taking care of some loose ends."

"You're off the case," he repeated, throwing the paper down, then thrusting a forefinger in front of her face like an exclamation point.

Megan wanted to grab his hand and bite him. Instead, she clenched her jaw and her fists. "I don't take orders from you, Wilhelm. Don't try to push me around. Better men than you have tried and regretted it."

A beeper went off like an alarm, shrill and piercing. They all flinched automatically in response, looking down at the little boxes on their waistbands. Wilhelm stepped back and unclipped his from his belt.

"If this is DePalma," he said, moving toward the door, "I'll tell him you're on your way, Megan, because you are *off this case.*"

Megan held her tongue until he was out the door and had closed it behind him. "The hell I am, Spaniel Boy."

"Megan, you're going to get yourself fired," Mitch said.

"I've already been fired."

"You've lost the field post, not your career. You jerk De-Palma around this way and he'll have your badge."

Megan stared down at the toes of her boots. She had been over all of this in her mind again and again. She had told herself her career was all she had, that she had to do everything she could to protect it—don't get involved with a case or with a cop. But she *was* involved and she couldn't walk away from this case for the sake of her career. A little boy's life was at stake.

"I'm not walking away from this until it's done. We're too close and it's too important. Now, you've got to get Christopher Priest away from Olie's computers."

"Why?"

"Because everything we just said about Albert Fletcher could apply to him, too."

"Megan, get a grip. He's been nothing but helpful on this case from day one."

She nodded. "And most arsonists return to the scene of the crime to watch the firemen. Listen to me, Mitch. I know it sounds crazy on the surface, but it could fit. The kid behind the wheel of that car was a student of his," she reminded him, refusing to back down. "Priest told me he had sent him out to run an errand. He had to know the kid would take Old Cedar Road."

"What possible motive would Priest have for taking Josh?"

"I don't know," she admitted, wishing she had more to go on than the uneasy feeling in her gut. "Maybe it's not about motive. We've said all along he's playing games with us. Taking Josh was the opening move. Then came the taunts, the messages, the notebook, his conversation with Ruth Cooper. Maybe it's just about winning, outsmarting everyone."

"And yesterday it was a personal vendetta against Hannah and Paul. And the day before that Paul did it—"

"What's that supposed to mean?"

"It means you'll beat your head against a wall until the wall moves."

"I'm doing my job," she insisted.

"And the rest of us aren't?" he said, spreading his hands.

Megan scowled at him. "I never said that."

"You've been taken off the case, Megan."

"And you think I should just back down and drop it?"

"I think you should have a little faith that someone besides you can do the job," he said, ticking his thoughts off on his fingers one by one. "I think you should realize DePalma's got you by the short hairs. I think you should take a look in the mirror and see what you're doing to yourself. Yesterday you couldn't even stand up!"

He reached out to touch her, to touch her forehead, where pain was gathering in a tightening knot.

She stepped back from him. "I'm fine now. I sure as hell don't need you—"

"That's what it comes down to, isn't it?" Mitch snapped, dropping his hand. "You don't need anybody. Mighty Megan O'Malley taking on the whole fucking male-dominated world!"

"Yeah, well," she jeered, "it's an ugly job, but somebody's got to do it." She gave a bitter attempt at laughter. "Like you want me to need you."

Megan stared up at him, wary and defiant. She had spent her whole life learning not to trust emotions, not to be vulnerable, not to put her heart in someone else's hands because she got it back when they found out she wasn't what was really wanted.

"I can take care of myself," she said, chin up, eyes glittering. "I've been doing it my whole life."

And she would go on doing it, Mitch thought. She was afraid to need and he had spent the last two years afraid of being needed. Where did that leave them? Squaring off in the war room. How apropos.

"Fine," he said, focusing past her head to the slick white board where the kidnapper's messages mocked them in bright-colored marker. "Then go do it. I don't have time for this bullshit game of yours, knocking the chip off your shoulder so you can pick it up and put it right back. I've got better things to do with my time. I've got a legitimate suspect at large."

"Yes, and since he's *your* suspect, he's the only suspect," Megan sneered. "Good luck finding him with your head up your ass." She ignored the dangerous glint in his eyes. She felt something dangerous herself.

"You're a great one to talk about playing games," she lashed out. "I told you from the first I didn't want to get involved with a cop, but you pushed and pushed, and now that you've had what you wanted, the game's over. How nice and neat for you. You don't even have to bother foisting me off on some other guy. I'll just be gone and you can have your town back and put your ring back on and go back to—"

He jerked a finger up in front of her face, cutting her off. "Don't," he said, his voice nearly a whisper, and yet stronger, more frightening than a shout, vibrating with emotion, sharper than steel. "Don't you dare. I loved my wife. You don't even know what that means."

No, she didn't know what that meant. Nor did she stand a chance of finding out, Megan thought as he turned and stormed out of the room. He left her standing there, slamming the door shut on her, on them. She stood there, the sudden silence pounding in her ears; angry, hurtful words echoing in her head—her words, his; the aftertaste of heartbreak bitter in her mouth.

CHAPTER 35

Christopher Priest was not at the station. Megan stuck her head into the little room assigned to Olie's computers, to find a brush-cut, bow-tied pencil neck from headquarters who had obviously been told not to share with her. He offered no explanation for the professor's absence and gave no indication as to whether or not Olie's machines had turned up anything of interest.

The carrion feeders were waiting for her as she tried to slip out a service entrance to the City Center. The mob lunged at her with microphones, hand-held tape recorders, cameras.

"Agent O'Malley, do you have a comment on your firing?"

"Not one you can print," she snarled, shouldering her way through the crowd.

"Do you have any comment on the lawsuit?"

"Do you have any proof Paige Price is sleeping with Sheriff Steiger?"

From behind the mirrored lenses of her sunglasses, she shot a glare at Henry Forster. His beetle brows were drawn together in a furry V as he stared back at her through the smudged lenses of his crooked glasses. The wind had blown his comb-over into a spike that stood straight up from his liver-spotted head like a horn.

"You're the hotshot investigative reporter," she snapped. "Dig up your own dirt."

They trailed her halfway across the parking lot, then gave up, disheartened by the lack of usable sound bites. Vultures.

Megan scowled at them as she wheeled the Lumina out onto Main Street.

No one at the volunteer center had seen Christopher Priest since Friday. Classes began again at Harris on Monday. She might try his office there, suggested one of Priest's student volunteers, while other members of the volunteer staff shot her looks from the corners of their eyes. A copy of the *StarTribune* lay on the end of a table, where fliers were being stuffed into envelopes, Henry Forster's headline jumping off the page— *O'Malley Strikes Out.*

"I haven't finished swinging yet, Henry," she muttered. She climbed back into her car and for the second time that day headed through the snow toward Harris.

Priest's office, she was told by a perky young woman in the administration building, was on the fourth floor of Cray Hall. Megan trooped across the Harris grounds. She tried not to breathe too deeply; the fresh air seemed to knife right up behind her eyes. Brain freeze—like swallowing too much ice cream.

"Just let me get through today, God," she mumbled as she climbed the stairs of Cray Hall. "Just let me get a good lead and then you can nail me. Just one solid lead. Don't let me go down in flames here."

One lead that might come from a man no one would ever suspect—or want to suspect. Professor Priest. Quiet, unassuming, more enamored of machines than of people. Fascinated and bewildered by the vagaries of fate and human nature. *Is it fate or is it random? What brought Mike Chamberlain to that corner at that moment? What put Josh Kirkwood on that curb alone that night?*

Had he been toying with her that day at the hospital? Trying to plant clues in her mind without her ever suspecting? Or was she grasping at straws, so desperate for an end to the case that she was beginning to see suspects every time she turned around? Megan's gut told her no, and her gut was seldom wrong. Unlike her mouth, which blurted out the wrong thing at the wrong moment with regularity. Or her heart . . .

The fourth floor of Cray Hall was a warren of offices and narrow halls the color of mustard. The building was old, the kind of place that would feel dank and clammy year-round. The sharp clack of her boot heels against the old brown flooring carried down the hall like the report of gunshots.

The door to Priest's office stood open, but it was not Christopher Priest who looked up at her from behind a mountain of books and papers on the desk. Todd Childs, the clerk from The Pack Rat, looked up at her with surprise in his sleepy, drug-dilated eyes.

"Hey, it's Dirty Harriet!" he said with a grin. A strand of rust hair fell in his face and he swept it back. Behind him, Garrett Wright looked up from browsing through a file cabinet.

"We seem destined to cross paths, Agent O'Malley," Wright said, smoothing a hand over his trendy silk tie as he came around the desk. "What brings you to the hallowed halls of Harris?"

"I'm looking for Professor Priest," Megan said. She glanced around the office. "This *is* his office, isn't it?"

"Yes. I think I told you—Chris and I are conducting a joint project dealing with learning and perception. It involves a computer program designed by his students," he explained. Slipping his hands into the pockets of his dark pleated trousers, he rocked back on his heels. "It's fascinating stuff. We're gearing up for the next phase of testing. Todd and I are going through some of the data we compiled last semester."

"It's way cool," Todd said. "How individuals perceive the world around them. How different personality types perceive and learn. The human psyche is a fascinating creature."

"Is Priest around?" Megan asked, her interest in learning and perception limited to the case.

"I'm sorry, no," Wright said. "He told me he had to go to St. Peter. Is this about the case?"

"I just wanted to ask him a few questions," Megan said, her face carefully blank. St. Peter. The call from Josh had come from St. Peter. "I'm fuzzy on a couple of things I thought he might be able to help me with."

"Ah . . . excuse me," Wright said, hesitant and a little awkward, "but didn't I read something in the *StarTribune* about you being taken off this case?"

Megan flashed him a phony smile and lied. "Can't believe everything you read, Dr. Wright."

He didn't believe her, but he gave a shrug as if it made no difference to him. "Oh, well . . . He told me he would be home about two-thirty. I'm sure he'll be eager to help. He's been so involved with the case, he hardly talks about anything else."

How involved was what Megan wanted to ask, but if Priest was in fact the man at the heart of the mystery, she doubted he shared that information with his college colleagues. *What did you do over winter break, Chris? Oh, I kidnapped a little boy and held an entire community hostage to the whims of my madness. How about you?*

"I've wanted to take a more active role myself," Wright continued, rocking back on his heels again. "I feel so bad for Hannah and Paul. Such a perfect family," he said with a tight little smile. "I haven't been able to contribute much to the effort, I'm afraid. The media grabbed me because I teach psychology. I keep telling them I don't have any degrees in criminal behavioral studies. They don't seem to grasp that."

"Yeah, well, they're that way," Megan said, backing toward the door.

"They don't see the big picture," Todd said, wagging his shaggy head sadly.

Megan forced a polite smile and directed it at Wright. "Thanks for your help, Dr. Wright."

"Any time. Do you know where Chris lives?"

"I can find it."

He nodded, smiling. "Right. You're the detective."

"For the moment," Megan muttered to herself as she retraced her route to the stairs.

Outside, the snow had begun to fall, fine white flakes sifting down like flour from the sky. Pretty. Clean. The Harris campus looked like a postcard setting. Winter wonderland. In the parklike square across the street, a group of young women were on their backs making snow angels, their laughter clear and pure as it rose into the naked branches of the trees.

Megan walked to her car and sat behind the wheel for a few moments with her eyes closed and her forehead pressed against the cold window. She turned off the incessant crackling of the police radio and tuned the car radio to a light rock station that always promised the latest weather updates.

Mariah Carey told her to look within herself and find

strength. "Hero." Good advice, but what happened when the strength ran out, or time ran out, or the villain was too damn smart? What happened to heroes then? And what happened to the people who counted on them? Like Josh.

Mariah blasted out the final note, turning it into a dozen notes with vocal gymnastics.

"It's going to take a hero to make it through this weather," the deejay said. "A word of advice for travelers—don't. We're looking at eight to ten inches of the white stuff in the metro area before it's all over tomorrow. Outlying areas are already reporting poor driving conditions. So bundle up and keep your dial on KS95, where it's always ninety-five and sunny."

The Beach Boys launched into "Kokomo." Megan cut them off with a twist of her wrist, put the car in gear, and headed for Deer Lake Community Hospital.

Mike Chamberlain wasn't able to add any pieces to the puzzle. While his injuries incurred in the car accident hadn't been critical, he had developed a serious bacterial infection that was threatening his life. He had been transferred to Hennepin County Medical Center, where he was in surgical intensive care with no visitors but family members allowed.

Megan took the news with resignation. He probably couldn't have helped. If he had played a part in this drama, he was an unwitting pawn. If the accident was indeed the first move in this madman's game . . .

She drove through town with her headlights on and wipers slapping ineffectually at the windshield. Main Street looked like a ski run for automobiles, tire tracks cutting through the heavy snow in a series of trails that told tales of control problems and fender benders. A team of city workers struggled to bring down the Snowdaze banner that spanned the street, the painted oilcloth billowing and snapping like a sail in the wind.

As she drove out of the business district toward the lake, she encountered more snowmobiles than cars. Yards that should have been overrun with children building snowmen and forts were mostly empty. With Albert Fletcher at large, the children of Deer Lake were being held captive in their homes by fear of abduction.

Gossip down at the Scandia House Cafe had it that he

might have poisoned poor Doris and that he had always taken an unnatural interest in the altar boys at St. E's. Some of the regulars nodded over their coffee and said they had always thought he was "a little funny." They were all angry and wary and afraid, and they all grew quiet when they realized the person sitting at the front table eavesdropping on their conversations was "that BCA woman."

Megan didn't blame them. Josh's abduction had cracked the placid surface of their quiet town and revealed a nest of worms. Betrayals and secrets, twisted minds and black hearts, all tangled together so no one could decipher the knot. Olie Swain had been transformed from a harmless loser to a wolf loose among the lambs. Albert Fletcher had metamorphosed from deacon to demon, Paul Kirkwood from victim to suspect. She wondered what they would say if she told them she was on her way to question the mild-mannered professor who had worked with juvenile offenders. Christopher Priest was a source of pride for Deer Lake. Would they turn on him or on *her*?

She thought she knew the answer. One more reason not to stay here, she told herself as she drove past the beautiful old Fontaine, past the courthouse, taking a left at the stoplight to drive past City Center. It was just a town, like a million other towns. If the bureau let her go, she could move to a better climate and find a town as nice as this. Her father could come with her or rot. He could live with Mick in L.A. and gush over him in person, and she could be free to start a new life. Alone.

Christopher Priest's home was on Stone Quarry Trail, a fraction of a mile north of the Kirkwood house, but not so easily reached. Especially not on a day when the country roads were fast becoming covered with pristine blankets of new wet snow. Megan navigated with the extreme caution of a city dweller, letting the Lumina creep along what she hoped was the center of the road. There was no other traffic. Woods crowded the shoulders of the road, the naked branches of the trees reaching overhead, nearly lacing together to form a bower. The occasional mailbox marked a driveway. Two to be exact. In the gathering gloom, with the snow coming down, the houses were hidden, crouching like giant forest creatures behind the cover of the woods.

The road simply ended. A yellow and black dead end sign stated the obvious at a point where the road crews had given up and let nature alone. The thick tangle of trees and brush belonged to the back reaches of Quarry Hills Park, the same park that ran behind Hannah and Paul's house. The park where Josh and his buddies had explored and played, never imagining that any of them would ever be in any kind of danger.

A simple black mailbox marked Christopher Priest's driveway, a signpost for a road no one had been down recently. The drive was narrow and thick with fresh snow. Priest hadn't made it back from St. Peter yet. If Garrett Wright knew what he was talking about, Priest would be at least another forty-five minutes—probably more with the weather—which would give her plenty of time to look around.

Not trusting the Lumina to make it up the driveway, let alone back out, Megan abandoned it at the end of Stone Quarry Trail and started up the drive on foot. The trees created a false calm, cutting the wind to innocuous puffs of air. They diminished what little light the day offered as well, giving the impression of a weird kind of twilight, a gray shadow kingdom with a small, dark castle at its heart.

The house sat in a clearing, like something from one of the Grimms' grimmer fairy tales. A shingle-sided Victorian painted the color of slate and ashes, a small turret squatted at one corner. The windows were dark, staring blankly at her through the falling snow. To the east of the house stood a double garage and south of it an old shed, both painted to match the house. Megan trudged up the steps onto the porch. She stamped the snow off her boots and knocked on the old glass-paned front door. With Priest gone, there should have been no one to answer. According to the background check they'd run on him, he was unmarried and had no children or roommates—unless he was keeping Josh locked up in the turret. No lights went on. No faces peeked out from behind the drapes.

She made the rounds of the first-floor windows, peering in to see no living creatures, only old furniture and books and computer equipment, everything as neat and tidy as if no one lived there. All doors were locked. Not that she would have dared go inside without a warrant or a damn compelling reason. She had no intention of tainting any future bust by breaking rules.

Crouching down in the snow along the south side of the foundation, she put her face up against a basement window as cold as a block of ice and strained her eyes to see into the gloom with the aid of her pocket flashlight. Nothing of interest. No sign of Josh.

The shoveled walkways to the garage and shed were filling in with several inches of fresh snow. Megan waded through it, cursing. The side door to the garage was unlocked and let her into a space that was disgustingly neat and clean.

Like Fletcher's garage, she thought. God knew he was a more likely suspect than the professor. She was probably just grasping at straws, desperate as she was to make something happen. The note Fletcher had left pinned to his wife's corpse scrolled through her head—*Wicked daughter of Eve: Be sure your sin will find you out.* Sin was a theme in the messages. Being fixated on his religion gave Fletcher an automatic preoccupation with sin. The question that nagged her was the deacon's sudden trip over the lunacy line. If he was that close to breaking, could he have orchestrated a game a chess master would envy? They had been manipulated from the word go, led one way then another. Clues had been planted to taunt them. Could Fletcher have managed all that, then flipped out over something as trivial as Father Tom putting his arm around Hannah?

Megan backed out of the garage, closing the door behind her. The shed was an older building, maybe fifteen feet deep and thirty feet long. It had probably housed farm equipment at one time. What it housed now was a mystery that made Megan hesitate at the end door. Her cop sense tickled the back of her neck. Logic tried to argue. There was no one here. She would have seen their tire tracks on the road or the driveway.

Unless they had come on foot.

Stepping to one side of the door, she tugged off her right mitten and unzipped her parka. The Glock slid out of her shoulder holster and filled her hand with its familiar weight and shape. Security. Protection. She snicked the safety off. Albert Fletcher had to be hiding somewhere. Christopher Priest's shed was as good a place as any.

Heart thudding slow and hard, she moved along the length of the shed. Her left hand traced over the big front doors. Her right hand held her gun, business end to the sky. Despite the temperature, perspiration filmed her skin beneath the layers of clothes.

At the far end of the building she saw the tracks. Footprints in the snow that came out of the woods of Quarry Hills Park and led across Christopher Priest's backyard to the door on the end of the shed. Her pulse picked up a beat. She stood to one side of the door and knocked with her left hand.

"Police! Come out with your hands up!"

No one answered. The only sounds were the wind singing through the treetops and the creak of old buildings. Her pulse throbbed in her ears, pounded inside her forehead. She blinked to clear her vision as it blurred around the edges.

She pushed the door open, staying to the side.

"Police! Come out with your hands up!"

Silence.

Megan scanned the yard. Electrical wires ran from the utility pole to the house and to the garage. None ran to the shed, meaning no interior lights. Only a fool would go into a dark building alone after a suspect. The dark diminished the advantage the gun gave her. The best thing she could do would be to go back to the car and radio for backup, then sit and wait. If it was Fletcher in the shed and he decided to run, he couldn't get far on foot. If it wasn't Fletcher, they had a trespasser to deal with, and she would rather turn it over to a local.

She flexed her numbing fingers on the handle of the Glock, took a deep breath, and stepped quickly past the open door and around the corner of the shed. Thirty feet and she would be clear of it.

She only made it fifteen.

He hit her from the side. Bursting out through the front doors of the shed, he struck a blow that sent Megan sprawling headlong in the snow. The gun flew out of her hand.

Training and instinct spurred her. Move! Move! *Move!* She lunged ahead in the snow like a beached swimmer, arms swinging, legs kicking, gasping for air as she scrambled frantically toward the gun.

He was behind her. She could feel his presence like an ominous weight in the air. She imagined she could feel his shadow fall across her, a black apparition, the shadow of evil, as cold and heavy as steel.

One more lunge. Eyes straight ahead, staring at her fingertips as they scraped across the textured handle of the Glock. His weight came down on her. She gasped and twisted her body, rolling out from under him.

His image flashed on her brain like quick snapshots. Black clothing, ski mask, eyes, and a mouth. He dove toward her, swinging a short black club. Megan caught the shattering blow on her left forearm. She scuttled backward, fighting to get her feet under her, to get some balance, to swing her gun hand into position. He rushed her, swinging the club again and again, hitting her shoulder, hitting her a glancing blow off the side of her head, hitting her bare right hand so hard that the pain roared up her arm and exploded in her brain, dimming her consciousness.

The Glock fell into the snow. Her arm dropped to her side, useless. She stumbled back another step, trying to turn, to run. One thought dragged through her mind—*Oh, shit. I'm dead.*

CHAPTER 36

Father Tom's head throbbed in time to his footsteps as he made his way down the center aisle of the church, cassock swishing around the ankles of his black jeans. Every third step coincided with a booming bass note from the pipe organ.

Several people, including Dr. Lomax, who had tended his head, and Hannah—who had hovered over him in the emergency room—had advised him to skip the Mass that night. He could have called in help from the archdiocese. They would have sent a retired priest or a rookie from one of the large city parishes, where priests actually had assistants. But he had been stubborn in his refusal. He took another step as Iris Mulroony hit that blasted bass note and thought maybe *foolhardy* was a better word.

He had a concussion. His ears were still ringing with the sound of the brass candlestick bashing the side of his head. Double vision came and went like a camera lens that wouldn't hold its focus. Dizziness buzzed around his head like a swarm of gnats. But he was conducting Mass. He wouldn't stay home and be perceived as hiding out—not only from Albert Fletcher, but from those members of his parish who had jumped at the chance to spread barbed gossip about the circumstances surrounding the incident. He hadn't done anything wrong. Hannah hadn't done anything wrong. She had needed the support and comfort of a friend. The day offering compassion became wrong was the day he gave up on the world.

Guilt nipped its sharp little teeth into his conscience. He had wanted to offer Hannah more than his friendship. He wanted to offer his heart. Was that so wrong, or was it just against the rules?

He took his position behind the altar. Iris mashed down on the keys for a final note he felt in his chest. The small Saturday-night crowd doubled briefly before his eyes.

"The peace of God be with you all."

"And also with you."

"Heretic!"

The shout echoed over the crowd. Tom looked up at the balcony, where Albert Fletcher stood on the railing, crucifix in hand, ready to jump.

5:07 P.M.   23°   WINDCHILL FACTOR: 12°

Mitch winced at a knot in his shoulder as he settled in behind the wheel of the Explorer. He had spent the better part of the day beating the bushes for Albert Fletcher with Marty Wilhelm dancing around him like a hyperactive border collie and the press swarming along behind them.

"Chief Holt, do you have any comments on the firing of Agent O'Malley?"

"Chief Holt, your truck was allegedly parked outside Megan O'Malley's apartment all night. What do you have to say about that?"

"That it's none of your goddamn business."

He supposed that remark would warrant more calls from the city council, but he didn't care. His personal life shouldn't have been an issue. The issue here was Josh. He couldn't believe anyone was bothering to zero in on irrelevant details.

Irrelevant. Good word for what had gone on between him and Megan. *Finished* was another.

Life had been so much simpler when good old Leo had the office down the hall. He had been safe in his emotional cocoon, insulated by the scar tissue of old pain.

He wondered how long it would take to seal himself back into a life that consisted of work and Jessie and fending off the matchmakers. Emotional purgatory. The life that hurt less and punished him more.

He looked at himself in the rearview mirror, his eyes narrowed with contempt at what he saw. Oh, well, he would go home to Jessie, who was too young to realize what a jerk her father was. He could choke down some supper with her before he took her back over to the Strausses so he could spend the rest of the night looking for Fletcher.

They had covered better than half the town in a house-to-house search. They'd been in basements and potting sheds and back-alley Dumpsters and found not a trace of the man. The choppers had hovered over town like birds of prey until the weather set them down. The most exciting report they turned in was that of a nude hot-tub party going on in the backyard of a Dinkytown frat house.

Mitch found himself giving some thought to Wilhelm's theory of Albert and an unknown accomplice splitting town. The deacon could have been a hundred miles away before they'd even gotten the roadblocks up outside of town Friday—and he could have had Josh with him.

The radio blasted out a staccato burst of garbled static as he reached to turn the ignition.

"All units: 415 in progress at St. Elysius Church. Repeat—disturbance in progress at St. Elysius Catholic Church: Possible 10-56A. Repeat—possible attempted suicide. Be advised: suspect is Albert Fletcher. Chief, if you're listening, they need you."

We have a treat for you, clever girl."

The voice was soft, a whisper, disembodied, unrecognizable. Megan opened her eyes and saw nothing. Blackness. The irrational thought that she might be dead went through her like a lightning bolt. No. Her heart wouldn't race if she were dead. Her head wouldn't pound. She wouldn't feel pain. Then light as faint as shadows slipped beneath the blindfold. She looked down. Her lap. A small wedge of concrete floor on either side of her. She was sitting on a chair. Correction—she was tied to a chair. Her arms were tied to the arms of the chair, her ankles bound to the legs. She didn't think she would have been able to sit on her own. She felt woozy, as if her soul and her body were attached by only the thinnest of threads. Drugs. He had given her something. *They* had given her something.

We have a treat for you, he had said. Odd, but it didn't feel as if there were more than one other person in the room. Her captor was standing close to her, behind her, but she didn't sense anyone else.

"Clever girl," he whispered again, tracing his fingertips around her throat. She swallowed, and he chuckled to himself, a sound that was little more than a breath. "You think we're going to kill you? Perhaps."

He tightened his hands slowly, fingertips pressing on her larynx until she coughed. He allowed her half a breath, then pressed harder. Her head swam and what vision she had went dim. Panic spurred her to struggle. She jerked and choked. When he released the pressure, she sucked in a wheezing breath, and another and another, while he laughed his breathy laugh.

"We could kill you," he murmured, his mouth brushing against her ear. "You wouldn't be the first by a long, long way."

"Did you kill Josh?" she mumbled. Her mouth felt as if it were coated with rubber cement. Saliva pooled beneath a tongue that felt bloated. Effects of the drug or the choking.

"What do you think?" The voice floated around her like a cloud. "Do you think he's dead? Do you think he's alive?"

Megan struggled to focus, to use anger to keep herself lucid. "I . . . think . . . you're a lunatic."

He struck her right hand and pain shot along her nerve pathways, the shock of it taking her breath away. He struck her again, hitting her fingertips with what felt like the narrow edge of a steel ruler. The pain ripped through her and tore up out of her throat in a scream that trailed off into shuddering sobs.

"Respect." The voice seemed to come from the center of her forehead. "You ought to respect us. We're so far superior to you. We've fooled you all along, so easily. It's a game, you see," he said. "We've calculated all the moves, all the options, all the possibilities. We can't lose."

A game. A chess match with living pieces. Megan shivered. Her coat had been taken. And her sweater. Finally she realized she was clad only in the black silk long underwear Mitch had chuckled at. The .380 A.M.T. Back-Up she wore in her ankle holster must have been discovered and taken. Not that she could have used it if she had wanted to.

"Did you kill Josh?" she murmured.

Her tormentor let the question hang. Megan didn't know if two minutes passed or twenty. The drug had warped her perception of time. For all she knew, days had gone by since she had driven out to Christopher Priest's house. She could still be there, but she had vague memories of riding in a vehicle of some sort. The smell of exhaust, the rumble of an engine, the feeling of movement.

The dizziness swirled around her. Nausea crawled up the back of her throat and she swallowed it down.

"The game isn't over yet," he whispered. Winding a hand into her ponytail, he pulled her head back slowly. Megan opened her eyes wider, tried to see more of the room, but all she could see was a strip of gray the color of concrete. Basement. "We can't lose. Do you understand me? You can't defeat us. We're very good at this game."

Megan was in no position to argue, and antagonism seemed unwise after her last attempt. Killing her would be a simple chore. She wouldn't be the first, he had said. Not by a long way. Fear skittered through her—for herself and for Josh, wherever he was. They had known almost from the first they weren't dealing with the average criminal, but she had never imagined this—a multiple murderer who would play with the lives of people like a cat with a mouse.

He let go of her hair abruptly and her head fell forward, the motion bringing another wave of nausea. A shoe scuffed against the floor. A single black boot came into view beside her right leg, then vanished. The chair tipped back and spun around—or she imagined it did. She imagined parts of her flying out away from her body and snapping back in place like something from a weird cartoon. Her consciousness swam in a thick black morass and white noise pressed in on her eardrums like a clamp tightening around her head. She couldn't tell if she was awake or in a nightmare, didn't know if there was a difference.

Then everything went still, the sudden absence of movement and sound as disorienting as the assault of sound and movement. She was floating on nothing in a black void. Then came a lighted image, just a glimpse, so brief it registered in the subconscious and came forward into the conscious mind one detail at a time: a face, a boy, brown hair, striped pajamas.

"Josh?"

Another glimpse. Freckles, a bruised cheek, blank eyes.

"Josh!" She tried to move but couldn't, tried to reach out to him but seemed to have no control over her body at all.

The image flashed again. He stood like a statue, like a mannequin, his arms outstretched toward her, his face expressionless.

"Josh!" she screamed, but he didn't seem to hear her at all.

The blackness fell again like a curtain. She drifted on it. So tired, but her heart was pounding out of control and the pain came at her from all directions—*bam! bam! bam! bam!*—hitting her everywhere at once like a dozen rods wielded by twelve angry men.

The voice vibrated against the top of her head.

"You wonder who we are, clever girl?" he whispered. "You wonder why we play this game?"

He settled his hands on her shoulders and sensuously stroked the aching, knotted muscles. A shudder of revulsion rippled through her, provoking his laughter.

"We play the game because we can," he said, sliding his hands down over her breasts. "Because no one can catch us. Because no one ever suspected. Because we're brilliant and invincible."

He squeezed a breast in each hand until she whimpered. "You came too close, clever girl. Now you get to play, too."

Megan tried to think who or what she had come close to. Names and faces floated through her mind, but she could grasp none of them.

"What will I do?" she asked as she tipped forward again.

He leaned so close she could smell the mouthwash on his breath. When he spoke, his lips brushed her cheek. "You're going to be our next move."

5:15 P.M. 23° WINDCHILL FACTOR: 12°

Albert Fletcher stood on the balcony rail, his left arm wrapped around a column. In his right hand he clutched an ornate bronze crucifix, which he brandished high over his head as he shouted at the people below him.

"Beware false prophets who come in sheep's clothing! They are ravening wolves!"

The congregation had been ushered out of the church, replaced by police and sheriff's deputies. Father Tom remained behind the altar, his gaze fast on Fletcher, as if it would hold him in place. He prayed it would. Guilt twisted like a knife in his belly. This situation was his fault. Right or wrong, his feelings for Hannah had been the trigger.

"Albert," he said, the microphone clipped to his vestments picking up his voice clearly. "Albert, you have to listen. You're making a big mistake."

"Wicked spawn of hell!"

"No, Albert. I'm a priest," he said quietly, hoping he was punching the button that would make Fletcher listen instead of push him over the edge. "I'm *your* priest. You have to listen to me. That's what you've been taught, isn't it?"

Fletcher shook his crucifix angrily; the railing shook with him. "I know where Satan's throne is!"

"Satan's throne is in hell, Albert," Tom said. "This is the house of the Lord."

"I will cast you out, demon!" Fletcher's left foot slipped on the railing. Everyone in the church held their breath until he regained his balance.

In the silence Mitch could hear the nerve-tightening sound of wood cracking. Crouched low in the shadows at the head of the stairs, he had a clear view of Fletcher, and through the spindly carved balusters of the railing he could see the vast open space beyond the balcony. Slowly he straightened and moved out into the light.

"Mr. Fletcher? It's Chief Holt," he said, his voice low and even.

Fletcher's head snapped around. The railing wobbled.

Mitch's body tensed, ready to spring forward. The deacon's eyes were wild, bright with madness.

"You're right, you know," Mitch said. "We're onto Father Tom. We're going to arrest him. We'll need you to help us."

Fletcher stared at him, pulling the crucifix down to clutch it against his body. "Beware false prophets," he muttered. "Beware false prophets. Shapen in iniquity. Conceived in sin."

"You know about sin, don't you, Albert?" Mitch said, inching toward the railing. "You can tell us all about it. But we'll need you to come to the station. You can be our witness."

"Witness," Fletcher mumbled. He thrust the crucifix skyward again and shouted, "Witness! Witness the wrath of God!"

The railing groaned. Mitch was moving even as the sickening sound of wood breaking cracked in his ears. He lunged for Fletcher as the balcony railing gave way, catching hold of the deacon's left hand. Momentum yanked him toward the edge. His shoulder slammed into the support column and he wrapped his free arm around it, gritting his teeth against the pain, against the strain of holding Fletcher's weight. A fraction of a second later, the hold was broken and the deacon's fate was sealed.

"*No!*" Tom shouted.

He saw Fletcher's body dropping from twenty feet up. He ran as hard as he could, but his cassock caught at his legs, pulled at him, slowed him down. He could see the cops rushing in. They were all too late.

Fletcher landed like a rag doll tossed out a window, his body shattering as it fell across the pews. Someone called out to God. Someone else shouted an expletive. Father Tom fell to his knees, his hands trembling as he reached out to cradle Fletcher's fractured skull. Paramedics rushed in with a stretcher. Too late. He passed a hand over the man's face, closing the sightless eyes, and he murmured a prayer for the soul of Albert Fletcher . . . and one for his own.

CHAPTER 37

The drug was fading. The fog in her brain was thinning, letting the pain come through like a hot desert sun, searing, unbearable. Megan tried to focus on the questions that floated through her head like wisps of angel hair. He said she had come close. To what? She tried to think back. He had caught her at Priest's house. Was that coincidence? Had she simply stumbled into the wrong place at the wrong time and flushed Albert Fletcher out of hiding?

You don't believe in coincidence, O'Malley. Nor did she believe the disembodied voice belonged to the deacon. There had been no spouting of Bible verse, no promise for damnation. The voice was cool, controlled, frighteningly so. A voice without a soul.

Did it belong to the professor? He had gone to St. Peter. He couldn't have known she would go to his house. He couldn't have been lying in wait for her.

Unless someone had warned him.

Only two people had known she was asking after him—Garrett Wright and Todd Childs.

Todd Childs, the psych major who worked at The Pack Rat. He had known Olie Swain, had been in computer classes with him—and with Priest. He had helped out at the volunteer center—with Priest. He was working on a project with Priest. She had no doubt he knew all about chemical substances. He would have known what to give her.

"It's almost showtime."

The words were whispered against her lips, an obscene kiss.

Megan recoiled, earning a breathy chuckle. He had been silent so long, she had begun to think he'd left. She looked down, tilting her head to the side as much as she dared. A portion of the anonymous black boot came into view.

"Why Josh?" she murmured, her mouth as dry as powder. "Why his family?"

"Why not?" he replied, sending a chill straight through her. "Such a perfect little family." The softly spoken words were venomous with contempt.

Megan stared down at the boot as he rocked back on his heels, the action flipping a switch of recognition. She'd seen him do that half a dozen times. Just a habit, a quirk, a minor detail she filed away in the back of her mind like eye color or a mole. The words were familiar, too. *I feel so bad for Hannah and Paul. Such a perfect family . . .*

Garrett Wright.

He had seen her standing along the road where Mike Chamberlain had lost control of his car. The helpful Dr. Wright, offering roadside assistance with a benign smile, later offering all he knew about his colleague's whereabouts.

Hannah and Paul's neighbor. A man who molded the impressionable minds of the students at Harris College. Respected. Above suspicion. A man the media had chosen as an expert witness. For once they had struck pay dirt. The irony was that they might never know it.

8:41 P.M.   22°   WINDCHILL FACTOR: 10°

Mitch drove away from City Center for the second time that night. The rush of adrenaline that had pumped through him as he'd sped across town to St. E's was long spent. He had hit rock bottom with the death of Albert Fletcher. If Fletcher had taken Josh, they weren't going to hear it from him now. Fletcher couldn't tell them where Josh was, whether Josh was alive or not.

He wanted to hit something, hard. Or be touched by something soft. The first night he had gone to Megan, she had reached out to him and taken away his pain. She didn't think she needed anyone. Had it ever occurred to her that someone might need her? Someone like him. A beat-up, broken-up, bad-tempered cop.

He pulled the Explorer in along the curb in front of the big Victorian on Ivy Street and sat there listening to the wipers thump back and forth. The snow was coming down fast and furious. With predictions that the storm would continue through the night, city crews had made no attempt to clear the side streets. People had parked haphazardly. The cars wore blankets of snow four inches thick. Except Megan's car, which was nowhere in sight.

There were no lights on in the third-floor windows. The black cat sat in the front window, visible against the backdrop of pale curtains, keeping watch for his mistress. She must have gone to St. Paul after all. Mitch didn't know whether to be relieved or disappointed. He didn't know what the hell he was doing here. What was he going to do—tell her Fletcher was on a slab down at Oglethorpe's Funeral Home and ask her did she want to go to bed with him for old times' sake because he was feeling battered and lost? She'd pull that Glock and plug him right between the eyes.

The cellular phone nestled in his coat pocket trilled. Mitch dug it out, swearing under his breath. "What now?"

The silence was broken by a thin, shaky breath. The hair on the back of his neck rose.

"M-Mitch?"

His heart jammed at the base of his throat. "Megan? Honey, what's wrong?"

"G-get the sonofabi—" A strangled cry choked off the sentence.

"Megan!" Mitch shouted, gripping the steering wheel hard with his free hand. "Megan!"

The voice that came on the line was not Megan's. Whisper-soft, it skated like a razor along his nerve endings. "We have a present for you, Chief. Come to the southwest entrance of Quarry Hills Park in thirty minutes. Come alone. Not one minute sooner, or Agent O'Malley will die. Do you understand?"

"Yes." Mitch bit the word off. "What do you want?"

The eerie, breathless chuckle went down his spine like a bony finger. He tightened his grip on the phone and swallowed at the tightness in his throat.

"To win the game," the voice murmured. The line went dead.

Megan did her best to brace herself as she heard him set the phone down. He would punish her. She knew that. He was a control freak and she had broken a little piece of that control. If she was lucky, he would rage and shout and she would at least be able to testify she had heard his voice clearly and distinctly. If she was unlucky, he would kill her.

"We thought you were a clever girl." He didn't raise his voice even a fraction, but the anger was there, humming like a power line. "We thought you were a clever girl, but you're just another stupid bitch!"

The blow caught her in the side of the head. Not the club, but the back of his hand. So hard that the chair rocked sideways. Color burst behind her eyelids and the taste of blood bloomed fresh and thick in her mouth. Before that explosion subsided, he brought his fist down on her battered hand. The tears were instantaneous. As much as Megan hated them, as much as she hated to have him see them streaming out from under the blindfold, there was nothing she could do to stop them. Still, she bit her lip and held her breath against the need to sob aloud.

This was what he wanted as much as anything: to humiliate her, to prove his own superiority in every way. He had calculated every move, every possibility, but he hadn't counted on her defying him. She could only hope it rattled him enough that he would make a mistake, that the mistake would give Mitch an opportunity to nail him.

She wanted that opportunity herself. The chance to beat him at his game. The chance to beat him physically, the son of a bitch. She wanted to take that little baton of his and bash his head in, beat him until he told her where Josh was and then beat him some more.

He used it on her with expertise, knowing just the spots to hit and the perfect amount of force to cause pain but not to make her lose consciousness. Her right knee, her left shoulder, her left calf, her right hand. Again and again he hit the hand, until the slightest touch made her scream.

When his fury was spent, she could no longer distinguish one pain from the next. The pain had taken on proportions larger than she was, suffocating her, deafening her, breaking her. The only thing she clung to was the burning coal of hatred in her chest and the knowledge that he was the key to finding Josh.

The bindings around her arms and ankles abruptly loosened and the chair tipped forward, dumping her to the cold floor. His voice seemed to be in both ears at once.

"Rise and shine, bitch."

Megan made no effort to move. The baton cracked against her back, her ribs, her buttocks, and she fought to make her body move. She couldn't get her feet beneath her, couldn't tell which way was up or which way to go to escape the beating. He grabbed her by the hair and hauled her up, slamming her sideways into a wall.

"We could make you *so* sorry, little bitch," he whispered. He closed his teeth on her ear and bit her through the blindfold until she cried out. "If only we had more time to play. But we have a date with your loverboy."

CHAPTER 38

Mitch settled back in the trees to wait. From his vantage point he had a clear view of the southwest entrance—as clear a view as the snow allowed. He had come in from the west, from the Lakeside neighborhood, no more than six blocks from the Kirkwood house. Noogie had dropped him off and gone on in the Explorer to wait until the designated time, and Mitch had set out through the thick woods that edged the park, wading through snow that was nearly knee-deep, skidding downhill, tripping on hidden roots and fallen branches.

He crouched against the thick, rough trunk of an oak tree, fighting to catch his breath. The drive that ran a bent horseshoe circuit between the east and west entrances of the park was no more than thirty feet away, with the parking area less than fifty yards to the south. Mercury-vapor lights were spaced out along the parking lot and farther apart along the drive. Snow danced like thick swarms of fireflies beneath their light.

He checked his watch. Twelve minutes to spare. Twelve minutes to wait and sweat and wonder what the bastard might have done to Megan. Twelve minutes to worry that his hasty instructions to Dietz and Stevens hadn't been clear enough, that someone would somehow screw up and get Megan killed. There hadn't been time to formulate much of a plan, and he was only too conscious of the fact that the officers he had to work with had no experience with hostage situations. They didn't dare risk radio communications for fear of being overheard on a scanner—by their bad guy or a citizen or a reporter.

Twelve minutes to wonder who the bastard was. Was it Priest? Had Megan's hunch paid off? Damn her for going off half-cocked with no backup. She knew better. But there hadn't been anyone to go with her. She'd been relieved of duty. And when she had told him her latest theory, he had discounted it and blown her off.

He couldn't believe it was Priest. He'd been around the man for two years and never felt a bad vibration.

And you thought Olie was harmless, and that nothing bad would happen in broad daylight at the 7-Eleven.

He closed his eyes. Oh, Jesus, not again, not Megan, not right before his eyes. Not because he'd been wrong or stupid or too stubborn to see the truth. He couldn't have another person die because of him. Especially not Megan, who had badgered and bullied him from the start to open his eyes and see something besides the bland haven he had created for himself. Not Megan, who had been abandoned and neglected and harassed, and deserved so much better from life.

The pickup turned in the drive at 9:05, ten minutes ahead of schedule. A late model GMC 4X4, jacked up on heavy tires and sporting the latest in roll bars and a bug guard that read ROY'S TOY. It rolled past the parking area and crept along through the fresh snow. Crouching low behind the cover of the trees, Mitch plowed his way north, rushing to come even with the truck before the driver got out, hoping this was their man and not some horny teenagers looking for a spot to make out.

The heavy snow sucked at his boots, costing him precious seconds. He lunged ahead, breath sucking in and hissing out through his teeth, his eyes on the pickup as it appeared and disappeared on the other side of the trees. The brake lights went off and he fell against a walnut tree. He slid his hand inside his open parka and eased his Smith & Wesson out of the holster, never looking away from the truck.

The driver's door opened. A black-clad figure slid out from behind the wheel, featureless, anonymous, a ski mask hiding the face. Dark Man. He took a long look around, scouting for any sign of betrayal. Mitch willed himself invisible, pressing hard against the trunk of the tree, holding his breath as the faceless eyes passed over his section of woods. The air seeped out of his lungs as Dark Man went around to the other side of the truck and let his passenger out.

He marched her a dozen paces back toward the parking area. Mitch strained to make her out, an impossibility in the poor conditions. It could have been anyone about the right height with dark hair. It could have been a decoy. This could all have been a trick. Megan could have been in a basement somewhere, her fate hinging on whether or not he screwed up here.

He fought the panic. *Think like a cop. See like a cop. What do you see?*

She was leaning heavily against Dark Man, as if unable to walk on her own. Bending over slightly, the gait off-rhythm, a limp. She was in pain. If this was a trick being set up ten minutes ahead of schedule, there would be no reason for the decoy to put on a show. It *was* Megan, and she was hurt badly. Jesus, what had that animal done to her?

Megan hobbled away from the truck, leaning hard against her captor, not by choice but necessity and because she thought any hardship she caused him was a small point in her favor. Her hands were bound behind her, the blindfold still in place. She wore no coat, only the thin silk underwear and a sheet for a wrap. The cold bit into her, exacerbating her pain instead of numbing it. She couldn't straighten her right knee. It felt swollen and every step brought a small explosion of pain. She wasn't sure it would hold her weight, but she exaggerated the limp, stumbling into Wright and causing him an awkward step. In punishment he squeezed her hand, wringing a sound of agony from her.

"Play your part, little bitch"—he brought the nose of a pistol up under her cheekbone—"or I'll blow your brains out."

Her role in his game was Humiliation. He had outsmarted them. He had snatched Josh away from under everyone's noses, laid out his little clues and red herrings, and fooled them all. She was to be his grand gesture, the ultimate insult. He had taken her and beaten her and wrapped her in a sheet of evidence he believed would do them no good at all because he believed he was invincible.

That would ultimately be his undoing, Megan thought. He

believed his own delusions of grandeur. God only knew what he had gotten away with over the years, but he wouldn't get away with this. Not as long as she was alive.

He faced her the way they had come in, arranging the sheet around her to his satisfaction like an oversize shawl, the ends fluttering and snapping in the wind. He had draped it around her before taking her out to get in the truck. A bedsheet. White with red flecks. She knew what it was: bloodstains. Evidence, he told her. He would hand them this evidence wrapped around a cop and still no one would touch him.

Think again, you bastard.

She felt him lean close, his breath warm and minty on her face. "It's been lovely," he murmured, and touched his lips to hers.

Megan spat at him and won herself a backhand across the mouth with the butt of the gun. As she staggered, the taste of blood bubbled up in her mouth like a warm spring. She spat it out, concentrating not on this newest pain, but on the thought that Mitch would be coming. He had to have risked coming in early. It meant catching their monster. But it could also mean her life. Would he take that chance?

Come on, Mitch. Be here. Be here.

She counted the footsteps as Wright moved away from her. Two, three . . . Had he holstered the gun? She inched herself around, her limited gaze on the ground, searching for footprints to tell her she was pointed toward the truck. Bending her head down to her shoulder, she tried to dislodge the blindfold and gained another fraction of an inch of vision in her right eye. Enough to see his legs.

If she rushed him—if she could—would it delay him enough for Mitch to arrive? Or would she die for nothing? The thoughts and questions shot through her mind, all of them boiling down to a simple truth: She didn't want to die like this—in disgrace, with so much left undone and unsaid.

Mitch held himself rigid. He wanted to nail the son of a bitch now, tackle him and beat him senseless for striking Megan. But he would wait. Let him get in the truck and drive out. Count on Dietz and Stevens to stop him at the east entrance. Dietz and Stevens, whose biggest busts had been drunks and petty drug dealers. This asshole was the key to finding Josh. If they had him in their sights and let him get away . . . He was halfway back to the truck. Once he was in the truck, he could be gone.

In a heartbeat the decision was taken away from him. Megan turned and flung herself at the man. He wheeled and caught her head-on, and together they tumbled into the snow.

Mitch launched himself down the hill, fear and fury driving his legs, bellowing out of his lungs. "Freeze! Police!"

Megan's breath left her in a rush. She gasped for more as she struggled to free herself from Wright's grip, from the damned sheet, struggled to get her legs under her. The blindfold came off, but Wright's grip never loosened. He pushed to his feet, dragging her up in a headlock and bringing his gun up hard into her temple. He half dragged her, half pushed her toward the truck, snarling in her ear.

"Tell him I'll kill you! Tell him I'll kill you!"

"Tell him yourself, asshole," she snapped. "Kill me and you're a dead man right here."

"Bitch!"

He jerked her sideways, his forearm tightening against her windpipe.

"Drop the gun!" Mitch shouted.

He came to a halt ten feet from them, the Smith & Wesson in position, cocked and ready, his finger itching to take the slack out of the trigger and blow the bastard's head open like a rotten watermelon. But he couldn't chance a shot; Megan was too close, too good a shield. The nose of a black nine-millimeter was biting into her temple. Mitch knew if he did the wrong thing, made the wrong decision, she would be dead. Sweat dripped into his eyes and he blinked it away. The image of Allison dead and Megan dead alternated in his mind like freeze-frame shots. Allison lying on the gray linoleum, her blood spreading out in a pool. Megan lying crumpled in the snow, her blood soaking it like cherry syrup on shaved ice.

"Drop it!" he bellowed. "You're under arrest!"

Wright pulled Megan another half-foot toward the open door of the truck. The engine was rumbling, waiting.

"You'll never get out of here in that truck," Mitch yelled. "I've got unmarked cars waiting on both entrances."

"Tell him he doesn't play fair," Wright whispered.

Megan cut him a glare out the corner of her eye. "Fuck you."

She let her legs buckle abruptly. Her dead weight jerked Wright off balance, giving Mitch the opportunity to charge. Wright shoved Megan into Mitch, sending them staggering backward in the snow. Firing blindly in their direction, he vaulted into the cab of the truck.

Mitch rolled Megan beneath him, shielding her, flinching as the bullets struck within inches.

"It's Garrett Wright!" Megan shouted.

Mitch raised himself up on his hands and knees over her. "Are you hit?"

"No! Go nail the son of a bitch!"

He lunged to his feet as the truck lurched into motion, tires spinning in the fresh snow. The back end fishtailed, swinging toward Mitch, who grabbed the side panel just as his feet were knocked out from under him. His hands slipped as he struggled for a better hold, and the Smith & Wesson clattered into the bed of the truck. Then the pickup slid the other way, dragging him in its wake.

As it straightened out, Mitch heaved himself up and over the side, rolling into the bed with a grunt of pain. Instantly, he spotted his gun and dove for it. Scrambling into a crouch, he lurched toward the cab, then grabbed hold of the roll bar.

"Stop the truck, Wright!" he shouted, pounding the back window with his gun hand. "You're under arrest!"

Wright responded by jerking the steering wheel, throwing Mitch sideways. They slid into a curve off-balance, rocking violently, the right side wheels coming up off the ground. Mitch was thrown back in the other direction. He grabbed again for the roll bar, brought the Smith & Wesson up, and fired through the back window. The bullet cut cleanly through it but shattered the windshield into an intricate spiderweb of cracks.

"Stop the truck!" He smashed the bullet hole with the butt of the pistol, cracking the safety glass and bending it in.

Wright twisted around and fired over his shoulder, the bullet sailing wide as Mitch ducked sideways, aligning himself directly behind his man. Still holding the roll bar with his left hand, he reached in through the broken window with his right and jammed his gun up behind Wright's ear.

"Stop the goddamn truck! You're under arrest!"

Wright twisted the wheel sharply to the left and gunned the engine. The pickup roared off the path and into space as it sailed off an embankment. Shouting a curse, Mitch dropped to his knees. He jammed his gun inside his coat and grabbed hold of the roll bar with both hands.

The truck landed bucking, then skidded sideways and slammed into the trunk of a tree. Mitch bounced around the bed like a ball in a game of bumper pool. A wedge of snow-flecked sky flashed across his vision as he was thrown, then solid white, then color burst behind his eyelids when he landed.

He was on his feet and drawing the gun out before his vision cleared. He ran for the truck, trying to spot Garrett Wright, wondering if the crash might have knocked him out. Gunshots answered the question for him—three quick rounds that sent him diving for cover behind a fat spruce tree.

He crouched there for a moment, trying to catch his breath, trying to catch a glimpse of Wright from between the branches, but it was too dark. Staying low, he crept ahead from spruce tree to hardwood, moving toward the truck. It had come to rest in a small oasis of trees. To the south and east was nothing but open ground. To the west was a fifty-yard sprint to the thick woods that blanketed the hillside. If Wright was going to run, west would be his only option.

Mitch darted behind another tree, his eyes on the truck.

"Give it up, Wright!"

Silence. The wind. The groaning of the trees.

Taking a deep breath, he ran low for the passenger side of the truck. No shots. Nothing but the hiss of the pickup's wounded radiator. Slowly, Mitch straightened. The cab was empty. Through the windows he could see Garrett Wright running, no more than thirty feet from the edge of the woods.

"Damn, you're too old for this, Holt," he muttered, gathering his strength. Then he pushed away from the pickup and ran. He expected Wright to fire on him as he crossed the open ground, but no shots came. He charged up the bank, plunging into the trees and brush, leading with his gun.

A flash of movement among the tree trunks to the north sent Mitch in that direction. A bullet chipped a tree a foot to his left at the instant the sound of the shot reached him. He dropped to his belly and waited, scuttling sideways, ignoring the sharp broken branches that poked at him through the snow. His hand caught hold of something soft and warm. He jerked back instantly, thinking it was something alive, but it was a black knit ski mask.

"Wright!" he shouted. "Give it up! You can't win!"

A game. A goddamn game. That was what he called destroying people's lives. The hell if he would win this one.

Another shot zinged toward him. Mitch zigged right and ran on, returning fire. He caught another glimpse of Wright, a darker shape among the shadows, then he was gone again, leaving Mitch swearing.

The muscles in his legs and back were burning. The cold night air came into his lungs like needles. The toe of his boot hit something and he went down hard. As he stood, a bullet cut through the left sleeve of his parka, nicking his arm and spinning him sideways.

"Shit! Shit! Shit!" He ducked behind a tree. The wound stung like hell, but it wasn't debilitating and it wasn't his gun hand.

Carefully, he eased his head around the tree trunk. No sign of Wright. An aura of light limned the crest of the hill. Beyond the last of the trees lay the Lakeside neighborhood. Hannah and Paul's neighborhood. Garrett Wright's neighborhood. Garrett Wright, who taught psychology and worked with the Sci-Fi Cowboys and drove a Saab. Who would ever have looked at him and wondered if a madman lurked beneath the neatly pressed surface?

Another flash of movement cut through the falling snow. Mitch gave chase, keeping his eye on Wright's back as he hit the cross-country ski trail that ran along the lip of the hill. Mitch hit the path seconds after him.

"Wright! Stop! You're under arrest!"

His quarry ducked left and disappeared into a stand of snow-laden spruce trees. Praying he wouldn't be running into a bullet, Mitch bolted after him. On the other side of the trees the houses of Lakeside stood on their oversize lots, lights glowing softly in windows. He narrowed his eyes, scanning the yards for Garrett Wright. A shadow moved along the next house to the north. Just a shape along the back wall of the garage, running through an open back door.

"Freeze, dammit!" Mitch shouted, charging through the drifts, never taking his eyes off the door as it swung shut two seconds before he reached it.

He lowered a shoulder and hit the door running. It burst open with an explosive *crack!,* the wood frame splintering. Mitch's momentum carried him straight into Garrett Wright. They went down hard, skidding across the concrete floor, Wright grunting as his breath left him.

"You're under arrest, you son of a bitch," Mitch snarled, rising up above him, his lungs working like a pair of bellows. He held the Smith & Wesson half an inch from Wright's pale face, the barrel quivering like a rattlesnake tail. "Game's over, Garrett. You lose."

CHAPTER 39

W hat's going on?" Karen Wright stood in the doorway
that led from the garage to her kitchen, her expression
pale and horrified.

"It's a mistake," her husband said. He lay facedown on the
concrete floor of the garage, his hands cuffed behind his back.
He twisted his head around to glare up at Mitch, who stood
with the Smith & Wesson still trained on him.

"Yeah," Mitch snarled. "It's a mistake—and *you* made it."

Karen's big doe eyes brimmed with tears. She twisted her
hands in the bottom of her baggy pink sweater. "I don't understand! Garrett hasn't done anything! He doesn't even
speed!"

Mitch spared her a glance. He had read many cases where
a woman had lived with a man for years, oblivious to the fact
that he led a secret life as a rapist or murderer or child predator. That was undoubtedly the case with Karen Wright. She
had been working at the volunteer center, mailing out fliers in
the effort to find Josh, while her husband had been playing his
sick game. Still, she would have to be questioned to see just
what she knew and what she didn't, to see if she could corroborate or destroy her husband's story. Mitch couldn't imagine
she would hold up very well. She didn't look very resilient.

"Garrett, what's this about?" she cried. "I don't understand!"

"I'm sorry, ma'am," Mitch said. "If you could just wait inside—"

"Garrett!" she sobbed.

The big garage door was up, a huge open window to the street, letting in the wind and the snow, affording a view of the cruisers coming up the block with Mitch's Explorer right behind them. The vehicles turned in the drive. There were no lights or sirens. Mitch had given specific orders for silence when he had called the dispatcher on his cellular phone. No mention of a code or a crime, just a specific request for Noogie, Dietz, and Stevens, and one other patrol car to report to 91 Lakeshore Drive.

Wright's own house. Mitch supposed he had thought to take the Saab in the garage and escape, but there would be no escape. Tonight, justice got the win.

Megan sat in the Explorer and watched as Noogie escorted Garrett Wright to a police car. She stared at the face of the man who had beaten her, tormented her, tormented them all. No more than four feet away, he turned and looked right at her. No emotion registered on the face that was cast half in shadow, half in the grainy light that shone down from above the garage door. He simply stared at her. Then Noogie clamped a big hand on his shoulder and stuffed him down into the car.

Megan shivered. She couldn't seem to stop shaking, and it wasn't from cold. Noogie had bundled her up in wool blankets and left the motor running and the heater blasting. She had refused to let him call an ambulance. She had no intention of being whisked off to the emergency room without knowing that Mitch had caught Garrett Wright . . . without knowing that Garrett Wright hadn't shot him.

Dietz and Stevens came out of the garage, one at either elbow of Karen Wright, holding her upright as she sobbed. Wright's eerie whisper floated through Megan's head—*we . . . we . . . we . . .* Never *I,* always the plural. But she couldn't picture Karen as the other half of the team. There had been too much contempt for women in that disembodied voice. *You're just another stupid bitch!*

She jerked at the memory of the blow that had followed.

"Dammit, Megan, you belong in the hospital!"

Mitch had pulled open the passenger door and was scowling at her. But it wasn't anger she saw in his eyes.

"I had to know," she whispered. "I had to see that you got him."

Something twisted hard in his chest as he looked at her. Her right eye was blackening. Her lower lip was split and swollen. That son of a bitch had pounded her, yet she sat there with her chin up and defiance shining behind the tears in her eyes.

"I got him," he whispered. Stroking a hand over her hair, he leaned into the truck and coaxed her head to his shoulder. "*We* got him."

He shuddered at the thought that the outcome could have been very different. She could have been killed. He could have lost her. But she was here and alive. Relief left him feeling a little shaky.

They were both blinking furiously as he pulled back. He sniffed hard. A crooked smile canted his mouth.

"You're a hell of a cop, Megan O'Malley," he murmured. "Now let's get you to a hospital."

11:47 P.M. 17° WINDCHILL FACTOR: 0°

D id he tell you where Josh is?" Hannah asked.

Mitch had told her to sit, but she couldn't. She prowled the family room, her arms crossed tight. Her pulse was racing off the chart. She probably should have been lying down, but she needed to move and to keep on moving until Mitch gave her the answer she needed. And then she would sprint out the door and run to Josh. Conversely, Paul sat at the end of the couch, bent over with his head in his hands, seemingly unable to move or speak.

The call had come nearly two hours before—Mitch telling her Garrett Wright had been arrested and that he would come by the house himself to explain. She had asked him to notify Paul at his office, then waited, stunned and numb.

Mitch looked at his boots and heaved a sigh. "No. So far he isn't talking."

Mitch had asked him to show a little compassion, tell them if Josh was alive at least, but Garrett Wright held no compassion. He met Mitch's gaze straight-on, nothing showing behind his cold, dark eyes, his fine features blank, devoid of emotion.

"Garrett Wright," Hannah muttered. "You're certain . . ."

"There's no doubt in my mind," Mitch said. "He's been toying with us all along, teasing us with clues. He meant to use Megan—Agent O'Malley—to make his point tonight, to show us all how superior he is, but he danced a little too close to the flame this time. I chased him down myself, Hannah. He's our man—one of them, anyway. Whether Olie Swain was connected, or someone else, we don't know yet."

Mitch refrained from telling them a Harris College student named Todd Childs had been brought in for questioning. Nothing had come of it yet. Nor did he make any mention of the fact that he had issued a bulletin for Christopher Priest to be brought in. The professor hadn't returned from St. Peter, if that was where he had gone. The St. Peter police were checking motels to see if he was among the motorists stranded by the storm.

"My God, *Garrett Wright*." Hannah shook her head. It seemed inconceivable. He was their neighbor. Karen's husband. A teacher at Harris. He had called her just last night and given her the name of a family counselor. *"Why?"*

"I can't answer that, honey," Mitch murmured. "I wish I could."

"Why would he hurt us?" she said as if Mitch hadn't spoken.

"Because he's a lunatic!" Paul shouted, vaulting up from the couch. "He's insane!"

And he was trapped in a nightmare. This couldn't possibly be happening. Garrett Wright arrested. No. It couldn't be Garrett. He couldn't stand for it to be Garrett.

"Anybody who would do this kind of thing has to be insane!" he insisted. He turned away from the fireplace, where a photo of Josh stared out at him from a cherry frame on the mantel. On the VCR shelf in the entertainment center sat a stack of Josh's video games. Everywhere he turned were reminders. Inside his head, Josh's voice echoed and echoed.

Dad, can you come and get me from hockey? Dad, can you come and get me from hockey? Dad, can you—

"I can't believe this," he muttered. He stared at the carpet, afraid to look anywhere else. He couldn't stand the reminders of Josh. He couldn't look at Mitch Holt. He especially couldn't look at Hannah. He couldn't think about Garrett Wright. Guilt and panic and self-pity clogged his throat. "I can't believe this is happening to me."

No one heard him.

Hannah's attention was on Mitch. He looked as if he had run to hell and back, hair disheveled, coat open and hanging crooked on his shoulders. One sleeve was torn at the biceps, bleeding goose down. The strain of the night sharpened the angles of his face, darkening the shadows, deepening the lines. The worst of it was in his eyes—regret, sympathy, empathy.

"You think Josh is dead, don't you?" she said softly.

Mitch sank down into a wing chair. They had all prayed for this case to end, but no one had wanted it to end like this, with no sign of Josh, with one of their own neighbors in custody, with Megan in the hospital.

"It doesn't look good, honey," he answered. Hannah knelt at his feet and looked up at him. "There were bloodstains on the sheet. We have to think the blood came from Josh. We'll need both you and Paul to submit to blood tests so the lab can try to get a match on the DNA."

"He's not dead," Hannah whispered almost to herself. She rose slowly, touching the fingers of her right hand to her left inner elbow. "They drew blood," she murmured. "I saw a bandage on his arm."

"Hannah . . ."

Paul wheeled around. "Jesus Christ, Hannah, give it up! He's dead!"

She met his outburst with steely determination, strength rising up from somewhere deep inside. In a far, detached corner of her mind, she thought it was odd that she should find the strength now in the face of such devastating news. She had imagined this moment in her nightmares, had envisioned herself breaking into a million pieces. But she wasn't breaking. She wasn't giving up on Josh and she was all through putting up with Paul.

"He's not dead, and I'm sick of you telling me he is!" she said, glaring at the man who had once been husband and lover and friend. "You're the one who's dead—at least the part of you I used to love. I don't know who you are anymore, but I know I'm sick of your lies and your accusations. I'm sick of you blaming me for losing Josh, when all you seem to want to do is bury him and hope the cameras get your good side at the funeral!"

Paul splayed a hand across his chest as if she had plunged a knife into his heart. "How can you say that?"

"Because it's the truth!"

"I don't have to listen to this." He looked away from her, away from the contempt in her eyes.

"No," Hannah said, picking up his coat off the back of the sofa. She flung it at him, her mouth trembling with fury and with the effort to hold the angry tears at bay. "You don't have to listen to me anymore. And I don't have to put up with your moods and your wounded male ego and your stupid petty jealousy. I'm through with it! I'm through with you."

She tried to draw in an even breath. She wouldn't cry in front of him. She would shed her tears in private for what they had lost. He stood there, staring down at the coat in his hands. The man she had married would have fought back. The man she had married would have said he loved her. Too bad for both of them that man no longer existed.

"You don't live here anymore, Paul," she murmured. "Why don't you leave now. I'm sure there are still reporters around eager to get a sound bite from the grieving father."

Paul took a step back, her words hitting him with the force of a physical blow. *I've lost everything. I can't believe this is happening to me.*

Josh's words whispered in the back of his mind—*Dad, can you come and get me?* The guilt nearly choked him. He fought to contain it, to hide it. He could feel their eyes on him—Hannah's, Mitch Holt's. Could they see it? Could they smell it on him like the stink of sweat? He was losing everything—his son, his marriage, everything. And for the rest of his life he would have to live with the secret—that while he had been cheating on his wife, his mistress's husband had abducted Josh.

Nausea and weakness shuddered through him. "I have to get out of here," he muttered.

Hannah watched him go, listened to the door close and the muffled sound of a car starting. She could see Mitch sitting there in the wing chair, his face averted, as if he were pretending he wasn't there at all.

"I'm sorry you had to see that," she said.

He stood, at a loss, out of energy. "This has been rough on both of you. You need some time—"

"No," she said quietly, firmly. She reached up and tucked a strand of hair behind her ear. "No, that's not what we need."

Mitch didn't try to argue.

"What happens now?" she asked.

"We're conducting an extensive search for the place Wright took Megan. We figure it can't be more than seventy-five miles away. Probably less. We're checking to see if he owns any other property, see if he owns a van. As soon as his lawyer gets here, he'll be questioned. In the meantime, we bust our asses to build a case that'll put him away for the rest of his life."

Hannah nodded. "And Josh?"

"We'll do everything we can to find him." Him or his body. He didn't say it, but Hannah could read it in his eyes.

"Tell me you won't give up on him, Mitch," she said. "You know what it is to lose a child. Promise me you won't give up on Josh."

Mitch slipped his arms around her and held her for a moment. He did know what it was to lose a child, and, practical or not, he couldn't make Hannah face that pain if there was even just a sliver of hope.

"I promise," he whispered hoarsely. "He's alive until someone proves to me otherwise."

"He's alive," Hannah said with quiet resolve. "He's alive and I'm not giving up until I find him."

Mitch promised to call her if anything developed, to keep her as well informed as he could. She saw him to the door and watched him back his truck out of the driveway and head south, taillights glowing, the only color in a black and white night. The snow was still falling, driven by a wind that cut to the bone.

Hannah stepped back into the house, rubbing the chill from her arms, though she knew it went much deeper. It gripped the core of her as she stood in the family room and realized her family no longer existed. The house felt huge and empty. She felt alone, and she shivered at the thought that she would be alone from then on.

Except for Lily.

Lily lay on her side in her crib, curled around Josh's old teddy bear, her thumb just out of her mouth. Hannah looked down on her daughter. The thinnest edge of a night-light touched Lily's face, so sweet, so innocent, so precious, framed in golden ringlets. Long lashes against a plump cheek flushed with sleep. Her mouth a rosebud just opening.

"My baby," Hannah whispered, reaching out to brush her fingertips over Lily.

She could still remember what it had felt like to carry this precious life within her. She could still remember what it had felt like to carry Josh. Every moment of joy, of fear, of wonder at the miracle that would be her first child. Their excitement—hers and Paul's—at the news that they would be parents. The nights they had lain in bed and talked in quiet voices, planning the future, Paul's hand on her belly.

It broke her heart to think that they would never lie together that way again, that she would never plan a future because she knew how bitterly the present could turn on her. She felt as if she'd been robbed. Robbed of her son, of her marriage, of her belief that the world was a place full of wonderful promise.

"There's nothing left but us, Lily-bug," she whispered.

Lily's wide eyes blinked open. The baby sat up, rubbing a small fist against her cheek. She looked up at Hannah, frowning at her mother's tears.

"No no cryin', Mama," she murmured, raising her arms in a silent plea to be picked up.

Hannah scooped her up and held her close, sobbing for all she had lost, for the uncertainty of the future. Pain and fear raked through her, and all she could do was hold her child and pray for hope. It seemed so little to ask when she had lost so much.

Her strength waning, she sank down into the old white

wicker rocker. Lily stood on her lap and tried to wipe her tears away with her hands.

"No no cryin', Mama," she said.

"Sometimes Mama needs to cry, sweetie." Hannah kissed her daughter's fingertips. "Sometimes we all need to cry."

Lily sat down to ponder this. Silence filled the room, while outside the wind howled a hostile counterpoint. Hannah slipped her arms around her little girl and pulled her close.

"Where Josh, Mama?" Lily murmured, her thumb inching toward her mouth.

"I don't know, honey," Hannah answered quietly, her gaze on the empty crib and the ragged panda bear that had been her son's. She had bought it for him the day her doctor told her she was carrying him. He had slept with it near him every night of his life. Every night but the last eleven.

"Let's think he's somewhere warm," she whispered, breathing deep of Lily's sweet, powdery scent, rocking her gently. "That he's not afraid. That he misses us, but he knows we'll bring him home just as soon as we can. That he knows we love him. That he knows we'll find him . . . because we will . . . I promise."

She closed her eyes and held her breath and held her baby. She prayed for hope and for the strength to make good on the promise and for the belief that somehow, somewhere, prayers were heard and answered.

CHAPTER 40

DAY 13
5:54 P.M. 18°

She could see the boy's face, a pale oval with freckles like a sprinkling of nutmeg over cream. He stared through her, his eyes wide and blue and blank. Then he was gone, like a light switching off to leave her in total darkness.

We have a treat for you, clever girl . . . clever bitch . . . A voice with no body, as smooth and sinister as a snake. She trembled and felt herself tipping, twirling in the black void. Powerless. Vulnerable. Waiting. Then pain struck from one direction, then another, then another.

Megan jerked awake. The surgical scrubs Kathleen Casey had procured for her clung to her body like wet tissue paper. She took stock of her surroundings item by item, forcing herself to calm, to pull back her control inch by inch, to shake the disorientation and the fear. She was safe. Garrett Wright was behind bars.

She wondered if they had found Josh.

The calendar on the wall across the room said it was Monday, January 24. Tom Brokaw was talking to himself on the wall-mounted television.

She remembered Mitch bringing her to the hospital. Everything after that blurred together like images whirling inside a kaleidoscope. A little man with an Indian accent and an enormous nose, calmly giving orders and asking questions. Nurses murmuring to her as they moved around her bed on air cushion shoes. Needles. Pain. Visions of Harrison Ford looking down on her.

She supposed that had been Mitch checking up on her.

She had slept through Sunday and most of that day, knocked out by exhaustion and drugs. Now she felt groggy and fuzzy-headed. The pain cut through whatever it was they were giving her. Fine lines of it were drawn directly from her injuries to her brain. Her right knee. Her left forearm. Her kidneys. Her right hand—the hand that had helped fill out a thousand police reports. The hand that had held a pistol steady enough to win her half a dozen awards for marksmanship. The hand that was now encased in a temporary cast.

Dr. Baskir, he of the nose and accent, had been in earlier in the day, during one of her brief periods of lucidity. Humming and muttering to her various body parts, he had checked her vital signs and her sore spots. Many, many contusions, he told her back. He told her knee it would want physical therapy. He addressed her hand last. "Poor, poor darling little bones."

With a grave expression of sympathy, he told Megan he couldn't promise she would regain full mobility of the hand. He spoke in a near whisper, as if he didn't want the darling little bones to hear the bad news. He had done what he could as a temporary fix, but now that the weather had finally cleared, they would transfer her to Hennepin County Medical Center, where an orthopedic surgeon would begin the painstaking process of repairing the extensive damage to the delicate structure.

Fear cut through her like a machete as his words replayed in her head. A cop needed two good hands. A cop was all she had ever wanted to be. The job was her life. Now her life stretched before her with the possibility of her never being able to hold that job again.

Fighting the tears that threatened, she looked around the private hospital room. Flowers and balloons decorated the cabinets. Kathleen had read the cards to her. They were from the Deer Lake force, the bureau, her old buddies in the Minneapolis police department. With the exception of a beautiful miniature rosebush from Hannah, they were from cops. Nearly everyone she knew was a cop. What would happen if she ceased to be one?

She felt as if she were attached to her world by a single thin tether, like an astronaut walking in space, and the line was in danger of being severed. And she was absolutely powerless to stop it.

In an attempt to push away the fear, she pressed the volume button on the television remote control. Her right hand was immobilized in a sling against her. The left had hosted an IV catheter for eighteen hours, but that was gone now. Maybe she could teach herself to become left-handed, she mused as she punched the channel button, surfing through the stations as the six o'clock local news came on.

She flipped past *TV 7,* home of Paige Anything-for-a-Story Price, and settled back on Channel Eleven. A shot of Minnesotans digging out after the weekend storm gave way to the file photo of Josh in his Cub Scout uniform.

". . . but our top story tonight comes from Deer Lake, Minnesota, where, over the weekend, authorities apprehended a suspect in the abduction of eight-year-old Josh Kirkwood."

Videotape of a press conference filled the screen. The press room in the old fire hall, standing room only. Mitch stood at the podium, looking grave and tired. Marty Wilhelm stood to his right, looking stupid. Steiger sat at the table, frowning, his nose a triangle of adhesive tape. Mitch read a prepared statement, stating only the barest of facts about the harrowing events of Saturday, refusing to answer most questions pertaining to details of evidence, refusing even to confirm Wright's name, on the basis that releasing any information could possibly endanger the integrity of the ongoing investigation.

"Josh Kirkwood is still missing and all law enforcement agencies involved are still actively searching for him," he said.

"Isn't it true that evidence recovered Saturday night included a bloodstained sheet?"

"No comment."

"Is it true the suspect in custody is a faculty member at Harris College?"

"No comment."

"So much for protecting the integrity of the investigation," Megan muttered. The media weasels would dig and hunt and bribe and trick their way into getting what they needed for their headlines and damn the consequences.

"Is it true you personally chased the suspect on foot half a mile through the woods?"

Mitch gave the woman offscreen a long look. Camera shutters clicked and motor drives whirred. When he spoke it was in the low, measured voice he used when his patience was wearing thin. "You've all tried to make me out to be some kind of hero in this. I'm no hero. I was doing my job, and if I'd done it better, there wouldn't have been a chase. If there's a hero in this, it's Agent O'Malley. She risked her life, and nearly lost it, in the attempt to bring Josh Kirkwood's kidnapper to justice. She's your hero."

"Oh, Mitch . . ."

"It's the truth."

He stood in the doorway, tie askew, hair mussed, looking tough and tired, his shoulders sagging a little. Jessie stood beside him, a plush tiger-striped stuffed cat under one arm.

Natalie herded them into the room. "Don't you keep me standing out here in the hall, where any stray nurse wandering by could poke my big behind with a needle."

Megan sniffed and mustered a smile. "Hey, look who dragged a cat in. Hi, Jessie. Thanks for coming to see me."

"I brought you Whiskers," Jessie said, presenting the stuffed toy as Mitch hoisted her up and stood her on one of the lower side rails of the bed. "So you don't get so lonesome for your real cats."

The toy looked well loved. The ears lined with pink satin were a little worn around the edges. The long white whiskers were a little bent. Megan's eyes instantly brimmed with tears at the thought that Jessie would give her such a treasured possession. She rubbed her fingertips over the soft gray fur.

"Thank you, Jessie," she whispered.

"Me and Daddy are taking good care of Gannon and Friday," Jessie said, her attention on the toy as she stroked it. "They like me."

"I bet they do."

"And they like to play with string." She looked at Megan from under her lashes. "Daddy said maybe I could still visit them after you're better."

"I'm sure they'd like that." Megan's heart sank at the knowledge that Jessie wouldn't be able to visit her cats at the house on Ivy Street because they wouldn't be in the house on Ivy Street much longer.

"Daddy said you aren't going to heaven like my mommy did," Jessie said solemnly. "I'm glad."

"Me, too." The words barely squeaked out of Megan's mouth. She had never allowed herself to become attached to anyone because she knew it would hurt. It hurt to feel the emptiness and the longing for something she couldn't have, and it hurt to know the relationship would end. It hurt now, the longing to pull Jessie close and hug her.

"I brought cookies," Natalie announced. She pulled an enormous Tupperware tub out of her tote bag like a magician pulling a moose head out of a hat, and plunked it down on the bedside table. "Chocolate chunk. You need fattening up." She turned an eagle eye on Megan. "You hurry up and get out of here, *Agent* O'Malley. That puppy-faced boy the bureau sent down here is like to drive me crazy."

"I think you'll probably have to get used to him," Megan said with a rueful smile.

Natalie gave a harrumph. "We'll see about that," she muttered ominously. Fishing several cookies out of the tub, she gave Jessie a nudge and wink. "Come on, Miss Muffet, let's go see if we can scare up some milk and spoil your supper."

"Catch you later, Megan!" Jessie beamed as she leaned over the railing to give Megan an awkward high-five, then scrambled down and scampered out of the room with Natalie right behind her.

Megan looked down at Whiskers, rubbing her thumb over one tatty ear. "She's pretty special."

"I think so," Mitch said. "But I suppose I'm biased." Gently, he hooked a knuckle under her chin and tipped her face up. "How do you feel?"

"Like a sadistic psychopath beat me head to toe with a baton."

"That son of a bitch. I'd like to take a club after him."

"Get in line," Megan said. She turned away from him and eased her legs over the side of the bed to slip her bare feet into a pair of hospital slippers.

"Are you allowed out of bed?" Mitch asked with some alarm. He rounded the foot of the bed and hovered beside her, ready to catch her if she collapsed.

Megan did her best to ignore his concern. Shooting him a

look of annoyance, she hobbled toward the window, leaning heavily on a single crutch tucked under her left arm. "As long as I promise not to run up and down the halls shouting obscenities." She had never dreamed so many parts of her could hurt simultaneously, but she would get through it, tough it out, because she had to. "I need to stand awhile. Lividity was setting in." She propped herself up against the window well.

Night had fallen outside. Black over a blanket of pristine white. The snow lay in drifts over the hospital lawn, sculpted into elegant lines by the wind. She could feel Mitch standing behind her, his warmth, his energy, tempting her to lean back into him. She could see his faint reflection along with her own in the window, dark shadows with haunted eyes.

"But, life's not *all* bad," she said with cynical humor. "I'm getting a commendation from the bureau. I'm losing my field post, but I'm getting a commendation. Beats the hell out of a pink slip, I suppose. And Paige is dropping the lawsuit in light of the photos old Henry Forster snapped of her sneaking in and out of Steiger's trailer. Lucky for me she was too greedy for details about the arrest to keep her panties on."

"Greed is a great motivator."

"That's a fact," she murmured. "I wish that's all this case was about—greed. At least that's something everyone can comprehend. Garrett Wright's motive . . . How can anyone understand a game as twisted as the one he's been playing?"

Mitch offered no answer. She knew he didn't have one any more than she did.

"Is he talking yet?" she asked softly.

"No."

"You haven't found the place he took me."

"Not yet. It could take some time."

"And Josh . . ."

"We'll find him," Mitch declared as if there weren't hundreds of cases that went unsolved forever. "We'll go on looking until we do."

"I saw his face," Megan said slowly. "In between beatings. I saw him, but I don't know if I was conscious or if I was hallucinating. I don't know if what I saw was real. I wish I knew, but I don't."

It made her head hurt to try to separate the real from the

surreal. Knowing that Wright was a psychologist, an expert in learning and perception, only complicated the issue. Could he have somehow planted that image in her mind? Possibly, but that didn't explain the conversation she had had with Hannah earlier in the day.

Hannah had come in to deliver the rosebush herself. Pale and thin, looking as if she belonged in a bed instead of standing beside one, she presented Megan with the plant and with her thanks for all she'd done.

"I got myself caught and beat up," Megan admitted. "I don't feel like I deserve thanks."

"Because of you, Garrett Wright is behind bars," Hannah said simply.

Megan didn't ask her how she felt about the fact that her neighbor, someone she had trusted, had been the one to put her through this hell. Enough people would ask that question over and over, poking at the open wound in Hannah's soul.

"I have to ask," Hannah murmured, trying to hide the tremor in her voice. Her gaze darted from Megan's to the square of bed covers she continually smoothed with her fingers. She started to speak, stopped, took a breath, and tried again. "Did he say . . . anything . . . about Josh?"

"No," Megan whispered, wishing with all her heart she could offer something more, some concrete evidence that Josh was alive. But all she had was a vision that might well have been drug induced. She looked up at Hannah, at the dark rings around her eyes and the emotions she couldn't hide and made her decision. Slim hope was better than no hope at all.

"I did . . . see . . . something . . ." she started, choosing her words as carefully as picking her way through a mine field. "He drugged me, you know, so I can't say if what I saw was real. In some ways it seemed like it was. In other ways . . . I just can't say."

"What did you see?" Hannah asked carefully, her expression guarded. Megan could feel her tension level rise. Her fingers left the sheet and wrapped around the bed rail.

"I thought I saw Josh. It might have been a projection of some kind. It might have been something Wright planted in my mind. I don't know. But I thought I saw him standing across the room, just looking at me. He didn't say anything. He just stood there. I remember his eyes and his freckles." She looked back into her own memory for details, for some hint of reality. "He had a bruise on his cheek and he was wearing—"

"Striped pajamas."

Hannah finished the thought for her. Megan looked up at her, stunned, a chill running through her. "How did you know that?"

She breathed deeply and stood back from the bed. "Because I saw him, too."

"How?" Megan whispered, nearly dumbstruck with astonishment. Was this the reason Hannah had sounded so confident on TV about Josh being alive?

"In my mind I saw him one night, and he looked so real that it couldn't have been just a dream. What you've told me confirmed what I already believed. Josh is alive. I'll get my son back."

Megan wanted to believe it, too. That they would find Josh safe and sound and bring him home to live happily ever after. She stood there now in her room, staring out at the night, wishing, and knowing wishes wouldn't get them anywhere.

"I asked him, you know," she said to Mitch. "If he killed Josh. He wouldn't say. He told me the game wasn't over yet. He told me they had considered every possibility, that they couldn't lose."

Mitch's eyes narrowed. "He's sitting in a jail cell, booked on charges of kidnapping, depriving parental rights, assaulting an officer, attempted murder, auto theft, and fleeing arrest. Ruth Cooper ID'd him in a lineup as being the man she saw on Ryan's Bay last Wednesday, and she ID'd his voice. We've got him dead to rights. I'd say he's a big-time loser."

"No sign of a record on him?"

"No."

Meaning if Garrett Wright had committed murder, as he had told her, no one had ever pinned anything on him. The thought only deepened the hollow feeling in Megan's stomach. She tried to ease it with the thought that now every stone of Wright's past would be turned over. A vision of squirming maggots filled her head and she blinked to clear it away.

"Any connection to an accomplice yet?"

"Olie looks like a good bet. He sat in on some of Wright's

classes. He had the van, the opportunity, the history. Wright might have had some kind of hold on him psychologically."

"What about Priest?"

"Volunteered to take a polygraph and passed it with flying colors. Todd Childs claims he was with a friend most of Saturday. Says he was at the movies the night Josh disappeared." He blew out a breath, his broad shoulders sagging under the weight of it all. "I've been talking to Karen Wright, trying to find out if she might know something without realizing it, but she hasn't been any help. She's so distraught, she can hardly function."

"Yeah, well, that's a pretty ugly surprise—to find out you're married to a monster. Seems to be an ongoing theme since I came here—ugly surprises. Do you think that's a sign?"

She tried to smile, but it hurt too much that she didn't belong there—and it just plain hurt, tugging at the stitches in her lip. She looked down at the cast on her hand and felt that lifeline stretching thin. There was no promise she would belong anywhere. She turned a whiter shade of pale.

"I think you should lie down," Mitch said gruffly.

"Don't boss me around," she shot back with a fraction of her usual fire.

"What are you going to do about it, O'Malley? Hit me with your crutch?" The mock irritation did a poor job of covering his concern.

"Don't tempt me. I'm cranky."

"Get back in that bed or I'll put you there myself." He pointed the way for her. "Natalie is right, we need you better and back on the job. That Tom Hanks impersonator they sent down here is driving me nuts."

Megan gave him a look. "Like I didn't?"

"At least you're a good cop," he grumbled. "And I can kiss you when you make me mad."

"Marty might like that, too. Have you asked him?"

"Very funny. Come on, now, Megan, I'm not kidding. Get back in bed."

Megan ignored the dictate, turning her attention back out the window. Talk of work only made her more keenly aware of her tenuous position. The fear swelled inside her like a balloon. She told herself to handle it as she had handled most everything else in her life—alone. Mitch didn't want her burden. He had made it clear what he wanted from her—a brief affair, no strings attached, no complications. She was one big complication now.

Still, the pressure of an uncertain future built inside her, trembling like a clenched fist, and she couldn't seem to keep the words from leaking out.

"I might not be coming back to the job," she said in a small voice. "Here or anywhere. Maybe never."

She watched his reflection in the glass as he moved a little closer. He ran a hand over her hair and settled it on her shoulder.

"Hey, I thought you were a tough cookie," he said. "It ain't over till it's over, O'Malley." She turned wary eyes on his reflection. "I know about your hand, honey."

"Don't call me honey."

He slipped his arms around her with infinite care. He held his breath as he waited for her to lean back against him.

Megan held her breath against the need to let him hold her, waited for the need to pass. It wasn't smart to need that way. She'd known that all her life. *Stand on your own two feet, O'Malley. Hang on to your heart.* The trouble was, she didn't feel strong enough to stand alone, and her heart was already gone. She had nothing left to lose but her pride, and that was tattered and threadbare.

The tears came despite all efforts to fight them off. She didn't have the strength for shields and armor, the defenses that had guarded a too-tender soul for so long. She could feel everything she'd ever wanted, ever loved, sliding through her grasp, leaving her alone, with nothing, with no one. She'd been alone so much and it hurt so badly.

The words, like the tears, came grudgingly. "I'm . . . so . . . scared!"

She turned and pressed her face against his chest and cried. Mitch held her and whispered to her. He lay his cheek on top of her head and squeezed his eyes shut.

"It's all right," he whispered. "I'm here for you, Megan. You won't be alone."

He tipped her face up and looked into eyes that were wary and wide, that had seen too much disappointment. His hand cradled a face so fragile, so pretty, it took his breath away. At that instant he didn't see the black eye or the battered lip. The feeling that swelled in his chest scared the hell out of him.

"I'm saying I love you, Megan." He swallowed hard and said it again. "I love you."

"No," she said, stepping back from him. "No, you don't."

Mitch scowled at her. "Yes, I do."

"No." She shook her head, hobbling toward the bed, the rubber tip of her crutch squeaking against the polished floor. "You don't love me. You feel sorry for me."

"Don't tell me what I feel, O'Malley," he growled. "I know when I'm in love with somebody. I'm in love with you. Don't ask me why. You're the most stubborn, confounding woman I've ever known. That's how I know I'm in love with you." He lifted a finger to emphasize his point. "If I weren't in love with you, I'd want to wring your neck."

"What a romantic," Megan said dryly, covering her emotions with sarcasm. "It's a wonder women aren't hurling themselves at your feet."

"No, I have to pick a woman who'd rather hurl something at my head."

"Lucky you I'm crippled," she grumbled, struggling to get herself up onto the bed.

Mitch made a sound of boiling frustration between his teeth and came to her aid. "Let me help you."

"I don't want your help."

"Tough." He put his hands around her waist and lifted her like a doll. "Dammit, Megan, it's not going to kill you to say you need me or to let me know when something hurts you."

"*You* hurt me," she said. "Don't tell me you love me when you don't. I'm not what you need or want and you know it! I don't know anything about being in love. All I know is how to be a cop and how to be alone. So why don't you just get out!"

He heaved a sigh. "Aw, Megan . . ."

She narrowed her eyes at the look on his face. "Don't you dare pity me, Mitch Holt. And don't argue. Just leave."

"I don't pity you," he said quietly, stepping closer and closer. "I love you. And God knows I've wanted you from the minute I laid eyes on you."

"So, you had me. You should be happy."

"I'm going to have to knock that chip off your shoulder every damn day, aren't I?" he murmured half to himself. "I can't say I would have asked for this. You punch my buttons. You make me mad. You make me feel. Maybe that's not what I thought I wanted, but I need it. To feel again."

He brushed a knuckle against her cheek. "I almost lost you, Megan. I'm not going to walk away from you. Our lives can change so fast. In the blink of an eye, in a heartbeat. It's stupid to let a chance go by because we're too proud or too scared. That chance may never come again."

A chance at love. It hung in this moment between them, a pale, shimmering promise. A chance Megan had longed for in silence all her life. It terrified her now to think it might be a mirage, that it might vanish if she reached for it. But what if she didn't? What would she have then?

"Come on, O'Malley," Mitch goaded. "What are you—chicken?"

"I'm not scared of you, Holt," she returned. Her breath hitched in her throat and she scowled.

"So prove it," he challenged her, stepping closer, sliding his fingers into her hair, cupping the back of her head. "Tell me you love me."

Megan met his gaze, his tough-cop look, his eyes that looked a hundred years old. Eyes that had seen too much. She raised a hand and traced a fingertip over the scar on his chin.

"Break my heart and I'll kick your ass, Chief."

A crooked smile broke across Mitch's face. "I guess that's close enough."

He leaned down and pressed a kiss to her unbruised cheek, breathed in the scent of her hair and the faintest breath of perfume that clung to her skin.

"So I know you've got a rule against dating cops, O'Malley," he murmured in her ear. "But do you think you could marry one?"

Megan lay her head against his chest and listened to his heart beat in time with hers. "Maybe," she whispered, smiling. "As long as the cop is you."

CHAPTER 41

Boog Newton sat with his feet on his bunk and his back against the wall, picking his nose, his eyes fixed on his little television. He never missed the news. A lot of it seemed like bullshit to him, but he never missed it anyway. That was tradition. The fact that Paige Price made him horny as hell was just a bonus.

The top story of the night was the press conference on that kidnapping deal. Boog felt a personal connection to the case after what had gone on with that Olie character. He listened closely as Chief Holt told the reporters practically nothing.

"Digging for gold, Boog?" Browning, the jailer, sauntered past the cells. He was making rounds every fifteen minutes instead of every couple of hours the way he used to, which had to cut into his magazine reading in a big way.

"Take off, pork," Boog sneered, flicking a big fat booger at Browning's beer gut.

"Jeez!" The jailer jumped back as if he'd been shot. His face twisted with disgust. "Look at that! God!" He ducked out the door. Boog snickered and turned back to his news. The guy in the next cell was watching, too. He was creepy, sitting there all day, never saying anything, his expression never changing. Boog had caught him looking at him different times, staring at him as if he were a bug under a microscope.

"Hey, that's you they're talking about, ain't it? You're the one took that Kirkwood kid. That's sick," Boog declared, sticking out his bony chin. "You're sick."

Garrett Wright said nothing.

"Hey, you know what happened to the last guy they brought in here? They said he done it. They put him right in that cell you're sitting in. You know what he did? He took his glass eyeball right out of his head and killed himself with it. I figure he was nuts. Anybody who'd do that has to be nuts." He pressed his lips together and scratched at his greasy hair, figuring some more. "You must be nuts, too," he deduced.

The corners of Wright's mouth flicked up. "I teach psychology at Harris College."

Boog made a rude noise, eloquently expressing his opinion of teachers. On the television they were showing cops and lab guys from the BCA trooping in and out of a fancy house in Lakeside—Wright's house. A pretty woman with dishwater-blond hair stood by the front door, bawling her eyes out.

"Hey." Boog shot another look Wright's way. "What'd you do with the kid? Did you kill him or what?"

Garrett Wright smiled to himself. "Or what."

DAY 14
MIDNIGHT 12°

Hannah woke sharply from a troubled sleep. Sleeping alone triggered some internal alarm system that was oversensitive and went off at the slightest hint of sound or movement. She lay in the middle of the big bed and stared up at the skylight and the black rectangle of January night, listening, waiting, every muscle tense. Nothing. No sound, no movement. The house was still. The night was silent. Even the wind, which had been relentless for days, as cold and sharp as an ice pick, held its breath as one day passed and a new one began with the tick of the clock: 12:01.

A new day. Another day to face. Another twenty-four hours to wander through, trying to function, looking like a normal person, appearing as her former self, an impostor. Nothing about her life or herself was normal anymore. She would get through this day and the next and the one after that because she had to for herself, for Lily . . . and for Josh.

He's somewhere warm . . . he's not afraid . . . he knows I love him. . . .

She came out of bed before the sound even registered in her conscious mind. Her bare feet hit the carpet. She grabbed the old velour robe Paul had discarded. Doorbell. At midnight—ten past now. Her heart pounded. Possibilities flashed through her head: Paul looking for forgiveness, Mitch coming with news—good? Bad?

She hit the switch for the front porch light with one hand while the other clutched the robe together over her breastbone, over her heart. The bell sounded again. She pressed her eye to the peephole.

"Oh, my God."

The words came out in a strangled whisper. Josh stood on the front step, waiting.

In the next instant Hannah was on her knees on the cold cement. She pulled her son into her arms. She held him against her body as tight as she could, crying, thanking God, kissing Josh's cheek, kissing his hair, saying his name over and over. She didn't feel the cold or the scrape of the concrete step against her knees. She felt only relief and joy and her son's small body pressing into hers. The relief was so enormous, she was terrified it was a dream. But if it was a dream, she knew she wouldn't let go. She would stay on this step and clutch him to her, feel his warmth, breathe in the scent of him.

"Oh, Josh. Oh, my God," she whispered, the words trembling on her lips, mixing with the salty taste of tears. "I love you. I love you so much. I love you. I love you."

She stroked a trembling hand over his tousled brown curls and down the back of the striped pajamas he wore. The same pajamas she had seen him in. The same pajamas Megan O'Malley had seen him in, though she had not been sure whether what she had seen had been real or imagined. There were so many questions yet unanswered. They flashed through Hannah's mind. If Garrett Wright had taken Josh, then who had brought him home?

She opened her eyes and looked beyond her front step into moon-silvered night. No one. No cars. No shadows except those of the trees against the pristine snow. The town lay sleeping, unaware, quiet.

Josh squirmed a little in her arms, and Hannah pulled herself back to the moment. Such a perfect moment, the one she had held as a brilliant and fragile hope in her heart. She had her son back. She would have to call Mitch—and Paul . . . and Father Tom. She would call the hospital and leave a message for Megan. Josh would have to be taken to the hospital to be examined. The press would descend again . . .

"Honey, who brought you home?" she asked. "Do you know?"

She leaned back to look at him. He simply shook his head, then tightened his arms around her neck and put his head down on her shoulder.

Hannah didn't press him. For this moment she wanted to think of nothing but Josh. No questions of how or why or who. Only Josh mattered. And he was home and safe.

"Let's go inside, okay?" she said softly, fresh tears squeezing between her lashes as Josh nodded against her shoulder.

Hannah rose with her arms around him, barely noticing his weight as she carried him into the family room. Doctor's instincts and mother's instincts prompted a quick evaluation of his physical condition. The small bruise on his cheek—the bruise she had seen in her dream—was fading. He was thinner and pale, but whole, and he wanted to be held. Hannah complied readily. She wanted him with her, next to her, physically connected to her. She held him on her lap as she sat on the love seat and used the portable phone to call Mitch, then Paul's office. Mitch promised to be over in a matter of minutes. Paul's machine picked up. Jealously channeling all her emotions to Josh's return, she didn't bother to feel irritation toward Paul for not being there; she simply left the message and hung up.

"It doesn't matter, sweetie." She kissed the top of Josh's head, hugging him tight again as another wave of relief washed through her. "All that matters is that you're home, you're safe."

She blinked away more tears as she looked down at him. He was asleep. His head lolled forward as he breathed deeply and evenly. His thick, long lashes curled against his cheek. *My angel. My baby.* The thoughts were as familiar as his face, thoughts she had recited in her mind since before his birth and countless nights after it, when she had slipped into his room to watch him sleep. *My angel, my baby . . . so perfect.*

A sliver of pain pierced her joy. *Perfect.* Josh had always been a happy child, a joy to her. Who would he be now? What had he gone through? The possibilities had tormented her every hour he had been away. Now they gathered at the edge of her relief like a pack of hyenas. She chased them back as she carefully eased out from under her son and lay him down on the love seat. He was in one piece, whole and clean. She kissed his forehead as she tucked an afghan around him and breathed in the scent of shampoo. She wanted to push his sleeve up to see if there was a bandage on the inside of his elbow, but she didn't want to wake him. And she wanted him to have these few moments of peace before having to face an examination and answer questions.

She let her hand rest on his instead, her fingertips on his wrist. His pulse was regular and normal. She didn't count the beats, but concentrated on what they represented—life. He was alive. He was with her. The piece of her heart that had been missing was returned and it beat in tandem with his.

Has he said anything about Wright?" Mitch asked quietly. He sat in a wing chair with his forearms braced against his knees, his parka open. After Hannah's call he had literally rolled out of bed and into a pair of jeans and a sweatshirt. His hair stuck up in all directions. He wished Megan could have been here to help him ask these questions, to close the case she had fought so hard to solve.

"No." Hannah sat on the floor in front of the love seat where Josh lay sleeping beneath the folds of the red afghan. She touched him constantly in small ways, stroking his hair, rubbing his back, petting his hand, as if breaking physical contact would shatter the spell and he would disappear again. "He hasn't said anything. I asked him if he knew who brought him home. He shook his head no."

"He's in shock. It may take him a while . . ."

He let the thought trail off, not wanting to follow it. Of the paths it might take, most of them led to more unhappiness, and he wanted to spare Hannah for the moment. Still, duty dictated. Procedure had to be followed, questions had to be asked. Even now, in the dead of night, he had men knocking on doors down the block looking for anyone who might have glanced out a window and seen anything out of the ordinary.

"We'll have to take him in to the hospital tonight—"

"I know."

"And I'll have to try to get him to answer some questions. If he can tell us anything about Wright—"

Hannah's fingers stilled on Josh's hand; she looked up at Mitch. "What will this mean? Garrett Wright is in jail and now Josh comes home. What will that do to the case against him?"

"I don't know. A lot depends on Josh, on what he can tell us. But even if he can't tell us anything useful, we've still got the lineup ID, and we'll have DNA and trace evidence from the sheet. If Wright thinks this gets him off the hook, he can think again. We caught him, honey," he said, his gaze unwavering, his voice quiet but strong with conviction. "We nailed Garrett Wright cold, he's as guilty as sin, and we'll keep looking until we find his accomplice. Then we'll nail him, too."

He rose from the chair and offered Hannah a hand up. "That's a promise. Garrett Wright's next game will be in a court of law. I predict Lady Justice will kick his butt."

"I hope so."

Mitch gave her fingers a reassuring squeeze. "I know so. But I don't want you worrying about it. The only thing you should think about tonight is that Josh is home. That's all that matters."

"That's the only thing that really matters at all," she agreed, looking down at her sleeping child.

He could have been lost forever, vanished into a shadow world, as many children were every year, never to be seen again, leaving behind only questions and heartbreak for the people who loved them. For reasons known only to the dark mind of his abductor, Josh had been allowed to cross back out of the shadows. That was all that counted. The truth, justice, revenge, were distant and abstract thoughts for Hannah. Their world had been shattered, their lives irrevocably altered, but Josh was home. That was all that really mattered.

Josh was home. Their lives could begin again.

EPILOGUE

> *They think they've beaten us at our own game.*
> *Poor simple minds.*
> *Every chess master knows in the quest for victory*
> *he will concede minor defeats.*
>
> *They may have won the round, but*
> *the game is far from over.*
>
> *They think they've beaten us.*
> *We smile and say,*
> *Welcome to the Next Level.*

Dear Readers:

I hope you found *Night Sins* as compelling to read as it was for me to write. Sadly for all of us, child abductions have been in the forefront of the national news. Even where I live, in a place not unlike Deer Lake, tragic cases have turned our attention to ugly truths and raised questions in our minds about what it would be like to have to live through such a nightmare. At the same time I was watching these cases unfold, a dear friend of mine was dealing with a devastating illness. Being on the outside looking in at these heart-wrenching situations left me feeling helpless and wondering endlessly why bad things happen to good people. For a writer, questions are best explored in one way —through a story.

So began *Night Sins,* with questions such as: What would it be like to be a cop on a case with few clues and much pressure for a resolution? What would it do to the parents in a relationship already on shaky ground to be put under the kind of pressure a tragedy like this brings? What kind of mind does it take to commit a crime of such callous evil? How far will that evil go?

One of the great benefits of writing fiction is the ability to control the outcome of the story. In real life, happy endings are not guaranteed. The bad guys don't always get caught. Loose ends are not always tied up. Justice is not always done. Children don't always come home. I was able to bring Josh home at the end of *Night Sins,* although, as in real life, some questions remain unanswered, an intentional act on my part. So the pursuit of justice is not over for the people of Deer Lake. As in real life, the apprehension of the criminal at the end of *Night Sins* is only half the story. Exacting justice is the job of the courts. The challenge of prosecuting this case will fall on the shoulders of Assistant County Attorney Ellen North in *Guilty As Sin,* where I get to explore a whole new set of questions. How far will the game go? Will justice triumph? And for Ellen North, as she finds herself in a dangerous maze full of shadows and mirrors and players with hidden agendas, the most essential question of all: Who can you trust?

I hope you will all look forward to searching for the answers to those questions in *Guilty As Sin.*

Tami

All Orion/Phoenix titles are available at your local bookshop or from the following address:

Mail Order Department
Littlehampton Book Services
FREEPOST BR535
Worthing, West Sussex, BN13 3BR
telephone 01903 828503, *facsimile* 01903 828802
e-mail MailOrders@lbsltd.co.uk
(Please ensure that you include full postal address details)

Payment can be made either by credit/debit card (Visa, Mastercard, Access and Switch accepted) or by sending a £ Sterling cheque or postal order made payable to *Littlehampton Book Services*.
DO NOT SEND CASH OR CURRENCY

Please add the following to cover postage and packing

UK and BFPO:
£1.50 for the first book, and 50p for each additional book to a maximum of £3.50

Overseas and Eire:
£2.50 for the first book plus £1.00 for the second book and 50p for each additional book ordered

---

BLOCK CAPITALS PLEASE

name of cardholder ....

address of cardholder ....

delivery address
(if different from cardholder)
....
....
....

postcode ....

postcode ....

☐ I enclose my remittance for £...........................

☐ please debit my Mastercard/Visa/Access/Switch (delete as appropriate)

card number ☐☐☐☐☐☐☐☐☐☐☐☐☐☐☐☐☐☐

expiry date ☐☐☐☐   Switch issue no. ☐☐

signature ....

prices and availability are subject to change without notice